THE GUZZI LEGACY VOL 1

CORRADO – ALESSIO – CHRIS

BETHANY-KRIS

Published by Bethany-Kris

www.bethanykris.com

ISBN 13: 978-1-989658-37-6

Editor: Elizabeth Peters

Cover Design © Lee Ching at Under Cover Designs

CONTENTS

CORRADO

THE GUZZI LEGACY, 1

PART ONE: BEFORE

1.

Corrado

Koi no yokan.

Corrado read those words, inked in a script font and hidden on the inner elbow of his family priest's arm. It was the only time he ever noticed the tattoo, and that said something considering he attended this church since he was a newborn. They had christened him in this place. His first communion had been an interesting experience as a kid with a church of more than four hundred parishioners watching. Catholicism for the Guzzis was a second skin—the church, a second home. He recognized these walls inside and out.

But not that tattoo.

"What does that mean?" he asked.

The priest—Father Gene, they called him—looked up from the papers he'd been moving aside on his desk. The office, a mixture of dark woods, richly colored tapestries, smelled of old leather, and even older books. Compliments of the row of texts that looked like they had seen better days lining the shelves behind the priest's desk.

"What, Corrado?"

"That, there," Corrado said, pointing at the black script on the priest's inner elbow. "What do the words mean?"

Father Gene's hand came up to cover the small spot of ink as a smile curved his lips. "Something you wouldn't understand at seventeen, I assure you. And we're not here to talk about tattoos I had done before I joined the priesthood."

"How old were you, then?" Corrado tipped his head to the side. "When you joined?"

"I started the process at nineteen."

"So, you had the tattoo before then, but you won't tell me what it means because I won't understand because of my age?"

Father Gene stared at him from across the desk, silent. His father, Gian, would say this was one of *those* times. Out of all his siblings, including his identical twin, Corrado was the one who spoke when he should stay quiet.

He'd rather talk about other shit than what he came here for.

"Are we asking about my tattoo because you're attempting to avoid the conversation about your lack of confession for two years?"

Corrado stared at the cross over the window to his right rather than at the priest. "I don't need to do confession."

"But your father believes something is wrong … he's the one who asked me to bring you in for a session of counsel, didn't he?"

He was smart, so he stayed quiet when he had nothing good to say. Like right now.

The priest didn't miss it.

"I'm worried about you," the man across the desk admitted. "You graduated high school three weeks ago, and according to your father, you have yet to decide on a *real* path of what you want to do. And without getting into the specifics of your father's business, because without me explaining that to *you,* he knows I don't approve, I'm concerned you will flounder with no stability to hold on to. No work, no college … no *faith.*"

Corrado's gaze snapped back to the priest. "I have faith."

He was sure of that. The problem? His faith and doctrine had taught him that certain parts of himself weren't *right.* He found comfort in church, but he also found confusion, too.

"If you tell me why you stopped confession, and why you're struggling to move forward in your life, I will tell you what the tattoo means," Father Gene said, grinning. "And whatever you tell me, that will never go beyond these walls."

"Not even to my parents?"

"Not even to them, Corrado."

He stared down at where he'd clasped his hands in his lap. This way, he wouldn't fidget or distract himself. He didn't need his nerves on display. Another thing being a Guzzi had taught him—the appearance of calm and confidence was *most* important, but especially in their life.

Corrado was far from stupid, and he could tell what people assumed when they saw him. They assumed because he ran around with Guzzi blood in his veins, that like his older brother, Marcus, and even his twin, Chris, he would be the same and go into the family business.

La famiglia.

The mafia.

His last name said so. The legacy that came with it kept the demand alive. Tradition. Men in this life followed their father's footsteps, and even more so when one's father just happened to be *Gian* Guzzi—Cosa Nostra Don, controlling the largest and most powerful crime family in Canada. It was expected of Corrado; history said so.

Except his father. Gian never said a word about it. Not to Corrado.

"You're struggling," the priest said, his French clear. Maybe because he assumed it would comfort Corrado. The only person who spoke French to him now, besides associates of his father, *was* Gian. He didn't see his father's French-Italian side of the family enough to speak anything with them. "I can see."

"I'm not like them," Corrado said.

Father Gene raised a single eyebrow high as he leaned forward to rest his clasped hands on the desk. "Why would you say that?"

He'd been ready to spill his secret, to admit why he was, in fact, struggling between life and business. The reason for his lack of a decision, and his waffling.

"Corrado?"

He swallowed hard and stared down at his hands again. "I stopped coming to confession at fifteen because I had sex."

The priest sat back in his chair. "Oh." And then, the man added with a laugh, "That's not a reason to stop confessing, it's a reason *to* confess, Corrado."

"With another guy," he added lower.

That quieted Father Gene.

Corrado shifted in the high-back leather chair the longer the silence dragged on. "That's partly a lie. I had sex with a girl before that, but—"

"I understand," the priest murmured.

"This is not ... our way." Corrado shrugged. "I hear what people say—inside this church, and outside, about people like me. In business, it's a weakness. Here, it's a sin. Except I can't be different, and so, I don't fit in."

He'd always been this way.

At first, Corrado didn't know what to label his sexuality. In high school, the only gay kid he was acquainted with—at the time—got treated like a second-class human. Because he liked girls, too, that helped to keep his attraction to guys under everyone else's radar. He kept it to himself because if that was how people behaved with someone at school, what would happen outside?

And then a new student came in—a guy that Corrado watched from afar as he navigated the terrain of private, Catholic school. He wasn't sure what clued him in about the fact the guy was more like him than the other students, or even the one gay student in their school, but it happened.

Corrado learned a lot about himself from that. Bisexuality was fluid, and hard to explain to someone who wasn't like him. Being with a guy didn't change the fact he still liked the way the girl's legs looked in her skirt from the school down the road. Except to everyone else, it seemed like they didn't *get that.*

Gay was gay. Straight was straight. There was no in between. That's what people said.

Corrado was right in the fucking middle, trying to figure out what it meant, and what he should do. Stuck between a culture his family was deeply ingrained in that told him he would never *belong*—he couldn't *be*—and the choice of disappointing those around him when he didn't decide what they wanted for him.

He couldn't win.

Guzzis always won.

"Corrado, if you want me to say sex before marriage is not a sin, I can't do that," the priest said, dragging him from his thoughts.

"It's not the sex that worried me."

The man across the desk smiled softly. "No, I imagine you worried about the *other* bits."

He shrugged.

"If you want me to tell you homosexual attraction is not a sin, then I can't do that, either," the priest murmured.

Corrado let out a hard sigh, and readied to stand from the chair. The meeting was pointless. This wasn't news. He hadn't expected to get a different answer than the one he had.

He should have known better.

They all thought the same thing:

He was *wrong.*

He didn't belong.

He was different.

And because he was a Catholic, and the son of an Italian mafia boss, his problem was on a more prominent display for him about just how much he didn't fit in anywhere. He couldn't explain that to those around him without giving away his secret though.

"Sit down," Father Gene said.

Corrado passed the man a look. "I think we're good here, yeah?"

4

"If you didn't notice, allow me to point out to you what you missed about my statement," Father Gene replied, pointing a finger at the chair. Corrado sat his ass back down because he didn't have a choice, honestly. "I treated the sin of sex before marriage with the same tone and respect as I did homosexuality. Because sin is sin. And sin, no matter who is doing it, is all the same. The thing people seem to forget is that we do not get to weigh one sin against the other to bolster our own sanctity and pureness, Corrado. One sin does not trump another—sin is *sin*."

The man shrugged, adding, "And we are all sinners. That is what Christ teaches us. It is why Jesus died on the cross for *us*. Because He recognized we were all sinners, and we would all need forgiveness not once, but throughout our lifetime. People wrongly assume that their faith, and the way they live within the truth of their faith is the same way everyone else should, too, but they don't understand that isn't how it works."

Corrado chewed on his inner cheek. "How does it work, then?"

"Faith is a discipline for your own morality, Corrado, but it is not a right to dictate to others about *theirs*. And it would be ignorant for me to assume anything about someone else's relationship with God, or their right to faith. I know *my* relationship with God; it is strong, and I hear Him, drawing me to my path and calling. So, because of that, I share His words, and I celebrate them—I do not dictate His words like a tyrant from the pulpit. That defeats the purpose of the Bible, and of *Him*."

Corrado stared down at his lap, the gold Guzzi signet ring on his index finger glinting under the office light overheard. "So, what does that mean for me?"

"It means you are allowed to have faith, and your own relationship with God, and no one should expect to understand that relationship, or define it for themselves. They have their own faith to worry about before they need to even consider yours. It means you may be a sinner, and *no one* can or should tell you that your sins are worse than theirs because they don't sin like you do. It doesn't matter—sin is still *sin*. And yes, I believe you should aspire to live a life free of sin, but it's impossible. Even Jesus sinned, Corrado."

"Huh."

Out of the corner of his eye, he saw the priest smile again. "Not the answer you were expecting?"

"No."

"I'm sorry that people seem to interpret the Word in their own way without seeing the bigger picture. That's not your fault, Corrado. It is their own flaw."

He nodded. "It doesn't help me to make a choice, though."

Father Gene cleared his throat. "About your father, and business?"

"Yeah, all of that."

"Knowing Gian like I do, I think he will be happy as long as you are, young man. It is a matter of finding what makes *you* happy. Do you understand?"

Possibly.

"I think so," Corrado said.

"Good. Confession after the New Year. I expect to see you here. Also, I hear you're heading to Vegas this weekend—a trip for business with your father, yes?"

Yeah, a whole trip Corrado did not understand, if he were being honest. When Gian traveled for *la familiga*, he was quick to point out to his sons all the details of

5

the organization they would be seeing. He liked for his boys to learn, so they never stepped out of line when it counted or caused a problem.

This time, his father said nothing.

Corrado wasn't sure what to expect.

"Safe travels," the priest told him, "I'll pray for it."

"Thank you, Father."

Corrado pushed up from the chair, moving to leave. It was only Father Gene's voice behind him that made his steps hesitate.

"Don't I owe you, now?"

Seemingly lighter on his feet, and like he could do something with what he learned here today, Corrado had no idea what he forgot. Giving the priest a glance over his shoulder, he asked, "And what's that?"

"*Koi no yokan,*" the priest said, and Corrado's gaze darted to the tattoo on the man's inner elbow. "It's Japanese, and it doesn't have a meaning as much as *what* it is. A *feeling*, Corrado. It is the feeling upon meeting someone you know, eventually, you will fall in love with that person."

"Like love at first sight?"

"No. It's something else entirely."

"Is it a real thing?"

"It was for me," the man murmured.

He had a realization, then.

Like the priest said, they all sinned; their sins were simply different.

"You must tell me if it ever happens to you, too," Father Gene said. "Gian is waiting for you, isn't he? Have a blessed day."

2.

"What is this fucking place?"

Gian gave Christopher a look over his shoulder that quieted Corrado's twin *fast*. The oldest between the two of them, Chris, was far more likely to toe the line and behave. Corrado, on the other hand, seemed to find some sort of trouble wherever he went.

Life wasn't fun otherwise.

Today, both twins pushed their father's limits.

Chris side-eyed Corrado when their father's back was turned. If it were anyone else, he might have to ask what they were thinking in that moment. But it was his twin, and he never had to ask. When one shared the same face as someone else in the world, even their expressions could explain the things they didn't say.

The two took after their father in appearance—brown eyes flaked with gold, straight noses with a sharp slope, full lips that always seemed to be smirking, and dark brown hair that, when not cut into a shorter style, seemed to be fucking unmanageable. They took the angular shaped faces from their mother, Cara, though.

The rest?

All their dad.

Corrado shrugged to answer his brother's unspoken question about the building they were currently approaching. Deep in Nevada's rural, dry land, they might as well be in the middle of nowhere. There weren't even power lines out this far. It felt like they drove for hours after exiting their father's private jet only to turn off on a gravel road that still led to fucking *nowhere*. Until all of the sudden, a tan building—or rather, what seemed like several buildings, although it was hard to tell—started to form on the horizon.

A few trees towered around the building that, partly looked like a warehouse but also brought to mind the word *compound*, when Corrado thought about it. The plain cement walkway didn't give anything away about the place, but the very expensive cars parked any which way they wanted to stop next to the side of the building made him think something was happening here.

Out in the middle of the desert, apparently.

"Was that a fucking *tumbleweed?*" Corrado asked, his gaze drifting to the line of cars again and the dry item that skipped behind a black Hummer.

"If you two don't fix your mouths and questions," Gian murmured a few steps ahead. "Correct it before we go inside, *s'il vous plaît*."

"I'm just saying horror movies start like this, Papa."

Gian made a noise under his breath but said nothing else. At the front of the building, there were no windows. Just a wall of tan-colored brick and a black door. *Stark* black, really. One couldn't miss how it stood out blatantly compared to the rest of the yellow earth and walls surrounding it. Above the door rested a camera blinking with a red light.

Silently, Gian pulled a card from his pocket. Corrado glanced at it quickly, taking in the matte black cardstock, the wax seal on the back side with a cursive *L* stamped into it, and the white, classic lettering on the front.

What did it say?

The League, Corrado thought.

What in the hell was—

His thought process was interrupted by a buzzing noise that was loud enough to scare a scavenging bird sitting on top of the entrance door's eave. It squeaked before flying off to rest somewhere else. By the time Corrado glanced at his father, both Gian and Chris were already heading inside the dimmed corridor of the tan building.

Ha.

Just like how the fucking horror movies started.

"Are you coming?" Chris called back to him.

Corrado didn't think he had a choice, even if he didn't like the feeling this strange place left him with in his gut. Like a heavy weight had come to rest there, and he wasn't about to get rid of it anytime soon. He didn't pretend to understand all his father's business—being a criminal organization meant Gian did not dabble with just *one* thing. He had his hands in several pots, and Corrado was not aware of every single one of them.

Was this just another thing?

Why were *they* brought here?

Why not Marcus, their oldest brother?

He didn't consider Bene or Beni, his youngest brothers—another set of identical twins in their family; their mother's genes were strong, it seemed. Those two were wild, and there was no way they'd relax enough for something like this.

"Corrado!"

"I'm coming," he snapped.

Not that he wanted to. He had the distinct feeling that once he stepped inside this building, something was going to change. Maybe for him, or his brother or father, he didn't know. He just had that feeling, and Corrado wasn't the type to ignore his gut when it acted up.

Slipping inside the building, but not before shooting one last look over his shoulder at the outside world, his gaze took a second to adjust to the dim lighting just beyond the black door. A door, which, closed without prompting once Corrado was out of the way while doing that annoying buzzing sound again.

Gian slipped the black card he'd flashed at the camera back into his pocket before turning to his sons, his expression a mask of nothingness. He didn't give anything away before he said, "A couple of decades ago, I was approached by an old friend to … invest in something. He had a plan—he wanted a League of people who could do many things, and who had many skills. Did someone need a robbery done? He had a person for it. A hit in another country on a political figure? There was someone for that. A retrieval of someone that had been missing? He could make it happen."

His father rubbed his hands together and glanced down a long hallway that led to yet another black door with a camera blinking red overhead. "The idea was interesting because imagine what someone could do with that kind of ability at their fingertips. I invested immediately. I invested *a lot*. And it has been incredibly beneficial for me in the long run. Here is where those people are trained."

Beside Corrado, his twin blinked. "Like mercenaries?"

Gian chuckled, and waved a finger at the older of the two twins. "Mercenaries are choosey—they *pick* what they want to do or who they want to work for, and often, their work is for the greater good even if they are doing bad things."

"Assassins," Corrado said. "They train assassins here."

"Smart boy," his father returned. "We call it The League. This is the new complex that was finished three months ago, but I haven't had time to make the trip to see how it turned out. I thought the two of you might enjoy getting a peek at another part of this business because you're ... at an age to come into the folds more than you already are."

Gian said that like he honestly meant what he said—directed at *both* his sons—but he really only looked at Corrado. Was his father giving him another choice? Something other than what everyone else expected from him?

"This building is a living quarters, office, and training complex," Gian said. "Behave while we're here, *oui*, and try to stay out of trouble while I meet with my partner. Do you both understand me?"

Chris nodded first.

Corrado came second, but now, he didn't have that heavy feeling about this place like he did when he first stepped inside. He just wanted to know *more*.

• • •

Corrado was enthralled with the fact that the deeper they went into the complex, the more it seemed like a maze of living areas for *several* people. He saw those people, too, but they barely spoke as they moved from room to room, doing their business.

He stopped just outside of one room and peered in as his father headed further down the hall with a laugh.

"Dare," he heard Gian greet.

Corrado was busy staring at all the knives lining the wall inside the room in front of him. And when he meant a *wall* of knives, it was more like three walls. It wasn't all knives, he realized as he took one step inside to get a slightly better look. No, it was several different kinds of weapons, but all meant to be sharp and deadly.

At the far end of the room, which looked to be at least thirty feet long, if he were to guess, was a wall of targets. Wooden, mostly, with paper figures taped across them. One in particular still had an axe right through the head of the paper figure.

He swallowed hard as he neared the wall of black knives with sleek, shiny blades. He didn't know if his twin had continued to follow his father, or not. These knives were far more interesting to him than anything else at the moment.

Reaching up, he drifted his fingertips along the edge of a six-inch knife that he bet would be quite heavy in his hand. Wrapping his fingers around the hilt, he pulled the weapon down from its spot on the wall to get a better look at it. Eyeing the targets at the other end of the room, he wondered if he might be able to hit one—

"Careful with that. Rich hands aren't meant to throw those; they're meant to pay someone else to do it."

Corrado spun around so fast, the navy-blue walls of the room were nothing more than a blur to his eyes. He found the source of the voice standing in the doorway of the room. The man standing there took Corrado by surprise. Not because he was strikingly handsome—he was—but because he didn't look much older than Corrado's seventeen.

The guy arched a thick, dark eyebrow when Corrado stayed quiet. The action made his strong features and stormy blue eyes all the more intense. His thin lips pulled into a sly smirk, making his square jaw, covered with a few days' worth of stubble, tighten with the movement. A slight shake of his head made the shaggy hair that seemed a little too long around his ears fly in all directions. Corrado tried to shake off the strange hum buzzing over him the longer he stared at the guy. He wasn't the first good-looking person he'd run into, and he wouldn't be the last. He didn't need to feel stupid or speechless just *because* this guy looked half decent.

Except, that wasn't it at all.

It was the way the man *looked* at him. The way his gaze drifted over Corrado with the slowness that reminded him of a predator, maybe. Like this guy had just found prey, and he was considering whether the kill would be worth it.

It *irked* Corrado.

Irritated him like nothing fucking else.

He wasn't *prey*.

"What did you just say?" Corrado asked.

The guy laughed and tipped his head to the side as he pointed at the knife in Corrado's hands. "Be careful, we don't need you cutting yourself because you wouldn't know what to do with a knife unless you were paying someone else to do it for you. Clear enough?"

Okay.

Yeah.

Corrado wasn't even going to act like that was a comment he could brush off as though it hadn't been said at all. This guy wasn't even *trying* to be subtle about it; he was outright insulting Corrado, and with a fucking smile at the same time.

"Do I know you?" he asked.

The guy peeked over his shoulder, looking at something down the hall. "Not yet, but you will."

That humming sensation was back again. It kind of pissed Corrado off that the guy could be so dismissive and insulting to him, while at the same time, acting like he had better things to do than stand there and have a conversation with him. He remembered his father's warning about behaving, but he was *very* close to telling this guy to fuck off right before he busted his mouth for those comments while he was at it.

"How about," Corrado started to say, "you go find someone else to—"

"Alessio."

The guy's gaze drifted back to Corrado, his eyebrow still arched high like he didn't have a damn to give, as a new voice sounded right outside the doorway of the room. Almost as soon as the voice spoke, a new face came to the doorway, and clapped a hand on the guy's shoulder. Right behind him stood Corrado's father.

Gian stayed back a couple of steps, though.

He didn't intrude.

"Introducing yourself, Alessio?" the man asked.

Alessio.

Corrado decided right then that he hated that name. And the man it belonged to, as well. The problem was, when Alessio turned his gaze back on Corrado, the humming was back. He couldn't look away from the ocean of blue that stared back at him, or the way that as much as this guy rubbed him wrong … he wanted to know *why.*

Or anything about him at all.

"You're not causing trouble, are you, Corrado?" his father asked out in the hallway.

"Define trouble." Alessio chuckled. "Is he allowed to play with knives where someone can't keep an eye on him at the same time?"

The man next to Alessio smacked him in the back of the head, making him glower back at him.

"Fuck off, Dare," Alessio muttered.

"Play nice, Les."

He looked back to Corrado again.

"But why, though? This is way more fun."

Fuck him.

And the fact Corrado found he liked it.

Yeah, fuck that, too.

The other man, *Dare,* shook his head. "All right, Les, since you're feeling chatty today, you can take Corrado around and show him the rest of the complex while I talk business with Gian."

Alessio scowled. "I didn't volunteer to be some mafia *principe's* babysitter for the day."

Dare smirked. "I'm sorry. Did I preface that with, *if you feel up to it and it pleases your spoiled fucking ass to do it?* No, so do it."

"Fine."

"Did you introduce yourself properly?"

"No," Alessio said. "Because I didn't think there was a point."

Dare sighed and waved between the two boys. "Alessio, you already know Corrado Guzzi … or you know what I told you about today. Corrado, meet the pain in my ass, also known as Alessio Sorrento."

"Thanks for that."

"But not a lie," Dare replied. "And now my good deed for the day is done. Gian, do you think these two will be fine alone?"

Corrado's father smiled a bit, amusement playing in his gaze as he nodded. "I think they'll be fine while we chat."

"Good, let's begin."

Alessio passed Corrado another look as Gian and Dare drifted away from the doorway, disappearing altogether. "Are you going to stand there all day, or what?"

Corrado didn't move. "I'm not doing anything with you."

"Yeah, that's not going to work. Dare said what he said."

"Fuck him, *and* you."

"Oh, he *swears*, too."

Corrado's jaw flexed with his annoyance. "What is your problem?"

Alessio looked him over again, his gaze slow and deliberate. All over again, Corrado felt that same flare of frustration and interest all rolled into one. It warred inside his mind, clashing together and making him want to punch this guy in the mouth just because.

"Do you like what you see, or …?"

"Why, because I stare?" Alessio asked.

"Because your stare *lingers*. So, that means you either like what you see, or you're trying to decide if I'm a threat. I think you know who I am, and you think you know something about me."

Corrado replaced the knife on the wall, and headed for the door, only stopping directly in front of Alessio. He knew what this guy was doing—trying to size him up, but also make him feel out of place. Screw that noise. He didn't know his purpose for being here, but he wasn't going to run because of *Alessio*.

He leaned in close to Alessio, but the guy didn't move back an inch. If anything, he stayed firm in his spot, those blue eyes blazing with the same interest Corrado was sure reflected in his own gaze. "Let me be the first to fix that mistake of yours—you don't know fuck all about me, Alessio."

"I prefer Les."

Corrado tipped his chin up. "*And?*"

"And right now I'm wondering what your face might look like if I roughened it up a little. Do you box?"

He *blinked*.

"What?"

Alessio shrugged. "I didn't stutter."

He hadn't.

"Do you want to get your ass kicked?" Corrado asked. "Because that's what'll happen if we spar."

The man *laughed*.

And all Corrado could think was that he looked fucking amazing doing it. That smirk on his face? Entirely bad for him given the way his chest tightened at the sight of it.

Oh, yeah.

He was in a lot of trouble here.

It all started and ended with Alessio.

He knew it by the annoyance still trickling through his bloodstream, but also the humming that continued to buzz over his skin. A part of him wanted to tell his guy to fuck off somewhere, and another part wanted to find out all he could about him. He had a feeling the more he learned about Alessio, the less annoyed Corrado would feel, and the more interesting the man would become.

All it took were a few words, and blue eyes. Something about Alessio Sorrento drew Corrado in and made every single one of his nerves turn on in a good and bad way. He wanted to run away as much as he wanted to stay right there and do it all over again.

Was this what the priest meant?

Was this *koi no yokan*?

Because it felt like something.

It felt like change.

It felt important.

Well, fuck that noise.

Corrado didn't like it at all.

"Guess we'll see what you can do, *principe*," Alessio said, grinning just enough to show off his white teeth. "Or, I'll have a lot of fun watching you try."

3.

By the age of ten, Alessio had learned the most important lesson he figured life had to teach him. It wasn't an easy one, or even *nice*. Very little about life was easy or nice, though. That lesson was simple, too.

Blood didn't always make family.

When he was two, his father died from a heart attack. A man he never really remembered, and only vaguely knew from the stories of others. Maximo Sorrento—mafia Don to a Cosa Nostra faction controlling Vegas, who also seemed to have a taste for women who were a fraction of his age. Like Alessio's mother, Elizabeth.

His father dying wasn't the memory that stood out to him the most, but rather how everyone else treated his mother, the man's mistress, after the fact. She'd lived comfortably, Alessio had been told, cared for and kept because she was a favorite of Maximo's, and she had given him a son, even if the boy was illegitimate.

Then, he was no more.

No, Alessio didn't remember his father dying, and he didn't have many feelings about it, but he vividly recalled the years that followed the death. Like how his mother spiraled, her young life wasted with every pill she popped, and every needle she put into her veins. Empty bottles littering the floor and the faint smell of old cigarette smoke accompanied Alessio's dreams every time he closed his eyes.

That was how he remembered his mother.

And that he never mattered to her.

Whether it was because she was so entirely heartbroken that she had lost Maximo, despite the fact he was three times her age, or because she had lost her status and importance without him there to give it to her … she forgot about Alessio in the process.

He was ten when his mother overdosed.

Ten when he buried her.

Yet, it felt like he'd been in the process of burying her for years before that. Life had a funny way of reminding the forgotten and the neglected at the worst of times that they weren't worth very much to the people who weren't faced with their struggle every single day. That had never been more apparent to Alessio than after his mother's death.

That was when Dare came in.

And Cree, another high-ranking member of The League.

Alessio was never sure *when* they found him after his mother's death, because the days passed by in a confusing blur that he'd rather not revisit, but they were a saving grace for him if there ever was one. Dare, having known Alessio's mother *before* Maximo, took him in.

For all purposes, Dare was his family.

The League, his home.

Here, he struggled *more*. Here, he learned to be something and someone. Behind these walls, he was given a purpose and stability. He was not the forgotten bastard son of a man who he didn't remember, or the child of an addict who died not knowing her son would be the one to find her cold on the floor the next morning.

Here, he was better.

At seventeen, almost eighteen now, Alessio spent much of his life feeling as though he didn't belong to any one person or place. Until Dare, Cree, and The League. He held this place so close to that thing in his chest that people called a heart, no one would ever understand. If someone thought to fuck with it, he was going to *rip them apart*.

And so, it pissed Alessio off to see some privileged prick like Corrado Guzzi walking around the place with a curious eye like he had any business being there in the first place. Sure, Dare was smart enough to explain to Alessio the week before the Guzzis arrival that Gian would be visiting to check out the new complex, with two of his five sons, but it hadn't bothered him until he saw one of those sons in that training room.

One of many training rooms here, really.

People didn't get an *inside* look at The League. If someone was brought in, it was because they were a client using one of the assassins for a job, or it was a prospect who had signed on to be trained.

No one was allowed here.

It was *his* home.

Except, there came the fucking Guzzis like they owned the place, and that just rubbed him all kinds of wrong. But especially Corrado—who thought to speak to Alessio like the two were on equal footing in some kind of way. Like he wasn't any different from him.

They were not at all the same.

He doubted a rich, spoiled mafia *principe* like Corrado had ever understood struggle, and The League certainly wasn't a place made for someone like him. They weren't here to *coddle* men and women—they were here to break them.

So yeah, the guy just rubbed him wrong.

The other thing pissing him off currently?

The fact he found Corrado attractive, and that he might like the guy even more if he could shut him the fuck up by either kissing him, or stuffing something in his mouth. Like maybe his cock …

"Are we even supposed to be in here doing this?" Corrado asked from inside the boxing ring.

Alessio made a harsh noise under his breath—the only sign of his irritation, really. He suspected Corrado believed it was because he questioned Alessio's choice to have them spar for fun in the gym section of the complex, but that wasn't it at all.

It was that he'd interrupted a nice picture.

He wasn't about to admit that out loud, though. Thing was, just because *he* felt attraction to someone didn't mean they felt the same way. Sometimes, it was obvious, and he could tell when a guy liked one thing or the other—or *both*. Maybe it was the way a guy would look him over, or when a hand on his shoulder lingered a beat longer than a straight guy would when it came to friendly actions. But with Corrado, he didn't know.

It was fucked up.

He hated him on sight.

And he didn't hate him at the same time.

It didn't help that Corrado *was* attractive in a way most men weren't. Something that Alessio recognized about him straight away—an air of confidence and cockiness followed him around whether he knew it or not. Like he'd been *born* with it. Most people had to learn that shit. And that was before Alessio got too detailed in Corrado's physical features, from the strong lines of his face that made up an angular jaw line, to the dark brown eyes that didn't seem to give anything away, not even when he *smirked*.

Classically handsome.

Disgustingly so, really.

Add that to the whole confidence shit and Alessio had a big problem here. Mostly, the fact that he noticed *at all*.

Dare was always clear when it came to Alessio and relationships or sex. As long as it didn't fuck up The League and the shit they were doing here, he was free to explore and do what he wanted. He couldn't remember how old he was when he figured out he liked boys as much as he liked girls—nine, maybe?

He was lucky that he didn't find confusion or pain in his sexuality swinging both ways like he knew some did when they realized they were bisexual. Here, he had been free to explore and find out what it meant to be a sexual being with varied interests. No one ever stepped in to shame him as long as it was consensual, and he was being safe. That was all Dare ever cared about when it came to Alessio.

"Are you listening to me?" Corrado asked.

Alessio clenched his teeth to stay quiet as he finished wrapping up his fists before slipping the leather, fingerless gloves overtop. Turning to find Corrado lingering in the far corner of the ring, ready to go, he used his teeth to tighten the wrist straps on the gloves.

"Are you used to just saying something, and people *jumping* to give you what you want?" Alessio asked back.

Corrado's brow dipped before he scowled.

Fuck.

Why'd he look good doing that, too?

Alessio ignored the clenching of his gut as he stepped up into the ring and dipped under the ropes to get into position. He figured this sparring match probably wouldn't end well for Corrado, all things considered. He doubted the guy knew he'd been training with The League from the time he was twelve.

Weapons.

Fighting.

Recon.

Killing.

All of it, he could do.

And he was only seventeen.

He doubted Corrado could say the same.

"What is it that gets under your skin the most?" Corrado asked back. "The fact that I have money, or the fact you don't?"

Alessio sucked air through his teeth.

Damn.

That was a good one.

Pretty boy mafia prince could cut with words, and Alessio liked that way more than he was willing to admit. His respect notched up a bit—this would have been incredibly boring for him if after everything, Corrado just laid down and took the shit Alessio threw at him. When someone became uninteresting to him, Alessio was quick to move the fuck on.

Not right now, though.

"You assume I don't have money," Alessio returned.

He did.

Probably not as much as Corrado, but he had enough to be more than comfortable. The longer he stayed with The League, the more money he would have, too. Not that money had ever been a motivating factor for his choice to train here. He'd gone for years without money—it was just paper to get someone by, nothing more.

He'd be fine either way.

Corrado shrugged before he tugged his T-shirt up over his head, and then tossed it to the side of the ring. Even from all the way across the ring, Alessio couldn't help but admire the hard lines that made up Corrado's body—or how those muscles shifted as he moved from one foot to the other.

Shit.

Yeah, he needed to move away from that thought.

Now.

"I say it," Corrado returned, "because you keep needling at me like something about me pisses you off. Maybe it's my money, privilege … my last name. Which one is it?"

Nope.

He wasn't falling down that rabbit hole.

Alessio grinned, removing his own shirt and enjoying the way Corrado's gaze drifted over the ink on his arms, and the Bible passage written in script down his rib cage. His stare lingered a beat too long, but he wasn't going to point it out to the man, not when he still wasn't *sure.* He waved two fingers at Corrado as if to tell him *let's go.* "Don't worry, I'll go easy on you."

"No need. I have four brothers. If you think you're the first person who thought they could kick my ass because you had a problem with me, you're not even the *fourth.*"

"Do you annoy your brothers just by *being* there as much as you do me?"

Corrado smirked and cocked his head to the side. "Do I annoy you, or unsettle you?"

That irked Alessio like nothing else.

Because the asshole wasn't wrong.

Back to the sparring, he figured. It was better than where his mind was trying to go, not to mention the way he was sure Corrado was looking at him. Like maybe he didn't need to wonder if the guy swung both ways like Alessio did …

"No cheap shots," Alessio warned.

"But your face is fair game, right?"

"Just like yours, Corrado."

Corrado nodded. "Fair enough."

Alessio intended for this little sparring match to be a quick thing for him—a way for him to knock Corrado down a few pegs, and nothing more. Yet, when the two young men met at the middle of the ring and tapped fingerless gloves together, he knew this wasn't going to be easy or clean between them at all.

They'd barely even moved their hands apart before Corrado came in with a jab to Alessio's right kidney. Who the fuck knew, but maybe he thought Corrado wouldn't know how to throw a half decent punch to save his life.

Ha.

He'd been so wrong.

That knocked the wind out of him.

"*Shit,*" he grunted, backing up a quick step.

Corrado laughed, his tongue coming up in his sneer to touch his upper lip as he stepped back and forth from foot to foot.

He just looked *too* arrogant.

Too confident.

Too good.

It all looked *too damn good* to Alessio.

A challenge, even.

And fuck him, he liked those.

"Just one cheap shot," Corrado said, "don't fault me for doing it. You deserved it."

Alessio nodded and pointed his fist at his opponent. "You're going to regret that when I fuck up your face, asshole."

"But then what would you stare at when you think I'm not looking, Alessio?"

Yep.

So entirely fucked.

"I told you, it's *Les.*"

Corrado nodded. "That's nice."

All right, Alessio was done fucking around now. He wasn't wrong—Corrado didn't give up easily. And yeah, he didn't have the sharply honed skills with hand-to-hand combat like Alessio did, but he could still hold his own. He wasn't so stupid that he didn't know to protect his face, and he was quick on his feet, moving from one side of the mat to the other when he really wanted to get Alessio pissed off.

They were supposed to keep it clean, and Alessio fully intended on doing that until he realized *this* wasn't going to teach Corrado shit. So, when he had the chance and was close enough after tossing hits back and forth for a few minutes, he made his move. Spinning a bit on his left heel, he raised his right foot from the mat, and came back around with a roundhouse that landed flat to the middle of Corrado's chest.

The force of the kick sent him hitting the mat, all the air rushing out of his chest in a loud *whoosh* at the same time. Alessio might have enjoyed the sight of the other man on the mat, blinking like he was trying to gain his bearings and figure out how this happened to him, but he didn't get the chance.

Corrado swung his leg out, and swept Alessio's feet right out from under him. In the next breath, he found *himself* on the mat, too. A rookie mistake, really. He never should have gotten close to a man on the ground unless he was willing to get down there with him.

Lesson number *one*.

Not that Alessio had the time to reflect on his mistake. Corrado had rolled over just as fast to pin him to the mat as fists rained down on his face—one after the other; *smack, smack, smack, smack*. The guy was fucking relentless, never letting up for even a second. Through his gloved hands, Alessio was struck by the intensity that sharpened Corrado's features as he focused on his goal.

Alessio, that was.

And beating the hell out of him.

He'd be a damned liar if he said that hardness roughening the strong lines of Corrado's face as he clenched his teeth—blood dripping down his full lips from an earlier punch compliments of Alessio—and the muscles of his arms and shoulders flexing with every punch didn't *do something* for him.

Because it did.

Wicked things.

Sinful fucking things.

Godly things.

Alessio used a common maneuver that he'd been taught to flip the two of them over by wrapping his legs around Corrado's back. Now, with him on top, he focused his efforts on getting the image of Corrado on top of him out of his mind and replacing it with the sight of him beating the hell out of him, instead.

Not that it worked.

Of course, it didn't fucking work.

And unlike Alessio, Corrado didn't use a move to try and right himself again, or to get the upper hand. Because he wasn't trained, and he didn't know *how* to get out of this. Instead, his body arched upward, all of his weight pressing against Alessio as he tried to force the man off. It didn't work. Just like when he used his knees to push against Alessio's stomach, it too was a dead effort.

All it served to do was get their bodies closer.

His fists rained down.

Corrado protected his face and tried harder to get away.

Still, hard lines met hard lines. Alessio was hyper aware of the way Corrado felt moving under him, never mind the fact that *something* felt hard against the curve of the backside of his thigh.

Alessio pushed his fingerless gloves hard against Corrado's chest, his breaths coming out hard and fast because *fuck* … why was his body this tense—this *hot*? Beneath him, Corrado panted, too, his bloodstained teeth still clenched as he glared up at Alessio.

Corrado shifted again.

Alessio felt *that* again.

Time slowed, or that's what it felt like. There was no hiding the erection he was sitting on, or the fact that his own cock was pressing against the seam of his jeans. He swore if he moved again—or Corrado, for that matter—he was going to explode.

What in the hell just happened?

"I fucking *knew* it," Alessio whispered as Corrado tried to force him off again, but it only served to have the ridge of his erection pressing against his body again. "*I knew it.*"

Corrado's gaze darted away. "Get off me."

He would have.

But he leaned in close, instead.

A bloody sneer answered him back.

"Do you really want me to?" Alessio asked.

Corrado let out a hard breath. "*Fuck you.*"

He kissed him, then.

Brutal, and fast.

Unforgiving.

He didn't know what made him do it. God knew Alessio had more control than this, but here he was, and he couldn't really complain when Corrado answered him back with a kiss of his own that had his whole body feeling like it was on *fire.*

Corrado tasted like blood and *heat.* His tongue lashed against Alessio's without shame, his fingers coming up to drag against the muscles of his chest like he wanted more. He understood that need—it was currently driving him insane, too.

There was nothing easy about the kiss.

Nothing *soft.*

No sweetness.

It felt like war.

Teeth biting his lower lip, and stubble dragging across his skin. It all felt like a fight he wasn't going to win but fuck him if he didn't *try.* Kissing never felt like war before—it didn't feel like his body was going to rip itself in half if he didn't *get what he wanted right now.*

Until this moment. With *Corrado.*

It was then that Alessio should have known what was going to happen here between him, and Corrado when this was all said and done. Corrado Guzzi was a fucking problem. One he was never going to escape.

Then, someone cleared their throat.

Ah, fuck.

4.

A throat clearing would have made Corrado jump back from the man he was kissing *fast*. But not Alessio. No, he didn't jump to get off Corrado, or even act like whoever had interrupted them bothered him in the slightest.

Before he did climb off Corrado on the mat, he pushed his gloved fists one more time against his chest and cocked a brow like he was daring him to *do something*. More than anything, Corrado wanted to do exactly that, but given the fact he was still hard under his jeans, and his mouth now tasted like *Alessio* and blood, he didn't think it would work out very well for him.

Corrado drew in another sharp breath, because even as Alessio left him alone on the mat to go to the other side of the ring, it didn't matter. His body still felt the man—his weight keeping him down, hard lines pressing into his, and those lips working savagely against his own. His tongue snaked out to run along his lower lip, and he *willed* his raging erection to go down just a little bit before he moved.

Pride was a bitch.

Corrado had too much of it.

It was only the sound of footsteps approaching the ring that finally made Corrado roll over to his knees and stand up from the mat. He shot a look over his shoulder to find Alessio at the other side of the ring, slipping on a T-shirt like he didn't have a care in the world. That irked Corrado a bit, too. How could he be so flippant about what just happened?

His fucking heart was *still* racing.

Christopher came up to the side of the ring and rested his arms along the ropes. His brother arched one eyebrow at him, a mirror of his own reflection right there staring back at him. He didn't need his brother to ask the question to *know* what Chris was asking him. *What in the hell was that?*

Corrado could count on two fingers the amount of people who knew he was bi. His brother was one of them because one day, Chris outright asked, and Corrado had never been able to lie to his twin for some fucking reason. The two weren't very much alike despite their identical features—Chris was more reserved, and Corrado wasn't; his brother tended to think things through, and Corrado went in full steam on something if he wanted to do it.

But lying?

Nope.

He never could.

If Chris didn't know he was lying right away, then Corrado felt like shit and eventually just spilled the truth to his twin, anyway. Because wasn't life just fucking grand like that?

Chris cleared his throat when Corrado stayed silent as he reached for his shirt hanging off the ropes of the ring. "Was that supposed to happen?"

"Mind your business."

"I am—you're my business."

21

Corrado shifted from foot to foot, punching his arms through the shirt before yanking it down over his head. All the while, he avoided his twin's stare like the plague. "Just … forget about it, Chris."

"All right, whatever. Papa's down the hall talking with that Dare guy."

"What were you doing?"

"Trailing behind you and …" Chris tipped his head in Alessio's direction, but Corrado refused to look that way. Not when he was still attempting to calm the semi hard-on he sported. "That one there. Did you forget I was here, too, or …?"

"*Vaffanculo*," Corrado muttered.

Chris smirked. "No judgement, if you're doing what you wanna do and all, I'm just saying you're not usually that obvious about it, you know?"

"Would you fucking knock it off?"

Laughter echoed from his brother.

Chris was enjoying this too much.

Heat flooded Corrado's face. He didn't even know it was possible for him to blush, but he was pretty sure his face was red. It wasn't *what* he had been doing that embarrassed him, but rather, that someone was there to see it. His *twin*, for that matter.

Not that Chris ever cared.

A part of Corrado knew his family didn't give a shit because his twin was a good indicator of how the rest of them would react if he outed the fact he was bi. It wasn't so much *them* as it was the people around them that concerned him at the end of the day.

Being the son of a criminal boss meant Corrado had to factor other people into their lives, as well. People who didn't share their blood or live in their home but would still think they had some right to speak about his sexuality either way. And it was those people who he didn't care to let in on his business.

Because they wouldn't shut the fuck up about it. Or, they wouldn't leave his father alone, or worse, blame him for something that no one could help. Which just pissed Corrado off more because *he didn't need help*. He wasn't sick, and something wasn't wired differently inside his head.

To them, he would be wrong.

To them, he would be broken.

That's what they had taught him.

Except he couldn't be any of those things when he was just born this way. And so, he adopted his simple strategy about it all. If nobody thought to ask, then he didn't have fuck all to tell them. His family included. They could assume, and he was fine with that, but he wasn't offering the information up willingly.

"Round two another day, Guzzi?"

Corrado couldn't even hide the way Alessio's voice from across the ring affected him as it reached his spot. His back tensed, and all over again, he could feel the man's mouth coming down on his, and the way his fingers had dug into his chest as those fingerless leather gloves came down against his body. His jaw clenched, and outside the ring, Chris raised an eyebrow again, clearly not missing Corrado's odd behavior.

"Don't," he warned his twin.

His brother just laughed, hit the ropes of the ring with his hand, and stepped back like he was done with the conversation.

"Round two another day," came a new, deep voice.

Corrado spun around fast to find where the voice had come from. Parts of the gym were shrouded in darkness, the different lines of machines barely visible in the shadows as Alessio had only flicked on two light switches instead of the other fifteen. At the very far right end of the gym, a man leaning against the side of a treadmill watched Corrado.

His hair, a sleek black and braided, fell over broad shoulders. He'd hooked one leg over the other lazily as he used the machine to keep him upright, arms folded over his chest. Corrado couldn't see the man's eye color until he moved closer—a dark russet brown. It complimented the golden brown of his skin, too.

"Fuck, *Cree*," Alessio said, giving the man a look as he neared the ring. "You could have let me know you were in here when I first came in."

Cree didn't bother to give Alessio his attention. "But why, so I could miss the show?"

That time, it was Alessio's turn to flush with a reddish color. Corrado would have laughed except he realized while he had also been on the mat, in a very compromising position. So, that *show* included him.

He chose to shut his mouth.

Cree pointed at Corrado. "*You.*"

He stiffened. "What about me?"

"You have a lot of anger, no?"

"What?"

The man used a closed fist to hit the middle of his chest, coming to a stop right outside the ropes of the ring. "Here, you have a lot of anger. And no place to do anything with it."

Corrado quieted.

Cree wasn't wrong.

Chris cleared his throat on the other side of the ring, but Corrado wasn't paying any attention to his brother because now, something else had his attention.

"How do you know that just by watching me?" Corrado asked.

Cree grinned a bit. "A talent."

"That's a non-answer."

"Smart, too," he said, finally directing a comment at Alessio. "And someone willing to put up with your shit. Congratulations on finding *that*, Les. I never thought you would."

Alessio opened his mouth, but Cree was quick to put up a hand to shut the other man up before he could start. He snapped his jaw shut with an audible click, which made Cree smirk before he turned back to Corrado.

What just happened?

He felt like he missed something.

"Do you know, Corrado," he said, tipping his head in Alessio's direction, "that this one has a tendency to ... pick fights when he wants attention? Oh, he won't *say that*. He doesn't admit that's what he does." Cree pointed at his temple and narrowed his eyes with a suspicious smile as he added, "But I know because I watch him a lot. I watch *everyone* a lot. It's how I know what someone needs to break and make them."

"Would you fuck off some—"

"Quite enough from you," Cree told Alessio without even looking away from Corrado. "And *you*, Corrado, you have a lot of anger and nowhere to do something with it. I think you would learn a lot here."

Corrado blinked. "What?"

"I thought what I said was quite clear."

"Cree, you can't be fucking serious."

"I am," he returned to Alessio, "but it's not about you, so shut up."

"*Cree.*"

The native man didn't turn away from Corrado even as Alessio fumed at the other side of the ring. Corrado felt stupid—shocked, really.

"You mean here, at The League?"

Cree shrugged. "Why not?"

Alessio made a harsh noise under his breath, taking Cree's attention away from Corrado for a second. "If you think some privileged fuck from—"

The man waved a hand at Alessio like he was dismissing him as he said, "Yes, I can see you have some issues you need to handle, too, Les. I'll come back to you."

That shut Alessio up *fast*.

It almost made Corrado want to ask what it was about Cree that clearly put Alessio on edge, but really, he figured he already knew. The man just seemed to know what everyone's bullshit was before they could even open their mouth and try to lie about it.

Cree came back to Corrado. "Well, what do you think?"

"Corrado," Chris said from behind him.

He stayed silent.

Considering …

"And what's happening in here?"

Corrado didn't need to turn around to know his father had stepped into the gym. He continued staring at Cree, all the while, thinking about the man's offer. Cree answered for him.

"Actually," Cree said, looking to the side of Corrado's legs from his position on the floor below the ring to speak to Gian from across the room, "I was making an offer to your son."

Gian didn't miss a beat. "What kind of offer?"

"To join The League."

"Cree," came another voice.

Dare.

The guy his father had been talking to earlier.

Dare's simple statement of Cree's name sounded like a warning, but clearly not one Cree intended to heed as he only stared between Gian and Corrado.

"Corrado?"

At his father's call of his name, he glanced over his shoulder. For some reason, he was worried then that he might find disappointment in his father's eyes. Even though Gian never outright told Corrado what he had to do—be a made man like him, or anything else he wanted to be—a part of him still wondered what his father *really* felt about it all.

"Yeah, Papa?"

Gian smiled, though it was faint and barely there at all. "It's your choice. It's always been, *fils*."

Cree clapped his hands loudly. "Great. And what do you say, Corrado?"

It was only his twin speaking up from behind Corrado that broke his stretch of silence after the question

"If he does this, I do it," Chris said.

"Chris," Corrado muttered, not bothering to turn around to face his twin, "you don't have—"

"I said what I said."

He sighed.

Stubborn.

That's what Chris was.

Yes, they were different.

They were still the same, too.

Chris would *never* let his twin go into something without being there to do it, too. Even if the idea of that thing wasn't something that interested him at all.

Cree leaned to the side, just enough to get Chris in his sights before he straightened again to stare up at Corrado in the ring. The man nodded once. "All right, I've never trained twins before. This could be … interesting."

"*Cree*," Dare said again.

"Yeah, yeah." Cree didn't move, still *waiting*. "Corrado?"

"All right," Corrado said quietly.

Cree smiled widely and wagged a finger at him. "Remember this was what you wanted, okay?"

What did that mean?

5.

"Gian, I don't think you understand—"

"I understand very well what it means for them, Dare."

Silence echoed from within the office. Alessio, standing where the two men inside couldn't see him, used the wall as a prop for his shoulder to rest against as he waited for the conversation to continue on.

Dare sighed heavily, and hands smacked on something solid. "The training is intensive, and—"

"We've gone over the training. I know what happens."

"If you would stop interrupting me, that would be great."

"By all means …"

Dare grumbled under his breath. "The training—it's going to break them at *every* level, Gian. Mentally, physically … that's the purpose of it, for us to find their limits, shatter them, and then teach them there is no limit. They're seventeen."

"Nearly eighteen, but all right. And how old is the one Corrado followed around today?"

"That is not the point."

"How old?"

"Alessio will be eighteen soon, but—"

"Mmm, I know you're going to say he's been with you and Cree from the time he was ten, but you're not going to lie right to my face and say you've been training him since then, will you? I didn't take you to be an ignorant man, Dare."

"He started the intensive training at fifteen, but he watched others and participated in different things from the time he was about twelve, yes."

"And is he out on assignments yet?"

"No," Dare replied.

"Why?"

"My choice. Cree thinks he's ready either way."

"But again, *why?*" Gian asked again, his tone sharpening the word. "Because I am sure the fifty percent that I fronted on this venture of yours allows me the right to ask a question and *promises* you will give me a truthful answer. Unless I missed something in that paperwork, and if so, by all means … correct me, Dare."

"Gian, this isn't about Alessio."

"I think it is about Alessio in the way that you are looking at him the way I look at my boys. And as I understand your relationship with Cree—"

"Could we not? *No one* gets the right to discuss my personal business. You included, regardless of how much money you have in this company."

Gian cleared his throat. "You know that's not an issue for me. I meant to say, I know that with *that*, and the fact you both have had Alessio for so long, he feels like a son to you. I understand *why*. *You* have chosen to keep him here for as long as you can—yes?"

The sound of Dare swallowing was audible. "Well, you're not *wrong*."

A chuckle echoed.

"I didn't think so," Gian replied quietly. "When will he be put out on assignments?"

"Cree decided eighteen."

Gian made a noise under his breath. "*Cree* decided?"

"I don't want to talk about it."

"And what about the auction, then? What will happen to him with that?"

"Another fight—I settled that one. He'll make the choice for himself after he's done a few independent jobs. If he wants to go up on the auction for a term of four years to do jobs for a specific client, then he can."

"Yet, the other assassins you've trained here don't get that choice at all. Or did I miss something from the last time we talked about the process here? Because I am positive *every* prospect you and Cree begin training sign the same contract—they *will* go up for a term of four years in the auctions the company holds, and then it's renegotiated after, yes?"

"How did this fucking conversation turn around on me? Because I am sure that's not what we were discussing two minutes ago, Gian."

"Ah, so now you understand."

"I beg your pardon?"

"Now you understand, Dare." Gian laughed under his breath. "See, you became defensive as soon as I pointed out the emotional side of your attachment here—to a specific person, sure, but it's still there nonetheless. Because *that's* how you feel about your boy, blood or not. And you expect me to have the same reaction about mine, but you're wrong."

"I—"

"I'm not finished. You seem to think," Gian said, his tone remaining level, "that I would pull rank on my sons simply *because* they are my sons. While I don't actually expect their mother to be happy about this decision, if only because that means at least a year she'll be without them, I don't have an opinion one way or another. If this is what Chris and Corrado want to do, then this is what they'll do. They have independent minds, I made sure of that. I wanted all my boys to be able to think for themselves. I love them, but they have to make themselves into something. I can't do it for them."

"Well ..."

"Hmm?"

Dare grunted under his breath. "Cree says Corrado is the best fit here. Because of his temperament, and the fact he seems willing to learn."

"And Chris?"

A laugh answered that back.

"What?" Gian asked. "Just say it."

"He says Chris's reasons are clearly self—"

"Don't call Chris selfish. He is *a lot* of things, but out of all of them, selfish is not one of them. He is the most *selfless* of all my children, although I never understood why."

"Okay, then I will rephrase. He thinks he is only doing this because of his twin, and not because he actually wants to. Rather, because he wants to do what his twin does, if you get what I am saying."

"So again, selfless."

"I will let Cree know that *selfish* is the wrong choice of word for Christopher."

"*Merci.*"

"I won't ask again, but I want to be sure you understand what will happen after you leave tonight."

"I understand. It's what they want, Dare."

"Or is it—"

"Barring Christopher, let me point out something about Corrado I am sure you and *Cree* don't know—since he's the one who feeds you information, and you get in your feelings about it. Corrado has never fit in anywhere with the rest of us. He's been under my feet, and men like me, for his entire life, and yet … he's not found the space where he belongs. He's not a normal boy, and he won't live a normal life. He can't when he has just a little too much of me and my blood in him, if you understand."

"So, what does that mean?"

"He might find where he belongs here, and if he has to sacrifice to do it, then so be it."

"And the other one—Chris?"

Gian made a dismissive sound. "Selfless. It's his path to choose, Dare."

"I see."

"Have we said all we need to say, then?"

A chair squeaked before Dare replied, "It seems so. They've already signed the contracts, but I haven't yet. I will now. It'll begin tonight once you're gone."

"I expect the same for them that you have given to Alessio," Gian added. "Put in as an addendum to their contracts for me—I *will* look for it."

"Which is what?"

"Independent contractors for The League—they only choose the auction route if they want when training is finished. If they decline the auctions when it is all said and done, I will pay the training fees to recoup the costs."

"Cree does want to make a team that he can use for his contacts."

"So, that's a yes, then?"

"That's a yes, Gian. I will add it in."

Gian hummed before adding lower, "He's scared of water."

"Which one?"

"Christopher. He almost drowned when he was two—slipped off the side of the dock at the small lake at his uncle's vacation home. A relative jumped in after him, but it was touch and go. The tank and the dark room are phase one for training, correct?"

"You expect him to react badly."

"I'm explaining why he might, yes."

"And yet you're still willing to allow him—"

"It's what he wants."

"But without knowing what will happen, Gian."

"He's not stupid, like Corrado isn't, as well. He has to know *anything* is a possibility here. I think … it might help him to control that fear of his because I know it's overwhelming to him at times."

"All right. I'll be in touch, Gian."

"I expect it—regular updates, *oui?*"

"Absolutely."

Alessio didn't have time to move away from the doorway so that the men inside wouldn't find him eavesdropping on their conversation in the hallway. Gian's footsteps came toward the door far too fast for Alessio to figure out something, or somewhere, to hide.

So, he just stayed there leaning against the wall.

Like an idiot.

Gian looked him over as he stepped out of the office, the lack of surprise in his features telling Alessio that the man expected *someone* to be out here. And he wasn't all that shocked about who it was, either.

Silence accompanied Gian's presence. Alessio didn't have anything to say to the man when he was still digesting parts of the conversation he'd just overheard. He hadn't realized how much the romantic aspect of Dare and Cree's relationship affected their business together. Not that *anyone* knew a whole hell of a lot about the two men, and what went on between them behind closed doors.

Alessio had never been privy to that, despite living with them for the last seven, almost eight, years. For all purposes, Cree and Dare kept the private parts of their life *private*. Even to Alessio. He only knew about it because someone made a comment once. He put two and two together about their relationship because of things he'd seen but overlooked, and at the time, he'd also been too young to really understand the complexities of a relationship like the one Dare and Cree shared. Eventually, he did outright ask Dare who confirmed that Cree was his partner in more than just the business.

That was the extent of the conversation.

Nothing else was on the table.

It had taught him that love was coveted here.

It was *protected*.

In their life, love was weakness. Love was a fucking *target*. It was something people could use to hurt you, and when you loved someone *that much* … you did everything you could to keep it and safeguard it from whoever might try to take it from you. Even if that meant hurting the person you loved in the process, too. Because sometimes, one had to do what one had to do.

"I am sure I'll be seeing you again, Alessio," Gian said, dragging him from his thoughts.

Alessio frowned. "I doubt it."

Gian grinned, and something shined in his gaze that Alessio didn't recognize as the man looked him over again—a *fondness*, maybe? "I'm not so sure."

"What does that mean?"

Did he know what happened between Alessio and his son in the gym? Had Cree run his fucking mouth about it? It wouldn't be like Cree to do something like that, but Alessio couldn't be sure, either.

Gian didn't say one way or another, simply murmuring, "I guess we'll see."

And then the man was gone, heading down the hallway with his hands stuffed in the pockets of his three-piece Armani suit like he didn't have a care in the world. Or, that's what one might think by watching him, but Alessio saw something different. The way Gian kept his head tilted down, how his hands had been clenched a bit before he hid them away, and now, the fact that his shoulders seemed tense beneath his suit.

He was worried.

He should be.

This place broke men.

Repeatedly.

"Alessio!" Dare's bark had Alessio jumping in place before he glared at the doorway. "Get in here, I know you're out there spying like a little shit."

"I was—"

"Don't lie."

Alessio scowled and turned to enter the office. He didn't move further than inside the doorway, but he didn't have to, either. Across the office, Dare sat behind his large desk. With his fingers steepled in front of him, he leaned back in the leather office chair, and watched Alessio with a pensive eye.

Like he was *considering* him.

God, he hated when Cree and Dare did that.

It meant they thought they knew something that he was hiding. And usually, they weren't wrong.

"What?" he asked.

"Nothing. Do you have anything you want to ask me?"

Alessio's cheek twitched, because *yes*. Between Cree and Dare ... he didn't get away with shit. Cree was the person who knew when Alessio was up to something, and constantly kept him on his toes because it felt like the man had insight to his mind that even he didn't know. Dare, though?

Well, he was something else.

For all purposes, they were both family to Alessio. One might consider them his adoptive fathers, but he never called them that, and they never asked, either. Still ... in a way, Dare felt more like a father figure to him than anyone else ever had.

Cree, more like a brother.

He didn't want to disappoint either of them.

"You're the reason I can't go out on an assignment until I turn eighteen?" Alessio asked quietly.

"Apparently so. I told you spying was a bad thing."

"Cree says I'm ready."

"And I want you here. Guess who gets the final say?"

"That's unfair," he pointed out.

He tried not to sound like a whiney fuck.

And probably failed.

Dare arched a brow, not bothering to indulge Alessio further because that's also how this worked between them. If he said something, it was done. "And why were you spying?"

"I wasn't—"

"You did."

"I was coming to tell you that they're not good choices for prospects here," Alessio returned, "but Gian was in here, so I thought it would be rude to interrupt."

"Or you took your chance to *spy*."

Alessio gritted his teeth. "I don't want to talk about it."

Dare smiled a little. "Is it that you don't think they're the right fit—because you follow Cree around too much and assume you can think the way he does—or because you like one of them? Corrado, I believe. I heard about how the gym was put into use this afternoon, yeah?"

Fuck.

So, Cree *had* told someone.

"It's not about *that*," Alessio muttered, annoyed.

Although, part of it was. Alessio had never felt such a strong attraction to another person who he would need to be around almost twenty-four-seven before. Not to mention, the fact that same person also managed to get under his skin in the worst of ways.

It was going to be a mess.

"Are you worried *for* him, Les?" Dare asked.

"Could you not do that?"

"Cree isn't the only one who can see your shit for what it is."

"Well, *don't*."

"Mmm," Dare said, standing from his chair. "Them being here … the contracts for them to begin training … none of it is your choice, Les. If you want to help the young man be his best here, then do that, but don't do it by attempting to sabotage him. Now, if you'll excuse me, I have to call in the team to begin the training tonight. I assume you don't want to be a part of this one, right?"

"I …" He struggled to refuse, but knew it was for the best if he did exactly that. If he said he agreed to help the team, then he would need to take part in some of the training that would be *most* difficult for Corrado and his twin. He helped to train others; this one couldn't be the same because Dare wasn't wrong, and he did have *some* interest in Corrado. His feelings might come into play. Lamely, he muttered, "I don't think I should."

"That's what I thought."

Alessio glowered, but Dare couldn't see it because he had already turned to leave the room. Clearly, this was going to get him nowhere and he didn't want to sit here and bother with it any more than he already had.

He hated wasting time.

"Oh, and Les?"

Alessio tensed in the doorway of the office. "What now?"

"If you're interested in Corrado Guzzi, my suggestion is instead of trying to pick a fight with him to get his attention, you might want to … oh, I don't know, *talk* to him?"

"Fuck you."

Dare's laughter chased him out of the office.

Asshole.

6.

Corrado

"How are they running power to this place?" Chris asked.

Gian tapped a finger to his ear. "Listen for it, *fils*."

Corrado heard the humming in the distance—somewhere behind them, he thought. Maybe in the middle of the complex? When they'd first come up on it, in the light, he thought it was several buildings close together. After walking around a bit, he realized it was actually one building, but in varied sizes depending on location.

"Generators," Corrado said.

"Oh," Chris said.

At the driver's side of the black Mercedes they'd arrived in, Gian turned to face his sons. Corrado stayed close to Chris, their equal six-foot-two height putting them pretty close to eye-level with their father. He couldn't remember when that happened, really. A growth spurt came along, and suddenly, he was no longer looking up at his dad.

He was staring him straight in the face.

"Corrado," Gian murmured.

His gaze lifted to meet his father's. "Yeah?"

"I know you're looking for something here."

"You think?"

Gian smiled faintly. "I hope you find it."

A thickness tightened his throat, but he nodded and said, "Yeah, me too."

Then, their father turned on Chris. "And *you*."

Chris grinned. "What about me?"

"I hope you know what you just signed up for."

"Not really."

Gian released a slow breath. "This is not … easy, Christopher."

"I'm here until he isn't."

"You don't have to look out for your twin every day of your life. That's not why you were put on this earth. You understand that, don't you?"

Chris only shrugged.

Corrado knew there was no point in his father trying to explain to Chris that he didn't really have to be here with his brother if he didn't want to be. Once they made up their minds, it was done—a Guzzi trait they took from their father, whether he wanted to admit it or not.

"All right," Gian murmured, pulling the key fob for the car from his pocket. "You know the deal—very little contact for the first year of training, but we'll see if the rules are bent. Believe it or not, but this wasn't my intention when I brought you both here."

Corrado smirked. "Not *at all*?"

Gian shook his head. "I thought it might give *you* a chance to see that there were other options in the business, if you were determined to stay in the life, but no, I did not assume it would be here. And now, I get to return home without both of you … your mother will be pleased, I'm sure."

Next to him, Chris made a noise under his breath. He didn't even have to say anything for that one sound to speak volumes. *Yes*, their father was in for hell when he got back to their ma. *Yes*, they were going to miss their mother like no one would ever understand. It was just how they were raised—Cara Guzzi made their worlds go around, and now, where would she be?

Corrado stuffed his hands in his pockets, and eyed their surroundings now that it was dark. A lot of the cars from earlier were gone—the people had drifted out of the complex throughout the day, without much of a word to him. There were still a few scattered vehicles, but he didn't know who they belonged to.

"Enough of this," Gian said roughly, "I should get going. *I love you.* Both of you, huh? Be *smart*, Corrado." Then, to Chris, their father said, "Don't panic when it starts, okay? It only seems like you won't get out, but I promise it'll never go as far as you think it will."

Chris's brow furrowed. "What does that mean?"

Gian's shoulders lifted with his stress. "Just remember what I said, son."

"All right."

Corrado figured his father would get in the car, and drive off after that, but Gian surprised them. Then again, their father had always been different than the other men around him—more in tune to his children, and he actually gave a fuck about what they wanted or needed at any given time. He also wasn't sure when the physical affection started to lessen with his father, but as they grew older, the hugs and kisses slowed.

A part of him knew it was because of them—he didn't need that shit to know his father gave a damn, and so, he stopped *asking* for it. Right then, though, Gian stepped forward, and embraced each of his sons one at a time, used his hand to pat the backs of their heads, and pressed a quick kiss to their foreheads before moving back just as fast.

Like it hadn't happened at all.

"Wish me luck with your mother, hmm?"

"Good luck," the twins echoed.

He was going to need it.

No doubt about that.

Gian was careful not to look over his shoulder as he slipped into the car, and turned the engine over. It wasn't until Chris and Corrado could only see a very faint outline of the car's taillights in the distance did they finally turn away from their disappearing father.

"What happens now?" Chris asked.

Corrado had no idea. "Something, I guess."

"I don't like *not knowing* things."

"Yeah, you're probably going to have to work on that, Chris."

His twin made a disgusted noise, but Corrado didn't reply because he wasn't lying. Neither of them knew *anything* about what was going to happen to them now. Other than the small bag with a couple of changes of clothes, he didn't even know where that shit would be coming from. No one thought to tell them because apparently, they didn't need to know.

That's what they had been told.

Next to going over a contract—that in all honesty, didn't give them much to go on—which basically explained the next year of their lives would be essentially owned by The League, and what the company wanted to do with them ... that was all Corrado knew. *Training*, the contract said over and over again. Except nothing in the damn paperwork explained what exactly this training would include.

"You know," Corrado said as the two of them headed back toward the black door with the camera overhead, "Papa was right."

"That I don't have to be here for you?"

"Yeah."

Chris shook his head. "No, he wasn't."

Well, all right.

Who was Corrado to argue with what was basically his reflection?

He knew better.

• • •

Not that anything at The League's complex made sense to him—something he thought was intentional on their part—but for whatever reason, the sleeping quarters that had been designated to Corrado were an entire wing away from the one that had been given to Chris. The two had broken off as they realized the hallway lights were starting to shut off or dim significantly, and headed to their own rooms.

Trailing his finger over a simple three-drawer dresser that looked like he could probably put his fist through the thin, pressed wood if he wanted to, Corrado eyed the rest of the space. It wasn't much—fifteen feet by fifteen feet or so. A double bed rested along one wall with a stand beside it, and a very small window overtop.

Given his room was on the third floor of a certain area deep within the large complex, no one would even be able to see inside because they couldn't possibly reach the window. There were no pieces of artwork on the bare, tan-colored walls to give it a comfortable feeling, and other than a small desk with nothing on top ... the room was basically empty. Clean, gleaming hardwood floors, white sheets on the bed, and very little else.

Welcome home for the next year, Corrado.

His mind was a special breed of hell when it wanted to be. This might have been made easier for him had he understood what was going to come next, but no. He had to be left in fucking suspense, which only made everything far worse.

The building itself, he'd realized as he walked through its hallways and sections earlier, was a fucking maze. It looked huge from the outside, but that didn't *begin* to touch how large and confusing it truly was once you were inside the damn place.

"Bored?"

Corrado spun fast to find a familiar—and *annoying*—man leaning in his doorway. "What do you want, Alessio?"

"I still prefer Les."

"Yeah, and how's that mood of yours, anyway?"

Alessio grinned. "How's that mouth of yours, huh?"

"Fair."

He nodded, and then inched a bit into the room. Corrado thought to tell him to get the fuck out, but he didn't bother. Besides, Alessio might be able to answer some of his questions, and he couldn't pry information from the guy when he chased him off, right?

"How big is this complex?"

"In total?"

"Yeah."

Alessio rocked back on his heels. "Around a hundred thousand square feet, give or take a few thousand. The main floorplan, back when they first planned to build it, covered a full acre of land. Some things changed as they moved forward, third floors were added, like *here*. What about it?"

"Curious."

"You know, the less questions you ask here, the better it'll be for you."

Corrado passed him a look. "*You know*, humans are curious by nature, don't you? It's how we learn new things."

Throwing those words back at Alessio didn't seem to bother him in the slightest. If anything, that grin he sported simply grew a little deeper. Corrado might think it was *sexy*, even, if it didn't fucking infuriate him so much. A part of him hated how Alessio could treat everything so flippantly—like it was a damn joke to him, and nothing more.

Even *him*.

Corrado didn't want to be a joke to anybody.

"Don't worry," Alessio said quietly, "they'll beat the curiosity, and almost everything else, right out of you by the time they're done."

He stilled on the spot, tension tightening his shoulders. "Is that what happens next?"

"Partly. You have to break before they can make you into something better. Some parts of you take longer to break than others, you know? That's the hard part, though. Once you get through that, it's mostly smooth sailing. It's what they have to take from you first that just about kills you. Oh, and how they do it, I guess."

"How do they do it?"

Alessio didn't reply.

Corrado wasn't one to accept a non-answer, so he moved a little closer to Alessio until the two of them were only a few inches apart. He fully intended to get an answer out of him, but it slipped his mind when he noticed the way Alessio's gaze darted down to his lips, and then quickly back up to his eyes.

Like he was *remembering*.

That memory flooded Corrado's mind, too.

Fuck.

Not what he needed right now.

"Was Cree right?" Corrado asked. "About you, I mean."

"I don't—"

"That you pick a fight to get attention."

Alessio's eyes blazed. "*No*."

"Really? So, you didn't try to cause a problem with me today because you didn't want to just come up and say *hello*? I don't know, like a normal person might."

"Cree says a lot of shit."

"I noticed a lot of it was right, though."

Alessio's throat jumped when he swallowed hard. "Possibly. Doesn't mean all of it is."

"Sure."

"I don't know whether I like you or not," Alessio muttered.

"Same."

This time, it was Corrado that found his gaze drifted down from the shaggy hair covering Alessio's eyes to where his lips rested in what almost seemed like a smirk. Not quite, but *almost*. Like the guy just had a natural arrogance about him. That was something Corrado found *most* annoying in others, but with Alessio, it drew him in.

Another problem?

Probably.

It had been Alessio that kissed him earlier, and Corrado wasn't entirely sure why he felt the strangest urge to see if the man tasted the same *now*, but he made the move this time. It didn't seem to come as any kind of shock to Alessio when Corrado's mouth came down on his, and he backed him into the wall.

Alessio's fingers found the waistband of his pants, his fingers digging into the hard muscles there as his tongue swept the seam of Corrado's lips. Just like that first kiss, this still felt like a fight to Corrado ... like neither of them were willing to yield to the other. No softness; no careful exploration. It was just *war*. Tongues clashing against each other as he realized, *yes*, Alessio tasted exactly the same.

Like fucking *sin*.

His teeth caught Alessio's bottom lip, and then the man's fingers pressed harder into his skin *just because*. If anything, it only made Corrado lurch forward, so he didn't just have Alessio backed against the wall. No, he had his body *pinning* him there. Just like when the man had him pinned to the fucking mat of the ring earlier. He wanted him to know what that felt like—to be under someone else's control, and to *like* it at the same time.

And yes, he could feel just how much Alessio liked it.

Corrado let out a harsh exhale, his lips grazing down Alessio's jaw as he tipped his head back to the wall. "*Fuck*, so that's a yes on the whole picking a fight thing, then?"

"Fuck you, Guzzi."

He just laughed.

What else could he do?

A noisy buzz echoed throughout the room, sending Corrado and Alessio's gaze flying upward to find the sound. Above the doorway, a light turned from green to red, making Corrado even more confused than he already was. It was Alessio who seemed to understand what was going on as he cursed under his breath.

"Shit, I gotta go," Alessio muttered.

"Wait," Corrado said, refusing to move to let him get past, "what does that mean?"

"It's starting."

"*What's* starting?"

Alessio wet his lips, his gaze meeting Corrado's. "*Training*. I hope you fucking make it through what they're about to do to you and your brother."

Ice slipped through Corrado's blood stream.

What had they signed up for?

"Why that hope?"

Alessio flashed a grin, as small as it was. "Because maybe I want to know what happens next with us."

Corrado jerked fast away from the wall at those words. Alessio wasted no time slipping out of the room, leaving him alone to his racing heart, and his thoughts. Out in the hallway, he heard footsteps—Alessio leaving, maybe?

And *doors* shutting.

He stared up at that red light again.

No one—or very few people—were left inside the complex. Why did it sound like all the doors were closing one by *one*? Hadn't Alessio said it was all electronic? Someone could control the doors without physically needing to shut them by hand?

The footsteps got louder, though.

And closer.

Definitely not Alessio.

Not anymore.

Corrado looked down to stare out his still opened doorway. Except now, the hallway outside of it wasn't empty. Black-clothed figures stood there, their faces covered with masks, and their hands steady on the weapons they held.

"It's time to get started, Corrado," the one in front of the group said.

He recognized that voice.

Cree.

"Doing what?" Corrado asked.

"You don't get to ask questions. Make this easy."

Right.

That probably wasn't going to work for him. Not when he didn't know what in the hell was going on, and he didn't know what might come next. His heart ached from beating so hard, but he was positive there was no way out of here.

Was that what they wanted, though?

For him to *fight?*

Because he could do that.

"Where's my brother?" he demanded.

"Walk outside the room, Corrado."

"No."

"You do understand that this *will* happen one way or another."

"That doesn't tell me—"

"Easy or hard," Cree said behind the black mask.

"Tell me where my brother is."

"Hard it is."

They came in on him, then.

All of them.

Corrado couldn't ever remember being taken to the ground so fast or hard before. His bones *shook* when they put him to the floor, an ache radiating throughout his whole body. He let out a shout, and tried to fight back. It was fucking pointless, though. There were too many, and only one of him.

His gaze darted from one mask-covered face to the other, but they didn't speak. Five of them, he thought, but maybe six. It was hard to tell when they moved so fast, and he still didn't know what in the hell was going on. His arms were tied at his back, but hell, he hadn't even seen the zip ties come out for them to do it.

Someone dragged him up from the floor while someone else leaned in beside him, their eyes being the only thing he could see behind the mask as they said, "Don't make this worse for yourself, kid. You're already *in*, and there's no way out. Just let it happen."

Right.

Okay.

Damn.

"W-what happens now?" Corrado asked as he was pulled from the room.

"It's gonna hurt before it gets better."

Who said that?

He didn't even know.

7.

Hidden in the shadows of the hallway, Alessio watched from a safe distance as Corrado was pulled from his room by the team. The *team* being a small group of men and women hand-picked by Cree to help him train whoever had signed the contract. They were never easy about it—they didn't go in easy, either.

All or nothing.

Corrado's shout echoed down the corridor, his voice thick with panic and uncertainty. Not fear, though. *Not yet.* That would come soon enough, Alessio knew. The fear would come when he was either locked in total darkness, rounds of beatings marking the passing hours he spent in isolation to fuck his mind entirely up, or when they put him in the *tank.*

Fuck.

That fucking *tank.*

Alessio felt the pressure building in his chest simply remembering his own time in that cold, dark water. It never got any better in the tank, or the darkness. Long stretches of time where your mind was too awake—fear saturating your entire body because you never knew what was going to happen next.

And when it did happen …

"*Where the fuck is my bro—*"

Corrado's question cut off abruptly when the first hit came. The sound of flesh meeting flesh was sickening, and *unforgiving.* A grunt followed the hit before a second one came, and then another and another. Alessio tipped his head back so all he could see was the white ceiling of the corridor, and then he closed his eyes altogether when the beating continued.

They didn't want him to ask questions.

He wasn't *allowed.*

Orders were given.

He was to follow.

Alessio knew how this *worked*, but the problem was, he couldn't tell Corrado that. Maybe back in his room, but even then … it wouldn't have helped. This was something *all* The League's prospects had to learn on their own, in their time. It was the very purpose of the training—to take a man who was already set in his ways, break him, and then change him into a better version of himself.

Even if that better version was created from violence, darkness, isolation, fear, and *pain.* Alessio didn't make the rules here; he only knew how to follow them.

"*Stand up,*" he heard ordered.

That was the thing that made him open his eyes again, although he didn't try to peek around the corner to look down the hallway. Part of him knew it wasn't a good idea. Cree would be pissed off like nothing else if someone interrupted his training team, but especially at the very beginning. He needed to stay out of sight as much as possible.

Coming to this end of the complex to get a couple of minutes with Corrado before the training began was a fucking risk anyway. A stupid one, probably, but he wasn't going to admit that to himself. Alessio wasn't very good at denying himself something he wanted, as it was, and he kept being drawn back to Corrado when he shouldn't want anything to do with him at all.

And it's only been a day.

Fuck.

The beating down the hall continued on like Alessio wasn't having a whole fucking moment at the other end, just around the corner. Not that the rest of them could know that he was in the midst of his own goddamn issues.

Alessio had to give credit where it was due, though.

Corrado didn't beg.

He fought back, by the sounds of it.

He didn't take *shit.*

Some cried. That wasn't unusual, and no one said a thing when it was all said and done. Some puked. Fear had a funny way of making the body do things no one could possibly understand unless it was them in the situation. Others begged and pleaded, realizing their mistake in signing a contract for something they didn't truly comprehend. It was too late by then, though.

They were *in.*

There was no out until it was done, or you were dead.

But for now, Corrado wasn't like the others. Very little was said to him from the team—orders like *stand* or *move* or *stop asking questions.* But nothing deep, nothing that answered the questions he kept demanding be answered about his brother.

Even Alessio didn't know the answer to that.

Usually, one person was trained at a time because it *was* so intensive. Maybe Cree was going to try a new way of training the twins because it would happen side by side in time, essentially, but Alessio didn't think he could stomach it to ask the details.

Part of him just didn't want to *know.*

"You're going to *learn,*" Alessio heard a muffled voice say down the hall.

"*Fuck you.*"

Corrado's words were mumbled now—like he couldn't speak right, or he had to make a great effort to do it.

That was enough for Alessio.

He knew what came next.

Instead of standing there to listen to it, he slipped down the corridor to go in the opposite direction from the rest of the team. They were taking Corrado to the west side of the complex, deep into the basement where even the people who milled about the building wouldn't be able to hear the fucking *screams.*

Alessio went east, to *Dare.*

He suspected he would find Dare in his office, sitting at his desk and handling the paperwork of the day. People who *thought* they knew the inner workings of The League thought Dare was untouchable in a lot of ways because he never directly handled the assassins, for the most part. That was usually Cree, and his team of people.

They also assumed Dare was … the very top.

In a way, he was.

It was the same way people assumed Cree—his choice—was just another assassin with a bit more leg room to move in the organization than usual. They were cautious about keeping Cree's *real* hand in controlling part of The League quiet. Instead, a carefully constructed story and persona for Cree was spoon-fed to the prospects and clients of The League where Cree was concerned, making them think he was less of a *boss* and more like them. They were far more likely to trust him in that case.

Dare, though, also had people like Gian Guzzi who fronted a lot of money for this organization to become something no one could possibly ruin, which meant things never stopped around here. If it wasn't a new prospect being trained, it was the auctions selling off the assassins to people with deep enough pockets all around the world who might be in need of someone with a particular set of skills. And if wasn't *those* things, then they were working.

Instead of finding Dare in his office, Alessio wandered the halls until he came to the control room. Or, that's what they liked to refer to it as. Inside, standing in front of a wall of screens, Dare used a sleek, thin remote with a touchscreen pad to separate what was actually *one* giant screen—that looked broken into several different screens—to bring up specific cameras. Just as quickly, he switched to a separate screen on the wall of moving pictures that brought up something else entirely.

A wall of doors, it looked like.

His thumb raced across the touchscreen, and Alessio watched on the screen as the opened doors in the hallway began to close one by one. Then, just as fast, Corrado was brought into view by the team … close to the tank room, now.

Well, the dark room *and* the tank room.

They were right across from one another. The walls inside were so thick, one couldn't even *blow* them out with dynamite. The floors, a cold cement that constantly seemed to stay wet from one thing or another.

"Did you watch mine, too?" Alessio asked.

His chest *ached*.

He wasn't sure why.

Maybe it was the memories racing past his eyes—the idea that a couple of years ago, this had been *him*. He'd been dragged through those halls, had the shit beat out of him, and was then thrown into hell for a month or more to break him beyond recognition. He'd thought he was ready; he'd watched from afar for other trainings before his time.

He had not been anywhere near ready.

Dare turned slowly, realizing he wasn't alone as his gaze fell on Alessio in the doorway. "I'm sorry?"

"Did you watch my training, too?"

"I did not."

"Why?"

"I don't have … a good answer for that, Les," Dare murmured.

"Or you don't want to sound like a coward."

"Maybe I was wrong."

"What?"

Dare shrugged, and looked back at the screens. "I said earlier you only *thought* you could think like Cree does, but I might have been wrong about that."

It took Alessio a second to understand.

Then, two.

"Because you *couldn't* watch me go through the first phase, right?" he asked.

Dare let out a heavy exhale. "If you asked for it to stop even once … *and they all ask* … I would have dragged you out of there myself. Because I was weak—love does that to you, Alessio, and I want you to remember that. It makes you *weak*. And so, when something is for the greater good when it comes to someone you love, even if it means hurting them, you have to take a step back and let it happen. Or in my case, be forced to do it."

"What does that mean?"

Across the room, Dare waved the remote at the screens, saying, "Cree had the team go in on you for phase one, then he locked me in the office and wouldn't let me out for that first night. It … was not a good moment for me."

Alessio frowned. "What?"

"You heard what I said."

"Cree wasn't in on my—"

"Not for phase one. He was too close to it, too."

Alessio hadn't known that, mostly because the team had been very careful not to speak to him during the first phase of his training. Other than a barked word here to there to give him an order, which he knew better than to defy them.

It only made shit worse.

"Did you ask for it to stop?" Dare asked.

Alessio watched the screens, another hallway … the rooms were coming faster now. Soon, Corrado wouldn't know what daylight was for a long fucking time.

"Not until the third round in the tank room," Alessio said, scratching at the side of his arm because *that* memory made him anxious as fuck, and he knew better than to show it. That's what training had taught him—he didn't deal with any of that in the same way anymore. Fear, panic … it was all secondary to everything else, now. "I couldn't find the pocket to breathe, the water kept coming in my mouth, and—"

Dare made a dark noise.

"Sorry," Alessio muttered.

"It's what you wanted, no?"

"It was."

Ten feet away, he watched Dare nod at the screens.

"And it's what they want, too, Les. You'll have to remember that for the next little while."

"Where is the other one—Chris?"

"In his room, *fine*. That's why we put them on opposite ends of the complex for living quarters. If we put them in the same corridor, it was likely one would panic and do something outlandish when the other was removed from their room. A risk Cree didn't want to take, of course. It'll be only once Corrado is situated—we knew he would be the more difficult one at first—that we'll begin phase one for the other twin. Rotational trips between the rooms for them, of course. Instead of long spreads in each like we typically do. The one, he's going to need a break in-between the tank."

"Christopher, you mean."

"Scared of water, yeah."

"But even if he asks for it to stop—"

"We can't stop it once it begins, that isn't how training works."

"What if he reacts *really* badly to the tank?" Alessio asked.

Dare chuckled dryly. "The best way to deal with a fear is head-on."

"Except it's more than a *fear*. Everybody is scared of things like the dark when it's been too long, or of the unknown for something like the tank. But that might not be the same."

"Then, he will break sooner than his twin because of it, won't he? A healthy mind processes things like anxiety and fear, or pain and discomfort in a completely different way than a broken one does, Les. And so, we need them broken before we can begin to rebuild. You know this."

"I guess."

"You don't like it, though," Dare replied.

"Not this time."

"Hmm."

On the screens, a battered Corrado had finally made it to the basement. The team stood outside of the two large, metal doors on either side of them that would lead into the dark room, or the tank room.

"They're about to begin," Dare said. "You should probably leave."

Alessio didn't move.

"I think I better stay, actually."

"Don't say I didn't warn you."

• • •

Safely behind one-way glass, Alessio watched the scene that seemed surreal happening beyond cement walls. The light from the hallway in the complex's basement allowed *him* the ability to see inside the tank room, but no one in there could see him.

Well, the *one* person in there.

The straightjacket attached to a chain and cable keeping Corrado suspended over a square tank of water that was *just* big enough to drown a man when he was dropped into it—if he didn't figure out how to save himself the first couple of dunks—was tight to his body. His eyes drifted closed, tiredness from the last few days of being rotated between the tank and the dark room finally getting to him.

It happened to everyone.

That was when this became *most* dangerous.

Alessio's gaze darted to the chain as it jerked. At the same time, Corrado's eyes flew wide open, and for a brief second, he swore the man was looking right at him though the small window he was able to watch through.

He knew it wasn't possible, though.

It lasted all of a half of a second before Corrado was *dropped*. Like a sack of dead weight, really. Right into the tank, where freezing cold water awaited him, and a top attached to an automatic arm slammed closed right after.

Alessio dragged in a sharp breath and stared upward, knowing what was happening inside the tank room now. He didn't have to watch it happen to *know*. Fuck, he knew it all too well as it was, honestly.

Corrado would struggle.

Under water.

Straight jacket on.

The top wouldn't budge.

More water pumped in.

His body remained constantly cold, wet, and *aching*. From the rotational beatings, and the lack of food and water. His mind would be spinning and out of control—fear and panic welling and rushing like the waves of the water inside that tank, making sure he thought at all times, this was it. *This* was the moment he would die.

Every dunk became longer.

A second here.

Two there.

Until he was under water for up to three and half minutes, or so. Until his vision began to blacken, and he swallowed water because the body's natural reaction was to *try* to breathe at that point, even if it meant no air would be waiting for him.

He'd fight against all of it—his own panic, the water, the need to breathe, and even the walls of the tank surrounding him.

And then the top would flip up, the chain would drag him out, and he would hang again ... waiting to be dropped into the water for another round of hell.

Over.

And over.

And over again.

Until the dark room.

Currently, that's where Corrado's twin was being held. He was about due for a beating, too, come to think of it, which meant he probably shouldn't be down here. The rotational beatings and the occasional bit of food and water were the only markers of time passing down in these fucking rooms.

It seemed cruel.

Pointless, even.

Alessio, and every other person who had gone through this training, would be the first to say they came out better for it—physically, and mentally. They were the last to panic, and the first to face everything without fear.

When you'd been so close to death time and time again ... everything that came after was nothing compared to it, really. Everything else was just a *bonus*, he figured.

"What are you doing down here?"

Alessio didn't turn at the sound of Cree's voice, but he did look back through the one-way glass to see Corrado being pulled out of the water, almost entirely unconscious, but not quite. Just *almost*.

"Watching," Alessio murmured.

"You shouldn't be down here."

"I know."

Cree came to stand next to him and crossed his arms over his broad chest.

"He's going to be difficult … to break, I mean. His pride holds him back. All of that has to go … the pride, dignity … the harder it is to take those things from him, the longer this process goes on."

Yeah.

He knew that, too.

"What about the other one?" Alessio asked, glancing over his shoulder at the dark room where Chris was having his rotation. "How did that go in the tank?"

"He about broke the fucking top trying to get out, one of the jacket's arms came undone … I have never seen someone fight *that* hard against it, and I have seen some things happen down in these rooms."

"Adrenaline?"

"Likely," Cree returned. "His second rotation in the tank starts tomorrow. We'll see how it goes, or if we get a different result."

Of course.

Alessio knew how this went.

Break the body; break the mind.

"As for *you*," the man said next to him, "you don't need to be down here reliving your own time in these rooms because you feel something for one of the two currently experiencing theirs. You realize that, don't you?"

He did.

All Alessio could think to reply was, "But shouldn't I?"

8.

Corrado

"*Stay down.*"

Corrado didn't.

His knees ached, and his legs shook so badly he was sure they were going to give out the second he put all of his weight back onto them, but he still forced his body back up. Back to his feet, he didn't stand quite as straight as he did the last ten times, not when he couldn't breathe doing it.

The straighter his spine, the worse the pain became. He trembled from the top of his head to his toes pressing against cold, damp cement. The amount of effort it took to pull his body up from the ground that time was clearly more than he realized.

Would he be able to do it again?

Corrado didn't know.

Fuck him if he wouldn't *try*.

Keeping his hands resting against his knees to give him a bit more support so he didn't topple over entirely—*that* was not happening—he took a few quick inhales to try and soothe the pain flaring in his side.

Was that his fucking kidney?

His ribs?

A collapsed lung?

All of the above?

Likely.

"You're a stubborn fuck, you know that?"

Corrado didn't reply to the voice in the darkness because that was the thing ... he barely saw a flicker of them in the blackened room before they struck out at him again with those goddamn bamboo rods. Flexible, and *painful*, the rods didn't do serious damage to his body. Typically no blood, and nothing that was going to force them to pull him out of these fucking rooms, but they still hurt. They bruised, and they *broke*.

It didn't matter.

He'd learned early on during these rotational beatings when he was in the dark room—a far better place than the tank, as far as he was concerned—that they were looking for something from him. And maybe it was his stubbornness or his damn pride, but he refused to give it to them.

Today, they wanted him to stay on the floor.

Just *stay down*, they kept saying.

Corrado got back up. Every single time they put him to his knees, or on his back, he forced his body back up to his feet. If they wanted him down there on the ground like a *dog*, then they were going to have to make sure he *couldn't* get back up.

Simple as that.

It was stupid.

Part of him knew that.

The beating—their *lesson*—would end as soon as he continued to follow their directions. As soon as he lost himself in the darkness of the room where he wasn't sure where the blackness ended and he began, it would end because they broke him.

Corrado didn't want to be broken.

Not like *that*.

"*Stay down*," the order came again.

This voice was new—it didn't belong to Cree, or some of the others he'd become accustomed to joining him in the tank or the dark room. Then again, they barely spoke at all so he couldn't honestly say it was a new person. They very well might have been involved in this phase of his training for the entire time, but tonight was the first time they chose to spoke.

He preferred it when they didn't speak.

It pissed him off more.

Corrado dragged in a painful breath, one that hurt right down to the marrow in his bones—old blood made his tongue have a rusty flavor that seemed thick; the smell of piss lingered in the room, but he wasn't even sure if that was from him, or not; the stench of vomit clung to the walls, wherever the fuck they were.

This place was *hell*.

Dignity?

What was that?

Probably in that bucket in the corner where he was expected to use the bathroom, for fuck's sake. He still had his fucking pride. The pride was what was going to kill him here. Of that, he was most sure. If he could just give it up, right along with his dignity and everything else they had ripped away from him in these goddamn rooms, then this would *end*.

Corrado knew it.

He'd figured out the *trick*.

Pride was a bitch, though. The one thing he wouldn't give up to anyone for *anything*. Ever. He didn't know if that was the Guzzi in him—although, he wouldn't blame his twin a bit if Chris had already given up and given in to this process—or if it was simply the way his brain was wired.

It was pride that made him drag in one more quick breath, settle into the pain of what was going to come next when he made the move, and then he focused all his efforts into making his muscles do what he needed and wanted them to do. Which was stand—entirely straight again, not bent at the knees to give him support and rest from the ache radiating throughout his entire body.

No, straight.

All the way up again.

In the darkness, one's eyes might eventually become accustomed to it. Not so much so that they would be able to see everything like they could in the daytime, but just enough that where it only seemed like black space before, now there were shadows.

Corrado watched one of the shadows move. It came fast, the strike *hard*. Right against his chest was where it landed, the second coming right after to crack him against his knees. That one probably hurt the worst.

If he *never* saw bamboo again, it would be a great day for him. He'd decided.

Not that he had time to think on that for too long.

He was on the floor again, blinking up at darkness and choking on the laughter that crawled its way out of his throat. The sound of his own distress and sardonic amusement echoed in the space, reverberating back to his spot on the cold, damp floor to taunt him.

Except he liked that sound.

It was better than the hell he usually found here.

"*Stay down,*" he was told again.

Fuck that.

Corrado rolled over to his knees despite the way his entire body protested at the action. There was pain, and then there was agony. Some people liked to use those words interchangeably like they were the same things.

Here, he learned they were not.

He wished he felt simple pain, now.

Only pain.

Instead, he felt agony—straight, *pure* agony everywhere. And not just from the beatings … not just from the way his body felt broken, and ready to be done with this. No, because inside his mind, and in his heart, it was as though he were being torn in *two*.

The part that wanted to stop.

The part that needed to *continue.*

They would not break him.

He would not beg.

But *fuck* … were they going to kill him trying?

He didn't know.

"*God,* stay down," he heard somewhere behind him.

Corrado couldn't.

That wasn't how he was made.

They could take the rest of it from him—a lot of it, they already had. Should they want his dignity so he wouldn't understand what shame felt like? *Fine,* take it. If they needed his body to learn to enjoy pain and discomfort so it could never be used against him? *Great,* they had that now. Did they need to take his emotions and twist them like his dark thoughts, lost to blackened walls and the water that rushed into his lungs every time they put him in the tank? *Okay,* he no longer cared.

But not his pride.

That was his.

• • •

There were times when the darkness of the rooms seemed like an old friend to Corrado. He found comfort in the rooms when he was totally alone—when the time bled together because he no longer knew what day it was.

Ha.

That was funny.

He had no clue how long he'd been doing this.

Days?

Weeks?

Months?

It could be any or all of those things, he understood. There was no real thing for him to use to mark the time in these rooms. Not when the people came just enough to give him food, as little as that was, or to beat the hell out of him again.

Never mind when they switched rooms.

Hood over his head.

Rough hands.

Harsh orders in his ears.

Still, he found comfort in the silence and the darkness. Oh, it played tricks on him, sure. The darkness chased away his ability to sleep, making him wired and staring into black space until he was sure he fell asleep just like that.

Sitting there.

With his eyes open.

Some people couldn't take darkness.

Corrado found he liked it.

He'd started measuring his breaths to combat the pain he constantly battled, but even that wasn't helping *now*. Nothing helped.

A buzz speared through the silence of the room, but unlike before when Corrado was new to these rooms, he no longer froze in fear and panic at the sound. That buzzer meant one of three things, and none of them made him afraid anymore.

One, a room switch.

Two, a beating.

Three, food and water.

There was no fourth option, and he had become so used to it being either a room switch or a beating far more often than food that he no longer gave a damn. He wasn't going to start in fear every time they came into the room for him— maybe they wanted that, or perhaps they liked it too much.

Whatever it was, he wouldn't be doing it.

The door opening was the only bit of light he got to see now. Just a slate of bright yellow color that seemed so blinding when the door moved that he had to look away from it so that his eyes didn't sting. Although, the one thing that never changed regardless if they were bringing him food or there to deliver a beating was the fact that the whole team entered the room.

All five of them.

Or was it six?

Corrado wasn't sure.

It didn't matter.

All of them contributed to his *training*. In one way or another.

Except this time, only one person was haloed by the light of the door. His shadow stretched along the cement floor with the stream of color, dragging through wet spots and cracks only to stop right before Corrado's feet.

A part of him just *knew* who it was. Maybe by the body shape, or the shaggy hair that the figure pushed back with one hand.

"Les," he mumbled.

It was easier than saying Alessio's full name.

His mouth *hurt*.

It all fucking hurt.

Alessio crossed the floor with quick steps, and never once did the door close behind him. Something else that was entirely unusual. When the team stepped into the rooms, the door *always* closed behind them. Like they were worried he might try to bolt, and they decided to take the option away altogether.

Not this time.

Corrado blinked as Alessio kneeled down beside him, and set a couple of items to the floor. He tried to take in his features, but he was pretty sure one of his eyes were swollen shut, and he couldn't see all that well in the darkness anyway. Not with that added bit of light shadowing Alessio's face as he put together something he'd set on the floor.

"You called me Les this time."

Corrado chuckled, but that hurt, too. "Don't get used to it, okay?"

"Mmm, here," Alessio said quietly, "*drink*."

Corrado didn't even bother to ask what it was that the man offered him—but it was cool, had a fruity flavor, if not a bit *chalky*, too. Still, he drank it down, eventually taking the bottle directly from Alessio to hold it up himself with shaking hands that clenched too tightly around the plastic, so much so that he spilled a bit.

Alessio didn't seem to mind.

"It has vitamins, and ... other things," Alessio explained, even though Corrado hadn't asked. "It'll help; you've been down here too long, and you need *something*."

"How long?"

"A month."

That long?

Corrado tried to settle that, but he couldn't. Not that it mattered, as his mind wasn't working that well, anyway. Even there, it seemed like all he could think about was darkness and silence. Was that a part of the plan, too?

"Chris?"

Alessio, seemingly understanding his question even though he hadn't given much detail, said, "He started phase two last week."

But he was out of the rooms.

Out of the *tank*.

Corrado could breathe easier for that.

He hadn't startled when the door was open, or when he realized it was Alessio that came into the room, but he did jump a bit when something warm pressed against the side of his face in the darkness. Alessio's hand, he quickly knew. His palm curved against Corrado's jaw, and then his thumb drifted over the swell of his bottom lip.

Gentle.

Slow.

Kind.

All things he was not given in these rooms.

"You have to give them what they want," Alessio murmured, "do you hear me?"

"They want too much."

"You *have to*."

He didn't reply because he didn't feel like repeating himself.

Alessio's sigh echoed beside him, his thumb sweeping Corrado's mouth again. "*Stubborn*. That's what you are. It's a process, Corrado, you have to trust it."

"I gave them everything."

All that he could give, anyway.

"The rest, I'm keeping," he mumbled.

Silently, Alessio leaned in, and pressed his forehead to the side of Corrado's cheek. He didn't linger there for very long. Just quick enough for Corrado to feel his warmth, and know his presence was *real*. This hadn't been something that the darkness did to his mind—it wasn't another trick.

"I gotta go," Alessio quietly, his words whispering along Corrado's bruised skin.

"I know."

"*Trust the process.*"

He did.

Just not the way they wanted him to.

• • •

Another round in the fucking tank.

Another round in the dark room.

Corrado wanted it to *end*.

It was a mantra in his mind now—one that wouldn't leave him alone during his waking hours. Which was damn near constantly. He found it hard to sleep in the darkness now. Impossible, really. He was sure humans weren't made to go days and days and days without sleep, but somehow, he was doing it.

Or … he was falling asleep and waking up without realizing it. He closed his eyes to darkness and opened them to the same thing. Time was irrelevant, and he didn't even comprehend when it was passing him by.

The first time they put him in the dark room, he *hated* the floor. Sure, he liked it more than being dunked into the tank for several minutes at a time without being allowed to breathe, but he still fucking hated it. Cold, wet, and cracked … there was no way to get comfortable, and he was convinced that coldness soaked into his bones *constantly*. And the wetness? He was never going to get dry.

Now, though?

Now, he didn't care at all. The discomfort he used to feel at being on the floor of the dark room was a moot point to everything else. He didn't get chilled from the cold, and the wetness making his dirty clothes irritate his bruised skin further was a background thought.

He simply didn't feel it at all.

Even the tank didn't bother him so much now. That had been the worst— trying to overcome the realization that, yes, he was probably going to die in that fucking water if they kept the top on him for another ten seconds. His vision would blacken, and his lungs protested so much when he was under the water that he was sure death was imminent.

Now, he just wished it would happen.

If it was going to kill him, then *do it*.

Resting on his stomach in the dark room, Corrado's head rested on his arms, and he faced what he suspected was the door. He couldn't be sure because they still brought him in here with a hood over his head to confuse the hell out of him.

It worked, too.

Every damn time.

Still, he laid there and waited.

For a beating.

For food.

For *light*.

Drumming his fingers to the floor, a sharp thought sliced through his mind—something he'd not really considered before right *now*. He was bored.

The beatings wouldn't kill him.

The food would be fine.

The light didn't last.

And he was just ... bored.

Corrado blinked, but what else could he do?

He stayed on the floor.

Bored.

He wasn't sure how long he was down there like that, waiting for something that wouldn't come. Long enough that he realized, *somehow* without a sense of time, that they were incredibly late bringing him food. And it had been a span of time since the team came in to try and beat the pride out of him, too.

He was on the floor for long enough that he was sure he would die there, wasted and broken, but it seemed like The League had one more surprise for him. Once again, when the buzz rang out in the room to signal the door opening, he didn't move an inch.

A beating?

Food?

Les?

He doubted it would be Alessio.

It was actually ... no one.

The door stayed open, light spilling in to streak across the floor from the corridor. No one came to stand there. Nothing happened at all.

Corrado kept waiting.

Still, nothing changed.

The door stayed open.

Maybe it was because his body had been put through hell, and his mind was currently shattered into a thousand tiny pieces, but he didn't move, either. He stayed right there on the floor, watching the light spill in and waiting for something to happen.

Anything.

It was the not knowing that bothered him the most. He'd become accustomed to their routine down here, and what he could expect to happen to him. He found comfort in that—in the *knowing*. And right now, he didn't know a fucking thing.

Minutes passed.

Then, maybe an hour.

It took Corrado entirely too long to get up from the floor when he realized no one was coming, and the door had been purposefully opened. Or, he suspected that was the case. They didn't open it if they didn't mean to.

Stumbling, weak, and nauseous with every step he took, Corrado left the dark room. He couldn't properly process things in the light, but he forced himself to walk down the corridor. How long did that take?

Too long.

And then another corridor.

Stairs that made his bones ache.

At the top of those, he found a black door with a camera overhead. He stared up at it because the door didn't actually have a handle on it for him to open it. Tipping his head to the side, he waited for a second before a buzz echoed, and *that* door opened, too.

In the next corridor, he realized all the other doors stayed firmly shut. He was being *guided* through The League's complex. Only allowed to walk where they allowed him to, and granted entry to the corridors and stairwells where they wanted him to be.

The dark room taught him something else.

Trust them.

They could and would do a lot to him—everything and anything to break him, or take from him, but they wouldn't kill him. They wanted him to understand that. They *needed* him to trust their process, and *listen.*

Orders were not always verbal.

Requests, not always obvious.

Lessons, found between the *lines.*

They got their point across.

But he still had his pride.

Corrado followed whoever was controlling the doors, and guiding him. His steps were far too slow, and *painful.* But he pushed through it because if anything, those rooms downstairs taught him he could handle a hell of a lot more than a little bit of pain.

Pain would pass.

Or he would get used to it.

One or the other.

Soon, he started to recognize the corridors, even though the doors to the rooms were still tightly shut as he passed them. Only one—the first room he'd spent any amount of time in when he first arrived at The League—was open.

The knife room.

Corrado stood in the doorway, and watched the man standing about twenty feet from the target blocks. He either didn't care that Corrado was behind him, or he hadn't noticed his arrival. Flicking his wrist back, Alessio tossed a knife that spun through the air so fast, it was nothing more than a blur before it embedded itself directly into the middle of the red circle on the target.

"Good shot," Corrado mumbled.

Alessio didn't startle at his words, simply glanced over his shoulder with a kind gaze that drifted over him like he was taking him in without judgement or comment. "Takes practice—you'll learn, too, if you excel in it."

Huh.

Corrado swallowed the thickness in his throat, managing to ask, "Is letting me out to wander the halls part of the process, too?"

Alessio picked up another knife from the table beside him, but instead of throwing that one, he flipped it over and over in his palm. "Possibly. It all depends on the prospect, and what they need, I think."

Ah.

Corrado understood.

He didn't need to be explicitly told.

They were going to kill him down there trying to take from him what he wouldn't give, and so, someone decided that it was better to compromise. And here he was, *out.*

"Want to try?" Alessio asked, holding out the knife for Corrado to take.

He didn't move.

His body hurt too much.

"What happens now?"

Alessio arched a brow. "Phase two."

"What is—"

"Recovery for a short bit, then the tests begin to find where you excel the most, so they can focus, and hone your skills."

"Well, all right."

What could he say to that?

"Corrado."

He looked up, meeting Alessio's gaze across the room. "Yeah?"

"You did well."

"I feel like death."

Alessio grinned. "You look like it, too."

He cleared his throat. "I spent my eighteenth birthday in those rooms."

Silence coated the space between the two of them. Not for long, though.

"I spent mine watching you," Alessio returned.

"Oh."

Alessio offered the knife again. "You're probably too weak, but you can try, if you want."

"I thought rich hands weren't meant to touch those, only pay someone else to do it."

"I can be wrong sometimes."

"Can you?"

Alessio gave him a look.

"Can you *really*?" Corrado pressed.

"Don't get used to it," Alessio told him.

Corrado smiled. "Good to know."

9.

"I know what you said. *Eighteen*, Dare."

The current source of Alessio's irritation—although if he were being an honest man, he had a lot of those annoyances lately—didn't turn away from the electronic map that covered the touchscreen on his office wall. He waved a hand over his shoulder, like Alessio was a fly he was trying to bat away.

"Are you even listening to me?"

"Annoying, isn't it?" Dare returned. "You do the same thing to literally everyone else, Les. If you don't like when people ignore *you*, perhaps you should attempt to stop doing it to us. You're beyond the annoying stage where I can use your age as an excuse for your bad fucking attitude. Besides, what I need more than you out on an assignment is for you to listen."

"Yeah, well, we don't all get what we want."

"Keep thinking that way, and see where it gets you."

Alessio glared at the back of Dare's head, willing the man to combust right on the spot. Sometimes, it was the little things that inspired the worst kinds of reactions in him. This was certainly one of those things.

Again, if he were being honest, there were many.

This was a big one, though.

"I went through all that training for you to keep me—"

"I have several job offers on the table right now," Dare interjected, still seemingly unwilling to turn around and face Alessio in the doorway. "And while *some* will go to others, because they have the specific skills for those assignments, I am deciding which one might be best for you. I don't take every job that comes in from clients who don't have a contract with a specific League member, and a lot of these are exactly that."

"So, I'll have an assignment soon, then?"

"I didn't say that."

Fuck.

Frustration slipped through Alessio's bloodstream, heavy and thick. Like every other conversation he tried to have with Dare, he suspected this one was going to end the same exact way as it always did. Dare talking him in circles, Alessio getting pissed, and after he'd walked away, he would realize he didn't get shit that he wanted.

"I want an assignment," Alessio said.

"And you will get one when you are ready for one."

"I'm ready now!"

Dare pointed at the map he'd been surveying since the moment Alessio came to his office. "That's a mountain range there—do you think a complex *within* a mountain would be a possibility? A back up, we'll call it. Just in case something happened, and I needed to move out the main area of operation for safety reasons."

"I … *what?*"

"A complex *inside* a mountain range."

"What does that have anything to do with the fact I want to go out on an assignment?" Alessio demanded.

Dare glanced over his shoulder, his brow furrowing. "Oh, I thought you realized I was done with that conversation. So, if you don't want to indulge these new plans of mine, you don't need to keep standing there."

Alessio *balked.*

It took him entirely too long to come up with a suitable response to that, and it wasn't nearly as insulting as he wanted it to be. Shame, really.

"You're impossible," he snapped at Dare.

"But am I really, though?"

"*Yes.*"

"And you wonder where you get it from, no?"

The two of them stared at one another for a spread of time, neither of them moving an inch or giving a damn inch. Finally, Alessio's irritation spilled over as he made a disgusted noise under his breath and turned to leave the office.

At his back, Dare called, "And don't bother the trainees today, Les, they need to *focus.*"

"I want an assignment!"

"Soon."

Yeah, *right.*

To Dare, that could mean months.

Fuck it.

He'd go to Cree.

• • •

Prospects for The League were given one week to recover after phase one before phase two began in full force. A single week with whatever medical care they needed, all the rest that would put them mostly back on their feet again, and then it was back to business as normal.

If intensive, seven-day-a-week training was normal.

The prospects were shoved from one thing to the next—tested on every skill The League could throw at them within a few weeks, and once they figured out where someone *really* excelled, then that's where they started to focus.

For himself, it had been weapons.

Knives, guns, and more.

Any weapon they put in his hands, he could use. And he could probably use it in several different ways to kill someone, if that was the need. He could also *make* a weapon out of just about anything because to him, everything *was* dangerous enough to kill. He just needed to figure out he wanted to do it.

Corrado and Chris were still in their second week of skill testing. Which was why he wasn't very surprised to find Cree hanging a few steps back from the mats set out on the gym floor where the twins were currently working with a League member who excelled in weapons, and specifically, fighting *with* weapons.

"What do you need?" Cree asked before Alessio had even spoke behind him.

He sighed. "I hate when you do that."

"Do what?"

"*Know* where I am."

"Yes, it's a *terrible* thing that I concern myself with your whereabouts so that I can make sure you're not finding some trouble when I'm not looking."

Just like Dare.

Alessio decided he wasn't falling down *this* rabbit hole again today. He'd done that already with Dare, and he wasn't doing it with Cree. It would end *worse* than the first time, that was a fucking guarantee. Cree was even less likely to take his shit.

"So, what do you want?" Cree asked.

Alessio's gaze cut to the mat when a *smack* echoed. The stick of bamboo Oliver was using as a stand-in for a weapon—it still hurt like a motherfucker, but it was *safer*—cracked against the back of Corrado's legs, and sent him sprawling to the mat with a hissed *shit* falling from his cringing lips.

He flinched, too.

That one *hurt*.

On the other side of the mat, watching from a safe distance because it probably wasn't his turn yet, Chris clicked his tongue, and looked like he was ready to back away altogether. That was the thing about The League.

No one said the training was *stupid*.

The same shit they used to break them with were the same tools they used to train them later. No doubt, the twins had more than enough of bamboo sticks being used to leave bruises on their body after the rooms downstairs. So, that meant they were either going to learn *fast* how to avoid those fucking strikes, or they were going to get knocked down time and time again.

It was a mind fuck, really.

"Les," Cree said again.

Yeah, yeah.

The whole reason he was here, right.

He kept one gaze on Corrado who pushed up from the mat with a snarl under his breath to face Oliver once again. Only this time, Oliver was smirking a little too much for Alessio's liking. It was one thing to be trained, but it was quite another when someone took it a little too far, and began taunting you at the same time when you failed.

"Dare," Alessio said, "you need to talk to him."

Cree raised a single black eyebrow, but didn't look away from the mats. "Why would I need to do that?"

"I want an assignment."

"And he won't give you one?"

"Exactly that."

Thud.

Alessio turned in just enough time to see Corrado crash to the mat, only this time, on his back. His arms flew out wide, and his eyes squeezed shut as the air rushed from his lips with a heavy *whoosh*. Oliver's laughter echoed in the gym as he pointed the stick of bamboo in Corrado's direction on the mat, his sneer wicked and amused.

"Come on, now, get up," Oliver said, his hand tightening further around the middle of the stick as he rounded the mats to come slightly closer to Corrado's prone form. "I heard you kept doing that in the dark room, yeah? You kept getting up, didn't you? Even when you were supposed to stay the fuck down, so don't disappoint me now, shithead. *Get up.*"

Alessio scowled, ready to tell Oliver where he could shove his fucking taunts. After all, Corrado wasn't the only one who spent time in those rooms downstairs, and Alessio had been in the complex two years ago when Oliver was trained, too.

He remembered how the man begged.

How he *cried.*

"It's possible," Cree said, dragging his attention away from the situation a few feet away, "that Dare thinks you might be more useful here for a little while."

"Why in the hell would he think that?"

Cree's gaze drifted from the people on the mats to Alessio, and then back again. *Very* pointedly. "Do you think Dare would have allowed you down in that room when someone was actively in phase one—when you *weren't* part of the training team, mind you—if he didn't think you would help? Or when he was released from the rooms, the path he was allowed to take led him to someone he would immediately trust when he would need it the most?"

"I—"

"Not everything is about you, Les," Cree murmured, his attention going back to the training. "And that is something you should remember. If you are better *here* for a time, then here is where Dare is going to keep you. You think it's about you, and Dare's feelings, which means you're selfish because you automatically dismiss the needs of *others*. The League is about more than just you—something we have always made clear."

Well …

Damn.

"All right," he muttered.

He wasn't happy about it, though.

Another loud smack drew Alessio's attention back to the fight happening on the mat. Or rather, the ass-whooping Oliver was currently inflicting on Corrado. Not to mention, the taunts that followed every single crack of the bamboo against another part of Corrado's form.

He was going too far.

Alessio knew it.

No one was expected to pick up one specific part of training right away. It took time, and muscle memory for some of it. Other parts of it was all in someone's mind. Except, Oliver was acting as though Corrado should be on his feet, and able to duck and dodge that fucking bamboo like the rest of them could when he was wielding it.

"*Get.*" Smack. "Up." Smack. "Now."

"Cree," Alessio said under his breath, "tell him to knock it *off.*"

Cree said nothing, only tipped his head to the side like he was considering the scene in front of him. His gaze drifted from the twin at the other side of the mats watching, to the one currently on his knees with his arm raised to protect his face in case that stick came back down again, and then to the asshole with a God complex.

"*Cree.*"

"Is that what it is, Corrado?" Oliver asked. "You *like* getting knocked on your ass like a fucking idiot?"

Corrado said nothing.

He didn't even react.

Not a blink.

Not a word.

Not a scowl.

Nothing.

He simply tried to stand again because *that's* what he was supposed to do— Alessio knew it. He was supposed to keep getting back up, and trying again until he could dodge the attack, and then they would switch places for his twin to do the same. Except, Oliver didn't even let him stand before he hit him *again*.

Knocking him back again.

And then, Oliver pulled the rod back to swing before Corrado even had time to adjust to the fact that he was on the mat again. He was going to hit him *because* he was down; something he wanted to do, not because it would teach a lesson, or was part of the training.

Alessio moved before he could think better of it. Darting forward fast, out of Cree's reach who likely would have pulled him back had he understood what Alessio was going to do, he stepped onto the mats, grabbed the smooth end of the bamboo rod where Oliver had it extended, and yanked *hard*.

The surprise move—Oliver was only thinking about what was in front of him, not behind—allowed Alessio to snatch the weapon right out of the man's hand. He flicked his wrist, flipping the rod over to his dominant hand, where he caught it right in the middle. Flexing his arm once to swing it back, he let the rod fly, cracking Oliver right in the middle of the throat with enough force to send him to his back on the mats, and *without* the ability to breathe, too.

Then, he took one more step, the weapon already poised to strike again as he pointed it at Oliver's chest. The assassin on the floor stared up at him with fury, his fists balling against the mats as he tried to gain his bearings.

"Remember where *you* started," Alessio murmured, "and how you got *here*."

That said, he dropped the bamboo to Oliver's chest. He turned to step off the mat, done with putting Oliver in his place, and willing to see how the man treated his prospect *now*. It was the sharp edge in Corrado's voice when he called his name that made his steps hesitate.

"*Alessio.*"

Over his shoulder, he found Corrado glaring at him.

Scowl in place.

Fists clenched.

Body tense.

Angry all over.

"Don't do that again," Corrado uttered, teeth clenched.

Alessio said nothing because he didn't need to. There was one thing the rooms downstairs didn't take from Corrado, and while it may not seem important in the grand scheme of things, it might be the only thing that would get him through the training.

If only because he couldn't give up.

His *pride*.

Not bothering to respond—Corrado wouldn't want him to—he turned to leave the gym altogether. Dare had been right; he didn't need to bother the prospects when they were being trained. He *was* a distraction.

At least, for this particular one.

"Les," Cree said quietly as he passed, "you know better."

He shrugged, saying nothing.

Cree only nodded back.

10.

"Tomorrow, six AM, *sharp*," Oliver said to the twins, "make sure you are both down here, and ready to go again."

Corrado felt like telling the man to stick his early morning training session right up his fucking ass, but he didn't think that would do him any good. Except to maybe have Oliver riding *his* ass worse than he already did.

"Got it," Chris muttered, taking it slow as he bent down to pick up the shirt he'd discarded earlier. "Ass crack of dawn to get the shit beat out of me again—*perfect*."

"I can hear the sarcasm."

"I wanted you to."

Corrado might have enjoyed the rare sight of his twin being a smartass—Chris was far more likely to fall back and stay in line—but he was too sore and *way* too pissed for that. If his entire body wasn't a canvas of newly formed bruises, then he was going to be very shocked. He fucking hated bamboo now.

Hated it.

"And you, did you hear me?"

Corrado's back tensed, knowing Oliver was talking to him. The only thing he really wanted to do to that prick was bust his mouth, but he had other things to handle first. Eventually, he would get his chance to put Oliver in his place, but today was *not* that day.

Unfortunately.

Soon.

"*Corrado.* Did you hear me?"

"Yeah, I heard you," Corrado said, waving a hand over his shoulder.

Stepping off the mats, he didn't even bother to turn around to directly speak to Oliver—he was a background thought, now. This session was done for the day, the asshole would get to leave the complex, and Corrado wouldn't have to deal with him until tomorrow. That was fine with him.

"Cree."

"What, Oliver?"

"Next week ... I want Alessio down here to spar with them both. He's close to their height, give or take an inch, and build. We both know he's good with a weapon in his hands."

"That's fine."

"Good—"

"For Christopher," Cree added, keeping that same bored tenor as he spoke. "We'll have to find someone else for Corrado."

"Why? They're the same fucking *people*."

Their conversation wasn't all that important to Corrado. His thoughts were somewhere else entirely as he stepped behind the half partition wall in front of a line of showers that gave them *some* privacy from the rest of the gym. Not that it gave them any privacy when someone else was under the showers, too.

But that was the thing.

Here, there was no privacy. And if one *thought* they were having a private moment, then they were foolish. There was also no sense of a man—or woman, although Corrado had only seen a handful of those since his arrival—holding onto any shred of dignity, either.

After the *rooms*, what was the point?

Dignity was gone.

Corrado wondered if he might get his dignity back or even his sense of *shame* … but he didn't think so. At least, not while he was at The League. They made sure to remind them whenever it was needed that here, things like that were nothing more than a distraction. Lose it, get rid of it, hand it over, tuck it away … whatever someone needed to do to forget about it, that's what The League expected. They were here to mold them into what they wanted them to be, not to hold someone's hand because they were worried someone might see their cock when they showered.

Not that he was concerned about *that*.

If people wanted to look, they could look.

Fuck 'em.

Corrado *tried* to follow along with Cree and Oliver's conversation as he dropped his shorts, and slung them over the wall. He still wasn't even sure what the problem was, or why Cree was giving Oliver a hard time over his request that Alessio be in the gym next week to spar with both twins, but whatever.

"I just don't understand why we have to bring in a whole second member to train with the other—"

"Because I said so," Cree replied dryly.

"What's he on about?" Chris asked, slipping behind the wall.

Corrado shrugged, stepping under the spray of hot water after turning the dial almost as hot as it would go. There was nothing better on sore, aching muscles than hot water. Later, he might see if he could find a bathtub in this maze of *hell*.

"I mean, didn't you spar with Alessio the first day we were here?"

Water sluiced down Corrado's face, and he closed his eyes as he scrubbed his hands down his jaw to relieve some of the tension there, too. He wasn't even listening to his twin, not when the hot water was making him feel ten times better than he had just a few minutes ago.

Chris didn't seem to care. "Oliver is right. That doesn't make sense."

"Cree—"

"You cannot teach *affection* with your fists," Cree said, "and that is not a lesson either of them need to learn between one another, sparring or not. If it is okay one time, it becomes okay at other times. My decision is made—find someone else."

Corrado's eyes popped open.

Chris made a noise under his breath. "*Well*, all right … he ain't wrong."

He might have told his twin to shut the fuck up, but he was more interested in the fact that Oliver looked like a gaping fish, and Cree had turned away from the man now. Briefly, Cree looked his way, met Corrado's gaze, and then just as quickly, left the gym altogether without as much as a glance back.

He was done.

Said what he said.

Cree never offered more than what he gave, Corrado found, but it was usually *important* things when he did speak. A man of few words because he watched more than he talked, Cree noticed far more than people gave him credit for, and he considered *everything* because of it.

Corrado cranked the latch to stop the water, wanting to get the hell out of the gym and back to the other thing that was currently on his mind. He barely bothered to use one of the towels waiting on hooks to dry off, instead haphazardly running it through his hair before throwing on his shirt and shorts.

"Hey," Chris said.

He didn't look back at his twin. "I'll catch you later, okay?"

"*Corrado.*"

"*What*, Chris?"

Chris's shower was turned off then, too. Corrado turned to face his brother—who was still naked, and didn't seem to give a damn, much like he hadn't earlier—without a shred of emotion on his face. He didn't *want* people to know that it bothered him that his interest in Alessio was clear, or vice versa. Those were things he always kept to himself, and he wasn't interested in sharing them now.

"It's okay," Chris said, lifting one shoulder like it didn't matter, "you know that, right? It's *fine*, Corrado."

He was *so* fucking grateful that there was another person in this world who not only shared his face, but also his mind. Because apparently Chris could just tell what his twin was thinking without needing to be told.

Yeah, just *great*.

Perfect.

Except it wasn't.

"Leave it alone," he told his brother.

Chris sighed. "It's not a big deal that other people *notice* there's something going on. He didn't say something to make it a *thing*. He said it because he's looking out for both of you—he had a point, too. Don't get in your fucking feelings about it."

"Leave it alone, Chris."

• • •

Corrado *got it*.

He understood why his twin thought he was making a big deal out of nothing, but Chris didn't understand. It wasn't *just* about his sexuality for Corrado—it went beyond that, too. And it seemed just like with everything else in his life lately, the issue started and ended with Alessio. This problem was no different.

It wasn't only about his sexuality.

It was more than that.

Like the fact Corrado walked into The League, and people—Alessio, for one, but he suspected there were more—looked at him with an opinion already formed. About who he was, what he came from, and the things he was capable of. It wasn't *just* Alessio, although he had been the first to verbally make his opinion known to Corrado. It didn't matter; he'd heard *other* members make the same kind of comments when they thought his back was turned.

He was *spoiled.*

He'd been pampered.

He didn't know how to *work.*

As it was, Corrado already had *that* shit he was dealing with here. It showed him he would need to work twice as hard to prove himself here, and make a spot that was his which said he, too, was *worthy.*

Now, there was this, too.

This.

If the members of The League who milled about, or those who were actively taking part in training the twins, didn't already believe something was happening between Corrado and Alessio—they wouldn't be wrong—they probably had a good idea *now.* For one, because of Alessio's show earlier in the gym, and now because of Cree, too.

It was yet another thing.

Something else for someone to use and say, *he's only where he is because of this.* Or, *he'll always need someone watching his back because he wasn't treated the same as the rest of us.* Corrado knew how this garbage went, and he didn't want to be put in the same trash pile.

Once again ... his pride was still a bitch.

That was why Corrado found himself standing in the doorway of Alessio's private rooms instead of his own, where he should have been to change clothes before going to find something to eat. No, he had to deal with *this* first.

"What you did today—don't *ever* fucking do it again. You got me?"

Resting on the bed with his right ankle propped over his bent, left knee, Alessio slowly looked over the edge of the thriller in his hands. His stormy blue gaze drifted to the side as though he was considering what Corrado said, before coming back to the angry man standing his doorway.

"Sure, come in," Alessio muttered. "Why not?"

"Cut the shit."

An arched brow answered Corrado back. Alessio and his attitude was fucking *infamous* around this place. One could tell if the guy was going to be easy to deal with simply by the way he walked out of his rooms first thing in the morning. Head down, he was ready to *fight.* Head up, he'd be mildly pleasant. That attitude of his never went away.

The book in Alessio's hands pissed Corrado off more, though.

Alessio didn't move it, or set it aside. In fact, he went back to reading like he had better things to do than bother with Corrado. "All right, come back when you're in a better mood."

"*Les.*"

"Hmm?"

"What you did earlier in the gym ... that can't happen again. It's bad enough that I already have people who think I shouldn't be here to begin with. *You* were one of those fucking people, remember? I don't need you—"

"I was trying to help."

"It doesn't help. It makes shit worse."

"Corrado—"

"Don't step in for me again," Corrado said, his jaw tensing with every word.

"The last thing I need is that kind of help around here, and you know it."

His piece said—because he was sure he didn't need to say more now—he turned to leave. It was only Alessio's next words that made him hesitate to leave.

"Sorry I fucking gave a shit, then."

Corrado spun back around so fast, the room was a blur. The thing was, by the time he turned around to respond, Alessio had already tossed his book aside so he could stand from the bed. The two of them met toe-to-toe in the middle of the room, never once breaking eye contact, either. He didn't know what bothered him more ... the fact Alessio didn't *get it*, or that it felt like he didn't fucking care either way.

"What did you just say?"

Alessio cocked his head to the side. "I didn't stutter. If you want to make an issue out of nothing, then do that, but do it *somewhere else*, Corrado."

He moved closer one inch.

Alessio didn't back away.

That probably wasn't the best idea, if only because *now* Corrado was close enough to Alessio that their chests grazed when he breathed a little too deeply. He could feel the other man's *heat*—smell the woodsy aroma that always accompanied the leather undertones of his scent. Like this, so fucking close, he could see the flakes of dark navy that made his blue eyes rage like a storm, and the small scar that ran right through the cupid's bow on his upper lip. He could count the few scattered freckles that dotted the bridge of his nose, nearly the same tanned color of his skin, so they would be missed if one was too far away. Except, right then, Corrado wasn't too far away. He was *too* close.

And he noticed everything.

Things that made Alessio uniquely *him*.

Things Corrado liked.

He wanted to be *pissed*. It was easier for him to deal with Alessio and the shit he felt when the other man was around when his anger was present because that took over everything else first, and nothing else mattered.

Things weren't so confusing.

But it was.

Alessio made it confusing.

"That kind of help doesn't *help*," Corrado said.

"Or you got in your feelings because it was me."

"No—"

"I think that's exactly what happened."

"I think you don't listen as well as you *talk*."

Alessio blinked.

Corrado stood firm.

"If you want to help, that isn't the way you do it," Corrado said, reaching up to poke Alessio right in the middle of his chest hard enough that it moved him a bit. Slightly, and not much, but it still did. "Do you hear me?"

Alessio's gaze blazed with fury ... and something else entirely. "Don't put your hands on me unless you plan to use them in a way I'll like. Do you hear *me*?"

He hesitated, then, his mind snapping back to earlier. To important words, and a lesson he hadn't thought about, really.

Fists cannot teach affection.

Here, at The League, fists taught *a lot*. Violence kept them in line, and made sure they understood exactly what was expected of them. And yet, it had been made explicitly clear, even if the words hadn't been told to him directly, that between Corrado and Alessio ... violence should never be the first default.

Ever.

He didn't understand this *thing* happening between him and Alessio. Sometimes, it made him infuriated. Sometimes, he was drawn in again just because. It left him a mess, and that wasn't something he was accustomed to.

It didn't matter, though.

Something *was* happening.

He had to be mindful.

Corrado dropped his hand instantly. "Sorry."

"Good. And don't do it again."

"Same for you, then."

"Is that really a fucking problem for you?"

Corrado let out a hard breath, and it ached the whole way out. "Yeah, man, it *is*. It doesn't help me here, and if you gave a shit, you'd realize that."

It took a second.

Then, two.

Alessio's stance softened. "I do ... know that, I mean. I didn't think."

"*Try.*"

In a blink, Alessio's defensiveness was back. His gaze narrowed. "Is that what you want to do right now—*fight* because you've got a problem with your fucking pride? Didn't you get enough of that with Oliver beating the hell out of you all day?"

Corrado's fists flexed, but not because he wanted to hit Alessio. More because he was still quite aware of just how close the two were together, and *no* ... he didn't want to fight at all.

"No, I don't."

"Don't, *what?*"

"Want to fight."

He didn't mean for his voice to *roughen* like that—to come out husky, and thick, but it still did. There was no mistaking what that meant.

Alessio swallowed hard, his gaze darting to Corrado's mouth before coming back up to meet his stare. "All you gotta do is *say*, Corrado. If you want something, then you say it."

Yeah, okay.

"I don't want to fi—"

He didn't even get to finish. Alessio caught that hand of his, and curled it in his own before his other came up to grab Corrado by his jaw. Fingers dug into his skin in the best way a split second before Alessio's mouth collided with his. The force of the kiss pushed him back against the wall, but not once did Alessio let him go.

Not once did he *back off*.

Corrado didn't want him to, anyway. Not when Alessio's hand let his go so that he could shove his under the waistband of his shorts to find his cock. Tight, fast strokes had his dick hardening quickly as Alessio's teeth dragged across his lower lip. And then that hand was gone from his shorts, replaced instead by Alessio's body pressing into his—the hard ridge of *his* erection grinding against Corrado's while the wall kept him steady when he felt like he might fucking *fall*.

He couldn't think to stand right then.

He didn't trust himself.

"The door," Corrado heard himself mutter when that kiss drifted down to the line of his jaw, and then lower still to where his pulse raced in his throat. "*The fucking door.*"

"Close it."

The words were grunted against his skin—hard, and *hot*. The sound alone hit a spot inside that he didn't fucking know existed until that moment. A place that felt raw, and primal. Sex had always been fulfilling a need for Corrado, something he *did* because it felt good, and he wanted to. This right here, with Alessio …

Well, it felt like that first kiss had.

Like *war*.

With hands pulling roughly at clothes to get them *off*. Mouths that said very little, but couldn't stop seeking the other's out. Couldn't stop tasting and biting and *learning*. Skin rough from two-day stubble.

And then, when clothes were gone, and Alessio was on his knees, reaching for Corrado's cock, he tipped his head back and let out a hard groan. He felt the warm air hit the head of his dick a second before Alessio had him in his mouth, taking him down to the base, and coming up tight around his head with each suck.

He'd blow his load like that.

Just like that.

Seeing him on his knees like that?

Taking him like that?

Yeah.

And then Alessio had to go and fucking stun him—letting him go altogether, and standing fast to crash his mouth against Corrado's. He had to know, then, how fucking hard was he for him? Did his cock feel like it was aching as badly as his was?

Corrado stared down between them, reaching for the man's cock. Alessio's lips drifted over the side of his cheek as he watched while he stroked him in his hand. Hard, tight strokes that had Alessio cursing against his cheek in heavy exhales.

Tight against the head.

Looser at the base.

"Gonna make me come if you—"

"*Nah*," Corrado replied, letting Alessio go altogether, and pushing a hand against his chest to move him back a step. "Not like *that*—not yet." One step turned into two, and then three. Alessio didn't drop his stare, hands shaking at his sides. Corrado got that; he understood why when his own body *vibrated* too. With need—for whatever *this* was. "Is this what you—"

"Yeah, I want that," Alessio murmured. "*You.*"

"I need—"

Alessio tipped his head to the side. "Nightstand."

He didn't even have to get the words out entirely, Alessio just knew, and for some reason … the fact that the man wanted it that bad, that he wanted to be the one *fucked*, made the anticipation thrum deeper inside of Corrado. Until all he could feel was the bass of his heart thrumming right along with it.

Fuck.

Yet, Alessio didn't move as Corrado crossed the space to open the small drawer attached to the nightstand. He stayed standing even as Corrado pulled the items—condom, lube—out before dropping them to the sheets.

He met Alessio's stare as he stood straight again, inching in closer until their chests touched. It was in his eyes that he found the truth reflecting back to him—the truth that *yes*, what he wanted was to be the one beneath the other, he still had *fight* there. A battle that said he wanted to win, to control, to *fuck*. That same war Corrado found in their kiss, and their touches.

The roughness that spoke of a man, and who *liked* that, too.

Because that was the difference between men and women. In sex, women *could* be rough, and they could make it *hurt*, but those were far and few between. Sex, with women, he always found was soft, no matter how rough. Something that fulfilled an entirely different need for sex with him.

Men were not the same—that attraction, for Corrado, were two entirely different things. He wouldn't be so arrogant to say *every* bi or gay man felt that way, or perceived it the same as he did, but that's how he always found it to be. And right then, he was seeing the same thing in Alessio.

That fight.

This time, *he'd* give it.

Give *in*.

Next time was a whole other story, though.

So, Corrado gave him what he wanted. If he wanted *roughness* like he wanted the *fight*, then he could have that. He slammed a bruising kiss to Alessio's mouth as his hand wrapped around the front of his throat. Lips dragged over his savagely, determined to take the very breath out of him as he took Alessio down to the bed.

Hard bodies met, grinding as the two pulled harshly at what little clothes remained between them. Corrado didn't remember when that last piece of clothing hit the floor—when it was just warm skin and muscle meeting his, but there it was.

He felt Alessio's cock, already hard, slide against his own. Their hips moving in rhythm together to get that sensation, fast and desperate, he thought. That's what was thrumming through his bloodstream with his heart now.

Desperation.

"Fuck, *yeah*," Alessio groaned, mouth falling away from his.

Corrado's hand shoved between their bodies to get his hand where he needed it the most. He only leaned up just long enough to grab that bottle of lube before he popped the top open, and got the cool gel piled on his fingertips. He didn't keep the bottle, tossing it aside so he could get his hand back on Alessio's throat while his other started to *work*.

His fingertips pressed against the tight ring of Alessio's ass. Just two, at first, working in with slow, twisting strokes. His fingers curved tighter around Alessio's throat as the man let out another one of those sounds.

Those *groans*.

And fuck, his moans.

His moans.

He was so fucking glad he wasn't new to this—himself, *and* Alessio. Learning sex was fucking *messy*, and this wasn't that at all. Not that he'd known that before this started, but he'd *assumed*. He knew he was right just by the way Alessio moved under him and *asked* for more. Any hesitations he had now were gone for sure.

"*Christ*," Alessio hissed when Corrado had two fingers stretching the man out.

Stormy blue met raging brown when Alessio's eyes lifted to meet his. And as much as he liked hearing those sounds, he wanted to *taste* them when they came out of the man. He got the heat of Alessio's mouth against his as he worked that third finger into his ass as his palm flexed against his throat.

Alessio's hands left the fisted sheets to grab onto Corrado's wrists. He could feel it, the push and pull of his hold on Corrado, the way he wanted to keep him right there, but push him back, too.

That fight …

Against Corrado's roughness.

That's what he wanted.

He pulled his slick hand from Alessio and let go of his throat, too. Those fingers digging into the skin of his wrist hard enough to bruise loosened, and in a breath, Corrado had Alessio twisted around to his stomach on the bed. His teeth found the hard muscles of Alessio's back as he snatched up the packet on the bed. He made quick work of getting the condom open, and sliding it down. The lube on his fingers already soaking his length.

And *fuck*, he felt painful.

Throbbing and aching.

He stroked his dick, getting that lube all over as his mouth found Alessio's back again. The man pushed up against him, seeking *more*. His hands fisted into the sheets on the bed as Corrado fit the head of his cock against Alessio's ass.

He'd stretched him.

And he was still tight enough to hurt.

Alessio let out a shuddering breath, and Corrado slowed. He didn't need to hear his words to *know*—easy, easy. So, that's what he did, careful and fucking slow. Until his chest was so tight from holding back that it hurt, too. It was only when he was halfway to nine inches deep that he heard Alessio's voice, husky and *deep*.

"*Fuck*, yeah."

Corrado swore those two words rumbled along the bed, reaching his spot like a shot of heat right to his marrow. One hand splayed to Alessio's back, his other grabbing tight to the man's side.

It was only once he was seated entirely inside Alessio that *he* felt like he could take in a breath again. Still ragged and aching, though. His chest still felt too damn tight, and it wasn't going to get better until—

"Fucking make me *come*," Alessio murmured.

That.

Until that.

His hips pulled back from Alessio slightly faster than he'd worked his way in, and then flexed forward faster again. The rhythm became a little rougher with each push and pull. Alessio found Corrado's hand at his side, and yanked it under him.

He used Corrado's hand to tug at his cock, his own being the one that worked him. He used him to get himself *off*, while Corrado used him to do the same.

"*Shit, shit*," Corrado heard himself mumble.

He couldn't remember sex being so quiet. And he didn't want to remember it differently now.

So fucking intense.

Like it had turned into something else—something raw, a need that just had to be filled, and *now*. But *God*, where had this been?

His next thrust came *harder*, and Alessio let out a sound that felt primal. "Right there."

Alessio's back tensed. His fingers around Corrado's tightened, and pulled at his hand to work his length faster.

That sound came out of him again as warm cum hit Corrado's fingertips. "*Jesus*, Corrado."

He hadn't realized his own orgasm was so close until Alessio swore again, and his ass tightened around Corrado as he kept up his pace. But there it was, and he leaned down to splay his palm against Alessio's back, his teeth biting into warm skin as he came, too.

So fucking deep.

He couldn't speak. Didn't want to.

Alessio let out a slow exhale. "What the fuck was that*?*"

Oh, fucking great.

So it hadn't just been him that *this* felt new for.

"Something good," Corrado mumbled against his skin.

"*Yeah.*"

As the shaking started to wane, his mouth trailed higher over Alessio's back. His teeth found the junction of Alessio's shoulder and neck, biting just hard enough for him to react. And he did—his semi-hard dick jerking in Corrado's hand. He tightened his grip just to let the man know he felt that, too.

"*Fuck*," Alessio mumbled. "Easy."

Corrado laughed. "*Now*, you want easy?"

"And?" Then, quieter, Alessio added, "I know I fucked up earlier … I didn't think because I didn't like *seeing* it—him taunting you when you were already down. So, I reacted."

Clearing his throat, Corrado pulled himself carefully from Alessio before rolling to his side on the double bed. Using his arms as a pillow, he stared hard at the ceiling for a while, saying nothing. He heard what Alessio told him; he understood it was *important*. Sometimes, things people said didn't seem all that deep on the surface, but it was the shit they *didn't* say that mattered the most.

He figured with this … the things Alessio said and didn't say were both equally important, and he needed to keep the fuck up.

Glancing over at his companion in the bed, Corrado replied, "I get it—you can't do it again, though."

Alessio, still on his stomach with his hands twisting into the edge of the comforter, curled his upper lip like the idea *offended* him. "What, protect you?"

Corrado frowned. Was that what he'd thought he did?

"I don't think I can do that," Alessio said after a beat of silence passed between them. "But I'm not really sorry about it."

Yeah.

11.

"What do you think he said?" Chris asked, his sarcasm heavy. "It's *Cree*, you figure it out."

"So, he basically told you no, but spouted some Yoda bullshit while he was at it."

"Yeah, and—"

"You didn't have to be here, though." Corrado made a noise under his breath, adding, "We told you that, but you decided to stay. I don't know what you want me to tell you."

"It's not about *being* here."

"I think it is."

"Corrado—"

"I don't know what else to tell you, Chris. You chose to stay. *This* is what it means."

Chris made a disgusted sound. "Fuck all of this."

Something crashed against the floor—a metal *ting* ringing out—before a few seconds later, Chris came flying out of the room where he and Corrado had been working for a good portion of the afternoon. Alessio, leaning against the wall because he'd figured it was better not to interrupt the brothers and their work, avoided Chris's gaze when he came storming out. Not that it made much of a difference, as he still saw the glare Chris threw his way before he passed him by without as much as a *hello*.

Alessio wasn't offended.

He didn't know much—if anything at all—about Corrado's twin, and not really for a lack of interest. There simply wasn't a lot of time here to bother with making *friends*. At least, not during that first year, unless someone was training you with a partner, or to be part of a team. Then, it was pertinent that you became friends with the person who you would be forced to trust with your life at one point or another.

It was strange, in a way, how he could easily pick out the differences between Chris and Corrado, and without much effort at all, too. But everyone else seemed more interested in finding all the things that made them exactly the same.

Alessio liked what made them unique.

He waited until Chris rounded the corner at the end of the corridor before he pushed away from the wall. Coming to stand in the doorway of the room where the two had been working, Alessio quickly found Corrado in the room.

Sitting at a large metal table, surrounded by dismantled pieces of *several* guns, Corrado stared hard at the wall, lost in his thoughts. His brow, dipped in concentration, knotted further before he shook his head. Still, he kept staring like he wasn't willing to get back to work.

This was meant to be a fun task, too, for the most part. Or rather, something that most prospects enjoyed. Getting set in front of a mess of dismantled weapons

71

and being told to figure out what went with what was a hell of a lot easier than getting the shit beat out of you in the gym, after all.

"Problem?"

Corrado's head swung around at Alessio's question. He leaned against the doorjamb, arms crossed over his chest, and gave the man across the space a look. A silent, *well?*

"You spy a lot," Corrado muttered. "People don't like that, you know?"

Alessio shrugged. "Keeps me in the loop."

"Well, *stop.*"

Probably not.

He didn't tell Corrado that.

"What's going on? That's the first time I've seen Chris get that pissed here."

And it wasn't like the other Guzzi twin didn't have a reason to get mad at The League. Everyone here had one reason or another to get pissed at someone or something. That was the whole point of this goddamn place—to push one's limits to the breaking point, and then beyond.

"It's nothing," Corrado muttered, and then, he held up a tiny spring, "is this for the AR or the AK?"

Alessio arched a brow. "Neither."

"*Fuck.*"

Corrado threw the spring back to the table, clearly disgusted that he'd been wrong. Folding his arms over the white T-shirt stretched across his chest, he glared at the many pieces he still had left on the table. No one ever told them *how many* guns were on the table, but it became obvious once someone started counting the clips and magazines.

Usually six to seven. All in as many little bits as they could be broken down into so that it could be more challenging. Little nuts and everything. Yeah, it was like a whole puzzle.

But with *guns.*

"Are you avoiding what that was all about with your brother because you're in a mood, or ...?"

Corrado glanced up, his brow furrowing as he took Alessio in again. "No."

"You sure?"

Because wouldn't that be typical Corrado?

Alessio figured so.

Corrado shook his head, dropping Alessio's stare as he reached for more parts to begin his task again. Negative reinforcement was a popular tactic at The League—this task wasn't any different than the others. So, if he didn't get those guns put together, now made *more* difficult by the fact he was doing it alone, then he was going to be here all night.

No dinner.

No bed.

No sleeping.

Nothing.

He would be here until he *finished.*

That's how it worked.

Alessio didn't miss that Corrado was quick to work, though. That he didn't care he'd been left alone to do the task, or that he would probably be here for a few more hours because of it, either. He didn't complain; he simply got to work.

That meant *good* things.

"Chris is in a different place than me," Corrado muttered as he eyed a small clip. "That's all. He came here with intentions that were way different from mine, and they're catching up to him. It's not about *me*, or even him ... it just is what it is."

Alessio tipped his head to the side, considering that. "Because he stayed here for you, and you joined because—"

His words cut off, and he realized then that, in fact, he had no idea *why* Corrado chose to join The League as a new prospect. He'd never thought to ask. Then again, there was a lot he never asked a guy he now regularly woke up to sleeping next to him in bed, or even, found him waiting for Alessio when he went back to his rooms at night.

It seemed like that was just how the two of them transitioned. All it took was a moment in Alessio's rooms a month ago, and the next day, shit was different. Or, that's how it started, with different things between them, until the two of them found a routine that worked for them in their private, quiet moments. They didn't talk about shit—they just *did it*. Alessio liked it that way, and he suspected Corrado did, too. Otherwise, they wouldn't keep doing it.

As for everyone else ...

If someone noticed, they didn't say.

Dare never mentioned it to Alessio, and neither did Cree, but that wasn't unusual, either. As long as no one was being forced to do something, and it didn't affect what was happening at The League, they were willing to let whatever happen.

"Why'd you stop talking?" Corrado asked.

"I just realized, I never asked you *why* you joined."

Sure, he heard the things Corrado's father said in Dare's office that first night. Corrado *and* his twin had made passing comments. But he never outright asked, and got the information from Corrado.

"And you know, that there's a lot of other shit I don't ask you about you ... or your life away from here," Alessio added.

Corrado looked up from the table again. "You want my life story, or ...?"

He gave him a look.

Corrado replied in kind.

Rolling his eyes, Alessio muttered, "It was just a thought, that's all."

Corrado went back to work, seemingly pleased with himself when he found the *right* barrel for a specific body piece he'd been tinkering with for a couple of minutes. "Ha, fucking piece of shit, I got it."

Alessio smirked to himself. "Start with why you joined, then."

"Because I don't fit in anywhere else, and this seemed like the right place to figure out what I was made of without ruining my family's legacy, too."

"What?"

Corrado shook his head. "Cosa Nostra, what Guzzis *are*, is not a good fit for me and my ... lifestyle, as they would call it. Like it's a fucking choice that I like to fuck guys and girls. They act like you wake up this way, and decide *yes*, I am going to like both."

"Who said it would ruin a legacy to be bi? That sounds dramatic."

"The mafia is a lot of things—ragingly homophobic is sometimes one of them. Not so much my blood, but others … people around them. It would be bad for the people I do care about, and I just never felt like I fit in."

Ah.

Alessio scoffed under his breath, thinking how ridiculous that sounded. "Being bi never ruined anything for *me*."

"You're not one of us, either."

Okay, *that* stung a little.

Not because Corrado was wrong, but because he also wasn't *right*. That pendulum swung both ways, and Alessio's mouth worked to tell the man exactly that before he would think better of it.

"Not that you know, but I'm the illegitimate son of Maximo Sorrento." Alessio saw the way Corrado's shoulders tensed at those words, and he almost wanted to laugh at the sight, but he held back. "*Yeah*, now you get it, huh? Maximo, who went mad before he died … who almost ran his whole organization into the ground after having a stronghold on Vegas for decades. That's my father, and you can be sure there are enough people who didn't want to let me forget it, either."

He expected Corrado knew exactly who he was talking about, if only because Maximo, like Corrado's father, were *bosses*—or Alessio's father was before his death—of major Cosa Nostra crime families. That meant, business often exchanged hands between families when Italians were known for being distrustful to organizations beyond their own.

Corrado cleared his throat, still staring at the table. "Sorry."

"Doesn't matter. I barely knew him, I was two when he died. He was old enough to be my fucking great-grandfather, too, fucking someone who could have been the same age as his granddaughter. Everybody wears stains, you know?"

"Huh."

Shifting from foot to foot, Alessio added, "But it followed me *after* … probably didn't help that my mother made a mess of herself. Overdosed when I was ten."

Corrado never looked away from the table, but his jaw worked as he chewed over his words. Finally, he said, "It … wasn't like that for me and Chris. Never chaotic, and we weren't ever neglected. I sound like a selfish fuck to you, don't I?"

"Sometimes." Alessio laughed, adding, "But I don't fault you for it."

"Thanks, I guess."

"Are you going to tell me what your brother is pissed off about, or what?"

Corrado glanced up from the table, a storm brewing in his eyes. "He wants to speak to our father."

"Yeah, that's not going to happen for a while."

"But more our ma, I think, even if he won't admit it."

Alessio made a noise, dismissive and cold, although he didn't mean for it to sound that way. "Yeah, can't relate to that *at all*."

"Sorry about that."

"It's all right."

"It's not—I don't know what I would do without my ma."

Alessio eyed him, chewing on the inside of his cheek as a million and one thoughts tumbled through his head. "What's that like, anyway?"

"Hmm, what?"

"Having a mother that loves you. I wouldn't know."

Corrado shifted on the chair, never looking away from Alessio. "It's …"

"Yeah?"

"Hard to describe. I love my ma."

Alessio nodded. "Wouldn't know what that's like, either."

• • •

"Recon and retrieval—Siberia, in a prison camp, we believe." Dare tossed the folder to the desk, but Alessio didn't bother to reach out and grab it. He was more focused on the image of the man in question that had apparently been missing for close to a decade. A prominent Russian mobster's son, who had disappeared during a war with a rival family. "We've had eyes on who we trust is him. The *team* will go in with you after you've done your recon and sent information back for the plan to be finalized."

Alessio's brow furrowed. "How long is the assignment?"

"Three weeks to a month, depending on how things go."

"And the client is—"

"The father, obviously. He knows it's a risk to go in and try to get the son out, but one he is willing to risk considering the man will die inside the camp otherwise. You are not to get close enough without the team that you might get caught. Do you understand me?"

Alessio gave Dare a look. "I'm not an idiot. I know how to do proper recon."

"I'm just—"

"If *you're* not ready for me to do an assignment, then just say that."

Dare swallowed hard, but straightened where he was standing beside his desk. "I do think you're ready."

"I didn't say me. I said *you*."

"That's not the same thing. The assignment is on the table, and it was given to you. That's what matters. There is no whether or not you want it, or if you would rather stand there and argue with me over *my* feelings … you take that folder, and you do the job you were given. It's that simple, Les."

But was it?

He didn't think so, not after knowing he'd asked for a job since *before* he turned eighteen, and here he was almost two months later, still wondering why *now* was the time Dare finally gave him a job. It rubbed him the wrong way, and he wasn't entirely done with this conversation, but for now, he also didn't get a choice.

Dare was right.

The job was given to him.

The file was there.

He had to take it.

Alessio snatched the folder up from the desk, and turned to leave the office without another word. He didn't have anything else to say when it was already done, after all.

Dare made him hesitate with, "And the cameras to your rooms have been permanently turned off, by the way."

"Oh?"

"I didn't think to mention it, but ... you seem to be busy with something, you know."

Something.

Someone.

Same difference.

"I appreciate it," Alessio said, not turning around.

"You know the rules, Les."

Yeah, yeah.

Don't let it affect The League.

All that good shit.

"I got it," he muttered, leaving the office altogether.

How could he not?

• • •

What time did Corrado *finally* stumble into Alessio's room? Well, he wasn't sure, but it was far too early in the morning for him to be making *that* much noise.

The clock on the nightstand said four.

In the morning.

Alessio was still trying to grumble his way back to sleep when the bed dipped after the shuffling of Corrado shedding his clothes to the floor woke him up in the first damn place. "I *know* you have your own bed, asshole."

Corrado chuckled. "Yours is firmer."

Well ...

"Is it?"

"Maybe. And warmer."

Alessio grinned, and turned to his stomach where he could bury most of his face into the pillow. Cracking just one eye open, though, he stared at Corrado who laid on his back, a hand splayed over his naked chest, while he stared at the ceiling. He said nothing, simply reached over to drag the tips of his fingers through the longer bit of Corrado's hair where his high fade started to darken.

Just as quickly, he pulled his hand back, the need to touch him satisfied. He was *there*. All was good to Alessio—he simply needed the reminder.

He never spoke it out loud, though.

It didn't make sense.

Why bother?

Corrado glanced over at Alessio, his dark eyes drifting over him in the bed beside him before he stared back up at the ceiling. It was in their quiet moments where Alessio found *peace*. He had quiet before—time when he was completely alone, no distractions. And yet, it wasn't the same when it was just him and Corrado.

Here, they decompressed.

Here, nothing mattered.

Here, it was just *them*.

Silently, Corrado's hand slipped off his chest to find Alessio's against the sheets. His fingers curled tightly with Alessio's, and wove together, tucking their hands next to his hip where their bodies were close enough to hide the touch.

"If I *never* see another dismantled gun again, that would be great."

Alessio barked out a tired laugh. "Tomorrow, you'll have five new guns waiting."

"*Fucking bull—*"

"It's a good lesson to learn."

"*Right*," Corrado mumbled, scrubbing a hand down his unshaven jaw. "I'll remember that. What's that file for, anyway?"

Alessio stiffened.

Corrado didn't miss it.

"What?"

"The one on the stand?"

"That's the only one in this room, isn't it?"

Alessio's jaw clicked from how hard he clenched it to hold the words back. He wasn't sure why, all of the sudden, he didn't want to tell Corrado about his assignment, but the urge was *strong*. They were just starting to figure whatever this was out—if someone wanted to call it that, but he didn't know if he would.

Nonetheless, that didn't make it any less true. And here they were, at this unsteady point, and now he was about to head out to a whole different country for three or four weeks? That sounded like a problem waiting to happen.

"Les," Corrado murmured, waiting.

"It's ... uh, a job."

That time, Corrado stiffened. "A job?"

"Mmm."

A beat of silence passed.

Then, another.

Alessio waited it out.

"Can you say what it's for, or no?"

"Recon and retrieval—Siberia."

"Interesting," Corrado replied.

"Could be a month, maybe a little less."

"Huh."

Alessio eyed him, trying to find *something*. Corrado's tone gave nothing away, and neither did his shadowed features in the darkness. Still, something just felt off.

"Hey," Alessio said.

"What?"

"What are we doing? *Us*, I mean. What is it?"

That seemed important to ask.

Wasn't it?

Shouldn't they get that part figured out here?

"Nothing, Les."

Alessio didn't move a muscle. "*Nothing?*"

Corrado looked over at him, still as blank as paper. "Yeah ... I guess."

He wasn't sure if that was Corrado's pride coming out again to make another appearance at the worst fucking time, or if the man simply believed what he was saying. Either way, Alessio didn't like it, but he also wasn't in the mood to point out that for people who were doing *nothing* ... they did it an awful lot, and Corrado *still* found his way to Alessio's rooms far more often than he did his own.

But all right.

They could be nothing.

For now.

Alessio rolled over in the bed then, and sunk back into the blankets, ready to go back to sleep. Corrado let him, at first, but then Alessio still felt him tuck into his back when he rolled over, too. The softest graze of his lover's mouth drifted between his shoulder blades, reminding him that even when he wanted to *hate* Corrado, he couldn't.

Not even a little bit.

The air caught hard in Alessio's chest as Corrado's arms snaked around him like bars. And then just as quickly, warm, rough hands slipped under his boxer-briefs to find his cock. It took Corrado no time at all to stroke Alessio alive under the blankets.

His mouth, still hot at Alessio's shoulders, skimmed higher. Corrado's teeth found the back of his neck while his fingers tightened and stroked him faster.

Dark words hit his skin.

"Like that, yeah?"

He couldn't speak.

Not when he was already *this* close to blowing his load. Not when those words caught in his chest because *damn*, maybe if he said nothing, then Corrado would say *more*. And there was something wicked and dark in his voice when he was like this.

Something Alessio *craved*.

There was one thing he found in men that he didn't find in women when he was in bed with them. Women gave *sweetness* in their sex, even when it was anything but. Men only gave darkness.

And when Alessio wanted *that*, he found it. When he needed sweetness, he could find that, too. Right now, he just needed the one.

Corrado had it all.

"Come on," Corrado mumbled against his skin, "fucking give it to me—I *want* it."

Alessio could feel him hard at his back, the length of Corrado's erection grinding into him in time with the strokes of his cock. In the next breath, he hit that *numb* place before he was thrown into the orgasm.

There was no holding that back.

He spilled on Corrado's fingers, and the sheets.

"*Shit.*"

Sinful, rough laughter filled his ears, and Alessio wanted to swallow it right up. He wanted all those dark, hard sounds against his mouth as he did the same to Corrado that had just been given to him.

Those feelings.

Those *sounds*.

Corrado needed to have them, too, he thought, and he twisted in the bed. Alessio found him already waiting as he reached back.

12.

Corrado

"*Fuck*," Corrado hissed, lifting his gaze from the scope to glare down the barrel of the sniper rifle. He didn't need to check the sights again to know, in fact, he had *not* hit the goddamn target four miles away from the complex's roof where he was currently perched. Or rather, resting on his stomach with the gun in front of him. Behind him, Nathan, his current trainer, sighed loudly. "The wind is too—"

"The wind is fine."

"I adjusted the way you told me to."

"And inhaled when you *shot*."

Had he?

Fuck.

Again.

It felt like Corrado had been saying that *a lot* this last week. Propping himself up on his elbow, he used the tips of his fingers to massage at the spot on his temples that were throbbing. He'd woken up with a headache, the day was half over, and it still hadn't gone away.

"Fuck this," Corrado muttered.

Pushing up from the ground, he snatched up the gun to disassemble it the way he'd been taught. Nathan cocked his head, asking, "What in the fuck are you doing?"

"Not this. Not today."

"That's not your choice. Get back down there, and do it again."

Corrado laughed bitterly. "No."

"No?"

"That's what I said."

"Corrado, I don't know what stick got stuck up your ass this past week, but—"

Fuck that noise.

Corrado tossed the gun to the ground, uncaring that it was unsafe and *stupid*. He looked Nathan right in the face, so there was no mistaking what he said next before he got off that roof, and said, "Sometimes, people just need a goddamn *break*."

Right.

That's what he was going to tell himself.

It wasn't entirely a lie, either. From the point he came to this place, he had not gotten *one* chance to breathe. Not one day to do what he wanted. Hell, he still hadn't even spoken to his three brothers back home, or his parents. He'd been in Nevada for months, but had yet to see the lights of Vegas.

He didn't see anything but *this place*.

The League.

That was it.

And the fucking desert around it.

Screw that shit.

It was made slightly more bearable when Alessio was around because that took Corrado's mind off other things. Or rather, he looked forward to when the day and training was done, and he could head to the privacy of Alessio's rooms where *no one* bothered him. It was just him, and Les ... nothing else mattered.

Except Alessio wasn't here.

He was fucking *tired*.

And today was *not* the day for this shit.

It just wasn't.

"Where are you going?" Nathan shouted at his back.

Corrado didn't even answer.

He just flipped his middle finger over his shoulder. *There*. Let the man make of that what he wanted because he was sure that he would. No doubt, he would quickly run it back to Cree or Dare, too, which meant Corrado would have to deal with that eventually.

He didn't care.

Not right now.

This bad mood wouldn't go away, accompanying him all week like a stink he couldn't get rid of no matter how hard he tried. *And he did try*. The problem was, he knew exactly why he felt this way, and the fact that it all led back to Alessio being gone.

He didn't like that.

None of it.

Corrado didn't do emotional shit—he found it much easier to deal with life and other people when he kept a healthy distance from it all. Then, stupid things didn't get brought in to play, too. You know, like someone's *feelings*.

Climbing down from the roof, he could still hear Nathan bitching up above. Then, it turned to Nathan getting on the phone to shout at someone—probably Dare, but he didn't care to listen and figure it out. It took him another twenty minutes before he was walking the corridor leading to his rooms.

Where he would be alone.

And *irritated*.

A great fucking combination.

The first thing he did once he was in his rooms was head straight for the connecting bathroom. It wasn't big—hell, Alessio's bathroom was bigger than his, *and* had a bathtub instead of a standing shower—but that's all he needed. Stripping down to nothing, he stepped in under scalding hot water, letting it pink his skin as he attempted to scrub away his frustrations, and clear his mind.

It didn't work.

Nothing worked anymore.

He needed quiet nights.

Conversations in darkness.

Fingertips keeping him awake when they glided over the ridges of his muscles because for some fucking reason, his body felt like a live wire whenever Alessio was near. A man who was *nothing* like him. And yet, he found familiarity in that same man, too.

He needed those things to get back to a *good* place, except he didn't want to need those things at all. That was where he found his biggest frustration, and he didn't know how to deal with it at all.

It was only once Corrado stepped out of the shower, dried off, redressed, and exited from the bathroom that he realized, no ... he wasn't alone anymore.

Chris leaned in the doorway. He passed his twin a look, but when Chris didn't say anything, Corrado chose not to offer an explanation for his silence or tenseness, either. It was just easier that way. Life was always easier when he kept his problems to himself.

Besides, Chris had his own shit he was trying to deal with, but Corrado couldn't relate. He *wanted* to be here—even if he was struggling right now for reasons that he didn't want to face—but Chris didn't want to be there at all.

Not anymore.

You know, ignoring the fact Chris wasn't really saying that. Corrado didn't need his twin to say it for him to know it was true.

"You okay?" Chris finally asked.

Corrado let out an annoyed snarl under his breath. "What's it fucking look like to you?"

"Like you got a bad attitude."

"*Yeah.*"

"And nobody fucking likes it."

Corrado turned around to offer his twin a sardonic smile. "Then, feel free to leave, Chris. The door is right there, and *look* ... it's already opened for you."

Chris raised a brow.

He didn't change his stance, or attitude.

In fact, Corrado waved at the door and added, "Go on."

"Les has been gone about a week, huh?"

Corrado's jaw tensed. "What about it?"

"Don't you find it funny how a couple months ago, you could barely stand to look at him ... and now lately, it seems like you become fucking impossible to deal with when he's not around?"

"No, I don't find that funny at all."

Truly.

He didn't.

Annoying.

Strange as fuck.

Not funny, though.

"Hmm."

"Get out," Corrado uttered.

Chris shrugged. "I'm just saying, you're in a mood lately. You should probably get that figured out, Corrado."

"Nobody asked you."

"And yet, I still told you."

Fuck that noise, too.

• • •

His bad mood didn't go away.

In fact, it got worse.

Three weeks later, he felt like he could probably rip someone's face off if they looked at him the wrong way, but Corrado had somehow managed to convince his delusional ass that if he ignored his mood, then it wouldn't be a problem.

Wrong.

He wasn't willing to admit it, though.

His pride was a bitch.

How many times had he said that?

A lot.

Corrado heard the footsteps—several pairs, not just one—approaching his rooms long before the figures shadowed his doorway. He refused to glance up over the weapons magazine he'd snatched from the communal kitchen to greet the newcomers. This was supposed to be *his* day to relax, and he was trying his fucking hardest to do that.

Not that it was working.

Nothing did.

"What is it you want, Corrado?"

Cree.

He glanced up over the edge of the magazine, but instead of looking at Cree, his gaze drifted to the people standing just behind him. The *team*, it looked like. The same team that dragged him into those fucking rooms months ago.

He still didn't know who they were beneath their black masks. It could be Nathan, the sniper, under one. Or Oliver, the fighter, under another. Although, he doubted that simply because he figured now, he might *know* them just by being near them. He knew at least *one* was a woman considering her smaller build, and curves that were accentuated by the tight, black clothing. But that was as much as he knew—they didn't speak unless they absolutely had to, and he was sure their voices were not the same when they gave orders as it was when they were joking down in one of the communal areas of the complex.

Corrado tried *damn hard* not to show how seeing the team at his rooms made him feel—tight in his chest, and like a deadweight had come to rest in his stomach. He was not doing those fucking rooms again. He had news for them, if that's what they thought.

"Are you listening?" Cree asked.

Corrado's gaze cut back to the man in question. "No."

Cree's expression didn't change.

Nothing new there.

"The last month—three weeks, give or take, but who wants to be specific?— you've been struggling," Cree noted.

"And?"

"What is it you need, hmm?" Cree tipped his head to the side, considering Corrado as he said, "Your brother wanted contact with his parents … he needed motivation, we'll say. He earned it, and got what he wanted. Did you know that?"

"*And?*" Corrado asked again.

Because yes, he did know. And no, he didn't see what it mattered.

Chris was Chris.

Corrado, despite looking the same, was not actually *the same*. Why was that so hard for people to figure the fuck out?

"I have an offer for you," Cree said, tipping his hand over like there might be something waiting in his empty palm for Corrado to see; there was nothing, obviously. "I don't think it'll be exactly what you want, but some things can't be helped … and, if anything, it might help with the fact you're a little stir-crazy."

He looked to the people behind Cree again.

"What kind of offer?"

"The team—they'll drop you off about twenty-five miles from here, even further out than we already are. You'll have to the end of the day."

Corrado blinked. "*To do what?*"

"Get back alive."

What?

Cree smiled slightly, as though he could see the questions forming in Corrado's mind. "For one, it's a good way to put some of the skills you've been learning to a *real* test. Out in the real world, so to speak. The team will be near, or close enough to cause you trouble here and there. Think of it like a—"

"Hunt," Corrado interjected.

"Well, yes."

"And what do I get … if I make it back, I mean?"

Cree shrugged. "You'll make it back, that's a certainty. It'll be whether or not they need to carry you back, or if you'll walk in with your own legs that'll make the difference."

"That's not that I asked."

"A night away," Cree said. "Whatever you want to do, wherever you want to go … *within reason*, keep it to the state, you will be able to go. You'll be provided with everything you need—vehicle, fake identification, just in case, and whatever else. No babysitters watching you. Prove you've learned something these last two months, because the past three weeks have put you back several steps, and we'll see what we can do for you."

Corrado chewed on his inner cheek. "Hmm."

"There is an expiry on this offer. Ten seconds is what you have to decide."

"Where will they drop me?"

"I told you, twenty-five miles—"

"No, *where* exactly?"

Cree smiled. "Nowhere. It'll seem like nowhere because that's exactly what it is."

Huh.

Corrado looked at the team again.

"Three seconds," Cree said.

"All right," Corrado muttered, pushing off the bed and tossing the magazine aside, "what's it going to hurt?"

Cree laughed.

An unusual sound, considering the man *rarely* did it.

"That's what I want to hear," Cree said, slapping him on the back as he passed. "Try not to fight the team too much when they put the hood over your head, yeah?"

"*Great.*"

• • •

Corrado was shoved to his knees roughly, and he *felt* the fucking rocks on the ground dig into his skin and bones through his pants. Something dropped to the ground beside him with a heavy thud, and then that hood was ripped from his head. It took him far too long to realize he was surrounded by *cliffs*. Red dirt, dry plants, and a few towering trees keeping the sun shaded.

Where the fuck was he?

He focused in on the man kneeling in front of him. Ten feet away from him was a helicopter that had landed in the only spot that seemed safe and wide enough for it to do so, considering the rocky ledges that led hundreds of feet down into *more* rocks.

Fun.

"Hey," the guy said.

Corrado swallowed his nerves, saying, "Yeah?"

"Here's where I let you go, huh?" Without warning, the guy pushed the mask up over his face, giving Corrado the first peek at *one* of the people on his team—the team that trained him. Dane, one of the few members of The League that Corrado liked ... strange how that worked ... gave him a grin. "Everybody else got dropped off in vehicles at different points. Nobody is going to kill you, but it might seem like it when they get a little close. Don't stop moving, because that's when predators find you, find your way back—keep going east. Do you remember how to tell if you're moving east?"

Corrado glanced at the rocky ledge.

Yeah, he knew.

East meant going right over that ledge.

"I know how to keep going east," he muttered.

Dane chuckled. "*Now* you get it. This isn't going to be easy, but if you keep going east, you'll be fine. At some point, if you're going the right way ... you're going to start recognizing shit from things you've done in training, or whatever else."

He wasn't wrong.

Some training *had* taken place in areas around the complex. Miles into the desolate land that surrounded the area.

Dane pointed at the bag next to Corrado. "There's a satellite phone *if* you need it, and it's preprogrammed with the only number you can call from it. You want water? *Find some.* You've got one small blade in there—get it out, and have fun getting your ties cut. Then, start moving. Sound good?"

Corrado smirked. "Sounds like hell, really."

"Depends on who you ask. This was one of my favorites. How else are you going to learn to *survive*, Corrado?"

Something beeped.

Dane checked his watch. "And that's my signal. Stop wasting time, Corrado."

That said, Dane straightened to his full height, and turned to head for the chopper. Corrado had about a million and one questions he still wanted to ask, but he figured Dane was right. Those things didn't matter, and he was losing seconds right now.

He bet even those were going to count here.

Seconds would make the difference to him succeeding with this or failing. With hands still tied, he used his booted feet to drag the small bag back closer. Then, he used his teeth to rip the zipper down as far as he could get it.

Corrado had the knife balanced between a rock and his boots as he ran the edge of the blade against the zip ties at his wrists before the helicopter had even lifted from the ground again.

And then he heard it.

A *whistling*.

The dirt next to his knee exploded, peppering his body, and making him jerk sideways to protect himself. The knife slipped from his grip and hit the dirt. Not that it mattered, despite slicing his skin a bit, he also cut the ties enough to break them when he yanked his wrists apart.

He was more concerned with the fact a bullet just hit the ground next to him, though. Looking up, he found Dane resting along the side door of the helicopter, sniper rifle aimed right at him. The man looked up over his scope, winked, and waved two fingers.

Yeah.

It kind of was a hunt.

Except ... he didn't like to be prey.

Damn.

"Let's fucking go, then."

No one else could hear his mutter, sure, but that was fine. He grabbed that bag and the knife tight in one hand, and headed for the rocky ledge leading to the cliffs. But first, he had to fucking climb.

All the way down.

13.

"Now *why* would you put metal in your face?"

Stepping off the escalator leading in from arrivals, Alessio grinned, knowing *exactly* what Cree was griping about. Raising his hand while giving Cree a look from the side, his fingertips drifted over the two small, golden hoops he had put side by side—with about five millimeters of space between each—in his right nostril.

A bit of spare time on his hands, a tattoo shop across the road from where he was hiding out when he wasn't working in Siberia, and *yeah*. Shit happened. Things like that always happened when Alessio became bored.

That's how all his tattoos got on his body, too.

Besides, now he had something to remember this hellish month by—and since he liked his new body modification, he'd think about that instead of the rest.

Certain places were wastelands, okay?

That's what he felt like he just came back from.

Dropping his carry-on bag, which was nothing more than a black backpack that made travel easy but also had the essentials he needed should his luggage disappear, to the airport's tiled floor, he gave Cree a smile.

"Nice to see you, too," he said.

Cree chuckled, and folded his arms over his chest. "I already know how it went, but go ahead and tell me."

Alessio shrugged. "It was fine."

"That's all you want to say? Your first assignment, *alone,* too, and it was fine?"

"Yeah."

Boring.

A little too easy, all things considered. His main part of the job had been the recon mission, which was basically doing nothing except watching, looking for shit, and staying out of sight. Then, when he had confirmation the Russian mobster's son *was* in fact in the isolated prison camp, he could prove it, and also had a good idea of the man's schedule inside the place, he called it into the team.

It was up to The League's team leader on whether or not he would be allowed to take part in the retrieval, and he had. Not that it had been anything exciting, either. They went in at night, armed and ready, took out the main security that would be a problem, grabbed the guy from his building where he was housed, and then blew out the side of the cement fence that was also wired to electrocute people who touched it.

Simple.

"Well, come on, then," Cree said, tipping his head sideways a bit, silently saying the two of them should get going. No one from The League liked to linger too long in a public space like an airport after a job in another country. "Let's get out of here."

"All right."

Alessio picked up the bag he'd dropped before and followed behind Cree until they were at the luggage carousel waiting for his to come around. Cree stayed quiet as brightly colored bags passed them by on the conveyer belt. He didn't mind the silence, as it gave him a chance to relax a bit, more so than he had over the past several weeks.

Nevada felt like home.

In a way nowhere else did.

He watched the people gathered around the conveyer, some leaning close to talk, others laughing, and a few looking as though they were simply ready for the day to be over. It was funny because he related to every single one of them.

For different reasons, obviously.

Did it feel good to be out and finally doing a job?

Yeah.

It also felt good to be back here. For the past three weeks, he felt like that last conversation with Corrado had left a lot of shit unsaid between the two of them. They had unfinished business, and that's where Alessio's mind continued to go back to every time he had a moment alone to think while on assignment.

He didn't need that distraction.

Didn't want it.

But here he was, so …

Alessio wasn't going to dwell on the *whys* of it all, because a part of him knew that was obvious, but he figured now that he was back, the two of them could settle out some shit. Then, he could put that behind him and get back to work. He wouldn't be kept awake at night by thoughts of a guy who clearly didn't know what in the hell he wanted where Alessio was concerned.

Or, whatever.

Who knew?

"You're quieter than I expected you to be after coming back from your first assignment," Cree murmured as Alessio's bag finally came around, and he could pick it up from the belt. "I thought you'd want to tell me *all the things.*"

Alessio passed him a look as the two turned to navigate the busy arrivals area so they could leave the airport entirely. "Is that what you want me to do?"

"I want you to do what you *need* to do, Les. That's what I spent years teaching you, even if you didn't realize it."

He did realize, though.

He'd simply never said it out loud.

"I left some business unfinished back here with someone else," he said, refusing to explicitly state Corrado's name, not that it would have made a difference to Cree either way. Still, if there was anything Alessio learned from watching the men he was closest to, it was that things like relationships—and the fickler, *love,* if that's even what this was because he didn't know—was not something you offered out for public consumption. Not in this life. "And it's followed me for weeks."

Cree nodded. "That happens."

"I'm not a dweller. I don't *dwell.*"

"Except when it's important. Then, you dwell entirely too much, overthink, and usually … overreact about it all. That is what you do."

Well …

"You're not wrong," Alessio muttered.

Not *happily*, though.

He caught sight of Cree's amused smile, but the man was quick to hide it by looking away. He wasn't sure whether to be annoyed that his affections for someone else was so clearly on display for those he was closest to, or that he should be grateful someone knew him well enough to see it at all.

This shit was confusing.

A mess.

And he still didn't know if he liked it.

Once the two were outside of the airport and had found Alessio's smoky gray Mustang parked in the underground garage where he'd left it three weeks earlier, Cree turned to him with a sleek burner phone in his hand.

"Here, one more quick job for you … although this one can end when you're ready for it to, I suppose," Cree said. "My car is on the other side of the garage, and I can find my own way back to the complex, I'm sure."

Alessio took the phone, his gaze drawn to the red, blinking dot on the middle of the screen. "What's this?"

"Something I suspect you need."

"I don't—"

"Find the dot, Les, whatever happens after that is up to you. You know how to get yourself back, and besides, I'm not worried about you leaving. Where would you go?"

He gave Cree a look. "I wanted to go home."

"I know."

● ● ●

Alessio found the red dot.

Corrado.

He found him sitting at the bar of an upscale hotel in the very heart of Las Vegas. The drive following the little red dot move around the city wasn't exactly hard, except for the fact Alessio hadn't known *what* he was looking for.

That was annoying.

Until he found it.

Alessio suspected whatever phone Corrado had on hand was being tracked, which was where the red dot came into play. He almost wondered what Corrado had been doing all evening, and why he'd been allowed to leave The League's complex before his first year of training was up, but those thoughts quickly drifted away as he watched him from afar. Nursing what looked like a glass of whiskey on ice, Corrado didn't even notice Alessio just twenty feet away standing in the entrance of the hotel's bar.

Despite being *only* eighteen, and not at all legal to drink, Alessio didn't think Corrado looked out of place at the bar in his dark wash jeans, and leather jacket. He tipped that glass up for another drink and shook his head when the bartender came around like he was going to offer another round, if he wanted it.

Alessio bet—because of rare occasions, he knew Dare let people have a free day away from the complex—that Corrado had been given whatever he needed for the night. A vehicle, likely, and IDs to get him by; probably cash, too, if not black cards without a spending limit.

He was content to watch Corrado for a while, and not interrupt his time alone, but that idea quickly went away when he realized the man sitting next to him at the bar was leaning closer. To his benefit, Corrado wasn't paying the guy *any* attention.

Not a lick of it.

That didn't stop the man from trying, though. In a silk dress shirt, top two buttons undone around his throat, and a grin that said he was *interested* ... the man leaned closer still, his hand coming to smack Corrado's arm.

All things Alessio instantly *hated.*

The guy could simply be attempting a friendly conversation. He might have noticed another quiet man at the bar and decided to make a friend.

Or maybe it was something else.

An attempt at *more.*

It didn't matter.

Alessio didn't *like* it.

He'd felt a lot of things in his life; far too much anger and bitterness from his childhood, and the loss of a father and mother that had never really been his to begin with. Abandonment and loneliness sometimes felt like his best friends when he was alone with his own thoughts at night, in a cold bed. Pride was something he'd learned to let go of years ago because someone always wanted to take it from you. He knew affection and loyalty because those were some of the first things Dare and Cree taught him when they took him in at only ten, and those emotions *sharpened* for him over time, but especially to those he cared for.

Right then, though?

All he felt was a hot, burning jealousy searing through his chest. It cut right through his fucking ribs, and stabbed him in an organ he liked to pretend didn't exist a lot of the time—*his heart.*

And he'd never felt that.

Not like this.

Not *that* strongly.

It was so strong and piercing inside his body and mind, in fact, that it propelled him forward across the floor of the hotel's bar before he had even thought about it. His legs taking long, sure strides until he came up behind Corrado, and the man that felt way to close to someone that Alessio felt like was only *his.*

Corrado was *his.*

He wasn't sure when he decided that fact—possibly that day he saw Corrado in the knife room, and the man didn't care to take his shit like everyone else did. Or maybe it was that first taste of him, mouth bloody, but *damn*, he still found something perfect there. It could have been late nights in his rooms where conversation wasn't always present, but Corrado's *presence* brought him the closest to the feeling of security that he'd felt in years.

He didn't care when it happened.

It just *was.*

And that man was too close to something that wasn't his. It couldn't be his when Corrado was Alessio's ... even if he didn't think so.

Yet.

He would know soon.

The man beside Corrado saw Alessio approaching first, his eyes widening a bit. Maybe it was just the fucking aura Alessio gave off—a *back off* kind of vibe—or it could have been the severe expression he couldn't shake, not that he bothered to try.

At the man's obvious distraction, Corrado turned to look over his shoulder. His gaze slammed into Alessio's, and for a second, it felt like the world slowed down around them. Gone were the sounds of a busy bar, and chattering people. The music in the background was dulled, and he barely felt the floor under his feet.

None of it mattered.

Not when Corrado's gaze skipped over his face and the rest of him like he was trying to correlate what he was seeing to *real life*. Like he didn't believe he was standing there for a moment, and he needed to make sure it was really happening.

"That's new," Corrado said, pointing over his shoulder at Alessio's face.

At the nose rings, likely.

He arched a brow. "I guess so."

"What if they get ripped out?"

"That'd be shit, I bet," Alessio replied dryly. "Say goodbye to your friend here, we've got other things to do."

"Excuse me?"

Alessio didn't look away from Corrado, not even bothering to spare the man beside him any attention. He wasn't fucking around here, and if he didn't put some distance between Corrado and the stranger, someone was going to get hurt.

Because apparently, Alessio wasn't good at this. He didn't do well with jealousy. And since he was more than capable of causing some serious bodily harm to another human being, it was better if he just corrected the problem causing him the issue in the first place.

Like *now*.

By getting Corrado away from the man.

If it seemed like Alessio was being an asshole, then so be it. They could deal with that later. At least, people would remain *alive*.

Right?

Yeah, jealousy was not his friend.

At all.

Learn something new every day.

"Say goodbye," he murmured.

Corrado's brow lifted, clearly hearing the heat in Alessio's tone. Yeah, he couldn't even hide what he was feeling, for fuck's sake.

This was ridiculous.

Downing the rest of his drink, Corrado set the glass to the bar, and pushed off the stool to stand toe to toe with Alessio. Alessio had all of a half of an inch on Corrado's six-foot-two height. It wasn't a lot—barely there at all, really. For the most part, it still put them damn near eye level.

He didn't say goodbye to the guy, who was now slipping off the stool that had been beside Corrado's, and moved further down the bar away from them entirely.

Corrado only looked at Alessio.

"Better?" he asked.

Alessio wasn't going to lie.

"Not yet."

"Yeah, I can tell."

"Don't sound so fucking smug about it," Alessio returned.

Corrado smirked. "Kind of hard."

Jesus.

Alessio needed to get off this conversation. He didn't need his weaknesses available to the rest of the world for public consumption. "Do you have a room here?"

"And a fake ID, some cash … twenty-four hours to do whatever I want." Corrado shifted from foot to foot, glancing away. "I didn't know you were back."

"Clearly."

Okay, that came out cold as hell.

Even he heard it.

Corrado looked back at him, a fire blazing in his gaze. "Do you have something you want to say to me, or what?"

Why lie?

"Yeah, but I don't think you want to hear it."

14.

Corrado

"Which room?"

Alessio didn't even look over his shoulder when he asked that question. Corrado watched his hand flex tightly around the black bag that dangled from his fist, and the way his shoulders tensed with every step he took.

Pissed all over.

Or ... Alessio was something else altogether.

Jealous.

"Room *208*."

Alessio made a noise under his breath, still walking straight down the hallway without bothering to look at Corrado behind him. "All right."

He wanted to deal with the fact that Alessio randomly showed up when *no one* was supposed to know where he was—that was Cree's deal, right? If he made it back to the complex before the sun went down, then he would get one free night to do what he wanted *without* babysitters watching him the whole time. So, how the fuck did Alessio know where to find him?

At the same time, he didn't mind. Or rather, he didn't care that it was Alessio that showed up. Except going into that meant handling the fact Alessio was jealous. Because he didn't like what he found when he showed up.

Not that it had been anything.

Or meant anything.

Corrado didn't even know that guy's name, or what the fuck he wanted. He'd been trying to have a drink before he went upstairs, and passed out on the king-size bed. He'd wandered around the city for a while earlier, trying to decide *what* he wanted to do. And maybe, had Alessio been there with him, he might have picked a half of a dozen things just because.

Instead, he wanted to be alone.

Drink.

Sleep.

Feel fucking normal.

He'd been content to ignore the guy at the bar, whether his friendly attempt at conversation was just that—friendly—or whether it was a hint for something else. Which was exactly what he had been doing when Alessio showed up.

Not that Alessio realized that.

Or saw it.

Corrado could tell.

The bigger problem?

He liked it.

Corrado wasn't a liar, or he tried hard not to be. So, it'd be a damn lie if he tried to say the warning—one for him, and for the other man at the bar—that flashed across Alessio's face because he *thought* he knew what was going on there didn't make Corrado feel some kind of fucking way.

Not that he wanted to feel that way.

Or any way.

He didn't know what the hell he wanted.

Alessio stopped in front of the room that belonged to Corrado for the night. Stepping aside so he could lean against the wall while Corrado pulled the keycard from his pocket to unlock the door, Alessio asked, "Would you have done that, then?"

Corrado's hand froze at the card reader, hovering overtop but not pulled down to drag the keycard through the lock. "Done what?"

"That guy—*him*. Would you have brought him back here had I not shown up? Spent the night with him? *Any* of it?"

"Why don't you just *say it*, huh?" Corrado returned.

"Excuse me?"

"You're jealous, Les. *Say it.*"

"That's half the fucking problem, isn't it?" Alessio let out a dark laugh, making Corrado's chest clench from the sound. *God*, he loved that sound. "The fact you don't *want* all that shit to be out there, right? Because once it's out there, Corrado, we don't get to take it back. You get stuck in your fucking pride, because you don't know how to deal, and there we'll be. That is the *problem*."

Corrado's jaw flexed, holding back words and anger. Because frankly, Alessio wasn't wrong, and he didn't know how to admit that without sounding like a fool. Nobody wanted to be the idiot with a foot stuck in his mouth.

"Yeah, I know," Alessio added when Corrado continued to stay quiet.

Raging blue met dark brown when the two stared at one another in the hallway. The silence stretched on, heavy and loaded with *a lot* of shit Corrado had been leaving to the wayside where he and Alessio were concerned. Things like *feelings* and what the fuck was even going on between them. The labels he hated because once *you* labeled yourself, the rest of the goddamn world thought they got the right to do the same. Or even the fact that he'd never connected with someone on a level like he did with Les—like the man just *knew* the craziness in Corrado's mind without him ever needing to open his mouth to say it.

And he recognized those same things in Alessio, too.

These things?

It was too much.

Too deep.

Things that he figured, once they were said, there was no going back. And maybe that bothered Corrado because it scared him. He didn't like to be scared of shit—didn't *want* to be, either—but he didn't know how to tell Alessio that without the rest of the shit in his mind spilling out, too.

Like the fact he didn't know how to do this.

How to be *someone* to someone else.

How to be a *them*.

A thing.

And despite a part of him not wanting to admit he wanted to be exactly that, even if that meant he would need to deal with things he'd shoved down where *nobody* could find them, the other part was louder.

"You didn't answer my question," Alessio said.

Corrado arched a brow. "You didn't answer *mine*."

"I already said you don't want me to."

Right.

"And that's *your* problem," Corrado replied, shoving the keycard through the reader to unlock the room door, "because you don't listen nearly as well as you fucking talk, Les."

"What does that even mean?"

Corrado shook his head, opening the door and entering the hotel room. He dropped his jacket to a chair, kicked off his shoes, dropped his bag, and headed for the bathroom. All the while, he ignored Alessio behind him as he called after him.

"Hey, I'm fucking speaking to you. What does that mean?"

No.

He was done talking.

For one, this wasn't a conversation he wanted to have. And for two, because even if he did want to have it, he didn't know where to begin. Not without admitting he didn't know if he could ever *be* something with Alessio.

Maybe a part of Corrado was just broken.

Or *wrong*.

Who knew?

"Corrado!"

He let the slam of the bathroom door answer Alessio's shout of his name. Maybe he'd get the hint, then, and back the hell off. Corrado hoped for too much, because as he was tugging off his shirt while turning on the shower taps in the large bathroom, Alessio came right in.

Like he'd been invited.

"We're not done here," Alessio said.

Corrado made a harsh noise under his breath, shrugging off his pants, and yanking off his socks. *Fine.* If that's what Alessio wanted—an answer to his damn question—then he would get one. "No, okay? No, I didn't even know that guy existed until you made it into a thing. I was too busy thinking it would have been a *far* better day had you been here to show me around the city." He stood straight, fingers hooking around the waistband of his boxer-briefs to shove them down before he could step into the shower. "There, is that what you wanted to hear?"

"You think *that's* what this is about?"

"No, I think you want something from me that I'm not even sure I can give, Les. *Why* can't I give it to you? I don't know, so don't ask. But if you're looking for that, you're not going to get it."

"I—"

"Get out so I can shower."

Alessio stood firm. "No."

"Fine."

Fuck him.

Corrado shoved his boxer-briefs down, and stepped into the shower, closing the frosted glass door behind him to keep Alessio out. Not that it really would if the man wanted to come in, anyway. He didn't need *Alessio* to be done with the conversation to keep doing what he wanted to do. He was sure that frustrated the hell out of his companion, but whatever.

Even beneath the spray of heavy, hot water from a shower head that was the size of a dinner plate, Corrado could still hear Alessio when he spoke. "I keep thinking it's your pride that does shit like this, but I don't know anymore."

Staring at the brown and beige tiles, Corrado willed his ears to stop working. If for just a second because he didn't *want* to know he was fucking this up. He didn't want to know he was hurting someone he cared about.

Someone he *loved*.

Because he wasn't ready to say that.

It couldn't be *real*.

Once it became real, then he had a whole bag of other shit to unpack, too. Like the people in his life who would say he was wrong and *weak* for loving who he did. Like the people who would shame his father, his family … their entire legacy because he loved another *man*. That culture—the mafia—was caustic when it came to people like him, and it wouldn't matter that he wasn't *in* it. It wouldn't make a difference because there were still expectations for him, and his family, regardless if he was made or not.

He knew it.

He heard them his whole life.

People like him?

They were shamed.

Shunned.

Forgotten.

God knew he never wanted to put his family in that position—he never wanted to make his parents or his brothers feel like they had to choose between him, and the life they'd always known. It didn't matter that they would accept him because there would be plenty of others around them that wouldn't. And when they chose to fight *for* him, it would only leave them with a target on their backs because of it.

That's how the mafia worked. When one didn't fall in line, even if that *one* was the boss, then the rest seemed to take that as a sign of weakness. A problem that had to be culled before it could get worse.

He loved his family.

He loved where he came from.

Those were things Corrado was *not* willing to give up, not for anything. And if he was going to keep them, and maintain the delicate line he'd been walking his whole life, then nothing could change. He couldn't give more to Alessio than he already had without sacrificing something else. It would always be that way.

It was Corrado's burden to carry.

He didn't expect Alessio to understand these things. He didn't think the man would care, either. Because in reality, they weren't at all alike, and they didn't come from the same *world*.

That pride of his …

It was still a bitch, but that was only because pride was the only thing that kept Corrado sane a lot of the times.

"I should have listened, right?" Alessio asked outside of the shower, his voice muffled by the water pouring down on Corrado's tense form. He heard the shuffle of fabric before Alessio added, "I asked what this was, and you said *nothing*. Man, yeah, I should have fucking listened when you said that."

His teeth clenched, holding back words and *pride* and the truth. "Les—"

Corrado's back hit the tiled wall when, without warning, the shower doors were thrown wide open. Cold air rushed in with the man that stepped inside, too, both wrapping around Corrado, but in entirely different ways.

The cold *chilled* him, slinking around his skin and muscles with a featherlight touch that had him shivering just beyond the spray of water.

Alessio, though?

He made Corrado *hot*, taking away that icy air as Alessio's hands landed to either side of his head, smacking against tile and effectively pinning him in place. He wasn't even *touching* him, but Corrado knew there was no way he was moving, now.

Not with Les so close.

Not with that *heat*.

"Except you're a fucking *liar*," Alessio murmured, his lips coming dangerously close to Corrado's as he spoke low, "because we can't be nothing when from the start, we were *something*."

Shit.

He hadn't even taken his clothes off. Corrado was all too aware of that right *now*. The way the water soaked through Alessio's clothes, making the fabric mold to his body. And as much as he liked the way it looked, he couldn't focus on that when all he could see was an ocean of blue bearing down on him.

Ready to *drown* him.

"You're right," Corrado said thickly. "You are."

Alessio's stance didn't soften a bit. "*But?* Because I can hear that—even when you don't say shit, I hear it, Corrado."

"But this is what I can give you. I can't give more. Either this is good enough for you, or you get nothing at all. That's how it has to be for me, and for *this*."

Silence echoed.

Alessio's gaze blazed brighter.

Then, his palm slapped the tiled wall next to Corrado's head hard enough that he felt it vibrate through the back of his skull. Yet, he didn't flinch; he wasn't *ever* concerned that this man would strike out against him in a physical way—not now.

People didn't hurt things they loved.

Life taught Corrado that.

"*Fuck you*," Alessio muttered, his jaw tight, and his mouth twisting with his anger. "Fuck you for that, too, because you know, right? You know it's better to have a *piece* of what you love than to have none of it at all."

"I'm sor—"

"Fuck you for doing that to me."

As fast as Alessio had come into the shower, he turned and left.

"Les, wait," Corrado called after him.

He got nothing.

Not even a *noise*.

"*Fuck*."

He hit the switch on the shower turning the water off, so he could go after Alessio. The cold air slammed into him again when he stepped beyond the glass doors, but he barely felt it. He was more concerned with the fact that the bathroom was now empty, the only sign of Alessio's presence being the droplets of water on the floor leading out. Grabbing the towel on the rack, Corrado tightened it around his waist as he headed out of the bathroom.

Alessio hadn't gone far.

Across the hotel room, the other man stripped out of the sopping wet clothes, leaving only his underwear, with his back turned to Corrado. There was no way he didn't hear his approach because Corrado didn't bother to be quiet as he came up behind him.

Still, Alessio said nothing as he pulled dry clothes from the bag. He stood straight, shoving the boxer-briefs down around muscular thighs as he *finally* turned around to face Corrado. Like now he had enough give-a-damn to allow the man his attention.

"Aren't I always the one running away from you?" Corrado asked, bitterness coating every word. "Not the other way around."

Alessio chuckled, nodding as he fisted the dry clothes in his hand. Standing there naked, he didn't seem the least bit bothered by it. Not that Corrado expected anything different from him. Shame was not something Les was well acquainted with, to be honest.

"What, you don't like a taste of your own medicine?"

"Don't be a fucking *child*, Les."

"I'm not." Lifting his shoulders, Alessio added, "See, it changes *nothing* here, Corrado. You said what you needed to say to keep your pride right where you like it—but it isn't what you want to say. And it changes fuck all."

"What does that even—"

"We're still something, and you're still mine."

Corrado blinked.

Stunned.

Alessio smirked a bit, clearly liking the reaction he got for that. "Yeah, because if *you* get to decide shit just because without considering me, then I get to do the same. And I decided *that*. You're mine, and while we're doing this together, keep that in mind."

He stepped closer.

Corrado didn't move an inch.

Just like in the shower, Alessio crowded him until all he could see was an ocean of stormy blue coming for him. Those eyes of Alessio's always told the truth of things far better than his mouth did.

He was *hurt*—he wouldn't say it, though.

He was *pissed*—it was just an afterthought right now.

Corrado did that.

He hated it.

"How's that for you?" Alessio asked.

"Depends on what it means," Corrado returned.

"It means while I'm fucking you, or you're fucking me ... or we're playing this stupid game with each other, then it's *just* us. It's you," Alessio said, pointing a finger at Corrado, and then turning it around on himself as he added, "and *me*. That's it. No other man gets to have you while I do, you got me?"

That's what he wanted?

Corrado cleared his throat. "That's what you want? Exclusivity?"

"No, *loyalty*. Because if you can't give me anything else, then you at least owe me that. And if you can't give me that, either, then this isn't happening at all."

All right.

Corrado let out a slow exhale, both annoyed and amused. But wasn't that what Alessio had always done to him? Frustrated and fascinated him to no end? Challenged and tested him every step of the goddamn way?

Why would this be different?

"Well?" Alessio demanded.

He was so close now, his mouth nearly grazed Corrado's as he spoke. And yet, it was still the intensity in his eyes leveling on Corrado that kept him ensnared, unable to move.

"Just you and me," Corrado replied. "Any other rules you want to slap on this while we're here?"

"Is that what we're going to call it—*rules*?"

"Why not?"

Alessio sighed harshly. "Don't joke. This isn't a *joke*."

"I'm not. I'm *trying* to give you as much as I can. You want control here? Fine, you have it. What are the rules, Les? Tell me. I'm listening."

"Just that one, then."

Alessio inched closer. Not that there was much space between them left to close now. In fact, this put the two of them practically skin to skin, but he was fine with that. Closer was always better with this man. Like this, he saw more; *found* more that Les liked to hide. Maybe they weren't all that different, after all.

Corrado felt Alessio's knuckles as they grazed the line of his stomach just above where the towel rested on his hips. It was a soft touch—barely there at all, if he were being honest. Except it was there, and that was important.

That was *Alessio*.

It was him being okay.

Connection in his silence, and that's what he offered. Corrado would take it. Even if it was just knuckles stroking his skin. He'd always take what Alessio gave him. No questions asked.

"No other men, got it." Corrado grinned a bit, murmuring, "Women are okay, then?"

That touch stilled on his stomach.

Alessio's head snapped up, and his gaze leveled on Corrado at the same time his tongue peeked out to swipe along the seam of his lower lip. Maybe it was the way the blues of his eyes darkened a bit, or it could have been how that soft touch against his skin turned into rough fingers grasping tightly to his side.

Whatever it was, Corrado saw it.

Felt it.

He just wasn't sure what *it* was.

"What was that?" he asked quietly.

Alessio's throat jumped when he swallowed thickly. "I was just thinking about that." He made a rough noise, adding, "It was a nice picture, and ... yeah."

Huh.

He wasn't going to pretend like he didn't like the sound of that because he did.

Probably a little too much for it to be healthy, but now wasn't the time. Even if his cock, perking to life under the towel around his waist, had an entirely different idea.

"More rules, then?" Corrado asked.

"We'll work on that," Alessio replied huskily.

"All right. Where do we go from here?"

"*Forward.*"

Alessio's fingertips dragged along the line of Corrado's stomach, then curled into the line of the towel to pull it away at the same time his other hand came up to circle around his throat. The kiss that came after, as the towel was dropped to the floor, reminded him exactly why he was here doing this in the first place.

The *war* of it.

The fight in it.

There was passion there, stoked by pride and words unsaid, emboldened by a touch that made him feel like a live wire, and strengthened by a man who was willing to cut his own heart out and hand it over if it meant keeping what he wanted.

Corrado knew that too well.

Here he was, doing the same.

Even if it was for different reasons.

He'd keep Les.

He needed to.

It just had to be *this* way.

Alessio's hand grabbed the back of Corrado's neck, and he dragged him down closer to the floor even as he continued kissing him. He was lost in the roughness, too lost to understand that Alessio had grabbed a small bag from within his backpack on the floor until he threw it across the room.

The small bag hit the top of the bed.

That didn't matter, either.

Not really.

What mattered was the palm hitting flat to his chest, pushing him back while the hand at the back of his neck kept him right there, connected to that kiss until he felt like all he could taste and breathe was Alessio. It was only after his back had hit the bed, when Alessio had crawled on top of him, that Corrado realized this was *different.*

Up until this point in their fucking and moments, it had always been him that felt in control—the one making the demands. And this was not the same. Not when it was Alessio's rough movements and kiss that had Corrado arching up to get more when the man dared to pull away.

Because now he was fucking desperate.

Now he wanted this.

Soft sheets slid against his back, Corrado found Alessio watching him as he reached for that bag. It seemed that's what *he* wanted, to watch Corrado as he took him—as he was given what he wanted.

And he did.

Watched him as he sheathed the thick length of his dick in latex. Watched him as cold lube and deft fingers stretched him open while Alessio's mouth worked his cock until he felt like he was going to come from that alone. Watched him when he was ready to *beg* to come when Alessio started working the head of his cock against Corrado's ass.

Never had he let a man take him.

Until *now*.

That ache was deep—the pain sharp even as something dark and *fucking amazing* started licking at his nerve endings. Still, it was slow. Too fucking slow, maybe. It felt like that heightened the pain, but also sharpened the pleasure trailing right behind. Enough to make him want to *stop*, though that teasing promise of more kept him right there, lost in that place.

And still, Alessio watched him.

A hand splayed to his chest, and another sliding under the roof of his jaw. He pushed Corrado's head back to the pillow as he continued staring at him. It was only when that pain started to ebb, when it became *better*, and Alessio was fucking him until he felt like he couldn't breathe that the man finally looked away from him.

Alessio's forehead hit his chest, and Corrado tipped his head back to stare at the ceiling, his lips falling open with a hard moan.

Because there it was.

Fuck.

How many times had he come before?

Felt *that* pleasure?

More times than he cared to count.

It never felt like this.

Never took away his sight, his vision, and everything else, too. Like he was drowning in Alessio, and *sensation*.

"Jesus Christ," he heard Alessio grunt, lips grazing his chest as he stilled, coming almost in perfect tune with Corrado.

Jesus Christ was right.

Corrado still couldn't breathe.

He felt the soft glide of Alessio's fingertips drifting over his chest, leaving a trail of raw nerve endings as his hand left where it had been resting. It was only then that Corrado realized he'd been fisting the sheets at his sides.

"You should have told me," Alessio murmured. "Told me you'd never—"

Corrado looked down as that hand fell from his jaw, finding Alessio's chin resting against his chest as he stared at him. "Why ... I wanted what I got, Les. It didn't matter."

Alessio blew out a breath, the warm air skipping across Corrado's skin. "Yeah, don't I know that."

PART TWO: AFTER

Almost five years later ...

15.

Ginevra

"His name is Andino Marcello, and he is who I picked for you to marry."

She used to be a normal girl.

And then life happened.

Or rather, someone's life collided with Ginevra's, and she realized that, no, her small world wasn't at all normal. She had simply been living in a delusion that someone else created for her. A pretty bubble that was opaque, so she was unable to see the truth happening all around her.

Last month, she had been normal.

A twenty-one-year-old woman with two younger sisters, a mom she loved, a dad who was distant but kind when he came around, hopes and dreams, and a *life*.

This month, she was something else.

The daughter of a dead mobster, a half-sister to three new siblings, and a woman with a life that was no longer her own to do with what she wished.

"This is the way of *Cosa Nostra*," Kev told her.

Ginevra sat on her mother's couch, hands twisted into tight balls where she could hide them at her sides, *willing* herself to stay quiet, and say nothing. She saw what happened when her new half-sister, Siena, tried to speak against Kev, or even their other brother, Darren. They weren't kind about telling them to shut up, or simply striking out to *make* them shut up with a slap.

Beside Ginevra, her mother, Marie, stayed silent, too, staring at the wall behind the brothers standing at the other side of the living room. She was immovable, a statue, even.

Matteo died, and everything changed.

Everything.

"This is the Calabrese way," Darren added when Ginevra and her mother stayed quiet on the couch. "And whether you like it or not, our father gave you the Calabrese name when you were born, and so you're now expected to *own* it."

"The way we want you to." Kev raised his thick brows when Ginevra *almost* opened her mouth to tell them right where they could shove their demands. His look shut her up instantly. "This will be good for you, and for us. Surely, you've heard of the Marcellos? You must know the family, Ginny. It's a good match."

"She knows *nothing* about that life," her mother said softly. "Matteo didn't want me to explain, and we were removed from it all, Kev."

His gaze drifted to her mother, his lips forming a thin, grim line.

Disappointment.

There was no denying the fact that Kev was his father's son, Ginevra thought. God knew he looked just like their father, even if a different woman had brought him into the world than the one that gave her life.

Still, they shared similarities.

Like Ginevra to Darren, or even Siena.

The dark hair, the shape of their oval faces, and even the way they all *smiled* the same. She'd taken her brown eyes from her mother, though, and she was grateful for that in moments like these. Because when she looked into Kev's eyes, all she saw was *coldness*. She knew her stare was not the same as his.

"I just ..." Ginevra struggled to find her words, to say *something* that would make these men understand this was not what she wanted to do. It didn't matter to her that the blood inside her veins said she was the same as them. It didn't matter that her father—now dead—had once controlled a major mafia family. She wasn't *like them*. She never lived like they did. Their way was not her way. "This isn't my life; I don't want to do this just because you say it's what I should do. I'm allowed to make my own choices. I'm twenty-one, and—"

"It's been decided," Kev replied dryly.

"And you will see it through," Darren added for his brother, "whether we have to force you down the aisle, or you walk down willingly. If you think we don't have the means and the motive to see it through for you, test us, Ginevra. It is going to happen."

"It *will* happen."

She sucked in a sharp breath, using her fingernails to dig into the palms of her hands to keep her emotions under control. These men were *horrible*. They would enjoy seeing her tears all too much, even if they were simply a byproduct of her anger.

To them, it would be a battle won.

To them, she was just a *girl*.

A stupid girl for them to use.

"I know you think because you weren't brought up in the same life as us that you can somehow ... escape the same expectations that we were given," Ken said, making Ginevra wish he would just shut the fuck up, and get out of her mother's apartment, "but that isn't actually the case at all. With our father dead, *we* are expected to carry on his legacy, and make the choices that will further our family in the criminal world. That's how it works. And you are the thing we plan to use to do that."

"Do you understand?" Darren asked.

Ginevra bit the inside of her cheek hard enough to draw blood. "I won't do this."

"You will. Or we will make sure you do. You continue to think you have a choice here, Ginny—"

"*Don't* call me that."

Kev let out a sigh. "Now, be nice. It's just a nickname."

No, it wasn't.

It was the name her mother had called her since she was a girl. It was the name her sisters shouted from the other end of the apartment when they wanted her to come help them pick out an outfit so maybe they could finally get their crush at school to notice them. It was the name her professors—which she would no longer be allowed to attend classes, according to Kev—used when they directed questions at her in classes.

It was not, however, a nickname her father gave her. It did not come from the fucking Calabrese. And she didn't want the rest of them using it.

"Don't call me that," Ginevra muttered, keeping her gaze down.

Kev, seemingly reaching his level of patience with her for the day, smacked the wall with his hand loud enough to make Ginevra and her mother jump on the couch. "I won't say it again after this, but it *has been decided*. You will marry the Marcello man within a couple of months. We'll nail down an appropriate date, and let you know. If you run, Ginevra, we will find you. If someone here thinks that helping you get away will help your case, then they will be *removed*. I won't tolerate someone going against me—I don't give a fuck if you are my blood. Do you understand me?"

God.

She hated him.

All of them right now.

"*Do. You. Understand. Me.*"

Ginevra lifted her head, and met Kev's stare from across the room. She felt her mother's hand find hers on the couch, and grab tightly to keep her grounded. Right now, she just had to get through this day. They could figure out the rest later.

Surely.

"I understand," Ginevra lied.

Lied, because no.

She would not marry someone chosen for her.

She wouldn't do anything they wanted.

Kev's gaze narrowed. "You know, I can see that fight in your eyes, Ginny. All of us Calabrese ... it all looks the same, and I see it."

Good.

She said nothing.

"But don't worry," Kev added, smiling in that cold way of his, "you will learn, and I will break you like I did the rest of them. Remember, you were warned."

A cold chill slipped down Ginevra's spine, but she refused to show her fear. Like her anger or heartbreak, her fear would make them think they had won, too. They didn't deserve anything from her, not even the emotions in her heart.

It was only once her half-brothers had left Ginevra and her mother alone in the apartment—although, not before explaining they would have guards posted at the door to watch them—that her mother finally turned to her.

Teary eyed, Marie grabbed both of Ginevra's hands as the wetness slipped down her cheeks. Usually, her mother was a ray of happiness. Always smiling, so strong, and never sad. Lately, it seemed like sad was all she knew how to be.

That broke her heart, too.

Ginevra dragged in a ragged breath, and for the first time, a tear streaked down her own cheek. She didn't try to wipe it away, her mother's hands keeping her from moving. Not that she cared, now. Her mother could see the emotion. It was *them* that couldn't.

"It's okay," her mother whispered, nodding fast, "I promise it'll be okay, Ginny."

"It won't."

Marie shook her head. "It *will*. I will figure out a way to get you away from them, and this *marriage*. I will, I promise."

"Ma, don't—"

"They don't scare me. It'll be okay, Ginny."

Except it wouldn't.

It *really* wouldn't.

It was the quiet whispers from the hallway that made Ginevra and her mother pull away from each other. A quick check over her shoulder confirmed what she figured, her seventeen and fifteen-year-old sisters waiting at the end of the hallway, standing close together like they were the only things keeping each other up at the moment.

They probably were.

"It's okay," Ginevra whispered to her sisters, seeing the tears in their eyes. This was not *their* life, either. This wasn't what they knew, or how they expected to be treated. They shouldn't have to watch their *new* half-brothers force their sister into a marriage she didn't want with a stranger, but this was their new reality. And it was terrifying. "Greta, Giulia, it's okay, I promise."

It would have to be.

For them, for her mama … she was going to have to be strong. Because if not *her*, then would Kev or Darren go for them next?

Ginevra couldn't safely say no.

That left her to keep them safe.

"Come here," she told her sisters.

The oldest, Greta, came first. Giulia was quick to follow. Just a month ago, they had been normal girls, too. Experiencing high school, and their worries filled up by things like what jeans looked best with what shoes, and if they were going to pass their upcoming tests. Now, they had far greater worries.

That shouldn't be how it was.

Once her younger sisters were sitting with her and Marie on the couch, Ginevra felt a little better. It felt good to hug them, to promise that things were going to be okay.

"Why are they making you marry—"

"It doesn't matter," Ginevra said quickly, hushing Greta as she shot a look to her mom. "You don't need to worry about me. I am going to be *fine*."

And so would her little sisters.

Somehow, she was going to make sure of it.

• • •

"Ginny?"

"Yeah?"

Giulia looked away from the casket a few feet in front of them to stare at her oldest sister. "I don't know how to say goodbye to Mama."

Greta made a soft noise under her breath—it sounded like an agreement—but she didn't look up from her hands. She'd been doing that for a week, now. Staring silently, but saying very little, and not engaging.

Ginevra worried more and more for her sisters with every passing day. For now, though, she had to worry about getting them all through this horrible day. "You don't have to go up and say goodbye that way, if you don't want to, Giulia. Mama knows that you love her, okay?"

Her youngest sister nodded.

"But I'm going to say goodbye, now. Are you both okay here?"

The girls nodded.

She didn't believe them.

None of them were okay, now.

Ginevra left her sisters behind in the pew, and headed for the altar. She glided her fingertips over the chrome decals of the shiny, black casket sitting atop the altar. For now, the church was quiet ... but not for long. Soon, it would fill with grieving people who had known and loved her mother, ready to send Marie off to a better place.

They would *never* know the truth. Not her sisters, or the people coming to the church today.

They would never know that her mother was killed trying to save her from a fate nearly as bad as death itself. That those scars on Marie's wrists weren't self-inflicted, no matter how much money the coroner had been paid to say so. That Ginevra blamed herself *every single day* for this.

I'm sorry, Mama, she thought. *I'm so sorry.*

She stroked the closed casket again, wishing she was *better*. Because then, she might have been able to stand having the top opened, so she could look at her mother's face and say those same words out loud. Instead, she was stuck like this.

Wishing she could be better.

I love you, Mama.

Peering over her shoulder, Ginevra found her young sisters—still teenagers, and now left with her to take care of them—sitting in the first pew. The priest had suggested the girls be allowed to have a few minutes with their mother's casket alone before the funeral started. He thought it might help them to say goodbye, but Ginevra didn't know if it mattered.

They were still heartbroken.

Still crying.

Still *alone*.

And now, terrified, too.

Because their *brothers* had done this. People who were supposed to be family had taken away the one person they loved more than the world and life itself.

Ginevra needed to be better for them, too. For Greta, and Giulia. No one else would be here to take care of them, and make sure they weren't pawns for Kev and Darren's fucking games. For now, they were too young ... they couldn't be used in a way to further the brothers' agenda, but eventually they would be older.

Eventually, they too would be on Kev or Darren's radar. Ginevra needed to make sure that never happened. And she didn't want them to be used against her, either. Not like her mother had.

Marie thought to help her.

Kev made sure she couldn't.

That couldn't be her sisters, too.

"Ginny," came a soft voice to her left.

There, she found Siena standing a few feet away. For the most part, her half-sister, yet another sibling she didn't know existed until Matteo died, was *nothing* like her brothers. Siena was sweet, kind, gentle, and all the things Kev and Darren didn't know how to be. She showed true empathy and sympathy for the situation

Ginevra had been put in, and she constantly stepped in between her brothers and sister when she thought she might be able to help Ginevra in some way. Even if it meant Siena got in trouble for it, too.

At the very least, Ginevra thought she could trust Siena. That was saying a hell of a lot more than she felt regarding most *other* people in her life. She didn't feel anything at all for them, now, except her sisters.

Everyone else just fell in line.

Except Siena.

"Yeah?" she asked.

Siena offered her a small smile. "You okay?"

She shrugged. "Not really."

"Yeah, I … get that."

Ginevra put her attention back on the casket, knowing she only had a few more minutes to spend alone with her mother before the funeral would start. Once the church filled with guests, she would be expected to put on her mask, and keep up the charade. Kev and Darren would expect nothing less from her, now.

She would do it.

She *had* to do it.

For her sisters.

But it killed her inside. It was taking a piece of her every single day. The closer she came to the date her brothers chose for the wedding, the worse she felt. In her heart, and in her *soul*. This was wrong, and all kinds of bad.

This was not how it was supposed to be.

"Hey, hey," she heard Siena whisper. "It's all right."

Ginevra didn't realize it until she had been thrust right into the middle of a panic attack, but she bent over at the knees beside her mother's casket. One hand stayed on the smooth, shined wood, while her other pressed overtop her racing heart to slow it down. She swore that if it didn't calm, it was going to race right out of her chest. Or *explode* altogether.

God.

"It's all right, Ginny, it *is*," Siena said softly.

She felt her half-sister's hands on her shoulders, and then one rubbing across her back like she thought that might help, too. She bet her younger sisters were watching from the pew, seeing yet another horrifying thing to remind them that nothing about their life was normal anymore.

Everything had changed.

Again.

Now, with their mother's death.

It was all wrong.

"Come on," Siena murmured, forcing Ginevra to stare up at her through watery eyes, "look at me, huh? Don't let them come in here and see this, all right? Don't let them see what they're doing to you—they don't deserve that. I promise they don't."

Ginevra dragged in lungful after lungful of air. She willed her anxiety and raging emotions to calm, but while it helped, it still felt like a whole war continued to battle on inside her heart and mind.

"What am I going to do?"

Siena blinked. "What?"

Ginevra swallowed the lump in her throat.

It *ached*.

Like the rest of her, too.

"What am I going to do, Siena?" she whispered, lips trembling. "If I run, they have my sisters. *If* I can even run, because I never get the chance. And if I stay, then I have to marry a man I haven't even met yet. What am I going to do?"

Siena's fingers tightened around Ginevra's shoulders. "For right now, you're going to get up, let me fix your face, and then we're going to sit down in the pew like nothing is wrong. You're going to get through this day, thank people who offer their condolences, and make sure Kev and Darren think you're doing everything they want. Okay?"

"I *can't*."

"You can. You've been doing it. This doesn't change that."

Ginevra let out a slow stream of air. "And then what?"

Siena's eyes burned brightly. "Never worry about those girls, Ginny. *I* will look out for them, if you can't. I promise you that. Don't ever think you have to stay for them when there are people here who will take care of them, too."

"I can't just leave them to Kev and Darren."

"*Stop.*" Siena gave her a look. "They'll be *fine*. They are too young to be married off, and right now, they wouldn't even consider those girls for anything else. What we have to figure out is how we're going to get *you* out of this."

"You shouldn't help me," Ginevra mumbled. "Look what happened to my mama."

Siena nodded. "I know, but I can't stand back and do nothing, either. That's not who I am."

Which was why she was different, Ginevra knew.

It was why she could trust her.

"What am I going to do?" she repeated.

"Give it time. We'll figure something out."

But would they?

• • •

The first time Ginevra met her *husband-to-be*, Andino Marcello said very little to her. He was kind, of course, and polite, but that was as far as it went. He didn't seem interested in discussing the wedding with her brothers, and he certainly didn't care to talk about it with her.

Not that she minded.

Even she was doing the very bare minimum that she could regarding the planning. If someone asked her for an opinion, she gave one, but that was it.

It wasn't like she wanted it.

Why should she care?

The couple of meetings that happened after that first one with Andino were basically the same. Safe, kind conversation that didn't make Ginevra think he was anything different than the other men in the mafia life. The only obvious difference about Andino was the fact he was actually an heir to a criminal empire.

The next boss, she was told.

You should be grateful, Kev had taunted her. *We picked you a husband that women in this life would kill for, in a position they would give anything for. And you cry about it?*

Like she should be happy.

She wasn't.

It wasn't Andino as much as it was everything else. She didn't blame him, either, and she tried to be polite to him—not only because her brothers threatened her, but it was who she was, anyway—but that didn't mean she wanted any of this.

"Do you talk at all?" Andino asked.

Ginevra looked up from the gross salad in front of her, and frowned. "I do, I'm sorry."

Andino tipped his head sideways at that reply. "Why?"

It took Ginevra entirely too long to respond to that. Mostly because she didn't know *how* to respond. No other man around her, but especially not her brothers, seemed to give even one damn about *why* for anything in her life. They didn't ask her questions, they simply told her what to do, and expected her to follow through.

It was that simple.

Andino's question surprised her.

"Why, what?" she asked.

"Why are you apologizing to me?"

She focused her attention on her plate, using the fork to play with the salad as she spoke. "For not being … whatever you would like, I guess. That's what I was told to be today—whatever you would like. And with everyone else, that usually means staying quiet and out of sight, if possible. I can't exactly be out of your sight when I have to sit right in front of you at the table, so being quiet seemed like the way to go. Sorry if that's not what you want."

Ginevra didn't miss the way Andino glanced a few tables over at her brothers where they sat enjoying their steaks and potatoes, while she had been forced—by them—to order a salad. The other thing she didn't miss?

The *anger* in Andino's face.

What was that?

What did it mean?

"I neither want, nor need, for you to be a piece of art beside me," Andino eventually replied.

Her brow knotted as she met his gaze, confused.

"Pretty, but inanimate," he added after a moment, shrugging. "If that's what they expect, then that's another story. When they are around, you can behave however they deem appropriate as to not cause yourself trouble. With me, you can be whatever you feel like in the moment."

"Right now, I would prefer to be anywhere else."

Andino smirked.

That surprised her, too.

Mostly, this man seemed like a statue. Cold, and immovable. Like he didn't have emotions at all, or rather, none he outwardly showed to those around him. It was why she found it so hard to read him. It was why she didn't understand his motives here.

"I do appreciate a woman who isn't a liar," he said, "but for the sake of appearances, let's at least play nice."

Okay.

He didn't want a liar?

She could do that.

"I don't want to marry you, Andino. I don't want to be here, and I certainly don't want to pretend to give a damn about anything you want to talk about right now. So, if it's okay with you, I would much prefer to sit here and occasionally nod when you talk so that you might think I give a shit. But really, we'll both know I don't."

It took a second for him to reply, but when he did, it stunned her.

Silent.

"Oh, good. Then, we're on the same page."

He didn't want to marry her, either.

Then why were they here?

Ginevra didn't get the chance to ask.

Just as quickly, he asked, "Did they choose the salad for you, too? Because I wouldn't willingly eat that without some kind of steak to weigh it down."

She almost smiled.

Almost.

"They did—heaven forbid you thought I ate too much."

Andino made a noise, shaking his head. "I prefer women who enjoy themselves, actually. Not that it'll matter what I prefer from you. Some other man, perhaps, but not me. You would do well to remember that."

She met his gaze again.

Andino smiled back.

"What does that mean?"

Because she was *desperately* hoping it meant one thing.

That this wedding wouldn't happen.

But *how?*

Andino pushed his plate of chicken parmesan across the table for her to take, winking as he did so. "You'll find out when the time comes. And here, take my food. At least, you won't leave here hungry, and my mother taught me to always make sure a woman was happy when she left a table with me. Eat up."

She did.

Still wondering if she could trust him.

Or what might happen now.

16.

Alessio

"Holy Christ, *Les*."

Alessio licked the salty, heady flavor of Corrado's cum from his lips as he slinked over his lover's body, using his hands to fist into the sheets covering their mattress as he hovered above him. Corrado lifted to kiss Alessio, his tongue slashing against his like he was ready to take the taste of him back.

"Fuck," Corrado said, falling back to the bed.

Grinning like the asshole he was, Alessio flashed his teeth, letting that cockiness of his come out to play. Because that's what he did, and Corrado liked it. If only because he could challenge it.

Corrado was probably the only person in Alessio's life—and that had never changed in the nearly five years that they'd been doing this shit together, whatever *it* was—who could deal with his nonsense. Not to mention, give it back just as hard.

He needed that.

Craved it, really.

Alessio dealt with all sorts of people on a daily basis. People he couldn't stand, and people that drove him up the wall. He came across too many personalities to name, and very rarely did he find one that actually *interested* him, or kept his attention.

His job, still being an assassin for The League, meant he went from one person to the next, taking on assignments and seeing the world over and over again.

Yet, he still wanted to be *here*.

In this bed, or this penthouse.

With Corrado.

It was where he found peace.

And happiness.

"Why ..." Corrado let out a hard breath, his tongue snaking out to lick the corner of his lips as his hands drove through the longer bits of hair at the top of his head. Out of breath, his chest still heaved from that orgasm. Alessio like that sight more than anything else. He liked knowing he affected him. Why lie? "Why were we doing that again?"

Alessio dropped to the bed beside Corrado, propping himself up with his elbow, and resting his head on his hand. "That chick—the Poland job."

Corrado nodded. "*Yeah* ... shit, yeah, okay. She was a screamer. How did the talk of the Poland job turn into you sucking my dick, though?"

He chuckled.

"Good memories."

Mostly, Alessio wanted to make Corrado shout, too.

He'd done that.

It worked.

Why did he have to explain it?

"And I just got back," Alessio added, rolling to his back to stare up at the glass shard chandelier that hung above their four-poster bed. Tucked against floor-to-ceiling windows in the penthouse's master bedroom, they had ample view of the busy Vegas city, although they were just high enough that unless someone was watching their windows with fucking binoculars, no one was seeing what they were doing. And if they were watching ...

Well, shit.

Alessio hoped they enjoyed the show.

Nightly.

Corrado shifted to his side, and Alessio caught his gaze with his own. Not saying a single word, he reached over and pressed his thumb to the corner of Alessio's mouth. The pad of Corrado's digit dragged across his lower lip with the softest touch.

The silence stretched on, but that was okay. He'd learned after all these years with Corrado that, sometimes, quiet was better. It was in their stillness where they found the *best* connection.

They didn't always need words.

They just needed *moments.*

Quiet, soft moments.

Sometimes, they came when neither of them expected it, too. Between bursts of busy schedules, and chaotic careers that sent them both running all over the world doing jobs for The League, and different clients. After the danger waned, and the violence was gone, it was just the two of them again.

They ended up back here.

In their life.

Together.

Quiet.

Alessio knew that from the outside looking in, he and Corrado didn't make sense to other people. They didn't have a *label.* Far too many overlooked them, and assumed they weren't a thing together. Not that they ever gave people a reason to know the truth, either.

You know, beyond living together.

For nearly five years ...

Still, people didn't know.

They could only assume.

He partly blamed himself, and Corrado, too. Not that he ever said that to anyone, or his lover. A long time ago, they'd decided *this* was what they were going to be. Together, but only to each other. A thing, but it wasn't open to public consumption.

Alessio was willing to do that.

It gave him what he wanted.

Corrado.

Somehow, they found a familiar rhythm like this. He didn't push for something else, or for more, because what else was there to have when ... in a lot of ways, he had it all.

Or did he?

People wouldn't understand.

They shared *everything.*

A life.

Work.

A home.

Women.

Sex.

There was nothing in their lives that wasn't somehow touched by both of them. So much so, that those closest to Corrado and Alessio thought the two of them were often extensions of the other. Without one, the other wasn't *right.*

Nothing was right.

"What are you thinking about, huh?" Corrado asked, his voice thick with sleep and *bliss.* Probably still humming from that orgasm, and if all went well, Alessio would be the next one. "You're quiet over there."

"You like that, anyway."

"Sometimes."

Alessio grinned.

Corrado smirked right back.

Reaching over, he drifted his fingertips down the line of Corrado's jaw still shadowed with a few days' worth of scruff. "You do like it when I'm quiet. Admit it."

It was true.

Corrado thrived on attention.

Alessio just liked to *watch.*

"And when you're a shit," Corrado added.

He laughed. "Yeah, that, too."

"And don't deflect. What were you thinking?"

Alessio sighed, his gaze going back to the large, glimmering light fixture above the bed. Only Corrado would know something was going on in Alessio's mind when he was quiet. No one else saw him in his silent moments and thought, *something's happening there.* They were all too willing to let him stew, even if they didn't know that's what he was doing.

Not Corrado, though.

He often wondered, how, at eighteen—although now, just a month or so shy of his twenty-third birthday—had he found his *person.* He knew some people went their whole lives without ever finding that person that was meant to be only theirs.

He found his early.

Corrado was still there, too.

God.

And he loved him.

Loved him fucking *stupid.*

Loved him enough to still be here even when shit held Corrado back, and forced them into his strange place where they were something, but they weren't at the same time. Where they shared women in bed, and had a whole life together behind closed doors, but out in the world … they weren't anything. Where they dictated this thing between them with rules that had followed them from damn near the beginning, but neither of them said three little words to cement it.

I love you.

But that was too deep.

Corrado didn't do deep.

So, Alessio lied.

"I was thinking one of us needs to take the black Porsche out, and open it up," he murmured, swallowing the emotions in his throat, "it's been a while since it's been taken out."

Corrado glanced over at him, and if he knew he was lying, he didn't say. Not that he ever brought up that kind of shit; it might open a can of worms that he wasn't willing to face yet, and Alessio had a bad habit of letting Corrado have what he wanted.

Even if it hurt him.

"Yeah, all right," Corrado replied.

Crisis averted.

As per usual.

The ringing phone on Corrado's nightstand saved the two of them from saying anything more. Corrado rolled over, and snatched the phone while Les pushed out of the bed, and started grabbing the few clothes he'd discarded earlier. A shirt, his pants ...

Corrado had *nothing* on.

He tossed his clothes over, too.

"Thanks," he mouthed, answering the phone at the same time. "Marcus."

Alessio stilled, shooting a look over his shoulder. Not that it was unusual for Corrado to get calls from his family because that was all *too* normal. Usually a couple a day, really. If not his mother, then it might be the man's twin, his father, or any one of his other three brothers.

All of which Alessio knew.

And well.

It was one of the reasons why this thing between them didn't make any fucking sense, not that Corrado liked it when he pointed it out. Alessio wasn't *hidden* from Corrado's family like he was a dirty secret to be kept. He sat at their dinner table—he attended their parties, and celebrations. They knew him.

And he suspected, they knew why he was there.

But no one asked.

So, no one told.

He just didn't understand.

Why?

What did it matter after all this time?

"But can't they just—" Corrado sighed harshly, telling his brother, "Fine, Marcus. *Yes*, they can throw a double birthday party for us, and you."

Then, Corrado added, "I assume Les will come, why wouldn't he? Tell Ma yeah for that."

Alessio went back to pulling on his clothes, slightly annoyed. Not so much at the conversation happening behind him, but the *topic*. His family just expected Alessio would be around for something like Corrado's birthday party his mother and father wanted to throw in a few weeks—although his birthday was sooner than that—because they had to *know*.

They had to know what he was to Corrado.

Why he was important.

That this *thing* was a fucking thing.

Why were they still playing this stupid game together?

He also knew that at least a handful—or a couple, anyway—of people, like Corrado's twin, knew a lot more about Alessio and Corrado than anyone else did. Like the fact their poly lifestyle in the bedroom often had them sharing women, and otherwise.

But never men.

Those rules, again.

Although, Les was to blame for *that*.

It made him see fucking red to think of Corrado sleeping with another man, but it didn't bother him at all to know during his last job, his lover hooked up with a woman at a club he frequented. And it wasn't different for Alessio, either. He had the same benefits in this mess that Corrado did.

The only thing was no other men.

And they *always* told each other the truth.

Simple as that.

Alessio just didn't understand why they were still here, deeper into this mess together than ever before, when it seemed like the only people who mattered around them already knew the truth. Even if no one was saying it out loud.

"I'll see what I can do," Corrado said, "and yeah, I'll talk to you soon, Marcus."

The call ended.

Alessio kept his back facing Corrado as he headed for the walk-in closet where their collection of *everything* stayed safe behind glass counters and shelves. There, he found a particular watch he wanted—encrusted with diamonds around the face, with a black background, and gold hands to tell time. He affixed it to his wrist, adding a couple of beaded bracelets around it that cost a fraction of what the watch did. A black cross made up of miniature, worn metal skulls attached to a leather cord dangled from his hand before he quickly slipped it over his head, letting it hang from his neck.

On jobs, he didn't wear jewelry.

Nothing but *black*.

Nothing to distinguish him, or give him away. He'd just come back from a quick trip with the team over in Romania, but he doubted he would have another job for a while. Dare tried to space them out a bit, unless something came up that couldn't be helped.

When not on assignment, Alessio wore whatever the fuck he wanted, his style a mixture of dark grunge, and *excess*. Like the watch. Corrado, on the other hand, looked like every other fucking Guzzi that Alessio had ever met. Dripping in wealth, and carefully put together. Not a hair out of place, and suits were preferred to jeans.

Although, Corrado did like his leather jacket.

It worked, though.

"You good?" Corrado asked, coming into the closet to stand just beyond the doorway.

Alessio shrugged. "Why wouldn't I be?"

"I don't know, I just got that feeling, Les."

Right.

That feeling.

"This whole thing with us is all about that *feeling*, yeah," Alessio murmured.

"What does that mean?"

Corrado had his *thing.*

Nobody asked about what the fuck was going on with him and Alessio, so he didn't offer the information willingly.

Alessio had his thing, too.

He dwelled on everything, overthought it all, and when all else failed … he managed to overreact, too.

Corrado wasn't working on his thing.

Alessio was *trying* with his.

Like now.

"Nothing," he said, willing to drop it, "I'm just running off at the mouth, and—"

The phone in Corrado's hand rang again.

Alessio wasn't even offended.

He just got back home from a job that had him away from this place, and his person, for three long goddamn weeks; he didn't want to fight. Especially not about something that had never changed in nearly five years.

What did it even matter?

"Les," Corrado said, ignoring the call, "are we good?"

He looked back at his lover.

His.

That was the thing.

Corrado was still his.

Nothing else counted but that.

"Yeah, man, we're good," Alessio said "Answer your phone."

17.

Corrado

Keeping his gaze locked on Alessio, because Corrado figured this conversation wasn't over, he answered the call ringing through to his phone without checking the ID. Alessio ignored him all the while, confirming to Corrado that despite what his lover might be saying, there *was* something wrong.

He planned on figuring out *what*.

Right after this call.

"Corrado here," he said into the phone.

"What's it been, Corrado, two or so years?"

He stiffened at the unmistakable voice on the other end of the call. "About that, Andino. Can't say that time bothers me, though."

Alessio tipped his head up, and eyed Corrado curiously at the mention of a man's name who lived in New York. Way the hell across the country from them.

Andino Marcello chuckled. "That's fair. I could say the same for you."

Something like that.

"What do you want?"

"My uncle. Lucian, remember him?"

Shit.

Yeah, he remembered.

The way this conversation was going, Corrado decided here wasn't the best place to have it, all things considered. Turning his back to Alessio, he headed out of the large walk-in closet, and back into the comfort of their spacious bedroom.

"What about him?" Corrado asked, coming up next to the chair Alessio liked to use when he tied his combat boots back around the ankles. "And spare me any bullshit. I don't have the time."

"Still as moody as ever, huh?"

"*And?*"

Andino sighed. "A couple years back, you were in New York on a job, and one of his people ended up caught in the mess. Lucian stepped in to help sweep that under the rug, and you promised him a—"

"Favor," Corrado muttered, his hand curling around the edge of the chair. *No one* was supposed to know about that favor—Lucian gave his word. Corrado hadn't been *new* to The League when that fuck up happened, but it had been one of his first few solo jobs. He didn't want to go back, and say he'd caused problems with a crime family as big as the Marcellos, so he worked something else out. "Well, what does he want, then?"

"Oh, he's allowing *me* to cash in the favor instead of him."

Great.

"And what is it?"

"Seems I'm supposed to be getting married on the twenty-fifth of July to Ginevra Calabrese. She's twenty-one, new to this whole … mafia bit, and whatnot. Ever heard of that family?"

"A bit," Corrado admitted. "I don't see what you getting married has anything to do with me or this favor I owe, though."

"Oh, I don't plan on actually getting married. See, that's where you're going to come in. I need that girl to disappear."

Corrado blinked. "*What?*"

"I didn't stutter."

"You want me to take out a woman you're supposed to *marry?*"

Because *fuck*, that was kinda cold.

A little bit.

Then again, Andino was known for being a manipulative asshole when he wanted to be. He didn't give a shit who it was, either. Blood or not.

"No," Andino said, laughing darkly. "She needs to go away for a while. This *marriage* … it's a sham. A way for her family to try to get a place within the Marcello ranks, and I won't allow it to happen. And so, she needs to *go*. And by that, I mean somewhere else, out of this country, for a spell of time. A few months, maybe. I figure, you have dual citizenship to Canada, I'm sure you have homes to use there, and I *know* you have the means and motives to keep her safe and out of sight for a while. It's perfect for me."

"But not for *me*," Corrado returned. "I have a fucking job, man. People I answer to, and things I have to take care of myself."

For the most part.

But a few months away?

Could he even swing that?

It was hard to say. Dare would likely allow him time off from The League, if he asked. He hadn't taken any time since becoming a full-time member, whereas others usually took a bit of time off every year, and some, after every finished job.

Everyone needed something different.

But it was more than The League, too.

It was also—

Alessio came out of the walk-in closet with his combat boots hanging from his fingertips. Corrado moved aside as the man came to sit in the chair he was standing next to, and watched as he slipped his feet into the shoes before lacing them around the back.

He had someone else to think about, too.

A few months was a long time.

"And I need this kept *quiet*," Andino added after a moment. "No one can know the details—the less people that know, the more unlikely it is that she'll be found. I don't want to have to worry about killing the woman's brothers, while at the same time, have to think about whether or not someone has figured out where *she* is. Do you get me?"

Fuck.

"Yeah, I get you, but—"

"A favor is a favor in this life. You say you owe it to someone, then they can cash it in *whenever* they fucking want. Am I right, or no?"

"You're not wrong."

"Hmm."

Asshole.

Corrado scrubbed a hand down his jaw, and eyed Alessio from the side. He was done with his boots now, and leaning back in the chair with his hand resting at the line of his jaw while he stared out the large windows surrounding their bedroom.

"I was thinking," Andino continued, "that since they have her so protected, the *only* time they might give us the chance to get her away from them is on the wedding day. If you could drive in, because I don't want *any* paper trail attached to someone the Calabrese might recognize or know coming into the city, then—"

"I'm in Vegas. That's across the country."

"You have three and a half days. Drive *fast*."

Perfect.

This was just … great.

"She's dark-haired, brown-eyed. About five-ten, or so. She'll be wearing a large church hat that'll cover her face. She *will not* be in a wedding gown. Make sure your vehicle is in front of the church to grab her as soon as she comes down those steps."

Andino gave the name of a well-known cathedral in New York City, adding, "I need to know what vehicle you'll be driving to let her know which one to get inside."

No questions.

Just a demand.

So, they were really doing this, huh?

Seemed so.

Corrado thought about the Porsche, if only because Alessio had mentioned it earlier, it did need to be opened up—what better way than fifty over the speed limit on the highway—and it was probably the fastest car they owned between them. "A black Porsche."

"Good."

Alessio glanced away from the window at that, his brow furrowing. Corrado shook his head, not wanting him to worry. This didn't involve his lover, and he didn't want Alessio getting messed up in this, either.

It wasn't that the Marcellos were bad people—in the underworld of criminals, they were more like *royalty*. He simply figured it would be better if he handled this mess alone, and let Alessio continue on doing what he always did without worrying about Corrado at the same time. He'd been the one to fuck up, so he would be the one who fixed it.

Easy.

Clean.

Just how he liked it.

"Better get on the road," Andino told Corrado. "I'll be in touch."

The man didn't even wait for him to agree, or say goodbye, before he hung up the phone. That might have pissed Corrado off any other time, but he was now focused on the fact that Alessio was looking his way with a question in his eyes.

Because, of course.

"What's going on?" Alessio asked.

Corrado stuffed his hands in his pockets, keeping a tight hold on the phone at the same time to hide it away, too. "Something I have to do—last minute, it just came up."

"A job?"

It wasn't unusual for Dare to send Corrado or Alessio on a job without telling the other one. He left that to them to figure out between them, and whether or not the details were something they could or should share.

"Something like that," Corrado replied, "but more like a favor. Outside of The League's business. Nothing serious, but I need to head out."

"For how long?"

Yeah, *damn.*

He didn't want to lie.

He also didn't want Alessio asking too many questions.

"Could be a while," he replied, but then quickly added, "I can't really talk about it a lot."

It was the shadows that darkened Alessio's expression that told Corrado he didn't like that answer, and was more than willing to ask more.

"I have to look after someone for a while, keep them out of sight, and whatever else," Corrado explained, hoping it would be enough for Alessio, "but they don't want too many people in the loop about it. It's just a favor ... it won't cause trouble."

"Yeah, all right." Alessio cleared his throat, and looked up at Corrado, his blue eyes stormy again. That's where his emotions always showed, even when the rest of him was blank. "Where are you going, then?"

"Back to Toronto, I think."

"And it's going to take a while?"

"Seems so."

"Didn't Marcus say, when he called, that they wanted to have a birthday party for you, Chris, and him?"

Yeah.

"It'd be better if you stayed here, especially if I'm still taking care of ... this issue," Corrado murmured.

"Is that it, or is it something else?"

"What?"

Alessio shook his head, his jaw tightening as he turned to look out the window again. "Nothing, man."

"You're not good at deflecting, Les."

"Maybe not, but I also don't hide things people already know, Corrado."

Ah.

Okay.

Now he knew what was wrong.

Except he really didn't have time to do this with Alessio right now, not considering he had a very short window of time to get on the road, and start the drive to New York. It certainly wasn't enough time to sit here and argue about *this.*

Again.

"I have to head out," Corrado said, "so can we come back to that?"

"*Right.*"

"Les."

Alessio looked back at him, and shrugged. "Yeah, we can come back to it. Where the hell else am I going to be, Corrado? I'm always here, right?"

He was.

Sometimes, Corrado wondered if he wanted to be, though.

Well, he knew what he wanted.

He always had.

Leaning down, Corrado kept his hands on the arm of the chair as he dropped a quick kiss to the side of Alessio's jaw, feeling the man's cheek twitch under his lips. "*Cette partie de mon coeur est à toi, hmm*? I'll call you, yeah?"

There were things he should say …

Things he needed to say …

Corrado never knew how to say them without needing to deal with the aftermath of it when for too long, he'd been used to *this*. Them being like they were, it was comfortable.

Cette partie de mon coeur est à toi.

This part of my heart is yours.

Alessio swallowed audibly. "You know, Kass has been teaching me French whenever I go into the complex, huh? Thought it was hilarious that it bugged me you two could speak, and I didn't understand, so he started teaching me some things. I didn't think to mention it, or whatever."

Corrado stiffened.

Well, then …

Alessio let out a breath, and tipped his head to the door of the bedroom. "Better get on the road if you really need to go now."

"Yeah, I guess."

"So, go."

• • •

Corrado's fingers drummed against the steering wheel as his gaze drifted from the cathedral to his right, and then back to the street in front of him. The *NO PARKING ZONE* sign two feet away from the still running Porsche was like a flashing warning for him—God knew he didn't need to get a ticket when the whole point of him being here was to stay under the damn radar.

Not that it mattered.

He had to stay here.

Until someone else got here, too.

Sighing, Corrado dragged his hand down his jaw while keeping a tight grip on the steering wheel, and a foot on the brake pedal. Because yeah, if Andino wanted him to get out of here quickly after he picked up this Calabrese chick, then he planned on doing exactly that.

He hadn't given her—Ginevra, was it?—much thought during the long drive across country. She was a job, and something he had to do. He didn't plan on making friends with her, so he didn't see why it would matter if he considered her or her situation when he was just there to hide the woman, and keep her out of trouble for the time being.

Instead, his mind focused elsewhere.

On a man he'd left back in Vegas.

Alessio.

He'd left things unsaid, and business unfinished there. He knew, without a doubt, the next time the two of them were standing face to face, Corrado was going to be pushed into a conversation that had been a long time in the making.

Shit that hurt Les.

Him, too.

Both of them, really.

Corrado wasn't sure when his family and people started putting things together about him and Alessio, but a lot of them knew the truth. It was kind of hard not to when they had lived together for the last few years and were practically inseparable except for when they were on a damn job.

It didn't matter.

Nobody *asked*.

Maybe they didn't want to.

Corrado didn't know.

He still didn't *tell*.

A part of him found comfort in that—in not feeling like he ever needed to justify why he loved Alessio, or in not needing to explain the complexities of their relationship. After all, it was *theirs*, not everyone else's.

Why did they need to know?

Corrado kept circling back to the customs and culture of his family's connections to the mafia, too. The fact that his sexual orientation could be used against them as a way to shame or harm them ... well, that about killed him.

It wasn't his fault.

It wasn't *theirs*.

He just ...

Didn't want to put them in that position.

At all.

Was that so fucking bad?

Les wouldn't understand.

Corrado was so lost to his thoughts that, for a moment, he'd forgotten where he was and why he was there. So stuck in his mind, in fact, that he didn't see the young woman approaching the Porsche until she had practically ripped open the door, and threw herself into the passenger seat. He didn't see her face at first, although he heard the sob that ripped out of her chest. He didn't know what she looked like, but he saw her hands balled into fists against the leather of the seat, and *shaking*. The dress she wore—it looked like something someone might wear to a wedding, but not on the bride—had ridden up around her thighs in her haste.

And then she looked up.

The wide-rimmed church hat likely hid her face when she was looking straight on, or even down, for that matter. Her dark brown hair had been pulled back into a sleek chignon, and while the makeup on her face had taken hell from streaks of tears ...

He still had to look twice.

Take a breath.

Blink.

Soft, dainty features set off her whole face. Small lips, and a thin nose that curved up at the end just a bit. Oval face, with wide, doe-like eyes that made her

look entirely too *innocent*. Tanned skin, and curves that filled out that dress *perfectly*.
Shit.

Corrado didn't know what in the hell he expected from Ginevra Calabrese. He
hadn't given her a lot of thought—why should he?

He was looking at her now, though.

She was filling his thoughts *now*.

This felt like trouble.

A lot of it.

He just didn't know why.

"Drive," she snapped.

Angry.

Terrified.

So why did she sound musical?

"*Drive!*"

Corrado said nothing, simply checked his mirrors, and then let off the brake as
he hit the gas hard. *Time for the second part of this damn road trip.*

18.

Ginevra

How long had they been driving now?

An hour?

She checked the clock on the dashboard of the Porsche, still kind of stunned she was in a Porsche at all. About an hour and a half of driving, it seemed.

The man in the driver's seat continued his stretch of silence—he'd not said one word to her from the moment she got in his car. Or ... she suspected this was his car. Who else would it belong to?

Glancing over at him, *again*, Ginevra took in his profile. With the sun still high in the sky, she didn't have to imagine anything about the way he looked when it was all there for her to see. From his strong jaw dusted with a bit of dark facial hair, to the dusky olive skin tone with just a touch of tan. His fingers—long, and *deft*, she thought—flexed around the steering wheel in a rhythmic fashion, as though he was thinking about something, and his hands told the story of his thoughts.

She wondered if he had been stressed about something before she got in the car—maybe about picking her up—if only because where his high-fade hairstyle melted into the longer bits of hair at the top of his head was messy. Like he'd been running those fingers through it, and the strands fell out of place.

Not that it looked bad.

Nothing about the man looked bad.

What was his name again?

Andino said it when he brought her a *gift* for their wedding day to her private suite. Her *get out of jail free* card, she thought, sadly. A way out, he'd told her.

But what was his name again?

"Corrado," she said softly, remembering it all at once.

Just as fast, the man in the driver's seat reacted, his head swinging in her direction for the first time since she had entered his vehicle. His profile did *no* justice to his rugged features when he looked at her head-on.

Strong lines.

Brown eyes, flecked with gold.

Intense all over.

"*What?*"

His tone, as sharp as the edge of a blade, shocked her. He seemed angry, his jaw tensing as his gaze flicked over her, but she didn't know why. Maybe he didn't want to be here, or to help her. She understood that—who would want to help someone they didn't know?

A part of her didn't want to be here, either.

She left her sisters back there.

With *them*.

It made her heart ache.

She had to make a choice—her own freedom, or to sacrifice it. Except, when that freedom had been dangled in front of her fingertips, with the promise that it *might* be okay in the end, the first thing she had done was snatched it right up.

Greedy hands shaking, and all.

Was that selfish?

She didn't know.

"What?" Corrado asked again, his tone softening slightly the second time.

Ginevra swallowed hard. "Sorry, I just remembered your name, that's all."

"And who told you my name?"

"Andino."

Corrado nodded. "Don't trust very much *he* says, let me tell you."

"He's the one who gave me this chance," she replied quietly, "so all I have to go on about him is that he made the right choice for me."

The man glanced her way again. "Arranged marriage, was it?"

"Not one I wanted."

"One rarely does."

He'd said that so dryly, and yet, managed to sound amused at the same time. Ginevra found, the longer she stared at him, the more confused she was about him, and *who* he was. How did Andino know the man, and was he someone she could trust? Where was she even going with him; where was he taking her, and what in the hell were they going to do once they got there?

She had too many questions.

And no fucking answers.

Ginevra's heart grew heavier the longer she thought about it. Her sisters, without her *and* their mother ... the fact she was now a girl on the run with a man she didn't even know, that the engagement ring she had been made to wear was *still* on her fucking finger.

"*God*," she mumbled.

Corrado glanced her way again.

She was quick to wipe away the tears that slipped down her cheeks, but that didn't really help. The stupid things kept coming, like a floodgate had been opened, and now she couldn't control it. She went from silent tears to hiccupping *sobs* in a blink, and she felt foolish for it, too. Not that she could stop it, now.

"Stop that," Corrado muttered.

Ginevra dragged in a ragged breath. "I'm *trying*."

"Try *harder*."

His sharp tone was back.

It made her cry more.

What was wrong with her?

"I don't *do* tears, fix your face."

"Excuse you?"

"I can't handle a woman that cries all the time, so quit it."

Fuck him.

"Would you *shut up*?" Ginevra barked back. "You have no idea what my life has been like lately, or what happened to me today! Just ... shut up!"

Corrado blinked, murmuring, "You're kind of a mess, *donna*."

"And you're kind of an asshole. What about it?"

Those tears still hadn't stopped flowing. Corrado let out a harsh noise, but that time when he looked her way, a sympathy stared back from him. She didn't know what happened until the tires of the car crunched on gravel, and they slowed to a stop. He came across the seats after throwing off his buckle. He snatched a couple of napkins from the cup holder between them, and with a soft, but quick, hand, wiped the wetness from her face.

And likely what was left of her ruined makeup, too.

He kept stroking away those tears, never saying anything the entire time. Part of Ginevra liked that *far* too much—the way he looked as he focused on his task of wiping away her tears, and how he did it with such silent intensity that it struck her quiet.

And made her stop crying at the same time.

Finally, she whispered, "Thank you."

Corrado shrugged one shoulder. "Don't mention it."

"Where are we going?"

"Home. Or, a place I used to call home … I'm sure they'll be surprised to see you with me when I arrive."

She frowned.

What did that mean?

Who else would he show up with?

"For how long?" she asked.

"Apparently," Corrado drawled out, sitting back in his seat and buckling up again, "until I am told otherwise. Settle in, I'm sure it'll be fun."

Yeah.

But would it *really*?

• • •

"Home sweet home," Corrado muttered, dropping Ginevra's box—the one Andino had given her with the forged passport, and other things she might need—to the floor. "Feel free to find a room you like, except the master bedroom, it's … mine," he said, after hesitating. "And yeah, that's about it for now."

He didn't say anything else, simply headed down the hall without taking off his blazer, or removing his shoes. Ginevra didn't feel comfortable enough to walk through this Toronto penthouse without taking her manners into consideration. If he owned the place, then he could do what he wanted—she hadn't been raised that way.

Hanging up the hat that she had used to hide her face as she escaped from the church, Ginevra noticed the coats hanging along the rack on the wall. It wasn't that there were coats there that made her hesitate, but more the fact that they were two entirely different styles.

Leather.

Blazers.

She kicked off her shoes, and moved them into one of the cubbies underneath the row of jackets, noticing there, too, were different styles of shoes. And not *just* a selection of loafers, but rather, combat boots, a pair of Doc Martens, and then next to those, runners, Armani loafers, and a pair of shined, black leather dress shoes that would work with any suit.

And just with a quick glance, she could tell the shoes were two different sizes. Like they belonged to two people.

Two men.

Did someone else live here?

"Is this yours?" Ginevra called after Corrado. "This penthouse, I mean?"

He didn't answer her back.

She tried not to be annoyed.

Not knowing where he went after he disappeared past the large entrance, decorated in black and white marble, Ginevra headed down the hall. That same sleek and stylish décor followed her deeper into the penthouse. She passed by a sitting room with an entire wall covered by windows overlooking a busy part of Toronto's center, and another that held a television large enough to be a projection screen. The black leather sectional sitting atop a similarly colored rug looked inviting, and God knew she needed to relax, but she had questions.

Only one man could currently answer them.

Overtop the couch hung a chandelier made up of metal fragments that mirrored the light from the inverted lights in the ceiling. Hardwood floors gleamed under her feet. Artwork covered the walls, and fresh flowers rested in a vase that she passed as she moved toward the noise coming from a room over.

Did someone change them regularly?

A maid?

The place screamed *excess*.

Money.

From the sturdy, huge bookcases she found in what looked to be a library-slash-office, to the black marble standing shower and matching clawfoot tub in a bathroom directly across from a state-of-the-art kitchen.

The kitchen was where Ginevra found Corrado nursing a glass of amber liquid. Whiskey, given the bottle sat in front of him on the gray, granite countertops. Stainless steel appliances and white cupboards surrounded him in the large space, and yet, somehow, he still dominated it. Her attention was only on him, and that *haunted* look in his eyes.

What was that from?

"There were keys in the bowl near the door," she said.

Corrado looked her way. "And?"

"I just ... thought it looked like someone had recently left and planned to be back or something."

"Or something," he replied.

"Do you have a roommate here?"

Corrado laughed. "I own this penthouse, and we use it when we're in the city to visit my family."

"We?"

He cleared his throat, setting the glass to the counter a little harder than was necessary. She could tell just by the look in his eyes that *moody* Corrado was back— oh, he still looked the same, sure, still devastatingly handsome, but that attitude screamed back off without him even needing to say a word.

Was it because of this place?

Or her asking questions?

"Don't you have something else to do?" Corrado asked. "It was a sixteen-hour drive, find a place to sleep."

"So, no one else lives here, then? I don't want to wake up to someone—"

"I have to make some calls."

With that said, Corrado moved around the kitchen island, and crossed the space. He passed her by in the doorway without as much as a look in her direction, and that only left Ginevra more confused than ever.

He'd said *we*.

She heard it.

What did that mean?

· · ·

"Fuck, thanks, I'm sure she'll be grateful to have something to wear," Ginevra heard Corrado say, his voice muted from how far it was traveling through the penthouse. "I'll take her out in a couple of days, or something, and let her grab the rest, but at least she'll have something to wear until then."

"No worries."

At the new male voice, Ginevra left the safety of the library where she had been mulling over the events of her life that led her to this place, and trying to find a book to take to bed at the same time. She couldn't do anything to change her circumstances at the moment, so she was content to distract her mind until something happened.

She lingered in the hallway as the conversation near the entry of the penthouse continued on between Corrado, and the newcomer. He hadn't said anyone would be coming over, so she wondered if it was maybe the *other* person who lived here.

"You want me to let Ma and Papa know you're here, or what?"

"I'll call," Corrado said. "They were expecting me, anyway. I just showed up a little earlier, that's all."

"Right, and they won't ask questions at all."

"I can't answer all of them even if they do."

"Yeah, I get you. The League, or …?"

"No," Corrado murmured. "Do you want a drink, or do you have somewhere to be?"

"I could have one drink, but I need to head out soon. A meeting tonight with some of the Capos, you know. It never ends."

"You always were a better made man than you were an assassin, Chris. I'm glad you figured that out before it was too late."

Chuckles echoed down the hallway. Ginevra came to the end, and peered around carefully so she wouldn't be seen. For a second, she thought she was seeing doubles as she found the two men standing at the end of the entrance hallway.

Like mirrors of one another.

It took her a second.

Then, *two*.

Twins, she realized.

Corrado had an *identical* twin.

If she hadn't known the clothes Corrado was wearing earlier, she might have needed to look twice to try and tell the difference between the two. They stood the same facing one another, arms crossed over their chests, and features looking as though they'd been cut from stone. Corrado's brother—Chris, wasn't it?—wore his hair a bit longer, and his three-piece suit was a contrast against the simple black slacks and silk shirt his twin wore.

There were differences.

But not many.

And they were *surface*, things. Clothes, hairstyle, and so forth. Nothing really physical about them was different, or at least, not that Ginevra could tell from this far away.

"Does he know," Chris started to ask, "that there's a chick here, I mean?"

Corrado shook his head. "Didn't mention that ... yet."

"Probably should, man."

"Yeah, I will."

Ginevra was too caught up in the fact that the two looked so similar that she missed part of their conversation. She didn't really understand what they were talking about, now.

"We have a guest," Chris said, his gaze drifting to Ginevra.

She was quick to dart back around the corner, but not before Corrado turned, and laid eyes on her, too.

Shit.

She caught that look he had.

Intense, again.

Contemplative.

Like he didn't know what to make of her. It was the same stare he'd had in the car, and she didn't know what to make of it. Or how it made her feel, or *why* she felt anything about it at all, really.

Why did it feel like everything was changing? That this was going to end up being *more* than just her hiding away from her half-brothers while New York waged a mafia war?

"Yeah," she heard Corrado say, "I think I found trouble with that one."

"Seems like you find trouble a lot, man."

"That's unfair, and—"

"And you're not a liar, so."

"You know what," Corrado said, "fuck the drink, get out."

Chris laughed loudly. "I missed you, Corrado."

"Can't say the same."

"*Lies.*"

Ginevra slipped back down the hallway, and into the library.

No one came to find her.

She didn't mind.

19.

"How long do you think you'll need?" Dare asked.

"A couple months, maybe. I'll let you know if I need more time off."

Dare made a noise on the other end of the call, but didn't question Corrado on *why* he needed time off. That was thing about The League—being an independent contractor, essentially, allowed him more freedom than other members who went up on the auctions, and signed years of their lives away to buyers.

Corrado would never do that.

No one owned him.

"I thought you wanted to do that upcoming job with Alessio. The political hit in Albania, I mean," Dare said, "because this will fall in that time frame, according to the details I have for that assignment."

"It didn't need two people on it."

He just wanted to go with Les.

Things changed sometimes.

It couldn't be helped.

Dare cleared his throat, asking, "Things are fine, aren't they? You're not … having trouble with anything, are you?"

Corrado almost laughed.

That was about as *deep* as Dare cared to get with one of his people. He didn't care if they had personal shit going on in their lives as long as it didn't mess with The League, and what the organization was doing. On the opposite end of the coin, Dare and Cree were some of the *few* people who knew the complexities of Alessio and Corrado's relationship.

So, when Dare asked something like *that*, he was really asking about Alessio and Corrado without outright saying it. Corrado wasn't stupid.

"Why, so you could send Cree to set me straight?" Corrado asked.

The man had the decency—or gall—to laugh.

"I only send Cree when you give me no other choice."

"Right," Corrado murmured. "And no, nothing is wrong. I just need a break. Other things to handle for a bit, and then I'll be back to work."

"Noted." Keys clicked on the other end before Dare said, "That's it, then. Call me if you need to change something, yeah?"

"Will do."

Corrado lingered in the library, that also doubled as his office, for a while longer after he ended the call. Staring out at the busy city below, one of the only rooms in the penthouse that didn't have full floor to ceiling windows, he found a strange comfort in this space.

Designed to be useful to him—he liked the office area—and to Alessio, who needed a million and one books because he could never find enough shit to read, the two of them often found themselves in here more often than anywhere else in the penthouse when they were in the city. It wasn't lost on Corrado how Ginevra also seemed to favor this room since her arrival here. More often than not, she gravitated to the books, and settled into one of the sitting areas to crack it open for hours on end.

Alessio would enjoy that. Someone to entertain his need for words and knowledge until long after the fucking sun set, and the rest of the world was sleeping ...

Not that Corrado needed to be thinking about that *at all*.

Yep.

Quite enough of that.

Spinning on his heel, he left the office library before he could think better of it. He didn't need to be thinking about shit that didn't matter, anyway. Strolling through the penthouse, he rounded the corner at the end of the hallway, and came to an abrupt stop in the entryway that led to the sitting room.

The *hint* of a smile curved his lips as he found Ginevra standing in front of a television screen that was as tall as her, and as wide as the entire wall. With a game controller in her hands, she pressed a button and laughed when her tank on the screen blew up her opponent behind enemy lines.

For the most part, he tried to give her space. He liked his own, after all, and figured most people were the same. Since she didn't try to seek him out, he offered her the same respect.

Like now, he would usually walk away.

He *should* walk away.

Instead, he stood there in the entryway, watching her from the side as she fiddled with the game, and her features lit up each time she succeeded in doing something right. He was reminded again, then, as her bow-shaped lips curved with her happiness, and her brown eyes widened with joy, that she was an *exceptionally* beautiful woman.

If not innocent ...

It was a silly thing, really. *Simple*, and not at all something that he would find amusement in any other time. That was a game he liked to play to chill a few years back, but he hadn't touched it in a long while. It had been too long since he and Alessio came back to Toronto for a visit, anyway.

He shouldn't be watching her at all, or *caring*. Not that she found happiness in his games, or that she enjoyed spending her time with Alessio's books.

That didn't mean *anything*.

Right?

Except, Corrado wasn't that simple, and neither was his mind. He was detail-oriented. He liked to know *all the things* about people, and what made them tick. Ginevra wasn't an exception to that rule, and if anything, he found himself *more* curious about her than he had anyone. How did she feel to be twenty-one, and in the position she now was? Who had she left back in New York? What had she wanted to be or do *before* this?

All those questions, and no answers.

Unless he talked to her.

That could be a problem.

"Do you want to play, or are you going to keep standing there watching me?"

Corrado found Ginevra staring at him from the side, unbothered by his presence. "It's my home, Ginevra."

"I prefer Ginny." She smiled brightly—*sweetly*. "That's what my mom used to call me, and my sisters."

Corrado dragged in a heavy breath, feeling the sense of time he had never been able to forget because it was seared into his brain coming back in a flash. That time, and that man, it melted together in his brain with this woman.

He saw her face.

He heard her words.

And he also saw Alessio—heard him, too.

I prefer Les.

That memory hit him hard.

All at once.

Like a punch to the gut.

He'd been this curious once a long time ago. He remembered that day vividly—that knife room, and those few words he shared with a man that would change his whole life. This felt different in ways, and in others, the same.

Because the curiosity was *there*. God knew it was going to be his curiosity that got him in trouble. It always did.

Like fucking *déjà vu*.

Yeah, a problem.

That's what this woman was for him.

Corrado knew it right then.

Because he had *interest*.

Nothing was ever simple when he found interest in something, but especially because *nothing* interested him anymore. Nothing but the man back in Vegas, and apparently, this woman standing in front of him.

"Well?" she asked. "Do you want to play?"

"I don't think I should," he replied, honestly.

Her smile fell. "Oh. Okay."

"Don't let me stop you from enjoying it, though."

She didn't reply.

He didn't mind.

Corrado left Ginevra to her game, and he went back to Alessio's library. Shit felt easier there. He could breathe better in that space, further away from her, and the confusion he now felt.

Except that was a lie, too.

Nothing was easier.

• • •

"*Fuck.*"

Corrado glared at the digital clock on the nightstand that displayed a time *way* too early for his fucking phone to be ringing. Even if the sun was up, it didn't matter. *Nobody* needed to wake his ass up before seven-thirty.

Unless someone was dead.

And even then, it depended on who died.

"*What?*" he snarled into the phone.

132

"Woke you up, did I?"

Corrado's brow knotted as he took in the familiar voice, and then eyed the clock again. Seven o'clock in Toronto meant it was four in the morning in Las Vegas. "Why aren't *you* sleeping, Les?"

The man on the other end of the phone made a grunt. A good sign he didn't want to answer the question, but he was probably going to do it anyway simply because Corrado asked. So was their way.

"Well?" Corrado pressed.

Pushing over in the bed, Corrado rolled to his back while keeping the phone at his ear. He waited for whatever it was Alessio had to tell him as he sat up, and used the black velvet of the headboard as a place to rest his back.

He needed to wake up.

Alessio was still quiet on the phone.

Across the hall from his master bedroom—without Alessio, Corrado *rarely* closed his bedroom door—he found a familiar form sleeping. Apparently, Ginevra also didn't know how to close her door when she went to bed, although this was the first time Corrado had woken up before her in the week that they had been staying together in this penthouse. Usually, he had found other ways to distract himself when the woman was around, so then they both had their space.

He didn't know *why* he did that.

She didn't upset him …

He just felt odd around her. Like when she'd started crying in the car when he drove them to Toronto, and his first reaction was to be *rude*. And then just as quickly, he found he needed to fix that and her because he didn't want to see her cry.

He shouldn't care at all.

She was a fucking job.

"Corrado, are you listening?"

"Yeah," he muttered, coming back to the conversation at hand. Although, he was still staring across the hall even as he said it, half amused by the fact Ginevra slept *on top* of the blankets, and also slightly bothered by it at the same time. Not because he thought she might be cold—the penthouse was warm—but more because he noticed at all. Like he noticed the shape of her thighs, and the way her legs looked under the pair of cotton shorts she'd pulled on. *Fuck*. He needed to get back to Les. Now. "What's going on?"

"You asked for time off from The League?"

Corrado stiffened in the bed, scrubbing a hand over his face at the same time. "Who told you that?"

"Who do you think?"

"Dare, likely. Cree doesn't pay attention to that shit."

"You're not wrong," Alessio grumbled.

Across the hall, Ginevra rolled over in the bed, a soft sound escaping her at the same time. It *almost* sounded like a moan. Add that onto the fact that Corrado was still admiring the swells and curves of her body, not to mention, the fact he was *quite* aware that she was a beautiful woman, and he suddenly needed to ignore a raging erection under his own sheets.

Great.

That's just fucking perfect.

Another woman, under entirely different circumstances, and Corrado might have acted on his attraction. He would have let Alessio know the shit he was feeling, that he was attracted to the chick, and it would have been done.

That was their rule.

It was *fine.*

Except this was different. He wasn't *just* attracted to Ginevra—he was also interested in her, and what brought her here to him. Things he had no business feeling, and he didn't know how that factored into the way he and Alessio had always done things when it came to women. Not to mention, he gave his word about the job with Ginevra; he wasn't to tell people where she came from, or who she was. Including Alessio.

It was a fucking mess.

This was trouble.

That woman was *trouble.*

Why, or for what reason, or even *how* … Corrado didn't know those things, but he knew this. He could tell already, one week into watching Ginevra, that she was going to be an issue for him. For more reasons than he cared to admit, if he were being honest. Sometimes, Corrado just got a feeling about something or someone, and he was *rarely* wrong.

He'd had that same feeling about The League.

Or Alessio.

Different jobs.

He didn't ignore it now.

"It's for that favor, right?" Alessio asked. "Andino Marcello?"

Corrado cleared his throat and forced himself to avert his eyes from the figure across the hall. As it was, the guilt had already started to compound in his chest. "Yeah, that's what it is."

"And you still can't tell me what it is?"

"Not really. I gave my word, that's all."

Although, Corrado was starting to think that was probably a lame fucking excuse. There was no one he trusted *more* than Alessio. Life had taught him that, and Alessio only proved it time and time again.

He could, at the very least, explain the *gist* of the job, and the fact that he had a woman here with him. Except, then he was wading into dangerous fucking territory with that—he would still be omitting important details to Alessio.

Like his interest in her.

The attraction.

So, no.

Corrado refused to say *anything.*

Because he didn't plan to act on it.

None of it.

Simple.

Or that was the lie he was going to tell himself. He'd fucked up here. From the moment Ginevra got inside his car at that church, the first thing Corrado should have done the *second* he could was call Alessio.

Been honest.

Gave every detail.

But he didn't.

And now here he was, a week into this *thing* ... and he was just digging the hole deeper. It wouldn't be as simple, now. He couldn't just tell Alessio the truth, and the man shrug it off. That wasn't how *they* worked.

That's not how their thing worked.

The fact that he didn't tell Alessio *from the start* would be a nail in the coffin. Corrado didn't need confirmation from Alessio to know it was true—it was their goddamn rule. Except he hadn't done anything, and as long as he continued on that path, then there was nothing to tell.

Right?

Yeah.

The guilt compounded deeper.

Fuck.

So, yeah. He was going to say nothing. *Do nothing.* He wouldn't act on a damn thing—not his attraction, or his interest. He was going to get this fucking job done, and go back home to Alessio like he'd planned to from the start before he looked at Ginevra after she got in his car, and got *that* feeling.

That same feeling he had when he met Alessio for the first time. A feeling that said *this is going to change everything for you.* Because what else could he do? He'd already dug this fucking hole, he might as well keep digging until he was out of it, too.

"I'm just saying that I don't like finding out shit from Dare instead of *you*," Alessio said on the phone, bringing Corrado back to the conversation again. "And you know how Andino Marcello is—he doesn't care what shit you step in for him, so are you sure this *job* is even on the up and up with him?"

"Les—"

"Since when do you hide shit from me, Corrado?"

Yeah.

Shit.

"I'm not hiding anything," he said.

There was just nothing to tell.

Not yet.

Across the hall, Ginevra made another noise before she rolled to her back. He saw her eyes flutter open, and she stared up at the canopy above the four-poster bed.

"Corrado—"

"I have to let you go," he said quickly. "I'll call you back."

He hung up the phone, and tossed it to the bedsheets without waiting for a goodbye from Alessio. His chest became tighter—that pain, growing *sharper.*

But he probably wouldn't call back. Not when it meant needing to hide things from Alessio because now, Corrado just didn't want to *lie.* That guilt was a *killer.*

Corrado still wasn't sure how he got to this point simply by taking a goddamn job to pay back a favor. All he had to do was open up his fucking mouth. Tell Alessio the job was a *woman.* And because it wasn't as simple as it seemed, his dick decided to get involved, and maybe his curiosity, too.

That was it.

That's all he needed to do.

He was making it more complicated than it actually was, but he didn't know how to fix it. Nothing was ever simple with him and Les, even if on the surface, it might seem like it. Those were lies, too. They'd made this complicated.

Corrado blamed himself for that, too.

20.

Ginevra

Ginevra eyed the landline cordless phone charging on the counter as she stirred the sugar into her steaming coffee. It'd been a week, and not once had she considered using any one of the many phones throughout the penthouse to call out.

Except she was doing that now.

Maybe it was because she woke up, and realized this was the longest she had ever gone without speaking to her siblings. Even after she turned eighteen, and moved out of the house to begin classes at a community college, she still called them every single day. And her mama, too.

She'd made an effort *not* to think about it since coming here. She knew it was dangerous, and calls could *easily* be tracked. This morning, it was all she could think about.

Funny how that worked.

What was happening in New York, now?

Were her sisters safe?

Had Siena kept her promise?

What was happening?

Nothing could drive a person to do crazy things more than the unknown. She'd spent the last week acquainting herself with the penthouse, and the different things to do inside it. She bet Corrado paid a good amount for this place.

Ten rooms.

Three bathrooms.

A few thousand square feet.

There were lots to do, too. Like the gaming systems in the sitting room, or the library. There was also a small gym with the same floor to ceiling windows that overlooked the heart of Toronto. A hot tub on a balcony that was enclosed with more glass walls.

Despite the fact a maid came three times during the week to clean, and bring in groceries, she also had a whole stack of takeout menus for restaurants she could order from. Corrado had also taken her into the city to shop, and grab whatever she needed by way of clothing or personal items.

Mostly, she tried to stay busy because then, she didn't focus on those unknowns back in New York nearly as much.

And still …

Here she was, eyeing that damn phone.

Ginevra sighed, and *forced* her damn gaze away from the phone so that she could focus on something else. It didn't matter how much she wanted to call, the rules were clear—she *couldn't*. Not until she knew it was safe.

Because that was the thing, right?

It was more than just her.

It was her sisters, too.

She had to be smart—and strong—for them. She was sure they were terrified

137

and wondering what in the hell happened to her. She highly doubted their half-brothers were treating the young girls well, but at the same time ... they couldn't *hurt* them, either. Greta and Giulia were literally Kev and Darren's last thing to use to reach for the top, right?

That's what Siena said.

Trust them, her mind whispered.

Except, who exactly was she trusting?

A man who led her to believe he was going to marry her right up until the point she was almost ready to walk down the aisle? A half-sister she barely knew, but always seemed kind enough for her to let down her defenses?

Corrado?

A man who *barely* spoke to her.

Who was Ginevra supposed to fucking trust?

Maybe that was the thing that bothered her the very most. Beyond the fact she was in a whole new country, or couldn't speak to her sisters. Separate from the fact she felt stir-crazy here, and didn't know anything that was going on back in New York.

It was that she didn't know *their* motives.

Andino.

Siena.

Corrado.

None of them.

She didn't know their motives, alone or with *her*, and that bothered her. The very last thing she ever intended to be was someone else's pawn, but right now ... that's exactly what she felt like at the end of the day.

A pawn.

Being moved.

No control.

It was only once she had poured a bit of cream into the mug that she turned back around to sip on her coffee, and stare at the phone again. She didn't know what made her reach out to pick it up, but she did. Staring at it, but not deciding to make that call, she simply *held* it.

She didn't hear Corrado until he was right there, *grabbing* the damn phone from her hand. He moved like lightening, silent and dangerous. She jumped when he came up behind her, and nearly rammed right into his naked chest when she spun around fast to face him.

With the phone in one hand, he cocked his head to the side, and smirked a bit. "What were you doing?"

"Uh ..."

It was hard to focus—hard to *talk*—when he was standing this close to her. She could blame it on the fact he wore nothing but a pair of boxer-briefs, and she had a glorious view of the hard lines, and ridges of muscle that made up his lean, yet muscular, form. He reminded her of a runner in the way he was built, and the way the waistband on those boxer-briefs rested against the hard V of his groin had her gaze lingering before he cleared his throat.

Ginevra's gaze traveled back up his body.

Jesus.

Skin uninked.

Though he had scars.

A few.

Yeah, she could have blamed her inability to speak on the way he looked—because he was shamelessly gorgeous, and he probably knew it—but that wasn't what did it. No, it was the way Corrado *stared* at her that always seemed to silence her.

He did it when she was looking.

And when she wasn't.

Did he even know how intense his stare was? Like he'd found prey, and was ready to go in for the kill?

A part of her wouldn't mind that.

Being his prey.

Not at all.

Corrado's right eyebrow arched when Ginevra's gaze drifted over his strong features, and she couldn't stop that heat from rising up her cheeks. *This close*, there was no hiding the fact she just stared at him like a foolish girl for at least two minutes.

Just *stared*.

He was kind enough not to say anything.

His smirk deepened, though.

"Well?" he asked.

"I was just ... looking at it," she said lamely.

Corrado cocked his head to the side. "You know the rules."

"Yeah, but—"

"No calls out. Yes, I can take you out of the penthouse, we can go do things, and whatever else, but if there is *any* chance someone could track you back here, then that's a no-go. From what I understand, you were mostly unknown back in New York, being that you were only recently brought into the folds of the Calabrese family, right?"

Ginevra swallowed hard. "Yeah, my mom ... was Matteo's mistress for a time. We were kept a secret until—"

"They needed someone to marry off."

"Basically."

"So like I said," Corrado replied, shrugging one shoulder, "you're mostly unknown, and that means you'll be able to do other things here besides stay hidden away in this penthouse. But if you go off doing stupid things like calling people, which will make it *far* easier to track us, then we're going to have to move again. I doubt you'll like where we'll go, or the fact you won't be able to leave the place. Got it?"

Well, when he put it that way ...

She nodded.

What else could she do?

"I understand."

"*Perfetto.*"

Corrado leaned around Ginevra, making her entire body seize when heat shot through her gut at the feeling of his body grazing hers—*how?*—and he froze, too.

She felt the way he stiffened, and a jolt of *something* passed through her before he sucked in a quick breath, too.

Like he felt that, too.

Electricity, maybe?

A *shock*.

Ginevra lifted her stare to find he was staring at her again, his hand holding the phone hovering over the charger like he forgot what he was supposed to be doing again. She didn't know how long the two of them stared at one another like that—a few seconds, or more, but it could have been longer, too.

It felt like forever.

She found heat in his gaze.

Interest.

Something unknown.

And she liked it far too much.

Not that she understood that, either. She didn't know anything about this man.

"Are you like them?" she dared to ask.

Corrado's tongue snaked out to wet the edge of his bottom lip. "Like *them*, how?"

"Mafia. *Made*."

"No."

"I don't know if I believe that."

He felt like them, in a way. Dangerous, and dark. Like he held secrets in his eyes, and in his heart. He didn't feel *average*, and God knew she had met enough average men over her lifetime to know it.

No, he felt like something else.

"I'm not like them," he said, "but I am a little worse."

She hesitated to ask more.

What did that mean?

Corrado seemed to take her hesitation as a chance to break their moment. Whatever in the hell that had been ... that touch, the heat, that fucking *feeling*. She didn't know what that was, and while she might like it, it also terrified her.

Because she didn't know him.

And she still didn't know if she could trust him.

He placed the phone back on the charger. As fast as he was touching her, he was gone.

It didn't matter.

He still lingered.

She felt it.

Everywhere.

What in the hell was *that*?

Corrado cleared his throat, and wouldn't meet her gaze. She wondered if he felt that, too? God knew he didn't say much to her. For the most part, he'd spent the last week avoiding her as much as was possible when they were alone together in the penthouse.

"Would you like me to cook you breakfast?" he asked, a thickness roughening up his tone as he reached for the cupboard beside her.

Ginevra was back to feeling like she couldn't speak, so instead, she whispered,

"Sure."

"And you can tell me about your sisters," he was quick to add, shooting her a smile, "maybe then you won't feel like you need to talk *to* them, if you're talking about them."

"You want to know about my little sisters?"

Corrado shrugged. "Why not?"

Well, okay.

Like he said, why not?

"So, there's Greta," Ginevra said, "and she's seventeen. And then there's Giulia, and she's fifteen. They're typical teenage girls. We're all close ... I guess because us girls are all we really had growing up since our dad just came and went. Usually when he came around, it was to give our mom money. So, we all leaned on each other."

"What about your mom?"

Ginevra stiffened, and Corrado didn't miss it. He turned to look at her, raising his brow in question at her sudden silence. Something painful came to wrap around her heart, and she swore those tears wouldn't be very far behind.

Did he see that?

She didn't know.

Not when she was too busy trying to hide it.

"Don't do that again—those tears," he said quickly when she peeked up at him. "I can't do the tears, girl. You might as well stick a fucking knife in my chest, and finish the goddamn job while you're at it. It kills me."

Ginevra did her best to hold back the emotion. *Barely.*

"They killed my mom," she whispered, "Kev and Darren, I mean. My half-brothers. They made it look like a suicide, but I knew. They told me what they would do if she tried to help me, and that's what they did. Because she tried to help me get away."

Corrado let out a fast breath. "Hey, that's not your fault."

"Isn't it?"

"No. And I'm sorry. About your ma."

Yeah.

She still hadn't gotten the time to deal with that. It was like one minute, her mama was there, and then the next, she was gone. Except she had to move on to taking care of her sisters, and dealing with the upcoming wedding. Her *brothers*, the bastards. And everything else, too. The wedding day, Andino letting her escape, Corrado, and coming here.

One thing after another.

It didn't stop.

Not for one second had she really been able to handle her grief for her mother. Until now, really.

"It's worse at night," she admitted. "Maybe because that was the time I used to spend the most with her ... we would read, or talk."

Corrado made a noise under his breath. "I know, I hear you crying."

She kind of wished he didn't say that. It just made her feel worse to know that someone was a witness to her pain, and couldn't help.

Nothing helped.

"You're allowed to grieve," he said quietly, leaning against the island and giving her a bit of breathing room. "And you're allowed to do it however you need to. If that means crying at night when you're alone, then that's what it is."

"It doesn't make it better, though."

"I don't doubt it."

Ginevra glanced away. "Then, I ran away, and left my sisters there."

"Hey," he murmured, his hand coming up fast so that his fingertips could graze down her arm with a soft touch. That light stroke was enough to send heat licking up her arm, but somehow, she ignored it. "I think someone else made that choice for you, and you're doing the best you can with it. Because what were the options, huh?"

"Well—"

"What were your options back there?"

"To marry a stranger."

Corrado nodded. "And your sisters ... you were told they'd be taken care of, I'm sure."

"But what if they *aren't?*"

"And you think, what, calling them, getting tracked down, dragged back there, forced into a marriage, possibly being hurt for running away ... do you think that will help *their* situation at all?"

"When you put it *that* way."

"Perspective helps everything," he murmured.

Sure.

Still ... "That doesn't make the guilt easier to swallow."

"Yeah, you're not wrong." Corrado smiled crookedly. "I know that. All too well."

Did he?

"What makes you feel guilty, then, Corrado?"

He straightened in place, the widening of his brown eyes telling her that he hadn't expected that question. Still, he continued pulling items from the cupboards, before moving to the drawers where he found utensils. "I don't know what to make of you, Ginevra."

"I'm sorry?"

"You continue to surprise me."

"Is that a bad thing?"

"I haven't decided yet. People rarely surprise me anymore. I'm not sure what to do with the ones that manage it."

"You know, you didn't answer my question. About what makes you feel guilty, too, I mean. Instead, you deflected it back to me."

He pointed a butter knife at her, and winked. "You're absolutely right. And look at that, you're surprising me again."

That said, he moved around her with the grace of a predator, opened the fridge, and pulled a carton of eggs out along with butter. That gave her an answer, too, even if it wasn't the answer she wanted: he wasn't going to tell her what made him feel guilty.

She didn't mind.

Now, she could watch him cook.

21.

Alessio

"Why are you in New York?"

"Pretty sure," he replied to Dare, "that I didn't have the chip put in for you to track me *just because.*"

"No, it was for emergencies only, but—"

"This is not an emergency."

"You didn't pick up my last three calls, or reply to Cree's texts," Dare said quietly, "and *yes*, to me, that is warrant enough to check up on your tracker."

All League members had them—or most. It was an option they were given simply because it was one thing to be forced into having a tracker put into your body, and it was another to willingly accept it. That was just about one of the only choices The League allowed the assassins to make for themselves.

Alessio understood the need for it. In their business, they made a lot of fucking enemies. A client one week could be a problem the next when a new client came in to take out the previous, or attempt it. Their business was dirty, no doubt about it.

Sometimes, in an attempt to get back at The League, the first thing someone tried to do was go after the members. The trackers at least gave Dare and Cree a chance to retrieve their man or woman, and hopefully, still alive, if they moved fast enough or got the team out. It didn't happen often, but even once was too much.

Corrado opted for a tracker, too.

"I'm not on a job, right?" Alessio asked into the phone.

Dare sighed. "No."

"Then, I can be wherever I need to be."

"Answer my calls, and I won't check in."

Something *akin* to guilt stabbed Alessio in his chest. He should have picked up those calls, or at the very least, answer one of Cree's many texts over the last week or so. It was entirely unusual for him to ignore both of them, never mind the fact he hadn't been into The League's complex since Corrado headed out two weeks ago for that … fucking *favor.*

"What's going on?" Dare asked.

"Nothing."

Lies.

Alessio wasn't a liar.

He *wasn't.*

He would be right now, though, for Corrado. Because if this favor for Andino Marcello was something that might get him in trouble with The League—not that Alessio knew that was the case for sure—then he wasn't going to be the one who delivered the news.

"Then why are you in New York?"

Alessio gave the café he passed a quick glance, trying to figure out a way to end this conversation so he could get on with his plans, and the day. "I have something to handle."

"Corrado?"

"Corrado is in Toronto, which you know."

"That doesn't change the fact—"

"Everything is *fine*."

"Alessio," Dare murmured, "I am not asking about things for The League right now. I know you think that's all I care about most of the time, but you have been my priority from the time you were ten."

His walk slowed until he came to a stop altogether. People blew by him on the sidewalk, but Alessio simply stared up at the cloudy July sky. In Nevada, the heat would be *dry*, which he liked. Here, it was fucking humid.

Which he hated.

And still, here he was looking for answers because he couldn't *not* seek them out. When it came to Corrado, Alessio didn't know how to leave things alone, but especially not when something just felt *off*.

This favor?

Andino Marcello?

Yeah.

It all felt off to Alessio. Like something was going on, or whatever was happening might bring Corrado a world of trouble, and Alessio wouldn't even be able to help him because he *didn't know what it was*. For two weeks, he'd practically crawled out of his skin with the feeling that something was up here, and it was going to end badly.

So, here he was.

In New York.

Alessio was going to get those fucking answers one way or the other. He knew where to go, and how to go about doing it, too. If Corrado couldn't—or wouldn't—tell him, then he would go to another source to get the details.

Simple as that.

Because *God*.

What in the fuck would Alessio do without Corrado? That, more than anything else, was what had been keeping him awake these past two weeks. He didn't like not knowing things, but especially when it meant something could be wrong.

Add Corrado into that mix?

People were *begging* to feel pain.

Alessio didn't fuck around.

"Les—"

"I just have business to handle," he said, stopping Dare before the man could ask more. "That's it, and that's all."

"Business dealing with *him*, no?"

"Even if it is, that's for me to take care of."

Dare sighed. "I wish you would learn the difference between something *healthy* and something that … turns you into someone you don't recognize when you look into the mirror at the reflection staring back, Alessio."

Funny.

"I don't even remember who I was before him."

"I can tell."

Alessio smirked, though Dare couldn't see it. "And I'm fine with that."

• • •

If it were possible for the ground to combust simply from Alessio glaring at it, then the pavement would be ashes under his feet currently. No doubt, it was his mood and current surly expression that allowed him a wide berth of space on the New York sidewalk as he headed down the busy block. People avoided him, parting the crowd for him to walk straight through.

He wasn't going to complain.

This city *was not* Vegas. Of that, he was most sure. Even in the bright light of day, New York still had a dreary, dark quality to it. Now, that would typically be Alessio's style. He liked all things moody and *black*—it reflected himself, after all.

Not when he was in this mood, though.

Alessio came to a stop in front of a Brooklyn restaurant. The gold lettering on the windows spelling out the name, and the satin curtains pulled back to expose the lavish décor let him know he was not dressed appropriately for the place in his black jeans, combat boots, and leather jacket.

He tipped his head to the side, considering.

Fuck it.

When had he *ever* cared about that?

Never.

That's when.

Taking one last drag from his cigarette, he tossed it to the sidewalk, and headed for the entrance of the fancy restaurant. Taking the steps three at a time, Alessio yanked open the door, and stepped into the smells of rich sauces, and lingering spices. Something that, on another day, he might have stopped to appreciate.

Not today.

Today, he had other things to do.

The girl dressed in a tight, black dress behind the podium looked up and met his gaze when the bell above the door chimed at his entrance. With a tablet at the ready in her hands, she opened her mouth to greet him.

As she should.

It was her job.

Alessio simply passed her by before she could even ask her question. Her shout of *hey* at his back fell on deaf ears because he didn't give a shit. His task was simply to find the man who owned this place, and have a chat. All it took were a couple of carefully placed calls to the right people—everyone in this *life* had contacts to use, him included—and Alessio knew exactly where he had to go to find Andino Marcello.

He heard the woman's heels clicking against the floor as she followed him through the bustling restaurant, still hollering at his back like he gave a single fuck about her. He didn't. Not at all.

His contact said if Andino wasn't having business in the private dining section of the place, then he would be in the back office at the far end of the kitchen. Passing the private area with a quick glance said Andino was in the office, so that's exactly where Alessio went.

Cooks in the kitchen yelled at him, too.

Fun.

He ignored them as well.

"Sir, you can't be back—"

"Who the fuck are you?"

Alessio came face to face with likely one of the biggest men he had ever seen in his life when he turned the corner around a rack in the kitchen. At least four inches taller than Alessio's nearly six-foot-three height, and probably a good sixty pounds of extra muscle than him, too. He had more of a boxer's quality. This man looked like he needed to be on the defense line of a fucking football team.

The guy stood in front of the open doorway that led into the office, and directly behind his very wide shoulders, he found the man he wanted to see sitting at his desk.

Beside that desk sat a ruddy-colored pit bull.

More fun.

"Me?" Alessio asked.

The muscle—no doubt, an enforcer for Andino's crime family who kept him protected while he worked—cocked an eyebrow like he wasn't here for this shit. Well, *surprise*, asshole … neither was Alessio.

"Who else am I looking at?" the enforcer snapped.

"Well, I'm not important," Alessio said, smiling just enough to piss the man off. If the guy wanted to try to make a move on Les, then he was more than welcome to come right on ahead and *do it*. All he had to say about that was the bigger one was, the harder they fucking fell when Alessio punched them in the throat. He pointed around the man's large shoulder, saying, "That man right there is who matters at the moment, and I have a meeting to speak with him."

"No, you don't."

"I do, actually."

The enforcer's lips flattened into a grim line. "Listen, I don't know who the fuck you—"

"Pink, let him in."

Alessio had all he could do not to laugh. He grinned instead, staring up at the bigger man with all the cockiness he could muster as he said, "*Pink*, huh, that's cute."

"I will fucking kill you."

"Yeah, you could certainly try."

"Well, as amusing as *this* is," Andino muttered inside the office, "let him in, Pink. Stay nearby, of course."

"If you're sure, boss …"

"I am sure."

Pink stepped aside, and Alessio winked at the man which only made his brow furrow, before he took a second look at him. Like he wasn't quite sure what to make of Alessio, and it put him on edge.

Good.

It should.

"Don't stand out there and continue to taunt him," Andino said, sounding entirely bored behind his desk, "because then I won't be responsible for what he does once you're out of my sight. Like Snaps here," he added, gesturing down at the mean looking dog next to him, "Pink only minds when he is in my view. I'm sure you understand."

Noted.

Alessio gave the enforcer a look from the side before he entered the office and closed the door behind him at Andino's gesture to do so. The man didn't offer him a chair to sit in, however, but that was fine with him. He would much rather stand for this.

Eyeing the dog next to the desk who looked like he was considering whether or not he wanted to find out what Alessio *and* his leather jacket might taste like, he asked Andino, "What is your business with Corrado Guzzi?"

"What is *your* business with him?"

Ah.

That question.

Well, that was not simple.

Part of Alessio and Corrado's thing of not being public with their relationship dealt with the fact one of them hadn't truly dealt with his bisexuality. Not that Alessio was naming names, but it wasn't him. The other part of it came down to *this*—when they were open and people knew, it gave others the power to hurt Corrado and Alessio by using one against the other.

It was one of the only reasons, next to the fact as long as he had Corrado, then he was happy, that he kept this fucking game up between them for all these years. *No one* would ever have the control to separate or hurt them. If that happened, it was because they chose to do it, not because someone with a touch too much power decided to put their hands in the pot, too, so to speak.

Alessio took his gaze off the dog and leveled it on the man behind the desk instead. "The League—business, that's all."

Andino sucked air through his teeth and rested back in the chair. "What, did The League send out one of their dogs to check up on another one of their dogs, or …?"

"Step *very* carefully from here on out with your words," Alessio warned the man, "because I take insults as a challenge, Marcello, and you don't want to know how I answer those."

"He owed us a favor."

"Us as in—"

"My family—the Marcellos. What else do you need to take back so they'll let me cash that in, and fuck off while I do it, huh?"

Right to the point.

Alessio would have appreciated that on another day, or about any other topic *except* his lover. When it came to Corrado, he couldn't appreciate anything that might put him in danger that would take him from Alessio.

Not that Andino knew that.

"Details," Alessio said, "that's what we want, just to make sure it's not something that will overlap with the rest of our business. I'm sure you understand that could be dangerous for him, and for the rest of us at The League."

"*Right*," Andino drawled, "well, there isn't much to tell, and if he keeps anyone in New York that would know who Ginevra Calabrese is away from her, then none of us will have to worry about any trouble coming his way. Certainly not The

League, regardless of what happens. They arranged my marriage to Ginevra but as I didn't plan on following through, she needed to go away for a while—hence, Corrado watching her. I doubt *anyone* in Canada knows that woman I sent him off with. Most people here didn't know who she was, and her face is a dime a dozen in New York. Canada doesn't mix very much business with the Marcellos, so I assume she is essentially a ghost there with him. Something pretty on his arm, I would say."

Alessio blinked.

What?

"Excuse me?" he asked, his voice a murmur.

Andino arched a brow. "Did I not speak slow enough for you?"

"He's looking after ... a woman."

It wasn't even a question.

Just ... a statement.

Why wouldn't Corrado tell him that?

They had rules for a reason—those rules between them kept the men honest, and their relationship open and *safe*. Telling each other everything was more than just showing their trust but offering their loyalty.

It didn't make sense that Corrado wouldn't explain *that* detail. He could have simply said there was a woman with him, and at the same time, keep the rest from Alessio if it might mess with this favor he owed to Andino.

Except he didn't.

He kept *her* a secret.

Why?

How long would Corrado keep that information from Alessio?

How long would he lie?

Alessio wet the corner of his lip with his tongue. "Ginevra, you said?"

"That's her. If you wouldn't mind, I need that info kept quiet because she needs to stay out of sight for the time being. We have a situation here in New York, a little war, nothing big ... and I would prefer if she wasn't brought back before I kill her useless brothers, and all."

"That seems like a strong reaction to an *almost* marriage."

"No, strong would have been blowing up the church with everyone inside when they thought they could marry me to her without giving me a choice. *That's* a strong reaction. Instead, I figured out another way. And all I have gotten for it is grief, and since I don't know who the fuck you are, or why you give a shit, I won't be taking any of that grief from you for it, too."

"Huh."

Andino nodded at the door and lifted his hand to gesture along with it. "And if that's all, you can get the fuck out. Do be sure to leave Pink alone on your way out—I can't stand his attitude when someone pisses him off."

Right.

Sure.

The last thing Alessio gave a fuck about right now was Andino's enforcer. He had other things to consider, now.

22.

Ginevra

Thwack.

Ginevra's eyes flew *wide* open at the loud sound. It came again less than three seconds later, letting her know that no, she was not dreaming, and someone was making way too much noise at … she rolled over in the bed, and blinked at the digital alarm clock on the nightstand.

Five-thirty?

In the morning?

What the fuck was wrong with people?

Thwack.

Ginevra jumped in the bed at the noise again. What even was that, and *why?* Why at five-thirty in the morning was someone—probably Corrado—doing it?

She wasn't lazy. In fact, she was usually the first one awake and around doing anything in this penthouse in the mornings. A month into living here, and she had quickly learned that, if he could help it, Corrado didn't roll his ass out of bed before *nine.* She was usually up around seven, and ready entirely for the day, including breakfast, before he even stepped out of his room.

So, what changed?

Ginevra didn't know, but she sure as hell planned to find out. If that meant going down the hall where that noise was coming from to tell him to knock it the hell off, then that's exactly what it meant.

Who said she was pleasant in the mornings?

She wasn't.

That's why she woke up earlier than everyone else, so she could get over her shitty morning mood, and be her usual sweet self by the time she had to even think about looking at another person. Seemed simple, right?

So, why was Corrado making it *hard* right now?

Huffing, Ginevra climbed out of the bed, ignoring the cold hardwood floors pressing against her naked feet as she padded out of the bedroom. She didn't bother to close her door at night because from the time she was a little girl, she'd been terrified that something in her room would magically appear, and it would be the closed door that stopped her from getting out.

Stupid and silly, sure.

But it carried into her adulthood, too. Not so much the fear, but rather, the habit of sleeping with the door wide open just in case she needed to get out quickly.

Bleary-eyed, she rubbed the back of her hand against her face to wipe away any remnants of sleep as she followed that damn noise. Every couple of seconds, another *thwack* would make her startle again, pissing her off even more.

Too early. This is way too early.

Finally, she found the noise.

Ginevra had to blink to take in the sight in front of her, and make sure it actually *was* what she was seeing. Other than running on the treadmill in the gym once a day or so, she really didn't put the space to use. She was lucky that it took very little effort to keep her body healthy and fit, but she found that running was a huge stress relief.

And she ran at night.

Before bed.

It also acted like a sleeping pill.

Never in the morning, though.

Across the gym, Ginevra found the source of the noise. Corrado, turned to the side so she had a good view of his profile and the hard lines of his body in nothing but gym shorts, flicked his wrist back before he let *something* fly out of his hand. She only realized it was a knife when he flicked another from his opposite hand into his palm, and let it fly with nothing more than a jerk of his wrist over his shoulder.

Her gaze followed the path of the twisting, spinning knife until it embedded itself right into a wooden block at the other end of the gym about twenty feet away. Along with the other five knives that he had apparently already thrown into the middle of the target.

Nearly perfect shots every time, it seemed.

This one, though, landed a few inches to the right. Corrado tipped his head to the side, his eyes narrowing on the slightly fucked shot as he made a grunt. That disappointment flitting over his features only served to roughen his face up more.

She liked that.

A lot.

Kind of like the way she enjoyed watching the carved-from-stone lines of his body move as he prepped another knife, the last one he held, before he threw it, too. There was something about his focus, that intensity setting his lips into a hard line, as he worked that made her mouth a little dry.

And her body *hot*.

She'd seen him look like that before—when he thought she wasn't looking, and he stared at her. He held that same intensity, that same *fire*.

Huh.

Corrado let his last knife fly, and the weapon quickly embedded itself right into the middle of the target, between two other knives. A perfect shot this time. It was the tilt of his mouth at the corners that gave away his pleasure at having gotten it right that made her realize it wasn't just her dry mouth or hot body that loved the sight of this man.

She ignored the ache between her thighs, though. It was easier. God knew she wasn't innocent when it came to men—she'd had fun and experimented. A part of her didn't think Corrado would be the same *at all*.

One could simply tell.

All men were different.

He was certainly *that*.

"Say something, but don't just stand there and *stare*."

Ginevra startled at Corrado's sudden statement, his tone surly, realizing his blazing dark gaze had turned to the side, and leveled on her. She drew in a quick breath, unsure of how to handle this man when he was in one of *those* moods.

They came and went, she noticed.

More so in the evenings, though.

Despite being told to *stop* staring, Ginevra couldn't help but to continue. All over again, she found her gaze traveling down the length of his body, from the gym shorts hanging loosely around the hard muscles of his hips, to the way his stance didn't move an inch from his feet being firmly planted at shoulder width apart.

Like he'd been taught that.

Corrado made a sexy noise, although whether or not that was his intention, Ginevra didn't know. Part of her felt like she was constantly walking on egg shells around this man. Electricity followed them day in and fucking day out. The closer they became, the more it *snapped* all around them.

His gaze followed her.

Her attention focused in on him.

It never ended.

She simply didn't know what—or how—to do anything with it. If he was interested in her, and she was *clearly* interested in him, then why hadn't he done something about it? That's what *she* wanted to do.

Instead, she was waiting on him.

Ginevra was just about done waiting. If she was going to be stuck here in Toronto with this man until God knew when, then why couldn't she have a little bit of fun while she was at it? Besides, it wasn't *just* the attraction. No, it was more than that.

Something about Corrado danced like a flame.

She was the stupid moth coming a little too close.

What would happen when they met?

Something amazing, she bet.

"I think you like my staring," she replied.

Corrado's tongue peeked out to wet the corner of his mouth, showing off rows of white teeth that made her wonder what it would feel like if he used those teeth on *her*. Okay, wow. She went there quick.

Yeah.

"You don't know that I like anything you do, actually," he returned.

No, because he was very careful about that. Quick to put distance between them. Fast to give her space when he thought the two of them were getting too close. He always made sure that they never got *too deep* when they talked. Not since that morning in the kitchen.

She didn't like it.

"Right now, I know," she said.

Corrado arched an eyebrow in challenge. "Oh, tell me how, then."

"I don't think you want me to."

A laugh answered that back. And *God*, he sounded and looked so fucking good doing it, too. Except in her distraction at enjoying the sight of him carefree and sexy, she didn't realize he'd crossed the gym floor and came to stand in front of her until he was right there.

Right fucking there.

Brown eyes bore into hers.

He was close enough for her to touch.

Ginevra stared up at him, words catching in her throat as that heat shot through her nerves all over again. *Electric*. It really was the only appropriate way to describe what she felt whenever this man was near. Like something was buzzing around them—something different and important and *amazing*.

He seemed willing to ignore it.

She wasn't.

Not anymore.

"Tell me how you know, then," he said, his head dipping lower so that she could feel the warmth of his breath whispering along her lips. "I'm waiting, Ginny."

Her gaze dropped between them.

And then, it came back up.

She couldn't manage to feel embarrassed about the heat staining her cheeks as she whispered, "You're hard."

And he was.

Under the thin, satiny fabric of the gym shorts, the ridge of his erection was plain to see pushing against the material. She didn't think he was wearing anything else under the shorts, not that she minded. It gave her a good view.

It proved something, too.

She *affected* him.

Corrado blinked once, slow and considering, his stare drifting over her face, down her throat, and then back up again where his eyes lingered on her lips. The action alone was enough to make her wet her lips, and swallow hard.

"You shouldn't poke a monster," he murmured.

"I only see a man, Corrado."

"It's what's hiding in the man that might scare you, *amour*."

"Just how many languages can you speak?"

Corrado's mouth edged higher at the corners. "*That's* the question you want to ask right now."

"Why not?"

"Surprising me again, Ginny."

She finally figured out what he meant when he told her that, too. Everyone else would ask the obvious question, and she didn't. She asked the things he wasn't expecting, and it constantly kept him on his toes.

"How many?" she asked.

"I grew up speaking three," he replied. "French and Italian from my father's side of the family—French from the *Quebecois* side, and Italian from ... well, we're a touch more Italian than French. And also English, of course."

"Is that all?"

"I know a bit of Russian, enough to get me through a conversation. Some German, but not nearly enough. And I might take on something else, if it interests me."

Ginevra nodded, and her gaze dropped between them again ... *just to check*. "And you're still hard. Is that all it takes, just a conversation with me to get your cock up, Corrado?"

"I shouldn't be feeling anything about you at all, but certainly not *that*."

"But why?"

He inched closer, his body molding against hers all at once, taking away her breath, and making her incredibly aware of every nerve ending inside her. He smelled like leather and musk—maybe a touch of whiskey, too.

It stunned her.

"You are far too innocent to be playing that kind of game with a man like me," he said, his tone dipping dangerously again. "I promise you that, Ginny. The things I've done in bed would make you *run*. You're looking for something that's going to be fun for you, and I only like to ruin things, woman. I take beautiful things, and I wreck them."

She didn't think so.

That only made her hotter.

And *curious*.

"Would you tell me those things?"

Corrado let out a dark sound, a noise that seemed like it tore right out of his fucking chest. Except, she didn't get the chance to admire the sound, or the way his features shadowed because in the next breath, he was kissing her.

There was nothing soft about the kiss—nothing *sweet*. The roughness of his lips slamming against hers was enough to have her stomach clenching, and her heart racing. His tongue swept the seam of her lips, *demanding*. Like the rest of his kiss, and touches, too. One of his hands tangled into the waves of her hair, and the other landed hard to her hip, fisting into the thin cotton shorts she'll pulled on for bed.

He took and took and *took*.

Lips that worked harshly against hers, their tongues warring, though he controlled that, too. And then his teeth slid against her lower lip before tugging. His mouth moved lower, a sharp heat following the same path when his teeth grazed her skin. Just as quickly, he came back up to claim her mouth again with another bruising kiss that felt like he wanted to suck the fucking soul right out of her.

She'd give it to him.

If he asked, he could have that.

He dragged her closer, grinding her body against his, and making that heat travel lower. Until her thighs ached from it, and she was sure her shorts were wet, too.

Then, all at once, Corrado stepped back from her. It happened so fast, that she didn't know what to make of it, or the sudden stiffness in his body as he refused to meet her gaze. She could see the need vibrating through him, the way his jaw flexed as his tongue swept his lower lip, tasting *her* there.

Still, he kept that distance.

He stayed stiff.

"Corrado—"

"Don't," he said thickly, a shake of his head punctuating the words.

Something painful hit her in the chest.

It felt like rejection.

Why wouldn't he look at her?

"There'll be a box on your bed later," he said, turning away from her. "I trust that the girl at the shop picked out something appropriate, and that you'll like it. I know that you picked up your makeup and whatever else women like when we went shopping, so put it to use. Be ready for six—we have somewhere to be."

Ginevra, refusing to show the hurt she felt, asked, "For what?"

"A mutual birthday party. For me, my twin, and my oldest brother, Marcus. Our birthday already happened, but Marcus's is coming up. Our parents like to … do a big thing for it."

Oh.

"When was your birthday?"

Corrado looked at her, then, something unknown flashing across his face. "Huh."

She blinked. "What?"

"I just … wish you would quit doing that. Surprising me, I mean. You should tell me to fuck off right now, not ask when my birthday was. Don't *care* about me, Ginny."

"Why not? Is that such a bad thing?"

"Because I'm only going to hurt you."

She shrugged.

"But will you really, though?"

Corrado's jaw tensed, and he let out a hard breath that almost sounded like defeat. "Girl, you have no idea the mess you just walked into here. *No fucking idea at all.*"

Probably not.

A part of her still didn't care, either.

"Now, go," he uttered.

Ginevra did, but not because *he* told her to. No, she spun around and left the gym because the ache between her thighs was so deep now that if she didn't do *something*, then there was no telling what might happen. She was positive Corrado had been able to see the heat climbing in her cheeks, and the way she clenched her legs together in an effort to soothe that ache.

She didn't need to be *more* humiliated.

This was enough.

And yet, even as she put distance between her and Corrado—one step after another until she was inside her bedroom, and slamming the door behind her—it did *nothing*. Nothing to help the heat curling around her throat like it was his hand there, squeezing tight. Nothing to make the *need* coursing through her bloodstream go away. Nothing to help the clenching of her muscles, or the fact she couldn't catch her breath. Nothing to make that fucking stupid ache better.

How did a kiss make her that crazy?

That stupid?

That high?

God.

It was unfair.

And she just needed to feel better.

Ginevra's back hit the door, and she acted on her need, and nothing else. Slipping a hand under the waistband of her cotton sleep shorts, she found her pussy wet already. Not that she was surprised, she'd felt the fucking wetness back there with him. It'd been far too long since she'd had release, or even thought about it, really.

Life was more important.

Everything else came first.

She came last.

But not right now.

Ginevra's fingers worked that wetness she found at her slit higher, rubbing it into her throbbing clit with small, tight circles that had her whining, and grinding into her own hand. *More*, that's what she needed.

So much fucking more.

She thought about *him*, then, and the way he watched her when he thought she didn't see. The way his mouth felt as it worked against hers. How his hands felt splayed along her skin, or grabbing tight like he didn't want to let her go.

Those circles at her clit came faster.

Her noises became louder.

She could have tried to hide it ...

She *should* have tried to be quiet.

Ginevra couldn't.

And when that orgasm finally came, it felt as punishing as it did *good*. Like ice water down her spine, numbing her entirely as a broken cry fell from her lips, and a heat shooting straight down to her pussy to remind her she was still empty.

It had been entirely hollow.

Fuck.

Ginevra stared at the bed, and the mussed sheets where she had been sleeping not too long ago. Or rather, the comforter that had been pulled back a bit because she tended to sleep on top of the blankets instead of underneath.

Beds were always cold with only one person.

Too cold, maybe.

This whole place felt cold right now.

She didn't want to think about that, *or* what she had just done. Feeling sticky, and sweaty, she just wanted a shower, and to go back to bed.

Pushing away from the door, she turned to grab the handle, pulled it open, and froze right where she stood. Across the hall, leaning in the doorway of his master bedroom, was Corrado. He didn't look up at her; he didn't move at all.

But she could see it.

That tightness in his jaw, and the way his tongue peeked out to snake across his lips like he might still be tasting her there. The shadows on his face, and how his next exhale came out harder than the last. His eyes, lowered but *dark*, when he dared to look up just a bit, although still not enough to look her in the face.

And his erection, still straining against the line of his shorts.

He'd heard her.

He'd listened.

And she didn't know how to feel about that at all.

What did this man want with her?

Ginevra slipped down the hall toward the main bathroom. Corrado turned, and went into his bedroom, slamming the door loudly behind him.

Apparently, *this* was what they were going to do.

Say nothing, acknowledge nothing.

Perfect.

23.

Corrado

The sky, streaked with colors as it began to darken from the evening, was the backdrop to Corrado's thoughts as he waited for Ginevra to meet him at the front of the penthouse. He didn't quite know what to expect for her outfit, but for the fact he told the lady who sent it over from the private boutique what kind of party it would be.

A *Guzzi* event.

That meant something spectacular.

If he had needed Ginevra in a ballgown or something like that, then he would have let the woman know that, as well. Really, she just needed to look *good*, and as though she belonged on his arm for the evening. The rest, he was sure she could handle without help.

Still, as his thoughts drifted to Ginevra and the upcoming evening, he also thought about someone else. Or rather, the fact that his cell phone was quiet, and had been for several days. Other than calls from his family, and one to confirm yes, he wanted the white Maserati removed from storage for the night, his phone was silent.

Completely abnormal.

Alessio called *often*.

It could be possible that Alessio took on a last-minute assignment from The League that took him out of the country, or required him to drop off the radar for a while. Even then, though, he would always let Corrado know.

The silence bothered him.

Something felt wrong.

Corrado couldn't think on it for long. The click of heels coming down the hallway toward the penthouse's entrance had him turning his head away from the view at the window in just enough time to see Ginevra come around the corner.

And *damn*.

What a sight.

It would have been a shame to miss that.

The gray, silk dress with thin straps over her shoulders was tight around the bodice, and cut *low*. Showing off just a peek of the beige lace bra cups underneath that made her chest look fucking fantastic. His gaze traveled lower, taking in the tightly cinched waist of the dress, and the way it fell over her hips and came to a stop quite a few inches above the knees.

It was *short as hell*.

She showed off all kinds of leg, and he loved it. He *really* did. She held tight to a matching clutch in her hand. The strappy, five-inch heels put her at damn near eye-level with him, and every step she took showed off a little more of the olive-toned skin of her thighs. And apparently, a diamond garter around her right thigh that only peeked out when the slit in the skirt of the dress opened with her steps.

It matched the choker at her throat.

And the studs in her ears.

Christ.

Which took his gaze right back up to her face. There, he found her lips were a stark red, and she had somehow managed to paint her innocence away with dark strokes of kohl that smoked her eyes, and mascara that fanned her lashes.

"Beautiful," Corrado murmured.

Entirely unable to stop himself, too.

He just said it.

It *needed* to be said.

Like he needed more reminders of just how fucking attractive this woman was because apparently, his body didn't let him know enough on a daily basis. Like their little moment that morning in the gym wasn't a *huge* fucking mistake that he suddenly wanted to make again. Or the fact that as he stood across the hall from her bedroom doorway, listening to her as she got herself off, that he considered breaking her door down because *he* wanted to be the one doing that.

Guilt.

Lust.

It warred inside him.

He was so fucked.

Not that it mattered.

He was determined to do nothing—say nothing.

It was better this way.

"You think so?" Ginevra asked, coming to stand in front of him. "I didn't know if this was going to be appropriate for whatever—"

"It's perfect, and so are you."

Her stare lifted then to meet his, and he didn't quite know what to make of what he found there. Confusion, mostly, but desire, too. That was his fault—he pulled her in only to push her away, and she probably felt like a fucking ping pong ball, now.

He'd been wrong.

Ginevra was not a mess.

He was.

"Thank you," she whispered.

Corrado had to *physically* hold himself back from reaching out to touch her. Because if he did that, there was no telling what might happen next. He couldn't trust himself around this woman, and as it was, he had already crossed a big line.

Jumped it, really.

"And you look quite handsome," she said, her hand coming up to flatten the edge of the lapel on his suit. "Your vest and tie matches my dress ... was that planned?"

"Probably. I had it sent up by the same woman who picked out your dress."

Ginevra made an appreciative noise. "Just how much money do you have, Corrado?"

He laughed, grateful for the change in topic. "Me, specifically? Or my *Guzzi* money?"

"Is there a difference?"

Corrado smirked. "A little, yeah."

157

"Which has more?"

"The Guzzi side of me. Saying the Guzzi family is *vastly* wealthy does not even come close to describing how much money we have." Corrado tipped his head toward the door, saying, "Come on, then, and we'll get going."

Corrado couldn't help but put his hand to her lower back, all the while becoming painfully aware of the crisscrossed opened back of the dress she wore at the same time. Doing his best to control the darker urges climbing through his body, he directed them out of the penthouse, and toward the bank of elevators at the end of the hall.

Ginevra said nothing as the elevator dropped lower. He figured he should probably give her a heads up about what to expect for the night, or rather ... the rules he needed for her to follow so that she was safe, and so was her identity.

"If anyone asks, you give your nickname or first name," he said, "but absolutely not your surname, do you understand?"

Ginevra nodded. "Sure."

"Say you come from New Jersey, they won't know the difference. We're old friends. That's all you need to say. I will handle my family, if they ask, and I'm sure they will. Nosy bast—"

"Be nice."

His gaze cut to her.

She winked.

Corrado chuckled. "You say that *now*."

"Actually, I say it because I think you must have an amazing family that they're willing to throw you a birthday party when you're ... how old are you again?"

"I turned twenty-three twelve days ago."

Ginevra nibbled on her bottom lip.

Corrado's cock *felt* that.

Fuck.

Tonight was going to be hell.

Absolute hell.

He could see it already. Stuck between his fucking guilt, and the constant want he felt for this woman who had no clue what he had done here. Even as he conversed with her, or spent day in and day out with her, his mind was on constant loop of thoughts revolving around Alessio.

Back and forth.

Ginny.

Les.

One he missed desperately, and knew something wasn't right because Alessio hadn't called in days. And the other, he was desperate to know, and who he thought Alessio should know, too, but the way this had happened would be enough to end it before *that* could begin. Corrado was most sure of that.

More nails in the coffin.

Corrado didn't ask for this.

None of it.

Back and forth he went again.

It never ended.

Christ.

"Anyway," Ginevra said, oblivious to the battle in his mind and heart, "I think they must love you a lot, and your brothers, if they're willing to throw you a party at this age. And not just *any* party ... look at us, this feels like an affair."

As she said that, the elevator came to a stop, and opened up to the front lobby of the building. Parked right in front, in full view of the windows, was the white Maserati he'd had taken out of the Toronto storage unit where he kept it when he wasn't in the city visiting.

"And that's ours, I bet," she said beside him.

Corrado sighed. "It is."

"Like I said, a whole *affair*."

He really wished she would stop using that word.

But not for a reason she would know.

• • •

Corrado helped Ginevra step out of the Maserati, and her eyes widened at the sight in front of them. Parked at the very end of the long, winding drive that led up to the three-level, two-wing monster that was the Guzzi Mansion, they had a way to go yet before they properly *arrived*.

Not that it mattered.

She could see now.

The wealth was on full display.

"Is this your—"

"Childhood home, yes," he said. "It sits on several acres of private land, and the mansion itself could house a good hundred people or more ... living wise. It has a pool, ballroom, three dining rooms, a library that, in all honesty, is bigger than most public ones, and well, that's just scratching the surface."

"Who is the reader?"

Surprising him again.

Those damn *questions*.

Corrado almost said Alessio before he caught himself, and realized she meant in his *family*. Although, Alessio was his family, too. "My mother. And you should know, this place ... this night, despite being for my brothers' and my birthdays, and all of the rest of it, is my father's doing. Like the library, and the tiled rose design at the bottom of the pool. Anything my mother wants, my father gives her. She is the queen here, and expect that she'll be treated as such. If she wanted to sit on a throne during the party, trust that one will be provided for her to do that."

Ginevra smiled slyly.

He didn't miss it.

"What?"

"I was just thinking you don't sound at all bitter about that fact. Your mother being spoiled, and loved, I mean."

"I'm not. It's all I ever knew."

Knowing the cobblestone driveway might be a little tricky for Ginevra in her stiletto heels, he wrapped an arm tightly around her side, and pulled her close to him. He didn't miss the shiver that raced through her body, but he did his very best to suppress his own reaction to it. It wasn't like he needed to walk the rest of this very long driveway with a hard-on.

Right?

Apparently, he did.

Fucking hell.

"Oh, wow," Ginevra said softly, her gaze drifting over the pots of roses that lined the middle of the driveway about midway, leading the rest of the way to the mansion. Twinkle lights colored the grass on either side, and hanging from the maple trees were rows of silk and chiffon that matched the white roses and lights. "This is something else."

"I am sure the inside will be just as … excessive," he settled on saying with a laugh. "And all for a birthday party, too."

"Hey, it's something different than balloons and streamers."

Right.

Except the balloons were roses.

And the streamers were made of silk and chiffon.

Right.

"It's the Guzzi way," he murmured. "And you'll fit right in looking like you do tonight."

Ginevra glanced up at him, those brown eyes of hers reminding him of an ocean. Expansive, dark, and deep. Oh, so dangerous, but pretty, too.

Just pretty enough to drown him.

He swore the music filtering out of the mansion, and the low tones of chattering people as they neared the grand, marble entrance faded away. There were far too many things about this woman that continued to draw him in, and ensnare him in her web of *trouble.* And then there were parts of him that recognized things in her that didn't fit him at all.

Things that fit someone else in his life far better. Except she didn't know that, and neither did the man who needed to know what was happening here.

This was a mess.

How many times had he said that now?

It didn't make it less true.

Corrado cleared his throat, needing to break their connection.

Because they couldn't have that at all.

That *connection.*

Not *now.*

Not ever.

"Let's have a good time, hmm?" he asked, turning back to face the mansion.

Ginevra glanced down at the ground. "Sure, Corrado."

24.

Corrado

The *most* crucial thing to know about Corrado's mother?

Nothing and no one would ever be as important to Cara Rossi as her five sons, and husband. By most standards, one could absolutely consider her a *mama bear*. And yet, on the flip side of that same coin, she was also fiercely protective of her sons' freedom and happiness. She, like his father, Gian, had made every effort to ensure their sons thought for themselves. That they understood the right choice was sometimes the hard one. They gave them protection and privilege, but also space to grow, and figure out who *they* wanted to be.

Never once had Corrado felt pushed to be one thing by his parents. He knew, safely, that his brothers felt the same way, even if they had clearly chosen a path more like his father's. But his mother?

Cara was the voice of reason.

The *loudest* voice, too.

She made it her first priority to know that her sons were happy, even if she didn't pry for the details as to why. Maybe that was why, when Corrado called his mother's name across the hall, her soft smile stayed permanently affixed in place as she laid eyes on the *woman* at Corrado's side, and his arm tucked around Ginevra's waist.

She didn't act surprised.

Not *concerned*.

Cara simply smiled wider, and opened her arms to Corrado like it had been far too long since she had seen her third oldest son. He let go of Ginevra to hug his mother. She took him into her embrace—lest she find trouble somewhere she *shouldn't* be because someone pried too much, and she slipped up.

Behind his mother, Corrado found the hoard of his brothers waiting, and their father standing behind the Guzzi sons. Chris stood next to Marcus, and beside the oldest, the youngest at only twenty, Bene and Beni smirked at one another like they were sharing some kind of secret. The second set of Guzzi twins very well could be doing exactly that. Those two shared a bond with each other like even Chris and Corrado didn't have.

Sometimes, it could be unsettling.

He was used to it now, though.

Cara leaned back, her hand still pressing against Corrado's cheek, and he took that chance to pull Ginevra close again. *God*, he loved his ma. There was just something about her that felt like home in a way nothing else could. "Happy birthday, my boy."

Corrado smiled. "Little old to be a *boy*, Ma."

"Not to be *my* boy."

He knew better than to argue.

She would always win.

Another lesson from his father.

"And who is this?" Cara asked, her smile turning on Ginevra in an instant. For the first time, Corrado loosened his hold on Ginevra, but not by much. Just enough to allow her to lean away from his side and take his mother's hands that she offered. His mother looked back to him, asking, "A friend?"

Nice.

That was smooth of his ma.

Cara wouldn't outright ask about his personal business—she never did. He was sure his mother assumed things, and put two and two together when she could about him and Alessio, but she never verbally confirmed it. It probably helped that his mother was a therapist, and always had a knack for knowing—or being able to pry—all her sons secrets from them, sometimes without their help at all. He figured seeing him without Alessio at his side *would* be a surprise.

Hell, it was a shock to him, too.

"Yeah, Ma," Corrado said, "Ginevra is a friend."

Cara still smiled, unfazed. "*Ciao.*"

Ginevra's gaze darted to him, a silent question there, and he nodded. "*Ciao.* You have a beautiful home."

"A bit much at first, don't you think?"

To her benefit, Ginny didn't miss a beat.

"Not at all."

Cara shrugged. "I always thought it overwhelmed you a little coming up on it for the first time."

The first time ...

Corrado shot his mother a look, but she studiously ignored it. If that was his mother's sly way of saying Ginevra had never been here before, well, he heard it loud and clear.

"Actually, I thought it should be in a magazine."

His mother laughed. "Oh, it's been printed a few times. Not magazines, though. More the newspapers. Usually, from reporters trying to catch us coming in, or out."

"*Cara.*"

All it took was the dark call of his mother's name by his father, and Cara rolled her eyes upward like she thought it was ridiculous. Ginevra pressed her lips together, probably in an effort to keep from smiling. Corrado found he had to do the same when his mother muttered, "Yes, Gian, don't talk about *that* ... I know, I know."

Gian made a soft noise, and then turned to take a small flute of champagne from a server as she passed, but otherwise, he said nothing.

Corrado chuckled, knowing he should probably change the subject. "The place looks great, Ma."

"It better," she replied. "But back to this beautiful woman ... Ginevra, you said?"

And that, in a nutshell, was his mother.

Ginevra gave him a wink. "That's me."

He could plainly see that twinkle in his mother's eye—that *curiosity*. "I think you and I should spend some time together tonight, and—"

"Oh, Cara, there's the director for the hospital," Gian said, coming up to slip his arm around his wife's waist, directing her in an entirely different direction as he did so. At the same time, his father passed Corrado a look that said, *we will have words later.* He didn't doubt it. "We need to discuss that donation with him, yes?"

Cara made a face. "*Fine.*" Then, turning back to Ginevra, his mother grinned. "I will find you later, okay?"

"You got it, Cara."

And to Corrado, his mother added, "Make sure you dance with her—I taught you well, use it."

Well …

Gian gave Ginevra a warm smile over his shoulder. "It was very nice to meet you, Ginny. I'm sure we'll be seeing more of you."

Corrado blinked, but his mother and father were already gone. Next to him, Ginevra's brow furrowed. Clearly, she hadn't missed his father's slip, either. *Ginny*, he called her. Like he knew exactly who she was, because she *had not* told them her nickname yet.

He passed a glance to his twin, wondering … he'd given Chris a few details, about the same he gave to Alessio, about what he was doing in Toronto at the moment. The only added thing his brother knew was the fact that Ginevra was a *woman*, and that was simply because he had brought Corrado clothes for her to wear those first couple of days.

Chris tipped his glass of whiskey up to take a drink, seeing the question in his brother's gaze. A simple nod gave Corrado all the answer he needed. Yes, his brother had shared what he knew with his father. No doubt, Gian had then made some calls to connect the rest of the dots with the information he had.

Great.

"Where the fuck is Les—"

"Ginny, do you want to dance?" Corrado asked, turning his back to his twin, and his other brothers before Bene could finish that question.

She smirked up at him. "What, don't want to introduce me to the rest of the Guzzi bunch?"

"We're a *hoard*, really. And no, I am sure you'll get more than your fill of my brothers before the end of the night. I had to live with them for eighteen years, trust me when I say it won't kill you to lose two extra minutes with them."

She hit his chest, but he was already walking them away. A quick glance over his shoulder let him know Chris was taking care of *that* situation. A sharp shake of his head to the rest of their brothers quieted them all, and yet, every one of them turned to watch Corrado and Ginevra walk away.

Like they just knew, too.

Corrado had secrets.

One too many to name.

It kind of felt like his family probably knew some.

• • •

"What is *this?*"

Ginevra walked further into the hall of paintings, and spread her arms wide as she did a little circle. Corrado stuffed his hands in his slacks pockets as he watched her joyful moment. That, and he liked the way that dress draped over her body, and glimmered when she moved.

"This," he said, "is the hall of Guzzis."

Stopping under one particular piece of art in the hallway, she leaned a bit over the red rope to get a closer look at the name under the piece. The man in the painting, surrounded by his wife, and children when they were just toddlers, stared straight ahead like he owned the world.

At the time, it probably felt like he had.

"Frederic Guzzi and family."

"My grandfather."

Not that Corrado had ever seen much of the man growing up. He didn't approve of some of the things that brought Gian and Cara together, and so, the rest of them suffered for it. A part of him always thought that was quite selfish, but he didn't think Ginevra needed to know that family dirt just yet.

"Do you have one?"

Corrado let out a laugh. "Not quite—we have a portrait, or two, as a whole." He pointed at the end of the hallway where a painting featuring his mother, surrounded by all her boys in a forest as she sat on what looked like a throne, was on prominent display. "There's one."

"Oh, wow."

"But no, I don't have one of *just* me."

"Why not?"

"Our family's tradition has always been family portraits, or those featuring the head of the house, usually the male. My father made my mother an exception to that rule, though."

Like everything else between his mother and father.

"Ah," Ginevra said, grinning back at him, "so you aren't the head of *your* household yet since you don't have one, right?"

"Exactly, and I'm unmarried, without children ... so no portrait, either."

"Corrado, there you are."

He spun to the side fast, finding his father watching him from a separate entry into the large hall of portraits. Next to Gian, stood Chris, Marcus, and two other men who rarely left his father's side. His consigliere, and underboss for the Guzzi Cosa Nostra.

"I wanted a word, if you had a minute," Gian said, gesturing at the hallway.

Corrado opened his mouth to refuse—Ginevra, after all—and he didn't feel like getting the twenty-one questions from his father that were sure to come once Gian had him alone. Not that it mattered, apparently, because his father wasn't going to give him a choice.

Perfect.

"Chris will entertain Ginevra, I understand they've met before," Gian said quickly.

Corrado kept his face passive. "*Met* is stretching it. They've seen each other from afar."

"What, you don't trust your twin with the woman?"

He gave his father a scowl. "That's unfair."

"The low shots usually get me what I want, you know."

Of course.

"Corrado?"

Behind him, he found Ginevra smiling. "I'll be okay for a while. Go with your dad."

"You sure?"

"Yeah. Besides, Chris can probably tell me more about these paintings, right?"

Chris laughed next to their father. "I certainly can."

"Good. See? Everything's great."

So it seemed.

Ginevra gave him a wink over her shoulder when Chris stepped into the hallway, and took her arm in his before they both turned to look at another painting. Dismissed from *their* conversation, he was left with his waiting father, oldest brother Marcus, and the other two men.

"My office, then?" Gian asked.

"I guess so," Corrado replied.

• • •

Corrado's father stopped pretending to be *polite* the very second the office door closed, leaving him, his dad, and Marcus within. Standing just outside were Gian's other two men who had not been invited in.

Something Corrado was sure they were unaccustomed to, considering what he knew.

"I will give you two minutes," Gian said, rounding his desk and pulling out the large leather chair to sit in, "to give me every pertinent detail about that woman, and your business with her, Corrado."

He smirked. "Or, you could just save me the time, and tell me what you know."

Gian made a face. "That's less fun, though."

"But quicker, and I would—"

"Like to get back to her, I imagine," his father murmured, steepling his fingers over his desk. Corrado opened his mouth to deny that statement, and the *connotation* behind it, but Gian was quick to add, "You know, I watched you for a while ... the two of you. I could explain your hand constantly reaching for her, or staying on her, when I also know that you are supposed to be hiding the young woman from her family. Except ... you know she's safe here, and two feet of space won't really make *much* of a difference, would it?"

Corrado swallowed back his denial.

What would be the point?

"So," Gian continued, "the only explanation why you keep touching or reaching for her is because you *want to*. And then if I move onto the way you watch her ... the way you stare when you think people aren't looking, and I am left wondering something here."

"Or you could mind your business," Corrado replied.

His father shook his head. "I can't ... not when I'm concerned."

"About what? The fact I have a woman with me, and I seem interested in her?"

"No," Gian replied just as fast and still calm, "the fact that someone else isn't with you ... your brother mentioned, at the time he met Ginevra, you said Alessio didn't know she was with you, and I have to wonder if he does now."

Corrado stiffened.

Gian raised a brow in response. "What, son?"

"What would that matter to you—if Alessio knew or not?"

A flicker of confusion drifted over his father's features before Gian was back to that same, unbothered demeanor as before. "Because I wonder if something happened with Alessio, Corrado. Has something changed there, and you've not told me?"

A lot happened, then.

Or rather, Corrado realized a lot of things.

This moment that he'd wondered and worried about for most of his life was actually happening. His father might not be directly saying it, but he wasn't dancing around it purposely, either. Gian was *outright* asking about Alessio, and Corrado's relationship.

Because he knew.

And that was something else he realized, then.

His father knew.

His mother probably did, too.

All his brothers.

Of course, he knew that. And yet, a part of him had still thought, after all this time, that his family were fine and comfortable in their place of not asking. Because if they didn't ask him, then he would never have to tell.

Not because they didn't love or accept him *exactly* as he was, but because this was how he chose to live his life. Not offering his personal life out like it was meant for their consumption.

"Corrado?"

He blinked, coming out of his thoughts with a bang. "I have not told Alessio about her, no."

Gian let out a slow exhale. "I know you two ... have a different kind of agreement about your relationship and other people, specifically women. I'm not sure if she falls under that, and guessing by your behavior right now, I don't think—"

"How do you know that at all?"

"I asked."

Corrado's jaw ached from clenching so hard. "Asked who?"

"Alessio."

Huh.

"And not *me?*"

And why hadn't Alessio told him that?

When had that even happened?

In the corner of the room, pouring himself a glass of scotch, Marcus cleared his throat, but otherwise, paid the conversation no mind. His oldest brother was good for that—more like their father than the rest of them combined, honestly.

Marcus was fit for his position as the Guzzi heir.

Undoubtedly.

"Corrado," Gian said, drawing his attention back in, "I just want to make sure you're happy, son, and that everything is okay. Don't think this was me trying to cause a problem, or ... something like that. It wasn't. I just worry about you. More than I do the others, sometimes."

"I know I need to tell him," Corrado managed to say. "I just don't know how. It's not just *her* ... it's more than what's on the surface of it, Papa."

Gian frowned. "All right. I'm sorry."

Corrado wished his throat wasn't so tight when he asked, "How long did you know?"

"About what—that you liked boys, too, or that you and Alessio were living and sleeping together?"

Well ...

"Both."

Gian nodded. "From the time you were fifteen for when I knew you liked boys, too. As for Alessio ... I was told about the kiss in The League's gym shortly after it happened. Otherwise, I assumed on that based on the obvious fact you were clearly in a relationship with him."

Huh.

"How did you know since I was fifteen?"

"Cameras caught you kissing the boy from your school. I had the footage deleted, and your mother and I simply decided we wouldn't pressure you in any way. We knew about the women you'd dated before that. And so, when, or *if,* you wanted to tell us that you were bisexual, then that was when you would tell us. It wasn't for us to decide when it was your time to tell *your* truth, Corrado."

"I always thought—" He stopped abruptly, unwilling to say the words. It was the look his father gave him, willing him to speak, that allowed him to do it. "I thought you didn't ask because ... I thought you didn't *want* to know."

Gian rested back in the chair.

Across the room, Marcus set his glass down.

"Because of the traditions?"

The traditions.

Such a simple way to describe the culture of mafioso that his family was so deeply engrained in.

"Essentially," Corrado replied.

Gian let out a noise, dark and dismissive. "I almost burned the city down once for a woman ... could you imagine what I would do to it for a child that woman *gave* to me, Corrado? Because that is what I would do for any of you—the way God made you never mattered one way or another. This *life,* this legacy, and this name ... it means nothing compared to what you, your brothers, and your mother mean to me. It gave me nothing compared to what she sacrificed and gave to me."

"I should have told you."

He should have done and said a lot of things.

Not all to the people in this room, or house, either. But to Alessio, also, who still hadn't called. The man with the piece of his heart that Corrado left in Vegas probably thinking they were chasing a dead fucking end together.

Because how long had they been doing this together?

How long had Alessio put up with this shit?

How much more would he take?

Except *now* ... now it was more complicated because Corrado had feelings in the game for a woman he had no business feeling *anything* for, and all this without having done nothing more than *kiss* her.

He'd punched those nails in.

That coffin was closing.

Corrado had no one to blame but himself.

"I should get back to Ginevra," he said quietly.

Gian tipped his head to the side, clearly hearing the pain in Corrado's words. "Son—"

"I have to get back."

"Okay."

Gian let him go.

It was his wrongs that chased him out of the office, though.

25.

"So, what's that like?" Ginevra asked her companion as he directed them back out to the party. "Having another face in the world that looks just like yours?"

Chris chuckled, his hand patting the top of her hand tucked into the crook of his arm. "Depends on which one of us you ask, I think."

Her gaze darted to the other side of the dining room that was currently being used as a gathering area for the many guests. The long table had been used to set up another row of white roses, while silk and chiffon hung from the large, crystal chandelier overhead. People milled about, chatting and laughing as music filtered in from the next room.

It wasn't the décor or the people that caught her attention, but Cara Rossi. And the two boys sitting next to her, and leaning close like they were sharing a secret. The *other* set of twins. Because apparently, there were two sets in this family.

"There *are* a lot of twins in your family to ask, I suppose," she said.

Chris grinned. "And each one of us has a different experience about it. My mother is also a twin."

"Really?"

"Identical, too. Her twin died when she was … well, probably about your age."

Ginevra's smile slipped away. "That must have been terrible."

"She doesn't talk about it, so I assume so. Lea, that was her name." Chris turned his gaze on her, and grinned, saying, "But I'm not supposed to be making you sad, right? And I think my mother would like to sit with you for a few more minutes. You know, *without* Corrado stepping in on every question or deflecting."

"He's so moody."

Part of her liked that, though.

The other part squinted at him a lot.

It was a work in progress.

"Mmm," Chris agreed, "and I bet he's worse right now, too. He usually is when he doesn't have his extension around to keep him entertained."

"What?"

Ginevra peered up at Chris, but he didn't answer her question. She didn't exactly have time to press him for more, either. Cara caught sight of them coming her way, and with a wide smile, she waved them over.

"Be good," she heard Cara tell the younger pair of twins. Although, they didn't look any older or younger than Ginevra, to be honest. It was only once Chris had pulled up a chair for Ginevra to take, and sit beside Cara, that the older woman passed a look to the men on the other side of her. "Ginevra, you didn't get to meet these two properly earlier—Benedetto, and Benito, or Bene, and Beni, as they prefer."

The young men grinned, playful and mischievous. Their gazes drifted to each other, before coming back to her just as fast. Like actual mirrors of themselves, it was almost comical. *Instantly*, Ginevra knew two things about the twins. One, they

169

were probably a hell of a lot of fun to be around. And two, she bet they were absolutely *trouble*.

They just had that air about them.

"Why do the nicknames sound a bit different from how their full names are said?" Ginevra asked.

Cara laughed. "You ask strange questions, don't you?"

Ginevra shrugged. "Corrado says I surprise him with them. I think he likes it."

"He always did like *different* things," Bene said.

"Careful," Chris murmured, his gaze cutting to the twin on the right. "Be very careful there."

"I didn't mean it like a bad thing, I was just saying—"

"Shut up," Beni told his twin.

"*Fine.*"

Cara, still looking at Ginevra as though the conversation beside them hadn't just happened, smiled a bit. "My husband is French and Italian. Their full names are obviously the Italian side, but the nicknames ... we've always said them more with a French flair. That's all."

"I like that," Ginevra replied. "It's interesting. Unique."

"It's about the only thing that sets them apart from one another."

Cara wasn't exactly lying. Passing the twins a second look was like staring into a reflection of them—they sat side by side, their hands in the same position on their laps, their suits matching down to the cufflinks on their wrists, and even their smiles crooked up at the edges on the same side.

They didn't seem aware Ginevra was watching them, since they were too busy staring at something on the other side of the room, but it was ... fascinating. She wondered if they purposely behaved like mirrors of the other, or if this was just something they did from the time they were born.

Twins were like that, right?

Except, Corrado and Chris weren't. Ginevra had noticed that about the men from the first night she saw them standing next to one another. Finding their differences had been easy to her, but this was not the same. At all.

Chris laughed under his breath, gaining her attention. The shrug he offered to her said that *he* had been watching her, and probably knew exactly what was running through her mind. He nodded like he was saying, *yeah, I know, right?*

She understood what he meant earlier now when he said every twin probably had a different opinion about what it was like to have someone else in the world share your face. No doubt, the two next to her had a different perspective than their older twin brothers.

"Now, do you have any siblings?" Cara asked suddenly, drawing Ginevra back to the present.

"Uh ..." Corrado wasn't there for her to ask if that was okay, so she deferred to Chris thinking he probably knew the truth about why she was there. He nodded once, and then turned to grab a drink from a passing server. "I do—two sisters."

Well, *three*, if she counted Siena, now.

And she was not mentioning her brothers.

"Are you the oldest?"

"I am."

"Ah," Cara said, smiling, "and your mother must love that. Having all girls around her, I mean. People always think I must lack female attention with all this testosterone around me." Just as quickly, the woman winked, her perfectly applied makeup not showing a bit of her age, and her loose chignon making her striking red hair seem like a deeper maroon under the lights in the room. "Like having all boys somehow made me into one of them, too. Don't I look like that's a problem?"

Ginevra laughed.

Still, in her heart ... it hurt.

Cara hadn't known it, but mentioning her mother was still a sore spot for Ginevra. She had moments where she didn't think about her mother at all and passing time in her days where her sisters slipped her mind, too. And then, all at once, it came rushing back like a wrecking ball to devastate her again.

It happened every single time.

"*But*," Cara drawled, grinning slyly, "soon they will all be married, and then I am sure I will have *lots* of women in this house. Won't I, boys?"

Grumbles came from the twins.

Chris altogether avoided his mother's stare.

Cara looked at Ginevra and rolled her eyes. "They don't like to talk about that."

"I can tell."

"That doesn't make it less true, though."

Yeah, she liked Cara a lot.

She felt like a mother.

Ginevra *really* needed that right now.

• • •

"There you are."

Ginevra turned to find Corrado coming down the steps of the porch of the east wing of the mansion. He smiled, but it didn't reach his eyes. And it was there, in his gaze, that she found the darkness. Something was wrong, even if he was more than willing to pretend like everything was perfectly fine.

"Chris was showing me the back. It's beautiful out here."

"It is," Corrado said, nodding to his twin. "Thanks, man."

"Sure." At her side, Chris patted a hand against her upper back. "This is where I say goodnight, but it was great to properly meet you, and not ... you know, peeking around a corner at me."

She didn't even try to hide her snickers. "Yeah, I suppose."

"Have a good night, you two."

Corrado didn't say goodbye to his twin, nor did he turn to watch Chris walk away from them. In fact, he didn't take his gaze off Ginevra, and with every step Chris took away from them, she became more and more aware that they were alone. Sure, they were alone *most* of the time, but for some reason, it felt different.

"Are you about ready to go?" he asked.

Ginevra's brow dipped. "They haven't cut the cake, yet."

"I'm not in the mood for it tonight."

"It's not really about *you*, is it? Seems like this was more for your mother and father, Corrado, and since they threw the party for you and your brothers, the least you could do is make an effort to please them and stay."

His jaw stiffened at that.

Ginevra arched a brow to dare him to deny it. "Well?"

"Ginny—"

"Something is wrong. I can see it in your face. What is it? It's not … New York, right?"

Corrado cleared his throat. "Not even close."

"Then, what—"

She didn't get to finish her sentence before Corrado closed the distance between them entirely. All at once, the space she had to breathe was gone when his lips crashed down on hers. The soft curves of her body fit perfectly into the fold of his as he leaned over her, a hand falling to her lower back to keep her from falling to the ground entirely. As his lips worked against hers, his tongue seeking the heat of her mouth, she fisted her fingers into the lapels of his suit jacket, needing him closer.

The kiss felt like *heaven*.

And just like sin, too.

How could a *kiss* make her entire body wake up like fireworks had been set off inside her bloodstream? Because that's what it did.

It felt like a hello.

And a goodbye.

All in one.

Corrado's lips slowed against hers, then, kissing her softly once, twice, and then a third time to her lower lip, whispering, "I had to do that one more time."

Ginevra blinked up at him, feeling entirely too high. *Right then*, she would have asked him to take her anywhere. *Somewhere*. As long as there was a bed, or a useable flat surface, she would have been up for it.

Except it was the look in his eyes that kept her quiet. That *pain*—the storm she found warring in his gaze—stopped her from saying anything at all.

Because a part of her knew, then.

She just *knew*.

His heart was not *all in* with her. Maybe that was why he'd constantly kept a distance, even though he *clearly* wanted to get closer. There was a piece of him somewhere else. Maybe she had known it from the start, or perhaps she pieced together the pieces overtime.

What did it matter?

She knew now.

She felt it *now*.

"I'm selfish," he murmured, "so I had to do it one more time, Ginny, before I can't anymore."

Her lower lip trembled.

"There's someone else, isn't there?" she asked.

"There is. It's not as simple as it seems, and we've always been different and open in our relationship. *This* wouldn't have been a big deal except I fucked up and started feeling shit about you that I had no business feeling. At that point, I should have done the right thing, but I didn't and here I am."

Corrado dragged a hand down his jaw, shaking his head at the same time. "So yes, there is someone else. And I love them, but I haven't been good to them, either. They deserve far better than what I gave—I need to give that to them, now." Corrado didn't look away from her as he said, "I'm sorry."

All the air in Ginevra's lungs came out in a painful exhale. She felt his hold loosen on her, but he didn't step back. Not yet.

It was the buzz of a phone in his pocket that made him put distance between the two of them. It wasn't much, just a couple of inches, but he wasn't holding her anymore, and she could stare up at the black, inky Canadian sky dotted with the brightest stars.

For the moment, she was grateful.

She needed that space.

Corrado made a noise, and she looked his way. He was still staring down at his phone, but she caught the name on the contact and what the message said before he turned the device off entirely.

Les, the contact said. And simply, *I'm in the city—we need to talk, now.*

Who was that?

Corrado's head snapped up, his gaze landing on her. "I think ... would it be okay if I had Chris take you back to the penthouse? I have something to handle right now."

Ginevra nodded. "Yeah, sure."

What else could she say?

• • •

Chris was quick to help Ginevra out of the silver Mercedes, and into the building while the rain continued to pour down from the dark sky overhead. At some point during the drive back to the city, the sky had opened, and began to cry.

It felt appropriate.

The sky was breaking open.

Ginevra, too.

Despite how fast Chris moved to get them inside the safety of the building, it didn't matter. Her loose waves were soaked, and so was the silk dress. Likely ruined, now.

Yeah, *so* appropriate.

Like her in that moment.

"I can walk you upstairs, if you'd like," Chris said, making sure to keep his gaze on *only* Ginevra's face, and not the dress that would have to now be peeled from her body. "My job was to get you back safely, after all."

She shook her head.

No.

Right now, all she wanted was to be alone. She highly doubted Chris would understand why, as he wasn't privy to the things that happened between her and Corrado. She really didn't want to explain, either.

Why humiliate herself further?

"If you wouldn't mind, I'd like to take the elevator up alone." Ginevra flipped her hand over, showing the keys in her palm. "He gave me the keys, so I can get in."

"Okay."

"Thanks, Chris."

He flashed her a kind smile. "Don't mention it, Ginevra."

"Well, I'll …" She nodded at the bank of elevators across the brightly lit lobby decorated in soft, neutral tones. "… get going, then. I didn't get to see your mom or dad before we left, but you'll tell them I loved meeting them, won't you? They were great."

And considering that she now knew there was someone else in Corrado's life, that his parents and the rest of his family probably knew about, she was only now realizing just how welcoming they had been, all things considered.

More kind than they needed to be, honestly.

"Of course."

"Thank you."

Ginevra headed for the elevator, head down, but Chris's voice behind her made her steps hesitate.

"I know things might seem bad right now," he said, "but it's always been complicated with them, Ginevra. They act like it's always been just them, and in their private moments, I'm sure it was. But they made this mess together, and so now they have to clean it up, too. It just so happened that you were the one who got caught in the middle. Give them a chance to figure it out—you might have been *exactly* what the two of them were looking for without even knowing it, but they won't know if no one tries."

Her brow furrowed, and she looked back over her shoulder. "I don't know what that means."

Chris nodded. "I know, but you will. Try to have a good night."

Right.

Once she was hidden by the closing elevator doors, Ginevra tipped her head down, and dragged in an aching breath. She didn't want to cry—she wasn't *that* girl. And besides, she had no business being heartbroken over a man who had never been hers to begin with and was clearly involved with someone else.

Simple as that.

It didn't help.

She still wanted to cry.

Ginevra wiped away the one tear that escaped the corner of her eye as the elevator came to a stop on the highest floor. It opened to the hallway leading to the penthouse. She took another quick, deep breath; she had her weak moment in private, and now it was done.

Right?

Yep.

She decided.

Soon—*surely*—she would be back home in New York with her sisters. Back where she belonged, and far away from a complicated man, and whatever mess he had dragged her into here. That's what would happen.

Ginevra unlocked the penthouse and opened the door to the dark entry. She couldn't remember if Corrado had turned off the lights when they left, or not. Probably, though. Kicking off the heels and pulling down the wet straps of the dress around her arms, she tried to remember where the light switch was for the damn entry.

Then, the lights came on.

All at once.

She spun around fast, letting go of the straps of her dress as she froze in place at the sight of a stranger leaning against the wall at the very end of the hallway. A *man*, actually. His shaggy, dark hair hung over his eyes, and yet even through the dark strands, she could still see the stormy blue eyeing her from the side.

His lips, the lower fuller than the top, stayed affixed in a grim line as he chewed on something in his mouth—gum, maybe? Her gaze traveled over the golden hoops in his nose, his steel cut jaw line, and the few days' worth of facial hair covering his cheeks and throat. Even under the leather jacket he wore, and the black jeans that molded to his thighs and ass, she could plainly see he was fit by the way the material of his white T-shirt stretched across the bands of muscle that made up his chest.

He leaned against the wall like he didn't have a care in the world, his black, scuffed combat boots hooked one over the other, despite the fact she could clearly see the tension wrapping his body. Like he was forcing himself to stay right there, and not come any closer.

My God.

He was *devastating*.

That was the first and only word to come to her mind.

Devastating.

A lot like Corrado, really. That first look at him had made her silent, and took away her breath, too. This was no different.

Except she didn't *know* this man, and why in the hell was he here?

"Who are you?" she asked, her voice faint.

The man smiled.

Just a *ghost* of one, though.

He lifted his head a bit, giving her a better view of the planes that made up his handsome face, and the war that raged in his stare. "Alessio Sorrento—I like Les, though."

Les.

That text ...

"But it ain't about me, is it?" Alessio asked, his voice a deep bass that came off both edgy and dark. "Lately, it's been all about *you*, Ginevra."

How did he know her name?

She wondered ...

No one had said either way—man or woman, they didn't *say* who the other person was for Corrado. She hadn't assumed, but a part of her just figured it was a woman because that was the default. Not that she cared either way who someone loved or fucked behind closed doors. That was their business, and as long as people were happy, what did it matter?

But *now*, staring at this man, and the way he looked at her like he was both curious, but he wished she would drop dead on the fucking spot, too, made her think ...

This was him.

This man was Corrado's ... person. They were a *them* before Ginevra ever came into the picture, clearly. Those shoes with different sizes on the rack when she first arrived at the penthouse; the different style jackets, like they belonged to entirely different personalities; the offhanded remarks Corrado made without realizing it— *and we use it*, he'd said—and then ignored when she questioned him; or even his hesitations when he nearly slipped up like telling her the master bedroom was his, but he'd almost said something different.

She knew now.

It meant these two men had been a thing for a while. She was in the middle. He came *before* her. She understood what she had missed.

It hurt worse because of it.

"Yeah, it's been all about you, huh?" Alessio smirked, adding lower, "And I'm here to find out why that is."

26.

Above all things, at the end of the day when the sun went down, and he no longer had to pretend like he gave a shit, Alessio was still an asshole. Oh, he had people he cared about—those he *loved*, sure. He usually cared to make an attempt with those people not to be an asshole, but most others were fair game.

And even those he cared for, if he were being honest, weren't special exceptions to the rules when it came right down to it. When things began to feel like they were falling apart around Alessio, or like his life was spiraling out of control … that asshole side of him liked to make an appearance.

It became *worse*.

Like now.

The fact that he was an asshole was the entire reason why he happened to be standing at the end of that hallway in their penthouse in Toronto. It was every single fucking reason why he had come here to do this tonight.

Near the front door, the pretty thing he'd likely scared the wits out of— *whoops*—made a sound that drew his gaze to her again. And *shit*, she was pretty. Disregarding the rest of this shit that pissed him off about her, and her presence here, Ginevra was a beautiful thing.

He wasn't *at all* surprised she managed to catch Corrado's eye. He always did have a taste for pretty, delicate looking things when it came to women. Ones that looked innocent because he enjoyed finding all the parts of them that were far from it.

Ginevra was certainly *that*.

Pretty, that was.

Okay, he might have been being an asshole again. Pretty was a bit … *nice*. If he were being honest, he would say that he understood entirely why she caught Corrado's eye because Alessio couldn't stop his gaze from drinking her in from where he stood ten feet away, either.

Like the way that silk gray dress, wet from the rain pouring down outside, had molded itself to her body. Silk was *un-fucking-forgiving* against a body. Instead of accentuating beauty, it highlighted every single goddamn flaw it could, but especially when it was *that* tight. Not on her, though.

Because he couldn't find a flaw.

He couldn't find something to dislike in the shape of her hips, or the length of her legs, her skin golden with a sheen from the rain, but olive-toned, too. Her breasts, emphasized by the beige lace of the bra cups peeking out from the low-cut front of the dress, lifted and fell quickly with her breaths, which only drew his gaze higher. To the delicate column of her throat, tense with her nerves, and making that diamond choker glitter as it caught the light.

And her face.

Her face.

Small featured, wide eyes, stained-red lips, and *beautiful*.

Yeah, it was no fucking wonder to him why this woman had caught his lover's eye. Because frankly, it took very little effort for her to make Alessio pay attention to the way she looked, too. Although, physical beauty was one thing.

Anyone could be beautiful.

Lots of people were.

What was it about her that made Ginevra different?

That was his question.

He'd thought, maybe stupidly, that he would come here and find out *why* Corrado had been so willing to lie to Alessio for nothing more than a woman—if he wanted a woman, there were thousands of them all around him, he could go *find one*.

What was it about this woman?

Why lie for this woman?

And that just pissed him off.

A lot more.

"Where is Corrado?" Ginevra asked.

Her voice was musical, really. Soft, and light. Like a melody floating through the air to reach his spot down the hall. He could hear the nerves working in her tone, too, and yet, she still managed to sound polite.

Why was she being polite?

If she knew who *he* was—did she even know?—then she would have no reason to be nice. It made him wonder if Alessio wasn't the only person Corrado had been lying to lately. It wouldn't be such a stretch, all things considered.

"Well?" Ginevra demanded.

Okay, there went her politeness.

Alessio, who hadn't moved from his spot against the wall since she opened the penthouse door, tipped his head up a bit. He'd not *really* met her stare since she found him standing there. Oh, he looked her way, and she looked his. He took his time to check out what made up the woman that his lover seemed determined to hide from him, and he hadn't missed the way she looked him over, either.

Still ...

He hadn't met her gaze.

Not until now.

Through the longer strands of his shaggy hair, he met Ginevra's stare head-on, unfazed and calm on the outside. He wanted her to see *that*—needed her to think that despite her presence here, he was fine.

Even if he was anything but.

He felt like a war, really.

She wouldn't know it.

Ginevra stilled in place, her milk chocolate-colored eyes widening. *No*, she didn't know her presence put him on edge, but he absolutely could see what his company did to her. Not that the beautiful woman wanted him to know, he thought, because she was quick to clench one hand tightly around the clutch she held, and her other formed a fist at her side. That trembling in her shoulders stopped, and she tipped her chin up.

Staring right back at him.

Standing tall.

As beautiful as ever.

God.

Any other fucking time—*any other fucking woman*—and he would have really appreciated that spirit. That determination he found in her gaze, hell yeah, he would have liked it, and urged her on to show him more.

He loved when people surprised him.

Not this woman, though.

Not right now.

"Are you going to answer me, or not?" Ginevra asked.

Fine.

But he was having fun here, that's all.

She didn't have to know that, right?

"Oh, I tricked him," Alessio said, grinning.

He tipped his head to the side a bit to watch her from that angle. He kept finding new things about her to stare at depending on the angle, and the direction at which he watched. Like now, he could see the way the side of her smooth, creamy throat worked as she chewed on her words, and held them back.

Come on, girl, say what you wanna say to me, I fucking dare you.

She had to know who he was.

Had to.

He just felt it in his bones.

Good.

Because he wanted her to.

She'd came into this place after him; she came here when he'd already been here. His thing—his *person*—was not for her. And he wasn't going to hand it over; he would not give Corrado to anyone. They would have to take him from Alessio first.

"I tricked him," Alessio said again, shrugging one leather-covered shoulder. "See, I knew he wouldn't give me five minutes alone with you when, up until now, he seemed determined to keep you from me, for whatever reason."

"I thought he was with *you* tonight." Ginevra's fingers drummed against the side of her clutch, and she glanced away from him. All those nerves—he saw it all and took them for what they were. "I saw the message you sent—that was you, right?"

"That's how I tricked him."

He laughed.

Ginevra simply stared.

Alessio rolled his eyes, getting bored now. "See, if I got him away from *you* … then I wouldn't have to worry about him being over my shoulder when I came up here to find what I was looking for."

But, oh, he certainly planned to have a conversation with Corrado, and *very* soon. He suspected the man was realizing, if he hadn't already, that Alessio was not, in fact, at a bar two blocks away from this penthouse that he and Corrado frequented together to play pool when they were in the city.

It wouldn't take much for Corrado to put two and two together—it always made four, after all. He'd be on his way back to this penthouse soon, if he wasn't already, and then Alessio would move into the second thing he came here for.

Dealing with Corrado.

Letting him know he *knew*.

Simple, really.

"And did you?" Ginevra asked softly.

There was something about her lips that kept drawing his gaze in. The bottom lip was a bit fuller than the bottom, making her look as though her mouth was set into a sweet pout. Stained red from whatever lipstick she had been wearing earlier in the evening, the color took away the innocence her mouth might held and made him think of *dangerous* things.

Like how one might smudge what remained of the stain, or how it got that way to begin with. Was it the rain? Her tongue wiping at the line of her lips? *Corrado,* even? Had he kissed it off her—*licked* it off her?

All things Alessio didn't need to wonder.

Yet, he still did.

"Well, *did you?*" Ginevra asked.

"Did I, what?"

"Find what you were looking for here."

How simple that question felt.

The answer was far from easy, though.

Because *no.*

No, he had not found what he was looking for. Some crazy part of him thought he would come here, lay eyes on this woman, and just *know* what it was about her that had Corrado willing to hide her. Whatever it was about her that made his lover prepared to throw away the trust that Alessio gave to no one.

He still didn't know.

It pissed him off.

Pushing away from the wall, Alessio moved down the hallway faster than Ginevra could react to his oncoming form. She took a step back, though, but it was too late because he'd already come close enough to her that his proximity alone allowed him two things.

To see the darker brown flecks in the lighter tawny irises of her eyes. To see the splattering of freckles on the edges of her cheeks, closer to her hairline. To back her against the wall as she stared up at him.

And to feel the warmth of her body.

He was entirely *too* close.

Alessio still didn't back up.

"No," he said simply, "I haven't found it yet."

"Sorry to waste your time, then."

Alessio arched a brow, his teeth grinding against the piece of mint gum that had, for the most part, kept him calm over the last hour while he waited. "It's fine, no worries."

"Really? Because I don't think it is, Alessio. Fine, I mean."

Her voice?

Still musical.

Not that it mattered.

"Oh, it's definitely *not* fine," he replied, "but I won't be leaving until it is."

Ginevra swallowed audibly, and that tremor danced over the line of her smooth shoulders again. Still damp from the rain, and naked now, as she'd pulled the straps of the silk dress down over her arms when she thought she was alone ... he noticed entirely too much about this woman.

But he blamed Corrado for that, too.

This *obsession.*

He just wanted to know why.

Why *her.*

Why?

Alessio took a step away from Ginevra when he heard the knob on the penthouse door begin to turn. He glanced to the side, a grin curving his lips as it opened, and the man of the hour finally arrived.

Corrado looked to him first when he stepped inside, and then he checked on Ginevra, too. He didn't seem surprised to find Alessio in the penthouse, but more like he expected it. No one was better acquainted with the asshole in Alessio than Corrado, frankly.

Quietly, Corrado said, "We should talk, yeah?"

Alessio winked. "You think?"

"Les—"

"Yeah, let's fucking *talk,* Corrado."

Time to really get this show started, then.

27.

Corrado

"Where do you want to—"

"The office," Alessio said, taking two steps backward.

Further from Ginevra.

Corrado wasn't really worried on that. Alessio wasn't the type to get violent when he was feeling some kind of way. At least, not to *women*. Men, on the other hand, were an entirely different story.

Fair game, as Alessio would say.

"The office, then," Corrado said.

He tried to keep his tone calm, but it was harder than he thought it would be. Mostly because he'd figured out quickly that Alessio had fucked him over tonight, and that wasn't like him at all. The second he stepped into the penthouse and saw Alessio stepping back from Ginevra like he'd had her backed against the wall, well … Corrado simply wanted to put some space between the two.

Make Alessio *think*.

Corrado needed a second, too.

"Yeah," Alessio muttered, shooting Corrado a look.

Just like that, the other man turned in the hallway, and walked away without as much as a look over his shoulder. Not that it made a difference. He could just *tell* … Alessio wasn't happy, but honestly, neither was Corrado. This could have been done a hundred different ways, but he didn't have to come in like this, either. The tension was still far too thick in their air; Corrado could practically taste it, for fuck's sake.

Once Alessio rounded the corner at the end of the hallway, Corrado looked to Ginevra, but she stared at the floor between them. Like it was far more interesting than him, and maybe in that moment, it absolutely was to her.

Who was he to say?

Still, he needed to check …

"Are you okay?" he asked.

Ginevra nodded, her fingers tightening on the clutch in her grip. "Yeah, Corrado."

"You're sure?"

Her chin tipped up, and through her lashes, he saw the anger and pain staring back at him. It really showed through in the frown that marred her pretty lips, and the tightening in her jaw. *Jesus.* The girl was good at hiding it—no doubt about it, and he wouldn't deny her that truth. But fuck him, if it still didn't cut him deep to see that leveling on him.

He deserved it, though.

Corrado knew that.

All the hell that was about to come his way from two entirely different people … yeah, he earned every bit of it. He wasn't so stupid or selfish that he didn't recognize the fact Ginevra and Alessio were both due their thoughts about what he had done to them. And so, he planned to let them do whatever they needed so that he understood their feelings on it all.

Didn't he owe them that?

At least?

Corrado thought so.

"That's *him*, isn't it?" Ginevra asked, her voice barely breaking a murmur. She wouldn't look at him entirely, but she still watched him through her lashes. It was enough for Corrado. "The other person, I mean."

He nodded. "It is. And I know you don't want to hear it right now, but I'm so—"

"You're right, I don't want to hear it."

"All right." He gestured at the hallway, knowing Alessio was likely already waiting for him in the office. "I have to take care of that, but you're … it's been a long night, Ginny. You should relax."

She scoffed at his back when he passed. Corrado didn't acknowledge it.

Then, behind him, she said, "He's …"

He hesitated in his next step. "What?"

"He's overwhelming," she whispered.

Corrado shot her a look over his shoulder and laughed bleakly. "I know."

Because where was the lie?

Alessio had always been overwhelming.

In every sense of the word.

● ● ●

Corrado found Alessio sitting on the edge of the desk, using the arm of a guest's chair to rest his foot on as he sliced through the top of a letter with his favorite pocket knife. He said nothing as Corrado stepped into the office and closed the door just enough that there was a crack to see out into the hallway.

Mostly because he wanted to watch for Ginevra.

All the while, Alessio said nothing. He pulled the bill out of the envelope that he opened, looked it over, and then tossed it aside. Just as quickly, he picked up another from the pile, clicked his tongue as he slid the knife under the paper, and opened it, too.

"That's what you want to do right now?"

"Why not?" Alessio asked, reading over the paper in his hands. "It's not like *you* care to look at the bills—they fucking sit in a pile."

Well, he wasn't *wrong* …

Corrado simply preferred to let Alessio do those types of things because he found it mundane and fucking boring.

"The maid handles that here," Corrado said. "Because someone needs to keep up on it when we're not around, Les."

"Right, right."

As fast as the bill had been in Alessio's hand, it too was tossed to the desk. Discarded, and forgotten in a blink when his gaze turned on Corrado standing in front of the door.

And there it is.

That fury.

The *sting* of it.

A war raged in Alessio's eyes, and Corrado didn't look away. He couldn't. Alessio was still owed that, after all, and Corrado would let him have it even if every second of it hurt him, too. That's what one did when they hurt someone they loved, or so he thought.

Not that he figured Alessio wanted to hear that right now.

"We're going to talk now, right?" Alessio asked. "*Talk*, Corrado, which is something we probably should have done, oh, what … about a month ago, or so?"

He straightened a bit, stuffing his hands into his pockets at the same time. "I—"

"No, no, no," the other man murmured quickly, stepping down from the desk in one fluid movement, like his entire body was made of water, and he moved like it, too. "No, I don't want to hear you *talk*, unless you're going to say something I want to hear."

Corrado eyed that knife in Alessio's hand. "You going to put that away, or …?"

That was a low blow.

Even Corrado knew it.

Alessio's jaw twitched, and he flipped the blade around in his palm without even looking at the weapon. "Fuck you. Like I would *ever*—"

"I didn't say you would. I asked if you were going to put it away."

Without a word, Alessio snapped the switchblade closed, and pocketed the weapon. He didn't acknowledge he did it other than to raise his brow at Corrado like he was saying, *better?*

"I made a trip to New York, yeah," Alessio said, taking one step closer to Corrado, but coming no further than that, "worried about *you*—because that's what I fucking do, Corrado. I worry about you. I think about *you*."

He sucked in a heavy breath but kept quiet. It wasn't like he needed to be told to shut his fucking mouth right now. He could tell what Alessio wanted, which was to get shit off his chest, and *then* maybe he'd be willing to let Corrado talk.

But who knew for sure?

"And what do you do, huh?" Alessio asked.

"I fucked up."

"*Right.*" Alessio glanced away, staring out the one bay window in the office that currently overlooked a darkening sky and a city that was still awake. "Do you wanna know why I picked this room?"

"Because you always liked it."

"Not even close."

"Then, why?"

"Because there's only one goddamn room in this penthouse that you'll sleep in, and if you're *fucking* her, that's where you're doing it, Corrado."

He didn't reply.

Alessio's gaze cut back to him fast. "You won't even deny it, then?"

"Would you believe me if I did?"

"What—"

"I haven't slept with her," Corrado interjected fast. *That*, he wanted clear. "Yeah, I crossed a line. Yeah, I broke those fucking rules. And *yeah*, I got too close, and I didn't let you know from the start like I should have, but I didn't fuck her."

Alessio made a noise under his breath.

Dark.

And oh, so painful.

It cut Corrado deep. That one sound could have been a knife driving into his chest because he *felt* that. He felt that betrayal swimming in Alessio's mind, and heart. Felt it like nothing else, but it was done now.

He couldn't change it now.

"But you want to," Alessio said. "You've *wanted* to."

"Les—"

"Fuck you, don't give me bullshit, Corrado. Not right now. You give me the truth you should have given me a month ago, or you say *nothing.*"

If one was unlucky enough to see a snake right before it struck, they would know the serpent liked to coil its body tightly, saving all its energy, and letting the power of its muscles do the work before it attacked. And that was Alessio in that moment—coiled, prepping, *almost* ready to come at him, and barely holding back.

"Why not?" Alessio asked, his head turned just a bit so he could watch Corrado from the side. "You wanted to fuck her—still do, I bet—so why not do it? Just do it, right?"

He wanted to speak.

Wanted to tell Alessio exactly why.

His throat tightened, though, making the words hard to get out. To his companion, it only made it seem like Corrado was holding back, something that had always hit a raw nerve with Alessio when it came to them.

"Why the fuck not, huh?" Alessio demanded, blue eyes blazing. "Because the rest didn't matter—you didn't care to tell me anything else, so why not just *do it.*"

"Because I couldn't."

"That's a coward's answer."

"It's the truth," Corrado murmured, "and I know I should have told you, but it wasn't that simple, Les. I fucked up, *yes*, but it wasn't as easy as you're thinking. I didn't purposely decide to do this, or do it to you, okay, I—"

In a blink, Alessio closed the distance between them. Another person, no doubt, would have backed up at the sight of Alessio coming at them looking like he did right then. Dressed in black, leather and combat boots, his expression darkened from his rage.

But not Corrado.

No.

He stayed right where he was, letting Alessio get as close as he fucking could, until their chests touched, and they were eye-to-eye. Stormy blue irises could have nailed him to the floor, but he still wouldn't have moved.

"No?" Alessio asked, leaning in closer until their mouths were a breath apart. "No, Corrado? You didn't purposely do this, huh? You didn't *purposely* decide not to tell me that you were watching a woman, that you had something going on here I should have known about because that had *always* been our way? You really wanna say you didn't do that knowing what you were doing?"

Alessio pointed a finger at him, but didn't touch Corrado with it, and lost all his sense of decorum at the same goddamn time. His next words came *loud*, and sharp, because he clearly wanted Corrado to hear and feel every single one of them.

"I knew shit was up, and I went looking for it, Corrado. And I'm so fucking glad I found it before you could tell me, right, because I don't think you would have."

"I was going to tell you."

"When, tonight? A little late, yeah?"

Corrado shook his head as Alessio took a step back. "If you'd just let me talk—"

"I'm *sick* of hearing you talk," Alessio returned, "because you don't say anything new, and you certainly don't tell me what I want to hear anymore. You've been saying the same shit to me for the last five years, so why would this be any different?"

"Stop it," Corrado said lowly, his fists clenching at his sides. "It's one thing to be pissed about this, but it's another to act like this has been something that's happened time and time again. Because it's *not*. It's not, Les. And I didn't mean for it to happen this time. She wasn't supposed to *be* anything. She was just a fucking job!"

"A *job*, right. That's fucking rich." Alessio let out a laugh, bitter and aching, and moved closer to Corrado again. This time, Alessio coming forward forced him back a bit until his side hit the edge of the opened door and made the crack wider so that both of them were almost standing in the doorway. "If you had wanted to fuck her, all you had to do was tell me. It's the one and only thing I've always asked from this, but you couldn't even give me that. I shouldn't be surprised."

"And what in the hell does that mean?"

Alessio shrugged. "At the end of the day, I'll always be the second choice. To everything else, I come second, and you just made sure to really let me know here."

No.

If it were possible for a heart to split in two from nothing more than someone's words and their pain, then that's what Corrado's did. He wished Alessio could see himself through Corrado's eyes. He wasn't so good at this thing they had, and he screwed up, but that didn't change what they were at the end of the day.

It didn't change what he felt.

Alessio couldn't be his second choice when he had already been his first.

"That's untrue," Corrado said, refusing to back down on that. *Ever.* "Don't say that, because you know it's not true, Les."

"I know you made it clear here. With *her*, yeah, you made it look like fucking crystal to me, Corrado. I see it far too well."

"You don't know any—"

"I know enough!"

"You won't let me *talk*!"

"I told you why that is. I don't care to hear what you have to say." Alessio took one step back from him, but it still wasn't enough. A part of Corrado wanted the room to breathe, but another part of him wanted this man as close as he could get him. That heartache was still there, bright and clear, and vicious. Ready to *hurt*. "I came here looking for something tonight, but I haven't found it. I don't know if I will, or if I even want to anymore."

Corrado let out a shaky exhale. "Don't say that; you don't mean that."

Alessio rushed forward, pressed against him, and stared him down *again*. Teeth clenched, body coiled, and emotions ready to go to war.

Corrado didn't move an inch. "If all you wanted to do was *fuck her*, then you could have told me, but that's the thing, isn't it? That's not all you want from her—that's not all you want to do with her. And that's why you didn't tell me about her, Corrado. Just *say it*."

"I won't deny that, but it's more than that, too."

A nod answered him back, but Alessio wasn't hearing him. He was too fucking mad, and ready to strike out because of it. That was the thing about him—once he reached his point of no return, it was over. He couldn't be reached.

Corrado simply had to weather the storm.

And what a fucking *hurricane* Alessio could be.

Violent, destructive, and raw. Unforgiving, willing to devastate, and unrelenting as he tore whatever was in his way apart piece by fucking piece. Even if it meant tearing apart the thing that he loved while he did it. Anyone caught in his path when he was like this would be lucky to survive, and if they did, they certainly wouldn't come out of it the same as they went into it.

Corrado was not an exception to that rule, but he *earned* this. Alessio was due this. So, he let him have it. Corrado let him do what he needed. Even if it killed him by the time his lover was done.

It wasn't about Ginevra, really. It wasn't that Corrado found a woman he was attracted to, or felt something for. It was the betrayal in it—the trust Alessio never gave to anyone, but that he willingly handed to Corrado.

It was *that*, and not the rest, even if Alessio used everything else as a backdrop to spell it out for Corrado. He'd always been good at reading between the lines, and he didn't need help now to see it written like black ink on white paper. Alessio was the paper. His eyes, his words, and his anguish became the ink.

"I'm so glad you found *something* in someone else," Alessio murmured, that betrayal coating every word and each breath he took, "because God fucking knows you never found what you wanted in me."

Fuck him for saying that.

It wasn't even close to being true.

Corrado had *everything* he wanted in Alessio—he'd found things he never knew he needed in the man looking like he was ready to burn him to the ground right where he stood. And he loved him more for it, too.

That's what made this hurt worse.

Because he couldn't explain why this happened at all. He would never be able to explain Ginevra, the things he felt for her, or why it happened at all … not when he already had what he wanted and needed from Alessio.

Not that it mattered.

Corrado had crossed Alessio's one line.

It was already too late.

"So, is that what you need to do, then?" Alessio asked, dragging Corrado from his thoughts as lightening streaked across the sky in the window behind him. "You want to fuck her, Corrado? Then *fuck her*. Have her."

28.

Ginevra

"You want to fuck her, Corrado? Then *fuck her*. Have her." Alessio's bitter laughter filtered down the hall to Ginevra's spot where she leaned with her shoulders against the wall while she stared down to the dimly lit office. She could see them in the doorway, standing too close, both seeming ready to strike out at one another. "That's our deal, right? I just have to know about it, and now I do. So, you want her, now I know, and you can have her."

"Les, it's not like—"

"Not *what*, like I think it is?" Even if Ginevra were able to see more of Alessio's face in the shadows of the office, she bet he would be sporting a sneer. It couldn't be missed in his tone. "It's exactly like what I think it is, and you can't deny it."

"I don't want to deny it, but that doesn't change *us*, either."

"Us?" Alessio scoffed. "*Us?*"

"That's what I said, wasn't it?"

"What is that?"

Ginevra lifted her gaze again to watch the scene playing out down the hall. She had no business standing there, and it certainly wasn't her place to watch this whole thing play out like she was a fly on the wall.

And still, she couldn't move.

She was compelled to stay.

The two men stood toe-to-toe in the doorway of the office, their bodies angled toward one another like one was waiting for the other to strike, but neither knew which one would do it first. She didn't even think they realized their fight had been this loud, or that it had almost moved entirely out into the hallway.

"What is *what?*" Corrado snapped.

"Us—what is that, huh? Because you haven't known, or you sure as shit didn't wanna say before, so let's not pretend like you do now."

"Low blow, Les. That's a low fucking blow, even for you. You're mad, so you're saying shit you don't mean because that's how you deal. And I get that, but that's low. You're pissed—so *fine*. I crossed a line—*yeah*. None of those things are untrue, but it doesn't change what this has always been to me."

"But all of them mean one fucking thing for me, Corrado."

"Stop saying that."

"What, you don't like having your bullshit thrown at your feet for you to unpack?"

"That's not it at all. It doesn't matter how many times you say it, it won't make it true."

"Then, what? Go on, tell me. I'll wait. *Surprise me* for once, please. I've had five damn years doing this with you, so what's one more night, right?"

"*Stop it.* This doesn't prove shit about us, or some complex you've had about what we've been for the last five fucking years," Corrado said, his tone roughening enough to make Ginevra startle against the wall. She looked down their way just in time to see Corrado step forward fast enough to force Alessio back a step, making the man press against the doorjamb. "It doesn't change the fact that I love—"

Corrado didn't get to finish his sentence before the inevitable happened. She'd been watching it from the time they came into her view—the way both of them seemed like one was going to strike out at the other. Only, Alessio didn't strike out the way Ginevra thought he would.

This all felt *violent*.

Anger overflowing.

Pain spilling out in words.

And yet, Alessio struck out at Corrado with affection. If one could call the kiss that he leveled on Corrado as *affectionate*. Ginevra didn't know if she would, not considering the force of the kiss pushed Corrado back until he was the one with his spine against the doorjamb, and a hand was at his throat.

She heard Corrado hitting the wall, saw the way Alessio's lips dragged against his, fingers curling into a suit jacket, and another fisting into leather. Somehow, though she didn't think there was any room left between them, the men moved closer. Their kiss wasn't soft or *easy*. Certainly not slow, or sweet.

Vicious, maybe.

Bruising, definitely.

And oh, so painful.

Painful, she thought, because one of them seemed to be fighting to leave something behind while the other was refusing to let go.

Ginevra sucked in a sharp breath, her heart aching as a whisper of heat shot through her body at the same time. It would be impossible for someone to see that sight, those beautifully haunted men showing love in their hurt, and not feel something for it. She simply didn't think she *should* feel something for it.

This was not the time for that. God knew, she had her own reasons to be mad here, and that was enough to make her want to slip out of the hallway and leave those two to their … *mess*.

Because fuck, she could see it was a mess. Somehow, she'd been put in the middle.

But still …

She couldn't look away.

This wasn't for her to see. Their moment—their *fight*. None of it was for her, even if it had been brought on because of her. She didn't have any business being privy to something that felt *far* bigger than her.

Because wasn't that much obvious?

It wasn't *just* her.

Alessio pulled away first, his face still darkened by the shadows, but that didn't stop Ginevra from noticing the way his jaw trembled when murmured, "*Don't, Corrado.*"

Corrado dragged in a ragged breath. "Les—"

"Don't you fucking *dare* say that to me," he interjected, swift and harsh, his voice straining with every word. "Not right now, not after everything and all this time … don't you dare do that to me. You never wanted to do it before, so you don't get to do it tonight. You don't get to use it *now*. You don't get the right to use those words when you did *this*, too."

"I'm not trying to say it to use it like a weapon—"

"You *are* because you know what it means."

Corrado released a rough sound that echoed down the quiet hallway. "Let me explain, please."

"Except you can't, can you?"

"Or you don't really want me to, Les."

Alessio nodded. "Don't do that, either."

"If you're going to throw my shit at me, then at least look at your own."

"Fuck you, Corrado."

As fast as Alessio had moved to corner Corrado, he stepped away, moving into the hallway with his back facing Ginevra. Although, she didn't think he knew she was there. She *should* move—now would be the right time to do exactly that—but she couldn't. Her feet might as well have been cemented to the floor.

Stupid, foolish girl.

"Just ... stay," Corrado said, "calm down, and then maybe we can talk without *this*. It doesn't have to be like this."

"Nah, I wouldn't want to intrude, you know?"

Alessio said that, and the same time, tipped his head to the side. Ginevra stilled against the wall, her eyes growing wide when the man pointedly looked her way. He'd known the whole time she was standing there, it seemed.

He didn't appear bothered by it.

Corrado sighed, his stare following Alessio's path until it landed on her. Still, he said nothing, and he didn't move when Alessio turned around, and headed down the hallway. He met her gaze, and held it even as he came closer, and didn't drop it as he passed.

"You really found a mess here, girl, huh?" Alessio asked her.

Ginevra looked away.

He wasn't wrong.

Silence echoed in the penthouse long after the slamming of the front door reached the far hallway. The hardwood floor suddenly became a hell of a lot more interesting to her, because it was easier than watching Corrado drag the pad of his thumb over his bottom lip.

Like he was still feeling that kiss.

Too many things warred in her mind, and her heart. All the things she'd clearly missed, and others that still didn't make sense. Oh, she had questions that needed and deserved an answer, sure, but some of them probably weren't her place to ask.

She'd been lied to.

She'd been hurt, too.

And still, all she could think to ask in that moment was, "You didn't think you should tell me about him?"

A hoarse sound left Corrado, but she continued her perusal of the floor. It was still easier than looking at him when she wasn't even sure how she felt right then.

"You should have told me," she whispered. "Maybe then, this wouldn't have happened."

He laughed, then.

Hard, loud, and *bitter*.

God, so dark.

Like someone ripped it out of him.

Ginevra looked up to find him staring at her in that way again. So intense, and pensive.

"You think that would have changed what happened here tonight?" he asked, shaking his head as he turned to go back into the office. Over his shoulder, he added, "In case you didn't figure it out, *this* was a long time coming. This was years in the making—you just happened to help it along."

"You still could have—"

"I should have done a lot of things, Ginevra. I don't need someone else to point it out to me, and I certainly don't expect you to understand me, or him, or this."

Ouch.

That hurt.

"Or is it because I'm just a job to you, Corrado?"

His next step into the office hesitated, his shoulders tensing before they visibly dropped, the same way his head dipped down, too.

Did that hurt him?

Good.

He should know how she felt, too.

She didn't give him the chance to respond before her feet finally decided to start working again, and she slipped down the hall out of sight.

There, she could hurt.

And he wouldn't see.

29.

Corrado

"And how long has it been since you had contact with him?"

Corrado's molars ached from how hard he continued clenching his jaw through this entire fucking conversation. How Cree was even able to understand half of what Corrado said to him was a goddamn mystery.

Better Cree than Dare, though.

Dare would tell Corrado he was a fucking asshole, didn't deserve Alessio—he wouldn't be wrong—and then he'd likely refuse to help him, or try to pull information on Les's possible whereabouts. All the while, he'd make sure Corrado understood every single bit of this was his fault, and again, he wouldn't be *wrong* ... but it wouldn't solve the problem of finding Alessio.

"Corrado?" Cree asked.

"A week," he said quietly, pacing the length of the office as he spoke, passing rows of books and the large window, and then coming back again. "It's been a week since he showed up here, and then he left. He won't pick up calls, doesn't answer texts ... I just want to make sure he's good, you know? I know Dare has access to his tracker, but I didn't think I should call him."

Cree released a sardonic laugh. "*No*, I promise you, that would have been a very bad thing to do. For you, not for Les."

Right.

He didn't need to be told.

Dare didn't have children, and as far as Corrado always understood, Alessio filled that place for the man. He protected Alessio far more than anyone realized, and not for one second did Corrado think that his relationship or love for Les would make a difference to Dare at the end of the day.

"I can't go into the tracker data without alerting Dare," Cree said, "and I'm going to assume you don't want me to do that."

"I just ... I don't know if he's okay."

Because this worried Corrado, not that he had any fucking business worrying about Alessio at all. If the man wanted to fuck off somewhere, then he was due that. If he needed to take time away and figure out this shit, then it wasn't Corrado's place to deny him that.

And he *wasn't*.

But he didn't think that was it, either. He figured Alessio was doing this *to* him because that's what he did when he couldn't deal with shit. After all, this wasn't the first time Alessio had gone off the radar when things caught up to him. Usually, he made sure at least *someone* knew where he was, or what he was doing, but not all the time. Sometimes, he hid away purposely, made sure *no one* could find him, if possible, and when he was good and ready, then he would come back.

Only when he was ready.

Corrado didn't know if this was the same, though. That's what bothered him the most. That's where his concern came into play because how in the fuck was he supposed to fix this between them if he didn't even know whether or not Alessio was going to come *back?*

"Maybe ..." Cree trailed off.

"What?"

"Alessio always seems *one* way to everyone else looking at him," Cree murmured, "but you know in his mind, he's different. He's always been that way. There are very few things he holds close, Corrado, but if someone tried to hurt those things, well ..."

"He would slaughter a city for them."

"Exactly."

"But someone didn't hurt *me*, Cree, I hurt—"

"Him," Cree interjected. "I figured that much out. And so, what we're learning now about Alessio, because I don't think he's ever had to handle this before, is that when the thing he loves hurts him, well, he does the opposite."

"What does that mean?"

"He wants to slaughter *you.*"

Corrado stiffened, coming to a stop in front of the window. The late July sky was cloudy, and dreary. A mix of wetness, and heat had made a fog sit around the tops of the buildings surrounding his. It felt appropriate for his life right now.

Confusing.

Suffocating.

Messy.

Horrible.

"But he can't hurt things he loves, because he has so few of those, and he knows what it's like to be hurt by the things that are supposed to love him," Cree continued on like Corrado was actively conversing back with him. "Go back to his parents, his abandonment ... it's really not hard to put it together, Corrado."

"Well, it is for *me.*"

"Yes, because despite what you may think, and what everyone else likes to say about you and Alessio being shadows—or extensions—of the other, you are both actually *very* different people. Two people who lived entirely different lives and see things like love and loyalty and bonds in varying ways."

"So, what you're trying to tell me is that—"

"He's staying away because he doesn't want to hurt you right now, and if he's too close ... he might do just that. He can't trust himself, so he needs some time. All you can do is give it to him Corrado."

"Huh."

Didn't that mean this wasn't done, then?

It wasn't *over?*

Corrado thought so because Alessio wasn't the type to play games. If he was done, and he wanted this to be finished between them, then he would have made that clear. He wouldn't have disappeared for an entire week like this, he simply would have *said.*

He just hadn't come back yet.

Eventually, he would.

Corrado still didn't like it, though, because it put him on edge. He didn't know if Alessio was okay—probably not, in some ways—and he couldn't stand this heavy feeling pressing down on his chest that only seemed to grow day after day.

Cree cleared his throat. "I pulled the aliases I could and did a quick check. Nothing came up on any of the ones he uses, so he must be using one I don't know about. I know you only want to be assured he's okay, but I won't check his tracker. For one, because of Dare, and it's best he stays out of this until the two of you figure out this … problem for yourselves. And for two, because Alessio is allowed his privacy, even if I was willing to deal with Dare when I checked the tracker. Which I'm *not*," he added in a grunt about Dare, continuing on with, "But allow Alessio his privacy, Corrado."

"Yeah, okay."

"You don't sound like it is."

Because it wasn't.

He was fucking *breaking apart at the seams*.

Corrado wasn't good at this. He didn't do *this*. And if this shit was what heartache was, well, fuck that, he didn't like it at all. It felt like his entire world had come to a stop, and yet, all he needed to do was look outside the office window to see … no, in fact, everyone else's world was still turning.

But his?

His was at a standstill, gone somewhere out there, away from him, and it was all his fault. He had no one to blame for this but himself.

"And," Cree added, bringing Corrado back to the conversation at hand, "if I understand the situation properly … the young woman is also still with you, yes?"

"It's … not like I have a choice."

For one, because Ginevra still couldn't go back to New York. And for two, because if Corrado were being honest, he had unfinished business with her at the end of the day. The feelings he had for Ginevra did not negate or change the way he felt for Alessio. But that worked both ways, too. The thing he had with Les, and the last five years they spent together, didn't change or negate the situation he found himself in with Ginevra, either.

"Don't be defensive," Cree said, "what happens behind your closed doors is not my business, which has *always* been our stance."

Our, he said.

Meaning Dare, too.

That was about as much as Cree gave regarding his relationship with Dare.

"I meant," the man continued, "that at the same time, did you consider Alessio might be also giving you what you want by staying away?"

"Excuse me?"

"The woman, Corrado."

"What—"

"While protecting you from him, he may also be giving you the chance to figure *that* out where he isn't imposing or making it more complicated. You were clearly in a situation with her before he came into the picture, and by stepping back, he's allowing you to continue it whichever way you want."

"I'm not sure that fucking her after all of this is going to make him come back, if that's—"

Cree made a harsh noise under his breath. "Never understood the appeal of vaginas myself, really."

Yep.

Great.

This conversation was just perfect, now.

"Could you not?" Corrado asked, pinching the bridge of his nose. "Make your point, or just hang up the phone."

"Oh, I'm going to do that soon, too."

Yeah, he figured.

"The point is," Cree added quickly, "sex is like every other physical thing for Alessio. Eating, sleeping, fighting, or working … it's something he does because he either has to, he likes it, or it fills a need he has. He only gets emotional with sex when there are emotions attached to it—like with *you*. For her, he feels nothing. And he feels nothing about the fact you may or may not be having sex with her— that isn't his problem, is it?"

Cree wasn't wrong.

"No, I don't think that's his problem. More … that I kept her presence and my interest from him. He asks for loyalty, that's all."

"Because *loyalty* is what is most important to Alessio, and to him, faithfulness doesn't fall into that category when that's not what he asked for, right? When sex is just *sex* to him … then, you having sex with a woman is just that to him as well. He's complicated, Corrado, in ways you are not, although that may not be a bad thing."

"You know, it's almost disturbing how you understand people the way you do," Corrado muttered. "And with very little information to go on, too."

"Is it, though? I always thought it was like a gift."

"No, it's disturbing. Definitely fucking disturbing."

"To be fair, I have known Alessio since he was ten, and I have *a lot* to go on in order to make sense of his mess." Cree made a dismissive sniff. "And it being disturbing to you doesn't change the fact that I'm right here, and you know it."

"Well …"

"Hmm?"

"She's complicated to me, too," Corrado murmured. "Like him, but in different ways."

"I bet. That sounds like something you should figure out. If Alessio doesn't call me before he comes back to you, then you're to let me know he's safe. If he's gone for more than a couple of weeks beyond this, I want to know so I can make the choice to bring up the tracker data on his chip implant and let Dare decide what he wants to do."

"All right."

"Also."

"Yeah?"

"Stop fucking this up, Corrado. Despite how it used to be amusing to watch you stumble over your feelings and bury your issues so deep that even you can't find them, it's no longer funny. It's time you figured your bullshit out, and fix it. *All of it.*"

He blinked.

And Cree hung up the phone.

Fuck.

His frustration at *everything*—this week, Alessio, feeling like he was walking on eggshells, the conversation with Cree—spilled over as he stared at the blank screen of the phone in his hand. Before he could think better of it, he whipped the phone to the side. It smacked the arm of the chaise in front of the large window, causing the back and battery to pop out of place, and fall onto the floor in three pieces.

Good.

Better that than him breaking it entirely.

Because that's what he wanted to do.

A quiet noise at the opposite side of the office had him spinning on the spot. There, he found Ginevra standing with a book in her hands, watching him. A million and one emotions raged through him at the sight of her there.

Annoyance.

Concern.

Amusement.

Indifference.

Lust.

Anger.

He didn't know how to deal with it all, but he went to the easiest to handle first, which just happened to be his annoyance. This girl had a bad habit of *spying*. Being places she shouldn't and standing there for way too long to listen. Like last week while she watched him with Alessio in this same fucking office.

"What are you doing?" he snapped.

Ginevra's brow knotted, and she glanced down before lifting the book. "I just … wanted to get another book, that's all. I thought it would be rude to interrupt."

"So, instead you eavesdrop?"

"It's not like you were being *quiet*. I could hear you all the way down in my room, thanks."

Corrado sucked in a shaky breath, willing his nerves to calm. He was snappy because of the shit happening around him, and sure, Ginevra didn't help in a lot of ways, but it wasn't *her* fault, either. She didn't choose to be here, but rather, she had been thrown right in the fucking middle of it.

This whole blow out between Alessio and him had been years in the making, always one step away from it happening. They hung on together by a thread because of literally everything else in their life except Ginevra.

Sure, she was a catalyst.

She pushed them over the edge.

And it still wasn't her fault …

She didn't ask for this, but here she was. It also wasn't lost on him that there was an almost poetic irony to the fact Corrado had realized all the things he'd done wrong in his relationship, what he wanted with Alessio, and that he was ready to fix it … at the same time he was looking this woman in the face, and feeling *something* he couldn't explain for her.

He wouldn't say he was in love with her.

But it was something.

The only other time he had felt that for anyone was Alessio, and so, he didn't know how to correlate this *thing* he felt to anything else.

Koi no yokan, he knew.

Except … it only made this harder.

More difficult.

Compli-fucking-cated.

Ginevra hadn't asked for this.

Neither did Alessio.

Corrado didn't know what to do.

"I'm sorry," he murmured, "I'm just in a mood lately, is all. It's not your fault, and I shouldn't be short with you, Ginny."

She didn't smile.

She only shrugged.

"Doesn't even faze me now," she replied, "I think it makes sense, actually."

"I'm sorry?"

"Your *moods*. I thought it was just you before I knew about … him. But now I think it's really you *without* him."

Corrado's throat tightened, a lump forming there.

Why? Because she was right. Entirely.

What made it worse was the pain he could plainly see staring back from this woman as she stood just a few feet away from him, hugging that book close to her chest, and refusing to meet his gaze. Her stance, the aura she was giving off, it all screamed *one* thing.

She felt unwanted.

Discarded.

Secondary.

It only left him more torn.

"Do you think he'll come back?" she asked suddenly.

Corrado sighed and tipped his head to the side. "Eventually. It's a messy thing … me and him, I mean. We're not normal. Nothing about our relationship has ever been that, you know? We've had an open bedroom for years where women were concerned, but this was different. Things were different this time, and I can't expect you to understand it."

Ginevra nodded. "That's what you meant by loyalty, right? You weren't *unfaithful*. You were disloyal."

He stiffened, realizing just how much she had heard in his conversation with Cree.

She didn't give him the chance to reply before she added just as fast, "But you're right, Corrado, I don't understand because you never thought to tell me. You didn't give me the chance to *try* to understand. Instead, I get to be the person in the middle—the one *ruining* something for someone else. I get it, though, it's not about me for you, right? I'm not the one you want."

Instead of coming into the office to drop off her book, and get a new one, she set it on the stand next to the door. All the while, Corrado's heart *raged* because this woman didn't understand.

She didn't know anything at all.

Not about him.

Or Les.

And certainly not how he felt for *her.*

She deserved to know.

30.

"You're wrong," Corrado said behind her. "You are *entirely* wrong, but I don't know how to explain this to you because it barely makes sense to me."

The last thing she needed to do was stand there and let that man justify his shitty actions to people he claimed to care about. And yet, something deep inside her soul came to wrap around her heart tightly, keeping her still in the doorway, even if her back was still turned to Corrado.

"Try, then," she whispered.

"Ginevra—"

"Try, Corrado. That's all you have to do. *Try* to explain it to me. You owe me that much, at least. I think you owe someone else a lot more, but he's not here, so for now … we can deal with this. Me and you. Try."

"There's never been a *you*, Ginny."

The crown molding on the hallway took her attention as she considered his words. "I don't understand what that means."

"Exactly, and neither do *we*. But there has never been a you—oh, there's been women, yeah. Women he and I shared, or women we found separately, but there has never been a *you*. Someone like you who I felt something for, someone I was interested in beyond taking to bed. The more I tried to ignore it, because I *did* try, the worse it became."

Corrado sighed loudly. "And that makes this complicated thing *more* fucking complicated than it already is with Alessio and I. That's not your fault. You didn't make us complicated or create this mess. We did it. The bigger problem is I don't think this can be simplified down to who I want here, and that's what you want me to give you. Isn't it?"

Twisting her hands together, she wanted to say no. It would be a lie, though, and Ginevra wasn't a liar. So, because she couldn't say no, she chose to say nothing at all. It was just easier, and God knew there was enough about this situation that was hard.

Her heart felt like ashes.

It'd been burning down all week.

In her chest, a constant inferno raged on, searing her from the inside out. She didn't know how to deal with it because it wasn't only *her* pain that was the cause of it. Instead, it was him, too. Corrado, and the things she saw him dealing with.

His struggle.

How he didn't sleep.

Constantly watching his phone.

Running himself dead on the treadmill at night.

Day after day, and night after night. It never ended. He struggled all the time because he was without something he needed and wanted, and she didn't want to see him in pain. That hurt *her*. She shouldn't feel like that at all, though, because he didn't deserve that.

Right?

She should have been pissed that instead of him wanting her, he was obsessing over someone who wasn't even there. She shouldn't want to give him anything— not her time, her attention, or even *this* here.

Except … Corrado was right.

This was complicated.

Emotions were a tricky thing.

"It can't be simplified down to who I want," Corrado repeated, his voice a hell of a lot closer to her than it had been before, "because that's not the problem in the first place. I know exactly what I want here, but it's the rest that makes it a mess for everyone else."

She turned around slowly only to find he had come to stand right behind her in the doorway of the office. He was entirely too close to her, really, as she could feel the head of his body drifting to hers and smell that musky scent that he seemed to prefer. It only served to muddle up her mind and emotions more, but she chose to ignore it.

She was doing that a lot lately.

"But *why?*"

Corrado frowned. "Why, what?"

"Why can't it be that simple? Pick the person you want."

"And you want me to pick you."

Ginevra blinked. "I didn't say—"

"You don't have to. It's in everything you do. Everything you say, and the things you don't say. I see it in your eyes, and in your silence. But you're *good,* you know. In your heart, you're far too good. Better than me, that's for certain. Because in there," he said, pointing a finger at the spot over her chest where her heart was beating far too fast, "… in there, Ginny, you don't want to be selfish, so you say nothing, and you do nothing. That's who you are, but I can't say the same."

"Or," she countered, "it's because I think love is—"

"Love?" Corrado scoffed, grinning a little too sardonically for her liking. "Let me tell you what I know about *love,* yeah? I met a man once, and I knew from the start he was going to change everything for me."

Her eyes burned, but she refused to blink. Then, the tears that were starting to threaten her calm façade would fall, and he would know just how much this hurt. She didn't want to do that—didn't want to give him that.

"And he did," Corrado continued, "he changed everything. That's what I learned about love, but I wouldn't tell him that. I kept that for me, and it hurt him. And then I met *you.*"

Air pulled painfully through her lungs, but still, she stayed quiet.

What choice did she have?

Corrado stepped forward, closing the inch or two between them until the soft cotton of her sleepwear dragged against his slacks and button-down shirt with every breath she took. "So, here you are," he murmured, his head tilting down a bit as she stared up at him, "and I got *that* feeling again—that same fucking feeling like nothing was ever going to be the same because of you, but this time, I just ignored it altogether. Because that's what I do, Ginny. I ignore, I pretend … I just *don't.*"

"Corrado—"

"I take too much, I want too much, and I demand *too much* from people who only want to love me. And that's what you're standing here asking me to give to you. Do you understand that? You're asking for me—this *mess* who is selfish and ruins the people who love him—to give those same things to you."

Corrado shook his head, saying softly, "So, when you ask why I can't choose who I want ... it's because I don't deserve what I already have, and I'm sorry that you seem to think you're the person who doesn't deserve me. You're wrong, and I'm so fucking sorry for *that*. I'm sorry for this, and nothing I do or say is ever going to make this better, but you should know that before anything else. I'm *sorry*. I'll say it every single day. Every hour on the fucking hour. It won't change a thing, though. It won't change it because I won't give you what you want. I can't ... not the way you want me to."

"But ..."

"Hmm?"

Ginevra stared hard at him, trying to find that lie. *Anything* to tell her that he was saying things he thought she wanted to hear, and not the truth. Instead, all she found was a stark, harsh reality staring back at her.

He wasn't lying.

It broke her heart more.

"I think the choice should be easy for you," she said softly.

Corrado laughed dryly, tipping his head away from hers as he asked, "And why is that?"

Wasn't it obvious?

"You don't love me—you love him."

She could see it in Corrado's eyes before the words even left his mouth that he wouldn't deny what she said—because it was the truth. And like her, this man seemed to make every effort not to lie when he could.

"But I could," he murmured.

Her heart stopped.

She swore it did.

"Pardon?"

"Love you," he clarified, "I could, and the longer you're near, the stronger it's going to be for me. This happened to me already—I did this once, I know how it ends, Ginevra."

Ginevra laughed, but it was far too faint. Hidden in her chest, that traitorous heart of hers pounded like it was going to explode. She liked what he said *too much*. And the way he was looking at her again?

Intense, and *knowing*.

Like he was so sure.

And daring her to challenge him.

She'd felt that, too. From the second she stepped into his vehicle in front of that church, she thought ... *everything was going to be different*. Maybe then, she'd assumed it was because of her sisters, and everything that was happening around her. The chaos, and the unknown waiting for her.

But was it?

Or was it him?

"You can't know that about love," she said, her words slipping out on a breath.

"You *can't*, Corrado."

"Why not? I knew it about him, so why would you be any different? My life wasn't right before him, and then it was … but now it's tilted again, confusing— wrong *again*. I keep thinking it's because of you, because nothing else changed except here you are, and I don't know what to do."

"I'm sorry."

Corrado gave her a look, a sad smile curving his lips up at the edges. "Why on earth are you apologizing to me?"

"Because love shouldn't be that complicated or painful. It should be everything but those things."

"It could be," he agrees. "I want it to be."

"And you want him," she whispered.

"I do."

"And me. You want me, too."

Corrado's agonized stare landed on her again, causing her heart to clench from the truth she found waiting there. "Don't you know?"

"I thought I did, but I think that I don't know anything at all."

"Yeah," he muttered, chuckling darkly, "I have a way of doing that to things I care about. Fucking up, I mean."

"Don't say that, Corrado."

It hurt her heart more.

For herself.

For him.

For a man who wasn't even here.

It all hurt.

"But haven't I?" he asked, his hand coming up so he could tuck the loose strands of her hair behind her ear with the softest touch. That was all it took, just his skin grazing against hers, and heat shot through her every single one of her nerves, making her air catch hard in her chest, and her heart skip beats all over again. "Haven't I made this mess?"

God.

This wasn't fair at all.

He didn't play fair.

The bigger problem was that she didn't think Corrado was trying to play games at all.

"I told you once before," Corrado said, his head drifting lower until his lips nearly touched hers with his next words, "I ruin beautiful things. I won't be the one who pushes you away, Ginevra, so if you want to save what is left of your heart, you need to be the one to do it for me."

If heartbreak was a picture, it would be his face.

Handsome.

Devastatingly so, really.

And tortured.

It killed her.

"You have to do it," he said again, "do you hear me?"

She did.

But …

"I can't," Ginevra breathed.

She couldn't say the words loudly.

Not yet.

They meant she was going to hurt worse. This would have to be enough.

Corrado didn't move an inch.

That was okay.

Ginevra didn't need him to move when he was this close—not when all she wanted to do was kiss him, *have him* ... take him for herself. Even if that meant, all too soon, she was going to have to give him to someone else.

So, she did just that.

31.

Corrado

Corrado was a selfish fuck.

How many times had he said that about himself already?

Too many.

Thing was, it didn't make it any less true. Because that's exactly what he was. Selfish. Greedy. Immoral.

He wasn't all those things at once, sure. Or, he tried not to be. And yet, when Ginevra's lips found his in that office doorway, the same way Alessio's had done a week earlier, he realized he could, in fact, be all those things.

Selfish. And greedy.

So fucking *immoral.*

Because all he could think in those seconds was how goddamn *sinful* Ginevra's kiss felt, and how Alessio's had bruised beautifully, too. He felt her softness and felt Alessio's roughness. The memory warred in his mind, dragging him closer to a place he had tried so hard to stay away from. A place that, once there, he wouldn't be coming back.

He couldn't stop.

Ginevra seemed all too willing to let him do what he wanted, too, and so he did just that. Each kiss he landed to her lips, her jaw, and throat pushed them back a step. His hands were harsh, and demanding, yanking at her clothes and pulling them from her body as they moved down the hallway.

Those tainted emotions of his …

Those ruining hands of his …

She only asked for more.

He couldn't get enough.

Corrado didn't remember when they hit the bedroom, but he'd stripped her of her clothes except for the cotton panties hiding the last bit of her from him. His gaze dragged down her olive-toned skin, taking in collarbones he wanted to bite, and tits that heaved with every breath she took.

Her trembling fingers reached for him, undoing the buttons on his shirt, and working at his slacks as he reached for her. He let her feel the weight of his fingertips driving down her chest before he tweaked her nipples into hard peaks.

"Won't you fuck me?"

Corrado's stare snapped up, slamming into hers. "After."

"After what?"

God.

Who had this woman before him?

Did she not know that the best of sex happened when one *knew* a body they were touching? Didn't she know how good it would be when he learned all those spots and the things she needed to make her gasp, or moan, or *scream*?

"I have to learn," he murmured.

Ginevra smiled shyly. "What do you have to *learn*?"

"All of it, Ginny. All of you."

And he did, after she'd helped him from his clothes, and as her fingers closed around his hard cock to stroke him softly as he learned her body. He used his mouth on her shoulders, at the delicate column of her neck, and along her jaw line. And then his teeth and tongue followed the same path, drinking in every noise that slipped from her lips and the way her fingers would tighten or slow on his length when he found something she liked.

His hands worked, too.

Slipping under the waistband of her panties as his mouth sought hers to taste when he found the wetness between her thighs. *Fuck.* She was slick at the slit of her pussy, and hot to the touch. Silky, and needy, too.

"*Mmm,*" Ginevra breathed against his cheek.

Corrado grinned.

She liked that.

Slow touches, his fingers sliding against her slit, but not entering her pussy. He let the side of his fingers come high enough to drag against her clit, too, taking in how her hips jerked, and a higher sound fell from her lips.

"What do you want, huh?"

"To come."

"Yeah?"

"So bad," she mumbled, turning her face against his so her mouth shuddered along the seam of his own. "*So fucking bad.*"

He'd have done it with his hands.

Fingers working her pussy.

Sure.

But he wanted a taste.

Hadn't he earned that?

Corrado thought so.

He dragged Ginevra's panties down with one yank of his hand against the gusset. Her soft gasp came high above him, because he was already down on his knees, and burying his face at the crevice of her thighs as he pushed her legs wider. He got that taste of her—heady and *tart.* Hot, too, as her arousal coated his tongue when he dragged it through her slit.

"What are you doing—*God.*"

All that noise.

He loved that noise.

His thumb worked at her clit as his tongue lapped at every drop her pussy gave him. There was nothing quite like the taste of a woman when she was ready to crash into an orgasm ... just like there was nothing that compared to the taste of man when he found his.

All it took was his tongue replacing his thumb at her clit for a beat or two before he sucked hard on the throbbing nub ... and she *flew.*

Wetness slicked her further.

Heat pulsed against his tongue.

But it was the sound of her crying his name into the dark bedroom that had his control snapping. He couldn't stand fast enough ... couldn't get her to that bed quickly enough to satisfy the need coursing through him.

And then she was.

On her back, thighs spread.

He found the condom he needed in the drawer beside the bed, tore it open, and slid latex down his cock as he climbed between her thighs. She was already reaching for him, one arm snaking around his back, and the other along his neck. Her fingers threaded into his hair as their lips crashed together again.

She didn't submit to his kiss, now.

She demanded more from it.

Corrado needed that, too.

If he had a vice, that was it.

His hand worked between their bodies until the head of his cock found her slit. He only flexed his hips forward enough that she'd get the tip of him, but not much else. He had to let her know he was there—feel her tense and clench around him before he took the rest of her, too.

Or rather, she took him.

All nine inches.

"Please," she gasped against his lips. "Please, *now*."

That did it.

His hips snapped forward, and he was buried deep in the next breath. His hand splayed wide to her side, holding tight and pulling her back into every pull and thrust of his body. She couldn't get enough, and he loved it.

All her *yeses*.

All those *pleases*.

Every single *oh*.

He drank them up.

Swallowed them whole.

Devoured them like he was starved.

"Fucking take me, baby," he said throatily in her ear, as their bodies moved faster. "God, you fucking love that, don't you?"

"*Yeah.*"

Her whisper was barely there at all. So fucking high, like she was *right there* all over again, and ready to shatter around him. He wouldn't mind picking up those pieces, though.

"Give me it, then. *Fucking give me it, Ginevra.* Give it to me again, baby."

Her heart tipped back as his mouth climbed her throat, his tongue striking out to taste every fucking inch of her that he could. He felt like he waited too long for this, and at the same time, he was so fucking weak for giving in.

Still, he wasn't stopping.

He was taking all he could.

Every bit she gave.

He was *keeping it.*

"Almost," she whined, eyes flying wide to nail into him as he pounded into her. "*Almost, Corrado.*"

Oh, fuck.

There was something in her voice, and her stare. Something in the way she moved against him seeking to get herself off like she knew what she fucking wanted, and she didn't care if she used him to get it, really lit him on fire. It made him want to get off as she moaned and panted against him for more.

The salt on her skin skimmed his lips with every word, each fucking breath. Her thighs held him tight, her back moving against the soft sheets with his own rhythm as her fingernails dug into his sides to find purchase. She was *wild*, then, hair fanning through his fingers and spilling to the bed. Her lips found the stubble on his throat, and then her teeth found his jaw. All those noises of hers muffled against the trembling of his overheated skin.

And yet, he could still hear what she said.

Felt it in his bones.

"Please, please, *please*."

His hand on her trim waist glided over smooth, damp skin that shivered from his touch until his thumb grazed her clit between their tightly grinding bodies. He swiped at her clit once, then twice, pressing harder the third to really make her scream.

And that's when she came.

It was a beautiful sight.

He leaned back a bit just to watch it all unravel for her, too. The way her pussy was stretched full of him, her arousal soaking his cock as it slid out of her before slamming back in to feel those inner muscles of hers clenching around him. How her body trembled against the bed, her hands falling from his sides to fist into the sheets.

The muscles in her throat flexed and tensed with the shout of his name that fell from pinked, quivering lips.

And what a sound that was.

All throaty.

Broken.

High.

As fast as he'd come up to watch that sight, and sear it into his memories so it wasn't one he would soon forget, he fell back into her. His arm locked around her back, and his other found steadiness against her vibrating thigh. He worked his body harder against hers, soaking in every second of her orgasm as he came closer and closer to his own.

"Come," he heard her mumbled. "Fucking *come*."

It sounded so *needy*.

So desperate.

He just wanted to give it to her.

Soon, the thrusts of his came to a still with one final flex of his hips as he spilled into latex while he panted against Ginevra's heartbeat thrumming fast like a hummingbird's wings at her throat. He couldn't make sense of anything—couldn't *speak* beyond the dark cusses that fought their way past his lips.

"Fuck, fuck … *fuck*."

It was blinding.

That release?

Everything he needed.

And it changed everything.

Of that, he was most sure.

Ginevra dragged in lungful after lungful of air as she stared at the ceiling, and he stared at her profile. "Oh, my God."

"Stay in my bed tonight," was all he could think to say. "Sleep here with me. *Be here with me.*"

Because if he couldn't have one, then he needed the other.

She blinked. "Okay."

• • •

Corrado stared out the window of the office as he fixed the phone in his hands simply by touch alone. He didn't look down to check what pieces he was snapping back together. The battery, and the back. Holding the phone, he pressed the button on the side until he felt it vibrate against his palm.

Turned on.

He swore it was muscle memory that allowed him to swipe his thumb across the screen, pulling up the messenger app, and hitting the most frequent contact at the top. *Alessio.*

He was too busy watching his reflection in the window of the office because he thought part of him didn't recognize the man staring back in the glare of the city below. The shape of his body, and the way his undone pants rested low on his hips were all the same.

The face?

Identical.

But in his eyes, something was different.

He didn't know what to do with that.

Corrado glanced away from the reflection, not wanting to indulge those thoughts more than he already had, he peeked over his shoulder at the dark doorway of the office. Just down the hallway, sleeping in his bed, was a woman who, a month and a day ago, had meant less than nothing to him and his life.

He'd never known she existed.

But now that he did?

Corrado knew nothing would be the same.

He'd done this once.

Except it couldn't be as simple as it once was where there was now a *before,* and an *after.* A time when Alessio and Corrado were them before Ginevra, and this … what they had become after her. What came next would be now, but he didn't know what that was, or what it would look like for them.

The phone still in his hand waiting for him to just do what he had to do, his thumb danced across the screen, keying in a message he knew would be received, but that he couldn't predict the impact when it was delivered. He poured over the four words, taking them in until the black letters began to bleed together. And yet, even had he hesitated to send the text, he never once considered *not* sending it.

It was just a matter of *doing it.*

He sent the message.

As the phone beeped, and the tiny *delivered* popped up under the message, Corrado let out a breath he hadn't known he was holding. He waited longer, still staring at the screen for maybe fifteen seconds before the *delivered* message turned into a *seen* one.

I slept with her, he'd written.

Alessio needed to know, whether that was what he wanted or was waiting for … whether he was planned on staying away another week or coming back right this minute. It didn't matter, this wasn't about *that*, it was about the truth.

The loyalty.

The thing Corrado had already broken and failed to give Les. He didn't think the message would fix what he'd done—not by a long shot, really. Still, it was a step forward. A reminder that, he knew what he had done.

He was so fucking sorry.

It was all he could offer Alessio because he no longer knew what to do; he didn't think there was any right or wrong way to move forward here, and he couldn't decide alone. There were now two other people he'd dragged into this mess that had to make their choices, too.

The text was one.

The rest was in God's hands.

Or rather, Alessio's.

Corrado lifted his stare, and watched the lights of the city below dance as he thought, *well, what happens now?*

ALESSIO

THE GUZZI LEGACY, 2

PART THREE: NOW

1.

Pain taught Alessio Sorrento a lot of things.

A motivator, punishment, or a reward. In true pain, someone would find their boundaries, and the ability to go beyond their limits, too. Nothing reminded someone they were weak more than pain, and it was one of the few things that proved humans had the capability to be godlike at the same time.

Alessio hated pain.

Loathed it.

He much preferred numbness because it was a far more dangerous thing. Sure, pain made people do inexplicable, unexplainable things, but numbness? That was the flip side of the same damn coin.

In numbness, one found nothing. And one didn't have limits or boundaries, one didn't need a motivator or a reward when *nothing* was the goal. It was a vicious place to be, so numb that even happiness couldn't find its way through to one's heart.

And still …

Alessio would take numbness over pain any day. One allowed him not to care, and the other forced him to care too fucking much. He also felt like his entire life had been one huge mountain of pain, time and time again.

People said pain was growth.

Survival.

Well, fuck that trash. He'd taken enough pain to last him several lifetimes over, and now, he didn't want to feel at all.

The unfortunate thing about loving someone else was that love didn't afford the gift of numbness. Which was every reason, instead of sleeping like he should be at two in the morning, he sat on a wicker chair in the warm August air with darkness all around. A humid dampness clung to the air, reminding him where he was instead of where he might have been if this situation had been different.

The back property of the Guzzi mansion expanded a far ways into a line of forest under the moonlight. Manicured pathways veered off to a large fountain with dancing stone doves at the top, and then into the flower garden that would make anyone with a green thumb jealous. Mostly, the silence called to him late at night. He stared at the stars—had to be alone.

Things hurt less here.

There was a time when coming to this place—Corrado's childhood home— seemed awkward for a variety of reasons, and none he cared to list. Not that any one person here gave him that impression, but he wasn't used to … *this.*

They all loved.

They supported.

If someone needed something, then a few hands would be able help. The Guzzi family—just Corrado's immediate relatives—were enough to seem like a small army, and that was something else Alessio got used to. A part of him had been so used to taking care of himself for so long a family unit seemed like a foreign thing to him.

Sure, he had a family unit of his own, in a way. The situation Dare and Cree gave him wasn't the same as the Guzzis. Parenting hadn't existed for him, and his most important lessons from Cree and Dare had been learning how to take care of himself.

And still when he came here, Alessio found a sense of home. He forgot the rest of the world for a time and focused on what he needed to do the most. No one here would judge him with their *no questions asked* policy when he walked through the front door, unless he wanted to talk. He'd never told Corrado those things because he shouldn't need to, but it was true. Here, he found comfort that didn't exist elsewhere.

That was why, when he had a hundred other places to hide away and stay under the radar, he came here.

The voice coming out of the speaker of his phone dragged him from his thoughts at the same time he heard footsteps approaching him from behind. He didn't bother to end the conversation because he wasn't ready to.

"And I suppose I owe you something, don't I?"

"What's that?" Alessio asked.

"A happy birthday," Dare said.

Alessio *almost* smiled, but pain was a fucking bitch. Twenty-three years old today, and he'd forgotten. Someone else had to remind him. Appropriate for it to be Dare. At the darkest points in his life, Dare always remembered his birthday for whatever reason.

"Is it, though?" he asked.

"What?"

"A *happy* day."

Dare made a noise under his breath as Gian Guzzi came to sit next to Alessio in the wicker chair beside his. Corrado's father said nothing, dressed in his night clothes with a black robe tightened at his middle, he stared over the back property, and rested his hand along his jaw as he waited for Alessio to finish his conversation. It was late for the man to still be awake.

"Les."

"Ignore me," he muttered. "Thinking out loud."

But also not a lie.

This wasn't a happy day.

And tomorrow didn't look good, either.

Welcome to his life, lately.

"Why don't you take a break, come back here for a bit, and reset—"

"That's Alessio?"

Cree.

In the call's background, Dare confirmed what Cree asked. A shuffle of the phone sounded before more movement echoed through the speakers. Alessio heard the slam of a door before Cree came onto the phone.

"Where are you?" Cree demanded.

Alessio arched a brow over at Gian. The man didn't even glance his way. "Away."

"Doing what?"

"Thinking."

Cree let out a harsh sound. "You don't call people?"

"I'm a grown man, I can—"

"Tell the people who give a fuck that you're *safe*, Les."

His throat jumped as he swallowed back a biting retort that would have only saved his pride but hurt someone else. "I'm safe."

A second passed. Cree sighed. "Good." Then, after a brief pause, he added, "Corrado called two days ago looking for you. You should at least tell him where you are, Les. You don't have to go back—I understand things are going on that hurt you, but he's worried."

Good for him.

Because he hadn't given a shit about Alessio before.

As fast as the seed of doubt drifted through his mind, the pain following behind just as fast, Alessio tipped his head down, and shook it away. It wasn't true, and a huge part of why this happened was *because* Corrado hadn't wanted to hurt him.

Yet, here they stood.

The same result.

Alessio didn't do well with pain, and especially not if someone he loved caused it. He had a handle on this shit—this thing between them. He assumed they were comfortable, but this had taught him he had been lying to himself.

Complacent.

It took nothing to be ruined.

Nothing but a woman.

"I'm not calling him," Alessio said, "there's nothing for me to say."

Hadn't he said enough when he showed up to the penthouse over a week ago? He believed so. His words had cut with each one said—landing like knives against the man he loved to the ends of the earth and back. Alessio didn't need Corrado to tell him how much he hurt him with the things he said. He was aware.

But that was good, too.

Partly.

Why should Alessio be the only one to hurt?

He wouldn't be alone.

He needed to get his shit figured out before he went back for a second round. He didn't want to keep cutting into Corrado. As much as he hurt, it wasn't fair he continued hurting Corrado, too.

Because *he* loved.

He gave a shit.

He would have never done this to Corrado.

Ever.

"You tell him you're *safe*," Cree said, "so he doesn't do something fucking stupid, and make a scene."

"He knows, and he won't do anything. Relax."

"No, he—"

"He knows—shit he doesn't understand is what bothers him. That's Corrado, and it sounds like something he should deal with because I can't fix it."

A lot about this thing between him and Corrado couldn't be fixed by him. Too much shit had been left unsaid for years, and other things they shoved under a rug, ignoring while they pretended to be fine with the things between them.

All lies.

White lies didn't stay white when they became dirty with time.

"Les—"

Typically, he had more patience, especially with Cree or Dare, and yet he only wanted to hang up the phone. So, he did, not even bothering to say goodbye before he reached over and hit the *End Call* button on the lit up screen, ending the conversation whether Cree wanted that or not. He would pay for the decision later, but ... *worth it.*

With the phone call finished, and the conversation over, Gian turned in his chair to give Alessio his attention. Respectful, *always.* Never imposing or intruding unless they gave him no other choice.

"How much longer do you want to stay here?" Gian asked.

Alessio shrugged. "Not sure."

The answer didn't seem to bother Gian when he only nodded. "All right, you're more than welcome."

"Thanks. Shouldn't you be sleeping? Doesn't your wife get prickly when you walk the halls at night."

Gian grinned. "I have things on my mind."

"Me, too."

"Probably similar things."

Alessio scoffed and looked away from the man. "Doubtful."

"Don't. I have always worried about the two of you. I wouldn't be a good father otherwise."

"You're not my father."

Gian cleared his throat, but Alessio refused to take his gaze off the line of trees in the distance. "And yet, that never made a difference, Les."

Yeah, he knew.

"I'm *mad.*"

"Mmhmm," Gian murmured.

"I really want to just do something."

Something horrible and *bad.*

Something that would make Corrado *get it.*

"Strike out, act out ... *hurt.*"

Alessio grunted under his breath. "But I can't ... so, I'm here instead."

Gian let out a sigh, and the wicker creaked before the man came to stand in front of Alessio. He stared up at Corrado's father, but Gian looked off into the distance where the moon shone high and bright against the black backdrop of the sky.

"You are always welcome here, even if what you're here for is to hide, Alessio. But if he calls and asks me where you are—"

"You'll tell him the truth."

But that was the thing.

Corrado wouldn't call here.

He'd never think this was a haven for Les because he never told him. There was a lot of *that* between them. Secrets, and things left unsaid. And usually, when they were saying things, it was the wrong shit.

"Take the time you need," Gian said, "and go back *better*, Les."

"This doesn't get better from here."

"But it might. Go back better, and ready."

Yeah.

Right.

Ready for what?

And how should he do that when he only wanted to hurt Corrado? He could think of a million different ways to do it—ones to make the man feel the same cold ache in his chest that Alessio now had. Pain was always better when shared, right?

Did that make him a monster?

Alessio wasn't sure he cared.

And right there ... that's why he hadn't gone back yet.

Not ready.

He wasn't better.

The phone buzzed on the table between the wicker chairs as Gian turned to walk away. Alessio let him go, and leaned over to check the phone, thinking it would be Cree or Dare trying to get him back on the phone.

A text from Corrado lit up the screen, reading, *Happy birthday, Les.*

Apparently, he wasn't the only one up way too late. He might have appreciated the text, and that Corrado remembered.

He still didn't.

Not when right above it rested a text, one the man had sent only two days earlier. One Alessio had been waiting for—*I slept with her*, Corrado had said.

This had never been about the sex.

The physical shit meant nothing to Les. Sex was sex to him—another urge or need to fulfill, like eating or sleeping or whatever else he needed to live. The idea of *men* sleeping with Corrado fucked with Alessio's head, and they drew the line. Women, though? He didn't care, he got off on it, really.

Rarely did he attach emotions to having sex with females, and neither did Corrado. Together was different, of course. Emotions had always been attached to their fucking when it was just them in bed together.

So, no, he didn't have a single fuck to give about Corrado sleeping with Ginevra.

It was everything else.

Everything Corrado *didn't* say.

All the things he hadn't done.

That was the problem.

• • •

Alessio blinked, and a week passed him like nothing at all. He didn't know how it happened, but he blamed the haze of his mind.

The *war*.

To his left, he watched the quiet, dark city street and the people passing by the bar's large bay windows as he tipped his whiskey up for another drink. Two glasses in, working on his third, and he still didn't *feel* shit.

The fucking numbness had come.

Now, he wasn't sure if he wanted it.

On the bar, his phone buzzed. Alessio ignored the device altogether. The chime of a bell somewhere behind him said someone new had come inside, and five seconds later, a presence sat next to him at the bar.

"Since when do you drink whiskey?"

Alessio made a thick noise, tipping his glass up for another sip. "Since now."

He preferred rum.

Tequila.

Vodka.

Bourbon.

Beer.

Fucking wine.

Anything but whiskey. The spirit was Corrado's drink, and Alessio didn't see the appeal. Something about the liquor made him cringe, which was amusing when he could take shots of tequila like nobody's business. The only time he liked the taste of whiskey was when he licked it off Corrado's—

Nope.

Not going there.

Not tonight.

"What do you want?" Alessio asked.

"Are you going to keep staring out the window, or look at me?"

Well …

Alessio turned on the stool to face his guest, coming face to face with Christopher. Before then, Alessio never looked at Corrado's twin and first recognized all the similarities between them. He always found the differences first because that's what he liked about Corrado.

All the things which made him different.

Today, the first thing he saw in Christopher's features were all the things that made him and Corrado identical. Right down to the way his lips quirked up at the corner when he smirked, and the gold flakes in the browns of his irises.

All it did was *hurt.*

Just like that, the numbness left, and the pain was back. Alessio didn't know which one he wanted more.

To feel *everything.*

Or nothing at all.

"How did you know I was here?" he asked.

Chris shrugged. "Dad."

"What, worried I might do something rash because I left the mansion?"

"Who knows? You might want someone else to talk to."

Alessio nodded. "Well, I don't."

"And I'm still here."

Perfect.

The phone vibrated on the bar. Alessio's gaze cut to the device at the same time Chris's did, both seeing a familiar name flashing on the screen to say a text had come through.

Corrado.

"What's that about?" Chris asked.

Alessio sucked air between his teeth, hating the taste of whiskey on his breath but needing the annoyance to help keep the numbness at bay for the moment. "I told him I'm fine … around, or whatever."

"Ah."

"And to leave me the fuck alone," he added quieter, turning to stare out the window again. "Apparently, he didn't get the memo."

Chris sighed. "Or he's ignoring it because he's worried, and he *cares*."

"*Right*."

Cares.

A funny way to describe what Corrado had done.

"Do you want to talk about them—him and her, I mean?"

Alessio made a disgusted noise under his breath. "I don't give a fuck about them, Chris."

It was a lie.

He *did*.

He concerned himself with too much about them, what they were doing, and *why*. More than anything, he wanted to know *why*.

What was it about the woman that did it for Alessio and Corrado? Why *her*? Why was it her who finally broke *them*? After all these years, all this time, and every female the two of them had gone through over the years in their bed … why the fuck was it *her*?

"Yeah, you get like that, huh?" Chris asked.

Alessio shot him a look. "Excuse you?"

"Indifferent. You *act* indifferent. You get in a mood whenever you don't want to deal. Corrado knows how to handle it, but the rest of us think you're being an asshole, Les."

Huh.

He stared at Chris and quirked a brow. "How is that my problem?"

Chris rolled his eyes. "You give a shit about them … or at least, *him*. Otherwise, you would have left by now, Les. You don't have to be here. Nobody is keeping you in this city. If you wanted to go, or tell my brother to go fuck himself, you would have done so. It's who *you* are. So, cut the shit, drop the attitude and the pretense, and then we can find what the real issue is here."

Alessio already understood.

Corrado lied.

They had a thing, and he fucked up.

Alessio didn't want to *deal*—he didn't know how to handle the person he loved, the only one in the world who he trusted more than himself, doing something to purposely ruin the delicate balance they had.

"And you know …" Chris dragged in a heavy breath before clearing his throat as his fingers drummed to the top of the bar. "I think he likes her."

Really?

That wasn't news.

If Corrado didn't like the fucking woman, and he had done this, it would stun Alessio. Why would he even bother?

"Obviously, he likes her," Alessio muttered before taking another drink. There was not enough alcohol in this world to deal with the darkness in his heart, he would swear on it. "Give me something I don't know, Chris."

"I meant," Chris replied, giving him a look from the side, "it's more, Les. Different. Like … him with you."

"Don't say that."

"But—"

"Don't fucking say that."

The level of his tone drew the attention of other patrons in the bar, but Alessio didn't give a shit about anyone but himself right now. Hell, he'd been selfless for far too long. Time to be selfish for once.

Right?

Chris straightened on the stool but continued staring at the bar top. "Is it the fact he might care for someone else like he does for you, or that it's *you and him*?"

Alessio clenched his teeth. "Leave it alone."

Because it was both.

Except it wasn't at the same fucking time.

He didn't need this shit right now.

Chris nodded, adding, "I don't think he saw it until recently … why she made him—"

"Lie?"

Hide things from him?

Break their agreement?

Ruin them?

"I know you don't want to hear this, but she brings out the same thing in him as you," Chris said, turning to step off the stool at the same time. "And … because no one else will tell you … you should be aware. He's a happier version of him when he's with her, even if he doesn't see. It's the same thing I see when he's with you."

Alessio's jaw clicked from how hard he clenched. "Except that's not how it is for us. That's not how *we* work. It's us, not us and someone else. Not me and him, and him and someone *else*. This isn't how it goes."

"Les—"

"Just fuck off, Chris."

Leave me alone.

He'd rather be back with his pain or numbness instead of this.

It was easier.

"You will never understand why if you don't let him explain. And yeah, it's fucked up … yeah, it hurts, I bet," Chris added quieter, "but that doesn't mean you can't find something *right* somewhere in the mess. You can't do that here, though, not alone. Let him explain, or—"

"What is there to explain?"

It was clear to him.

"Why her?" he asked around the rim of his glass.

Chris chuckled. "You could always try to find out."

Right.

Not a bad idea.

He didn't think Chris meant so in the same way Alessio took it.

Yeah, he would find out.
All of it.
Whether or not Corrado liked it.

2.

Ginevra

You're a Calabrese woman—act like you know what that means and keep your eyes on the only man who'll ever be able to touch you.

Those words, said to her by her oldest brother when she first met the man she would be forced to marry, drifted through Ginevra's mind as she was reminded yet again why morning sex with Corrado was the *best* kind of sex. He had that energy—echoing around his being when he first cracked his eyes open. Like he needed to touch, and she was the closest thing he could find in his bed to do it.

She doubted her brother would approve of this.

Of this man, the way he was touching her, never mind the way she watched him as he did it all like there was nothing else he would rather be doing.

The sharp bite from Corrado found the junction of Ginevra's shoulder as she leaned down over his body, her hand pressing against his chest to keep her steady as she rode her way closer to heaven.

And what a beautiful heaven it would be.

"*Fuck*, you look good like this," she heard him say in a moan, his fingers at her waist tightening to almost a painful point. "Love it when you ride me, Ginny."

"I'm gonna—" Ginevra stiffened on top of Corrado, the wild rhythm of her hips moving against his stilling even as his continued driving into her. His fingers at her throat tightened, and she caught sight of his *oh, so pleased* sneer curving his lips as he watched her come on top of him. "*Corrado.*"

"Fuck, yeah, give me a taste of *that,* Ginny."

He only let her stay on his cock long enough to let her get the orgasm rushing through her bloodstream before his hand let her throat go. His fingers dug into her hips, and with a firm pull, he had yanked her up his body until her thighs were sitting on either side of his face. She didn't have time to appreciate the loss of his length stretching her out before his lips enclosed her clit, and he was sucking hard. She finished the orgasm off shaking while sitting on his face.

Crying loud.

Blinded.

And wishing the feeling would go on forever. She'd happily die like this. Almost numb all over, but with tingles racing up her spine, over her shoulders, and then danced over the rest of her body.

She couldn't breathe.

And it was glorious.

"Fuck, fuck, *fuck*," he groaned against her sex.

So sensitive.

Still trembling.

Way too sensitive.

Still, she couldn't move, instead rocking her hips against the lashes of his tongue taking whatever her body would give him. Fast jerks of his arm against her thigh said he was stroking his cock, and almost at his own release.

And even if she hadn't felt him doing it, she would have known by the sounds coming out of his mouth. God knew she didn't need to be in this man's bed, causing more of a problem than she already had in his life, but she'd found herself in it time and time again since the first—chasing a high, wanting to have what he gave her again.

She'd not been much for sex before—not an angel, sure, but she didn't have sex *just* to have sex. And yet, that's why she wanted to be here with Corrado doing this. Because this was so fucking good, and he kept drawing her in for more. *Sex is sex*, he'd say, and he wasn't wrong. Sex was physical, a release. It only had emotional weights when someone brought them along.

Was this emotional?

Right then?

God, yeah.

The problems those emotions might cause?

Well …

Fuck it.

Selfish?

Yes.

But why didn't she care again?

Oh, yeah, because of the man with his face currently buried between her thighs. Guilt was hard to comprehend when you still had the tendrils of an orgasm sliding through your veins. Or easier to fucking swallow.

"*You want this?*"

The gruffness of his tone dragged her back into the present with a shudder. Something about his voice changed during sex. But in a really good way. She loved the sound of his voice anytime, but it ramped up like this.

"Ginevra, do you want it?"

"Yeah," she mumbled.

She understood what he asked.

What he *wanted*.

"Now, kitten."

She slipped down his body, her hands steady against the sheets as she moved. Still spinning high, and loving the way he watched her as she took over at his cock once he'd pulled the condom off, she took him in her mouth and hands. She sucked and worked him as his fingers threaded in her hair to pull tight, and his hips flexed upward against her rhythm. Satiny and hot against her tongue, the hint of salt said he would blow soon.

Another one of those groans left his lips—heady, and deep. So fucking husky, too. Her name followed right after, and his tightening fingers stilled in her hair.

"Fuck, kitten …"

The pet name made her shiver. He'd used the name the morning after they first had sex. *Because you are*, he'd said, *as soft as a kitten during sex*. Because he was rough enough for them both.

"*Ginevra.*"

He came hard, and she took every drop he gave, letting her throat relax as she swallowed him down. She released him from her mouth, but kept her fingers tight to his base as she stared up at him from his cock.

Corrado grinned back at her. "Look at you, huh?"

She smiled back.

"What's that mean?"

"You ... There's something about you like that."

"Tell me when you figure it out."

Corrado laughed darkly. "I *will*. I definitely will."

She had no doubt.

"Let me clean up, yeah?"

Her lips curled up in dislike of the idea, but he only chuckled, and waved his hand. The action alone was enough to remind her that, yeah, he'd taken the condom off, and needed to handle it. She gave a little huff before rolling off him. The sound of his laugher colored up the bedroom. His hand landed to the palm of her ass with a soft crack, before grabbing the spot, and rolling her over in the sheets.

Corrado dropped a quick kiss to her lips as he climbed over her body to leave the bed. The loss of him seemed substantial as she watched his naked backside disappear into the bathroom. But that was a nice sight, too.

Very nice.

"I have something to do today," he said, voice filtering out of the bathroom.

Ginevra sat up into a cross-legged position in the bed, dragging the sheets to cover her nakedness. She needed to cover herself. Hide what she had done again. Corrado slipped out of the attached bathroom into the walk-in closet.

"Oh?" she asked.

In his tone she found the truth.

Relief, but wariness.

Love but anger.

"Are you going to see Alessio?"

There, she asked.

Ginevra figured if she had any business being in this man's bed after everything, then she at least needed to have the courage to ask him outright about the situation at hand. Right? That didn't mean she would like the answer.

Still, she *had* to ask.

All the noise in the closet quieted, and the silence echoed. A few seconds passed before Corrado came to the doorway, still naked except now he'd pulled on a pair of clean boxer-briefs. Dragging a hand through his hair, his gaze darted around at everything except for her before finally, he met her stare.

"Yes," he said. "He wants to meet up at a place two blocks away. A restaurant, my brother's."

Ginevra nodded and stared down at the sheets bunched at her waist. "Okay."

Her voice came out faint.

"Ginevra."

Her hands became interesting.

The sheets, too.

Anything but his face.

"I hope you figure ... whatever ... out."

"*Ginny*."

There were things she didn't want to ask. Stuff the two of them didn't need to talk about yet because she wasn't sure she would like what happened after. She needed to understand why Corrado would take her to bed again and again, but not seem to have an ounce of guilt. What kind of relationship did those two men have inside their bedroom?

Was *this* really okay?

She didn't have a good grasp on her own emotions here.

Dirty.

Blissed.

Ashamed.

Wild.

She felt all of it ….

That's what held her back; kept her quiet.

Ginevra dragged in a shaky breath and decided changing the topic might get them away from this for now. Oh, it wouldn't fix the deep ache in her heart, or how the bed suddenly seemed cold.

"Have you heard anything about New York—my sisters?" she asked.

Still, she stared at her hands on the sheets.

Not at him.

"Not yet," Corrado murmured, "but I can try to get a message through, and see what comes out."

She sighed. "All right."

At night, home filled her mind. About her *sisters*. When no one saw her struggle, or how she cried over things she couldn't control and the fears keeping her company, that's when she allowed herself to wonder.

All the things that might happen, and her helplessness. A rock and a hard place.

It was funny, though, how when she crawled into Corrado's bed at night, and he dared to tell her everything would be okay, she trusted him.

Her worries left.

Sleep came easier.

Or hell, maybe it wasn't funny at all.

• • •

"The building is secure, no one knows you're here," Corrado had told Ginevra before he left, "so you're fine to stay here alone. I'm trusting you not to do something to change that—yeah?"

And then he left.

For the first few minutes, Ginevra wandered the large penthouse, moving from room to room trying to find something to keep her occupied. She used to enjoy being alone, but not right now.

She didn't want to consider what Corrado might do with someone else instead of being there with her—where she wanted him to be. Because that was *most* selfish of her. She didn't have any claim here, and not over Corrado. She was the *other*.

She expected nothing from him.

Ginevra wouldn't wallow on the topic, either. It only hurt her more, and she shouldn't feel that, either.

Not now.

Eventually, she found herself in the office and library space again. Her fingers drifted along the edge of a shelf, taking in the spines of the books lined up by size. Not a single one was bigger than the other in whatever row she stared at—all matched. She often came back to this space in the penthouse because for whatever reason, this comforted her.

More than the books, and the escape provided by the words.

Something about here … she craved it; something she didn't even find in Corrado.

Soon, Ginevra found the book she had been looking for on the fourth shelf up from the floor. A book of poems by an author named only as *Anonymous*. That's what had drawn her to the book in the first place; someone didn't want to put their name on their words. As though instead of claiming their art, they wanted to *give* the words to people without the pretense of who created them, or why.

She kept coming back to the book of poems, all ranging in topics from everything like love, to the way sunlight looked on a sidewalk in the month of May. There wasn't rhyme or rhythm to them, but she liked that. She would come into the library, find the book, and read a few pages before sliding it back into the slot.

Someone else had read this *a lot* before she ever found the book. A cracked spine and the dog-eared pages told the story of someone else's appreciation of the words inside.

Opening to her last page, she always remembered the page number and didn't need to dog-ear to find her place, she became lost in words again. Time slipped by when she had a book in her hands, and nothing else to do.

She flipped to a new page—the start of a new poem—when a familiar voice came from behind her, almost making her drop the book.

Goddammit.

"What are you doing in here? Are you supposed to be alone where you might … oh, I don't know, *run?*"

Alessio.

He had a darker quality to his voice than Corrado's. She noticed that about him first. Both spoke with deep tenors that made her pay attention, but something was *different* about Alessio's.

Like he was always holding back.

Never giving *everything.*

Refusing to let the man behind her see he had scared her, Ginevra continued reading the poem as she replied, "Why would I run?"

"I'm not sure if you want to be here."

Ginevra almost laughed. "I didn't at first; I wanted to be with my sisters, but I also don't get a choice, so here I am."

"That doesn't mean you want to be here, though."

"Right now, I do."

He made a noise behind her—gruff, and *curious*. She didn't understand what to make of that, or why he came here again, although it was *his* home along with Corrado, so she focused on things that made sense.

Like the book of poems in her hand.

"Did you trick him again to come here alone?"

Alessio chuckled. "And if I did?"

"He won't like that."

"He doesn't seem to give a shit about what I like lately, either. Fair is fair, yeah?"

Ah.

Yeah.

Ginevra wouldn't argue that point.

"But what *are* you doing in here?" he asked.

"Reading."

"Why?"

"Because I like to."

Alessio made another one of those noises. "But *why?*"

"I like how others express themselves in words. Everyone is different. I'll read just about anything—*not* a standard textbook meant to teach me something; I learn more reading things that aren't being spoon-fed like I should fit in the same box as everyone else. You can tell a lot more about someone in the way they write than in the things they say."

"Huh."

She didn't expect the response.

Then, again …

"That's not the answer I expected you to give," Alessio murmured. "But still a good one."

Yeah, she was full of surprises.

"It's the only right answer for me. That's why I majored in English." Ginevra shook her head, laughing under his breath. "Not that college matters with me here, I guess."

"You'll get back to school, eventually."

"Who knows?"

"You will. I'm sure he'll make sure of that, if it makes you happy."

She stilled in place.

Did he mean Corrado?

Ginevra turned, only enough to watch Alessio where he stood in the doorway. Not much about him had changed in the time since she had seen him last. He still wore all black, from the jeans molded to his legs, to his leather jacket, and even the black necklace with a cross made of skulls hanging down from his throat. His face, still hauntingly handsome, seemed carved from stone. His eyes, hiding secrets and warring emotions, nailed into her from across the room.

She stayed quiet as he scrutinized her. Not because he bothered her. Oh, he unsettled her, sure, and made her fine hairs stand on end, but she didn't *dislike* it, though. She found something familiar in his gaze and recognized it. That intensity in his gaze as he surveyed her from a safe distance was the same way Corrado liked to watch her when he assumed she wasn't looking.

That was the unsettling part.

The only thing that had changed about the man in the doorway since the last time she laid eyes on him was his hair. He lost the shaggy mane he seemed to hide his gaze behind. Shortened around the sides, but still long on the top to push the strands back, if he wanted. A touch wild, still, but more tamed.

It suited him better.

Not that she had any business thinking that at all.

Then, all at once, Alessio rocked back on his heels, hands loose in his pockets, before he came forward, closing the distance between them. Ginevra didn't know if she should keep standing there or get the hell out of his way. That concentration stayed in his gaze like he wanted to burn her to the ground right where she stood, but as though he also found her *extremely* interesting.

Would he hurt her?

Would he do something to her to hurt Corrado?

Those were things she didn't know.

The closer Alessio came, the more Ginevra teetered on a sharp edge. He wasn't the only one curious and muddled in his heart and mind. She only had to *look at him* to feel those things.

What was it about him?

There was something about him that Corrado loved—something that made him get out of bed far earlier than he normally would to chase a *chance*. What was it?

She wondered ... how did they fall in love?

"What are you reading?" he asked.

Ginevra broke their staring contest to look down at the book. "*A Life Lived in Words* by—"

"Anonymous."

Swallowing hard, she peeked back up to find he stood next to her. She would still use *overwhelming* to describe this man, and his presence. Imposing fit, too, but she didn't feel like he was imposing on her or this space she adored so much.

"It's my book," Alessio said, "I found it at a used bookstore in Portugal. Figured it was ... strange, spine cracked, pages smudged like someone had read the words repeatedly. One of *five* English books in that store."

"Maybe someone lost it?"

"Possibly, but I bought it, and the book made its way into this library."

Ginevra blinked. "It's yours."

"I just said that."

"No, I mean ... the library here."

Alessio raised a single dark brow high, and with his new haircut, she realized how much *easier* she could see the things he had hid behind shaggy hair.

"Corrado only reads things that are legal, and he needs to sign."

Ginevra laughed. "That can't be true."

"Mostly, yeah."

"Someone needs to fix that. Did you dog-ear the pages, too?"

The corner of Alessio's mouth twitched. "And what if I did?"

"That's a crime."

"Well, it ain't your book, girl."

She narrowed her gaze at him, half-playful and yet still serious. "Or use a fucking bookmark. And you can call me *Ginevra,* or Ginny. But *not* girl."

His lips twitched *again.*

Then, he smiled.

A full-blown grin.

The first thing to come to her mind?

My God.

Because it was devastating.

Not sardonic, or sly. Not jealous, or angry.

No, just *genuine.*

And his smile was beautiful.

Ginevra's heart squeezed painfully. What in the hell was wrong with her? She had no place thinking something like that about this man.

Not at all.

Alessio's blue eyes flashed with something she didn't recognize. Another thing he was holding back.

Did he do that a lot?

Stop, Ginevra, you don't need to worry about this man.

"I didn't get the chance to finish the book," Alessio said, dropping her gaze to peek at the book again. "*And this thing, misunderstood and overlooked, vivid but understated, and which shatters and grows and is, will always be, at the heart, most human. For we love, we always love.*"

Ginevra blinked.

Stunned.

She said nothing as she flipped back the pages, knowing where to find those words he spoke. She found it easily. One of the *first* poems in the book. She remembered it, too, because she thought it was one of the best in the book. One or two, sometimes three, words to a line, three stanzas, of which he only spoke one, and yet, she felt every single syllable as it spoke of love being, at its core, *human.*

The last stanza of three stared up at her from the stark white pages, the corner dog-eared like Alessio had intended to come back to it, and the edge of the paper smudged like someone touched it often.

> *And this thing,*
> *misunderstood*
> *and overlooked,*
> *vivid*
> *but understated,*
> *and which shatters*
> *and grows*
> *and is,*
> *will always be,*
> *at the heart,*
> *most human.*
> *For we love,*
> *we always love.*

He had known it by heart.

How long had it been since he had this book?

And he *remembered that?*

"One of my favorites in there," he said.

His fingers drifted along the edge of the book in her hands. When his fingertips brushed the side of her palm as he was pulling away, Ginevra froze. Not *because* he'd touched her at all, but because of the way it felt and what it *did*. How it warmed her and shocked her all at the same time. An energy she couldn't explain, a shift that felt *visceral*.

So fucking real.

And not at all what she asked for.

She glanced up only to find he wasn't looking at the book at all, but rather, at her. Gone was that angry, dark glint in his eyes from earlier, now replaced with *only* that curiosity she had seen.

How did the saying go?

Curiosity killed the cat.

"I don't think I wonder *why* he found something in you," Alessio murmured, "I wonder what it *is*."

Ginevra swallowed hard, confused by this man. "I didn't ask for—"

"That doesn't change that it is—it's a thing now."

Yeah.

He wasn't wrong.

Alessio tipped his head to the side, his grin deepening to something more sinful. It was enough to take her breath away, but that only left her perplexed. "Would you like to read the next one?"

Needing to break his stare, she peered down, and flipped the page without thinking. The black words printed on the white paper stared up at her, and as her gaze took the poem in, she felt her cheeks heat.

Damn.

She'd forgotten what the next one was.

> *He sounds*
> *rough,*
> *when he needs you.*
> *There is*
> *fire,*
> *as he loves you.*
> *He discovers*
> *life,*
> *as he fucks you.*

Ginevra's voice grew faint, but *hot,* as she spoke the last word. It was all of one stanza, and twenty-one words. But it felt *purposeful*, as though he'd known what the next poem in the book would be, and he wanted her to read it.

"Another favorite," he murmured.

She desperately wanted to look at *anything* but him, and yet, her gaze lifted to see what he looked like right then. So, she might know if there was something to see there that he wasn't saying.

Instead, she found him staring at her lips.

"Did you like that," he asked, his tone roughening, "watching us from the end of the hallway that night? Did you know we shared women? Us together, I mean. It was *fun*—fair game. And then there was you, and he broke the fucking rules."

"I—"

"Yes or no suffices, Ginevra. You either *liked* seeing us like that—*together*—and you want to see more, or you didn't. Yes or no."

Fine.

If that's the game he wanted to play.

"Yes."

Alessio chuckled, his thumb edging along the page in the book before raising, so he could slide the pad of the digit against the seam of her *mouth*. She hadn't expected the touch until it was right there, but she couldn't find it in herself to back away.

Not when he was looking at her like that.

Yeah …

Entirely *overwhelming*.

That's what this man was.

"If you liked that," he told her, "then you should see us when we *fuck*."

She sucked in a sharp breath.

Alessio winked before leaning in and pulling his thumb away to drop a featherlight kiss to her lips. There was something *wicked* about the kiss. How his lips moved against hers, and then his tongue swept the seam of her mouth to coax it open for him. She didn't need to be *kissing* the man whose lover she had been in bed with that morning, but she answered his kiss back.

It felt natural.

And sinful.

Then, as fast as it had happened, it was over, and he stepped back. Not that it mattered.

She felt it.

Everywhere.

The same way she could still taste him—a minty heat—lingering on her tongue and lips. Ginevra took a step back, too, needing the distance, and holding the open book closer to herself like that might stop him from doing it again. And why did she want that?

Because she liked the kiss.

As quick as it had been.

She still *liked it*.

"Why would you do that?" she asked, airless.

To hurt Corrado?

Or confuse her?

To make *this* worse?

Alessio lifted one shoulder, the hint of a smile creeping in. "I wanted to know if your lips were as soft as they looked, that's all."

She still couldn't breathe.

"That was why?"

"Does there have to be another reason?"

Ginevra wished her throat wasn't so tight, or that her heart would calm. "I think there is when the circumstances here are not—"

"If I wanted to cause Corrado pain, because I know that's what you think, I wouldn't use you to do it. I know the best place to hit that man to make it hurt, and I promise it isn't *you*. Not yet, anyway. We'll see if that changes."

"What does that even mean?"

"It means, I kissed you because I wanted to. Nothing else, so don't make it into something when it's nothing."

It didn't feel like nothing.

She was sure, to him, it couldn't be *nothing*.

"But you shouldn't—"

"I shouldn't do a lot of things I do, and here I still am, doing it."

Ginevra ran the tip of her tongue along the edge of her lips, finding more of his flavor there. "You're a complex man."

Perplexing.

And difficult, likely.

She had that feeling.

Alessio hummed low and waved a finger at her. "You're not wrong."

Well, at least he knew what he was.

That was a start.

"You should go back to the spot where I had to stop reading, and start from there," he said, turning and dropping into a nearby chair like his body was water, and it all moved at once. Hooking his combat boots one over the other at the ankles along the arm of the chair, he nodded at her. "Go on, it's been a while since someone read me poetry."

"You want me to read to you?"

"Why not?"

Yes.

That was a good question.

Why not?

Ginevra didn't have an answer.

So, she found the page he'd left dog-eared toward the middle of the book, the last marking he had made, and read. Alessio watched her the whole time, and she felt that, too.

His gaze?

Yeah.

She felt that right down to her bones. Like he was trying to figure her out, or learn what made her tick by staring at her. But what did he think he would find?

That was the better question.

3.

Corrado

What the fuck are you nervous for? It's Les. Les.

Corrado's thoughts were a special brand of his own personal hell as he parked his vehicle along the side of the restaurant that belonged to his twin. One of the few businesses Chris cared to use on his investment portfolio.

Cutting the engine on the black Porsche, he stared at the windows lining the side of the business, but the glare of the sunlight kept him from seeing inside. Where would Alessio be sitting in there? Near a window to watch people—he liked doing that—so did that mean he could see Corrado right then? Or was he sitting nearer to the front?

He drummed his fingers to the leather-wrapped steering wheel, trying to shake off that edginess. It didn't work, instead burrowing even deeper into his heart. How long had it been since Alessio showed up in Toronto now?

Two days shy of three weeks.

Nearly three weeks Corrado had spent wondering, and worrying, and … too much. He knew Alessio needed his time, but that didn't make it any easier on Corrado even though he still tried to give his lover space.

And *now* …

Now he wanted to close that space.

Fuck it.

Refusing to over think this more than he already had, Corrado pulled the fob, that also acted as the key, from the starter, and opened the Porsche's suicide doors to step out into the bright daylight. The humid August air wrapped around his three-piece suit, reminding him that black had been a bad choice for the day, but screw it.

He liked a good suit.

Taking the walkway along the side of the building, he entered the restaurant at the front, stepping under the entrance enclave that welcomed patrons with gold and black drapery that spoke of the truth behind this place.

Mob owned.

Specifically, Guzzi owned.

All one needed to do was look at the color scheme, gold and black. The Guzzi family colors, they showcased them on their coat of arms, throughout their businesses, and anywhere else they might be able to sneak it in. One of the few things someone was able to count on where his family's legacy was concerned. Before the Guzzis had become synonymous with crime, they had made their riches in black gold.

Oil.

Inside, Corrado greeted the woman behind the podium, but didn't bother to let her direct him inside the restaurant. She recognized his face—it matched her boss's, considering it was Chris's place, and she was accustomed to the Guzzis coming and going. Beyond the entrance, Corrado found a busy restaurant waiting for him.

Tables full.

Booths at the windows busy, too.

The breakfast bar had patrons milling around.

Exactly as he thought. It wasn't what he expected to find that irked the hell out of him, but rather, what he didn't find.

Alessio.

Corrado's gaze searched the large main floor of the restaurant, but he didn't find Alessio's familiar face. There was a small private dining area that Chris liked to use for private meetings, but he didn't think Alessio would be back in the area.

Which meant one thing ...

"Fucking hell."

Alessio had tricked him again.

Corrado was tiring of that goddamn game.

A quiet chuckle at his left had Corrado turning to see who was laughing, because for some reason, it felt like they were laughing at him. The universe seemed to enjoy having a laugh at his expense, so why would this be different?

To his left, he found his twin.

Chris drank from a cup of coffee with steam rising around the rim where he sat in a booth next to the window. "Looking for someone?"

"Were you aware he planned this?"

"I had breakfast with him this morning, so yes ... and no."

Corrado's jaw tensed. "And you didn't give me a heads-up, or ...?"

"He showed up here, Corrado. He knows this is where I do business in the mornings, and where I take my breakfast. I figured out his plan after he asked if I would be around because you might show up. Right before he left."

A sigh passed his lips.

Chris shrugged. "But hey, at least he's out of the mansion now."

That made Corrado pause. "Excuse me?"

"Ma and Papa's place—that's where he was staying."

"What?"

And his mother and father didn't think to tell him?

That irked him, too.

Sort of ...

To be fair, he hadn't called his parents and asked them anything about Alessio, or his whereabouts, because he figured they probably didn't know. Why would they? And, he also didn't want to bother them with everything going on in his life, but especially the personal shit. Didn't they have enough to deal with?

Another part of Corrado found it comforting that Alessio went to his parents', out of all the places he might have hidden himself away. Like *that's* where he thought would be safest for him. *Corrado's family.*

Huh.

Chris took a drink from his coffee. Corrado figured that looked like something he should do, too. Relax for a minute and rethink this whole thing before he headed back to the penthouse to deal with the frustrating man waiting for him. Waving at a server passing with a tray of dishes she'd bussed from a table nearby, he was quick to say, "Another black coffee over here, if you wouldn't mind."

He'd add in his own sugar and cream from the table.

The server gave him a bright smile. "Sure, sir."

Chris eyed him from the side. "You're not going right home? I figured you would, knowing he's with her."

Corrado shook his head and dropped into the booth opposite of his brother. "He's not going to hurt her. Not Les's style, and all."

"I didn't assume that, either." Chris cleared his throat and dropped his brother's gaze. "I meant, more that you might be jealous the two of them are alone together."

"Why?"

"Because if someone I was fucking was alone with someone else, and the circumstances were ... like yours, I might get irritated about it."

Corrado nodded. "And you're not me ... or him."

Or her, but Ginevra was still a wild card here.

"I don't understand how your relationships work at all."

Corrado laughed. "You don't have to. It's not *your* relationship, and you're not the one they're fucking, Chris."

"That's probably a good thing."

Right?

"Besides," Corrado said, pulling the sugar and cream bowls closer to him as the server neared their table with a carafe of coffee ready, "the more time they spend with one another, the better it'll be for me."

Chris arched a brow at the statement, but waited until the server had poured Corrado's cup of coffee, and then left them alone before he spoke. "Why would that be good for you?"

That seemed obvious.

Corrado lifted his shoulders. "Then, perhaps I can get what I want."

"Which is ...?"

"Both."

Chris let out a sigh across the table, giving his brother *the* look. They both used it—identical twins and all, right? It said he was annoyed and amused all in one breath. "That's a little selfish, yeah? You made a mess in your relationship with one, and then you dragged the other one into it without giving them the benefit of knowing what you were doing first. And now you want both like they should just ... fall in line?"

"That's fair." Corrado stirred sugar into his coffee first, following up with the cream. "But it still feels right."

That's what mattered to him.

Besides, he wanted what he wanted.

Guzzis always got what they wanted.

• • •

Corrado didn't want to return to the penthouse pissed. He took his time going back. He figured ... Alessio clearly wanted to do something there, or whatever. He wanted *something*, and Corrado would give him the chance to find it. It wouldn't hurt Ginevra to spend time with Alessio, if she was able to handle his swinging moods.

Corrado wasn't any better in that respect, and hell, she handled him fine. He had no doubt Alessio would be the same.

So, when he stepped inside the penthouse to *laughter*, he took a second to soak it in. It confused him, sure, and he had to listen again to make sure he heard what he thought he did … but yes, they were laughing.

Together.

Corrado didn't bother to kick off his shoes, or remove his jacket before heading down the entrance. He came to a stop at the end, staying beyond the entryway to stare into the sitting room, finding the laughter.

The first thing he noticed?

Alessio had cut his hair.

Gone was his almost *a-little-too-long* shaggy dark brown, almost black, style, only to be replaced with a shorter, but still wild, style. It never escaped Corrado's notice how Alessio was, in many ways, his opposite. Corrado was the calm to Alessio's storm. From the way they styled their hair, to the clothing they wore.

Corrado would never ink his skin.

Never pierce his body.

Alessio did those things and more.

Regularly.

He liked this new hairstyle though. It showed Alessio's eyes, even if all Corrado could see was the man's profile. Now, Alessio didn't have dark strands of hair to hide behind when he didn't want someone to look in his gaze—which was where Corrado always found the truth hiding.

Sitting opposite to Alessio on the couch with her legs thrown over the back as she rested on her back, and played the game on the television, Ginevra laughed again as Alessio shook his head.

"That's what he's saying here, okay, it says right there in the line. That's how you know he's talking about sunlight in this one. *Streams shooting high, blinding and bright, yellows and—*"

"It could be a sh*e,*" Ginevra replied, never looking away from the game as she conversed. "You're *assuming* it's a man, and you shouldn't. Anonymous might be a woman. A lot of the poems in the book reference *men,* anyway. Sex, relationships, love … many discuss men, and not in *first person,* either."

Alessio made a noise under his breath. "It could be a man talking about all of those things with another man, too."

Corrado blinked.

Were they talking about …

Poetry?

"So, what you mean to say is your *bias*—because you're a bisexual, and in a relationship with a man—clouds how you interpret poems written by someone, who for all we know, is genderless, faceless, and … well, personless."

Alessio stared hard at Ginevra, even though she wasn't looking back at him. Corrado found himself all too amused at the concentration knotting Alessio's brow as he took in Ginevra like he was trying to figure her out. *Finally,* someone to challenge this man and his need for words.

Corrado could never do it.

Reading wasn't his thing.

"How did we go from talking about whether this poem is referencing sunlight to you deciding I'm biased on the author of it?" Alessio asked, cocking his head to the side as his gaze narrowed on the woman who was still playing her game like this wasn't at all a big deal to her. "Because maybe I like to put pronouns on things, Ginny. It doesn't have to be that *deep*."

"Oh, but it does, because everything is deep, Les. *Everything* when you read, or how you interpret it, but especially poetry, has meaning. The things you find between the lines, for example. Word play. It is all important. That is the author's intention, but more so one who wrote an entire book of poetry under the name *Anonymous*, because they wanted you to consider them, or perhaps ..."

"What?"

"Perhaps it was written with the intention to put yourself in their place."

Ginevra paused the game and turned to give Alessio all of her attention. A small smile curved her pretty, pink lips, and the sly glint in her eyes only added to the appeal. Alessio stared back, engrossed in the conversation, and unwilling to back away.

Good, Corrado thought. *Now he can see why ... maybe.*

There was something about Ginevra.

Something that *fit*.

Not just him.

Alessio, too.

"Maybe, it was written like it was," Ginevra said, "because the author wanted to write it for you, for me, the man walking down the street, or the woman sitting on the bench in the park ... for my friend at college, or the professor at the front of the class. For *anyone*. So, every person could see the words and put themselves there. Because once a name gets attached to a book, whether we mean to, we put a face and a person to who wrote it, or what we *believe* about the person who wrote it based on the penname they chose, and what it means. Like this, we read it differently."

Alessio relaxed into the couch, considering. "Huh."

"And they could still be talking about the color yellow, and not something else, so ..."

"It's sunlight, Ginevra."

"Says you. Not once, in any of the four stanzas, does it reference the sky, clouds, the color blue, and it doesn't even use words like *overhead*, or *up above* to make us think *high*, like the sky. So, no, it doesn't have to be the sun just because you want it to be."

Her argument made, she went back to her game, unpausing it and clicking away at buttons on the remote.

"Jesus Christ," Alessio muttered, turning his attention away from her only for his gaze to land on Corrado in the hallway. For a brief second, something unknown flashed in Alessio's eyes, almost like he didn't know how to feel about the fact Corrado was there, watching them. Just as quickly, something else replaced it. *Cunningness.* "Looks like we have a visitor, Ginny."

She peeked around the edge of the couch, craning her neck just enough to see

Corrado in the hallway, before going back to the game. "Seems so."

Corrado put his focus on Alessio, for the moment. "The haircut is new."

"I like to come back with something new, don't I?"

Ginevra passed a look to her companion on the couch. "What does that mean?"

"It means he changes his appearance with different things when he's away on …" Corrado considered his words, and how he wanted to say *that*. "… a job. That's how he got the piercing in his nose, the ones in his nipples, the second sleeve of tattoos, and more. Sometimes, he keeps them, and other times, he doesn't. All depends."

Alessio grinned over at Ginevra. "Reminds me of where I've been."

"Except you didn't *really* leave, did you?"

Just like that, Alessio's smirk faded away as his gaze turned back on Corrado. "I wasn't *here*. Same difference."

"According to you. How are my parents?"

"Fantastic."

Corrado nodded. "Good. And, if you want to be here, you don't have to trick me away, Les."

"Or you shouldn't keep falling for it."

The snickers from the woman on the couch made Corrado narrow his gaze. Alessio's smirk was back in place, like he enjoyed this.

"What are you two doing?"

"Reading poetry," Ginevra said, although he couldn't see her now she'd slid lower on the couch.

"And gaming," Alessio added, "or she is … she beat your score, too."

Corrado glanced at the television.

Ginevra had done that, playing the online version which connected her to his account which he'd been working on back in Vegas.

Dammit.

He worked *months* for the score.

Oh, well.

He couldn't be mad.

Right?

4.

"Could we chat for a minute?" Corrado asked, stepping closer to the two on the couch as he nodded his head toward the back hallway leading deeper into the penthouse. "If you're ... not busy here, I mean."

Alessio might have enjoyed the sight of seeing Corrado confused—but also amused?—but he figured, this was going to happen, too. Them *talking*, like it would change what needed to be said.

It wouldn't.

Alessio wasn't ready for that.

"Why not?" Alessio tossed the book of poems to the couch before standing. Then, to Ginevra, he said, "And it's still talking about sunlight."

She grinned but didn't look away from the TV.

"Probably," she returned, "but we don't know for sure, do we?"

He arched a brow, considering those words. She wasn't wrong, but he thought she also didn't realize how her words could be applied to a lot of other things in his life currently. Like *this*, and Corrado. Them, and whatever the hell they were doing.

He was here because he needed to be.

A part of him searching for something.

Another part wanting to *fix it*.

Yet, he wasn't sure if those things were possible. Would he find what he was looking for here, and could they fix the mess they were now in? He was going to try for both, but he didn't know anything for sure.

"Also," Ginevra said while Alessio rounded the couch, "if you two could just *talk*, and not ... you know, do what you did before while I sit out here alone, that'd be great. I would appreciate it."

Alessio passed Corrado a look, smirking a bit at the sight of his lover's face brightening with his surprise at Ginevra's frankness. Did he not get that from her a lot? Because Alessio found Ginevra was straightforward when she wanted to be, and he enjoyed that.

More than he should.

"Oh, she's sassy," Alessio said, heading for the hallway, "and you know how I like that."

Corrado's sigh echoed.

Alessio's laughter chased behind it.

He took the first door in the hallway, to the master bedroom. Not five seconds later, Corrado followed behind Alessio, although he didn't close the door. The sheets on the bed had been thrown aside. Rumpled and messy.

Two people slept here.

Fucked there.

"I thought you didn't want to be in here because I was—"

"It's not about the sex," Alessio said, turning fast to face Corrado where he

236

stood just beyond the doorway. "It was never about the fact you wanted to fuck her, Corrado."

"Yeah, I know." Corrado stuffed his hands into his pockets as Alessio took a seat in the chair near the far window. There, he could watch Corrado's reflection, but also enjoy the cloudless sky overhead. "Did you want to be alone with her today—this was purposeful?"

"Yep."

"Could you try *not* being an asshole, or make any trouble, because you're in your feelings right now? This is bigger than us—it's about her safety, too. That's why she's here in the first place, to stay out of sight, and be somewhere safe while Andino Marcello handles her family in New York."

Alessio's brow dipped. "Do you think I'm that petty?"

"Pardon?"

He stood from the chair, deciding he could do without comfort while he handled this *thing* Corrado was dancing around. Closing the space between them with wide strides, Alessio came toe to toe with Corrado, and only then did he speak again.

"Do you think I am so petty I would put her in danger because you *like her*? Is that the man you believe I am, Corrado? Because if so ... we need to have a different discussion."

He let that hang between them.

It was Corrado's move now.

God knew Alessio didn't come here because he wanted to shout and fight again. They'd done that already—he said enough shit to last them a lifetime. That's not what this was about, now.

He was *trying*.

Corrado needed to try, too.

"I know *exactly* what kind of man you are," Corrado murmured, holding Alessio's gaze, and refusing to drop it, "but I also know when you're hurt, you act out even when you don't mean to, Les. So, if you're still working on *that* ... let me know. Her safety here—not from *you*, not like that—is a priority for me."

Alessio made a noise, deep and dark. "And what other priority does she have?"

"See, like *that*."

Okay, so Corrado wasn't wrong.

Alessio put his attitude in check.

"I'm working on it," Alessio said simply. "It's the best I can do."

"All right."

Alessio broke their stare first, instead finding a spot on the wall to focus on as he said, "I'm here because it's more than just her right now. It's us, too. You owe me that—to decide this, and what we're doing together. You owe it to me, Corrado."

"I do."

"That's all you want to say?"

"That should be all I need to say. Is it confusing and a mess? Yeah, Les, I know. But you're *here*, so I can deal with the rest, and we can figure that out as we go. I can't change the circumstance, and even if I could ... I don't know if I want to."

"Right, because you're *happy* with what you did. You're pleased with what you've got here right now. A woman you want to keep, and a man you can't let go of—with you in the middle, huh?"

"And you seem to think that's *easy* for me. Like this mess doesn't keep me up at night wondering what the fuck happened, or why, and you're wrong. Because I know what I did, but I'm the only one trying to figure it out or fix it right now."

"No, I'm here. *I'm here.*"

That should mean something.

Shouldn't it?

Alessio thought so.

"I just … want to know why," Alessio said, shrugging one shoulder and still focusing on that spot on the wall. It was easier than looking at Corrado because when he did that, his emotions came into play, and he couldn't compartmentalize the anger and sadness and betrayal with the parts of him that didn't want to feel any of those things at all. "Why her, and why *this*. But also, why she has you like this … why you did this *now* … after five fucking years, you did this now."

"Do you want to know?"

"*Yes.*"

He figured that was obvious.

Or it should be.

"But do you *really*," Corrado pressed, making Alessio's attention snap back to him at the deeper tenor his tone took on. "Because you've always been touchy, Les, about me, what's yours, and when you think someone is encroaching on things that belong to only you. Yeah, you don't make it obvious sometimes, but you still do it. And don't act like you didn't come here because you felt like someone was *encroaching* on me, and you didn't like that."

It was the challenge in Corrado's stare that kept Alessio silent—the unspoken *I dare you to lie right now* that Corrado wouldn't say.

"Well?" Corrado asked.

Alessio swallowed the thickness in his throat. "You're not wrong."

It was his favorite way to say someone was right *without* showing his whole ass even if it irritated Corrado to no end.

"She's not a man," Alessio said, "so I shouldn't have felt that way at all, but I did because you *hid her* and your intentions. You put me in this position, in this fucking head space I don't want to be in, and I can't jump right out of it because you snap your goddamn fingers and tell me to."

"I don't expect you to."

"But I don't know what I want to do now, either," Alessio muttered, "and that pisses me off more. You didn't give me a choice here, Corrado. I'm here, or I'm *gone*. Those are the options I have … five fucking years with you, and those are the options I'm left with. To stay here, and watch you *be* with her because you want to, or walk away alone. It should be an easy choice—I'm tired of what we've been doing, but I've still got *you*, right?"

"Until I die, yeah."

Alessio sneered, angry again just like that. "So, yeah, you put me back there like you did five years ago. Where I have to make the choice between keeping you, because at least I get a part of what I love, or walking away and having none of it. So thank you for that, really."

"Les—"

"Just, don't."

Corrado dragged in a heavy breath and dropped Alessio's stare. "It's only like that because you don't want me to tell you what you want to hear right now because she's involved. If she wasn't here, you'd let me say and tell you *all of it*. The shit I didn't say five years ago, the issues you kept running from, and I ignored ... I'd say it but she's here, and that changes it for you again."

Again, he wasn't wrong.

Alessio shook his head. "I want to understand why it was her. Why now?"

They weren't even questions.

Mostly because, he didn't know if there were answers.

"I can explain it, but once I do, when it's all out there, everything will change again. Is that what you want to happen? Because I will, Les. I'll say what you wanted me to say for the last five years, but I will say something about her, too, and it will change things. So, if that's what you need, and you want to handle all of it, then let me know."

Alessio stayed quiet.

He heard what Corrado said.

He knew what it meant.

And fuck ...

"Not yet," he said under his breath. "I don't think I can understand yet, and I know it's important to you, and *this* ... I need time."

"Just tell me when."

Time for Alessio also meant space—he needed *both*. Which was fucking hilarious, the world was laughing at his stupid ass, because at the same time ... he didn't want to leave here. He needed to *be* here. Something inside told him he wouldn't find what he needed *away* from Corrado, and this home.

"I'm staying here, though. In this penthouse, I mean."

Corrado shrugged like he expected nothing different. "Our names are on the deed. It's your home, too. You good?"

"Not even close."

"I'm sorry."

But all it took was Corrado's hand coming out from his side so that his fingertips could glide along the inner skin of Alessio's wrist. A *soft* touch, something he wasn't at all used to with this man when they were doing their thing. He expected roughness ... but never in their quiet moments, he knew.

Never then.

Alessio let out a slow stream of air, flipping his hand around, and let his fingers weave with Corrado's. The touch was brief, with featherlight pressure, and he didn't look at his lover, but he needed that.

A *them* moment amid everything else.

It was good.

Right.

Then, Alessio let Corrado go, and moved to head out of the bedroom, but stopped beside him first to say, "And I kissed her earlier, so you know."

Corrado cleared his throat. "Did you?"

"I did."

"Hmm." Corrado glanced to the side, cocking a brow when his gaze met Alessio's. "Was that because you wanted to hurt me, confuse her, or something else?"

Alessio smirked.

Really?

"One—I don't need to use her to hurt you. *Ever.*"

"Fair," Corrado replied.

"Two—that woman is a lot of things, but confused isn't one of them when she's getting something she wants. And she wanted that."

"Be careful with that, she's not used to this thing like we are." Then, Corrado nodded, his tongue peeking out to run along the edge of his bottom lip. "So, your reason for doing it was the *something else?*"

"I wanted to kiss her. That's all."

"And you always take what you want, don't you?"

Alessio winked. "That I do."

Back in the living room, Alessio took his position on the couch he had vacated earlier. Ginevra looked his way as he picked up the book, too, but continued playing her game like nothing was happening. Corrado hung back in the hallway like he hadn't decided whether he wanted to join them.

"So," Ginevra said, still watching the screen, her tone playful, "where is everyone sleeping?"

· · ·

The black Cartier watch on Alessio's wrist ticked past twelve at night as Corrado stepped into the penthouse's home gym. Corrado found Alessio perched on top of the bars they used for chin-ups. The single, smooth bar of metal secured between two beams wasn't the most comfortable place to sit, but it gave him a better view out of the windows, and made him seem unavailable to conversation.

Which he was because—

"Is that the book Ginevra was reading?" Corrado asked.

Alessio rolled his eyes and peered up from the words on the page. "The poems, yeah."

"Didn't she take that to bed with her?"

Why was he asking questions?

It was easier *not* to ask.

Alessio didn't want to explain that he'd felt the strangest urge to sneak that book from Ginevra's bedside table and take a peek at where she left off before falling asleep.

"I'll put it back before she wakes up," he muttered.

That was way too defensive, asshole.

Corrado's brow lifted, but he said nothing in reply to that. "Just curious."

"I noticed she's not in *your* bed," Alessio said.

"You're here," Corrado replied. "I left the option open, if she wanted, and I think her conscience sent her across the hall."

Right.

"Or her morals, yeah?"

Corrado sighed. "Are they not the same thing?"

"Not really. One means she might feel guilty, and the other says she thinks it's wrong to have sex with someone in a relationship with someone else, Corrado. Guilt is a byproduct of an action."

"I don't think the latter is the problem, all things considered."

"Or it becomes a problem when the other person is using the bedroom down the hall."

"I didn't come find you to talk about where Ginevra is sleeping," Corrado said sharply.

Ah. Who's defensive *now?*

"Well," Alessio said, shifting and dropping to the floor eight feet below soundlessly, "I suppose that means you're sleeping alone then, doesn't it?"

Corrado gave him a look.

Alessio just shrugged.

That was his way of telling his lover he wouldn't be joining him in bed, either. And if there was anything Corrado hated the most, it was sleeping alone. Maybe it was because he'd become used to Alessio sharing a bed with him over the years, or because he woke up ready to fuck as soon as he cracked his eyes open.

It could have been a lot of things.

"You should suffer a *little,*" Alessio murmured as he came to stand in front of Corrado in the doorway, "for what you did. Take your penance, Corrado."

"You're an asshole."

"Do you have something new to tell me?"

"I have a question."

Alessio tipped his head to the side, tucking that book under his arm as he shoved his other hand into his pocket. "Give it to me, then."

"Why did you go to my family when you needed time alone? I think I know … I want to hear you say it."

Alessio's shoulders tensed at the question, his heart thundering with sharp beats that ached all the way through his bloodstream. If Corrado owed him certain things, then he might as well admit there was shit he should give back to the man, too.

"They remind me of you."

Corrado's gaze drifted over Alessio with slow intent. He wanted *something.* To be close—*closer*—to touch, or to fuck. To have the thing he wanted, or one, which was Alessio. It was his gaze that always told the truth when his mouth didn't.

"Oh?" Corrado asked, his stare coming back up to meet Alessio's.

"And even when I hate you, Corrado," Alessio said, his words a whisper before he leaned in to press a quick kiss to Corrado's mouth, pulling away just as fast to add, "I still love you."

He left Corrado alone in the gym.

It was for the best even if it was the last thing he wanted. They could fuck this out like they did other fights they had in the past. They could find a familiar comfort in the physical side of this together. The thing was, it would only work for so long. More shit swept under a very dirty rug. It wouldn't *fix it.*

Sometimes, the right choice was the hard one.

Including walking away.

5.

Ginevra

Tucked into the checkered pattern bucket chair, with her feet resting on the ottoman, Ginevra was more interested in the two men across from her rather than the movie. Alessio, comfortable in a chair, set his arms along the recliner, and Corrado, on the couch next to him, kept glancing over at the other man.

Something was bothering Corrado ... She could tell in the way he kept shaking his head subtly, and his gaze kept narrowing back on Alessio every twenty or so seconds.

Ginevra couldn't figure out what.

It could be anything, really. A week after Alessio decided he was *staying* in the penthouse, and she wasn't sure what any of them were doing together, or what was happening. They all gave each other a wide berth of space, safe conversation was a must, and nobody stepped on anyone's toes.

She was back to sleeping alone.

So were they.

They all moved around each other like they were familiar strangers, as if that was possible. Nods in the mornings, and hellos at the table. Little else, though. She was sure Alessio and Corrado hadn't worked out their issues, and *she* hadn't settled herself with everything happening here, but for now ... this was what they did.

Nothing.

It was awkward.

"Jesus Christ, will you give me those?" Corrado snapped.

Alessio turned his attention from the television, a smirk playing at that edges of his lips as he did so. "Does it bother you that badly?"

"*Yes*, it's annoying. You know I hate it when you let them get like that."

What were they going on about?

Ginevra tucked herself tighter under the blanket she was using while watching the movie. This way, she could hide her grin because for a brief second, Alessio and Corrado looked like lovers arguing with one another, and not ... whatever in the fuck they had been for the last week.

She liked this sight of them more.

And that only left her confused.

"Fine," Alessio muttered.

In a blink, he flipped his wrist over, placing it across the arm of the couch where Corrado was sitting at the end. Ginevra watched, fascinated and amused, as Corrado seemed too pleased while he untangled the thin, black braided bracelets on Alessio's wrist. Maybe fifteen. All twisted into a mess of a knot because of the delicate design.

Corrado worked in silence, his gaze lifting to check what was happening on the movie, before he went back to untangling again. Alessio, as though this was normal and something Corrado did, paid the other man no mind.

Did they do this often?

Sometimes, she thought they forgot Ginevra was in the penthouse with them. They often had silent conversations, even when standing across the room from one another. Shared looks, and quiet noises she didn't understand, but they seemed to comprehend from the other just fine.

It was yet another testament to her about just how long these two men had been together. That their lives, even if on the outside they seemed entirely different, were very intertwined. They fit better together, but for now, they were still too far apart.

And she was right in the middle.

It took all of five minutes.

Alessio pulled his arm back when Corrado released his wrist, all the braided cords sitting nicely against each other instead of the mess they had been. "Better?"

Corrado shrugged. "Getting there."

"Hmm."

Ginevra raised a brow, wondering what in the hell she had just watched. "How did you two meet?"

Corrado stilled on the couch, but didn't take his gaze away from the screen. Alessio tipped his head sideways as he peered over at Ginevra.

"Work."

"Easy," Corrado muttered.

"She asked."

"That doesn't mean she needs to know."

"Except that's exactly what it means."

Corrado let out a sigh and pushed up from the couch. He didn't even bother to say goodbye, or explain what he was doing before he left the sitting room, and disappeared into the hallway. Ginevra was still staring at the spot where he'd left when Alessio grunted under his breath, gaining her attention instead.

"What was that about?" she asked.

Alessio clicked his tongue. "He doesn't *talk* well."

"He talks perfectly fine."

"Okay, his communication is sometimes shit."

Ginevra considered it. "Yeah, that's fair."

"And he's in a mood."

"I figured. It's the whys."

Alessio chuckled. "He's sleeping alone, and he isn't getting to fuck first thing when he wakes up. He doesn't have quiet time in the morning because when he does roll his ass out of bed, there's already two other people in this house that have been up for hours. Oh, and he doesn't like to run on a treadmill, but he hates jogging on a city street, so all he has is the gym here. He ran out of his favorite whiskey he likes in his nightly coffee three days ago and hasn't gone out to get more. The current ringtone on my phone irritates the hell out of him, but he won't tell me to change it. You sat on the chair instead of next to him when we started the movie. Pick one, Ginevra."

She blinked.

He ... *knew* all of that.

Like he'd been keeping a tab.

"I'm very out of place here," she murmured.

Alessio's amusement faded. "Or you need time to learn." He waved a hand, adding quieter, "He's moody, difficult, and *fickle*. Constantly. His mornings often determine how the rest of his day is going to go, and God knows it's better for everyone when it goes well. And yet, he puts up with my shit, too, or the fact he has to turn on the heat in the penthouse at night because you won't sleep under a blanket."

Ginevra guffawed. "That's—"

"The truth. Everybody's human, and it's not the flaws that make up the person … we all have those, and it's only a small portion of what defines us. Corrado isn't easy to deal with, but I'm not perfect, either, and neither are you. If you want to know why he gets into his moods, then pay attention. You'll figure it out, too."

They stared at each other, but neither spoke. He had offered her something— the confirmation she was *wanted* here, by at least one. And she was kind enough not to point it out to him.

Alessio had his pain, after all.

"So, will you tell me how you met?"

She figured a change in subject was needed.

Alessio let out a steady stream of air, his smile growing again. "The League."

"What is—"

"An … organization," he interjected carefully. "Do you want me to be frank, or color it up with goodness for you?"

"I'm sorry?"

"I know where you came from—who you are. So, you're aware of *some* things about this world, and how it works. You recognize things are not always black and white because some of us, like me and Corrado, or the people you come from, live in shades of gray."

"Corrado told me he was worse than them once. Made men, I mean. The mafia."

Alessio nodded. "He's not wrong, either."

She stilled, a chill running down her spine. "But what does it mean?"

"The League trains people—we walk in one way and walk out another. Think of it like this … a man comes back from a war, he has a *very* specialized set of skills that is no longer useful to his country, and won't help him in civilian life. What's he to do?"

"I'm not sure."

"The League does. They'll train him, and he'll either become an independent contractor for the organization, or he'll be auctioned off to a buyer who will decide, depending on his skill set, what kind of jobs he might do. Recons, hits, robberies, recoveries … more. It all depends on what someone needs, and what the person with the skills is capable of. The training takes place over a year, it's intensive, and it's *hard*."

"That's …"

"Overwhelming, isn't it?" Alessio asked, chuckling. "It's a lot to take in. Sounds like a fucking movie, huh?"

"Like it's not real."

"Except it is, and from the time I was ten, it's what I've done with The League.

I've been to twenty-eight countries, I have taken out the potential leader of a major rebellion for a government who couldn't have it on paper, and I have been on a team that went after a politician's daughter to remove her from the traffickers who took her from a family vacation on a cruise. I killed a mob boss's rival because he was causing too many problems, but he couldn't be attached to the hit. What do you think I do for a living, Ginevra? Or Corrado?"

"Hitmen doesn't sound like the right word."

Alessio scoffed. "Not even close."

"What would you call it?"

"Well, everybody likes to call it something different, but The League likes to say they train assassins. Highly skilled, dangerous, and useful depending on who has deep enough pockets to buy one of us."

Oh, wow.

Ginevra had another inkling even as the chill in her spine grew colder. "So, why is Corrado *guarding me,* then? Seems like a waste of his time if you all do ... other things."

"He owed a favor."

"Oh." Ginevra pulled the blanket down and eyed Alessio. "Ten, you said?"

"Yeah, it's about when I first came to the people who started and control the organization."

"That's very young."

"My father had been dead for years, and my mother might as well have already been six feet under what with the way she needed drugs to get her from the bed to the floor on an hourly basis. The League was a far better choice for me, trust me."

God.

Her heart hurt.

No child should feel unloved by their parents. Ginevra missed her mother more than anything in the world, and thoughts of Marie filled her mind late at night when she couldn't sleep. The pain of losing her mama would never go away, but she realized as she stared at Alessio, she would much rather deal with this kind of grief than the type he faced every day of his life.

They both hurt.

One seemed ... more painful.

"Your mom, well, you don't talk about her with fondness."

"Because I felt none."

"I'm sorry."

Alessio shrugged and grinned again. "Thing is ... I'm grateful for her, which puts me in a strange place, right? She might as well have abandoned me, like my father, and everybody else around me, too. But if not for her, then I wouldn't be here. I wouldn't have The League."

Ginevra cleared her throat. "Or Corrado, right? You said it's where you met him."

"Yeah, and him, too."

Ginevra heard his wariness. Like he wasn't sure whether meeting Corrado had been a good thing, but he didn't sound like he wanted to change it, either.

God knew she understood the feeling.

Far too well.

• • •

From her position on the chair, Ginevra was able to see the credits for the movie scrolling past, but Alessio was the most fascinating thing. She wasn't sure when he'd rested his head in his hand, and closed his eyes, but at some point, he fell asleep during the movie.

Usually, the man gave off an intensive vibe. Like he was vibrating with energy, some of it dark and enthralling, but it had nowhere to go. A simple conversation with him left her doing a deep dive through her mind and heart because even talking to the man was overwhelming.

She wasn't sure what to make of him.

What to think …

Alessio hadn't touched her since the day in the library. He hadn't even tried, really, but he observed her all the time. Similar to the way Corrado did, too. Like he both enjoyed what he was seeing, and, there was something about her that he couldn't quite figure out.

It put her on edge.

And she liked it.

Which only confused Ginevra *more*.

Like she needed this problem.

Wasn't being entangled with one of these men bad enough? For her, yes. She had enough shit to consider about Corrado without adding Alessio on top of the mix, too, but that's what a single kiss had done.

A kiss.

A few words.

Poetry.

Sharing the same space.

All of this made her consider Alessio.

Refusing to go down the damn rabbit hole again, Ginevra stood from the chair, gathering the blanket into her arms. Corrado hadn't come back after he left the living room, and she wasn't sure how to turn off the movie using the game system remote, so she let the credits play as she headed out of the space.

Not that she needed *more* shit to wonder about before bed, Ginevra still lingered in the doorway of Corrado's bedroom. He milled about the room, shedding his clothes, undoing his wristwatch, and leaving the bathroom like he wasn't at all bothered about her staring.

Finally, he turned to give her a look as, in nothing but boxer-briefs, he came up to the side of the bed, ready to get in. "Are you sleeping in the room across the hall again, then?"

Ginevra blinked.

His frankness never failed to surprise her.

"I shouldn't be in here," she said truthfully.

Corrado raised a brow. "I would prefer you in my bed."

Wow.

And he didn't pull punches, either.

"And if you think," he continued, not giving her the chance to speak, "you

246

sleeping in my bed is a problem for Alessio, you're wrong ... you're not giving this enough consideration, Ginevra. He doesn't care if you're in my bed, or if I'm fucking you in the shower first thing in the morning. It's not about *sex* for him— oh, he fucking loves that, yeah—but it's something more for him about this.

"The physical side of a relationship is probably the easiest thing for him to deal with, if I'm being honest. He can compartmentalize and comprehend all the *whys* I want to fuck you, doesn't see a problem, and because of that, doesn't care. It's not the real issue."

"Seems strange. I would imagine that part of this would be the hardest to deal with."

"Not for him, or me." Corrado shrugged one shoulder, pulled the blankets back, and slipped into the bed as he said, "It's not about the sex, and it doesn't matter how much you *think* it is, it won't change that he doesn't give a shit."

"He told me about where he came from, his mom, and stuff. After you left earlier, I mean."

Corrado made a noise under his breath, dark and irritated. Over what, though, she didn't have a clue. It could have been something hurt Alessio, or that they had a conversation. Because frankly, Alessio was right.

This man was *shit* at communication.

He needed to work on it.

"Stem it back to that," Corrado said, gesturing between them, "for this, huh? You want to understand what his problem is here—it's *that*. It's about being vulnerable to someone else for Alessio, him giving something willingly when he doesn't give it to fucking anybody."

"Loyalty. Trust."

"That, yeah. And I abused it, in a way." Corrado leaned back against the headboard, using his arms crossed behind his head as a pillow while he watched her with that stare of his, so penetrating and vast. All it took was a look, too. "So, again, if you believe this is about sex, or the fact you're in my bed might piss him off, you're wrong. It's not even a fraction of the problem."

"It's good to know, but it's not why I came in here to talk, either."

Corrado nodded at her. "What do you want, then?"

"I want to ask some things."

"*About?*"

She shifted on her feet, tightening her hold on the blanket like it might make it easier to say the words drifting through her thoughts. Because, if she wanted to *think* about two men, their relationship, and her interest in both, then shouldn't she voice those same feelings, too?

What was it her mama told her years ago?

If you suppose you're mature enough to have sex with a man, Ginevra, then you best be ready to talk about it, too.

Right.

"How long have you been together?"

Corrado smiled a little. "Five years, or so. Almost from the day we met, but it was a shaky thing for a while."

Huh.

"And you ... love him?"

"Even if he doesn't want me to say it, yes."

"Is what he told me true?"

Corrado gave her a look, murmuring, "I have no idea what he told you, Ginny."

"That you ... share women and—"

"Yes."

"Often?"

Corrado laughed. "I mean, not as often as you might assume. We didn't prowl the streets every night looking for someone to take home to fuck, kitten. If it came up, then it did. We did our thing together, too, and we slept with different women alone without the other involved."

"Sounds ... messy."

And *intriguing.*

She had so many more questions about that part of Alessio and Corrado's relationship, especially where other women came into play. But she didn't want to mull it over right then, not that her body was giving her much of a choice. She was glad she had the blanket hanging from her arms, so Corrado wasn't capable of seeing the way she shifted on her feet because the spot between her thighs was hot and aching for reasons she didn't care to admit.

"And that's what you want to keep doing with him?" she asked.

Corrado stilled on the bed, his gaze drifting from the black and gold trimmed comforter to where she still stood in the doorway. "No, not at all."

"I don't understand."

"I found what I want, even if I didn't realize I was looking for it. I don't need to look elsewhere when it's all right here, I need everybody else to figure it out now."

Well ...

That only made her more confused.

"He kissed me," she blurted. "The day he came back, I was in the library, and he kissed me."

Corrado nodded like he already was aware. "And did you like it?"

What?

She stayed quiet.

Corrado gave her another pointed stare. "Well, did you?"

"I did."

"Good, think about that, and what it means," Corrado said, gesturing at her doorway to add, "And if you're not sleeping in here tonight, then leave the door open when you leave. Good night, Ginny."

That was it—*done.*

Not that it left her with any more answers.

And she still didn't know what to do.

6.

Alessio

Are you sure you want to do this, Les?

Dare's words from their earlier phone call drifted through Alessio's mind as he flipped over another sheet on the contract spread out across Corrado's desk. Placing his hands to the edge of the curved, smooth wood, he took in the words in black ink, their ramifications not lost on him should he put his name on the dotted line.

It will require Subject One to commit to four years under contract with WHICHEVER bidder wins the bid on his or her person. No circumstances will void the contract before the four-year term is up unless or until the buyer is deceased, and in which case, Subject One may be transferred to someone of the buyer's choice, if made before passing.

Four years of his life.

Auctioned to the highest bidder.

All the skills Alessio worked to hone over the years with The League came down to a ten-page contract that laid out every detail for him so that he had no questions left to ask. Until now, his career with The League had been as an independent contractor. A choice Dare and Cree allowed him to have because of their attachment to him, and it meant a lot.

Others didn't get the same treatment. Mostly, people came to The League knowing what their fate would be—one year of training, and then the auctions came up where very rich and dangerous people bid on the members for four-year contracts. That's how The League's *real* money got made.

Alessio never had much interest in the auctions. Working alone, or with The League's team that Cree had made, gave him enough freedom to do whatever he wanted. Something had changed over the last year, though, and he leaned towards the auctions as the yearly date neared for them.

Hence, the contract.

And his need for a decision, considering in two months, the auctions would happen. Dare would need to get his paperwork settled and put him on the roster for potential buyers to peruse before they went into the auctions. It was typical for a buyer to settle on which member they wanted before they ever even stepped foot inside The League's building.

"With your varied skills," Corrado said from the doorway of the office, "you'll cause a bidding war, likely."

Alessio had known Corrado was standing there from the moment he entered the room even if the man hadn't made a noise. So was their fucking life together. He wasn't able to even consider this alone because he had to consider everything else, too.

"Yeah, possibly," Alessio muttered, "but that's not a bad thing. Thirty percent of the final buyer's cost goes to me, and the rest to The League. After four years, I wouldn't have to take another job, if I didn't want to. I could do ... anything."

"You have enough money to do that now."

Another thing that wasn't a secret between them. Alessio didn't even hide how much fucking money he had spread across several portfolios because Corrado had details for all that shit, too.

"What do you want?" Alessio asked.

"To know if you will sign that and go up on the auctions."

"Considering it."

"I don't want you to do it," Corrado said.

Alessio's shoulders tightened at that. "I've been saying for a year I wanted to do this, Corrado. It shouldn't be a surprise now that I have the contract in front of me. If you had an issue with it, then you should have said something *months* ago. Not now."

"Months ago I would let you do whatever you wanted to make *this* better for you. And sometimes, that meant you running away from me, right? Fucking off to work, or staying away from me because you didn't want to deal with the shit you didn't like at home."

"Where in the fuck do you—"

Alessio turned to tell Corrado to go fuck himself, but stopped when he realized the man had crossed the office to stand right beside him. With Corrado *this* close, there was no mistaking that look in his eye.

That *glint*.

He wasn't hiding shit.

It was all on the table, now.

"You only want to do this to get away from me," Corrado said, not pulling any punches with each word he threw at Alessio, "the same way you take extra jobs, run with the second team when Cree allows it … you have to keep running away, Les, because you're scared of what might happen when *I* catch up to you—when this shit between us comes to a head, right?"

Alessio straightened to his full height, realizing his pride could sometimes be just as much of a bitch as Corrado's. "Or I want something *different*, yeah? Not everything is about you, Corrado, even if you want to make it that way."

Low blow, Les.

He knew it.

That was the thing, though, if Corrado wanted to say shit that hurt Alessio, then the man better be damn ready to have it thrown right back at him, too. Alessio no longer understood how to survive the mess they'd created together, otherwise.

Was it healthy?

Not at all.

Not that it mattered.

The words were out there, now.

He blamed his attitude and mood on the fact he had been tiptoeing around Corrado for almost a week and a half. Shit was always better, *and far easier,* between the two of them when they were together, and close. Sure, those issues still existed, but at least he was able to tuck them away when they had each other to focus on.

Right now, they were focusing on the wrong shit.

Or it was right.

It just wasn't easy.

Corrado didn't seem bothered by Alessio's words. He came back stronger for the second round, saying, "It's true, you didn't want all of this—our problems, the shit you weren't getting from me—to come to a head, either, because you're terrified of what might come after. So, you keep busy, you keep running … it keeps a distance between you and me, yeah. But then, you come back, and we have two weeks together."

He let out a bitter laugh, so fucking dark and hurtful, adding, "But then we're too busy focusing on being *together*, Alessio, because neither one of us like being apart, instead of all the shit that weighs us down. That's why you want to do it."

Fuck.

More than anything, Alessio wanted to deny what Corrado said to him. He wanted to tell him to shove his fucking assumptions up his ass and get out of his face. Except he couldn't say any of that shit at all, even if he was mad—and *Christ*, he was so mad—because Corrado wasn't wrong.

Nothing he said was a lie.

"You want to do the auctions because you need a new way to run, instead of staying here and handling the issues we've unpacked from the baggage we've been carrying for five fucking years," Corrado uttered. "If you can do it to me, then the least you can do is *say it*, too. Just admit it."

God.

Alessio dragged in a lungful of air that burned all the way in. "And if we didn't have all this shit going on if we were *good*, Corrado … then what would you say about these auctions, and me going up for a buyer?"

Because that mattered, too.

"I would still ask you not to do it."

Alessio's jaw ached from how hard he was clenching his teeth. "Why?"

"Because they won't give a *fuck* about you. You will be a tool, something for them to use. They will tell you where to go, and what to do. They will determine your worth, and the value of your life, by how valuable you are to them. You might die because someone figured you were just collateral, and that contract says it *doesn't matter.*"

"Corrado—"

"That contract says someone can take you from me, and there's not a fucking thing I will be able to do about it because you signed your goddamn name on it. And right now, the only reason you want to take that risk is because as much as you like to throw my bullshit at my feet, you're still not ready to deal with your own."

Why did he have to be like that?

Why did he have to be *right*?

"Okay?" Corrado asked. "Was that what you wanted me to say? Because fuck knows you still won't let me tell you I love—"

Alessio's hand hit the papers on the desk, sending them scattering everywhere. He didn't let Corrado finish his statement before he spun on his heels and left the office without a look over his shoulder.

No, Corrado didn't get to say those words.

Not yet.

They still struck like a fucking weapon.

Alessio wasn't ready for the impact.

$$\bullet\ \bullet\ \bullet$$

The music filtering out of the tiny speaker on the middle of the kitchen island had Ginevra dancing to the beat, a wooden spoon swaying with the rest of her body in her grip. She didn't seem to care at all that Alessio sat at the right side of the island, a thriller opened in front of him, while she cooked and danced.

In fact, she barely paid him any mind at all.

He was sure Corrado had found the speaker for her and let her steal his phone for the *massive* music playlist he kept on the damn thing. Not that he cared to ask at the moment, because despite how interesting his book actually was, Alessio was far more concerned with watching Ginevra.

A curious thing.

Smart, and quick.

She didn't miss a beat.

Innocent, but sinful.

Sly, but sweet.

He found it odd he was able to sit down and have an intellectual conversation with her about things that no one else ever wanted to talk about—like his appreciation of the written word. She calmed his constant, *excessive* energy, and brought him back down to earth with nothing more than a conversation. On the flip side of that coin, he watched her handle an uptight and stiff Corrado, and make him more playful than Alessio had ever seen.

He had yet to grasp how to deal with it. Unlike everything else, compartmentalizing this woman was impossible. It was how Alessio liked to deal with anything in his life. Things fit in neat little boxes inside his mind, and he handled them accordingly.

Ginevra was not the same.

At all.

There were too many facets to her personality, and he couldn't unveil them all before another one came along to make him do a double-take of her yet again. He was still trying to find that *thing* in this woman that had made Corrado change the landscape of their relationship, but the longer he searched for it, the more Alessio realized something else.

He liked Ginevra.

Finding the parts of her that had Corrado spun up in the woman became *almost* insignificant when suddenly, Alessio had his own interests in her.

And that was a goddamn problem.

He didn't ask for that.

None of it.

"Want to try it?"

Alessio blinked to find Ginevra had stopped dancing and came to stand on the other side of the island from where he sat. On the wooden spoon in her hand, a red sauce coated the concave tip. A rich red, and smelling like spices, his mouth watered as she held it out like it was a treat she might tease him with.

That cunning smile on her lips said the same.

"Well?"

"Who taught you to cook, hmm?" he asked.

Ginevra grinned. "My Mama."

"Oh?"

"She worked a lot, so I had to look after my little sisters. They didn't like things that came from a box when our mom wouldn't dare feed them something like that, so I had to learn how to make them what they liked."

"And you liked that."

She arched a brow. "What do you mean?"

"Taking care of your sisters."

He didn't miss the way her throat jumped, or how a sadness dimmed her eyes. "Of course, I did. I love them, Les."

"You haven't seen them in a while, huh?"

"Too long. I don't like to think about it. There's nothing I can do about it. I can't talk to them, they can't be told where I am, so … I don't bother."

Yeah, he could tell.

The emotion in her eyes, and the thickness in her tone, that made him lean forward to take her sauce. Perhaps then, she would go back to smiling and dancing, and his chest wouldn't feel like a fucking elephant was sitting on it because she was *sad*.

Yeah, fuck.

He didn't ask for this.

Alessio shouldn't have *any* emotion for this woman.

Yet, he did.

More and more each day.

He did.

That would be a problem.

Alessio took the sauce on the tip of the wooden spoon Ginevra held out to him, surprised at the richness and varying notes that glided across his palate from just *one* taste. Leaning back on the stool, he nodded.

"It's good."

She gave him a look. "*Just* good?"

One breath in.

Another breath out.

He had to remind himself to breathe with her, too.

"It's wonderful," he murmured. "Really."

A lot like her.

And that's enough.

Alessio liked this woman—did he need to say that again?—and he hadn't planned for this at all. It wasn't why he came back here, not even a thought until it stared him right in the face and *laughed* at him.

The universe having another joke.

He wasn't ready for it.

He was pissed, but not at her. Ginevra hadn't asked for this situation, and mostly, she gave him and Corrado as much space as she could to work out their issues *without* her stepping in. That's why she still slept in a separate bed even though he didn't give a fuck if Corrado was fucking her.

Because she had a heart.

She gave a shit.

Even though this hurt her.

Alessio needed to be *mad*. Mad this became less and less about why the fuck Corrado had done what he did—more about why Alessio thought he was doing the same fucking thing.

He pushed off the chair, despite Ginevra's confused expression, and turned to leave the kitchen without an explanation. Corrado, standing in the entryway, and watching their exchange with an amused smile *really* sent his blood pressure spiking.

Like the man just knew what was happening—expected this.

And he *liked* it.

Fuck that noise, too.

"Les," Ginevra said, a question lingering in her tone, "are you okay?"

Not at all.

Not one fucking bit.

He left the kitchen in a rush, sliding past Corrado who met his stare, before he tried to put distance between him and them. That was the problem with him deciding to stay here.

There was no space.

Only an illusion.

"I didn't mean to upset him," Ginevra said, her tone quaking but faint. "What did I do?"

"Nothing," Corrado replied. "I doubt it was you, Ginny."

"But—"

"Everything is all right, keep cooking."

Alessio didn't want to see them—didn't want to smell, or hear, or *feel* them. He went to the only place which might give him some sense of privacy, if only for a short time, to clear his fucking head. Maybe that was his biggest mistake; he thought he could stay here, and not change anything.

He found the solace he needed in the attached bathroom of the bedroom he'd been using. Three bedrooms, and three bathrooms, the penthouse gave them all their own personal spaces, if needed.

Not that it helped.

Clearly.

Alessio wanted to do and be nothing. He wanted to be able to ignore the fact his cock was hard as he stripped out of his clothes, all because he'd enjoyed the sight of Ginevra dancing in far more ways than one.

Another goddamn problem.

Stepping under the too-hot water after he'd spun the taps on, Alessio let steam and heat drag him from the hell of his thoughts. Except, it didn't last. Once the sting of the hot water dulled beating down against his head and back, his mind filled with nonsense again.

Of *everything*.

Them.

This mess.

His *feelings*.

Fuck, he hated that the most.

"*Les.*"

Corrado's voice had him tensing under the water, but he didn't answer the man back. Instead, he kept his hands pressing against the cool tiles of the shower, happy with pretending like he had gone deaf.

It was easier than explaining his behavior.

Making sense of *this*.

"Les," Corrado snapped again.

Still, he said nothing.

And *shocker,* that wasn't good enough for Corrado, because when the man didn't get what he wanted verbally, he yanked open the frosted glass doors of the shower, and stepped inside, fully clothed. At his side, Corrado stared hard at him, barely fazed at all by the large shower heads raining down on them from several directions. Soaked to the bone, and *waiting,* Corrado said nothing. Alessio didn't move or speak, either.

Finally, he uttered, "Get out."

"No."

Alessio let out a dark sound. "Get the fuck—"

"Not until you tell me what that was about."

"You fucking *know.*"

"Maybe I want to hear you say it."

"Fuck you," Alessio mumbled, shaking his head under the water, droplets sliding down his face to fall to the tiled floor. "I didn't come here for *this*—for her. We're supposed to be figuring shit out, but we haven't even done that, and you know what's happening with me because that's what you fucking wanted to happen."

He would not spell it out for Corrado.

The asshole could read between the lines.

"It wasn't *us* with someone else, Corrado," Alessio said under his breath. "That's not what this ever was, but you didn't let me choose—*you did.* And you knew what would happen if I stayed here long enough ... if I was around her long enough, so fuck you for that, too."

Every word he threw at Corrado cut like knives. He was sure when they stabbed into Corrado, it hurt like hell. He wanted that clear, though, because it's how this shit felt to him. Someone decided something else for him, and he didn't get a say either way.

He could be pissed about that.

That, he could choose alone.

"Get *out,*" Alessio snapped at Corrado when the man just kept standing there.

"Les—"

"*Go.*"

Corrado didn't leave like Alessio wanted him to. He never had understood boundaries, or possibly, a part of Corrado sensed when Alessio struggled, even when he said he wanted to be alone, he needed someone there more.

He'd been alone for most of his life.

A vicious circle.

Corrado often reminded him he wasn't navigating life by himself so that just made this worse. It made the pain of it all amplified because *God* ... Alessio handed him everything, and he ruined it.

Instead of leaving, Corrado backed him against the shower wall. Alessio tipped his head back to the tiles, letting the coolness of the marble press along his jaw and cheek when Corrado buried his face into his neck. His lips touched his skin, soft and quick, silent apologies following the featherlight kisses.

He didn't need to have it said.

He knew what Corrado didn't say.

"I didn't *find* her," Corrado muttered against his skin. "I didn't seek her out—she just *was*, and I didn't get a choice, either. You don't want this to change, and I get it, Les. You get too close, you give a shit, and then what happens, huh? It's someone else that can leave you, right?"

"Fuck you," Alessio mumbled.

Fuck him for knowing.

For being right.

For doing all of this.

It wasn't fair.

"It's like you fucking tricked me, like you manipulated me," Alessio said, his voice a rumble under the noise of the shower. "This is what you wanted, right?"

"I did nothing. I let shit happen."

"No, you did."

"Les—"

"That's what it seems like, Corrado. And it makes it harder, it makes this worse."

"Why would I do that to someone I lov—"

Alessio turned his head fast, his lips crashing against Corrado's. He still wasn't ready for those words, still didn't want to hear them, not when he was trying to deal with everything else too. It made it more difficult, because part of him wanted that more than anything, he wanted those words for so long, and now, Corrado *needed* to say them, too.

But all it took was that kiss, the hard work of their lips moving against one another's, and they lost the words. Oh, the anger was still there, visceral and vicious. Tinging every swipe of his lips against Corrado's. That anger colored the roughness in Corrado's hands when they slid down the sleeves of tattoos on Alessio's arms.

Still, it was a background thought.

Fading away with the flavor of Corrado when Alessio's tongue teased the seam of his lips. He had far more he wanted to say, all those warring emotions battling for a presence, but he didn't want to feel anything at all.

Instead, he found somewhere else to go—a better place to be. He found it in the wet clothing covering Corrado's hard lines as he crowded closer to Alessio. He reveled in letting the anger drift away when a firm grip found his cock and stroked him fast. Teeth cut into his lower lip, giving him a shock of pain with the hot licks of pleasure climbing his spine with every pull of Corrado's hand along his length.

It'd been too long.

Hell, he hadn't even touched himself in *weeks*.

Too caught up in their shit, this mess, and everything else. Sex came secondary, and he didn't care for the release when it would only be fucking *empty*. And yet, he was begging for it, now. *Craving it*, so bad.

"Jesus Christ," he growled against Corrado's kiss.

That palm on his dick tightened.

God, yeah.

"Let me say it," Corrado murmured, "just fucking let me *say it*, Les."

"*Shut up.*"

"Stop using that to *punish me.*"

Never once did Corrado's hand slow. Those strokes came faster, and the next kiss bruised. It's what Alessio needed, what he wanted more than anything, and when he came … *fuck*, it ached as much as it relieved. His semen spilled between them, hitting the tiles just long enough for the water to wash it all away. A broken sound tore from his chest, breathless and harsh, as Corrado's hand slowed but his fingers tightened at the same time.

Corrado's gaze lifted to meet his, but Alessio was already turning his head to look away again. Now, they had switched places, he thought. It wasn't *him* that wanted something from Corrado that his lover wouldn't give.

The shoe was on the other foot.

He didn't mean for it to punish; love wouldn't hurt anymore.

Corrado released his hold on Alessio, his palm coming up to snap hard against the tiles of the shower when he still wouldn't return his stare.

He couldn't.

Not when he was mad again.

"So, what if this thing of ours has to change?" Corrado asked. "What if it makes it better?"

Alessio didn't reply.

Corrado stepped back from him, letting the cold air wrap around Alessio as he moved out of the shower. He left behind a mess on the floor from the water dripping off his clothes, closed the shower without a word, and exited the bathroom with a slam of the door.

Only then did Alessio breathe again.

What if it makes it better?

Right.

Because it sure as hell couldn't get worse.

7.

Corrado

Rolling over, because Corrado could no longer ignore the sun coming in through the windows of the bedroom, his hand slid across the top of the bedside table. Soon, he found the device he was looking for.

His cell phone.

He dragged a hand down his face, willing away the grumpiness he *always* felt first thing in the damn mornings, and pulled the phone closer to his face. He blinked, making the screen come into focus when he turned it on to check for something.

A missed call.

Any texts.

A fucking *smoke signal.*

Not that the last one was possible, but anything would be better than what he had been getting, which was nothing. Anyone else, he called or sent a word to, and they were quick to get back to him.

Andino Marcello was an asshole.

And he did not care.

Out of everything Corrado knew about the man, he was quite aware that Andino being an asshole was the most truthful. It was obvious Ginevra was missing her sisters, and that she worried about what was happening back home in New York. Regularly, Corrado had sent a message to check in with Andino just to make sure he was still where he needed to be, so was Ginevra, and that nothing had changed.

He never got a response.

Ever.

Corrado didn't know why that was except to say Andino was being his usual asshole self and didn't want to return a fucking call or message. What other excuse did the man have? Through the contacts Corrado had with his twin in the Guzzi Cosa Nostra, if Andino or any other Marcello was dead, then he would know it.

They were alive and well.

Except that one's husband.

Cella Marcello, was it?

A bystander, Chris had told Corrado. Wrong place, wrong time, but it looked purposeful, too. Not that it made any fucking difference to Corrado either way.

If the Marcellos wanted to go to war in New York, then they could do that. He would rather keep Ginevra here with him while they did it, so she wasn't another innocent bystander in their goddamn feud with her half-brothers' organization.

And even so, she continued to worry.

Silently.

So, he kept sending messages.

Frustrated at the lack of a response from Andino—yet again—Corrado threw the phone to the blanket and rolled over so his back was against the headboard. Through the opened door of his room, he could see the empty bedroom across the hall from his. That wasn't unusual, either, considering Ginevra was often up and around long before he ever was.

Same with Alessio.

He was not rolling his ass out of bed before nine if he wasn't doing it to fuck someone. He didn't make the rules of life—like needing sleep to survive—but he could sure as hell decide what he did about it.

It took Corrado too long to get out of his bed and make his way to the attached bathroom. He did his business, wishing he had just stayed in bed the entire time. Mornings were not his thing, and the less time he spent around other people, the better the rest of it went for him.

Why pretend?

The only exception to that rule was when someone was in the bed *with him*. And since that wasn't happening, either, because both people he wanted to fuck decided they would rather sleep in their beds that weren't his, then his ever-present pissy mood was a constant in the mornings.

What could he do?

He dressed, opting for gym shorts and runners because once he stuffed his face full of something suitable for breakfast, he would hit the gym in the penthouse. Corrado slipped out of the bedroom with his head down. He expected to find Alessio and Ginevra in the kitchen, making their usual noise and waiting for his moody ass.

Instead, he found it empty.

Well, mostly.

A plate of eggs, bacon, and toast waited for him in the warming rack of the oven. Still hot, and ready for him to eat. *Huh.* He pulled it out, ignoring the nagging sensation in his chest because *fuck*, he was selfish as hell, and yet, one of those two still thought about him and made sure he would eat.

Probably Ginevra.

Alessio didn't cook—he ordered.

Corrado, balancing the plate in his palm and using a fork to stab into the eggs, he decided to go find the two. He figured they were likely in the library, pouring over a book because that's what they enjoyed first thing in the morning, and it let him have quiet time after he woke up. Something he needed when he first woke up.

Bad moods, and all.

Corrado entered the hallway leading to the office, main bathroom, the gym, and the one spare bedroom Alessio was using at the far end. The connecting hallway led to the other bedrooms, his and Ginevra's. He'd focused on getting out of bed, he hadn't bothered to look around the corner when he came out.

Alessio leaned against the doorway of the gym, staring inside. Corrado set his fork to the plate, and picked up a strip of bacon, shoving half into his mouth while his brow furrowed at the sight of the man standing there, dressed, staring into the room like he was considering whether he wanted to enter.

"What are you do—"

Alessio waved the hand at his side, never looking Corrado's way. He made an annoyed noise, passing the office library and realizing, it was empty. Ginevra wasn't in there, either.

He figured out where Ginevra was when Corrado came to stand next to Alessio's side. Inside the gym, the woman had slipped on the headphones Corrado liked to use when he was running in the mornings—it helped to distract him from the fact he wasn't running on a trail—as she jogged on one of the four treadmills lining the far windows. *Four* treadmills, because each one served a different purpose, and did different things.

"So, she jogs," Corrado said to Alessio.

Alessio nodded. "But for an hour or more?"

Corrado raised an eyebrow as he took in Ginevra again. *No*, that was unusual. Typically, if he woke up early enough to see her go into the gym, she jogged for twenty to thirty minutes, jumped in the shower, and then went about her day.

Oh, he liked watching her run, sure. He would not pretend like her lean form didn't have his cock perking under the satiny cloth of his gym shorts, but he figured Alessio was trying to tell him something right then, and his lust could wait.

"That long?" he asked.

Alessio let out a hard breath. "Yeah."

Huh.

"Something is on her mind—it's bothering her," Alessio murmured.

Corrado gave the man a look from the side. "Les, her whole life is a mess. Congratulations, you're just realizing she is *really good* at compartmentalizing shit like you do. She tucks it all away, lets no one know she's having a rough go, and continues on with her life. Between this here, New York, being without her sisters … I would be shocked if she wasn't one step away from a nervous breakdown."

"So, we … let her do this?"

He looked back in the gym, noting Ginevra's pace hadn't changed. She focused, working through whatever nonsense was in her mind by making her body tired, and pushing it to its limits.

"Because I don't like that," Alessio added quieter, "I don't like it when she's upset, even if she doesn't say that."

"That's a step forward, ain't it?"

Alessio scowled. "Could you not?"

"I'm just saying."

"Well, don't." Alessio sighed, shaking his head. "It bothers me she's—"

"Hurting," Corrado interjected, handing his plate over to the man, which Alessio took with a question in his stare. "You figured out what my problem has been these last three weeks."

"What?"

"With you. Excuse me."

Corrado left Alessio in the doorway, and entered the gym, still hungry but willing to put it off for a little while. He crossed the space, and jumped onto the treadmill beside Ginevra's, turning it on and starting a pace good for a warmup.

She peeked over at him.

"Faster?" he asked.

Ginevra grinned, faint as it was. "Yeah, sure."

Five minutes later, Alessio joined them, too. On the opposite side of Ginevra, he started the treadmill he preferred because he'd pre-programmed paces into it, from a slow jog, to a sprint, and then to a full run before switching all the way back again.

She didn't want to talk.

Fine.

They would still be there.

They would still do this.

• • •

A month was a blink in time for Corrado, but especially when he wasn't doing anything. Days melted into one another, turning into weeks, and then changing into a month before he even realized what had happened.

An entire month with the three of them sharing the same space. And hey, nobody had ripped anybody's head off yet. He took that as a win.

Corrado only realized the date because his father said it in his ear, and he checked the calendar on his desk to confirm that Gian was correct. Surprise, he was.

"How is everything over there?" his father asked on the call.

"Better."

Gian chuckled. "You know, I never realized how nosy I was until one of you five boys had something … interesting going on in your personal lives."

Corrado wasn't stupid—that was his father's sly way of asking about their situation. Mostly, his father allowed all his children their privacy and space.

Sometimes, though, he didn't.

Like now.

"It's a complicated thing," Corrado said quietly, eyeing the open doorway of his office. Ginevra had been playing a game in the sitting room, and Alessio was in the gym again, beating the hell out of a punching bag. "But then again, it was a complicated thing before she ever showed up, too."

"And delicate, I imagine."

Corrado cleared his throat. "Yeah, that, too."

"I'm sure you'll get it figured out. You got that message from your mother, *oui?*"

"I did. She's like you—*elle est trop curieuse.*"

He only got to speak French with his father, and Corrado tried to sneak it because he could. None of his brothers, except for Marcus, had picked up French from their father like he did. Just bits and pieces, but not enough for him to hold a proper conversation. He liked to use it when he could.

"She is not *too* curious, Corrado. That is not why she asked for lunch."

"Right," Corrado said fast before his father could make up another excuse for Cara, "not at all."

"Maybe that's the case, but she also gets whatever she wants, and what she wants right now is to spend time with—"

"Oh, I'm sorry."

Corrado's head snapped up, and he found Ginevra standing in the office's doorway. Her gaze drifted from him to the bookshelves lining the wall at the left of his desk.

"I'll just give you a minute," she said. "I didn't mean to interrupt."

"It's fine," Corrado told her, and then back on the call, "I will call you back, Papa, and *yes*, tomorrow is a go. Tell Ma."

"Will do, son."

Once Corrado had ended the call, he gave Ginevra his attention. She continued standing in the doorway not coming further into the room or moving away.

"You need something?"

She pointed at the bookshelves. "I picked out a book yesterday, but I didn't take it with me. I hadn't finished my other one, so ..."

Corrado nodded and gestured at the shelves. "Go ahead. This space is as much yours as it is ours while you're here."

She passed him a curious glance, but Corrado didn't bother to ask what for. He figured it was better he talked like Ginevra had to share the same spaces he and Alessio did daily because it was true.

She belonged here.

With them.

They needed to figure it out, too.

Ginevra moved into the office, and crossed the space with quick, quiet steps. She bent down to pull a book from the third shelf, like she had known where she left it, and straightened back up with it in her hand, ready to leave.

Before she did, she flipped it open to the title page, and a soft noise of surprise escaped her. That gained Corrado's attention again, but she wasn't even looking at him. Instead, her focus was on the book in her grasp.

"Something wrong?"

Ginevra glanced up, a soft smile curving her cheeks. "No, I ... there's a note here, is all."

"Pardon?"

She turned the book around so that Corrado could see what she meant by *a note*. There, a yellow sticky note with familiar handwriting scrawled across it stuck to the page. He was unable to read what Alessio had written on the note, but he still recognized the bold cursive lettering.

Corrado felt his smirk growing. "From Les."

She shrugged. "Seems so."

"What does it say?"

"That I will like the second half more, and to skip the first," she said, laughing. "He gave me the page numbers of his favorites, too. It's another book of poetry—that's all."

Not at all something Corrado enjoyed.

Or appreciated.

Yet, Ginevra and Alessio shared that, and he found it fascinating. "Did you show him that book when you picked it out yesterday?"

"No, I came in and looked it over before putting it back."

Right.

But those shelves ...

All those books.

They were Alessio's. He'd picked every single one and decided where they should go on the shelves. He recognized them front to back because not a single book went into his library if he didn't read it cover to cover. If one of those books moved, Alessio would know about it.

Which meant …

He'd been watching for which books Ginevra picked out on her own.

"I'm sure it seems silly," Ginevra said, rolling her eyes, "But … it's nice."

He didn't think it to be silly. No, he didn't appreciate books and words and poetry like the two of them did, but he grasped what Alessio had done here.

"It means he likes you," Corrado murmured.

She scoffed, giving him a roll of her eyes. "Lately, he barely speaks to me. He keeps a distance, not that I blame him. Oh, he watches me sure, but so do you. But *likes me*, Corrado, that's a stretch."

Oh, it was way deeper than that.

"You should have figured out by now that nothing with Alessio is simple or obvious. Think about it," he said, leaning back in the office chair to watch her over the steepling of his fingers, "you hadn't told Les about the book which means he sought what you read, so he would be aware, and keep up with you. It means he's thinking of *you*, Ginny, in his own way."

Corrado shrugged, adding, "So, he keeps a distance, and he's quiet. *That's Alessio*. He's working through his own shit, and when he does that, he isolates as much as he can. It's not about you, even if it is *for* you."

He didn't miss the way her fingers tightened on the edge of the book, or how her throat jumped at his words. She shifted from foot to foot, too, refusing to meet his gaze. All those nerves of hers, he saw it all.

And Corrado *hated* that.

Out of all the things happening here, he did not want her nervous about this. Not about Alessio, or him, or what might come of it. Some things should be *easy* and them falling into step together needed to be one of those. There would be more than enough of it that would be hard, surely.

"Come here," he whispered, tipping his head to the side.

"What?"

Corrado pointed at his side. "Get over here."

Still tittering in her anxious way, Ginevra closed the book, and came to stand next to Corrado's chair behind the desk. Staring down at him, he thought she looked sweet, and a little sinful. Expectant, but hesitant.

Exactly as she should, really.

Reaching up, he caught one of her stray waves of hair between his fingertips and twisted the strands around his index finger. "I like you closer, Ginny. You understand that, don't you?"

Her tongue peeked out to wet her lips when he tugged on the strands of hair, making her lower until she bent over at her middle, and the two of them were at eye level with each other. Here, he only had to lean forward and *kiss her*.

Still, he held off.

For a moment …

"Do you?"

"Hmm?"

"Like me closer."

"More often than I get you, *chérie*."

Her gaze dropped to his mouth before snapping back up to his eyes. He didn't miss the way her lower lip trembled like she had something to say, but held it back.

"What is it?" he asked. "Say it, kitten."

"You still call me that."

"Because you are, soft but with sharpness. It's perfect."

Like her.

Ginevra let out a slow breath and glanced away. "I'm not sure what to do here, Corrado."

"With what?"

"You, and … him. I don't know what to do, or how to act. I didn't ask for any of this, and it's hard enough handling *one* man who has an interest in me, let alone two. It's confusing and—"

"I get it," he interjected. "He knows that, too."

She gave him a look again.

That look.

Annoyed, and amused at the same time.

"What?" he asked.

"It doesn't bother you at all?"

"I need more to go on, Ginny."

"To think someone else might want me—to touch me, *fuck* me? Or I might want to do that to someone else that isn't you?"

Corrado blinked.

Straight to the point, then.

That's what she worried about?

God.

That was the last thing he worried about with the three of them. It would probably be the easiest part of it all. Sex was sex, and when that was good, shit, everything else came a hell of a lot easier.

"No, actually," he said, smiling as he leaned in closer to her, nearly able to kiss her as he spoke, "the idea of that, the person I love, and the one I'm falling in love with might love each other, too … why would that bother me?"

She blinked.

Still and quiet.

Corrado wasn't sure if he liked that more than her frankness in this discussion, or not. Quickly, he added, "And it turns me on."

Ginevra made a soft noise.

Airless, he thought.

And hot.

"A bonus for you, I bet," she said.

"Or the way it *should be.*"

"I don't think this is that easy, Corrado."

"No, some of us want to make it hard, I suppose." His gaze dropped to her pretty, pink lips and their natural pout. "I'd like to kiss you."

He hadn't touched her.

Gave her space.

Didn't *push.*

It stopped now, but he needed her okay, first. Their game had becoming tiring.

He'd sacrificed and suffered because of what he'd done, and he took that penance, as Alessio had once said.

He'd gone without.

Waited.

He wanted from afar.

"Do you?" she asked.

"I do."

Ginevra swallowed audibly, her lips pressing together before she said, "Then, do that, Corrado."

He didn't need further permission. The second those words slipped out of her sweet mouth, he closed that inch of space between them. Catching her lips with his own, he reveled in the softness of her mouth against his own. It'd been far too long since he had a taste of this woman, and he soaked in every single second.

The way her lips worked against his, slow but *sure*. How her tongue struck out first to tease at the seam of his lips, asking for more. The little gasp she gave when he nipped at her with his teeth, and how her tongue slashed with his, not giving him even an inch of control in this battle between them.

He loved it all.

Wanted it all.

Corrado stroked the side of Ginevra's cheek with the pad of his thumb when he pulled away, although part of him wanted to just stay right there, with her caught up in him and those thoughts of Alessio running through her head.

Because yeah, he knew that's what was happening.

And he was fine with that.

"My mother called this morning," he said, holding her gaze strong, "she wants to have lunch with you tomorrow."

Ginevra's gaze widened. "Why?"

"Because she found out you were still in the city with me, that Alessio is also here, I imagine she has questions, and she knows better than to ask me. Oh, and because she thought you made quite an impression on her, which means she *likes you.* Surprise, someone else that thinks you're amazing."

"Corrado. Stop it."

"But it's not a lie."

And it wasn't.

"We Guzzi men try to give our mother what she wants," he added, "or we have to deal with our father. You're safe to leave the penthouse, even if you haven't asked to go further than a shop for clothes. No one knows you're here, so if you want to do lunch tomorrow—it's not negotiable, Cara decided, so—then you can do that. Chris promised Ma he would come to pick you up, so you wouldn't be late because they don't trust me to let you out of here, apparently."

Ginevra grinned slyly. "Oh?"

"Seems so."

He let her go, and Ginevra stood up straight. A happiness lingered in her smile, but he found something else dimming her gaze.

"What's wrong?" he asked.

She shrugged. "I just … have you heard anything about back home, or my sisters?"

He didn't tell her about the calls and messages he'd made because Corrado didn't want to get Ginevra's hopes up only to watch them crash and burn when he got no response from Andino. She had enough to deal with, and that didn't need to be something else on her plate.

"No," he said.

"Will you try?"

Corrado sighed.

Ginevra frowned. "*Please?* I haven't tried to leave, or use the phones or your laptop to contact anyone. I've followed all the rules, haven't I?"

Jesus.

Why did she think he would say no?

That it depended on her behavior?

He would do it because he cared—he had been doing it because of that. Nothing else.

"I'll see what I can do," he said.

"Thank you."

Quickly, she leaned down and pressed another quick kiss to his lips, winking before she turned away from his desk, and headed out of the office without a look back over her shoulder. She was gone all of four seconds before someone else came to stand in the doorway.

Alessio.

"Were you spying?" Corrado asked, never looking up from the papers on his desk. He had things to do. "Because you know, you're more than welcome to *join* the conversation, Les."

"And if I was?"

Corrado chuckled. "The door is open. I leave it like that for a reason."

He met Alessio's gaze.

Questions stared back.

Curiosity.

How much had he heard?

Corrado didn't mind waiting to find out.

8.

Alessio

"Give Ma my love, yeah?"

Chris nodded at his twin where he stood next to a waiting Ginevra. "I will." Then, the man's gaze lifted over Corrado's shoulder, drifting to where Alessio stood leaning against the wall further down the hall. "Les, it's been a while."

Had it?

A little more than a month, he supposed, since he sat with the man in that café.

"Chris," Alessio replied. "Get her there safely, yes?"

He hadn't meant for the statement to sound threatening, and yet somehow, it did. Except there wasn't anything he could do about the looks coming his way now because the damn words were already out of his mouth.

Ah, well.

Corrado cleared his throat, passing a pointed look over his shoulder at Alessio. A quiet, *hey, now, that's family.* Alessio only shrugged back.

"No worries," Chris said, shaking his head as he turned to offer a hand to a grinning Ginevra. "She'll come back in one piece."

She better.

At least, that time, Alessio kept the thoughts inside his head. It wasn't lost on him that his sudden protectiveness over Ginevra was for more than just him. He also felt protective of her for Corrado, and he didn't want to get into it.

Not yet.

Once Ginevra and Chris had exited the apartment, Corrado turned to face Alessio with a raised brow. "You don't need to go full-on asshole to Chris, right? It's *Chris*, Les."

"Gotta make an example out of everybody, or nobody will care, huh?"

It reminded him of that whole saying *if you stand for nothing, then you'll fall for everything.* In a way …

"It's still *Chris*," Corrado said, laughing under his breath.

Yeah, yeah.

Alessio didn't need his nonsense pointed out to him when he was glaring at him right in the face every time he looked in the fucking mirror. He changed the conversation, because all too soon, the two of them would go right back to shit that had them snapping at one another's throats again.

Wasn't that the way, lately?

Well …

"I've been here a little more than a month," Alessio said.

Partially passing him in the hallway, Corrado's walk came to an abrupt halt. He looked over at Alessio and nodded. "Yeah, I figured that out yesterday. Passed quickly, didn't it?"

He hadn't realized he had been here with Corrado and Ginevra that long, and he'd barely left other than to take his morning jog, and pick up a coffee from that

267

place he liked down the street.

He took a second.

And then another.

Alessio couldn't remember a time when he had stayed in one place for longer than a month. Or rather, two weeks. The longest was for a *job*, and he had been alone on that one. He stayed home for a while, and then he took off again. And sure, he recognized why he did that, but it was still the urge he had.

Well, the urge he *didn't* have.

Not here.

With them.

He didn't want to run like he'd been doing for years—trying to out run his problems, their issues, and just *life* because it worried him what might happen when it caught up to him. He wanted to be here with them, even if it meant pain and facing his own baggage because God knew he'd been throwing Corrado's at him for so long, now.

Alessio wanted to be here.

Even if it wouldn't be easy.

Even if it didn't end well.

He still wanted to be *here*.

"Les," Corrado said.

He lifted his gaze from the top button on Corrado's dress shirt he'd been using as a focal point to ignore the man's stare. There, in his lover's eyes, he found an understanding reflecting at him.

Corrado always had known Alessio better than anyone, and he wasn't fucking perfect ... that was one thing about Corrado that Alessio had never denied.

This man in front of him wasn't perfect.

He was *flawed*.

So difficult.

Selfish, sometimes.

But he was still Alessio's.

And he loved him, regardless.

He always would.

"Are you going to call Andino for her?" Alessio asked.

Corrado smirked a bit. "So, you're admitting you spied yesterday on our conversation instead of joining?"

"Are you going to answer the question?"

"I have been calling. Three times this last week, in fact. He ignored my calls and messages. You're informed on how Andino Marcello can be."

"Rivals you for the biggest asshole, doesn't he?"

Corrado flashed his teeth when he laughed. "Yeah, a bit. I asked Chris to see what he might find for her, and about her sisters, though. I figured ..."

"Cosa Nostra, made ... connections to New York, yeah," Alessio said, "I get it."

"It's the best I can do right now."

"Is it?"

Because if Corrado really wanted to, he would make a trip to New York himself, pay a visit to Andino, and get business *done*. Like Alessio had done when he wanted details about what in the hell Corrado had gotten himself into here.

It's who they were.

Rules be damned.

Corrado sighed and glanced away. "For once, my pride isn't playing a part here, Les. She needs to be safe more than she needs to be informed on what's happening there ... doesn't she? *Yeah,* I could go there, get what she wants, and come back, but it's a risk. I don't take risks with people I love."

Alessio blinked.

Corrado stared back, silent.

Alessio thought hearing Corrado say those words would have more impact when they hit him with their reality—their blinding truth. Though he had been watching this man fall in love with that woman for an entire month ... a month after Corrado had already spent time alone with Ginevra before Alessio even showed up, he still hadn't allowed himself to *think* Corrado loved her.

He didn't want to think it.

Not when he *wanted* to hear Corrado say it.

"I expected a different reaction when I told you that," Corrado murmured, "something other than ... silence."

"I already knew because I saw it coming, and I understand why."

Corrado nodded. "And you're not hurt or—"

"Was I the first person you told? Not *her?*"

"Of course, you were."

Alessio's brow dipped. "Why?"

"Because that's what we do, Les. That's what we're supposed to do, and I didn't do that before. *I'm sorry.* So yes, you were the first person I told. Anything else you want to hear me say right now? Anything else you want to ask about that conversation I had with her yesterday, or no?"

A lot.

But he was still trying to unpack all that shit he'd compartmentalized over the years. One thing at a time, and he was trying to handle this *thing* in the present. He couldn't go back to the past.

"I want to talk about now, *really* talk," Alessio said.

"Her, you mean?"

"Why you did this, yeah. You said when you told me, there would be no going back. That it would change everything. I want to know—so talk."

"*Koi no yokan.*"

"I have no idea what that is."

Corrado smiled, staring down the hall. "You wouldn't unless you favored Japanese writings, and you don't."

"Because I can't understand the language."

"*Anyway* ... I learned what the phrase meant days before I came to The League with my father and brother; when I met *you.*"

"That doesn't tell me what it means."

"It is the knowledge upon meeting someone that, eventually, you will fall in love with them."

"Sounds like bull—"

"Except I felt it with you," Corrado interjected, his gaze snapping back to

Alessio's in an instant. The truth he found staring back kept Alessio from saying anything more. "And somehow, I believed you would change everything for me. You did, by the way."

Alessio dragged in a hard breath. "And you mean to tell me … what, you felt it with her, too?"

"Almost instantly."

Huh.

Alessio ran his tongue along the seam of his lips, considering and unsure of what to say. Mostly because *yes,* he was still angry this had happened. He became so attached to this thing they had created between *only* them; he didn't know what it would be like after.

Because this would change.

Corrado's feelings, even if Alessio's were not there yet, determined that for them. Would the rest come along, too?

That was yet to be determined.

"You get she's not like us, right?" Alessio asked in a murmur. "She hasn't been in this kind of relationship, Corrado. This *poly*—"

"Or are you scared she might be perfect for us, but then that leaves you vulnerable again, Les?"

"Unfair."

Not everything boiled down to Alessio's *issues.*

Sometimes, shit just was.

"Why, because I understand your baggage like you get mine? Is it only okay when you want to throw my baggage at my feet for us to unpack together, but not when I throw yours back at you to do the same?"

"All of this still doesn't change you didn't tell me from the start about her, Corrado. The one thing I asked for with us, and you abused my trust."

"I understand. I'm trying to fix it."

"It's still hard for me."

"I didn't assume otherwise."

"As long as you're aware."

Corrado laughed huskily. "And nice deflection—you *still* haven't answered my question. Anything else you want to ask me about my conversation with Ginevra?"

"Good catch."

Because the man wasn't wrong.

Alessio just figured this was something he should work out on his own, but especially his darker urges that seemed to want to come out to play more often. It'd been too long since he'd fucked, and he sat on an edge like never before. It was strange how something like sex could drive him up the wall, becoming a focal point in his thoughts.

"I get you—you already have me. Despite all of this, that hasn't changed. I swear, we won't ever fucking change, Les."

Seemed not.

"Okay," Alessio said. "Did you mean that when you told her it didn't bother you at all to think of me being with her—*fucking* her, Corrado, or having her with me?" Corrado opened his mouth to speak, but Alessio was quick to jump in with, "She's not the same as when we shared women before. This is *different.* Feelings are at play here—emotions. She's not the same to you."

Corrado remained quiet.

Alessio continued on with, "Can you mean what you said knowing that?"

"Yes."

There was the truth again.

Staring him right in the face.

Corrado grinned in his way—cocky and dark. The sight alone was enough to get Alessio's cock perking to life. How long had it been since Corrado leveled the look on him, and *fuck*, he'd missed it.

The man inched closer to Alessio, closing the bit of small space between them until they were eye to eye, one with his hands in his pockets, and one with his arms folded across his chest. Corrado looked calm with his easy, arrogant stance, and Alessio was trying to keep a wall built up around him with his.

They were hard to let down.

"What do you want to hear, huh?" Corrado asked. "About her, Les. What she tastes like after she's come a few times? The sound of her screams in the morning when she's still hoarse and raw? The way she looks on her knees when she's got you buried down her throat?"

Fuck.

"*Ask*," Corrado added, his tone dropping, "and I will tell you."

He could ask a lot.

So many fucking things.

He fantasized far more than he should. To punish himself, and because he *wanted* it. Wanted her, wanted her with Corrado, and wanted her between them. Everything else was hard.

That would be easy.

"Well?" Corrado asked.

"What does she look like when you're fucking her?"

Corrado flashed a smirk. "Of course, that's what you ask."

"You've always known what I like."

"Watching me work."

Alessio shrugged a shoulder.

Why deny it?

"She looks like art," Corrado said, "she always looks like art."

A centimeter closer, and he'd be able to taste the lust right from Corrado's mouth. He was a breath away from closing the distance, but the ringing in his pocket broke their staring contest, and the conversation.

A familiar ringtone.

Dare.

The League.

Corrado dropped his stare, and so did Alessio. "You should get that, yeah?"

Alessio nodded. He needed to breathe. To reflect again.

Corrado's presence made those things hard. Even when it hurt.

"I have calls to make," Corrado said, stepping back as Alessio fished the phone out of his jeans pocket. "Say hello for me."

"Probably not."

"Yeah, Dare is likely in a mood, anyway."

Where was the lie?

Alessio answered the call as Corrado disappeared down the hall. Not that he sensed the man's loss, because it was still imprinted on Alessio's entire soul. Corrado never left, even when he wasn't seen.

"Dare," Alessio greeted, putting the phone to his ear.

"Les, how are things?"

"Better."

It wasn't a lie.

"Oh?"

"Yes."

"That's ... good," Dare replied.

Didn't sound like he meant his statement, though.

"I have information, or rather, confirmation," Dare said.

"On what?"

"The upcoming Albanian job. We were waiting for the call, the *right time*, as the client said. They're nearly ready to give the okay, and it should come up anytime over the next few weeks. You need to be ready to pick up whatever and leave. All right?"

Shit.

This hit had been years in the making, according to the client. Alessio had taken the job a few months back even though the client wasn't ready to see it through back then. Semantics, and details wouldn't line up quite right.

"Any way we can change the member for the job?"

"Not possible," Dare said, "I have signed the contract to you. Those are rules I don't bend or break, not even for you, Les."

Right.

"Got it, Dare."

"Are you sure everything is well?"

"Yes."

Or it would be.

Soon.

"Oh, and Les?"

"Yeah?" he asked.

"I need the contract for the auctions signed and faxed over soon to include your portfolio for the potential buyers."

Yeah, damn.

"I, uh ... I'm not going to the auctions, actually."

Dare was silent for a moment. "Because of him?"

"It doesn't matter why."

"Whether I want you to do the auctions is not important, but I don't want you *not* doing something you've wanted to do because Corrado Guzzi has more control of your life than he should, Alessio."

"Dare—"

"You seem to forget you're not an extension of him, Les. You're not his shadow. Don't forget you were somebody long before you even knew he existed."

Yeah, but Alessio liked life better *now*.

He could never go back to *then*.

9.

Ginevra

"Ma," Chris greeted, leaning over the table to kiss a waiting, smiling Cara on her pinked cheek. Ginevra, standing next to the man, wasn't offended that he said hello to his mother before he even considered pulling a chair out for her at the table. "Corrado sends his love."

"I bet he does." Cara's gaze turned on Ginevra and lit up even more. "And I managed to get you away from that penthouse, hmm?"

A laugh escaped her.

"Thank you for asking me to lunch."

Cara waved a hand. "Oh, it's a little thing. Chris, help her sit."

"Right, right."

Chris pulled the chair across from Cara at the table out for Ginevra, and she made herself comfortable at the table. Once he was sure she and his mother were fine, he said his goodbyes, and said he would be back later before disappearing around the partition wall keeping them hidden from the rest of the restaurant.

And what a place it was.

Gold draperies, matching tablecloths, napkins, and dark-colored rugs under each modernly decorated table. Large golden chandeliers hung above every table, making Ginevra think she was underdressed in the simple black dress she had thrown on for the lunch date with Cara Guzzi.

"This place is …" Ginevra trailed off, unsure of how to describe it.

"A little much, yeah?"

She passed Cara a look.

The other woman only shrugged.

"My husband likes to go over the top," Cara explained, "and since this restaurant is one of a few he owns, you can always tell when Gian has had his hand in the design. Lots of gold, a spattering of black, the sense of wealth all over … it all screams Guzzi."

Ginevra hadn't considered that, but now Cara had said it, she realized the other woman was correct. Like their mansion, or even the aura the couple and their sons gave off, it very much appeared like she was sitting in an excessive show of wealth.

Not that it was uncomfortable.

Just … very *there*.

Present.

Unashamed, maybe.

Cara waved a hand, and the woman that had been standing at a table nearby, but without staring at them, made her way over with the crystal pitcher of a pinkish liquid. She poured the juice—at least, that's what Ginevra assumed it was—into the two glasses on the table, and then turned to give Cara her attention.

"The usual, Mrs.?"

Cara nodded. "Yes … gives us a few options."

"Sure."

It was only once the server left around the partition wall that Cara turned her attention on Ginevra again, a glimmer in her eye as she asked, "And how are the boys?"

Boys.

As in, both.

Ginevra didn't miss that.

Cara smirked when Ginevra didn't answer right away. "I know about them, you know, and about things I am sure Corrado would tell me are none of my business, too."

Great.

Ginevra's cheeks heated, but still she answered with, "It's complicated with the three of us."

"I imagine."

"I'm not sure what else to say about this other than that."

"Nothing," Cara replied, winking. "Complicated sums it up pretty well."

Didn't it?

Conversation turned to a safer topic as they waited for their food. The designer of the dress Ginevra was wearing, one of the many outfits that were delivered to the penthouse from the same boutique that Corrado seemed to favor when she needed something special to wear.

"Why all the gold?" Ginevra asked.

"Oh, that's just a Guzzi thing." Cara shifted in her chair, flicking out one napkin to ready it on her lap. "Blood made of dirt and gold, they like to say. It's been a thing for a few generations, and started before they were ... a *famiglia*," she said, choosing her words carefully, "the family had made their money in black gold."

"Oil."

"Yes." Cara peered around their private section with a soft fondness in her gaze. "And as much as this restaurant seems like too much, I still love it the most out of all the ones in the city."

"Why is that?"

"My husband bought it after a date we had here, although back then, it didn't look like it does now. They had the best poutine I had ever tasted, and Gian took that to heart. As he does with most things."

Ginevra laughed lightly. "Really?"

"Yes. Have you ever had it—poutine?"

The memory of the one time she had tried the French dish of fries, cheese curds, and dark gravy seemed to come to the forefront of her mind with a heaviness, taking with it all of her happiness.

Cara didn't miss Ginevra's change in expression. "Something wrong?"

A typical mother.

Caring.

Concerned.

Loving.

Like hers.

"I had poutine once," Ginevra said, "with my mother and sisters. Mama made it because Greta saw a recipe on the internet—looked fun, I guess."

Cara quieted for a moment. "Ah."

"I liked it."

"Ginevra."

She peeked up through her lashes, but Cara's soft smile faded. Instead, she found sympathy and understanding in the older woman's gaze. "I'm aware of your current circumstances, and what brought you here."

"Oh."

"I'm so very sorry about your mother's passing. You are too young to be without your mother, and I bet that because you have two younger sisters, you feel you need to fill that role for them now. Except being here makes that impossible, doesn't it?"

"Entirely." Ginevra shrugged. "And thank you. I try not to think about it … it's easier."

Well, mostly.

"Once," Cara said, "there was a time when I, too, was a woman who did not want the legacy of the mafia following me, or the life I was just *given* and told I belonged to. I know what this world can sometimes make you sacrifice for this, and I'm sorry that they took your normalcy from you for the benefit of men who do not care what will happen to you because of their choices."

Ginevra dragged in a burning breath, surprised at the ache in her chest. "I didn't ask for what my half-brothers did. But I had no choice—if not me, then my sisters. I was willing to be whatever they needed for me to be so that my sisters didn't have to."

"And you worry for them now because you're not with them to stand in where they might have to," Cara replied. "I can hear it in your voice."

"Every single night. I worry for hours. I can't sleep."

Cara sighed. "I am not supposed to talk about the things my husband knows, or his contacts with other crime families outside of his own. Not our way, you see."

"I suppose."

"*But* … I will make an exception for you, Ginevra." Cara smiled, that twinkle back in her eye as she said lowly, "From what I understand, and from what Gian has gathered, New York will be a better place for you and your sisters when this ends … one side is winning, and it's the one you want to win."

Ginevra straightened on her chair, taking that statement in, and what it meant.

"And for now," Cara added, "no one will blame you for focusing on yourself, and your own happiness. Because there is nothing else you can do when these men … they make our choices. We make the best of it and say to hell with them when we can. You didn't ask for this life, but you can do amazing things with it, Ginevra. I hope you're aware of that."

The server came around the table, stopping the two from saying anything more on the topic. Food piled high on a silver platter that the woman balanced on her arm had Ginevra's stomach rumbling.

She could absorb Cara's words later.

When she was alone …

• • •

"Have you pried as much information from her as you could, Ma, and can I take her home with me now?"

Ginevra and Cara spun around from the piece of artwork they had been admiring behind the restaurant's bar. Done with their lunch, Cara had called, so Chris could come back around to pick up Ginevra anytime he was ready.

Someone else came instead.

Cara grinned at the sight of Corrado standing behind them with his hands tossed into the pockets of his suit's slacks. "Is that the only reason you assume I wanted to have lunch with her?"

Corrado's gaze drifted to Ginevra; his usual intensity colored by a clear affection. "Of course not, Ma. She's amazing without all the other interesting bits with me and Alessio. She doesn't need us for *that*."

"And you would be right," Cara said.

Ginevra smiled and stared down at the floor.

"And yes, we're done," Cara added, "so you can sneak her back, and hide her away from the world, Corrado."

"Thank you, Ma."

Cara pointed a finger at him, her gaze narrowing. "I do, however, want to see more of *you*, if you will be staying in this city. It's not acceptable for you to be here for two months, and I see you all but *one* time. I don't like that."

"I will fix that."

"Make sure. Oh, and Alessio, too. Although, I have seen far more of him than you … pick up the slack, huh?"

"Noted, Ma."

Ginevra hid her grin at Cara chastising her son by continuing to stare at the floor. She only looked up when Cara touched her arm with a soft touch.

"Thank you for joining me today," Cara said, winking, "and we will do it again soon. I promise."

"I can't wait."

It wasn't a lie, either.

"Your driver is outside, if you're ready to leave, Ma," Corrado said. "I chatted with him before I came in."

Cara nodded. "Good. I have errands. Take care of this woman, Corrado."

"Will do."

Corrado leaned down to press a quick kiss to his mother's cheek when she stopped at his side before passing him by. A simple wave of her delicate hand over her shoulder was all Ginevra saw of his mother before Cara disappeared out the front of the business.

Just like that, her focus was back on Corrado.

And that sly grin of his as he stepped closer to her until she had to walk backward from his closeness. Not that she went far—her back hit the edge of the bar, and she was cornered. Except it didn't *really* feel like he cornered her, not when she liked being caught by Corrado.

He stared down at her, his brown eyes darkening before he dropped a quick kiss to Ginevra's mouth without asking if he could or should. She didn't mind that, either, taking his kiss and reveling in the way he owned her.

All too soon, he was pulling away.

But he didn't move away.

Corrado's thumb stroked her bottom lip, and then drifted over the edge of her jaw as he asked, "Did you enjoy yourself?"

"Very much."

"Good. My mother loves you."

"She's ... amazing, too."

Corrado cocked his head to the side with a curious eye. "She is, and so are you."

"Do you lay that charm on for every woman that catches your eye, or am I a special case?"

"I never tried."

She appreciated his frankness.

"And you're quite special," he added, winking.

Ginevra laughed. "You came to get me alone?"

"I did. Today has been long ... Alessio needed time alone. I'm giving it to him."

"Did something happen?"

"Nothing that didn't need to happen."

Ginevra wasn't sure if that was a good thing, but Corrado also didn't seem like he would give her the chance to figure it out. Not before he leaned in, and found her lips with his own again in a soft, slow kiss that had her entire body heating as sparks lit up all of her nerve endings.

Damn this man.

"And I wanted to spend time with you," he murmured against her lips, his forehead touching hers, "because I don't do that enough."

"We spend all day together. We're living in the same place, and we don't leave it often, if at all."

"It's not enough. It's easy to be with you, Ginevra. *Too easy.*"

Yeah, she understood the feeling well.

And still when she looked in his eyes, she was sure something else lingered there, too. His need to have someone else with them, too, but that person wasn't there.

Which was also strange ...

Because she felt that, too.

What were these men doing to her?

10.

Alessio

"I want coffee."

Alessio didn't bother to look up from a new set of knives Corrado had laid out across the desk for him to admire. "Then, make one."

"No, from that place down the street."

Corrado peeked up at Alessio to smile. "Ah, the café down the block. She thought it was cute when we drove past yesterday."

"Yeah," Ginevra said in the doorway, "that place. Can I walk down—"

"No," Alessio said.

"But … it's a block away. And no one even knows I'm here."

Alessio turned away from the knives all at once, done with them now that something better had his attention. Ginevra, that was. "If you want to walk down to the café, then that's what we'll do. Let's find your coat."

"You're busy."

"And Corrado's middle name is Paul," Alessio said, because it was as ridiculous as her statement. "What does it matter? Now, I'm not busy. Let's go."

He didn't give her the chance to argue it further before heading past her in the doorway with a wave that demanded for her to follow. He wasn't so busy that he couldn't come back to the damn knives another day, no matter how nice they were. If she wanted coffee from the place down the block, then that's what they would do.

"Pick me up one of those Danishes!" Corrado called after him.

"Diabetes in a paper bag, got it."

"Fuck off, Les."

"But not a lie."

"Wait for me," Ginevra muttered, jogging to catch up with Alessio in the hallway. "I'm just saying, I could have walked down by myself."

"And then if something happened—"

"It wouldn't."

Alessio shrugged. "Well, it won't *now*. Will it?"

She huffed in the front hallway.

He pulled her coat from the hook and handed it to her with a grin.

"Besides," he added, "I need a walk."

"What, like a restless puppy?"

His grin turned playful in a blink.

"Exactly like that."

Mostly.

"Really?" she asked.

Alessio made a noise under his breath. "Listen, if I can't fuck my issues out, I might as well walk them out, huh?"

Ginevra's cheeks pinked.

God.

He had no clue how this woman was both innocent and sexy.

"Let's go," he said, yanking open the penthouse door.

"Should we get you a leash?"

Her teasing tone had him shaking his head. The sassiness, though? Definitely his favorite.

• • •

"Les?"

"Hmm?"

The sky, a bright blue for the second of September, stayed clear overhead. He hadn't been spending enough time outside.

When Ginevra didn't respond to his prompt, Alessio gave her all of his attention. He didn't miss how she tried to avoid his gaze by using her to-go cup of coffee as a shield in front of her face when she sipped from it.

"Ginevra, what is it?"

She peeked over at him. "Well ..."

"Say whatever, woman."

"Why haven't you kissed me since the day in the library?"

Alessio blinked, surprised at the question. "I'm ... not sure."

"Oh."

Her dimmed tone made a tightness clench in his chest. Mostly because, to him, the sound echoed with rejection. She had to realize that was the furthest thing from the case with him and her, *and* Corrado.

"Is that what you want?" he asked.

Ginevra laughed and glanced away. "I asked *why*, if you might have a reason."

"And that's not an answer to my question, Ginny."

"Because I don't know, either."

Alessio chuckled, stepping closer to her side as they continued their walk down the street. Close enough to wrap an arm around her side, hold tight to her waist, and pull her into his body. Like this, he was able to press a quick kiss to her temple, which he did to have the softness of her skin and her scent against his lips.

Only a *tease.*

A promise.

A hint of what he wanted to do.

"I've been busy unpacking my shit," Alessio murmured against her skin, tightening his hold on her waist, "and it had nothing to do with you on a *personal* level. Your presence, yes, but not you. But yes, I think about you, and what I would like from you, often."

"Do you?"

"More than I should—feelings make things dangerous, Ginevra."

"It always comes back to that for you, right?"

"Pardon?"

"How you *feel*, or what feeling something might do to you."

He stiffened.

She wasn't wrong.

"Yes," he said, "and I needed to make sure what happened here, with *you*, had nothing to do with him."

"I don't understand."

"I don't want to have you only because he does, Ginny. And I wasn't sure if that's what was happening here, or not."

She stopped their walk, turning, so both faced each other. He didn't mind because now he saw her eyes, and she had all his attention. His truths were always in his stare.

He wanted her to *know*.

All of it.

"Maybe I lied," she whispered.

Alessio arched a brow. "Oh? Hard to believe."

"I want you to kiss me, and *more*, but this is overwhelming, and confusing for me. It's easier for me to do the simple thing because I don't have to overthink, or worry about the consequences of what this all means. And—"

Quite enough of that.

Her rambling.

He only needed *I want you to kiss me*, and would happily give her what she wanted. Right fucking now, honestly. Alessio liked to give everyone their space, but especially this woman and Corrado because shit was easier.

He was tired of easy.

The only way the three of them might figure this out was if they closed all the distance and opened every single door. *Wide open*, right?

Yeah.

Alessio leaned down and grazed his lips against Ginevra's with a gentle kiss. *At first.* Enough to taste her, and the lingering bitter sweet coffee she'd been sipping on during their walk. And that's all it took for her to inch closer, for her hand to snake up against his stomach before her palm laid flat to his chest, pressing hard.

Not to move him back, no.

To keep him right *there*.

The russet stare of hers locked on his as his tongue snaked out to strike against the seam of her lips, testing and promising. *Give me a little more*, he wanted to say, *and let's see what might happen here, Ginevra.*

Instead of talking, he let the kiss say what he needed to, and what she *wanted* to. God knew he found more than what he expected in the way she stood there on the sidewalk, tight to him, her tongue slashing against his as their lips worked a familiar beat together.

Somehow, the kiss seemed familiar. Like it *should be*, as though it had always been.

Ginevra pulled back from the kiss first, her ragged exhale whispering across his lips when she breathed, "You should do that more often."

"I will."

"And you know ..."

"What?"

"Those feelings, Les," she whispered, "It's not just about me, but Corrado, too. If being here has taught me anything ... well, loving someone is not a *vulnerability*—it's courageous."

"What makes you say so?"

"What else would you call handing over a part of yourself to someone else when it means also accepting that being alone is a possibility? And yet, you're still willing to take the risk. Loving may make you vulnerable to being hurt, but it's courageous to love all the same."

"And you think that's what I should do here?"

Ginevra smiled, her fingertips drifting over his jaw with a soft touch. "Not with *me* … no one but you knows what you want with me. I meant with him—it hurts you more when you're not doing what you want to do with Corrado, when you're not *with* him."

"How can you possibly—"

"All someone has to do is watch. I have had a lot of time to do that, haven't I?"

Why should he argue?

Right was *right*.

"You realize me being with Corrado means we would be—"

"Loving again?"

Alessio wet his lower lip. "You think that man and I have *love* in the mess we made together?"

"You two might not love the way everyone else does, but it's yours. That's what matters, isn't it?"

"I still haven't decided if that makes it right, though."

Or *healthy*.

"I think it's where you're meant to be," she said, shrugging one shoulder, "together, Les. When you're apart, even when you're standing in the same room, everyone else senses the distance, too."

"Or only you do."

"Doesn't change that it's true." Ginevra sighed, dropping his gaze. "I haven't figured out yet where I fit in here."

"I know exactly where you fit in."

Her head snapped up, and those wide eyes of hers, always so expressive and deep, found his with a million and one questions reflecting back. "Do you?"

"Yes."

With them.

She belonged with them.

Except this was all on her, and she had to make those choices on her own. It wasn't something they could do for her. He only controlled what he wanted to do with Corrado, and Ginevra was right. Closer had always been better for Alessio with Corrado. Being *together*, despite the things separating them, would forever be right when everything else seemed wrong.

Alessio leaned in and pressed a quick kiss to Ginevra's lips again. "Thank you."

"For what?"

"Being you, Ginny."

• • •

Alessio knew exactly how he'd found himself like this—his back straight against Corrado's leather-wrapped headboard, a hand tight around his throat to keep him pinned in place. Corrado's mouth worked against his, kissing him hard and deep as his cock fucked him the same way.

Strange, that.

And fucking wonderful, too.

Corrado's kiss was the same as his beat with every thrust and pull against Alessio's body. Brutal, and *so fucking good*. Each snap of his hips had the firm lines of their forms driving against one another. Alessio's cock, painfully stiff, felt the brunt of their weight, grinding against his length in the best way possible.

It was too much.

It wasn't fucking enough.

How long had it been since the two of them were like this? Since Alessio just *woke up* in the night, needing Corrado? Far too long, he realized. He'd understood that better than ever tonight when he woke up, alone again, in a bed that didn't belong to him. Like one side was far too empty, and he needed to fix it.

Nothing was ever right like that.

He could still remember the cold floors chilling the pads of his feet as he drifted through the penthouse, needing to find that thing he'd been missing. *Corrado, Corrado, Corrado.* It had become a mantra in his mind, until he slipped into Corrado's room, then his bed, and finally ... *this*.

"Too long," Corrado mumbled against his mouth.

His thrusts were coming faster, now.

Harder, too.

Like the hand at Alessio's throat, those fingers tightening and loosening almost rhythmically. His voice was fucking hoarse, so deep, full of air and lust and *love*. He'd realized that, too, now. He didn't need to be told those words to know they were true.

They were *words*.

Not actions.

Or behavior.

Or their *life*.

It was just words.

Alessio had put far too much weight into words, and less trust in the man he had known from the time he was seventeen years old. So, no, he didn't give a fuck about words.

Not tomorrow.

Not yesterday.

And not right now, either.

"Look at me."

Alessio's gaze snapped up, pleasure racing through his bloodstream with every pounding beat of his heart, to find Corrado's eyes locked on his. His lips hovered above Alessio's, ragged exhales coming out fast between them, their kiss broken.

"Fucking missed you," Alessio said, words husky.

"God, yeah."

He was going to come.

Soon.

The sensation teased in the tightness of his balls, and in the heat shooting up his spine. Every slam of his lover's body into his, stretching him open in the best way as fingers dug achingly into his thighs, and he tangled his into Corrado's hair.

He couldn't stop it.

"Jesus Christ, Corrado."

Alessio stiffened, a loud groan escaping from his lips before Corrado slammed his mouth against his to swallow it up. Their tongues clashed, warring like their hands pushing and grabbing far too tightly as his come spilled between them.

"Come on," Alessio urged Corrado, his tongue snaking out to taste the salt on his lover's jaw as those words tumbled out. "Fucking give it to me, then."

"Fuck."

Teeth scraped against his stubble, a sting following the same path. The ache of Corrado's hands, one still at his throat, and the other now pushing firmly against the hard ridges of Alessio's abdominal muscles, only want more.

"Come," Alessio goaded. *"Fucking come."*

The control Corrado always had snapped, and nothing was better than that, too. The wild darkness he found in the man's gaze under the dim lighting of the one bedside lamp which was still on. The way he bared his teeth and met that challenge staring back.

After all these years that was still the same.

Sex was still their war.

There were no losers here.

It didn't matter if he was *fucking*, or the one being fucked. This was their battle that only got better with time. The one place they found the most solace together. Quiet, alone, lost in each other, and nothing else.

Fuck, he forgot how much he missed that.

How much he needed it.

The husky moan that escaped Corrado as his next thrust brought him to a full stop against Alessio, his grasp stilled before it trembled like the rest of his body, brought him out of the remnants of his own orgasm to watch his lover fall into his.

Corrado's head dipped down, his forehead pressing to Alessio's chest over the tattoo of a crowned heart, as his back tensed, and a curse fell from his lips. Nothing sounded better, and nothing would ever calm him more than this.

Of that, he was most sure.

Seconds passed.

Silence echoed.

Alessio sighed. "Too fucking long, Corrado."

"Yeah."

"Shit still won't be perfect," Alessio warned.

He figured, the man needed to hear that.

He did, too.

"But it is right now," Corrado replied, tone low.

"It is right now."

Their reminder.

They could have this. It would be there, present and effective like they needed it to be. That didn't mean it would fix everything. Sex didn't work that way, not for them. But it helped.

Alessio stared at the ceiling above him, body thrumming and sensitive in the best way. "I could love her."

His words were soft in the darkness. Like maybe if he didn't say them loudly, then they wouldn't come true yet. He wasn't sure if he was as ready for that as he had been for this.

He heard Corrado's swallow.

Audible, and weighted.

Like the rest of this, too.

It was all too fucking heavy.

"I could," Alessio said again.

"You should. *You should.*"

11.

Alessio shifted around Corrado in the walk-in closet, reaching past to grab the folded pair of black jeans sitting in a pile of other plain, black jeans. It was almost amusing because even Alessio's clothes had remained in Corrado's room, although the man didn't.

Corrado slipped a watch onto his wrist, already mostly dressed after their shared shower. He wasn't soon going to forget that, or the night before, either. It always led to far better mornings when he woke up next to the person—people, now—he wanted. Last night seemed like it was for him *and* Alessio, and this morning ... well, it was only for Les.

From the second the man backed him against the shower wall, to the way his teeth had found the back of Corrado's neck when he fucked him.

Like that, they connected better.

It was *easier*.

"Yeah, this is gonna have to do," Alessio muttered.

Corrado eyed him from the side, smirking. "You're practically naked."

In nothing but black jeans, showing off inked, tanned skin, nipple rings, and the hard-cut V of his groin, Alessio stared back at Corrado like he didn't see the problem. He hadn't even bothered to pull on shoes or socks. He worked on affixing his row of bracelets and his favorite watch to his wrist as he asked, "*And?*"

Corrado shook his head. "And nothing."

It spoke to their differences again.

The things which make them unique.

Corrado was up and dressed in slacks, his usual silk button-down, and ready for the day, bad mood not included. He couldn't be in a bad mood after a night and morning like the one they had. It had been a long fucking time coming.

Alessio liked a bit of laziness when he first woke up after a night like the one before. Half-dressed, partially awake, still happy, all things considered, but not sure if he wanted to start the day or not.

Leaning against the row of shelving in the walk-in closet, Alessio said nothing as Corrado pulled a silk tie from the rack that matched the navy blue of his shirt. He didn't mind the man's attention, because it wasn't unusual, but he still figured after the night before, maybe Alessio had things to say.

"What?" Corrado asked.

"Nothing."

"You sure?"

Alessio grinned. "Just thinking I missed this, is all."

Corrado stilled as he threw the tie around his neck, the ends hanging down. He peeked up, meeting Alessio's stare to hold it as the silence echoed all around them. Not that he needed to repeat or confirm what Alessio had said because he heard it fine. He didn't think Alessio needed Corrado to say he felt the same, either.

Wasn't it obvious?

And yet, he still murmured, "Me, too. Every fucking day, Les."

Because this was *them*.

Their life, routine, and *thing* together. Morning, noon, and night. For five years, there were things about them that had never changed. And when one became comfortable in the mundane parts of life with someone else at their side, like getting dressed together first thing in the morning, it was like missing your left hand when you had to do it alone.

Corrado *hated* that.

He needed Alessio to feel right.

Normal.

"Yeah, me too," Corrado said again, moving to leave the walk-in closet.

Alessio stopped him with a hand that shot out fast to slip around Corrado's neck to stop him. His fingers threaded into Corrado's hair line at the nape of his neck, tightening just enough, before he yanked him forward for a kiss.

He took that, too.

Happily.

It was softer than their moments had been the night before, or even that morning. Slower, too, like Alessio wanted to enjoy it.

Corrado didn't mind at all.

His teeth dragged along Alessio's lower lip as he pulled away with a wink. "We're good?"

Alessio nodded. "We're *better.*"

He'd take that.

It was something other than what they had been.

"And I'm still not fucking getting entirely dressed yet," Alessio grumbled when Corrado turned to leave the closet. He laughed, hearing the pattering of Alessio's footsteps following behind him. "I want pancakes."

"Cook them."

"I don't ... *cook.*"

"You should learn. Why do I always have to feed *you*? It should be the other way around occasionally, yeah?"

Alessio made a noise under his breath.

Corrado just chuckled.

"Fine, I'll cook them, but if you die from it, you can't blame me."

"I'll help."

"Thought so."

He ignored the smugness to the man's tone as he found the shoes he'd slipped off next to the bed before climbing in the night before. Sitting on the edge of the mattress, he shoved his feet into the supple leather loafers, glancing up to find Alessio leaning against the small dresser between the bathroom and closet doors.

"I'm not signing the contract for The League's auctions," Alessio said without prompting.

Corrado took those words in before responding. It was Alessio's choice, but after saying his piece that day in the office, he decided there wasn't anything else he needed to do.

Like everything else in their relationship.

Corrado didn't have to like it all.

"And how does Dare feel about that?" Corrado asked.

Alessio shrugged. "It's not his choice."

"That's not what I asked."

"I'm aware."

It didn't matter, Corrado decided.

Alessio was right.

No one else but Alessio got the final say.

Standing from the bed, ready to start his day in a far better mood than he had in a month or more, Corrado turned to face the doorway of the bedroom.

The *opened* door, he realized.

He blinked, staring across the hall to the open doorway of the bedroom just across from his. There, Ginevra slept on top of her blankets, like usual. There was nothing strange about that, and yet, it still seemed like he was missing something.

"Hey," Alessio said behind him. "We cooking food, or not?"

Corrado didn't move. "Did you close the door last night?"

Alessio didn't answer.

Because he didn't need to.

A sound escaped Corrado, wary and curious at the same time. "*Les?*"

"I can't remember, and I don't, no. That's *your* thing, not mine. Someone is in the bed, you close the door. I came in, Corrado, and we didn't get out of the bed."

"I didn't open it this morning."

"Me, either."

They had yet to leave the bedroom. So yeah, the door had been open all night.

Had Ginevra's also been open?

Fuck.

• • •

"If your first ten calls and messages went unanswered," Andino Marcello said, his tone cool in Corrado's ear on the other end of the call, "then maybe that should have been a clue to you about the fact I wasn't willing to chat."

Corrado stiffened, trying to subdue the urge to tell this asshole where he could fuck himself, and with what tool to use to do it. "Despite this ... *favor*," he said, choosing his words carefully although he wanted to make himself clear, "I don't answer to you, Andino. When this is all said and done, remember that, yeah?"

Alessio peeked over his shoulder, arching a brow in silent question. Corrado shook his head in response, not wanting the man to worry about it. They would talk about this after. Alessio needed to focus on *not* burning the pancakes.

Because apparently, standing next to the stove while he cooked was too big of a hassle. That was every reason Corrado was standing behind him while on the call to make sure Alessio didn't move from his spot.

That, and he wanted to be close.

"I have nothing to tell you," Andino snapped.

"She would like to speak to her sisters."

"Absolutely not. As far as they know, she is missing, and dead. I want them to keep believing that. They are too young to understand the consequences of outing the fact she's still alive."

"They think *what?*" Corrado hissed.

Alessio's hand drifted behind him, his fingers twisting into the fabric of Corrado's shirt like he assumed holding onto the man would keep him calm. It helped; he wouldn't lie about that. So much so that Corrado moved closer to Alessio. Close enough to share the warmth of Alessio's sculpted back molding against his silk-covered chest.

"You're not serious, right?" Corrado asked, his tone calmer.

Not by much though.

"I need people to rely on what I tell them," Andino said, sounding as though he was just about done with this conversation. "And I don't care if you, or she, or anyone else, fucking likes it. As long as I get what I want that's what matters."

"They're teenagers. You're *traumatizing* them, likely. Their father died a while back, then their mother, and now they think their sister is—"

"Is there something I can do for you, or did you keep calling me so you could bitch about shit that won't change soon, Corrado?"

His jaw ached. That's how hard he was clenching his fucking teeth. It was likely the next time he had a face-to-face moment with Andino, well, it would not end well. Corrado would guarantee it wouldn't end badly for him, though.

"Easy," Alessio murmured as though he was reading Corrado's mind. It was far more probable he was feeling Corrado's body cues that spoke of his anger, and he was reacting to that. "Try to get *something* you want from him. Something to give her, Corrado. It's the best you can do. We can handle his stupid ass another day."

Right, right.

When had Alessio become the voice of reason?

It didn't matter.

"Just …" Corrado cleared his throat and pinched the bridge of his nose to settle the fury swimming in his bloodstream. Some people just had that effect on others. Like instant anger right to the fucking vein. Andino was one of those. "How much longer before she might come home?"

Although that thought alone was enough to make Corrado want to rage all over again, but for different reasons. Ginevra had a life away from here … people to take care of. And God knew he would never deny her those things, even if he had fallen entirely in love with the woman amidst this mess with him, the favor to Andino, and Alessio.

Still, he loved her.

At some point, she would go back.

Corrado didn't like it, but that didn't make it any less true. He figured, when the time came, then they would all handle it together. Him, Les, and her. However they wanted to work that out, then they would.

"When?" he asked again, firmer the second time when Andino said nothing.

"I'm not sure."

"Jesus Christ. And they want *you* to be the next boss of that organization there?"

"Out of line," Andino murmured, "and now you're pissing me off."

Oh, really?

That was nice.

So fucking nice.

And Corrado didn't give a shit.

"You've been pissing me off since—"

Alessio pivoted and snatched the phone right out of Corrado's hand. He put the device to his ear at the same time his palm came to rest flat against Corrado's chest, a silent order for him to stay. He wasn't even pressing down to keep him from moving, and Corrado's blazing gaze didn't seem to bother him in the least.

"Andino," Alessio said into the phone, never looking away from Corrado's severe expression as he did so, "it's Alessio—yeah, you remember, right? Say hello to Pink for me, I'm sure he needs the reminder, too."

A beat of silence passed.

Alessio grinned. "And your point is? Because here's our fucking point—we need a timeline, something to *give* this woman here who did everything you asked of her even when you gave her fuck all in return. She followed *your rules.* She did what you wanted. Not once has she stepped out of line, and every single day, she continues to do these things hoping that back there, the people she loves—who no worries, we know you don't give a shit about—are still okay. And so, if you can't tell me things I need to know here, I will come find it."

A hum sounded from the speaker.

Loud and dark.

Alessio seemed unaffected. "That's nice, and I also don't care. Because while we're aware that to you, Ginevra is a means to an end, *here* ... here she means something. So, you give me something to tell her, or I will come cut it out of your fucking mouth. You hear me?"

Corrado grinned, glancing away because *right,* he was the one who needed to keep himself in check. Not at all Alessio.

No.

Alessio's fingers tapped against Corrado's chest, drawing his attention back to the man as he nodded. "Within a couple of months? Not firm, but likely. Got it."

He hung up the phone without a proper goodbye and handed it out to Corrado accompanied by a pointed look. Corrado took the device, shaking his head at the same time.

"He's hoping to have *everything* finished within a couple of months," Alessio said like Corrado hadn't heard the conversation already. "We'll see how that works out."

"Still nothing for her to have about her sisters, though."

Alessio shrugged. "They're alive, Corrado. You can tell her they are still alive."

Yeah.

What good would that do, though?

"It's the best we can do."

"Right," Corrado agreed.

Not that it made him feel better.

Alessio turned back to the stove, his pancake bubbled in the center to say it was ready to flip.

"Turn it over," Corrado said. "And try not to make a mess."

"I am doing *fine.*"

"I didn't say you weren't."

Alessio made a noise under his breath but did flip the pancake. Corrado wasn't sure how long the two of them stayed like that, close together against the stove as Alessio made an entire stack worth of pancakes that were decent, and not at all burned, but the minutes ticked by.

In their closeness, he found home.

In their silence, comfort.

A part of Corrado hoped the two of them were getting back to what they had been before this whole thing happened. Oh, he wasn't stupid enough to think it would be the same, but it could be better.

He wanted that just as badly.

Corrado pressed a quick kiss to the top of Alessio's wide shoulder. His head turned, his gaze finding Corrado, but he said nothing. Not that he needed Alessio to say anything—all he ever needed was the man to be *there*.

In Alessio's stare, he found familiarity.

Understanding.

Corrado figured Alessio still had shit he needed to work through here, and he was more than willing to allow him whatever he needed to do it. Now, at least, they could get back to *them* while he did it, and that made all the difference.

It always had.

Alessio turned his attention back to the last pancake on the frying pan, saying, "Someone should go wake Ginevra up. She'll want to eat, too."

"She's up."

Corrado glanced to the side, and sure enough, found Ginevra standing in the kitchen's entryway watching them. He'd sensed her presence from damn near the moment she came to stand there, even though she hadn't made a single noise the entire time. She hadn't been there long enough to overhear the phone conversation with Andino, but she had been watching Corrado and Alessio interact together for quite a while.

Alessio looked her way, too.

Ginevra's cheeks heated as her stare drifted between the two. He didn't find shame there … at least, not to say she might be embarrassed despite her blush. A bright curiosity blazed in her eyes, and he bet she didn't have the first clue what to do with that at all. And then she turned to dart out of the entryway, leaving air and shadows in her wake. Corrado let out a hard breath, a heaviness climbing up his spine.

Her reaction was all he needed.

The door had been open.

He bet she knew what happened the night before and had a front-row seat for at least *some* of it.

Alessio dropped the spatula to the counter. "Let me go talk to her, yeah?"

That … wasn't a bad idea.

"You should."

Alessio sidestepped Corrado to leave the stove. "All right. Keep the food hot."

"Sure. And, Les?"

"Hmm?"

Corrado shrugged one shoulder. "*Be easy.* You're a bit overwhelming at first, but especially like *that.*"

A sinful smirk curved Alessio's lips in the most wicked way. "You don't know that's what—"

"Be easy." Corrado pulled open a drawer on the island, and in a flash, tossed an item to Alessio that he caught without hesitation. He stuffed the foil packet into his back pocket. Alessio didn't know whether he was offended or aroused that Corrado was sure enough about what would happen between him and Ginevra that he pulled out a condom from one of their many stashes, or if it should irk him. "A *just in case*, yeah?"

"Right."

12.

"Ginevra."

Oh, God.

Alessio's voice calling out behind Ginevra had her wishing she could crawl into a hole and disappear. She thought, *surely*, she could act like nothing had happened the night before. Like she hadn't woken up in the middle of the night to the sounds of two men *fucking*. Like she hadn't been able to tip her head up and see *everything* happening across the hall because Corrado slept with a goddamn lamp on.

Not that it bothered her.

That was a lie.

It *bothered* her.

But in strange ways she hadn't expected. For one, because a part of her wanted to join them. For two, because she was out of her league here with these men, and their brand of love. Not only had she found that she couldn't look away the night before, a part of her hadn't wanted to, either.

That wasn't *her* moment.

They weren't fucking *her*.

She had no business watching them together, and yet, she hadn't been able to stop, either. Somehow, she'd went back to sleep ... but not until they finished. And not without an ache between her thighs she was sure wouldn't *ever* be satisfied.

"Ginevra!"

A few more steps that's all.

Then, she could tuck herself away in the bedroom, close the door, and pretend like this hadn't happened at all. She wasn't ready for what was happening here if she couldn't stare those two men in the face the next morning without reliving every single detail of the show she got the night before.

So, she needed to avoid it.

Entirely.

Right?

"Would you *stop*? Christ, woman!"

Ginevra didn't make it to the bedroom before Alessio caught up to her in the hallway. His hand snagged her wrist and grabbed tight before she found herself spun around *fast*. The walls were a blur until everything stopped, her back hit the edge of the decorative table a couple of feet away from the bedroom doorway, and Alessio closed in on her.

She felt like a caged animal.

This man had *that* effect.

When he loomed over her, when he got close, and those eyes of his were only on her. Yeah, she felt just like a caged animal, and he was the predator that found his prized prey. Not that she minded it, but right then ... Ginevra wanted to hide away.

"I want to go to my room," she whispered.

Alessio's brow dipped. "Ginevra—"

"I didn't mean to see that last night, and I'm sorry. I know I shouldn't have spied. Please, let me go."

He didn't.

In fact, he moved closer.

Pinned her harder.

Ginevra dragged in a ragged breath. "What are you doing?"

"You think we're *mad* at you?"

"I—"

"The door was open, Ginny."

She blinked at how he said those words. Like it just was, and she should have realized that a long time ago. She didn't think he was talking only about the bedroom door, either. She only had to consider it, and this last month with the three of them living in the same place.

Rarely did they close doors.

In any room.

Alessio and Corrado didn't tamper their tones when they spoke, either. It didn't matter if they were talking about the weather while running on the treadmill or shouting at one another in the office like they had when Alessio first came back.

The doors didn't get closed.

They let her hear everything.

She saw *everything*.

Her gaze lifted to meet Alessio's, and there, she found a raging blue storm staring at her, but in the middle of it all, she found truth. They'd purposely done that—never once had they hid themselves, their baggage, or the rest. To her, they stayed *way open*.

Alessio, too, she now realized. Even when he had been so mad, closed off, keeping that distance, and dealing with his own mountain of problems, he'd not shut her out physically. It was disconcerting.

Because she liked that.

And it terrified her, too.

"Ginevra," he murmured.

Still staring at him, she swallowed the nerves in her throat, saying, "I still shouldn't have done it. I … you didn't invite me to do that."

Right?

She didn't think so.

It didn't matter she liked it, or they left their door open like they had a silent understanding between the three of them that she only now realized … that was them, and their private moment together.

"I didn't feel like an intruder, but I still think I intruded."

Alessio shook his head. "Not at all, sweetheart. That's one thing you couldn't do with us, but especially not when we're fucking. Do you hear me?"

God.

That heat climbed in her cheeks again, and shot right down to her pussy, too. It was easier to admire the grain in the wood floor than his handsome face, so she did that. His words shouldn't have sounded as sinful and inviting as they did, and somehow … he still pulled it off.

"You know," she said, her nervous energy falling out in fast words, "before you two, I used to say I was open about sex, and what people liked, or … all of that. Someone else's bedroom was theirs, and it's fine."

"And now?"

"I still think that, I just didn't consider it would be *my* bedroom someday, either."

Alessio chuckled. "Ginevra, look at me."

When she didn't do what he wanted right away, his left hand shot up to catch her under the jaw. A simple tilt of his hand, and she was staring into his eyes again, frozen in place by the intensity she found there.

"It's okay to be overwhelmed and confused," he said, shrugging one bare shoulder, "but never *hide* when you want it, too. That's the only way you can find out if what you want is worth it."

"Oh, that I don't doubt."

He raised a brow. "Hmm?"

"That this will be worth it."

It was the aftermath that made her wonder, but even then, she would brave it for them. She wasn't sure she wanted to find out what life would be like after these men had come into hers to change it irrevocably.

"Did you see me go in last night?" he asked.

Ginevra shook her head. "I woke up *during* …"

The memory flashed in her mind, thick and heady. Part of it hadn't seemed real, and yet, every inch of her body knew it was vivid and true.

Corrado had put Alessio on his knees, a hand tangled into his hair, and the other wrapped around his chest to keep the man suspended higher off the bed as he fucked him from behind. Their voices, their *sounds*, all came out husky. And even as it seemed like one had more control than the other, she found power in Alessio, too. In the way his body moved, how his hands tugging and grabbed to Corrado, seeking what *he* wanted.

She'd blinked, stunned at what she was seeing, and after they had rolled over, Alessio's back against the headboard, and Corrado was above him. They stayed close, movements frantic, and beauty covering every action between them.

And their *fucking?*

She found it familiar. Or rather, she recognized it was familiar to them. So rough, and vicious, yet she found affection in between, too. Maybe that was what had drawn her in the most …

"There's *always* affection," Alessio said.

Ginevra flew from her thoughts in a bang, her stare still locked on Alessio's, although she had been seeing him differently just moments ago inside her mind. Now, she found something hotter staring back at her, not that the night before, she would have thought anything would be more wickedly tempting than seeing those two men fuck.

Now, she'd say it was the way Alessio was looking at *her*. A lot similar to the way Corrado did when he had her pinned under him, making her beg and scream in all the best fucking ways.

"Intense, and beautiful," she said, her voice a breath, "that's what it was."

Alessio's gaze blazed with lust. "Was it?"

"I wondered …"

"Tell me."

"Does he fuck me the same way he fucks you—will *you*?" Ginevra dragged in a hard inhale, letting the air ache in her lungs at the thought. "Would either of you ever be able to love me the way you love each other?"

Alessio never blinked.

Didn't *breathe*.

"And how do we fuck—and love—each other, Ginny?"

"Savagely," she whispered.

It was true.

They hurt each other loving. Survived from it, *killed* with it, or become better for it. Was that not the most primal aspects of being *human*? Of loving as a human? And so, it seemed appropriate to say at their most base of being, in their moments of rawest need, they savagely loved.

"Savagely," Alessio echoed.

Ginevra nodded. "And I don't know if I could ever be the same to—"

"You only have to say yes."

"What?"

"*Say yes.*" His hand on her thigh squeezed, making her all too aware of how close his fingers were to the tiny cotton shorts she wore to bed. The matching top rested higher above her navel, and she had on nothing underneath. There was no hiding the way her nipples had pebbled under the thin top, or the way her throat jumped when her gaze darted down to his mouth.

Not that her staring stopped there. She had never gotten the chance to admire Alessio without a shirt. He even worked out with one on, and he didn't leave a bathroom unless he was fully dressed after a shower, not that it mattered because he had a private bath in his room.

But *now* …

Now, she admired the strong muscles that made up the man's chest, and the hard lines that showcased his abs, and the way his pants rested low on his defined hips. He seemed chiseled from stone, a lot like Corrado. She'd watched him and Corrado put the gym to use day after day enough, so she knew why they looked like they did, too.

She took in his tattoos, the double sleeves, and the start of the chest tattoo that showcased a crowned heart. Corrado hadn't been lying, either. Straight bars pierced through both his nipples. They were opposites in that way. One showcasing his calm strength in a body that was uninked and unmarked in other ways. And the other taunted the world with his wildness through colorful designs, and piercings.

It wasn't obvious.

Then again, they'd been subtle from the start.

But she saw it.

She recognized it all.

They were Godly.

Both.

Why her?

What God had she pleased?

"I like your staring," he said, chuckling, "but I would *love* an answer more, Ginevra. A yes, or a no."

Right.

"And if I do? Say yes, I mean."

"Then you can learn what we both can do," he replied, his tone husky.

Like last night.

That memory swept in again.

She was *wet again.*

"Say yes," he urged.

How could she not?

Temptation had ruined the world before.

And she was only a woman.

Ginevra stood no chance.

Her hands shook against the table when he set her on it, yet her next word same out clear, and sure. There would be no mistake about what she wanted. "*Yes.*"

She was grateful for the sturdiness of the table—its thick, long curved legs and strong, shiny top more than capable of handling their roughness.

Alessio closed all the distance between them in an instant. His mouth collided down on hers as his hand at her thigh slid higher up the leg of her shorts. The way he kissed her matched the way his fingers explored her. Soft strokes at first, his lips drifting over hers damningly the same way his fingers drifted over her bare pussy. Tentative at first, *seeking.* All it took was her moan, and the widening of her thighs as her lips parted for his kiss to deepen, and she found a whole *new* heaven.

There was something wicked about the way Alessio kissed her as two of his fingers slid into her clenching sex. His tongue curled around hers as his fingers twisted into her G-spot. At her jaw, his hand still keeping her head in place, so he watched her while he came up higher, and his thumb slipped into her mouth as he pulled back.

He watched her like that, too.

Sucking on his digit.

Riding his fingers.

Jesus Christ.

She would come fast.

It didn't matter he wasn't kissing her now, either. He cocked his head to the side, a sexy smirk curving the edges of his lips as he pulled his thumb from her mouth with a *pop*, and his hand slid down to her throat. Those fingertips of his drummed against her racing pulse as he spoke. "Right there, huh? Your pussy is holding onto my fingers so tight, Ginny? *Fuck*, are you gonna rain on me, sweetheart? Soak me?"

"Oh, my God," she breathed.

"Come, and give me some of you, yeah? Let me suck you off my fingers before I see my cock stretch you out, Ginevra."

Yeah.

That did it.

She came hard, a broken cry escaping her, and a rush of wetness pooling between her legs which she *might* have been embarrassed about with someone else, but not with this man. Alessio's gaze dropped between their bodies, and his grin deepened salaciously, pride coloring up the throaty noise he made as his fingers slipped out of her pussy.

He liked that.

"Fuck yeah, that's what I wanted to see," he murmured. "You try."

His hand came up fast, and unquestioningly, she opened her mouth to take the single finger he offered for her. Her heady flavor coated her tongue as she sucked herself from his digit, surprised at the tart undertones of her arousal.

She still trembled from that orgasm when he pulled his hand away to clean his other finger, the one still wet with only her, too. *God.* Nothing looked better than him enjoying the flavor of her.

Those next few seconds came like a blur. He moved fast, tugging her shorts down her legs so fast it stung her skin, not that she cared. Her hands worked at his jeans while his slipped under the cropped tank she wore to cup her breasts. Her gasp filled the hallway when his fingertips tweaked her hard nipples.

"Still yes?" she heard him ask.

"Still yes."

Undeniably yes.

Alessio's hands disappeared from her shirt to speed up her attempt at shoving down his pants. Although, not before he grabbed a foil packet from his back pocket.

Oh. And did she mention he went commando? Because he did. *Yep.*

Fuck.

Her fingers circled around his length, already so fucking hard and weighty in her palm. She stroked his length, letting her fingertips drift over the vein on the underside of his cock that pulsed from her touch.

"Easy," he was quick to say when her grip tightened, "let me fill that pussy before you try to make me come, woman."

Ginevra grinned.

She got his kiss again, after they rolled latex down his length, and he widened her thighs enough that her muscles ached deep. His lips found hers as he positioned the head of his cock at her slit. His tongue stroked hers when his hips flexed forward.

She was so wet.

So beyond ready.

And still the first thrust took her breath away. Her body tensed, the width of him stretching her open fast, and hard. She loved it, though. So much.

Still, he didn't stop kissing her, lips warring with hers as his tongue seemed intent to lick the fucking taste right off hers. His pace came swift, and deep. A brutal rhythm that held no reservations and didn't hold back.

Not for a second.

His hands were on her body again.

Pinning her in place.

Tightening to take her air away.

One on her chest.

At her throat.

Ginevra whimpered, words becoming impossible. It surrounded her in *him*. His taste, his scent, and all of him inside and on her. It was overwhelming, and exactly what she needed.

"Let me have this pussy suck me dry, sweetheart," he uttered against her cheek. "I want it, so you better give it to me, huh?"

Her desperate cry tangled with his thick groan.

That pace didn't let up.

Ginevra's peak climbed higher and faster than she expected it to. Still soaked between her thighs from that first orgasm, she fell over the cliff again. His blue eyes stayed locked on hers, and pleasure darkened Alessio's stare as he watched her come from him fucking her that time.

His hands slid down to grip tight onto her thighs, his strokes coming shorter, but still as rough even as he fucked her through that orgasm. She couldn't breathe, her vision tunneling from the intensity.

And then his head tipped down, his forehead resting against her chest as his thrusts came *faster*. Shaking, her peak waning but bliss racing through her bloodstream, as his fingers dug painfully into her thighs.

God, it felt good, though.

Still.

He had the best view like that, she realized. Looking down, watching himself fuck her. His next three thrusts came slower, but deeper than before, the final one making him still as her name tumbled from him with the rawest sound.

"*Ginevra*, fuck ..."

He shook, too.

He lost his breath, too.

And she was still spinning high.

Ginevra wasn't sure how long the two of them stayed like that, tucked close, saying nothing, and letting it all sink in. A minute, or maybe two.

Hell, it might have been more.

She didn't care to know.

A throat cleared further down the hall, and Ginevra's eyes squeezed shut, *knowing*. Against her chest, Alessio let out a dusky laugh that still somehow sounded airless as his shoulders lifted with his breaths. She turned her head, unsurprised to find Corrado lingering at the end of the hall, half around corner, and half not. He didn't directly look at them, but he didn't keep his focus off them, either.

The ridge of his erection straining against his slacks was impossible to miss, never mind the way his tongue snaked out to wet his lips like he'd seen something he liked. She might have been embarrassed another time, but not then.

The doors were open here.

And she wanted to do this again.

All of it.

With both.

"Food is hot," Corrado said, "whenever you would both like to join me."

That said, Corrado turned, and left her view.

Ginevra made a sound under her breath. "What happens now? What do we do now?"

Alessio laughed again. "Nothing. Everything. *Anything*."

Well, that told her all she needed to know, didn't it?

298

13.

Alessio

Sex was sex to Alessio, and he rarely, if ever—because he couldn't remember a time when it happened—felt awkward afterward. He understood why other people might feel that way, though. Which was why after he'd tucked himself away, and slid Ginevra's cotton shorts back up her legs, he helped her down from the table in the hallway, and with a press of his palm against her lower back, directed her into the nearest bedroom.

Hers.

She twisted her fingers, fidgeting as he moved around the room to pull clean clothes from the dresser before setting them on the edge of her bed. Not that she had a lot of clothes—a few things, he supposed. Enough to get her by here as Corrado told him.

"You need more clothes," Alessio muttered.

Ginevra let out a soft laugh. "And what would you know about that? You only wear black; everything looks the same."

He tossed her a heated look over his shoulder, and he liked the way she stilled when his gaze landed on her. All over again, the taste of her seemed to flood his mouth, and every sweet sound that came out of her when she was being fucked filled his ears again.

Yeah.

Alessio was screwed.

"Really, I just *always* look the same?" he asked, arching a brow.

Ginevra grinned, some of her nervousness bleeding away. "You're far too cocky for your own good."

"But *with* reason."

She didn't deny it.

Alessio pulled a white, cotton thong from the top drawer in the dresser, and tossed it to the pile of clothes, too. Coming to stand in front of Ginevra, he found her nerves made an appearance again when she wouldn't look up at him.

That was fine.

He could fix it.

Sliding his hands under her jaw, he tipped her head up, so she *had* to look at him. Those wide brown eyes of hers reflected everything she wasn't saying, and he saw it as clear as day staring back at him.

"Hey," he murmured.

Ginevra wet her lips. "Yeah?"

"Everything is *fine.*"

"I know that."

"Nothing happens unless you want it to."

She nodded. "I know that, too."

He grinned. "That's all that should matter, then. Everything else is details, and noise. Don't overthink it. That's my job."

Her soft laughter had his semi-hard dick perking in his jeans again, making him all too aware that he still needed to go dispose of the condom, and clean himself up. *Fuck*. He'd much rather stay right here with her and handle whatever she needed.

Still, the bigger deal they made about this, the harder it might be for Ginevra to see *this* was all normal. Perhaps not for other people, but for them … it was fine.

"I just … what if I mess up?" she asked.

Alessio frowned. "How would you do that?"

"I'm not sure." Her fingers tittered in the air when she waved her hands. "Maybe I give him more attention, or I sit beside one and not the other. Or—"

"Stop. That's ridiculous."

Ginevra blinked, hurt coloring up her expression. "It's not ridiculous just because *you* already know how to handle something like this. *I* haven't, Les."

Okay.

"So, that's the wrong word," he said, dropping a kiss to her lips that lingered as he continued quieter, "these aren't things that matter here, I swear. Corrado and I … we can handle each other, or get what we need. Whether that's from each other, ourselves, or from you. This thing isn't a tit for tat, sweetheart. We're not keeping score."

"So, I can just … keep doing what I'm doing."

"If that's what you want. The only things that change are the things you want to be different."

"Okay."

Alessio smiled and pressed another kiss to her grinning lips. "Get dressed—you need to eat, huh?"

"Yeah."

It might not fix her nerves, but he hoped it helped a little. His fingers drifted over her cheek, tucking the wild strands of her dark brown hair behind her ears before he left her side, and headed out of the bedroom. She needed time by herself, he figured.

And he needed to get cleaned up.

After doing that in his own room, Alessio arrived back in the kitchen alone, although Corrado was already there, sitting at the large dining room table with the newspaper spread out in his hands. To his benefit, Corrado didn't look at Alessio as he came to sit on the left side of the man and reached for the plate of pancakes in the table's middle.

That didn't mean he stayed silent though.

"And?" Corrado asked, his voice a murmur, his gaze still taking in the paper.

"Give her a minute. Let her absorb it all."

Corrado hummed his agreement, then turned to peer at Alessio as he smothered a pancake in maple syrup. The thing he loved the most about Canada, next to the fact it was Corrado's birthplace, was that they didn't do that fake syrup shit *flavored* like maple.

"And what about you? Are you good?"

Alessio arched a brow. "You're right."

"Oh? I usually am, but do tell. It's not every day you say *you're right* and not *you're not wrong*. Because one is you outright admitting *you* were wrong, and the other is your way of trying to keep from showing your whole ass in a conversation."

"Fuck off," Alessio muttered, chuckling.

He peeked up from his plate, but Corrado hadn't looked away from him. Their gazes met, and Alessio relaxed in a way he hadn't before.

"Not a lie, though," Corrado said, shrugging.

"Not a lie," Alessio echoed. "And I meant … about her. You were right. She's like art."

Fucking her had been a privilege.

And not one he was sure he deserved.

Corrado made an appreciative noise under his breath, and his attention quickly went back to the paper. "I know, now so do you."

Right.

He was a quarter of the way through his plate when Ginevra darkened the entryway of the kitchen. She hesitated only momentarily before joining the two at the table, taking a seat at Corrado's right, across from Alessio.

Ginevra didn't reach for the food.

Alessio continued eating, and Corrado didn't turn his attention away from the paper in his hands. It was like any other morning, except it wasn't.

He could *feel* the change, now.

It was palpable.

Corrado flipped the corner of the paper down and winked at Ginevra. "Eat, kitten. Food is better when it's hot."

"Oh, I like that better," Alessio said more to himself than anyone else at the table. "Kitten—it's appropriate."

"Right? That's what I thought."

"Makes sense."

Ginevra let out a breathy laugh. "You two are horrible."

"But are we?" Alessio asked.

"We are a *little*," Corrado said, and then to Ginevra, "Unless you want a plate made for you. All you have to do is ask."

For anything, Alessio added silently.

He was sure they'd figure out a way to give it to her now.

Ginevra smiled. "I do like being spoiled."

Corrado tossed his paper aside before Ginevra had even finished her sentence and was already getting up from the table to do her bidding. Alessio met her gaze across the way, and winked.

See?

Fine.

Everything would be fine.

• • •

"Cree," Alessio greeted, standing from the couch and giving the other two a wave of his hand as he left them alone while he answered his phone. "What can I do for you?"

Alessio was on the other side of the large sitting room from Ginevra and

Corrado when Cree finally responded. "You're not picking up Dare's calls."

"I have nothing to say to him, he doesn't need me for a current job, and I don't like listening to him bitch at me because he's in his feelings."

Behind him, Alessio heard Corrado clear his throat. Okay, so he hadn't been quiet about saying what he had to say, even if he was twenty feet away. Not that anything he said was a goddamn lie, either.

"He doesn't want to talk about the auctions, if that's what you're worried about," Cree said.

"I have no doubt it'll lead into that, and I made my decision. It was mine to make."

"I agree, and so does he."

Alessio stuffed a hand in his pocket, turning to watch Ginevra sitting in Corrado's lap on the couch while the two of them battled one another on their war game. She whooped his ass all over the screen which amused Alessio to no fucking end. Even Corrado seemed to enjoy it, and usually, he was a sore loser.

He wanted to be back there.

Not here, doing this phone call.

"What do you want?" Alessio asked.

Better to get straight to the point.

"To make sure you are okay," Cree said. "Because otherwise, you don't fill us in."

"Because I'm handling shit I need to handle. And since at least one of you are of the opinion you get a say on how I handle my personal business, I no longer want either of you in on it."

Cree cleared his throat. "He didn't want you to do the auctions. Dare, I mean. He wanted to let you do what you wanted. He's only in his mood now about it because he believes you backing out had to do with—"

"Corrado," Alessio interjected. "And he's not wrong, but that doesn't change it's still my choice to make. I don't want to do it, and regardless of what happens here, I still won't be doing it."

"Les—"

"The only reason Dare is in his feelings about Corrado and I is because *you* took the information I shared with you back to him."

"I don't hide things from him."

"Oh, I get that," Alessio said, "and I don't blame you, but you also can't fault me for keeping my private business *private* from here on out, yeah?"

"We worry."

"Don't bother."

"Alessio."

"Any news on that Albania hit yet?" Alessio asked.

Cree made a noise under his breath. "That's what you want to ask me?"

"I'm not talking about anything else with you, or him. Not until you both learn that taking me in when I was ten doesn't mean you're owed everything I do now, Cree."

"We don't assume that."

"I beg to differ."

Cree sighed. "Are things better there? That's all I want—that you're *happy*, Les."

A loud, happy holler drew Alessio's attention back to the other side of the room. Ginevra's hands flew high in the air as she tossed her head back and laughed in her triumph. On the screen, the words *Mission Accomplished* flashed across her character, while Corrado's only had a red *FAILED*.

"How did you beat me again?" Corrado groused.

Ginevra grinned, turning her head enough to catch his scowling lips in a kiss that had Alessio's own smile growing. He wished he was over there, sharing their moment with them, instead of on this damn call.

Because they were happy.

He was happy.

"We're all happy," Alessio said. "And you can tell Dare, too."

"I'll try to rein him in, Les. It's the best I can do."

"I would appreciate it."

He had to get back to his life.

• • •

"Stop it."

Alessio's words came out in a mumble given that his face had buried in the pillows on the bed, and he was half asleep. *Nearly there*, but not quite. He couldn't fall into sleep like he wanted when a foot away from him on the large king-size bed, Corrado kept tensing every few seconds.

It wasn't the movement, or even Corrado's sighs in the darkness, but rather, the fact his lover was annoyed. Or bothered … likely both.

Alessio didn't like that.

"Am I keeping you up?" Corrado asked.

Alessio twisted his head around, so he could stare at Corrado, or what he could see of him. "Yes, and if you want something different, go *do that*. Don't lay there and fret about it. That drives me fucking crazy."

"You don't—"

A quiet shuffling echoed outside of their bedroom, because *yeah*, Alessio was back in here a couple of days later. This was where he wanted to be, he had a better night's sleep, and didn't give a fuck about the details. Those only held him back. Corrado left the door open in case the woman across the hall wanted something other than to sleep alone in her bed. Not that she had taken the invitation yet.

But at that sound, the noise Ginevra made when she rolled over in her bed *again*—for what, the millionth time since she had gotten out of the bathtub two hours ago?—Corrado tensed again. The woman wasn't sleeping, but she was far enough away that she probably couldn't hear their quiet conversation, and he wasn't sure she had a clue that they were aware she wasn't sleeping.

Her choice to sleep alone was hers.

They said nothing.

"At night, she worries," Corrado said.

"About home, you mean."

"What else? When does her brain shut off? About her mom, I suspect, and her sisters. She doesn't tell us because who knows why … but it's what she does. I don't like it."

Alessio sighed, and scrubbed a hand down his face, willing that sleepiness to *go*. "Just go do what you want to do. If you're going to lie beside me wondering about it, and keep me up all night, too, then I will need you to do that somewhere else."

"Well—"

"*Go get her*," he grumbled in the darkness.

"Or this is her time, no? At night, that's when she can actually be alone without *us*, Les. It's how she deals with all the shit going on—her anxiety, and the rest, you know?"

"Except it's not dealing with it when she does the same thing night after night, is it?"

Corrado didn't reply.

"Fine," Corrado snapped.

Alessio smirked to himself as Corrado kicked the blankets off and jumped out of the bed without another word to his lover he left behind. He listened as footsteps padded across the room, out into the hallway, and faded into the room next door. A quiet *hey* echoed from Ginevra, followed by a *what are you doing* before Corrado was back in the bedroom.

He lifted his head from the pillows in enough time to see Corrado set Ginevra on the bed right in the middle. His hands scooted her over as she still looked confused before Corrado got back on his side and found his comfortable position on his side again.

Ginevra blinked. "I was fine over there."

"No, you weren't," Corrado muttered.

"I *was*."

Alessio grunted under his breath. "Lies. You twist and turn half the night, and when you fall asleep, it keeps going. Just saying, you could sleep better over here."

"We're only *sleeping*?"

Alessio would have laughed at the question she hinted at, but he didn't think now was the right time. Corrado saved him from having to say anything.

"This isn't about sex," Corrado murmured. "It's about something you need … sleep, rest, or a recharge—letting someone else take care of you because you're dealing with shit alone when you don't have to, Ginny. Just because you think you're handling it alone doesn't mean everyone around you isn't still affected."

Sleepily, Alessio said, "Exactly." His tone deepened as he added, "But if it was about sex, though, we'd *all* be good with that."

"*Les*," Corrado warned.

"I'm not wrong."

Ginevra let out a soft laugh, but it was the *heat* lingering behind her nervous energy that took his attention the most. He looked up to see her staring back at him. The same curiosity and lust lit up her gaze.

All right.

"Is that what you want?" he asked her.

Ginevra sucked in a tentative breath. "It wasn't."

Corrado made a dark noise from the other side of the bed. "And now?"

"*Maybe*."

"I don't do maybes, kitten."

Consent always mattered here.

Clear, unquestionable consent.

It *had* to.

Alessio rolled to his back, deciding he would settle this for all. He figured it had been one thing for Ginevra when she was dealing with these men one at a time, but when they were close like this, both near with her in the middle … she had to get stuck in her head.

It wasn't that deep.

"Think about it," Alessio murmured, "he will tuck you against him on your side, get his hands between your thighs, make you crazy, and after, he's going to fuck you while I enjoy the show, Ginevra. That's it, that's all. And you get to fall asleep fucked, happy, and on top of the blankets the way you like. But if you would prefer to overthink it until you think it to fucking *death,* fine, we can do that, too."

Corrado chuckled. "There you go."

"I thought …" She trailed off, her voice faint.

"What, both?"

That seemed like the obvious answer.

"A little," she whispered.

Alessio dismissed that with a grunt. "Not yet."

"Not yet," she echoed.

"Soon," Corrado added, a wicked promise lingering there. "But not yet."

That took time.

A *readiness.*

A certain level of trust and need he didn't think Ginevra was ready for yet. Oh, they would get her there, certainly, but not tonight.

Ginevra made a soft, hot noise. "But tonight—"

"If you want," Corrado said, "but that's not why I brought you over here. It's not why you're in this bed at all, and as long as you get that, then whatever you want, you get."

"You only have to ask," Alessio said.

"Okay."

Alessio peeked up at her where she still sat between their resting positions. "*Okay,* okay, or okay we will sleep?"

Ginevra grinned in the darkness. "Sleep … later."

Yeah, that's what he thought.

"Corrado, then?" Alessio asked, wanting to be sure that was *who* she wanted. "Because I have a kink, and I like to *watch.*"

All it took was Ginevra's subtle nod, and her soft *yes,* for Corrado to reach for her. Alessio didn't plan to touch, but he reached over to drift his fingers through Ginevra's hair when Corrado kissed her. He hadn't been wrong, either.

Corrado used his hands first—stripping her of clothes and shedding his own; he did his best work between her thighs, hands spreading her legs wide before his fingers stretched out her pussy, too. All those sounds that crawled out of her throat as Corrado circled her clit with the pads of his fingers while his other hand stuffed her full had Alessio harder than ever.

Still, he didn't touch.

He didn't need that to get what he needed here.

"Fuck, yeah," Alessio murmured, "you should see what I see, Ginny. How wet your pussy is, and how you're already soaking his hands. So fucking good. How bad do you want his cock, huh? *Tell me.*"

"Jesus," Corrado grunted, "killing me here, Les."

He grinned.

Yeah, he knew.

He loved watching Corrado work.

Corrado liked hearing all the details.

"Use your words, kitten," Alessio urged Ginevra.

"*Please …*"

Her eyes flew wide, landing on Alessio when Corrado's teeth found the junction between her neck and her shoulder. She came hard, gasping into the dark room and twisting against the bar-like hold Corrado had on her body.

Alessio enjoyed every fucking second. There was nothing better than watching someone get off unless you were the one making them do it. And even that … well, he didn't mind this.

For now.

He'd get the rest later.

Her next words came out breathless, and high. "*Fuck me. Please, oh my, God … please, fuck me.*"

Alessio might have gotten his own cock in his hands just to get his own while he watched them get theirs, but she reached for him across the bed. Her fingers tangled with his to hold tight as Corrado left her long enough to grab what he needed from the bedside table. Alessio slipped across the bed, his mouth finding Ginevra's in just enough time to swallow her hard moan when Corrado filled her from behind.

And *God …*

That did sinful things to him.

Wicked things.

He inched closer, but only because her soft hands pulled at him to do it. He tweaked her hardened nipples and tasted the salt on her skin as she whispered for *more.*

Corrado's hand slid through Alessio's hair, threading tight, while Ginevra's drifted lower to slip under his boxer-briefs.

Sex was always *just* sex to Alessio. He liked it, and so he did it. He needed that connection with Corrado, and he found it. Anyone else, though, and it was just a need he fulfilled.

Now, though, he couldn't get enough. This—them with her—would quickly become an addiction for him. A habit he couldn't kick.

Alessio didn't mind.

14.

Ginevra

"We're taking you out. A date."

Those words of Corrado's, ones he'd spoke in her ear after she was drifting in and out of sleep between the two men in bed while her body hummed from one of the most erotic things she had ever experienced in her life, rang through her mind as she surveyed the items on the bed.

The silver boxes rested open on the bed as she eyed each item set out in front of her.

Black, patent leather, peep-toe stilettos with red soles rested in one box, and a black dress with a designer tag that made her blink rested in another. The layered necklace, glittering with red gems—were those real?—would hang low in the deep neckline of the dress.

And the matching earrings were just as beautiful.

Not to mention expensive.

"Miss?"

Ginevra glanced over her shoulder at the woman standing just behind her, full of styling tools, makeup, and whatever else the woman needed to pamper her. Because to Corrado and Alessio, a date could not be *just* a date.

It had to be a whole experience.

One Ginevra *needed.*

Or that's what they explained.

This was a lot.

Then again, so were those men.

"Would you like to begin?" the woman asked.

"Where do we even start?"

Cassidy—that was the woman's name—grinned. "Well, wherever you like? They told me this day was *your* day. So, it's all up to you."

Right.

"I'm not used to being spoiled," she admitted.

"That doesn't mean you don't deserve it, though."

Ginevra liked this woman.

And those men.

"I'll let you pick," she said, giving Cassidy a smile.

"You got it."

• • •

A low whistle cut through the penthouse as Ginevra turned the corner. The appreciative sound from Alessio had Ginevra grinning, and standing beside him at the door looking just as good in his suit as Alessio did in a blazer and black slacks, was a smirking Corrado.

"Look at you, huh?" Alessio said, his gaze drinking her in.

Corrado did the same—his deepening sexily. "I should send that boutique and their people a bonus, yeah?"

Alessio nodded. "Definitely."

"That's enough from the two of you," Ginevra said, unsure of how to handle their attention when it was on her like *this*. Some things just took time to get used to, she supposed. This was one of those for her. "And I think you went a little overboard today."

"We didn't do enough."

"Agreed," Alessio replied.

Ginevra sighed, coming to a stop in front. Brushing her fingers over the shoulder of Corrado's suit jacket, her gaze turned on Alessio. "I think this is the first time I have ever seen you wear something that isn't black jeans, a leather jacket, and a plain shirt. I like it."

"Don't get used to it."

"I like you as you are, too."

"You better."

"He cleans up well," Corrado murmured.

Alessio flashed his teeth in a tempting grin. "But only when I'm forced to."

"See," she said, "overboard."

"Not at all." Corrado's hand slipped around to her lower back, and with a gentle nudge, they headed out of the penthouse after Alessio opened the door. "Besides, this was just for *fun*. And you don't get enough of that here, do you?"

"I think I'm wearing about five thousand dollars between these clothes and the jewelry—"

"About fifteen, actually."

Ginevra balked. "How is that *fun*?"

Because now she was just worried that she might lose the goddamn necklace or earrings. That was before she thought to ask just how much of that fifteen thousand belonged to the dress, the lingerie she wore under it, or the shoes on her feet.

Damn.

"For a Guzzi," Alessio said behind her as he locked the door, "spending money *is* fun."

Corrado shrugged. "Yeah, mostly."

All Ginevra could do in response to that was laugh because it seemed *so* excessive. And yet, she wasn't at all surprised.

"Besides," Alessio said, coming up to her other side as they waited at the bank of elevators, "the best part of having a beautiful woman at your side is getting to show her off."

"And reminding everyone else that she is not theirs."

Alessio chuckled. "Exactly that."

Ginevra shook her head. "Terrible. Both of you."

"And yet, you like it," Alessio returned. "Does that say more about you, or us?"

Well ...

"That's fair," Ginevra said softly.

Alessio pressed a quick kiss to her temple as the elevator doors opened.

Corrado let his fingers dance up the low cut back of her dress. Both actions did different things to her body.

Tempting.

Both *lovely*.

This would be an interesting night.

Of that, Ginevra was most sure.

• • •

Ginevra learned that it was one thing to deal with Alessio or Corrado *individually*. The two of them were a handful when it was just them, smirks and cockiness included. But when someone had to handle these two men *at the same time?*

A woman didn't stand a chance.

Ginevra was not an exception to that rule. All it took was Corrado murmuring in her ear, leaning forward from the back seat to tell her the history of a building they passed, while Alessio's hand stayed curved around her thigh as he navigated the Mercedes-Benz into a parking spot.

They were two different men, and that's what enthralled her the most when both of their attentions focused in on her, even if they did it in different ways. Despite their uniqueness, she was very much present for *both*.

"It's a bar, restaurant, club … everything, really," Corrado said. "Depends on the day of the week, and what they've had planned."

"And private," Alessio added.

Corrado winked at Ginevra. "Members only, for those with deep enough pockets to be invited to join."

"And you two are members, hmm?"

"We are. They invited us through my oldest brother, Marcus, who likes to use this as a meeting hub when he doesn't want to have those in a more public place."

She didn't see a sign on the side of the old brick building they parked beside, and she hadn't noticed one at the front, either. "What's it called?"

"The Clubhouse."

Ginevra snickered. "That doesn't sound … innocent."

"It's not meant to," Alessio teased with a grin. "That's why it's private."

"But today," Corrado added, giving Alessio a look that quieted him, "we're having dinner, getting out of the penthouse, and having fun. Nothing crazy."

"Right."

Because they made her crazy.

A little.

They were still close.

Still touching her.

That was enough to make *any* woman insane when her body was constantly ready … hyperaware and finding a sinful temptation in every grin or word tossed her way.

She was the lucky one between Corrado and Alessio right now. And if she could help it, she would stay there. For now, her heart couldn't stand being apart from them, not now.

• • •

They broke the restaurant portion of The Clubhouse into several small rooms, which made it comfortable and caused the people eating to sit closer together than they might at the round table.

They weren't alone in the place—murmurings came from down the hall, and dishes clattered before laughter rang out, echoing to their spot. But with the four walls, and only a doorway to peek into their room, they had privacy.

And she appreciated that.

"I want that," Ginevra said, pointing her fork at the cheesecake Corrado had been teasing her with for ten minutes. She had her own, a different kind because she didn't want to order two, but he had to order the other kind for himself. "Let me have a bite."

"But you didn't want it when I ordered it a half hour ago."

"I do *now*. And you're not even eating it. It will go to waste, and *no one* wastes good cheesecake, Corrado. If it's not a crime, it should be."

"Like dog-earing books?" Alessio asked.

"Use a *bookmark*, Les."

"They're still not your books."

She gave him a look.

He winked and grinned back in a way that had her stomach clenching. Ginevra now understood the effect these two men had on each other, too. Oh, they were infuriating and amazing and *perfect*, yes. How they interacted, loved, and lived that made them so fascinating to her. Especially now that their attention and affection was also being put on her.

"I'm only saying to use a bookmark, that's all. It's not hard, but you seem to think it is."

"Or I keep doing it my way because you're terribly cute when you're worked up."

Ginevra scoffed. "That's—"

"Not a lie," Corrado interjected.

Ginevra let out a hard breath, knowing there were fights she would not win. Chances are, these would be some of those.

Alessio chuckled, nodding at the man across from him. "Corrado doesn't even like cheesecake—he's more of a pastry type."

Corrado glared across the table. "I'm having a teachable moment here, Les."

"Right, sure."

Ginevra grinned. "You just ordered it, so I would have it and not be guilty, didn't you?"

"Maybe … or not."

Alessio, leaning back in his chair so it balanced on only two legs while his foot propped itself on the edge, had his arm slung around the back of Ginevra's chair. It allowed him to play with the edge of the low neckline on her dress and drift his fingers through her hair at the same time. He seemed all too content with watching Corrado tease Ginevra, instead of finishing the dinner on his plate.

Well, it was mostly gone, anyway.

Corrado picked up the fork, swiped it through the top of the soft cheesecake, and offered it to her with a sly smile that showed off every ounce of his arrogance. "Bite?"

Alessio clicked his tongue, chiding and amused at the same time. Still, he stayed quiet and watched them.

Ginevra eyed the sweet on the fork. "Will you admit that you only ordered it for me?"

"I don't need to confirm things you already know, kitten. Take your bite."

She did.

And loved every second, too.

Corrado's thumb came up to wipe at Ginevra's lower lip while Alessio's fingertips danced along the column of her throat. Distracting and enticing. All of it—both. She didn't know which way to turn, so she settled herself on enjoying *both*.

Besides, wasn't that what they should do?

Sticking the tip of his thumb between his lips, Corrado sucked the bit of cheesecake off, and shrugged. "Tastes better coming off you, undoubtedly."

"Well, thanks." Ginevra took the fork from him and stabbed it into the cheesecake for another bite. "Now, what's the teachable lesson, again?"

Corrado laughed, tossing his head back as he did so. On the other side of her, Alessio hummed a low, sexy sound.

"Never *ever* feel guilty about doing something you enjoy," Corrado said, leaning in close enough for her to see those gold flakes in his irises. "Be it food, fucking, or living. You're only going to be on this earth once, Ginevra."

"Better enjoy it," Alessio agreed.

They had a point.

15.

"Here."

Corrado took the jacket Alessio held out, already turning to help Ginevra slip it on. September in Toronto was mild, but the sky had darkened, and he didn't want her getting cold between The Clubhouse, and the car.

Ginevra smiled sweetly back at him when he placed the blazer over her shoulders—Alessio didn't give a shit he had to give it up for her. God knew the man would much rather be in a leather jacket, anyway.

"Thank you," she said.

"Always, *mia cara*."

Corrado pressed a kiss to the middle of her forehead, enjoying her fingertips drifting over his unshaven jawline with a tender touch. A few feet away, a couple waited with the girl who manned The Clubhouse's entrance, never allowing entrance to someone who didn't have the credentials to enter. Corrado didn't care who came in and out of these doors most of the time. Usually, he never noticed.

This time he did because the woman dressed in deep red continued to glance back at the three while they waited for their turn to take their leave. People stared at him and Alessio, anyway … maybe it was the vibes they gave off, or someone liked the way they looked. Either way, he didn't mind it.

Right now was not quite the same.

He didn't like someone staring at Ginevra *at all*. Especially not when she didn't notice they were doing it because she was far more concerned with him and Alessio.

Call it instinct …

Whatever.

He didn't like it.

Corrado arched a brow at the woman over Ginevra's shoulder where she couldn't see him do it. The woman saw it clear as day, however.

Which was the damn point?

At his stare, challenging her to continue watching them, she was quick to look away, but not before rolling her eyes.

Fuck it.

As long as she stopped staring.

"Do you want me to hold on to this, sweetheart?"

Alessio waved Ginevra's small clutch, and she shrugged, taking it from him when he offered it to her.

"Is Camden around?" the man at the podium asked the woman manning the entrance.

"He is," she said. "In his office."

"Does he have a minute to chat?"

"Let me call through."

Corrado passed Alessio a look who shook his head. The rules of this place was one of the few things Corrado disliked about it. Like needing to check in and out, which could take a while if there was someone ahead of them.

Like now.

The woman—Kasie, was it? He couldn't remember, and he didn't care to—spoke into the Bluetooth speaker in her ear, nodding once before smiling at the man on the other side of her podium, still waiting.

"He's got a few minutes, but your ... guest will have to stay here," she said.

The man and the woman in red shared a quick word before he passed by Corrado, Alessio, and Ginevra to head back into the main section of The Clubhouse. With the podium free so they could check out, retrieve their electronics that everyone was required to drop off upon entering, Corrado stepped up to finish their time here.

As soon as he left Ginevra's side, Alessio was quick to take his place, sliding an arm around her waist to keep her close to him. Corrado didn't miss the way the woman in red narrowed her eyes at that, or how her lips pursed when the two he left behind shared a quiet word, and Alessio kissed Ginevra's temple.

Not that he could say anything about her staring *again*. The chick at the podium was now pulling the phones out of a small drawer behind her and had the tablet on their information to remove them from the current patrons list.

"Camden wanted you to be aware that, should you bring your guest again," Kasie told him, "she will need to be made a member. You know the rules, Mr. Guzzi. Once is fine—twice, she'll need a card."

Corrado nodded.

He understood the specifics.

It was all about safety here.

"What is it, three members who need to vouch?"

"Correct."

Corrado tapped a finger against the podium, saying, "Me, Les, and Marcus ... we'll add him to it, have Camden call him to get it done. Does that work for you?"

"Sign here."

He took the stylus the woman held out and scribbled his unintelligible signature to the bottom of a form she'd brought up on the tablet. There was one on him, and one on Alessio, too.

"And he must sign it, as well. I can email the one over for Marcus after Camden calls first to make sure he's fine with it."

Corrado waved two fingers at Alessio, and his silent demand for the man to come over worked. Alessio left Ginevra's side, coming to stand next to Corrado so he, too, could sign the document. There were a few others things they had to fill out—standard information that The Clubhouse kept on file for all members.

It took five minutes.

It would allow them to bring Ginevra back, though, and she seemed to like it here. Or rather, the restaurant portion, anyway. There was a hell of a lot more to see.

"That's all," Kasie said.

"*Merci*," Corrado said.

Alessio handed the stylus over as he had been the last to initial a part of the document. "Are we good?"

"Perfect."

"Great."

The two of them turned, ready to take Ginevra home.

"I'm just saying, it's *interesting*," he heard a woman say.

The woman in *red*.

Somehow, with their backs turned, she stood next to Ginevra. Which wouldn't be such a big deal, or a problem at all, if not for the fact Ginevra looked like she was about to *cry*. She avoided the woman's stare next to her, her jaw tight, and her arms folded over her chest. If it wasn't clear, by the fact she wasn't talking, that she wasn't interested in a conversation, then her body language sure as hell should have done it.

Still, the woman in red continued, saying, "If you know what I mean."

"I don't, actually."

Ouch.

The venom in Ginevra's tone wasn't missed.

"Huh," the other woman said.

What the fuck?

"Ginny," Corrado said, stepping forward while shooting daggers at the woman next to her with his gaze, "are you good?"

He offered his hand.

She didn't take it.

Alessio cleared his throat, but stayed quiet.

"Are you ready to leave?" Corrado asked.

They could figure out the problem later. He wanted to get her away from the bitch beside her. Whatever the issue was, it started and ended right there.

"I am ready to leave," Ginevra said stiffly.

She still didn't take his hand.

And she sidestepped Alessio, too.

They followed her out.

What else could they do?

• • •

"Ginevra, will you talk now?"

"I would rather *not*."

"Ginny—"

"Leave me alone for a minute, okay?" She kicked those Louboutin shoes off in the hallway, the red-soled shoes smacking the wall hard. "I need five seconds to think."

"About *what*?"

"Corrado," Alessio murmured.

He ignored the man behind him.

Mostly, because he didn't understand what happened back at The Clubhouse in five minutes that turned their *fantastic* evening into ... whatever the fuck this was. She had been having fun—enjoying her time with them out of this goddamn penthouse, because fuck, she didn't get that enough.

And somehow, it was ruined.

Corrado wanted to understand why.

He needed to fix everything.

That was his *thing*.

"Give her a second," Alessio said when Corrado moved to follow Ginevra down the hall.

He shook off Alessio's hand that came to land on his arm. "Don't."

"Corrado—"

"What the hell happened, Les? Don't you care about what went wrong?"

Alessio shrugged, his face unreadable. "Sometimes, people need to work through shit."

Right.

Well …

"That doesn't work for me," Corrado said.

"That's half your problem. You don't let shit go, man."

"And we wouldn't be here if I did."

Alessio nodded. "All right, but don't say I didn't warn you."

"Noted."

Not that it made a fucking difference to him.

Corrado didn't bother to take the time to remove his jacket or shoes before following Ginevra. He stood in the doorway of her bedroom and watched as she struggled to pull the zipper down on the back of her dress.

She didn't ask for help, so he stayed back.

Finally, she got the dress down. Yanking the expensive fabric down her body, the dress fell to the floor in a heap, forgotten. Standing in black lace that hugged her curves in the best way, he had a view that showed all the parts of her that had his dick standing at attention in a breath. And yet, all he focused on was that anger written across her pretty features.

She let out a harsh noise, pulling the drop earrings from her ears, and shaking her head at the same time.

"Do you want help with the necklace?" he asked, staying put in the doorway.

"*No.*"

He straightened, her sharp tone taking him by surprise. Rarely did Ginevra get heated with her tone, even in her anger. She didn't need fury to get her point across, not when she wanted to.

"What is wrong with—"

"I said to give me a minute, didn't I?"

Corrado stayed put and shrugged as he tossed his hands in his pockets. "And yet, here I still am. Something clearly upset you back at The Clubhouse, and I want you to tell me what."

"You don't get to *know* everything because you want to, Corrado. That's not how life works, okay? People have feelings—*private* feelings."

"Right, but since, chances are, this has to do with me, or Les, or that chick who talked to you, I think you could at least tell me what happened."

"Or you should leave it the fuck alone."

Oh, cusses, now?

Yeah, she was *pissed*.

Leaning his shoulder against the doorjamb, Corrado settled himself on not moving unless she spoke up and told him what the hell was wrong now. "I'm not going anywhere unless you talk to—"

"*God.*"

Ginevra spun around fast, looking like an angry angel in her black lace, that ruby, white-gold necklace hanging low between her pert breasts covered *just enough* by the cups of the bra against her chest. At her sides, her hands balled into shaking fists.

But what hurt him the most?

The tears that formed in her eyes.

"You want to know what she asked me?" Ginevra asked.

Corrado swallowed hard. "I do. It upset you."

"How much you two paid for me."

What?

Corrado blinked. "I don't ... what?"

"Yeah," she snapped, scoffing, too. "That's what she asked, Corrado. How much did you and Alessio pay for me—*hard enough for a woman to find* one *man that looks like that, let alone two? So, how much are they paying to fuck you tonight?*"

"Ginny—"

"Is that what will happen every time I step out in public now? The first thing someone thinks when they see me with you two is *oh, she's a whore.* Because that's hard for me to swallow, okay. Before Andino shoved me in your lap, I was able to count my partners on one hand. And now, I'm fucking two men. So, forgive me if I need five seconds to *breathe.* All right?"

He blinked *again.*

Like an idiot.

"You let her comment bother you *that* much?"

Okay, that might have been the wrong thing to say. Or even, a little cold of him. Still, this bothered Corrado that the first thing Ginevra felt when someone thought to place judgement on her choices or relationship with him and Alessio was something *bad.*

That she was a whore.

Or the suggestion she was a slut.

None of which was true.

It pissed him off.

"That's what it was?" he asked.

Ginevra stared back at him, unmoved. "Yes."

"Just that."

"It's not *just* that, Corrado. Think about what it *means.*"

"To you," he intoned, "what this means to you, Ginevra."

"I don't get what you're trying to say here, but—"

"No, because you're stuck in your goddamn feelings about what *one* person said to you about your private relationship that has fuck all to do with them."

She stilled, her back straightening fast at his harsh tone.

Corrado didn't back down.

He wouldn't.

This needed to be clear.

"You need to figure out what you want here," he told her, pushing out of his lean to stand straight in the doorway. "Decide whether what makes you happy in private is worth the shit you might take in public, because *shocker,* this isn't only you here, Ginny. We're here, and we have to deal with it, too. Just because you have some complex about sex and relationships and monogamy, I suppose because society and religion and the rest of your life has spoon-fed what they consider to be appropriate and acceptable to you regarding our relationship or sex doesn't make this *wrong.*"

Ginevra opened her mouth to speak, but he was quick to stop her with, "The way we love, or fuck, or *live* with each other behind closed doors, or out in the world, still will not be wrong just because someone else has a fucking problem with it. This is ours, and it doesn't have to be the way someone else does *theirs.* Figure whatever out. We can't do it for you."

He turned to leave, but a scoff left his lips before he added, "And guess what, the man you wanted to fuck and liked before you ever knew about Les, and the rest of our life, is the same man you're looking at right now. Just because none of that was staring you in the face before doesn't change the fact we still existed. We are who we are—you either want to be a part, too, or you don't. Simple."

Corrado didn't wait to hear what Ginevra had to say to that before he headed out into the hallway. He wasn't at all surprised to find Alessio at the end, waiting for him and listening to the argument. Alessio arched a brow before following Corrado to kitchen.

Fuck.

He needed a drink, now.

Pulling a beer from the fridge, not his first choice, he slammed the door shut harder than was necessary. A black card stock he hung on the front of the fridge with a magnet fluttered to the floor, the gold flake detailing on the corners and white font staring up at him from the floor. Alessio was quick to come up beside him, and pick it up, reading over the invitation to a club opening coming up soon for his brother, Marcus.

"When did you get this?"

"Yesterday."

"We should go. Get out of this penthouse again where we're all stir-crazy."

He wasn't lying.

"I told Marcus I would go," Corrado said, sighing.

Alessio gave him a look, leaning against the fridge. "Except, if this is an opening for Marcus, then there will be a handful of made men around, too, yeah?"

"Likely."

"So, I'll go, too."

Corrado sucked air between his teeth. "You don't have to."

"Yeah, but you get twitchy around some older fucks, so ... I'm going."

"Which means she'll need to go, too, because she won't want to stay here alone."

Alessio didn't miss the heat in his tone if his frown was any sign. "Give her those few minutes she asked for from the jump, Corrado. People need time alone to work through their shit, and you need to accept that."

Right.

"And how long is that going to take?"

Alessio made a noise under his breath. Either he didn't have an answer, or he didn't want to give one. Corrado understood that all too well.

Until that night, apparently.

That's how long it took Ginevra to get out of her feelings and decide she didn't want to be without the two.

She darkened their bedroom door as Alessio drifted out of the bathroom with nothing but a towel wrapped around his waist. His footsteps hesitated, he made a noise in Corrado's direction, and that was how he realized Ginevra was standing there.

The girl looked smaller than ever with her gaze turned down, and her arms crossed over her chest, making the over-sized T-shirt draped over her body tight around her trim waist. Still, Corrado said nothing as Alessio headed into the walk-in closet to pull something on for bed, and she stayed in the doorway, not coming an inch closer.

"I'm sorry," she whispered.

"For?"

Ginevra let out a steady stream of air and shrugged her delicate shoulders. "Letting someone else upset me about this."

"All right."

As long as she understood *that* was what happened. It wasn't her that did this— she let someone else affect her feelings. Someone who wasn't here doing this with them. Someone who understood nothing about this thing of theirs.

That was all.

Those people didn't matter.

If they weren't in their life, their bed, or their home, then they didn't get an opinion on what Ginevra, Corrado, and Alessio did together. Simple.

"The door is still open," Corrado said.

Ginevra smiled as she tipped her head up, her gaze landing on him across the room. "It always is anyway. Like I didn't listen to the two of you in the shower for—"

"Should have joined," Alessio returned as he came out of the closet, having pulled on a pair of boxer-briefs, and nothing else. "You get more that way, kitten."

Corrado chuckled. "I mean, *yeah*."

Ginevra shifted from foot to foot. "I'll keep it in mind."

He gestured at the bed, feeling the tips of Alessio's fingers drift over his lower back as the man passed him by. "Sleep?"

"If you want me in here."

Corrado smirked. "When do we *not*?"

16.

Alessio

Why, when things were going good in Alessio's life, something had to come around to fuck it up?

He didn't need to answer the ringing phone in his pocket to know whatever that call was about, it would fuck up the balance he had found with Corrado and Ginevra. Sure, it was touch and go after the whole *Clubhouse* incident, but after a couple of weeks, they found a comfortable routine he liked.

He didn't want to fuck it up.

"Are you going to answer that, or …?"

Alessio grunted under his breath. "I'd rather not."

"That's the ringtone you use for Cree."

"And?"

His sharp question drew in the gaze of several people inside the café, and even Ginevra who now waited closer to the cashier in line. Alessio and Corrado had opted to stand back to let the line weed itself out—she didn't need them standing beside her twenty-four seven even if that's what they both wanted to do more than anything.

The phone rang again.

Corrado sighed. "Stop ignoring him, Les."

"It's not about ignoring him."

And it wasn't. It would have little to do with Dare, or the fact Alessio still wasn't calling them to keep him and Cree updated like he did.

No, it wasn't for that.

The fucking Albania job.

Which meant as soon as Alessio picked up the call, there would be a timer ticking down. The job had been years in the making, and he would have a tiny window of time after being given the okay to begin before he would have to get on a plane, and travel to a different country.

Away from here.

Away from them.

After his last conversation with Cree, well, Alessio doubted the man would call just because. Cree wasn't the type to push Alessio's lines, and he'd certainly done that during their chat.

So, it could only be for one thing.

"If you don't pick up the damn call," Corrado warned when Alessio's phone continued ringing in his pocket, "I will call Cree back myself."

Jesus.

"Fine," Alessio grumbled.

He pulled the phone from his pocket, giving Corrado a look before turning his back to him and the rest of the café as he answered the call. He stepped over to the window, putting some distance between himself and Corrado, not to mention the others lingering in the café.

"Les here," he said into the speaker.

"Nice of you to *finally* pick up my call," Cree muttered.

Alessio sighed. "I was busy."

"But were you?"

"Listen, I picked up the call, Cree."

It was the best he could do right now.

Anything else, and they asked too much.

Alessio kept his eye on Ginevra who was now giving her order at the front of the line to the cashier. Her bright smile had his own growing, not to mention the way she kept glancing back to check on Corrado and Alessio.

The woman … was something else.

And Corrado had been right.

She fit *them*.

"What did you need?" Alessio asked.

Although, he had a good idea.

It was just a matter of saying it, now.

"The Albania job is a go," Cree said.

Alessio figured it would be pointless to ask, but he still had to try. "And we're sure there's no possibility of them allowing another member to do the hit?"

"I've told you no."

Right, right.

Alessio's gaze drifted to Corrado who looked his way with a sly grin, pleased he'd gotten his lover to answer the call from Cree. It was too bad Corrado didn't understand yet what Alessio picking up the call meant.

He needed to be *here*.

More than anything. He wanted to be here. They were still figuring this out, between them, and Ginevra. Yeah, shit was better … but they were all still walking a very thin line with one another. He wanted to believe it wouldn't take much for them to get to a better place, but right now …

Anything could happen.

It was all in the air.

"I just think it's ridiculous they wouldn't allow someone else to take it, if there's no reason *why not*," Alessio said under his breath.

"You want to tell me what that mood is about, or no?"

Alessio scrubbed a hand down his face and turned to stare out the window. Then, Corrado wouldn't be able to see the displeasure on his face if he was still watching Alessio on the phone. "It's nothing—me voicing my thoughts out loud."

"Right," Cree murmured, "but I think it's more."

"And we're still not discussing my personal business. That hasn't changed."

"Les, I get I crossed a line."

"So?"

"Cut the shit."

Alessio pulled in a lungful of air, wishing it helped to settle his nerves, but it didn't. Nothing helped with it anymore, it seemed. Not unless he was in bed with Corrado or Ginevra, because then, he only had to think about one thing, and none of this shit factored into that at all.

Another reason to be here.

"I want to take fewer jobs," Alessio said.

Cree made a soft noise. "Oh?"

"I used work and keeping busy as a way to run from my issues, and I don't want to do it anymore. So, I understand what I need to do to fix that."

"Take fewer jobs, stay home more."

"Exactly."

Something shuffled on the other end of the call before Cree replied, "There's no reason you *can't* do that, Les. And you always did well training the new prospects with the occasional job thrown in with the team. If you want to go back to that, you can."

"But not right now."

"No," Cree agreed, "you have to do the Albania job. Within seven days, you need to be on a plane to contact the client within the proper time frame we previously agreed upon. I will send his details over, and you'll have everything you need once you land in the country."

"Great."

Except it wasn't great.

Not at all.

"Within seven days," Cree repeated, "call me to confirm you're on the way, all right?"

"Yeah, sure. A week, I got it."

Without a goodbye, Alessio hung up the phone. Cree wouldn't give a damn, really. He'd only slid the phone back into his pocket when Corrado saddled up to his side, arms folded over his broad chest. He spoke to Alessio as he continued watching Ginevra.

"A week for what?"

Alessio's jaw clicked from how he clenched his teeth. "The Albania job—we were going to do it together, remember?"

"I backed out because of the favor for Andino, yeah."

"Well, guess who doesn't get to back out?"

Corrado stiffened beside him, but replied, "It's a job—what, a couple weeks at the most? You'll be back soon."

"Some things are more important than The League."

"Yeah."

"And stop glaring," Alessio added.

Corrado glanced his way, raising a single brow. "Pardon you?"

Smirking, Alessio nodded toward the front of the café where Ginevra chatted with the man behind the counter who now handed over her coffee, and donut. Alessio hadn't missed how if Corrado's glare could burn someone to the ground right where they stood, the man who had the nerve to talk to Ginevra would be a pile of fucking ashes.

"You know what I'm talking about."

Corrado grinned. "Hmm."

"Do you do that for me, too?"

"What?"

"Glare at people who get too close."

Corrado didn't reply.

Alessio didn't need him to.

Yes, he did.

Corrado was *very* good at hiding his possessiveness. At least, to the people he was possessive over. He didn't have a problem with making people aware they stepped out of line.

Not at all.

"So, where to now?"

Corrado and Alessio broke their staring contest to find Ginevra had left the counter, and the chatty man behind, to come stand in front with a smile that reached her bright eyes. Honestly, she was probably happy to be out of the penthouse again.

"To get you a dress," Corrado said.

Ginevra sipped from the to-go cup of coffee. "I have dresses."

"No, a *new* dress."

"You have heard of reusing things, right?"

Alessio scoffed. "You have high hopes, woman."

Corrado scowled. "I can spend my money however I want to."

"Yes, you can," Alessio agreed, "but most people don't spend money like you do."

"Why do I need a new dress, though?"

"We have a club opening to go to in a couple of days," Corrado explained, "and because I want to. Also, something for dinner tonight with my parents, too."

"I miss Cara," Ginevra said absently.

"That's why we're having dinner. And because she demanded it."

Alessio reached out and snuck a piece off her donut ... which ended up being a quarter. Well, she noticed.

Ginevra gave him a look.

He winked as he popped it into his mouth.

"Are we shopping, or no?" Corrado asked.

"Right after someone gets me another donut," Ginevra replied, not looking away from Alessio. "Since they don't know how to ask for their own."

Funny how she didn't share food well.

She shared them perfectly fine.

Win some, lose some.

"Well?" Ginevra asked him, looking entirely offended he dared to take a bite of her donut she now held out of his reach. "Because I'm not leaving until I get another."

Corrado chuckled. "You heard her."

Alessio groaned. "*Fine.*"

17.

Corrado

"And," the older woman who handled the patrons of the upscale, private boutique said, "we're closed for the next two hours to make sure you find what you need, Ginevra."

Ginevra's wide eyes turned on Corrado and Alessio. Although, just him because Alessio was busy leaning over the glass counter to pull an item out from behind it. Something that was a no-no, but he didn't follow the rules. Or, how to act like he had any sense of decorum.

"Les," Corrado snapped, "leave it alone."

"But it's perf—"

"Would you like me to get that out for you, Mr. Sorrento?"

Alessio came back up with a sly grin. "The blue choker, if you wouldn't mind, yes."

The woman—Mandy—nodded. "I will do that for you."

She left Ginevra's side, who was still wide-eyed and taking in the large and modernly decorated boutique with high class designer names hanging from every tag, to slip behind the counter. Bending down, she found the particular blue-gem choker that Alessio had been admiring through the glass, and then decided he needed to touch because why not?

It was Les.

Sliding it across the counter, Mandy shrugged. "Sapphires imported from India, designed in Russia—seven thousand for the choker. It's not an accent piece, but a solitary. There is no matching designs, it's better—"

"On its own," Alessio said, picking the choker up from the black velvet where it was displayed. "Add this to the bill, yeah?"

"Absolutely."

"That's too much," Ginevra whispered at Corrado's back.

He chuckled, amused at how she lowered her voice so the other two wouldn't overhear. She was trying her best *not* to become overwhelmed by the boutique, and the items inside, but she was still wide-eyed and stunned.

He liked that look on her.

"It's a good price, actually," Corrado returned, turning to face her. "And it's going to hug your throat nicely."

Ginevra balked. "But—"

"We should look for something blue to match."

"You're ... *impossible*."

Corrado arched a brow. "I didn't pick the jewelry, I'm just saying the rest should match."

"The more expensive things are, the worse it is to wear them."

"Why?"

"Because I worry it might break, or get ruined, or—"

"I don't want to tell you those feelings are nonsense, because Alessio likes to tell me that all too often, I dismiss others' experiences and emotions, and I shouldn't do that."

Ginevra glared at him. "*But?*"

"But this is ridiculous. Last year, I pulled in four million doing jobs for The League, but that's only spending money," Corrado murmured stepping closer to her, so she had to look up at him with those big, brown eyes. Her lips fell open in surprise, but Corrado continued on with, "It was spending money because my trust fund, for being born a Guzzi, which is spread between four investment portfolios, made me two times that in profits and interest last year. That's before I talk about the money that is just sitting there *working* to earn that profit and interest. A *trusted* money manager handles things like taxes, my major donations to several charities, and whatever else, but those cards in my wallet I swipe every time we go out?"

Ginevra's throat jumped when she swallowed. "What about them?"

"They have no limit." Corrado bopped her on the tip of her nose with the tip of his finger, adding, "And that's before we talk about the money Les has. So, can we shop, wear beautiful things, and be happy that we're lucky enough to do this?"

"That's a lot of money, Corrado."

"I can't be buried with it, Ginevra."

Her gaze flashed with an understanding. "You have a point."

"I understand that my wealth, to others, can seem excessive, and a little overwhelming."

"It is."

"So, I won't dismiss what you think, but I won't change how I live, either. I would rather you learn to be comfortable with wealth than afraid of it."

Ginevra let out a light laugh. "Well …"

"Hmm?"

"As long as it's not *my* money that's being thrown around, I guess."

Corrado grinned. "Compromise. Now you're talking my language, kitten."

Her cheeks pinked, but she didn't hide it.

"Now, what are we shopping for again? What kind of event?"

Mandy's voice had Corrado turning to face the woman. She was still standing behind the counter, and Alessio was already looking their way with a lazy smile.

"A club opening for the Guzzis," Corrado said, "but we can handle finding something on our own, if you wouldn't mind."

Mandy waved a hand. "The shop is yours for the next two hours. If you wouldn't mind, I might take my lunch. You won't need me hanging around, and I can pop over to the café across the street."

"We'll be fine," Alessio assured.

He left the counter to join Ginevra and Corrado, his hand sliding around her lower back while Corrado turned to check out a rack of large church hats. His mother liked those, and she might like to find a gift here waiting for her when she came to shop the next time.

"Oh, and that royal purple hat," Corrado said, "box it up for my mother, would you?"

"First thing when I get back, Mr. Guzzi."

"*Merci.*"

"That was sweet of you," Ginevra said as Mandy picked up her coat and purse, readying to leave. "Does your mother shop here often?"

"A few times a month."

By the time Mandy had locked the shop's door as she left, the three of them were already closer to the back of the store. Corrado remained closer to Alessio's side as Ginevra reached up to admire a glittering blue clutch hanging on the wall.

"So, which Guzzi is opening the club?"

"My oldest brother—Marcus."

Ginevra peeked back at them, her nose crinkling in *that way*. It only did that when she had something on her mind. "Huh."

"What?"

"Your family … they're Cosa Nostra, right?"

Alessio cleared his throat and gave Corrado a look from the side. One he did his best to ignore because Alessio was quite aware this was a goddamn touchy topic for him.

"The majority are," Corrado replied tightly. "I expect there'll be a handful of important made men there considering Marcus is my father's current right-hand, and while it's never been explicitly said, the next Guzzi to take over the *famiglia*."

Ginevra turned to face him. "What was that about?"

"What? Nothing."

Her gaze darted to Alessio and then back to Corrado. "No, there was *something*. In your tone, like it annoyed you."

"It was—"

"Something," Alessio put in.

"Don't," Corrado warned the man beside him.

Ginevra nodded. "Okay, now I *really* want to know."

God.

Why couldn't people leave him to stew about his issues alone? Not every piece of baggage he carried around needed unpacked.

"Some people in the Guzzi organization," Alessio said.

"Could you *not?*"

"No," the man murmured to Ginevra, "some of them take issue with the fact Corrado didn't join the family business and went outside of the organization instead. And this is before we deal with the fact that Cosa Nostra isn't kind to boys who like boys."

Ginevra blinked.

Corrado sucked on his teeth, annoyed again.

"Thank you," he told Alessio.

The man shrugged. "Better to just handle it, I guess."

Right, that's what it was.

"And they understand you two are …?" Ginevra asked, leaving the rest of her question unsaid as she raised her brow.

"For the most part, no," Corrado said. "We're always very careful about how we present ourselves outside of our private space, and not *just* because of the opinions of people who might not like we're together, but also because emotional attachments in this business can sometimes be a target for those who would think to use it. I never wanted someone to use Alessio against me, or vice versa."

Alessio cleared his throat. "You never explained this to me like that."

"Yeah, well …"

Shit left unsaid, *again.*

"But yes," Corrado added, shrugging one shoulder, "I didn't care what people from my father's *famiglia* thought about the fact I sleep in bed with a man, either. They're not the ones living my life, so their voice counts for very little."

"Oh."

Corrado smiled at Ginevra's soft reply. "It doesn't matter, anyway. If most of them aren't already aware, they suspect, anyway. I am at a point where I don't say, and they don't ask. I no longer care what they think though."

"Was that another rule?"

Alessio grinned. "Pardon?"

"Like the not sleeping with other men thing, or that women were okay as long as one told the other," Ginevra said. "Was the whole not talking about your relationship another rule?"

"No, more like an unspoken agreement."

Ginevra nodded. "Are there still rules?"

Alessio tipped his head to the side. "That kind of got blown out of the water when Corrado broke the important one."

Yeah.

Ginevra frowned.

Corrado sighed. "We handled that, right?"

"Mostly," Alessio agreed.

"Well," Ginevra said, picking a blue dress from a rack she passed before heading toward the back of the shop, tossing her words over her shoulder, "while I'm here, nobody better be fucking *anybody* else but the people standing right here. Got it?"

The heat in her tone couldn't be missed.

That possessive glint in her eye?

Clear as day.

Corrado appreciated that.

Alessio chuckled beside him.

"Yeah, we got it," Corrado said.

"Absolutely," Alessio agreed as Ginevra disappeared into the back hallway where the large changing rooms were situated. "But that means we get what we want, too, right? And *when* we want it, yeah?"

Ginevra peeked back around the corner, an eyebrow cocked in curiosity. "What does that mean?"

"How long do we have?" Alessio asked him.

Corrado glanced over his shoulder, his gaze finding the café across the street where Mandy had gone to be full with people lined up close to the door. "A safe while, I'd say."

"*Good.*"

"What does that mean?"

Ginevra's voice was a little higher, now.

Anticipation, Corrado thought.

"You know what it means," he said.

She disappeared into the hallway again, and they were quick to chase after the sound of her laughter. Alessio darted past Corrado by *jumping* over a rack. Not that Corrado minded as Alessio had always had the benefit of speed between them. He could outrun Corrado on his *worst* days, and that was saying something because he sure as fuck wasn't *slow*.

They turned the back hallway corner into the section of changing rooms in just enough time to see Ginevra drop the dress she had worn out that day to the floor. Then, she slipped into one of the six-by-six changing rooms with a wink over her shoulder, and that fucking blue dress from the wall in her hands.

"Too slow," she called out.

Corrado made a thick noise in the back of his throat. Alessio, at his side, tipped his head to the side with a cunning smile growing.

"She thinks we're teasing her, doesn't she?"

"Yes," Corrado murmured.

"She doesn't think we're at all serious, huh?"

"Nope."

Alessio laughed darkly, a sound that had Corrado's cock perking, and his chest tightening in the best fucking way. "She's in for a surprise."

Fuck yeah.

"I'm gonna need someone to help me zip the back of this up," Ginevra said, her words muffled behind the door. She didn't seem to have heard them—*good.* "But just a second, I might be able to do it myself."

"You got it," Corrado replied, his gaze settling on Alessio at his left.

"I want that woman between us," Alessio said under his breath.

"Here isn't the best place for that, Les."

"I know, but it needs to happen *soon.*"

Corrado agreed.

Entirely.

"But that doesn't mean we can't show her a little," Alessio said, looking Corrado's way. "Just a little, yeah?"

God.

Corrado nodded. "A little, then."

"See what happens, yeah?"

A groan fell out of Corrado's throat without his permission. "Killing me."

"Not quite," Alessio returned, winking.

Prick.

He knew his words turned Corrado on as much as they would Ginevra. That was, if she could hear them.

"Okay," Ginevra called out, the door to the changing room door opening. "I got it."

Alessio drifted past Corrado, but he was right behind him. Ginevra's sweet gasp rang out when Alessio slipped into the changing room before she could even come out. By the time he got past the door, Alessio already had Ginevra backed against the wall. Corrado took a second to take in that sight—oh, he'd seen it a couple of times over the last two weeks ... they tempted and loved her as much as she wanted, and yet, it still *stunned* him.

The way Alessio handled her.

How he *kissed* her.

The way the man just seemed like he couldn't get enough, and God knew Corrado understood that far too well where Ginevra was concerned. Everything about her, from the way her skin heated under their hands, to the way she sounded, and even the sensitivity of her skin was addicting.

And that was before he mentioned how he ached to fuck her, or to get her flavor coating his tongue while she shook and called out his name.

Or Alessio's.

Fuck.

"Yes, then?" Alessio asked. "Tell me yes, and we'll make it so fucking good, Ginny."

Corrado moved in beside them to tilt Alessio's head back by tangling his fingers into the hair at the nape of the man's neck. His lips crashed down on Alessio's, tongue slashing against his that was already waiting to war in their familiar way. He reached for Ginevra, his fingers drifting down the fabric of the dress covering her chest, hearing her soft whimper.

Something about that did it for her.

He learned that, too, over these weeks. They could find her soaking fucking wet after she watched them do anything—fuck, kiss, *touch*. It didn't matter, for her it was hot as hell, and he fucking loved that.

Les, too.

Alessio's teeth caught Corrado's lower lip as he moved to pull back, that sting hardening his cock to a painful point as Ginevra whispered, "*Yes.*"

The stormy blue of Alessio's gaze locked on his for a brief second, he took that connection for what it was, those silent promises of *yours is coming too.*

He wanted that.

As much as he wanted Ginevra.

But her first.

Alessio kneeled down, his hands shoving the blue satin of Ginevra's dress higher as Corrado focused on her lips, and getting her kiss, too. The shuffle of fabric, thin lace being yanked away, sounded over her hard breaths. She shifted against Corrado's side, and how he was leaning over her, her legs widening for Alessio down below. He knew the *second* Alessio had his face buried between Ginevra's thighs, because even if the man's hard moan wouldn't have been enough to tell him he found heaven, the broken cry Ginevra echoed against his kiss would have done it.

Shivers raced through her body. His hands chased after them, yanking the straps of that dress down her arms, and past her chest, making her lace-covered tits spill out to his waiting palms. He dragged those lace cups down, too, still lashing his tongue against hers as she whined into his kiss.

Corrado pulled back, thumbs tweaking her nipples as he peered down. Alessio stared up, their eyes locking again as he worked between her thighs, his tongue beating a fast rhythm against her clit as the sounds of his fingers sinking into her wet pussy filled the surrounding space.

"Come, and he'll fill you," Corrado told her. "Stretch you out nice, Ginny, while I get a taste of you both, and show you how good it will be when we're both filling you full, kitten."

"Oh, my God," she breathed.

"That works, too."

She choked on her next cry.

Corrado watched as Alessio bared his teeth, giving him a silent warning, not that he needed it. He could sense how close Ginevra was to coming, and the right move on Alessio's part would throw her right over the edge. All it took was the scrape of Alessio's teeth against the hood of her clit before he sucked it between his lips, and she flew.

His hands ghosted up from her chest, her racing heat thrumming into her throat, as his fingers wrapped around the column of her neck. He took in all those sounds of hers with kisses dotting across her trembling lips, over her jaw, and back to her mouth again.

"I ... I ..." Ginevra couldn't get words out, the air of her voice pulsing along Corrado's mouth as she tried. "*Please.*"

"Easy, easy, *breathe*," Alessio murmured as he lifted, and Corrado moved aside for him. "Fuck, doesn't she look good like that?"

"She does," Corrado agreed. "So fucking good, Les."

"You hear that, Ginny? How much we love watching you come for us, huh?"

Her darkened brown eyes, hooded with lust, focused in on Alessio. His hands were already working to undo his pants, and shuffle them down. He took the condom Corrado handed over as he held out two fingers to Corrado, wet with Ginevra. *Fucking hell.* Corrado took that offering *happily*, getting her hot and tart arousal on his tongue as he watched Alessio give Ginevra a taste with a kiss.

Alessio took his hand back, but only to get his cock sheathed in latex. Ginevra, though, reached for Corrado with one hand, and Alessio with the other. Her fingers drifted through his hair, fingernails dragging over his scalp to pull him in for a burning kiss while she laid her palm flat against Alessio's chest.

What came next was fast—a blur to Corrado's eye because he felt like they moved out of need, and nothing more. In a blink, Alessio had pulled Ginevra away from the wall, and Corrado's hands skipped up her back as he followed behind, making sure she didn't fall from the rushed movements.

She sat down in Alessio's lap when he fell onto the plush white leather chair in the corner facing the mirror.

"You got a nice fucking view," Corrado said as he keeled down behind Ginevra, between Alessio's widened stance, his hands palming her ass. "You can watch it all, Les."

"And you," his lover murmured.

Yeah.

Corrado did. The perfect view of Ginevra's wet, pink cunt hovering above Alessio's cock. He got his fingers wet with her arousal, letting the digits slide through the lips of her sex, and teasing the entrance of her slit before sliding further back.

Alessio wasn't the only one who liked to watch.

"*Now,*" Ginevra said, her body vibrating. "Fuck me *now.*"

"Whatever you want, kitten."

Corrado pressed a single finger into the tight ring of Ginevra's ass as Alessio brought her down on his cock. Her loud cry echoed, but Corrado focused, now.

Watching the way Alessio's cock slid in and out of Ginevra's pussy, stretching those sensitive tissues of hers open as his dick came out coated in her with each thrust.

And then his fingers.

One, at first, working her ass. And then a second, making her feel a little more full. He went slow, using her body's natural cues and the wetness he'd been able to gather from her sex to make it easy. He didn't want it to hurt.

Sex *shouldn't* hurt.

Not unless someone wanted it to.

"Like this, Ginny," Corrado murmured, his tongue sliding along the curve of her ass as he spoke. Her noises climbed higher as Alessio continued pulling her up and down on him with a brutal pace, something he *loved*. Sex was always better for Alessio when he could let go of his control. "It's going to be like this when we're *both* fucking you—but better. You'll be so full, kitten, *too fucking full*. And then it will drive you crazy, make you fucking high, baby. Imagine, huh?"

"*God*," she whimpered.

Alessio chuckled, and Corrado peered up to see him pull her in for a deep kiss. At the same time, he added a third finger, and let his teeth drag against the curve of her supple ass. She tensed, just a split second, before a low moan crawled out of her throat.

So raw.

And loud.

Jesus.

"It'll ache so goddamn deep," Alessio told her. "But it'll be so fucking good, too. Do you want that—both of us fucking you?"

"I do."

"Oh, you'll get that." Even Corrado heard the promise in Alessio's tone—*soon* was coming far sooner than Ginevra thought. If they got this woman through dinner tonight before they said fuck it and took her home to bed, it would be a fucking miracle. "Are you going to come like this?"

"Y-yes."

"Give it to us, then. *Give it.*"

It took Corrado widening his fingers on the withdraw, and Alessio pulling her in for another kiss before Ginevra fell over that cliff into her second orgasm. She stilled on Alessio, sitting down on him entirely as her shoulders shook violently.

Corrado took that chance to lean in, his lips finding the base of Alessio's cock where the condom didn't quite reach all the way down, but where Ginevra was still stretched around him. Her pussy, and his cock against Corrado's mouth, their tastes blooming across his tongue, was enough to make him think he was about to blow.

"*Shit*," Alessio muttered.

A familiar pulse thudded in the base of Alessio's cock, and the way Ginevra's muscles at the same time around him, her sex still flexing from the remnants of her orgasm.

Alessio's next words came out in a groan, his hands slipping down around Ginevra's ass to widen her for Corrado as he licked them both again. "Holy fuck, Corrado, you made me—"

He pulled back, grinning as he countered, "Come, yeah."

Ginevra's voice was airless as she whispered, "Did we even have time to do this?"

"Oh, we had time—still do," Alessio replied.

"*Still?*"

His gaze darted to Corrado as he stood, and then drifted lower to the outline of his erection pressing against the leg of his pants, the lower portion of the zipper biting into him. "Yeah, Ginny, now we get to see how much Corrado can take."

She peeked back at him, a demure smile playing at the edges of her lips. "We do."

Fuck, yeah.

Corrado was up for that.

18.

The thing Alessio wanted to be doing?

Well, it certainly wasn't what he was doing.

"You're quiet down there," Cara said, drawing Alessio out of his thoughts.

The loud chatter at the table continued like she hadn't called him out on the fact he wasn't feeling the conversation tonight. To his benefit, Alessio turned his attention away from Corrado and Ginevra sitting across from him. He wanted to be over *there*—or rather, get both home, and in his bed.

That's what he wanted.

Instead, he smiled at Cara, tipping his wine glass up for a quick drink. "Things on my mind, that's all."

Corrado's mother returned his smile, her gaze drifting across the table from where he was sitting to the other two, but came back to him. "So, what you're saying is I should thank you for making time to leave the penthouse for us, hmm?"

Alessio laughed. "Anything for you."

He loved Corrado's mother. There was something warm and inviting about the woman. She comforted without trying at all, and he never felt unwelcome here. And, through watching her with her small army of sons, he had learned how a mother should love their children. He respected her for that, more than anything else.

"Well, I'm glad you're all getting it figured out," Cara said, winking.

Alessio shrugged. "Getting there."

"Figuring out what, now?"

Corrado's voice drew Alessio's attention back across the table. He would have sat over there, on the other side of Ginevra, but he didn't trust his control to do that right now. Corrado had a *far* better handle on his needs and keeping them tampered down until it was an appropriate time.

No doubt, his hand was on Ginevra's thigh under the table. He'd have the soft skin of her thigh against his palm, warm and shivering. Despite having ate dinner here, he bet Corrado could still taste the woman on his tongue, too, because Alessio sure as hell could.

And he wanted *more*.

If he was over there, like Corrado, they would have already left. So, he took the seat across from them, and settled himself with his fucking imagination. Which frankly, was just about as bad as *having* them.

Alessio shifted in his seat, ignoring a raging erection because *now was not the goddamn time*, and his body didn't care.

"Figuring out what?" Corrado asked again, grinning.

Alessio gave him a look as Ginevra turned into the conversation, her conversation with Bene over. He gestured between them with a flick of his wrist. "This."

He wondered how Corrado would take him outright saying that at his family's dinner table. Sure, they'd come here a lot over the years. Both had sat at this table, ate meals with his parents and siblings, and were together through it all. Yet, never once had they said those words.

Oh, sure, he told Corrado's father when Gian asked.

That wasn't the same.

Corrado nodded, unbothered at the silence stretching over the table, and glanced his mother's way. "Yeah, that's about right."

"How?"

Both Alessio and Corrado's attention snapped to the youngest of the second set of Guzzi twins. Bene, who Ginevra had just been conversing with moments ago. At the lift of Corrado's brow, a silent order for his brother to clarify, Bene did just that.

"How does that work?" he asked.

Corrado cleared his throat. "Bene."

The warning was clear.

Don't ask.

"I get how *that* works," Bene muttered, "I'm not a fucking idiot, Corrado."

"Then don't ask."

Bene looked only to Ginevra. "No, how does that work? Because Corrado was like a sixteen-year-old girl with her heartbroken throughout high school—in a fucking mood, and you just wanted to punch him in the throat and tell him to suck it up. And Les? *Yeah*, in case you didn't get the memo, he's a fucking asshole on his good days, too. How does she put up with it all the time? Because I had to live with one for a long while, and that was enough for me."

Ginevra's mouth popped open, but she said nothing. Maybe she didn't know what to say. Light laughter drifted down the table, from the other twins, Marcus at the end near his father, and the heads of the household, too. Not nervous laughter, either, but genuine. Because well, none of what Bene said was a lie, and he always had the biggest fucking mouth at the table.

Alessio wasn't even offended.

Corrado grunted under his breath. "I am not *that* bad."

"I am," Alessio said, nodding in his seat, "and Corrado is ... well, Bene isn't wrong."

"See," Bene said. "I wanna know *how*."

All eyes turned on Ginevra again. Alessio was sure this was not what she had planned for the dinner, but hell, one had to expect anything with the Guzzis. Well, everything except judgement or problems. As long as they gave a shit about you, then that's what mattered. They would be the first to jump in and support whatever someone needed or wanted even if it meant everyone else would back away.

Her cheeks tinted with pink as she said, "Well, I learned to like it, I guess."

"But *how?*"

Ginevra's stare drifted between Corrado at her side, and Alessio across the table. "Kind of hard not to with those two, that's all."

Bene opened his mouth to speak again, but it was Gian who spoke up to stop him at the other end of the table. "That's enough, Bene, you understand the rules. Unless someone offers, you mind your own."

The youngest twin scowled. "I can't help I'm curious."

"Be curious privately and allow others the same respect."

"*Fine.*" Bene muttered to Ginevra out of the corner of his mouth, "But they're still moody as fuck, and I'm not sure how you do it."

Alessio smirked at Corrado's mother, shrugging as he took the final drink from his wine glass. "So yeah, it's good."

She laughed. "That's all I care about."

Right.

Him, too.

. . .

Alessio whistled low, admiring the twin Ducati super bikes parked in front of the large garage. "Damn, I will need to get me one of those."

Matte black.

Chrome detailing.

Speed like nothing else.

"Yeah, I need one," Alessio said.

Beside him, Chris chuckled and shook his head. "Ma saw them, and the first thing she said was it was just another way for Bene and Beni to kill themselves."

"Well …"

"She had a point," Chris muttered. "They have no concept of fucking danger, and if anything, they chase that shit. Usually together."

"You're aware I like you, right?"

"Mostly, yeah."

Alessio nodded and gave Corrado's twin a smirk. "But I'm also grateful you're not as close to Corrado as those two are with each other. I couldn't handle your ass in front of me every single day."

Chris chewed on the piece of gum in his mouth before muttering, "You know what? Same."

Yep.

He respected Chris a great deal, like the rest of Corrado's family, but he also wasn't lying. He wouldn't appreciate and like Chris as much as he did if he was around twenty-four-seven.

Facts were facts.

"And what are you two doing out here, hmm?"

Chris and Alessio spun around to see Gian crossing the driveway, coming their way with a knowing smile. The man tossed his hands in his pockets, looking unconcerned that they had snuck out of the house, and away from the noise.

Mostly, Alessio just needed to breathe. Corrado should enjoy dinner with his family—they had tonight planned for a week, now. Ginevra was having a good time, too. It didn't matter that Alessio wanted to take them home, and move onto *far* better things.

His needs could wait.

So, he needed distance.

A *breather.*

"Admiring your sons' bikes," Alessio said, spinning back around to look over the Ducatis again. "I hear your wife doesn't appreciate their beauty."

"No, she doesn't appreciate that they stunt on them, and regularly break two-hundred kilometers an hour on the highway. Because she knows, when they hit the pavement, there will be nothing left."

"And yet, here they still are."

Gian chuckled darkly. "Only because Cara has not gotten mad enough to tell me to get rid of them, yet."

"They're not kids anymore, Papa," Chris said. "They're adults, with their own money, and they can do what they want with it."

"Except you all will always be *my* kids, regardless of your ages. And you keep thinking you can do what you want, Christopher, we'll see how that works out for you."

Chris sighed.

Gian smiled as he came to stand in between the two. He gave Chris a nod and then tipped his head back toward the house. "Give us a minute, would you?"

"Sure. Later, Les."

Alessio tipped his chin in Chris's direction, his silent goodbye. It was only once the front door of the mansion slammed shut that Gian turned his focus on Alessio next to him.

"I'm glad to see things are better for you three, but I didn't think you—or him—wanted me to mention it in there," Gian said.

"We're getting there. Still complicated, but—"

"There's three people," Gian interjected, chuckling, "the complications can't be helped."

"It's good complications, though."

"I bet." Gian rocked on his heels, surveying the bikes in front of him, and then staring up at the dark sky overhead. "On another note, I had a phone call with Dare earlier."

Alessio made a noise under his breath, bitter and annoyed. "Right, well, I should go find Corrado and Ginny."

"Or you can accept that when people care about someone else, sometimes they make bad decisions or say things without thinking them through *because* their feelings sometimes get in the way. All things considered, Alessio, I think you should be able to understand that better than anyone else. Stop ignoring his calls—he's the only father you've ever had, blood or not. Attempt to keep what you have, regardless of what your pride thinks about it."

Jesus. Alessio let out a harsh sigh. "I have a job I need to do—sometime over the next week, I need to be on a plane for it. I planned on seeing him before I left, or when I came back, considering I have to make a stop at The League before I head out."

"Good."

"And he doesn't need to use you as his messenger. He has Cree for that."

"Right," Gian said, turning to face the house with a knowing grin, "but sometimes, it's better to go to someone who can make more of an impact when it counts, you understand?"

"Not really."

Gian patted him on the back. "You don't have to."

19.

Ginevra

"Where did Alessio go?" Ginevra asked, peeking up at Corrado over her shoulder where he stood close to her back. "I didn't see him sneak out."

All Corrado had to do was tip his head down, and as he spoke, his lips whispered over her skin. It was enough to get her body *humming* again. From that moment in the changing room earlier that day, she had been on a high. Her mind knowing where this would lead, and she wanted it more than anything. That anticipation had curled around her nerves; she felt like she might snap.

"Careful," she said quietly enough that the people laughing a few feet away wouldn't hear them or notice their distraction. "You will start something we can't finish here."

Corrado's dark chuckles pulsed against the back of her shoulder. "Patience is a beautiful thing to learn, but you get me best when I have none, Ginevra."

God.

Well, he wasn't wrong.

"And he snuck out with Chris a while ago," Corrado murmured. "I suspect he needed a second to relax … get his mind off things. He's another one, you know? Alessio doesn't have a fucking ounce of patience in him."

That dark, suggestive tone of his had her stomach clenching. All husky, and deep. Like he already had the taste of her on his mouth, and he was ready for more. It was enough to make her wish they were anywhere but here, and that Alessio was with them.

As though he could read her mind, Corrado's hands tightened on her hips. Those fingers of his pressed firm enough to make her breath catch, reminding Ginevra how good it was to have his fingers filling her ass while Alessio had been fucking her on that chair.

It also reminded her they were not at all in an appropriate place for her to be having those kinds of thoughts.

"We should go," she whispered.

Corrado's lips curved into a smirk as his mouth drifted along the line of her shoulder to the junction at her throat. "We should. Let's say goodbye, and go find Les, huh?"

"Please."

A thick noise fell from his throat, and those fingers of his flexed at her hips harder, promising the best of their night was yet to come. She couldn't wait.

"Leaving, are we?"

Ginevra smiled, tipping her chin down to hide the reddening of her cheeks at the familiar, sexy voice behind them. Why wasn't she surprised that Alessio had sneaked up on them in the family room while they were distracted together and then stayed quiet, so he could watch them.

336

He loved that.

It made Ginevra hotter.

"Well?" Alessio asked, stepping up beside Ginevra. "Are we leaving?"

She heard the other question in his statement he didn't outright ask. That simple *yes* or *no* they always waited for her to give. It was their reminder, even when their movements were rough, and she felt like she was spiraling down to crash between them, that ... she still had the control here.

Even when it didn't seem like it.

"Yes," Ginevra said. "Yes, we're leaving."

• • •

They knew *her* so well.

They knew each other so well.

And maybe that was what captured Ginevra the most when she was between Corrado and Alessio. That even in the simple things, as they undressed her, they were so aware what the other did that in their rushed movements, they didn't clash. Their hands *knowing* and sure, like they had mapped these paths out on her in their minds a million times before they had ever gotten her on her knees on the bed.

It was how they moved with each other, how they *worked* that took her breath away first. Even as their attention focused in on her, she stared up in enough time to watch Corrado lean over her from the front, reaching for Alessio. His thumb caught the other man's lip while Alessio drew soft circles against Ginevra's clit.

Corrado's other thumb slipped past Ginevra's lips for her to suck on the tip even as he kissed Alessio.

Still, her body hummed.

Still, she had to watch.

She barely remembered the drive home. Not when Alessio had settled into the backseat with her while Corrado drove *far too fast* down the highway. She didn't think about the blur outside their windows from the speed when Alessio was between her thighs, his hands holding her down against soft leather while his tongue found a spot on her body *no man's* mouth had ever been. And his fingers were there, too, pressing into her ass to stretch her open.

In the front seat, Corrado told Alessio, "But don't let her come."

Yeah.

Alessio followed the direction, too. Throughout the drive, on the way up to the penthouse, and now she was in their bed, one standing on the right of the mattress as he worked her pussy and clit with his mouth and his fingers, and the other in front of her ...

She still hadn't come.

Oh, they brought her *so fucking close.*

To that edge where blissed numbness came in, the seconds right before they would push her into the abyss of an orgasm ... and they stopped. Corrado would kiss her, his hands driving over her spine, and under to her chest where he tweaked at her nipples. Alessio would back off from behind her enough to let her shaking subside.

And then they would begin again.

Like *now*.

And Ginevra?

Fucking *crazy*.

If there was a raw, pure version of her, this was it. She didn't recognize the sounds climbing her throat every time they denied her another orgasm. Her begging had started three denials ago.

"*Please, please,*" she mumbled.

Corrado's hand curved her cheek, the tender touch about the only thing that didn't make her ache in the best way from the rest of their roughness. "Not yet, kitten. See, you're almost there … he will edge you again and again, until you want to scream. And then it's going to feel like *nothing* will sate you except everything."

"And don't you want that, Ginny?" Alessio asked behind her.

Why did their voices sound so *hot*?

Throaty.

It drove her crazy, too.

"Almost," Alessio murmured. "She's shaking good."

Corrado peered down at her, a glint staring back at her. "You can see it in her eyes, too. They darken when they widen."

She didn't understand their words, not when another orgasm was so fucking close as Alessio continued circling her clit at a much faster speed than before. And yet, she was scared they would take it away from her, too.

Deny her *again*.

Corrado kept his touch at her cheek, his thumb roving over her trembling lips as he freed his cock from the confines of his boxer-briefs. A grunt escaped from his mouth when she leaned forward, her mouth encasing the head of his cock even as he stroked the base made her wetter.

It seemed like it.

Then again, it might have been when Alessio's mouth found her pussy as his fingers kept working her clit, his tongue lapping at her sensitive tissues and flicking at her entrance for more sensation added to the rest.

Or it might have been all.

"Fuck, *Ginny*." Corrado's words sounded like they ached coming out. "*Les*, at this one, yeah?"

Alessio's hand at her ass flexed roughly against her muscles, and he pulled away from her sex, making her whine low. "You s—"

"*Yes*."

Ginevra sucked in a loud breath as the numbness came, the orgasm *right there*. She was sure Alessio would pull his hand away from her clit like he had so many fucking times before, but he didn't.

He didn't.

"Oh, my—"

Ginevra didn't get to finish the cry before she slipped into the beginnings of her orgasm. Further than they had allowed her to go before. *Edging*, Corrado had called it. She didn't know whether to hate it, or love it.

And then, Alessio pulled away.

His hands, his mouth, and his body. All of him drifted away from her, taking every bit of sensation with him. Corrado kneeled down, pulling his cock away from her as the disbelieving yell left her mouth.

"*No*," Ginevra gasped, "*no, no, no … why?*"

The orgasm of hers, with no sensation to aid her through it, was ruined. A waste, really. Weak as fuck, and it left her almost empty inside, somehow. Her vision blurred as Corrado got close, tipping her head back to drop hot kisses to the seam of her trembling lips.

"What do you want *now?*" he asked.

"*Why?*"

Why hadn't they given her that?

Why had they stopped?

She couldn't breathe or *think*.

"Why?" she mumbled.

"*Kitten*."

Ginevra's gaze snapped to Corrado's, her entire body acting like a live wire because *goddammit*, if she didn't come, and soon, then she might lose her mind. She hungered for the release like they would never understand.

It was the basest urge she'd ever experienced in her life.

Deep in her gut.

Thick in her blood.

Harsh in her heart.

Hot in her mind.

Something cold slipped against her ass, but it relieved Ginevra. Something to help her overheated body. The sting of Alessio's two fingers pushing into her ass only made her shake and want more. Because even the pain seemed too fucking good to be true.

Corrado swallowed thickly, his nose skimming hers as he murmured, "Now you get it, kitten. And it's about to get *so fucking good* for you."

The only thing Ginevra could say was, "It fucking *better*."

Corrado's rich laughter drifted over her skin with hot intent, a lot like the way Alessio's behind her added to the hard slap he leveled down on her ass.

Christ.

These men would kill her.

Surely.

It would be worth it.

A rustle sounded, and Corrado's hand flew up to catch the condom tossed across the bed. Alessio added a third finger to her ass, making Ginevra fist the bedsheets harder as she whined from the lovely sensations.

Except she needed more.

Now, after everything, that would not be enough to make her come.

Corrado slid the condom down his length, stroking his cock as his free hand caught her under her jaw. He tipped her head back and then drifted lower. Behind her, Alessio stepped back, withdrawing from her body as she found herself drawn up to her knees.

They were back to those rushed, but *knowing* movements again. Warm, rough palms sliding down her sides, and two more down her back. Corrado settled her onto his lap as he came to rest on his knees on the bed. It allowed her to straddle over his body as he filled her pussy full of his cock, lips attacking hers.

Shaking all over, Ginevra was hyperaware of Alessio fitting in behind her. How his knees tucked in under her ass, and his hands came lower to spread her ass as the lube still soaking her ass and pussy met the head of his cock.

"Easy," Corrado murmured.

Behind her, she heard, "*Breathe.*"

Wasn't she?

Ginevra had no clue.

Still wild.

Still out of control.

And yet, in the back of her mind, she understood all she needed to do was say *one* thing to stop this, if it's what she wanted. She had the power here, and they had given it to her time and time again to prove it.

One of her hands landed on Corrado's shoulder as he filled her, seated deep on his cock while the head of Alessio's dick pressed at the tight ring of her muscles. Her other reached back, grabbing to Alessio's hand at her hip, while his other kept her ass spread wide for him.

The pain she thought would come was there, too, but brief ... and diluted. Because still the pain was something *good.*

Something to get her there, *finally.*

"Fucking *beautiful,*" Alessio muttered, his kiss grazing the back of her damp neck.

"Perfect," Corrado said, his gaze locking onto hers. "Good, kitten?"

Alessio had started slow, short strokes at her back. His cock entering her just enough to stretch her out while Corrado stayed still inside her pussy. Not that it mattered because both filling her made her tighter.

"So good," she breathed.

Alessio's teeth found her shoulder.

Corrado's found her jaw.

Ginevra's fingernails scored red lines across Corrado's shoulder, and Alessio's hand as they worked her body against theirs. Corrado used his hands to move her against his cock, while behind her, Alessio flexed his hips against her ass while he worked his way in.

Her body burned.

Hummed again.

"How good is he in your ass, Ginevra?"

Her cry came out raw.

Broken.

"So fucking good, yeah?" Corrado grinned wickedly. "You're gonna want it so much now—getting your ass filled while one of us is eating your pussy or fucking it the way you like. Do you want to come?"

Her throat clenched with words wanting to spill out.

Alessio gave one more hard flex of his hips and settled all the way inside her ass as Corrado seated her down entirely on his cock, too.

That forced the words out.

"*Corrado* ... please, I have to ... come. Les ... *please.*"

Stilted, fractured, and rushed.

"*Yeah*," Alessio said hoarsely, "I fucking need that."

Corrado groaned. "Me, too."

Their pace turned into a rhythm that matched the other one would fill her as the other pulled away. Every single one of her nerve endings snapped and twisted as their cocks worked her body to the peak.

Because even if it was too much, she needed it.

Ginevra came *screaming*. Shocked the orgasm came at all because she hadn't felt it until it slammed on her at once. More than fucking relief, if heaven existed, she saw it—sensed it deep in her bones. She wanted nothing more than *that* … and when they gave it to her, it was surreal.

Blinding.

Impossible.

But it was possible.

It was real.

Like them.

That final peak, so high and unbelievable to her, reminded Ginevra of the men who had given it to her. They'd been out of her reach, and almost unreal to her before.

And she didn't know if she could ever let them go.

20.

Corrado

"You got her?"

"Mmm."

Corrado peeked over his shoulder as he yanked a pair of cotton sleep pants up—enough to keep him decent for now. That's all he needed. Behind him, he found Alessio had picked Ginevra up from the bed in a cradle hold as he waited for Corrado to finish getting dressed.

Ginevra smiled sweetly when Alessio winked down at her. "Oh, do I get special treatment now? Because I thought the sex was it."

"Not even close," Alessio returned.

"The big bath, yeah?"

Alessio nodded his way. "Sure."

Corrado led the way out of the bedroom, and Alessio followed behind without a word. He couldn't help but to check behind him as he headed for the penthouse's main bathroom where a large clawfoot tub waited.

Alessio's head tipped down, and he nuzzled his nose and mouth along the line of Ginevra's hair, murmuring words too quietly for Corrado to discern a few steps ahead of them. Ginevra's soft smile and hooded eyes were more than enough to tell him that she liked whatever he said, though.

It wasn't lost on Corrado the affection Alessio showed to Ginevra without even thinking about it, really. Sure, they *always* took care of a woman after she allowed them to share her between them. It was only right, after all. Alessio never, however, showed affection very much while doing it. Always kind, but he wasn't *loving*.

Not like right now with Ginevra.

For a brief second, Corrado wondered why he experienced no jealousy at the sight of two people he loved showing ... well, love to one another. Because that's the thing, wasn't it? It had been inevitable, something he expected would happen with enough time, but he still only realized was a reality now.

Alessio loved Ginevra.

He might not say it.

He didn't have to.

Not when he showed it.

As for her ...

Corrado didn't have to wonder if Ginevra loved them. She did. Otherwise, she wouldn't be still doing this with them at all. He had thrown her in this mess between him and Alessio, but she didn't have to continue to indulge it.

And yet, she did.

She *wanted* to.

More than anyone else ever had—including the two of them—she helped them. Probably more than she would ever know.

In the bathroom, Alessio set Ginevra down on the toilet with a raised brow

342

when her cheeks pinked. "I don't have to p—"

"Yes, you do. UTIs are a *bitch*."

He wasn't wrong.

Ginevra sighed when Alessio left her to come stand next to Corrado as he leaned over the claw tub and turned the levers on the rose-gold tap to start the water running. They worked together at the tub, keeping their backs turned to Ginevra while she did her business, and the running water masked their quiet conversation.

"You should tell her," Corrado murmured.

Alessio glanced his way. "Pardon?"

"That you love her, Les."

"I—"

"You should tell her."

"Have *you?*"

Corrado hesitated when he reached for the bath salts Alessio handed out to him. "No."

Not because he hadn't wanted to, but rather … the time never seemed right. Maybe a part of him still felt like, after all this time of him not saying those words to Alessio, it might be a betrayal, too. Didn't he at least owe that to Les, or did it even matter anymore?

He didn't know.

Alessio never defined the lines, either.

Corrado wasn't sure where to go from here.

Alessio shrugged. "It'll happen when it happens."

Right.

Ginevra made a quiet noise, making both men straighten to their full height at the tub, their attention going to her where she stood next to the sink. Her stance was careful, and when she stepped closer to the sink, her walk was measured.

Because *yeah*, he didn't doubt she was tender.

Sore.

"It's time to relax," Alessio told her.

"I have to wash my hands, don't I?"

"Fine." Alessio left Corrado's side, so he could slip in behind Ginevra at the sink. His chin rested on her naked shoulder as she washed her hands. As soon as she finished, not that her hands were dried because it wouldn't matter, he picked her up in that same cradle hold and carried her to the bath. "It'll help the muscles, Ginny."

"Is someone getting in with me?"

Corrado chuckled as he placed her in the hot water. "Better that we *not.*"

"You should rest," Alessio agreed.

Ginevra sunk lower under the water, all of her curves and lines available for them to admire as some of her tension drifted away. "This is nice."

Corrado kneeled down, resting an arm along the edge of the clawfoot tub while he tucked stray strands of her hair behind her ear with his fingers. She turned her head into his touch, tucking her cheek into his palm, and smiling.

"It's your turn to be taken care of, huh?" he asked in a murmur. "You're always so busy worrying about *us*, Ginevra. We're fine … we've been driving each other up the wall for years."

"Not a lie," Alessio said behind him.

"Point is," Corrado continued, "it's our turn to take care of you. Whatever you want, you ask."

Her gaze drifted between him, and then to Alessio.

"I have what I want *here*," she whispered.

Right.

Corrado heard what she didn't say.

It was outside of this place where she was missing the important parts of her life.

"I miss my sisters," she said, shrugging. "But I know—"

"I might be able to help with that."

Now.

It was a risk, and Chris had been quick to refuse the first time Corrado asked for help with his plan a couple of weeks back. Corrado was done trying to get something from Andino Marcello for Ginevra related to her sisters.

The man wasn't giving anything.

So, fine.

Corrado would go elsewhere.

Ginevra's gaze lit up. "Really?"

He smiled. "It might not be *everything* you want, but it is something. Will that help?"

"*Yes.*"

"All right."

Good enough for him.

Corrado stood straight and turned to Alessio with a shrug. "You good for a minute?"

"Of course."

Alessio was quick to take Corrado's previous place at the side of the tub. Although while Corrado had been fine to let Ginevra rest in the water for as long as she wanted with no interference from him, Alessio was more practical.

He pulled a folded up wash cloth sitting on a stand next to the tub and dipped it into the water before dragging the soft terry fabric along the column of Ginevra's throat. Her sweet smile turned on Alessio, and Corrado decided to slip out while he distracted her, and he wouldn't be missed by either of them.

Unlikely, but whatever.

He missed them constantly—whether they were five feet away, or five miles. It didn't matter, a part of him felt their loss. Which, if he were being honest, was one of the most terrifying parts of this thing they all shared.

And not something he wanted to think about.

Corrado headed for where he'd dropped his coat, earlier. He found it draped over the back of the couch, and funnily enough, couldn't even remember putting it there. They focused on getting into bed and clothes went wherever the fuck they went.

Like Alessio's jeans in the hallway.

Corrado's shoes at the end of the entrance.

Yeah.

He found what he needed in his coat—a small scrap of paper that Chris had written a phone number, and a name on.

Siena Calabrese, it read in his twin's familiar scrawl. Apparently, Siena, the full-blood sister to Kev and Darren, and half-sister to Ginevra and her siblings … was tasked with looking after Ginevra's younger sisters. Oh, and from Ginevra, Corrado knew Siena had been the person to help her get away that day of her arranged marriage, alongside Andino's plans.

Not to mention, it seemed Siena had a taste for a certain Marcello herself. A very *important* Marcello, considering the man she was messing with, Johnathan, happened to be the nephew to Dante Marcello, the organization's Don. It was no wonder Siena had helped Ginevra, and was now taking care of her sisters when, she had her own secrets to keep hidden.

She had things she wanted, too.

Chris figured, if anyone might be able to help Ginevra's worries, it would be Siena. Was it a risk? *Yeah.* That's also why Corrado picked up a burner cell phone—which he also pulled from his jacket—on their way to the dinner at his parents' mansion as a *just in case*. It wouldn't be traceable, and he could dispose of it when Ginevra finished her call.

Simple.

Mostly.

Or fuck, he hoped, anyway.

Corrado made his way back to the bathroom, but instead of going all the way in, he lingered in the doorway to watch Alessio and Ginevra chat. Alessio had sat down on the floor next to the tub, resting his chin on his arm sitting along the edge. Their quiet words, and soft laughter, had Corrado smiling to himself.

It didn't take long for Ginevra to see him standing there though. And once her attention shifted to him, Alessio's did as well.

"Find what you were looking for?" Alessio asked.

Corrado nodded and waved the paper and phone in his hand. "I did."

Ginevra tipped her head to the side, considering the items he flashed at them. "What is it?"

"Something you've been asking for."

Corrado crossed the space in the bathroom keeping a distance between them. Kneeling down beside Alessio, he took his time turning the phone on for the first time and getting it ready to use with the card that was attached to the back with a set number of minutes. Anymore, and he would have to buy another card.

Not that it mattered.

He'd grab a second phone instead.

Swiping his thumb along the screen to unlock it, he brought up the call icon, and typed in the phone number written on the paper. Instead of hitting the bottom to make it call through, he held the phone out for Ginevra to take after Alessio had dried her hands with a small towel.

She took the phone, glanced at the number on the screen, and froze. Her breath caught in her throat, and Corrado dragged in his own, anxiety slipping through his veins for reasons he didn't understand.

Well, that was a lie.

He knew.

Perfectly well.

What happened when this was over here? When Ginevra had to go back to New York, and they left this penthouse behind? Where would that leave the three of them?

Corrado didn't like to think about those things.

He wasn't sure what she wanted.

And he'd learned, with Alessio and all of this, that he shouldn't influence their choices. In order for them to be happy in this thing they had together, everyone had to make their own decisions, and be sure about them. *Pleased* about them. What he wanted didn't always factor into their wants, too. They were all different people.

So, he said nothing.

Especially not on this.

If Ginevra wanted something, then she would have to speak up and tell him, or Alessio. It was as simple as that.

Even if it killed him.

"Siena?" she asked.

Corrado nodded. "Supposedly, she would be someone we could trust to talk to, yes?"

"Yeah, of course. She only ever helped me."

"Call her," Alessio murmured. "I'm sure she'd be willing to chat about your sisters and fill you in on what she can."

"Right, yeah."

Still, Ginevra hesitated.

Her hands trembled.

"Call," Corrado told her. "It's safe."

Or as safe as it would get.

Ginevra nodded and pressed the call button before putting the device to her ear. Alessio and Corrado were quick to give her privacy but not much. They drifted just outside of the bathroom, their backs turned to the door.

Not that it mattered.

They could still *listen.*

"Siena?"

Her voice ached.

So close to tears.

Corrado stared at the floor.

Alessio leaned against his side.

"Yeah, it's me," Ginevra whispered. "How are my sisters?"

"Who takes care of her?" Alessio asked.

Corrado glanced at him. "Hmm?"

"She takes care of everyone else, but who takes care of her?"

"I think it's supposed to be us."

21.

"Ah, they let you out of the penthouse again to spend time with the rest of the world, did they?"

Ginevra grinned at Marcus's teasing. He ignored Alessio and Corrado behind her, who no doubt, were glowering at Marcus for his comment. Not that it was a lie.

"I came to dinner last night, too," she pointed out.

Marcus nodded. "Right, but does a dinner really count?"

"They're working on it."

"Well, that's what counts." Corrado's oldest brother laughed, and stepped in close enough to press a quick kiss to each of Ginevra's cheeks. "Thank you for coming—drinks are on the house, yeah? Have fun, Ginny, I am sure you deserve it with those two."

She smiled. "They're not so bad, actually."

"I'm sure." Marcus kept an arm around Ginevra's waist as he turned them both, so he could greet Corrado and Alessio behind her. "Behave tonight, huh?"

Corrado smirked. "When do we not?"

Marcus arched a brow. "You want a rundown?"

Alessio tapped his temple with one finger. "No need."

"Listen," Marcus said, his gaze drifting over the people lingering near the bar, "I'd like for this opening to go off well, if you wouldn't mind. So, if someone opens their mouth about something the two of you don't like, let me handle it."

"I'll try," Corrado murmured.

Marcus looked to Alessio displeased with Corrado's answer. Alessio only shrugged like he didn't have an opinion one way or the other, saying, "It's a sore topic."

Right.

Ginevra understood now.

Made men.

The *famiglia*.

Corrado joining The League.

Him and Alessio.

Yeah.

"You would think the two of you would try to keep each other *out* of trouble more often than you do," Marcus muttered.

Alessio made a dismissive noise under his breath as he rocked back on his heels. "You *would* think that, but no."

"Marcus!"

His arm slipped away from Ginevra as he turned to see who was shouting his name behind them. Quickly, he found whoever he was looking for, raised a hand, and then shot a look over his shoulder at the rest.

347

"Business calls," Marcus said. "We'll be in the VIP section upstairs when you're ready to join us."

Corrado reached for Ginevra as he replied to his brother, "Got it, Marcus."

Ginevra found herself tucked into Corrado's side with Alessio on her other side as Marcus walked away from them.

"He's just like your father, you know?" Alessio asked.

Corrado sighed. "Too much, sometimes."

"Just enough, maybe."

"Yet to be determined," Corrado muttered.

"I'd like to dance," Ginevra said, peeking up at him.

Corrado made a face.

She laughed.

"What?"

Alessio chuckled. "Someone doesn't *dance*."

"Not unless it's a waltz," Corrado said under his breath.

"Why not?"

"Never cared to bother, *but* ..."

Ginevra pouted. "But what?"

"Alessio loves to dance."

"*Yes.*"

Corrado's heady laughter drifted all around them, over the music in the club and the loud people, as he stepped aside so Alessio could take his place at her other side.

"Ah, see, now she's happy," Corrado told Alessio. And then to her, "And he likes to make those he loves happy, Ginny."

The words were said almost *carelessly*. Just tossed out like they shouldn't have meant very much at all, and she shouldn't take them too seriously. It didn't matter. Their weight upon impact still took her breath away as the word *loves* kept ringing around in the back of her mind. Not that she could think about it or dwell for too long. Alessio was already pulling her out to the floor.

Later, she thought. She would deal with that word, what it meant, and her own feelings later. Surely, they would have enough time for that. Besides, she thought they should be aware.

They *needed* to know how she felt, too. That nothing in her life would ever be the same because of these two men, and she didn't want it to be. There wasn't a single part of her that wanted to be without Corrado and Alessio. She wasn't sure how that happened, but she understood *why* it did.

Them.

Simply put—because of them.

How could someone not love those men?

Yeah, she suspected things would be tricky when she had to go back home, but shouldn't they at least *try*? She winked back at Corrado while Alessio pulled her further away, waving two fingers as her silent goodbye.

He grinned back.

Turning her attention on Alessio, she said, "They won't bother him, right?"

"Who?"

"His father's people."

Alessio's hand at her waist tightened at her words. "Corrado is grown—he knows how to handle that nonsense."

"Yeah, but *still.*"

Their walk came to a stop on the dance floor after they had weaved in and out of the moving people, so they were closer to the DJ booth on the other side rather than the tables and bar at the opposite end. Alessio spun around on her, a faint smile playing at the edges of his mouth, although she could still see the wariness in his gaze.

"No, they rarely make it a point to say anything directly," Alessio explained, shrugging his shoulders under his leather jacket. "Mostly, it's underhanded comments that people overlook because nobody wants to cause shit for something like that. And *never* when his father is around to hear it."

Ginevra swallowed the lump forming in her throat. "Gian isn't here tonight, though."

"No, he isn't."

"So, a quick dance, we get drinks, and then we go back to Corrado. Right?"

Alessio's gaze drifted to somewhere behind her, searching the crowd. Probably for where Corrado had gone after they left him. He didn't bother to mask the concern flashing in his gaze. Oh, sure, he *acted* like he wasn't worried, but he was.

Because it was Corrado.

Otherwise, he didn't give a shit.

That was his line.

"Sounds good," Alessio murmured, his attention coming back to her with a sly smile. "Now, someone wants to dance, huh?"

Ginevra laughed. "Very much."

• • •

"Two fingers of whiskey," Ginevra told the bartender—for Corrado—before adding, "spiced rum on ice, and—"

"Try the house drink," Alessio said in her ear, "it's the same one across all the Guzzi clubs. Like a signature drink, it's how you can tell when you're in one of their spaces."

He winked over her shoulder.

"Fine," she said. He leaned in and kissed her lips, but backed away so she turned to the bartender and add, "and one of the Gold Dreams."

"Coming up."

"Thanks."

"Turn around," she heard Alessio murmur along the shell of her ear.

Ginevra grinned, but didn't move. "Many people are watching, Les."

"*And?*"

"And we're supposed to get drinks, and find Corrado again, remember? You're a bad influence, and a distraction."

Not a single bit of that was a lie, either.

"We're *waiting* for drinks. And I don't see what the problem is."

Of course, he didn't.

Under the urging of his strong hands, Ginevra found herself turned around to face him. He had her pinned against the bar, his fingers tightening deliciously around the curve of her waist, so she was unable to move.

Not that she wanted to.

Not when he was looking at her like *that.*

Alessio tipped his head down, and caught her mouth with a slow, searing kiss. He was soft at first, his tongue teasing the seam of her lips until she parted them to allow him entrance. Then, at the taste of her, that kiss turned a hell of a lot hotter. All the while, he kept her steady against the edge of the bar, unbothered by the people around them or the noise.

His focus was on her.

That's all that mattered.

All too soon for Ginevra's liking, Alessio pulled away. Sure, he didn't go far, only enough that his lips grazed hers as he spoke, but it was enough for her to sense his loss, and wish he was kissing her again.

"I have to tell you something," he said.

Ginevra tensed, knowing nothing good *ever* came from those words. "Oh?"

"Relax."

"What do you have to tell me?" she asked.

Alessio sighed, his tongue snaking out to drift along his lower lip before he muttered, "I have to leave soon—The League business, and whatnot. A job that has been in the works for quite a while now, and they have the okay for it. I was the contractor put up for it, and we're not able to change those details."

Ginevra blinked, taking in those words. "How soon?"

"Likely within two or three days, we'll see how long I can stretch it. I got the call yesterday when you were ordering at the café; that gave me seven days to get my shit in order before I have to head out."

"Oh."

Alessio made a dark noise. "Don't do that."

She peered up at him. "Do what?"

"Sound so fucking sad, it kills me."

"Should I be happy?"

"Well … no."

Ginevra gave him a teasing glower. "I can't feel *nothing*, either, so you get one or the other. And sad was the one you got."

Alessio chuckled, his hands flexing against her waist again. "I get it, sweetheart. I need to go to Vegas first and grab things I need there. And if I play my cards right—or rather, work the flights right—I'll have a daylong layover in Toronto before I head out on the assignment, but still, it'll be soon."

"Soon," she echoed. "What kind of job?"

"Better not say for that."

Ginevra shivered.

"But that wasn't why I wanted to tell you," Alessio said.

She met his gaze again. "No?"

"No, more like … if where you want me to return to is wherever you are, and him, too, that's where I will be. Is that where you want me, Ginevra?"

Didn't he already know?

"Yes, this is where I want you."

22.

Alessio

A bouncer for the club led Alessio and Ginevra upstairs to the VIP section. He suspected that's where they would find Corrado, considering he no longer lingered on the lower floor of the club.

"Aren't you hot in that?" Ginevra asked, fingering the neckline of his leather jacket.

"Yes."

"Why not take it off, then?"

"Discomfort doesn't bother me that much."

He thanked The League for that.

And training.

Ginevra looked like she would say more, but he pointed across the room to distract her instead. Her gaze followed Alessio's movements, and a playful smile curved her cheeks at the sight of Corrado sitting beside Marcus in a booth.

"Better take the *principe* his drink, yeah?"

"What does that mean?"

"Hmm?"

"*Principe*," she said as they crossed the floor.

"Oh, don't call him that, it makes him pissy."

Ginevra arched a brow at Alessio.

He shrugged.

"They like to call sons and daughters of mafia Dons *principes* or *principessas*," Alessio said, shrugging one shoulder. "And I only say it when I want to get a reaction out of Corrado."

"Because he doesn't like it."

"Exactly."

"That's terrible."

Alessio made a noise. "Well, it's not terrible when it ends with him fucking you."

Ginevra shivered.

He laughed.

"Now you get it," Alessio told her.

"What are you two grinning about?"

Corrado's question had Alessio turning to wink at his lover, forgetting for a moment about the people around them, and *who*. Although, as soon as that thought drifted through Alessio's mind, it left with one look at Corrado.

He was unbothered.

He grinned back, in fact.

Ginevra had changed more than she realized for the two. Things that had once been a source of discontent for Alessio between him and Corrado now became a background thought because it didn't factor into what they shared, not when everything they had together proved it unimportant.

He probably should tell Corrado that.

There was never a good time.

"Well?" Corrado asked.

Alessio ignored the other people milling about—the ones at the booth with Corrado and his brother, and the others around surrounding booths. "I told her there will be a lot of *principes* in this club tonight, yeah?"

Corrado's features flashed with darkness.

A *warning*.

Alessio smirked. "All the Guzzi *principes*, in fact."

Ginevra smacked Alessio with the back of her hand, but he didn't even flinch. "That's enough of that."

Corrado chuckled and waved two fingers at her. "Come here, you."

He didn't mind that Ginevra left his side to slip in the booth beside Corrado because Alessio quickly slid in after her. There, she was between them. He had his hand on her bare thigh, just under the skirt of that short dress of hers, while Corrado slung an arm behind her on the booth.

Conversation turned on the club, and Marcus. An easy, *safe* topic. It allowed Corrado to join in without having to bring *himself* into it, which Alessio figured the man appreciated. With Guzzi mafioso, it could go either way.

For now, Corrado relaxed, but Alessio kept an eye on him because that could change in a blink. An offhanded comment from one of the many men who just wanted to point out *again* that Corrado didn't wear the Guzzi legacy the same way his brother did, or his other brothers who hadn't arrived yet. Or perhaps someone who wanted to share their opinion about what they believed about Corrado and Alessio's relationship.

Although, now, it was different.

A woman stood between them.

Alessio *highly* suspected a comment would come because of that if nothing else. And if he could shut it down before it turned into something that might cause a problem, then that would be far better for all of them.

He'd become used to this game with these people. They were careful when their boss happened to be around, but other than that ... Corrado became fair game. Like he had been for most of his life.

Alessio wouldn't stand for it.

For the most part, Corrado ignored the shit they threw at him from people who, as far as it concerned Alessio, didn't deserve to breathe the same air as either of them. He didn't want to cause issues for his brothers, or father. God knew Alessio could understand that, but it left Corrado as the proverbial punching bag.

Which he was *not*.

Anyone else, and he'd cut their throats.

Just not these people.

It irritated Les to no end.

"He's not wrong, though," Ginevra said.

It didn't take Alessio and Corrado long to figure out what she was referring to. Across the VIP section, the rest of the other Guzzi brothers had arrived in a trio. Chris, and the other twins didn't waste time greeting the people closer to the stairs before crossing the floor, and joining the rest of their family.

Bene and Beni busied themselves with Marcus, congratulating him on the club before turning their attention on Ginevra just long enough to greet her the same way their older brother had earlier. Chris laughed as he leaned over the booth to give his twin a one-armed hug.

"Got them both out tonight, huh?" Chris asked.

Corrado flashed his teeth in a grin. "Careful."

"I'm just saying you're in a far better mood when one of them happens to be around. That's good for all of us, Corrado."

Alessio glanced at Corrado from behind Ginevra, nodding as he did so. "He's right, though."

"Fuck off, all of you."

Someone had to tease Corrado, but they did it in such a way that didn't make him the lesser man in the room because his choices didn't match their own. All in good fun, and Corrado knew, too.

There was no malice here.

Only respect.

And of course, love.

They were simply careful about how they showed it. Alessio doubted they would change that about their relationship. He didn't *want* people to see the depth of this thing between them. Oh, he believed Ginevra understood, but that was different.

She should.

She was in it, too.

Everyone else?

Fuck them.

Corrado caught Alessio's stare again, but he didn't find playfulness reflecting back. Instead, he found the same silent intensity that had accompanied their relationship from the beginning. A conversation that wasn't had with words because they never needed to say things to make sure the other heard what they wanted said.

Alessio gave Corrado a half smile. In response, Corrado's hand lifted from Ginevra's shoulder, and two of his fingers ghosted along the side of Alessio's neck. Barely there at all, and yet he still somehow felt it all over.

Fuck.

He needed to get this goddamn Albania job done, come back home, and settle out all the shit they had left to work on. Which wasn't that much, but more … things left unsaid.

They needed to be *out*.

Tonight, however, wasn't the right time.

When would it ever be?

Or there wasn't a right time for this. Timing didn't matter when something should be said, full stop. As long as they put it out there, wasn't that all that mattered?

Alessio didn't get the chance to think on that for too long. A sound behind him—someone's disgust at *something* coming out as a harsh noise. Like a cross between a scoff, and a grunt, he thought.

Turning his head, his gaze landed on an older man. With a middle as wide as his shoulders, and his gray hair thinned on the top. Still, the fitted suit he wore, the lit cigar dangling from his fingertips, and the smug look of utter arrogance on his face told Alessio all he needed about the man.

Likely a Capo.

His choice in dress, and the attitude wafting from him gave it away. They all acted the same fucking way, but especially the older generation.

Alessio's gaze darted to Corrado when he turned to look for the sound behind them, too. He hadn't recognized the man, but clearly Corrado did what with the way his jaw tightened at the sight of the prick staring at them. Apparently, their chat and Corrado's touch wasn't missed by that fuck.

He didn't even try to hide his disgust.

"Do you have something you want to say, George?" Corrado asked, his hand coming to rest along the side of Ginevra's shoulder when she thought to turn around to join the conversation, too. His hand kept her facing the rest of their booth which had now gone silent. Alessio's attention went back to the Capo in the booth behind them. "How long has it been, anyway? Three years since I last saw you? Could have done with another three, to be honest."

George smirked, flashing yellowing teeth. "I feel the same way, Corrado. I prefer it when your father keeps you out of sight, if I'm being honest."

Alessio tensed at that.

Where the fuck did this guy get—

"And why is that?" Corrado asked, stopping Alessio's train of thought.

What was he doing?

Purposely trying to bait the asshole?

Why?

"Fucking *queers*," George uttered, his gaze darting away from Corrado and Alessio. "Gian Guzzi ought to be fucking ashamed of what he's allowed to happen with you, Corrado. Had you been my son, I would have beat your ass until you understood what I expected from you."

Yep.

This time, the comment hadn't even been underhanded, but right fucking out there. Alessio drifted away from Ginevra in the booth.

Alessio didn't get offended at being called a queer, frankly. He was bisexual— he fit the bill of queer perfectly fine, even if he didn't use the label. Some people needed labels because it gave them a sense of belonging.

Words were important.

People forgot.

"What did you fucking say?" Alessio asked, straightening to his full height as he exited the booth. George looked his way, gaze narrowing and still looking too fucking arrogant for Alessio's liking. The man likely figured nothing would happen to him because of who he was, and his position. "Say it again ... *go on.*"

George sneered. "I said *fucking qu*—"

"*Les*," Ginevra whispered, her hand reaching out to grab him.

Her, and those words, had him glancing her way. Not that it mattered, his attention flew back to the Capo behind their booth when Corrado turned, and launched himself over the back of the seat.

Nobody saw it coming.

Nobody planned for *this*.

Not when Corrado had always been the one with the calmer head between the two. He'd resigned himself for years to turn his cheek, and ignore the shit people liked to say about him, or them.

Not this time.

And nobody had time to react.

By the time Marcus decided to climb over the table at their booth, and head for Corrado, it was already too late. Someone else tried to jump in, too, but nothing helped.

Alessio stood *stunned*.

He heard every fucking punch.

Smack, smack, smack.

Bone hitting bone.

He saw the blood.

Spewing to the checkered floor. Spraying across Corrado's silk shirt. Dotting his busted knuckles every time his fists slammed into the face of the Capo again and again. Marcus tried to pull his brother back by grabbing onto the back of his shirt, but Corrado would not move.

"*Fucking help me here!*"

"Corrado, stop! *Stop it!*"

Marcus's shout echoed.

Ginevra's *ached.*

Alessio cared nothing for Marcus's demand, but Ginevra's had him moving. And only because she looked like she would get out of the booth any fucking second, and Alessio couldn't have that. She didn't need to get in the middle of this mess.

Already a whole group tried.

And failed.

It was chaos. Men shouting. Corrado's brothers holding back those trying to get to him to save the man on the ground. Pointless. In the background, Alessio seemed removed, somehow.

As though this had been inevitable.

Why were they surprised?

Alessio shoved between the semi-circle of people trying to yank Corrado from the man on the floor—who was no longer moving. He would have been fine to let Corrado get out *years* of frustration, hurt, and anger on the face of the asshole, but it only took one peek at a *terrified* Ginevra for Alessio to realize this wasn't good.

"*Corrado.*"

His first shout did nothing, not that he expected it to. Alessio got down, wrapped his arms around Corrado's chest, and pulled back hard enough to send them both tumbling to the floor.

"That's enough," Alessio muttered, forcing them over so he had Corrado pinned under him to the floor. The daze hadn't left—*fury* stared back at him, written in heavy lines all over Corrado's strong features, and exhaling in every hard breath he let out. "*Fucking stop.* That's enough, Corrado."

He didn't fight him, though.

Didn't shove him off.

No, he *stared* at him.

So goddamn angry.

And yeah, Alessio got it.

"*Fuck*," someone—Marcus—hissed behind them. "He's dead; someone call in the cleaner, this mess needs to *go*."

Someone else cried.

Ginevra.

Alessio looked her way.

Corrado did the same.

That, more than even Alessio dragging Corrado from the dead man on the floor, brought him back to reality. Alessio sensed the change in Corrado's body, how all the fight and tension and anger bled away when his gaze landed on where she stood just five feet away.

Shaking.

Crying.

Scared.

She could be frightened of them, or of Corrado, or just what he had done. Alessio wasn't sure, but when Corrado reached out a hand to her, a *sorry* already falling off his tongue, she took a step back.

A whole step.

Away.

"Get him out of here," Marcus said, blocking Ginevra from Alessio's view when he came to kneel beside them. "Calm him the fuck down, I need to handle this and fast."

Right, right.

Mafia business.

Can't kill made men.

All *trash*.

"Ginevra," Corrado said.

Marcus gave his brother a glance from the side. "She's fine for now."

Except she wasn't.

Even Alessio understood that.

23.

Alessio shoved Corrado through the exit door, making him stumble into a back alley that was cold, and yet still somehow smelled of garbage and piss. *Fucking perfect.*

Not that it mattered.

The cold air helped to soothe some of that rage inside his soul—that bitterness making the beats of his heart faster. And not in a good way, either.

It barely helped, though.

Alessio stayed back by the door, sticking a rock in the track to keep it from closing before he turned to face Corrado. He didn't need to look at Alessio's face to see the disappointment staring back from him.

Corrado wasn't the hothead here.

He didn't *freak out.*

Over the years, he had become rather good at pretending like people's bullshit didn't bother him, and ... tonight had been more than enough to make him fucking snap.

Oh, sure, Alessio would have taught the guy a lesson, too, but just differently than Corrado. Like taking him outside and beating the piss out of him where people couldn't stand there and watch.

People like *Ginevra.*

Corrado let out a heavy breath, his back hitting the brick wall opposite to Alessio. Still, his companion said nothing as he snarled under his breath, dragged his palms down his face, and stared up at the inky sky with bright stars dotting its surface.

He still missed the stars.

They didn't see them enough in Vegas.

"Corrado—"

"Just don't," he muttered.

Alessio sighed. "That was bad."

"I don't need the memo."

"No, I mean ... that was a mess, and what the fuck?"

What was it?

A lot of things.

Nothing, too.

Everything.

Five fucking years of comments under people's breath about what they thought with Alessio and Corrado, like they had any fucking business opening their mouths to say anything at all.

It was *more years* of him always being told *famiglia* should be the only thing Corrado did—he would only ever be useful as a man, if he was his father's clone.

The frustration.

His anger.

A *reaction*.

Corrado finally reacted, and surprise, it came out badly. Why on earth was anyone surprised? Because he wasn't.

This felt like a long fucking time coming.

"He didn't give a fuck, you know?" Corrado asked.

"Who?"

"That *fuck*—George."

He still stared at the sky and willing that hatred in his heart to disappear, loathing the emotion—it had no place in his life. He felt a lot of ways about a lot of different things, but *hate* terrified him.

Hate made people do awful things to one another. Fear bred in hate, and people had killed for nothing more than their hate of someone else, or for their hate of *something*.

Be it differences, sexualities, religion, or skin color … hate caused pain. That's all it was good for, and he proved that tonight, hadn't he?

His hate came out in *violence*. How did that make him any worse or better than the man who was dead on the floor upstairs?

Corrado didn't think he was better.

"I don't understand," Alessio said quietly.

Of course, not.

Because Corrado hadn't explained.

All that shit unsaid.

"He didn't give a fuck," Corrado repeated, "because he didn't know anything about us, and that's what pissed me off, okay. All he sees are two men who are affectionate, and that made him uncomfortable enough to say something about it. Not because it hurts him, or affects his fucking life, but just because he *didn't like us*."

"There are millions of people like him, Corrado."

Yeah, he understood.

Clearly.

"Does that mean they should open their stupid fucking mouths and spew their bullshit, though?" Corrado asked, lowering his gaze from the sky to stare at the man across the alley from him. Alessio stared back with his face an expressionless mask, not that Corrado took offense to that. They *all* needed a few seconds to deal with this, and what it meant. "When they know nothing—not what we are, what it's been like for us *together*, or what you mean to me. And they sure as fuck don't have a clue how much I fucking love you because they're too worried about the fact two men might kiss where they can *see*."

Silence echoed between the two in the alley.

Finally, Alessio cleared his throat and muttered, "You drop that bomb, huh?"

"What?"

"The *love* bit."

Corrado gave him a look. "*Cette partie de mon cœur est à toi*—this part of my heart, it's *yours*. I have been telling you this for years, but you only wanted to hear it in the way you wanted me to say it, Les."

Alessio's throat jumped, and his cheek twitched. Corrado waited him out because now, he didn't have a choice. He did what he did—it'd been *said*. The rest would be determined by the man across from him.

"I figured out something over the last while," Alessio murmured.

"Do tell."

"You don't have to be an asshole."

Corrado checked his attitude. "Sorry."

Alessio shrugged, stuffing his hands in his pockets as he looked up at the sky above them while he spoke. "I figured out I clung to that—to *words*, Corrado, putting too much faith and weight in what words meant, and not what's true. I thought, if you said those words, then it would mean this was *real*. I held onto a need for words when literally everything else about us and what we are is the definition of what I wanted. It's love, and I'm sorry I didn't tell you this sooner."

Corrado blinked, quiet again.

This *thing* that had been such a fucking problem ... now wasn't one. Like that, it was done, and he wasn't sure if he understood what it meant.

"And you know I love you, so," Alessio added. "I've always loved—"

Corrado crossed the alleyway before Alessio could even finish his sentence because *no* ... no, that could not be an afterthought. Not when he was aware, regardless of what Alessio decided he had figured out about all of this, that those three little words had meant a lot to him when he felt like they weren't freely given.

Alessio might have understood *now* Corrado wasn't like him, and he didn't show his affection and love in the same ways. That didn't mean he couldn't do it, anyway.

Because that was love.

Corrado crashed into Alessio hard enough to send them both into the wall beside the propped open door. Alessio's fingers threaded into Corrado's hair when their lips met, moving to a fast, familiar rhythm as his frustration and anger started to bleed away.

All the hatred?

Gone when he got a taste of Les on his tongue.

Because that was the thing about hate, too.

Love always won.

Corrado flexed his hands, the pads of his fingers scraping against the brick wall as his mouth ghosted over Alessio's when he whispered, "I fucked up tonight."

"You had a moment. We all have them. He's a prick, and so fucking what if he was made, they'll handle it, Corrado."

Right.

But no.

"I meant with Ginevra, not *la famiglia*."

Alessio let out a slow stream of air. "It scared her."

"Of course, she was."

"She comes from violent men. She's sensitive to this kind of thing. Give her a second to come back. We're not them, and it might take a bit for her to figure that out."

Corrado looked away, the reality a little too sharp for his liking. It stung. "I—"

"We're not *saints*, Corrado. This is our life; we are who we are."

No exceptions.

No apologies.

He heard what Alessio didn't say. This had always been their way.

"And what if it's not the life she wants?"

"You always want what you love, even when you're not supposed to."

The door beside them swung open before Marcus stepped out into the alley. Corrado didn't bother to step away from Alessio at the sight of his oldest brother—he no longer cared to make others comfortable by hiding the best parts of himself.

Because that was another thing.

Alessio?

Ginevra?

They were the better parts of him.

His better *pieces*.

"What?" Corrado asked.

"The cleaners have arrived. They will take the body out the back here." Marcus fixed his suit jacket and shook his head. "You made a mess—I have to call Papa and make him aware."

"Whatever Gian wants," Alessio blurted before Corrado was able reply, "we'll be happy to do for him."

Marcus nodded, turning to head back into the club. "And Ginevra … she asked to leave, and so I had someone take her home."

"Home as in our pent—"

"Home as in *my* home," Marcus said. "She asked for some time, Corrado. Let her have a moment."

Right.

Yeah, he expected that.

It still fucking *hurt*.

Corrado went cold all over.

Alessio's hand tightened on his shirt. "It's *fine*."

No. Not at all.

24.

Ginevra

Knowing something was different from it being *your* reality. Out of everything Ginevra learned since being put in the lives of Corrado and Alessio, that seemed to be the most important lesson to stick with her.

She'd known about *many* things before them. For life, about herself, and even the bad parts forced upon her. And then she met them—one by one, everything changed into something else.

About life.

Herself.

And even the bad parts.

Still, a piece of Ginevra had been hiding one aspect of who those men were and what it would mean to her. She understood what Alessio and Corrado did for a living—they were *connected*. They were more like the people who hurt her, and less like the boy who sat next to her during her first class of the morning at the community college.

She understood it, but knowing those things was different from seeing it. However, being shoved in her face, a man capable of violence that scared her and did it *without* retribution, reminded her she was not like these people.

Her life had been different.

She hadn't seen their version of life through their eyes and experiences, and she'd been shaped differently because of it. And yet, she chose to turn her cheek.

That wasn't right.

Even she got that.

And yet, that other part of her was clear, so much so it became impossible to ignore. Knowing might not be the same as seeing, sure, but she had still known and still stayed.

In fact, she *wanted* to stay.

Ginevra realized far too late, as she sat staring out the bay window of Marcus Guzzi's beautiful townhome the morning after the night at the club, that she was not having an internal dilemma about Corrado and Alessio.

Of them, she was *most* sure.

Them, she wanted.

It stuck her in this dark place because of her own complex about who she thought she was, and how much changed. Ginevra never said she was a saint, but she had *some* morals. That in the end, she was the person who understood where right and wrong fit in her life.

The mafia came for her when she barely knew it existed.

She'd almost been forced into an arranged marriage.

Her mother had been murdered.

All those things meant Ginevra should have made the easy choice—with freedom at her fingertips, she should run from these people, and those like them,

361

that had done to her what they did without as much as a blink about it.

Because they were made differently.

And somehow, Ginevra found herself inexplicably and irrevocably in love with men who, while they'd not done bad things to her, had done them to others. She overlooked it before, but not so much now. The man they killed, she bet like others in their business, said awful things—he was not a good man, and to some, he deserved to die for it, and for other reasons.

But to someone?

That man had probably been a father—maybe a good one. A husband. He'd been a son, perhaps a brother, a grandson, and more. He was a *person*.

Her dilemma in a nutshell

For herself—just her.

After knowing what they could do ... what had been done to her ... After everything, Ginevra still found that need deep in her bones that she wanted to be with Corrado and Alessio more than she had wanted anything in her life.

Ginevra was not who she assumed she was before them. And she would never be the same after, either.

That terrified her.

And changed nothing.

"Ginny."

Turning on the bench seat in front of the window, Ginevra found a *very* familiar face in the living room's entryway room. Chris smiled, but the sight didn't quite reach his eyes.

"How're you doing?" Chris asked.

Ginevra shrugged under the oversized sweater that Marcus found for her. "I'm not sure."

Chris cleared his throat. "Hmm. Corrado called—Les, too."

She swallowed the ache in her throat. It only became even more painful with every beat of her heart, making it impossible to ignore. Somehow, she talked through it. "I just ... need a bit of time."

To keep thinking, and to realize, *this* was the life she wanted. To get over herself, in a way.

After the time she had spent with either one, or both men in the past months, they should at least give her a day to herself.

"Let them explain," Chris said.

Ginevra's brow furrowed. "What is there to explain?"

She understood perfectly well what happened. The mess in her heart and soul needed dealt with now, and they couldn't help with that. This was on *her*.

Right?

Chris's features went stony, leaving Ginevra confused. "I will let them know, then."

"A lot was taken from me," Ginevra tried to explain, "and I've shoved it aside while I was here ... so it's catching up in different ways."

This was one.

Chris nodded. "I understand."

It didn't sound like he did, though.

Then, he asked, "Anything else you want me to tell them? I'm about to meet up with them at the mansion in a couple of hours, so I can pass it along face to face."

All over again, she considered the conversation with Cara in the restaurant. How she told her, in so many words, to always make the best of this life.

She didn't have to *make the best* of anything.

Not when she had Corrado and Alessio.

"Ginevra?" Chris asked again. "Anything?"

"Yeah. Tell them I lo—"

Marcus stepped into the entryway beside his brother, making her words stop short as he held out a phone with a small smile. "Someone would like to speak to you from New York, Ginevra."

Her gaze darted to Chris, but he stepped back to let Marcus offer the phone still outstretched for her to take. She did but didn't look down at the screen right away to see if she might recognize the number.

She wanted to thank Marcus first.

He had been kind to her.

Even if he didn't have to be.

"Thank you for everything," she said.

Marcus shrugged. "No worries, this is what I was taught to do."

She looked past him to finish her conversation with Chris, but she found the entryway empty. He already left.

Damn.

Ginevra would have time.

Later.

She would go back to Alessio and Corrado and say what she wanted to say face to face. They would get it from her mouth, and not from someone else's.

She loved them.

They deserved to hear it from her.

"Take your call," Marcus said, bringing Ginevra back to reality.

She laughed under her breath, and nodded, pulling the phone up to her ear as she said, "Hello?"

"Are you ready to come back?"

Ginevra stiffened all over. "Andino?"

The man on the other end of the line chuckled darkly. "That would be me, yes."

"Why are you calling—"

"I am the one who sent you away," Andino said fast, "and I should have access to call you if I need, even if I am in jail, right?"

He really was an asshole.

And ... "*What?*"

"I'm sorry?"

"You're in jail?"

"Semantics, and I have access to a private cell, so my business, like you, is still being handled."

Ginevra moved onto another topic, then. "What did you mean—about home?"

"Exactly what I said."

"You mean—"

"I heard you spoke to Siena," he noted, a slight hum in the background of his call lowering to nothing at all as a door shut on his end. "But what she didn't tell you was just how close we were to the end the night you called. A few days before you spoke to Siena, Darren got caught in an unfortunate situation—a bomb that did quite a bit of damage."

Ginevra dragged in a breath, surprising herself when she cared nothing for a man who shared at least half of her blood.

"And a while ago," Andino added quieter, "they buried Kev—did they tell you?"

"No. Is Darren alive?"

"Barely. Life support most of the way. He won't come out of it, and Siena only has to sign paperwork after filing to take over his next of kin as their mother is missing, and can't do the job of pulling the proverbial plug. No one is left who will give a fuck, or can change the fact, that you didn't marry me, and ran off instead. Not anymore."

Jesus Christ.

"It's over, Ginny," Andino said, "and you can come home. Siena said your sisters have been told the truth about you recently, and they ask for you every chance they possibly can. I will be emailing Marcus with the name and contact of a pilot who is willing to overlook a hidden passenger on his private jet when he makes the trip across the border today, where he will land in a safe, private strip to drop the passenger off. *You,* I mean."

It was over.

She didn't know how to feel.

"But we are running on a short timeline," Andino said, "because I was barely able to call in that favor and contact today. Just my luck that my old friend is making the trip this morning. So, otherwise, we'll have to wait and pull strings to get you back home soon. It's up to you."

Ginevra didn't have to think about it.

She wanted to be here.

Should be here.

But she missed her sisters. She needed to go back to them.

The boys would understand.

Surely.

"Well?" Andino demanded.

"I'll be on that plane if it's waiting for me."

25.

Corrado

"Stop obsessing."

"I'm not."

"Corrado."

He glowered at the phone in his hand. "What, Les?"

"It doesn't help to sit there and—"

"Or you could leave me the hell alone?"

Alessio sighed.

Corrado shrugged.

"Fine," Alessio muttered, "I need to pack up my shit, anyway. I got the new flight set for this afternoon, so we can head over to your parents together, and I'll leave for Vegas after."

Great.

Just perfect.

Corrado said none of that out loud because his pride kept him quiet. That stupid bitch of a thing seemed to follow him no matter how hard he tried to forget about it. He didn't want to speak up and tell Alessio he couldn't leave—right now, he was the *only* person here that Corrado wanted besides Ginevra, and she wasn't calling.

All she had to do was use Marcus's phone.

Except she didn't.

And his phone was still in his hands, no calls or texts.

The very last thing he needed was for Alessio to leave. But they didn't get a choice because of that fucking Albania job, and Corrado's pride kept him quiet. Instead of saying what he needed and wanted in those moments, he kept his mouth shut.

It wasn't easier.

It made sense.

"Give her some time," Alessio said, "to process whatever it is she's got going on in her head, and then we'll go from there. That's all you can do—she asked for it, Corrado."

"*I get it.*"

All too fucking well.

And it killed him.

"All right," Alessio muttered, stepping out into the hallway out of sight.

Just like that, Corrado was alone again. He was all too aware that soon, he would be far more alone than he was right now. Alessio would be gone—for a week, maybe two, who fucking knew? Ginevra was ... out of reach.

Not taking his messages, or calling back.

He'd not told her how he loved her. That, more than the rest, he regretted the most. The time had never been right to say that, but he realized now, far too late ...

there shouldn't be a right time for love.

Too little, too late.

His mind was hell.

Far too dark.

Frustrated, Corrado glared at that phone in his hand, and before he could think the action though, tossed it to the hardwood floor harder than he should have. Was it smart? Not particularly, but it felt better than feeding the hot fury flooding his veins in another way.

Too bad he hadn't figured that out the night before.

Getting off the side of the bed, he scooped the phone up in one hand, popping the broken back into place before turning it over to see a large crack across the screen. The battery hadn't come out, and the screen blinked black and white.

Shit.

The screen wouldn't react to his touch, and it wouldn't bring up the home screen. Turning it on and off did nothing for him, and neither did restarting the device.

It was good and fucked.

A lot like him.

Fuck it.

Corrado tossed the ruined phone to the comforter on the bed, settling himself with the fact he would have to get a new one. Right then, though, he didn't want to do *anything*. He was feeling entirely too much, and that never worked out well for him.

Shit was out of control.

Things he wanted, gone from his grasp.

His heart hurt.

Corrado never did well like this. He wasn't weak, and he didn't want something like *love* to make him that way, either. That might have been his pride talking again, but it was the only goddamn way he protected himself.

Heading to the bathroom, he stripped down and turned on the shower. Stepping under the spray, a hiss left his lips as the hot water stung when it beat down on Corrado's back. He should turn the water temp down, but at least like this … he focused on the pain of that, and not the fact that he was losing something important.

He didn't want to lose anything.

"Hey."

Corrado heard Alessio's voice outside the shower, but he didn't reply. Alessio continued talking like that didn't bother him.

"Your father called the penthouse—he's ready to see you whenever you are."

"Great."

Except it wasn't.

Not at all.

"What happened to your phone?" Alessio asked, the shuffle of clothes following his question.

"Les, just leave—"

Corrado didn't get the chance to finish his statement before Alessio had opened the shower and was stepping inside with him. *Naked*, too. One second, he had been alone with his thoughts and fears, and in the next, he wasn't. It only hurt him, though, even if he loved the way Alessio backed him into the wall with a rough, demanding kiss … because this distraction wouldn't last forever.

He was leaving soon, too.

And what would Corrado do then?

Not that he was able to think about that for too long with Alessio's kiss demanding attention from him, the clashes of his tongue against Corrado's hardening him. He found the friction he wanted for his erection along the hard lines of Alessio's form shoving his into the wall, and the ridges of firm muscle that somehow fit perfectly alongside his own.

Alessio's mouth left his to skim along the line of his jaw, lips dragging over Corrado's stubble as words drifted over his skin. "You want to feel good, then— not think?"

"Yeah. Just for a bit, Les."

"Whatever you want."

And Alessio was so fucking good at *that*—at just giving Corrado what he wanted.

That knowledge was written in the way his hands ghosted confidently over the slopes of his body. How he found Corrado's cock with a rough palm to stroke fast while his teeth dragged across his lower lip to leave a sharp sting behind. Alessio worked him high, and as fast as possible, so that Corrado was aching by the time he was done, when his strokes slowed, and his legs were shaking from the intensity …

Corrado had never been more grateful. Just like that, Alessio had taken his mind from a bad place, to somewhere else. He pulled him from the edge of one insanity to take him right to the cliff of another one.

He could handle this one, though.

Corrado reached for the small bottle of lube they always kept in the shower— one of their favorite places to fuck because it made clean up *easy*. Alessio took it from him as he kneeled down, making quick work of popping it open to get what he wanted from it before he was back to making Corrado think he was going insane again.

This time, it was Alessio's mouth sucking down his length, and the fingers that worked into his ass with the help of that lube. There was always something about the sight of Alessio sucking him off that did it for Corrado—maybe it was the way he always looked so fucking contrary and cocky at the same time staring up at him with something akin to a smirk dancing in his gaze.

Like he was *daring* Corrado not to come because Alessio was all too aware how goddamn hard it was for him like this. And like when he jerked Corrado off, he used his fingers to stretch him open, and his mouth on his cock to get him ready to blow in barely anytime at all. It was Alessio's teeth dragging gently down his length when he sucked him in again that about had his knees fucking buckling as the sensation of an orgasm drew near.

His balls tightened with his.

Shoulders tensing.

Corrado's groan threatened to bubble out of his chest, and Alessio let him go all at once. *Everywhere*, he was hands-off, letting hot water and cold air beat down on Corrado instead of allowing him to come.

Fuck.

But it was always so much better when Alessio did that, and Corrado was well aware what would come next because of it, too. Alessio lifted to his full height, lips crashing down on Corrado's for just long enough to have his cock jerking between them before he was spun around to face the shower wall.

One of his hands hit the tile, the other went back to grab onto Alessio's side as the man's hand came down to smack Corrado hard on his ass before he grabbed hard to the same spot. Heat flooded to the bits of his skin where Alessio's fingers dug in, holding him still while the head of his cock pressed against the tight ring of muscles at his ass.

"Jesus Christ," Corrado grunted against the wall.

Alessio's teeth found the junction between Corrado's shoulder and his neck. His gaze pinned onto Corrado's, lips curling upward. That ringing pain from the sharp bite took away the bit of sting from Alessio working his way into Corrado's ass with quick flexes of his hips.

They had been doing this for years.

Working each other to their limits.

Alessio knew what to do, and how to do it without Corrado needing to stop, or even wanting to.

"Fucking *yeah.*"

Alessio's words murmured along Corrado's shoulder as he *finally* worked his cock to the hilt. His hand wrapped around Corrado's front, his fingers snaking along his length to stroke him in time with his next thrusts.

They came *hard*—fucking deep, fast, and brutal.

It was exactly what Corrado had needed.

He couldn't breathe, but he didn't think he needed to. Not when it was far better to focus on the way Alessio felt fucking him, and the ache spreading through his muscles.

From the bites and rough kisses Alessio kept peppering over his neck and shoulders. To the way he stroked him faster with his hand, tightening enough at the head of Corrado's dick to make a moan fall between his clenched teeth. And even his fingers digging into Corrado's hip while his hips met Corrado's ass again and again at a pace that made it impossible to hold back the orgasm.

Not that Alessio seemed to want him to hold it back. "*Come on*, fucking give it over."

Corrado did, coming fast and painting the shower wall as a thick moan followed, every part of him growing hot and tense from the relief that swept through his system. Alessio wasn't very far behind, those pumps of his hips working faster for a moment before they stilled all together, and his hands tightened on Corrado again.

Alessio's groan echoed.

Corrado still had trouble breathing because the pain flooded back in, so air came second. It was worse, too, taunting him for daring to forget it.

Alessio held him tighter.

Somehow, that helped.

• • •

"You good?"

Alessio nodded at Corrado's question and took the cigarette Bene offered him next to the bright red Lambo his brother loved. "Yeah, I'm fine out here. This asshole will keep me company."

"Nice," Bene muttered around his own cigarette as he attempted to light it. "Papa's waiting in the kitchen, Corrado, don't fuck around."

Right.

"I'm running low on time," Alessio said as he turned to head for the mansion entrance, "I have to be on the road in twenty minutes to make my flight."

Loneliness stabbed at Corrado's back.

He didn't turn around, though.

"Yeah, I got it."

Inside the mansion, Corrado navigated the familiar halls until he stood in the kitchen entryway. It wasn't only his father waiting. Cara sat on a stool at the island, flipping through a home décor magazine while she sipped from her tea. On the other side of the island, his father stared his way.

Gian cleared his throat. "Cara."

Glancing up from the magazine, Cara peered at her husband, who nodded in Corrado's direction. His mother didn't smile at him, but in her stare, he still found love. The same as his father. That was the thing about his parents—he might fuck up, and he had, but they still loved him.

Unconditionally.

Wasn't that love?

"Where is Marcus and Chris?" Corrado asked.

He'd thought his twin, and oldest brother would be around. Or, that's what he had been told about this quick meeting.

Gian set his coffee down. "Chris got stuck in traffic—an accident, apparently. Marcus had to handle something else. He'll come later, but I assume you'll be gone by then."

"All right."

"Care to tell me about last night, and why I now have a dead man—a *made* man—to bury, and explain to the rest of my organization what happened that caused his death, Corrado?"

No.

He still did.

Corrado talked through the events of the night before in a monotone, not bothering to justify his actions, or where they led them to now. He'd done wrong—crossed a line. Oh, sure, he wasn't the least bit fucking *sorry* for it. But yes, he had gone too far.

So, he was here.

He expected to be punished for it.

"I apologize for putting you in a bad position," Corrado finished.

Gian sighed, his fingers drumming against the countertop. "That's a careful choice of words, yeah?"

"He deserved what he got, Papa."

"Perhaps, or he might have been another old fool with an opinion to share because of his raising, Corrado."

He scoffed hard. "People don't get to use age or their raising as a reason for their bigotry or homophobia—they just *are* those things, and they don't want to change. Don't excuse him, or people like him, thanks."

"I didn't mean it like that, but ... point taken."

Cara made a noise under her breath and peered at Corrado over her shoulder with a sharp stare that pinned him in place. *All* mother's had that one look. That stare that put the fear of God into her children, even if she had never raised a hand to them, let alone her voice. When his mother turned that look on him, Corrado wouldn't be stupid enough to open his mouth and make it worse.

"And what about others?" she asked.

"What?"

"He is—was—not the only person in this world who will have an opinion and something to say about your life, the choices you make, or the way you love, not to mention ... the *people* you choose to love, Corrado."

"I'm aware."

"So, what about them?" Cara demanded. "Are you going to beat the life out of every person who dares to say something you don't like? Because that's the thing, son. He's one of many, and the next comment that hurts is right around the corner. You cannot *kill* every person who has something to say about you, or them."

"Why, because you agree with them?"

Cara's expression didn't change. "You know *far* better than that."

He did.

"Sorry, Ma."

Cara turned more on the stool, resting her hands in her lap as she spoke to say, "The world is full of close-minded people who will have no problem opening their mouths. It's up to you whether what they say or think matters to your life or choices. It's up to you to decide if what they say *matters.* You have been fine to stick your head in the sand and hide your activities before now ... but that can't continue, and it's not going to work after last night."

Corrado's chest ached from the tightness. Nothing his mother said was untrue. That didn't mean he liked it pointed out to him like this, not that he was being given a choice. Hell, perhaps that was it.

Someone needed to say it.

And he needed to hear it.

"Figure out a better way to deal with people like that, and your issues," his mother finished quieter, "and a way that doesn't involve your hands taking their life."

Right.

Easier said than done.

"I will handle my people," Gian said, "because there isn't much someone can do when you're not made, and you don't belong to this organization, Corrado. Being a member of The League saved you retribution for this, and I hope you know that."

"I didn't. I still expected something."

"And you're ready for it."

Corrado lifted his shoulders. "I did what I did."

"Be careful when you come home to visit," Gian said, waving a hand. "Respectful, and mindful of your words and actions. They will watch to make sure you're not stepping out of line against them after this. Do you understand me?"

Everything about the mafia came down to semantics.

Theatrics.

"I got it," he replied.

Gian tipped his chin in Corrado's direction. "Then, that's all I have to say. I know Alessio is catching a flight soon, yes?"

"Too soon."

That's all he offered.

Corrado tried not to think about it.

"Better spend the time you have with him, then."

Yeah.

Cara pushed off the stool before Corrado turned to leave, and he waited as his mother joined his side.

"I'll walk you out."

"You don't have to."

"But I want to."

Corrado *almost* smiled. His mother wanted something, and so, she would get it.

Cara grabbed a shawl hanging from a hook in the entry hallway and took her time wrapping her shoulders. She smiled over at her son, a familiar softness coming back into her eyes as she murmured, "I would ask you to stay for lunch, but …"

"Les has to leave, and I'm not in the mood, Ma."

"I bet. Your father didn't want to mention it because he didn't want to upset you more but I'm sorry. I'm sure this'll work out, Corrado."

His brow dipped. "Sorry for what?"

"Ginevra—Marcus told us she's on her way to a private airstrip to catch a flight to New York today. I assumed that would upset you."

Sure did.

A lot.

He hadn't known until now. He couldn't call Marcus to ask anything because he ruined his phone. He could use *anybody's* phone to do it, but he didn't want to.

If Ginevra needed to leave, why should they stop her?

Yeah, it fucking hurt.

Life took from him again.

"Corrado?"

His mother's hand came up to rest on his arm, letting him know how stiff and quiet he had gone after she delivered her news. He forced a smile on his face, not wanting to worry his mother, and shook his head.

"I'm fine, Ma," he said softly.

Cara frowned. "Are you?"

No.

Still, if Ginevra wanted time and space, well, it was hers to have.

"It will be."

She sighed. "Let me see you out, then."

"Sure, Ma."

Outside, on the front steps of the mansion entrance, Corrado kissed his mother on the cheek to say goodbye before leaving her to approach Alessio standing under the maple tree with Bene. One look from Corrado, and Bene gave Alessio a shrug before he darted off to join their mother.

"What's wrong?" Alessio asked.

He just knew.

Because of course, he did.

Corrado's life took a nosedive.

Fast.

"Nothing," he lied.

Alessio arched a brow. "Really?"

"Yeah, just some news."

"And?"

"Ginevra is on her way back to New York today."

Alessio stiffened all over, but returned with, "So, you catch a flight, and meet her."

"Why?"

The two of them stared at one another, saying nothing.

"If that's where she wants to be, Les," Corrado said.

"You know nothing she wants. You didn't *ask*. Neither did I, Corrado, not really. She asked for *time*, not for us to fuck off."

"You have a flight to catch, don't you?"

"Corrado." Alessio's phone buzzed in his pocket, and he scowled. "She's supposed to be with *us*."

"Answer your phone."

Alessio continued ignoring it.

"Cor—"

"If she wants to be with us, she will, but I will not force her," Corrado said, letting that be his final word on the topic. "And answer your phone."

"It's Cree. Or *Dare*. I'm supposed to be on a flight this morning, but changed to one this afternoon instead. They got a notification for the change, I imagine— doesn't matter."

"The world doesn't stop for me, Les. I learned that a while ago. You still have a job to do, people are still waiting on you, and I have to figure shit out on my own."

"Don't start."

"Start *what*?"

"This," Alessio snapped. "*Run* because you don't like to deal. You've been doing this for years, and I've chased after you the entire time. Stop, Corrado."

"I'm not running."

For once, he came to a standstill, and he didn't have the first clue how to fix it. He was one of three people here—he couldn't help if Alessio couldn't understand that, not to mention, that he didn't think he wanted more pain from this.

Because she left.

Ginevra *left*.

And that's all leaving meant to Corrado.

26.

Alessio

The phone continued to ring in his ear; the call went unanswered. Alessio didn't want to let that bother him, except it did. It wasn't like Corrado to ignore his calls. For another, he could tell Corrado was in a bad headspace before he left, and wanted to check in last minute before he headed out of The League's complex to catch his second flight of the damn day.

That night-long layover he was supposed to have after leaving Vegas in Toronto before flying off the continent had changed to *two* hours. People didn't complain when a long layover was shortened, but Alessio was the first to do exactly that. Not that he understood why the flight schedules had changed, but it meant he would barely have enough time to get to the penthouse and back to the airport in enough time to catch his flight.

But fuck him if he wouldn't *try*.

The ringing in his ear clicked before Corrado's standard message came on for him to leave a message. Cussing under his breath, Alessio ripped the phone away, and hit the end call button. His calls hadn't been going straight to voicemail, but rather, ringing through to it. Which meant Corrado didn't have his phone shut off, at least.

He was just ignoring calls.

Including Alessio's.

Great.

The one thing that Corrado was ridiculously good at which Alessio couldn't stand? *Wallowing.*

"No phones on the job—hand it over to Cree, or leave it on my desk before you head out, all right?"

Alessio stiffened in front of the safe he had been opening in Dare's office. Not that he had been avoiding the man since he arrived back at The League, but his flights and the shit he had to do didn't allow him time to seek Dare out.

Dare hadn't been in his office after Alessio came over from the Vegas penthouse he shared with Corrado, and so he figured the man was giving him some space to get his shit done before he headed out. Apparently, he had been wrong.

Nodding over his shoulder, Alessio muttered, "Yeah, I know. Just some last-minute shit."

He tried dialing Corrado again, but once more, the call rang through to the voicemail. *Jesus Christ, this is the hill you wanna die on, huh?*

Corrado was a shit.

So stubborn.

"Les?"

"Yeah?"

He pulled documentation he needed from the safe. A file with a plain silver stripe across the front, color-coded to him so he knew which one was his. Inside, he would find identification to get him through customs regardless of which country he was traveling to. A whole set of IDs that would be destroyed once he was back on American soil, and the job was done just in case he attracted attention in Albania.

Not that he should do that.

It wasn't the job.

He also pulled out a stack of cash—ten-thousand, nothing more, and nothing less. All in small, unmarked bills. He could take ten thousand in cash through customs, and they wouldn't say shit about it. One dollar more, and they would confiscate it, and arrest him for attempting to smuggle money.

Because right, *that's* what he would do.

Fun times.

"Are you listening at all?"

"No," Alessio said.

Dare sighed. "Listen, I understand you're still pissed at me and everything. I know I overstepped my bounds, Alessio. You don't need to continue giving me the silent treatment as a way to punish me, okay?"

Standing straight, and closing the safe, Alessio kept a tight grip on that folder, and the stack of cash as he turned to face Dare in the doorway. "First, anger doesn't work that way—I can be mad for as long as I fucking want, and you don't get to decide when that changes. Not that it matters because I'm *not* pissed anymore, I'm just *busy*. I have a solid two hours to make it back and catch my flight."

Dare nodded, shoving his hands in his pockets as he did so. A sign of his nerves. Growing up under this man's feet from age ten allowed him to recognize all of Dare's *tells*.

"Sorry, yeah, you're right. And I noticed all those flight changes."

Alessio shrugged. "I tried to work something out, that's all. It didn't … well, work."

"I see."

"Second," Alessio continued, because he wasn't done yet, and now seemed like the best time to get it out because he wouldn't have time when he got back from this job, "you're right, you overstepped your bounds."

"And I'm sorry for that," Dare added.

Right.

Alessio was aware.

That didn't change a lot, though. At least, it didn't change what he thought or had to say about all of this, anyway. He wanted his line to be clear between him and Dare, and in case the man hadn't got the memo, that line was *way* before Corrado. Someone getting too close to Corrado, or the life Alessio shared with him, and his walls would go way up again.

Simple as that.

"If you have an opinion, *and* I care to hear it, then I will tell you. About Corrado and me, though? You could at least give me the same respect for him I've given you about Cree for the last decade. I never asked because it was not on the table. This is the same thing—or when you wanna stick your nosy ass into our issues, anyway. Just stay way the fuck back. Got it?"

"Understood."

"And I get it's because you *care*," Alessio added quieter, softening his stance, "and I love you for that, but please stay out of it."

Dare shifted on his feet, glancing away from Alessio as he did so. "That's the first time you've said that—the love thing."

"I'm doing a lot of new shit."

"Huh."

"I need to get going. Can you do me a favor?"

"I can try."

If what Alessio thought about Corrado was true, then the man had shut himself off. He was powering down and putting a distance between himself and everything that might penetrate his *very* high walls.

That's how he protected himself.

Not that there was anything Alessio could do about it right now. Not only did he need to get rid of his phone in the next minute, and he likely *wouldn't* get to the Toronto penthouse when he got back for that two-hour layover because traffic was a bitch in the city. He would have no contact with him for the next week or two ... depending on how long this job lasted.

To Alessio, that all said one thing.

Corrado wouldn't fix this mess—not the one made of himself, or the one he made with Ginevra because she had gone back to New York. Alessio would fix it because that's just what he did.

They were all human.

They all made mistakes.

Alessio would let Corrado make his.

And he would fix them.

"Ginevra Calabrese, lives in New York, and she's the illegitimate daughter of a dead Cosa Nostra boss," Alessio said to Dare. "She has two full-blood sisters, if that helps to narrow it down. And her half-brothers were recently killed. Her half-sister, Siena, is still alive, same last name. You'll find her somewhere around the Marcello family now, I think. I need as much information on her as you can pull for me by the time I get back. *No one* can be aware you're pulling it and leave it in one of my folders for me to grab when I come back."

Dare cocked a single brow. "That's a woman."

"*And?*"

"Why are you doing a check on a woman?"

"Because she's ours," Alessio explained, "and I don't like waiting for other people to figure shit out that should be obvious."

Dare didn't reply.

Alessio was fine with that.

He had a fucking plane to catch, now.

• • •

Somehow—by the grace of God—traffic in Toronto hadn't been bad. He went twenty over the speed limit to make it back to the penthouse with lots of time to still catch his flight on the way back, though. Not that it left him very much breathing room for minutes to stay … because it didn't.

Alessio had a whole …

He checked the dashboard, the digital clock spelling out the time for him as he pulled the car he'd left at the airport when he first left the city to a stop in front of the building. Right in a *No-Parking* zone, too.

Fuck it.

Tow it, motherfuckers.

Ten minutes.

It's all Alessio had to spare right now. If in that time he wasn't able to convince Corrado to pull his motherfucking head out of his ridiculous ass, well, he would go to plan B. Which unfortunately, would have to wait until he got back on the continent.

Perfect.

Life loved him.

Sarcasm was Alessio's best friend.

He left the car running at the curb, knowing he would be back down here and speeding through the city in no time to get back to the goddamn airport. Ignoring the look the doorman passed him when he didn't even wait for the older gentleman to open the door, Alessio headed into the building.

He didn't bother with the front desk—rarely did, anyway—instead opting to head for the bank of elevators at the other side of the entrance. A lady behind the desk calling his first name made Alessio hesitate in his steps.

He shot the redhead a look over his shoulder. "What?"

She smiled, waving a white envelope for him. "I'm supposed to give this to you, if I saw you come through."

What?

He felt like a parrot.

Even inside his head.

Alessio glanced back and forth between the elevators, and the waiting woman. He didn't have time to fuck around here—it would take him a few minutes to get upstairs, and inside the penthouse anyway.

"I'll grab it on my way out," he told her, going for the elevators.

"The penthouse is empty, sir. That's why I have this."

Alessio's back stiffened.

Of course.

Fucking Corrado.

He loved the man.

Loved him stupid.

But he did dumb things.

And this was probably one of those.

Alessio spun on his heel and crossed the space to the front desk in six long strides. He took the envelope from the woman with a tight smile and turned his back to her as he ripped it open. Pulling the piece of white stationary from it, he found familiar handwriting staring back at him.

Something else people didn't have a clue about Corrado?

He didn't like to *talk*. Communication wasn't his thing because he'd never been good at it when he was in a mood, and he would avoid it at all costs.

Corrado had known Alessio was coming back. It didn't surprise him all that much that the man had done this—left him a small note—instead of sending him a message or answering one of his many texts.

I need a couple of days, it read. *Sorry, Les. I'll see you when you get back. Love you.—Corrado*

Alessio tapped the paper against the palm of his hand, aware he had to get back to the airport soon.

Fuck it.

Plan B, then.

As soon as he got back.

27.

Ginevra

Andino had lied.

Sort of.

Ginevra could not immediately see her sisters when she arrived back in New York. *Details*, someone thought to explain. Yes, the girls knew she was coming back, and yes, she could see them soon, but first they had to finish out a few things.

Just in case.

Those *things?*

Pulling the plug on Darren's life support. Apparently, with her half-brother still technically alive, though no one believed he would make it through considering the doctor's prognosis on his condition, people on the Calabrese side of things were still holding out hope. Like that would make a difference.

Ginevra didn't pretend to understand the way Andino Marcello's mind worked, or why the man seemed to enjoy pulling the strings of the people around him in a way that showed he was the only person who was in control, but here they all were.

Because of him.

Instead of being granted access to her sisters, Ginevra was tucked away in a fancy room at the Waldorf in Manhattan for the better portion of three days. *Without* a phone, or any other way to communicate with someone outside of the hotel.

There had even been two men who worked in twelve-hour shifts that guarded the hotel door. They were also the ones who took the phones from the Waldorf suite and only allowed room service in when she let them know ahead of time, so they could order it.

They're not for you, she was told, *but for someone who might want to hurt you.*

Right.

Ginevra wasn't sure if she would accept that shit, or not, but she hadn't been given much of a choice. If she wanted access to her sisters, then she had to follow the rules. Hadn't the last several months proved she was more than willing and capable of staying in line when it meant getting something she wanted?

Still …

Ginevra could have stayed in Toronto for just a couple of more days if this was what Andino had planned for her when she arrived back in New York. Then, she might have fixed the mistake she made by leaving the club that night. No doubt, Corrado and Alessio assumed her leaving was about them when she hadn't given them a reason to think otherwise.

Sure, Marcus could have told them she had gone home for her sisters, but if they had been told … wouldn't they come to her?

Ginevra thought so.

Hoped so.

And yet, here she was.

Alone in this goddamn room.

"Miss?"

Ginevra looked away from the bay window positioned across from the large seating area. She found one of the two men tasked with guarding her room standing just beyond the entry that led between the kitchen section, and the sitting room. He gave her a tight smile when she stared at him, waiting.

She had nothing to say.

What did they want from her?

"The boss just called—"

Ginevra frowned. "Who?"

"Andino, Miss."

Oh, right.

So many things had changed in her time away, and that was only *one*. Not that she had understood the mafia, or how it worked before Andino sent her to Toronto, but since she came back, things she didn't understand were different again.

Andino now controlled the Marcellos. Johnathan, Andino's cousin, headed the family that used to belong to her half-brothers.

They acted like she was supposed to already be aware of these things, and she was still trying to catch up with what happened before she left, let alone what was going on now. Ginevra would not apologize for needing a minute to get herself together.

"And what did he want?" she asked.

The man—Tim, was it?—nodded once. "He wanted me to let you know your sisters are on their way here ... or they're almost here. About ten minutes away, now."

Her heart stopped.

She was sure it did.

"Yeah?"

"Yep. I will let them in when they get here."

So that must mean ...

"Darren is—"

"They shut his life support off days ago," Tim said, shrugging. "I assume Siena will get the information together for his burial."

"Huh."

"You okay?"

She gave the man a second look. He hadn't bothered to care before if she was fine, or not. He was there to do his job, and she respected that. They all had roles to play in this life, and she was all too aware of that fact.

"Fine," she blurted. "I'm fine."

"Good. Your sisters will be here shortly."

"Thank you."

Tim left her to resume his post outside the room, and Ginevra *paced*. Next to wishing Corrado and Alessio were there with her, she wanted nothing more than to be back with her sisters.

But would they be resentful because she had left them here alone? Would they be angry that she run off without them? Might they feel like she fed them to the wolves to save her own skin?

Those were things Ginevra wasn't sure.

And it hurt her heart.

Ginevra continued to pace, unaware of the minutes ticking by, until the hotel door's knob jiggled. All at once, she turned into stone, her gaze darting to the opened doorway, and there they stood.

Greta.

Giulia.

Looking too much like younger versions of their mother, with water in their eyes as though they feared what would be waiting on the other side for them, too, and yet, still searching for *her*.

"Ginevra?" Greta asked first.

Ginevra sucked in a ragged breath. "*Hey.*"

And yet, she didn't give a fucking damn, either.

Giulia smiled widely, the first tears making lines down her cheeks when Ginevra took a step toward them. "I missed you so much. I tho—"

"*No, no, no.*"

She didn't want to hear those fears. She wanted to take these teenagers, not quite women yet, away from those that wanted to take her from them. No one would ever take her from them.

She decided that.

Not again.

Ginevra quickly crossed the floor then, her arms already opened to hug her younger sisters. Greta stepped forward first, slamming into Ginevra at full speed, but Giulia came right after. She kissed the tops of their heads, trying to search them at the same time for any changes.

It was just a couple of months.

There shouldn't *be* changes.

Still, she wanted to check. Were they taller? Greta changed her hair to a stark red that looked beautiful against her olive-toned skin. A change from brown, and their mother once *loved* the color red.

"God, look at you," Ginevra said quietly, her hands skimming over both her sisters' faces to wipe away their tears. "Don't cry, okay? It's all going to be better now—I'm not going away again."

"Promise?" Greta asked.

Almost eighteen, but right then, Greta sounded *small*. Childlike, even, and it killed Ginevra a little. They'd all been nothing more than pawns to a bigger game played by people who didn't give a single shit about them at the end of the day.

"I promise," Ginevra whispered.

Giulia hugged Ginevra again, and Greta followed her lead. She let them, and the hotel door closed by Tim when the tears fell once more. Was this the reunion her sisters expected? It was still good.

They loved her.

She loved them.

That's all that mattered.

She wished two other people were here, too.

• • •

"Here we are."

The car rolled to a stop in front of an apartment complex that was decent, considering the area and location.

"And what am I here for?" she asked.

In the driver's seat, Andino chuckled. "Well, you need a place to live, and your old apartment is gone."

"Gone *how?*"

"Kev and Darren forced the girls' into Siena's care—not that she minded," he added when Ginevra gave him a sharp look from the side. "But she has things to take care of with John, and starting their life, so I figured you would want the girls with you. The apartment is furnished, and ready for you to use."

He leaned over and opened the glove compartment. There, he pulled out a manila envelope that looked to be two inches thick, or more. "Here—*cash*. It'll take care of whatever else you and your sisters need for a time while we wait for Siena to settle out your brothers' estates, which she has decided will be divided between you, and the girls."

Ginevra swallowed hard, trying to take all that information in. "And how much is their estates worth?"

"A lot."

Huh.

Did that mean she would go back to college? Buy a house? Could she pay for Greta's college next year, or put Giulia into a private school? What did it mean?

Ginevra didn't have the first clue, and she didn't care to ask. She took the envelope, nodding as she said, "Thanks."

"No worries. Least I can do."

"No, you didn't need to let me think I would have to marry you right until the last second, Andino."

He made a noise under his breath, amused. "Everyone needed to believe the ploy. Even you, and I won't apologize for it, either."

"People aren't pawns on a chessboard for you to move as you deem fit."

"They are if it gives me what I want."

Ginevra had the strangest urge to hit the man beside her because that *might* make her feel better if only for a second. "And what's that, Andino? What you wanted, I mean."

"A woman."

His frank answered stunned her.

"A woman," she echoed.

"And I got her," Andino said, offering nothing else. "So, I care very little about what you or anyone else says about how I did this when I get to spend the rest of my life apologizing to her for the things I did ... and trust she is the *only* person in this world I will apologize to, and mean it. As for you, the girls will be brought over by Siena later, and then you are free to do whatever."

Go back to normal.

That's what she would do.

Make sure her sisters were able to resume their normal life before *all of this* happened. It would be hard without their mother, and nothing would ever be the same, but that's what she planned on doing. And somehow, amid that, try to get back to the men she left behind in Toronto.

Speaking of which ...

"Has anyone tried to get in contact with you to speak with me?" she asked.

Andino passed her a glance. "I don't understand."

"From Toronto, I mean." Ginevra didn't want to *out* her relationship with Corrado and Alessio because that wasn't anyone's business, but she still had to ask. "Corrado, maybe, because he watched after me. Or ... Alessio?"

It took Andino a second.

Then, two.

He gave her a curious glance when he said, "I heard rumors about those two, but I didn't know if they're accurate. People say they're *together*, but they share women, too. How true is that?"

Nope.

She wouldn't do that.

Not with this man.

"Has anyone tried to contact me?"

Andino shook his head. "Anyone in Toronto has been quiet since you left. That's all I can tell you."

Why did that sound like a door closing? Like an *end*—an answer she didn't want, but one she now had. What should she do with it?

28.

Corrado

It was almost strange how when Corrado needed something to relax him, or pull him out of the hell that was his mind, he often found himself back at a place that *rarely* allowed him those things in the past. The League, that was.

There was little about the complex that allowed Corrado happy memories. In fact, his training had been some of the worst months of his life. Demanding, intense, and often mind-breaking. Although, that had been the point. They had to break all the pieces of him to put him back together better.

Maybe that was why, now, his mind didn't work the same way. He didn't find *normal* things relaxing—not the shit other people liked to use to chill them out, anyway. Now, he needed the familiarity of a space that had humbled him in more ways than one, and gave him something he hadn't known was possible in Alessio.

Love, that was.

Even if love wasn't here now.

Corrado spent a few days at his family's lodge in Quebec, hiding away from the world, focusing his attention on taking care of himself, and doing what *he* needed. He didn't have a phone to answer, and he didn't use the landline at the lodge to call out except once to let his father know where he was, if needed. He hadn't stayed on the call long enough for his father to ask questions, and he informed no one else about his whereabouts, either.

Should anyone at The League need him, Dare could use Corrado's tracker. His brothers had their own life and business to handle, so they didn't need to worry about Corrado.

Alessio left—the fucking *job*.

Ginevra …

Well, she made her choice.

Didn't she?

Corrado was letting her make it.

Simple as that.

Except it wasn't that simple.

The one thing he never experienced with Alessio in all their years together was heartbreak. Not because there hadn't been opportunity or things that came up between them that might separate them. They always chose each other first, and everything else second.

Usually.

For the first time, Corrado learned about having his heart broken by someone he loved, and he realized that, no, he did not react well to it. In fact, he took it so badly that he wanted to hide away from the world.

That was the problem, though.

It wouldn't be over.

He would not be okay.

And that's why, when the trip to Quebec didn't work, he made his way back to Vegas, to sleep in a familiar bed that still smelled like one of the people who still held a piece of his soul and heart in their hands. To walk familiar halls he once walked with Alessio; to focus on *anything* except the ache in his heart.

Not that it helped.

His mood became worse.

Hence, Cree inviting him for a sparring round in the ring that morning. Had Corrado been a smarter man—apparently, he wasn't today—he would have refused the offer. Anyone with any brains understood sparring with Cree was pointless because he either beat the shit out of someone, or he nearly did so. Besides, this was him substituting one pain for another.

"*Fuck*," he hissed, ducking back to miss a punch Cree threw his way. "If you don't break one of my bones, that would be great."

"Or get quicker." Cree bounced on the balls of his feet as he said that, fists already up and ready to go with Corrado again. He carefully measured every single move he made, and never without an intentional impact when he fought. It made Cree one of the more difficult opponents in a match. "Besides, if you didn't want this, you wouldn't have gotten up here today, right?"

Well, he had a point.

Not that Corrado would admit it.

"Fuck you," he muttered.

Cree raised a brow. "Your mood is about as bad as Alessio's this morning when I saw him."

What?

The word rang so loudly in his mind that everything else around him came to a standstill, including his desire to defend himself against Cree's oncoming attack. Corrado froze—like a fucking *cafone*.

Cree, never one to miss out on an opportunity, used the chance to swing back with a roundhouse. The kick landed hard against Corrado's ribcage and sent him flying back to the mat with enough force to take the air right out of his lungs.

Pain bloomed in three of his ribs as he sucked in a gulp of air, and stared at the ceiling of the complex's gym, trying to let his mind catch up to what he learned. Cree said *when I saw him* and *this morning*. Meaning, Alessio had to be back in the country, but not just *back* ... no, *here*. In Vegas.

And he hadn't told him? Didn't come to the penthouse?

"What?" Corrado asked, still looking like an idiot on his back.

Cree's figure came into his view when he moved to stand next to Corrado's prone form. "He got back this morning—job finished two days ago."

"Well, where the fuck is he now?"

"Doing something he wants to do, I imagine. You know how he is."

Very well.

And whenever Alessio came home, he came back to Corrado. So, what was different this time? Hadn't the last week, and a half been bad enough for him dealing with the Ginevra thing alone while Alessio had to go out of the country?

"You look confused," Cree murmured.

"I'm fine."

Corrado wouldn't let them see his pain.

Cree kneeled down next to Corrado on the mat and rested his arms along his bent knees as he spoke. He didn't look at Corrado, and yet it still seemed like the man stared into his mind even so. "There was a time, and I still think it's possible—if I cared to try, which I don't—when I believed I would *beat* the pride out of you. It's something you couldn't get rid of, and it still holds you back in your life when it shouldn't. Alessio has accepted it is a flaw in your character he has to love like the rest of you. So, where I want to fix it, he will work around it."

Corrado's brow dipped. "What?"

And *damn*, his ribs ached now.

Fucking Cree.

The man reached over and *patted* Corrado's head like he might for a goddamn puppy. "I'm sure you'll figure it out. You're a smart man."

Annoyed, Corrado waved his arm to knock Cree's hand away from his body, lest the fool pet him again. "Knock it the fuck off. Either tell me where Alessio is, or—"

"Or *what?*" Cree cocked his head with a slight smirk that rivaled the devil's. "Because one of us can make threats and demands, and one of us cannot. Guess which one you are, Corrado? Go ahead, I'll wait."

Fucking asshole.

"I'll go speak with Dare," he muttered, pushing up from the mat to stand. "And see what he can tell me."

"Wise choice," Cree replied, "not that he will tell you anything, either."

Right.

Well, Corrado would try.

Cree lounged at the edge of the ring, resting his arms over the ropes as he eyed Corrado while he gathered his things. All the while, he said nothing, but he didn't wipe that amusement off his damn face.

Corrado headed out of the gym with his phone in one hand, and his discarded cross-body bag in the other. The bag wasn't his style, but neither were the jeans and faded T-shirt he'd thrown on that day to go with his runners, either.

He didn't come to The League to look like he walked out of his parents' mansion, though. He came here because he needed to work out some of his frustration, and there was only one person who might help with that in a short amount of time.

Cree.

Or rather, he *usually* helped with that. Today, he only pissed Corrado off and left him with more questions than answers.

Speaking of which …

Swiping his thumb over the screen of his phone, Corrado woke the device up, and typed his pin in. Pulling up the call icon, he selected the top contact highest on his list.

Alessio.

He hadn't bothered to call the man for the last week and a half because he assumed it would be pointless. Being on a job meant Alessio needed to leave his phone behind, and when he was back, *then* he would call Corrado, or show up at home.

This time, Alessio did neither.

He was *back*.

But where?

Despite being back in Vegas for the last week, Corrado had a flight to catch tomorrow that would take him back to Toronto for the weekend. His parents annual Halloween party, something they threw every year for all the kids who lived in their gated community, was on Sunday evening, and if he didn't show up …

He'd never hear the fucking end.

Which meant if he didn't get ahold of Alessio, and let him know where he would be, if the man wanted to see him, it was going to be several more days before they got together. Corrado didn't like that at all.

The past while had been hell on him. He didn't like being alone, and if he couldn't have both people he loved, then he needed one.

Where the fuck was Les?

In his head, the phone rang and rang. By the fourth ring, Alessio's voicemail would pick up because the man wasn't answering his calls. Or maybe it was just Corrado's number he didn't want to pick up.

But *why*?

That heaviness came back in his chest.

Hard.

Thick.

And *aching*.

Actually, it hadn't left him since he got the news Ginevra headed back to New York, but he got better at ignoring it. Now, it was back with a vengeance.

Fuck his whole life.

The call clicked, and Alessio's standard message to leave a message came through the speaker. Corrado gritted his teeth, yet still left a simple message that said, "Les, call me."

Stuffing the phone back into his pocket, Corrado navigated the halls of The League's complex until he stood in the doorway of Dare's office. He never understood why the man rarely closed his door, but he didn't.

Not unless Cree was in there.

"What can I do for you, Corrado?"

Dare, with his back facing Corrado as he watched a screen on the wall showcasing a news reel, hadn't even twitched a finger to let him know he was aware of his presence.

"Alessio arrived back from his assignment today?"

"Apparently."

"What does that mean? Either he did, or he fucking didn't."

"It means yes, he was here, and no, I didn't see him."

"Well, where is he?"

"I'm not sure, but if he's not picking up your calls, and he didn't let you—"

"Try not being an asshole for five minutes."

Dare shook his head. "*Eh*."

Corrado clenched his teeth so hard his molars ached. "Dare—"

"I made a promise to Les—I would stay out of his business for you, and other personal issues. That's what he asked, and that's what I will do. But understand, Corrado, that if he's taken off again because of something you did, I will cut your heart out and mail it to your father with blood still in the chambers. Do you hear me?"

He blinked.

Dare continued to watch the screen, unbothered.

Well …

"I'm not even sure if it's about me, or not," he muttered.

"Yes, well, that happens when you choose selfishness over selflessness."

Right.

Dare made a good point.

And Corrado *hated* it.

29.

"Thank you."

Siena's head popped above the island counter, so she could see Ginevra on the other side. Slowly, she stood, a casserole dish in her hands she planned on using to cook their dinner. "For what, Ginny?"

"Everything you did, I guess. For me, but also for the girls when I couldn't."

"But ..."

"Yeah?"

"That's what a family *should* do," Siena said quietly.

Ginevra nodded. "You're right, they should. I think because me and the girls were so used to depending on each other, and our mom, that we got used to it. We learned not to expect kindness from others because if we ever needed something, we could just go to each other for it."

Siena set the dish down to the counter and offered a smile. "You probably don't see me as your *real* sister, even if we are, but I hope you can someday, and that you'll come too. I didn't have a close family unit growing up, either. Dad preferred the boys, too."

"Well ..."

"What?"

"I wanted life to go back to normal for Greta and Giulia. Before all this happened, when the mafia hadn't touched us, and we were just ... *normal.*"

Siena let out a soft laugh. "Doesn't work that way, huh?"

Not at all.

Ginevra tried to put as much distance between their life, and the people affiliated to the mafia as she could, and yet they still kept drawing her in. And while she understood people like Siena—or the woman's boyfriend, John—were safe, she knew that didn't matter.

All it took was one connection to become a target, and she never wanted her sisters to be that for anyone ever again.

"I just want them to be safe," Ginevra whispered.

"And they will be. We made sure."

Right.

For now.

Ginevra didn't say that out loud. "And you love them, don't you?"

"The girls?"

She nodded.

Siena smiled. "I do. And I never had sisters growing up—just a pair of asshole brothers that only cared about me when I was doing something for them. I was always the one expected to look after everyone else, and I do that with the girls, too. Except now, I don't mind it. They don't *demand* that of me, they need someone who gives a shit."

"Yeah, they do."

"And now they have you home, too."

Greta and Giulia flew into the kitchen, their laughter high and breathless as they watched whatever loud video was playing on the tablet they were using. They had been the first ones to jump at the chance to have dinner at Siena's place when she called earlier to ask. The girls fell into the chairs at the table, unaware or uncaring about Siena and Ginevra's conversation. Not that she minded all that much.

She preferred them close.

She needed her family.

It had more people now.

"I had been so settled on what I wanted to happen when I came back for them that change scares me," Ginevra admitted. "And I might seem a little too protective, but after everything, how should I be? So, I apologize in advance if I come off strong."

Siena shrugged. "I get it."

"Do you?"

"Of course, but you should know it's easier to be open to change than to live with an ache in your heart because you'd rather things stay the same, Ginevra. That's all."

Ginevra had to laugh at that.

Heartache.

"I can't find more heartache and trouble than I already did in Toronto."

The words slipped from her lips before she could stop them. Maybe it was because Ginevra didn't have anyone to talk to about the craziness going on in her life—things she hadn't shared with her younger sisters because for one, she didn't think it was appropriate, and for two ... because she didn't want to worry them. Without Corrado and Alessio, she became hollow.

Instead, she handled it alone.

Lonely.

Siena cleared her throat, and her gaze drifted to the girls at the table behind them, distracted with a tablet. "Andino had hinted to John that you found someone in Toronto that you became close to."

Close.

Right, that was a good way to put falling in love.

And *someone?*

"More like two *someones,*" Ginevra replied.

She had to be mindful of those younger ears behind them. She wasn't sure how to appropriately explain the relationship she found herself in with two men when in general, all society showed as respectable couples were a pair of *two* people. Not that society was right—love came in many forms, she had learned.

It wasn't easy to explain.

"Huh," Siena said. "Really?"

"They were together before I came into it with them, but I fit there ... with them, between them, and with each of them. It wasn't easy, but it was right—somehow, it was right, and now everything seems wrong."

Siena let out a slow breath, her gaze reflecting only sympathy. She opened her mouth to say something, but one of their sisters at the table spoke up first.

"What does that mean, that they were together before you?" Giulia asked. Apparently, those young ears had been listening.

Great.

"What do you think?" Greta asked. "Guys can like other guys, Giuls."

"Yeah, but—"

"No *buts*. It's true."

Greta wasn't wrong.

"That's kind of like cheating, isn't it?" Giulia asked, not knowing Ginevra's face was heating from their conversation as they pondered her private life. "If they were with someone else—even if it was Ginny, right?"

"Poly, Giulia," Greta said, like it should have been obvious.

"What?"

"*Poly.* Polyamorous. There are lots of people in committed relationships who go outside to sleep with other people."

Ginevra sighed. "Could we not talk about this right now?"

"Well," Greta asked, "how is she ever going to know about that kind of stuff if no one takes the time to explain?"

She had forgotten that although Greta was younger than her, and she had helped to raise the girl, she was still almost eighteen. The world was not so rose-tinted to her anymore, and she had noticed boys and things like sex a while ago.

Siena giggled, but popped a hand over her mouth when Ginevra shot her a look. "Sorry," she mumbled.

"So, it's not cheat—"

"Look at it like a triple Venn diagram," Ginevra said, not wanting to keep letting them *assume* what they wanted about her relationship with the men. It would be better if they understood what it was, and that was it. "We are all individual people, but there are parts of me that overlap with one, and then another part that overlaps with the other. And there are parts of them that only overlap with each other, too, but there is a piece of all of us that overlap together. *That* is how it works, for us. Not everyone is the same, and no, it is not about sleeping with anyone you want."

Or she assumed she had made that clear to Corrado and Alessio.

Now, nothing was clear.

That's what killed her.

"Okay, so I was kind of right," Greta said.

Giulia made a noise under her breath. "Sounds complicated."

"Funny," Ginevra replied.

Siena gave her a look across the island. "What is?"

"It never seemed complicated at all. Easy, really."

More like ... it was where she was meant to be.

And now, she wasn't there at all.

Where were they?

Siena whistled. "Props to you, though, because I have a hard enough time keeping up with one man let alone *two*."

Ginevra grinned at that, her cheeks heating all over again. "They ... made it worth it."

Giggles echoed from the table behind her.

Damn.

Young ears, again.

Because even if she had been *very* careful to explain the relationship without making it seem tawdry with sexual innuendo and details, those girls were still fifteen, and seventeen. They were still teenage girls.

"What's their names?" Greta asked.

"Are they cute?" Giulia put in right after.

To Siena, Ginevra mouthed, "*Help me.*"

Siena shook her head. "Nope—on your own here."

Perfect.

"Thanks."

"Well?" Greta demanded.

"I'm not sure it matters. I kind of left them high and dry, and—"

"That doesn't tell me their names."

"Or if they're cute," Giulia added.

Ginevra turned around to eye both her sisters with a curious eye. "Corrado and Alessio."

"*And,*" Giulia said, eyes wide.

"They're both ... very handsome."

That was putting it mildly.

Giggles lit up the table again.

Ginevra figured, this would be a long night.

"Not that it matters," Ginevra said, "because I am here, and they're not."

"But is that how you want it to be?" Siena asked behind her.

That question was easy to answer.

No.

She wanted both with her. That didn't mean she would get what she wanted, though. As far as she understood, neither of the men had tried to contact her, and she didn't have a way to get ahold of them, either.

It was what it was.

Even if she hated it.

• • •

"Okay, but like how does it work, does one get mad when you don't spend enough time with them, or—"

"Could you save some of your questions for another day?" Ginevra grumbled as her sisters followed behind her in the hallway of their apartment building. "Because that would be great, Greta."

"I'm just curious."

"You have asked me a lot of questions in the last three hours."

Too many questions.

Their dinner with Siena turned into a game of twenty-one questions with Ginevra. All focused around things she didn't want to explain to her younger sisters, but also a topic that made her heart ache.

She couldn't win.

"And," Ginevra said, coming to a stop in front of their apartment door to pull the keys from her bag before sticking it in the lock, "while I get you want to understand how it works, it's also none of your business. Some things are private unless I offer the information to you, Greta. Respect that."

Greta leaned against the wall and rolled her eyes. "Fine."

"Thank you."

"Still think it's complicated," Giulia muttered next to Greta.

Well ...

"I guess that means it's probably not for you, huh?"

Greta considered that for a second before she nodded. "That's fair."

Ginevra waited just long enough to decide that the girls had finished with their questions for the evening—thank God—before she twisted the key in the lock and opened their apartment door. The first thing she noticed was the lights. They were on when she had shut them off before leaving.

The second thing she noticed? A leather jacket hanging over the arm of the couch just beyond the hallway.

The third?

His scent.

Leather, smoke, and man.

Distinct to Alessio, and Ginevra swore every nerve in her body lit up when she dragged in another lungful of the smell. There wasn't enough, and she might never taste it on her tongue again.

The girls, seemingly unaware of their sister's frozen stance, pushed past her to enter the apartment. They didn't notice the familiar cologne Alessio preferred lingering in the air, or his jacket tossed over the back of the couch.

She might have spoken up ...

Might have told them to wait ...

Her words wouldn't come.

The girls didn't even reach the end of the hallway before Alessio stepped around the corner, directly in their path. Giulia, with her head down to watch whatever she found interesting on her phone, rammed into the back of her sister when Greta came to a full stop in front of Alessio.

He tipped his head to the side, amusement lighting up his gaze when the two teenagers lifted their heads to meet his stare. His lips quirked into a wicked grin, too, almost making Ginevra laugh at the sight.

"Hello," he told them.

Giulia squeaked.

Greta said and did *nothing*.

"Do they not speak?" he asked, his gaze lifting to find Ginevra at the end of the hall. She found affection staring back.

Her heart beat again.

"They do, you shocked them, Les."

"Les—*Alessio?*" Greta asked.

Giulia made another one of those *squeaky* sounds.

"That is my name," Alessio told her sister.

"Oh, wow," Greta mumbled.

Alessio cocked his head to the side again. "Uh, what?"

Ginevra pressed her lips together and decided the wall was a far more interesting thing to stare at because it would not make her laugh out loud.

"Greta, Giulia," she said, still keeping her attention on the wall, "this is Alessio. Les, these are my little sisters."

"They don't talk well," he noted.

Ginevra let out a sigh.

Greta huffed. "How did you even get in here?"

"Picked the lock."

"*What?*"

Ginevra looked their way again only to find Alessio had arched a brow when he drawled, "I picked the lock with a tool in my pocket—I'll show you sometime."

Greta glanced back at Ginevra and pursed her lips before she nodded. "Okay."

Okay. Just like that.

Giulia giggled under her breath, likely because she wasn't sure how to handle this situation.

"Would you two give us a few minutes alone? Close your bedroom doors, too, please."

Giulia looked like she would argue, but Greta pulled her away from Alessio as they slipped past him in the hallway. Once they had left around the corner, and the sounds of a bedroom door slamming shut—they each had their own room, but must have gone into just one—Alessio's attention came back to Ginevra.

And *shit*. She felt that.

"You left," he said, "and you didn't even say goodbye. You *left* ... and you haven't even tried to call, or anything."

She swallowed hard, and he took one step closer. "Andino called—he said I could come back. My sisters needed me. I figured you and Corrado would understand ... I didn't have a way to contact either of you. I don't have your phone numbers; neither of you gave me them and I never needed them before now. Who am I supposed to ask to help me? The same people who sent me away, who didn't give a shit about what happened to me? Who?"

Alessio tipped his head back. Ginevra held firm.

"You left," he repeated.

"Where were you?"

"Albania."

All at once, the air left Ginevra's lungs.

Right. The job.

He'd told her the night at the club.

"What about Corrado?" she asked.

Alessio smiled, but *damn*, it was bitter all over. It made her heart go crazy when he took another step closer to her, leaving only a few feet between them now.

"Corrado is the ..." Alessio considered his words, adding lower, "... well, he's the difficult one here. See me, I'm used to being abandoned, Ginny. I can take it."

"I didn't abandon either of you."

"You left," he returned, "and when you leave, this is what it feels like when no one explains anything to us, and we're all just ... *stuck*. Wondering."

Alessio shrugged. "Corrado ... he's not like me. When something seems like it will hurt, he shuts all the way down. Almost everyone in my life has left me, so I can handle this, but not him. I don't like to see things hurt him, either."

"I didn't *leave* like that, Les."

"But he thinks you did. It's a pride thing for him, Ginny … because that's who Corrado has always been. Despite how much it pisses me off sometimes, it's also one part of him I love the most. You can't fault him for his flaws, just like he didn't want to fault you for yours, either."

Ginevra hid her shaking hands at her sides, balling them into tight fists when Alessio took yet another step toward her. *Careful.* Holding himself back because that's what he thought *she* wanted.

He had to know … She wanted him so fucking close.

"I missed you," she whispered, "and I miss him. All the time. Every single day. I wasn't sure what to do, and I'm sorry."

Alessio dragged in a hard breath. "Yeah, me too."

"I'm still not sure what to do."

All at once, Alessio closed the distance between them, and Ginevra had never been more grateful. She found herself wrapped up in his strong, familiar embrace. She pulled in lungful after lungful of his heady scent, letting the comfort take her back to a happier place.

Alessio's hands slipped under her jaw, and he tipped her head back. First, he kissed her soft, and tentative. So unlike him though she loved the gentle press of his lips against hers. But then, the kiss turned into something else when his tongue snaked out to tease the seam of her lips, seeking more.

God.

She gave him that. And took what she wanted, too.

Nothing was like kissing someone you loved. Everything was … perfect. Her world almost tilted back on its proper axis. Except she missed someone else, now. *They* missed someone else.

Alessio pulled away, but his thumbs stroked her cheeks, taking away the tears that had escaped from her eyes. "Don't cry, sweetheart."

"I … this has been a lot."

"We'll fix it."

"How?"

Alessio chuckled, and pressed another quick kiss to her mouth before saying, "By not giving him a choice—making a *statement*."

Ginevra gave him a raised brow. "What, like a grand gesture? Cliché, yeah?"

"Maybe, but it *is* Corrado. And as much as he figures he's hard to understand, he really isn't. Sometimes, show him where he's wrong while you also admit to your own. Those flaws of his again, and you have to love them, too. Not just *parts* of him."

"I do, and you, too."

Alessio's throat jumped when he asked, "Do you?"

"What?"

"Love me?"

Ginevra reached up and stroked the underside of his jaw. "*Too much.* I love you too much."

"How else would this work, huh?"

Exactly.

Now, she had to let Corrado know, too.

30.

Corrado

I'll see you there.

Corrado stared at Alessio's last text after he'd cut the engine to the Porsche in the driveway of his parents' mansion. He hadn't wanted to come to this goddamn Halloween party at all, but he wasn't able to come up with an acceptable excuse to get him out.

He couldn't even use *Les.*

Not considering Alessio was here, or if not, was on his way, if his last text to Corrado was any sign. He had no idea where Alessio had been for the last couple of days. He hadn't come back to Vegas, he wouldn't pick up Corrado's calls, and he only answered back one of his texts.

The one about the Halloween party in Toronto.

That was it.

Corrado wasn't sure what in the hell was going on, but he didn't like it. At all. It felt like Alessio was hiding something from him, and he needed to find out what that was. Which was what he planned on doing tonight.

He couldn't do that if he continued to sit in this damn car, so he shoved his phone into his pocket, and stepped out of the vehicle onto the driveway. He took in the fake strings of a spider web hanging from the trees lining the driveway, and the pumpkins decorating the cobblestone. He didn't know what it was, or *why*, but his mother never went half-assed for decorating.

Cara didn't understand the meaning of *subtle.*

When he was younger, Corrado used to love that, he thought as he headed for the mansion. Every single holiday had been a memorable experience with his family because his mother and father made sure of that, no exceptions.

Given the time of night, closer to nine, he suspected all the neighborhood kids had come and were long gone. The damn bylaws in the gated community made sure all the parents knew their kids had to be home by eight-thirty, sharp.

Now, given the cars in the driveway, and the music filtering out of the mansion, it was time for the adults—and older teens—to have their fun. The invitation went out to anyone who was a friend of the Guzzi family, and anyone in *la famiglia.*

Corrado tried not to miss it—or any big party his parents threw. This one hadn't been quite the same, though, because the last thing he was in the mood for was to entertain other people when he could barely stand to look at himself in the mirror.

Yet, here he was.

Doing that.

And why?

Corrado wasn't sure. Maybe because he was trying to be a little less selfish for one—God knew it had been pointed out more than enough to him over the last while that he could be a self-serving prick when he wanted to be, and this party was about his parents and family. So, he could show up for them, right? Put on a suit, because he was not wearing a costume, a smile, and be the good son for an hour or two.

Or maybe it was because this was the only place Alessio seemed to be willing to meet him, and so Corrado had to do what he had to do.

End of.

At least, tonight, he would get *one* person he wanted. The other? Well, Corrado was refusing to even let himself think about Ginevra at this point.

It was easier.

"You look *really* pleased to be here, yeah?"

Corrado's walk came to an abrupt start, and his fucking heart was ready to explode in his goddamn chest at the same time. *That voice.* All calm, cool, and unbothered. Like it didn't bother him at all he hadn't seen Corrado in two weeks, and nothing had changed at all.

He turned his head, finding Alessio standing under a canopy of fake spider web hanging from the largest maple tree on the property. He wasn't sure what it was about those specific trees, but they were Les's favorite.

"Waiting for me?" Corrado asked.

"Or I stepped out for a smoke—it doesn't have to be about *you*."

Yeah.

Right back to normal.

Corrado smirked, giving a pointed look at Alessio's hand. "Except there's no cigarette, and we both know you only smoke here with Bene or Beni."

"You can't ever just let me *have* a moment, can you?"

"Where's the fun in that, Les?"

Alessio shrugged, stuffing his hands in the pockets of his black jeans. The leather jacket he'd thrown on was new—different from the last one Corrado saw him wearing. This one had a dozen buckles, and small, silver spikes on the shoulders.

Very … *Alessio.*

And he looked good.

Too good, really.

"Why are you smiling like that?" Corrado asked.

Alessio's sly grin drifted away. "Like what?"

"Where have you been the last couple of days? I knew when you got back, and you just … fucking *took off*. You couldn't call me, or—"

"I had things to handle."

"Oh?"

"Yeah, shit to take care of that you wouldn't."

Corrado stiffened, his throat growing tight. "And what does that mean?"

"This," Alessio said, pointing between the two as he met Corrado's gaze, "it's not all about you. It's about *me*, too. And someone else because *you* brought her into it. You keep thinking you're also the only person here that gets to decide about it—like the choice to say fuck it, hide away, and pretend like nothing is wrong. The rest of us here aren't always going to just fall in line with you, Corrado. That's not how love works."

That ache was back in his heart.

"You don't get—"

"Yeah, I get you don't like shit that hurts. Don't worry."

"I needed a minute to figure out what I was doing, Les."

"Well, you got two weeks, and I'm fucking tired of waiting."

"*What?*"

Alessio grinned and gestured at the mansion. "Do you know why I didn't call you or come back home the last couple of days since I got back?"

"Because you wanted to punish me?"

"*Really*, that's what you think it was?"

"That's what it seemed like."

Alessio's smile drifted away. "I'm sorry."

"You're all I have, Les."

"No, I'm not. I am *one* of two people for you, Corrado. And I'm fucking sorry that life gets in the way, and you're not sure how to deal, but you gotta learn. Like the rest of us did, okay? You can't run when shit gets rough. You *can't*."

Corrado nodded. "Yeah."

"I didn't call or come home because I didn't want to lie to you. I *don't* lie to you, no matter what. And so, if I didn't see you or speak to you, then I wouldn't have to do that, not even by omission."

He stared at Alessio as still as stone.

Alessio stared back, *waiting*.

"What did you do?" Corrado asked.

"I brought her back for us. Ginevra is here tonight."

He hadn't been ready for that.

He also wasn't *at all* surprised.

"She *left*."

"Yes, because not everything in her life will always be about *us*, Corrado. We had a spread of time with her *away* from her life—without her responsibilities, and the things she left at home. She didn't have to worry about that during *our* time, but that time ended. And she needed to get back to reality, but that doesn't mean she didn't want to stay."

"If she wanted to stay—"

"It is possible she both wanted to leave and stay but with only those two choices … someone will always get hurt."

"I don't understand what you're talking about."

Alessio gave him a look. "Because you never *asked*."

• • •

Corrado heard Ginevra first. Her soft, tinkling laughter—unmistakable to his ear—seemed to stand out from the feminine laughter of others as it filled the hallway he walked down with Alessio at his side. It did something to his heart, still racing hard and a little too heavy in his chest, but he didn't wish it away.

A part of him had been wishing too much away.

Right then, he wanted to *feel*.

Corrado wasn't pleased with the way Alessio did this, but he stepped back and *shut up*. He didn't go to Ginevra after she left, and he hadn't given her the chance to explain anything.

So, regardless of the heaviness on his shoulders, the tightness in his chest, or the ache in his heart ... he would see her, and listen to her explain.

Because Les was right.

As he usually was.

Corrado figured if he admitted that fact a little more often, they wouldn't have as many of these issues as they did. His pride was a real bitch.

Time to let it go.

A good portion of the main entrance, the first dining room, and one of the sitting rooms inside the mansion became a haunted house for the kids that was now ... well, empty of children, anyway. A few adults lingered in the spaces, drinks in hand. Some still dressed in costumes, and others, not. Corrado had no interest in them, though.

Corrado rounded the corner at the end of the hallway, Alessio still at his side, and came to a full stop at the sight of Ginevra in the middle of what his parents used as a ballroom when they held parties. In the middle, a fountain with an embracing nude couple carved from stone with water pouring from their outstretched hands that seemed to reach for each other.

And right in front of it?

Ginevra.

Like him, and Alessio, and most of the other people in the room, she wasn't dressed up in any costume. Instead, she wore a black dress that hugged her curves with a slit down the middle that showed off all kinds of leg, and black, strappy heels that made his throat tighten again.

She smiled at something his mother said next to her, nodding back at the younger girl standing close to her. Cara leaned in closer to Ginevra, her gaze conspiratorial as she said something in a whisper, pointing to someone across the room.

Ginevra, though, looked *happy*. Perfectly content in her place, enjoying the party, and not at all bothered by the fact she was in the middle of the room, the center of attention next to his mother where they stood just a few feet away from the rest of his brothers, and father.

Like she was meant to be there.

Because she was.

Corrado had known from the start—sensed it in his heart the very second she looked him in the eyes that day she fell into his car in New York outside of the church. It'd been him and his *pride* that fucked this up.

The same way it messed with everything.

"Ginny!"

Corrado watched an older girl, although still younger than Ginevra, dart across the ballroom floor, away from a young man who was staring after her like his favorite thing had been ripped out of his hands. Ginevra turned away from his mother, laughing at whatever the older teenager rushed to tell her, while the younger girl who had been beside her the entire time rolled her eyes.

"Her sisters," Alessio explained next to him. "Greta is the older one—she'll be eighteen in two months. Giulia, the youngest, is fifteen."

Right.

Her sisters ...

Corrado felt like shit.

That was the best way to describe it. He didn't have the right words, otherwise. He said it—*entirely selfish*. So caught up in his own wants, that he never even considered the people around him, or what they needed to handle.

Like Ginevra.

And her sisters.

"I do not deserve you or her," he murmured.

But fuck him if he didn't want them, and he would make damn sure both understood for the rest of his life *they* came first to him. Always, no exceptions, *ever*. That would be Corrado's promise from this day forward, he would make sure.

Once he fixed this ...

Alessio glanced at him from the side, letting out a quiet sigh. "You're not wrong, but ... we still want you."

"Have you figured out why that is?"

"Love," Alessio said. "It's because of love."

Right, because even until this point, Corrado's own love had still been—in many ways—an extension of his own selfishness. It came back to *him*, and what would best serve his needs to wants.

No more.

Ginevra gave her sister—Greta?—a nod before turning away. Her gaze skimmed over the crowd. She bypassed him not expecting him to be standing there with Alessio, but she tensed, her stare darting back to him.

She *smiled*.

Soft, sure, but still ...

Corrado smiled back.

He didn't wait for her to make the first move to cross the distance between them. He figured she and Alessio had been doing enough of that for all of them, and he had to try now. Alessio trailed behind Corrado when he closed the space keeping Ginevra too far away from him, and not as close as he wanted her.

She took only *one* step forward. Just enough to say she finished the conversation behind her and entered a new one. Not that it mattered because her sisters and his mother watched him and Alessio come closer with curious gazes that also seemed too *knowing* for his liking.

"Ginny," he said when he came to a stop in front of her.

Not close enough, though.

A foot away.

He itched to touch her, but he didn't reach out to do it. *That* would be her choice, always.

Ginevra's gaze darted from Alessio a foot behind him and then back to Corrado in a flash. "No costume?"

"Where's yours?"

"Big wings—they wouldn't let me bring them on the plane."

Corrado smirked. "Really?"

"No."

"Damn, that might have been nice to see."

Ginevra shrugged the delicate line of her shoulders, saying, "I didn't have time to grab something for me and the girls. Alessio didn't give me much notice about this. He told me when to be at the airport, and that's it."

He swallowed hard.

And she just *came*.

She didn't question it.

"Thank you for coming," he said.

Ginevra smiled in *that* way again. "I love you, Corrado. Why wouldn't I want to be with you … wherever you are?"

He had a million reasons she *shouldn't* want to be with him. The same way he could list the whys that Alessio shouldn't be his, too. And yet, here they all were.

They didn't fit alone.

They only worked together.

"Corrado, right?"

Behind Ginevra, he found which of her two sisters asked the question. The tallest, and oldest, of the two.

"Greta, right?" he returned.

The girl flashed her teeth in a smile. "That's right." She jerked a thumb toward the girl next to her, saying, "And this is Giulia."

Corrado nodded. "Very nice to meet you."

Greta arched a brow. "You're very different from the other one."

"*Greta*," Ginevra admonished.

"What, he is. I thought he would be like Les, Ginny."

Alessio chuckled behind him. "Where is the fun in two people who are the same?"

Giulia's cheeks turned red, but Greta glanced between the two men like she wanted to take in all their differences, from the different style of clothing, to even the cut of their hair.

Corrado understood, then. Ginevra must have explained about this situation to her sisters, and they had to process all of it. That meant awkward questions, or comments at the wrong time.

He didn't mind.

"Alessio is the fun one," Corrado told Greta.

"Is he?"

Alessio scoffed. "*Yes.*"

"Girls," Cara called behind them, saving Ginevra from saying anything, "do you want to see which rooms you'll be using for the weekend?"

Just like that, Ginevra's sisters were thoroughly distracted. It let Corrado take all her attention again.

"You're staying?" he asked.

She nodded. "I left some unfinished business here. So, yes, if you'll have me."

"We both will," Alessio said.

Corrado tipped his head in Alessio's direction. "What he said, of course."

31.

Alessio

"The girls—"

"Are fine in the mansion with Cara and Gian," Alessio said quickly.

Corrado unlocked the front door to the Guzzi guest house, adding, "My mother *rarely* has girls she can spoil, so you'll be lucky to get them back tomorrow."

Ginevra let out a little laugh, but Alessio could still hear the stress there. Corrado didn't miss it, either, if the look he shot Alessio over his shoulder when he pushed the door open was any sign.

Sliding an arm around Ginevra's waist, he pulled her in close while keeping the overnight bags he held back so they didn't get in the way. Then, he pressed a quick kiss to the side of her temple, saying, "Really, they're good. And if they need you, then you're not very far away. But better for us to do all the talking we need to *away* from everyone else, right?"

She smiled up at him.

Alessio winked back.

"Right," she whispered.

He didn't fault her for wanting to keep an eye on her sisters, though. She had been forced away from them for so long, now, that she tried to make up for lost time. Already, Greta was now in her senior year of high school, and Giulia asked to go to Siena's almost as much as she wanted to stay with Ginevra.

Alessio didn't think Ginevra was jealous of the girls' affection for their half-sister, but change could be tough. And in some ways, people had a habit of holding onto the past.

It would get easier.

Eventually.

Alessio supposed him and Corrado could help with that occasionally. By being there, or with whatever else she might need to make her life easier. And the girls, too. He liked her sisters, even with their desire to make sure he understood not to touch their things on the bathroom counter, and including all their attitude first thing in the morning.

He'd forgotten what it was like to be a teenager. Then again, he had never been a *proper* teen, anyway. A moody prick, sure, but he hadn't had the same experiences as Ginevra's sisters.

Ginevra took a minute to admire the inside the Guzzi guest house, which frankly … was larger than most normal homes, but as Alessio had spent time in it before, he was more interested in watching her.

Well, her and Corrado.

"So, you're where Les has been, huh?" Corrado asked.

Ginevra turned away from the painting she had been admiring over the fireplace to give Corrado a sly grin. "For a couple of days, but then he left a day early to come here."

Corrado gave Alessio a look.

He shrugged. "I thought people here might like a heads-up on what I was planning, that's all."

"I see."

"Are you *jealous*?" Alessio asked.

Corrado arched a brow. "Over what?"

"That I was with Ginevra."

"I slept *alone*, Les."

Right.

And he so hated that.

"But that was my fault," Corrado muttered, facing Ginevra again. "I wish you hadn't left—at least, not without telling me *something*."

"I thought Marcus would explain," Ginevra replied.

Corrado laughed darkly. "He would have, likely—except I didn't answer my calls."

"And then you broke your phone," Alessio added, "before you headed off to … where was it?"

"The lodge in Quebec."

"And then Vegas," Alessio said. "Where you still didn't bother to answer anyone's messages."

"I know what I did, Alessio," Corrado murmured. "I understand how I made it worse, thank you."

"Always helps to have it pointed out, though."

"It also doesn't matter," Ginevra said, "because we're *here*."

Alessio drifted past Corrado, tipping his head toward him as he shrugged off his jacket to set it along the back of the couch in the main room. He dropped the three small overnight bags he'd carried for them all over the side. "She's right."

Ginevra laughed. "Women are *always* right. I can't help it that neither of you are used to that—having a woman between you as the voice of reason."

Corrado chuckled.

"Nice," Alessio told her.

She winked.

Alessio dropped into the corner of the couch, settling himself on watching the two of them work their shit out. After all, he had two days to do that with Ginevra, and he was good. He knew what he wanted from all of this. They were the only ones left, now.

"A drink?" Ginevra asked.

Corrado nodded as she neared the small wet bar next to the couch. "Sure, why not?"

Ginevra didn't even ask which drink he wanted. She already knew and reached for the bottle of whiskey before pouring three fingers of the tawny-colored liquor into a low-ball glass. As she passed it over to Corrado, her gaze on him like she was waiting for their talk to continue, she didn't forget about Alessio by reaching over with her other hand to let it drift through his hair, and then her fingertips ghosted over the side of his cheek.

Second nature.

He'd realized it a while ago, but this woman was perfect for them. There were parts of her that were better suited to handle Corrado, and other pieces of her soul seemed to just fit Alessio. She was the calm to the storm, and the light to the darkness.

He'd used to think the thing between him and Corrado—whatever that was, as strong as it was—needed to be the sun in their life. Something they revolved around. The thing that kept them *alive*, and together.

He was wrong.

Ginevra was the sun.

They just hadn't found her until now.

"I'm where I want to be," Ginevra said before Corrado could speak. "Here, *with you*. And with Les. I am where I want to be, and where I should be, so let me say that first. Is this where you want me to be, Corrado, regardless of the rest?"

Corrado didn't hesitate. "Yes."

Alessio tossed an arm over the back of the chair. "That settles that, doesn't it?"

"But not *all*," Corrado returned. "What happened at the club scared you, and you ran off, Ginny. Which would have been fine, except it seemed like you kept running."

"I don't like what you sometimes do," she said simply. "That scares me for a lot of reasons, and it makes me question who I thought I was when I have to face the fact I love people who also do bad things, but I am where I want to be. And that's what matters."

"Is it?"

She stared hard at Corrado. "*Yes.*"

"Even if it happens again?"

"Even then," she whispered.

She was still touching Alessio, her fingers skimming over his jawline as she took a minute to consider whatever it was running through her mind. He knew it was something in her mind keeping her quiet because that knot formed between her brow which said she was thinking too hard.

She always did that.

Ginevra focused on details.

Alessio dwelled.

And Corrado ... well, he *shut down*.

They were three imperfect people who had somehow found a way to fit together. Life would be far more boring without them there to share it with him, though, flaws and all. Of that, Alessio was most sure.

"I always take care of everyone else," Ginevra said, her hand leaving Alessio so she could fix the bottle on the wet bar. "I was the friend my mother didn't have because she had been so isolated and dependent on a man who only used her for years; a caretaker for my sisters, and even when our mother was still alive, I filled in where she couldn't. And I was willing to marry a man I didn't know and didn't want to protect the people I cared about. In every other aspect of my life, I still take care of other people because it's what I do. It's who I am. I want to say sorry for making you think I was leaving you behind, but I can't because someone else needed me more for a bit."

Corrado cleared his throat. "You shouldn't have to apologize for being selfless, Ginny."

"Except you didn't see me that way, did you?"

"What do you mean?"

Ginevra frowned. "*Selfless.* You didn't see me the way I am because I don't have to be that with either of you—I never have to sacrifice for you or Les. You don't ask for more than I give, and you take care of me far more often than I take care of you."

"Debatable," Alessio spoke up, "but I think the way you *take care* of us, as you say, is so ingrained in who you are, and how you fit us, that you don't feel like you have to do it. It just is, but we notice it."

Corrado nodded. "We do, and when it was gone, well … it went badly, didn't it?"

Alessio glanced Corrado's way.

A crooked smile answered him back.

Where was the lie?

"So, how do we fix that?" Corrado asked. "This, I mean, how do we make sure it doesn't happen again? Because this is where you want to be, with us, and you are where we want you to be … so we need to make sure this is where you stay, Ginny. I love you, and I need you to *stay.*"

"A rule," Ginevra said.

Alessio made a noise under his breath.

She looked to Corrado for an explanation, and he grinned when he murmured, "Those are what got us into trouble."

Exactly.

Alessio stayed quiet.

"All right," Ginevra said, "an *understanding,* then. Better?"

Alessio tipped his chin down to agree.

"We don't shut out people we love, and we don't shut off from them, either," Ginevra said. "*Ever.*"

"Just like that?" Corrado asked. "That's all you want from us?"

She met Corrado's gaze, unafraid and *so sure.*

Alessio smiled—life was right again.

Or it was getting there.

"And we stay together," Ginevra said quieter. "*No matter what.* Because I'm not me without the two of you, and I might be selfless to everyone else, but I am selfish enough with my happiness that I want to keep both of you."

"Do you?"

"How could I not when I love you?"

Yes, Alessio thought, *life was most definitely right again.*

Corrado stilled at Ginevra's statement, his gaze skipping to Alessio for a split second. Alessio hadn't missed it, and he was quick to ask, "What?"

"I just …"

"Corrado," Alessio murmured.

"Weren't you the one who said we put too much weight into those words?"

"*I* did."

"And yet," Corrado hedged.

"The impact is still unlike anything," Alessio said. "And doesn't it sound so fucking good coming out of her, though?"

"It does."

Ginevra passed a soft smile back to Alessio. "You are something."

He winked. "And you love it."

"Lucky for you."

"It is," Corrado said, "lucky for him, I mean ... for both of us."

Ginevra's laughter colored up the space, but just as quickly, it was drowned out by Corrado closing the distance between them to kiss her. A few steps had separated them, then she moved around the edge of the couch to stand in front of Alessio, when Corrado caught her. Alessio had the privilege of being able to see it when the two let down the rest of those walls.

He understood Corrado's need—that undeniable urge to just *kiss* Ginevra and have her close—because he sensed it, too. He'd felt it when he first saw her in her New York apartment, and it had taken *everything* in him to wait long enough for her sisters to be gone before he closed the distance one fucking step at a time to get what he wanted.

Hell, Corrado had lasted longer.

Props to him.

There was something stirring to Alessio to watch the two—it didn't matter if they were cooking side by side, kissing like they were now, or waking up to see them fucking next to him in the bed. It all brought on the same hurricane of emotions. It still thundered deep in his chest, something that went beyond his heartbeat.

Love.

Lust.

Need.

Want.

Amazement.

Terror.

Appreciative.

Selfishness.

Because that was all his—both people. And that thing between them they shared. It was his, too. Individually, with each of them on a one-to-one basis, and them together as a unit with him.

People who are lucky get one great love in their life. Many more never even get the chance to meet theirs.

Alessio?

He was given two.

Two.

The hand Corrado had tucked clasped onto Ginevra's side drifted away from her to reach for Alessio. He didn't question the want for touch, simply answered it by reaching back, his fingers threading with Corrado's before he leaned forward enough to press his forehead against the side of their clasped hands.

For a single second before this moment turned into something else—he figured it would; they needed the physical side, too, with each other—he soaked that in, refusing to let anything seep into his mind so he wouldn't forget it.

That feeling.

Would it ever be the same again?

He wasn't sure.

It didn't matter.

He'd never forget it now.

But he also wasn't wrong on what he believed, either. All it took was a soft, "I need you—both of you." That whisper from Ginevra was so quiet, and yet, there was an unmistakable heat in her tone. A *want*.

And he swore it was second nature for he and Corrado ... an uncontrollable urge they both had to *give* this woman what she wanted, when she wanted it. It didn't matter what it was, pancakes at nine in the evening, or fucking at two in the morning, they would give it to her because she asked.

A lot like each other, too.

Ginevra fell back into Alessio's lap, her loose hair spilling over his shoulder as his arms locked around her waist. He took that chance to dip his hands lower while Corrado pulled his suit jacket off and worked on the buttons of his shirt. Alessio wasn't the least bit surprised to find Ginevra hot and wet under the lace panties hidden between the skirt of her dress. He bunched the skirt around her hips. His hand under her panties moved fast, stroking through the seam of her sex to take the wetness he found there up to her clit.

All she needed to get off were the pads of his fingertips against her clit in fast back-and-forth strokes at a steady pressure, and he would make her come like *nothing at all*. He did exactly that, wanting her worked up. No flavor was better than Ginevra's pussy right after she came, no doubt about that.

There was something sweeter tasting to her skin, he would *swear* on it.

"Yeah, *fuck*," Corrado said when he buried his face into Ginevra's neck to breathe her in as she squirmed against his hold, "make her come, Les. Let me see it."

"Oh, my *God*," Ginevra choked out, the sound raw enough to make his cock impossibly harder beneath his jeans. And with her tight little ass grinding against his groin to get more friction of his hand against her clit, he damn near blew his load like a fucking teenager. "Please, don't stop. *Please, Les.*"

He laughed against the heat of her skin, and her pulse thrummed under the spot where his lips grazed her throat. "Not this time, sweetheart."

Alessio realized Corrado had kneeled down between the two of them when the warm roughness of the man's tongue lapped at his fingers running across Ginevra's clit. The heady moan that Corrado let loose was enough to have Alessio clenching all over—but in the *best* way.

"Do you hear that, Ginny?" Alessio asked her, his mouth drifting up the side of her trembling jaw before coming to a stop at her ear. He found the flavor of salt on her skin already, but also that strange sweetness, too—it would be a good fucking night all around. "That sound means he likes the taste of you on me, woman. Do you want him to eat your pussy while I make you come?"

A whine echoed from Ginevra. A clear *yes* following right behind it. Corrado did what she wanted, and Alessio intensified the pressure and pace on her clit for her. Everybody had that button to push, and this was Ginevra's. As soon as he hit it, and Corrado was feasting on her pussy she shouted loud as she came.

Trembling all over.

Hot to the damn touch.

Sobbing their names.

Fuck.

It was sacrilegious.

It had to be.

If sin was a physical thing like people believed it to be, it had to be the sound Ginevra made when she was coming like that with both of them touching her. And if heaven truly existed, it was also this.

Alessio grabbed a fistful of Ginevra's hair to turn her head enough to kiss her. His tongue clashed with hers, their kiss a familiar war he found had his heart pounding even as his fingers slowed between her thighs. He wasn't sure when Corrado stood up, but the rustle of a bag had Alessio pulling away from the kiss to find what was happening. He didn't wonder for long, though.

Corrado was back, leaning over Ginevra to take a kiss, too, his hands locked onto her thighs. Next to Alessio on the couch, he found what Corrado had been digging for. One of their small, black travel bags where they kept anything they might need to stay overnight. And as a *just in case*, condoms and packets of lubrication.

"Turn around," Corrado demanded.

Ginevra hurried to obey, letting Alessio drag those ruined panties off her legs before she twisted around on his lap to straddle him. He dragged the straps of her dress down her shoulders, thankful she'd picked the tight bodycon one he'd liked in her closet because the material had give.

Once he had that dress pulled down enough to get his hands on the lace bra that was covering her chest, she arched into his touch. Her lips fell open, and her tongue snaked along the outer edge as Corrado lifted her higher so that her ass was thrust out for him.

Alessio, though, focused his attention on getting his palms under Ginevra's bra. Skimming his fingertips over the tops of her nipples, he hardened them into peaks. He took one in his mouth, his teeth teasing her nipple as Corrado worked behind her. The rustle of the bag echoed again, and the sound of foil ripped open.

He knew when Corrado slipped his cock into Ginevra's pussy because her body jerked against his, and another soft whimper fell from her lips. Alessio stared upward, Ginevra's nipple still tight between his teeth to see Corrado biting the top of her shoulder as the echo of skin slapping skin sounded in the room. He got his hand between her thighs long enough to graze the hard length of Corrado sliding into Ginevra's wet heat before he moved higher to work her clit between his fingertips with a massaging motion.

Different from before, but more intense.

His other hand came up to grab her jaw as he let go of her nipple, tipping his head higher to watch her face when she came a second time.

"Almost?" he asked her.

Ginevra swallowed hard. "*Almost.*"

"You want more?"

She nodded once.

Good.

Because what she wanted, they gave.

Corrado tipped his head to the side, making Alessio aware he thought the same thing and was ready for it whenever he wanted to move. Alessio pushed his hands against Ginevra's thighs, and Corrado slowed behind her, removing himself from her body, and helping her to stand against the couch. It was long enough for Alessio to move over, and Corrado put Ginevra back on her knees on the couch, already slipping his cock back into her to fuck her from behind while Alessio stripped of his clothes.

He took all of thirty seconds to get rid of the shit in his way and find a condom in that bag to put on. Bottle of lube in hand, he handed it to Corrado as they let him resume his previous position, except this time, Ginevra's hot pussy came down on Alessio's cock.

The groan that came from him sounded foreign to his own ears, but he'd forgotten how much he loved this woman's cunt. He let Ginevra ride him at the pace she wanted for, his hands skimming around to her ass to spread her wide. It gave Corrado easy access to work her from behind.

First, with his fingers. Stretching her wide and wanting to fill more and more with each twist of his digits inside her ass. The lube would ease the tension curling her shoulders as her breaths came out a little faster with each finger Corrado added. Her rhythm on him never changed, though, because *damn*, she wanted that.

It vibrated through her.

In every single inch of her.

"Tell me," Corrado said where he kneeled behind Ginevra. "Tell me what you want, kitten."

"*Just ...*"

Air rushed from Ginevra.

Alessio leaned in and kissed her hot mouth. "Say it for him. He wants you to use words, kitten."

And so did he.

"Fuck my ass," she whispered. "I need ... I need ... *Please.*"

Corrado's next moan came out *thankful* and husky at the same time. He stood, his hand finding Ginevra's shoulder as he fit in behind her. Alessio's fingers squeezed on Ginevra's ass, slowing her to a stop. He could tell by the tightening of Ginevra's muscles and the low cry that fell from her trembling lips when Corrado pressed his cock into her ass.

Alessio distracted her with kisses, swallowing all those sounds she let loose, and soothing the tension in her body. But that noise she made when Corrado fit tightly against her, cock buried deep, and she sat all the way down on Alessio again ...

Primal, he thought.

So fucking raw, really.

Her pussy flexed all around him, taking his breath away when she mumbled, "Please move ... *fuck me.*"

Corrado's hand found one of Alessio's on Ginevra's ass. Their fingers wove again, tight together as they both found a steady, fast rhythm that allowed one to flex into Ginevra as the other pulled off her. He used the hand he still had on her ass to lift her on his cock, and to yank her down harder with each thrust.

But her like this?

Perfect.

Undoubtedly.

Free with her back arched, and ass curved out. Head thrown back, and waves of dark hair falling over her shoulders. Those tits of hers pert and pink nipples hard from his handling. She'd have their marks by the morning, both seen and invisible. She'd ache from them, even sitting down, they would linger on her ... and that drove him fucking crazy.

He loved it.

Ginevra's hand on his shoulder grabbed harder, those nails of hers scoring lines across his skin as she came with a broken cry. He didn't catch that one with a kiss like he had the others, but he didn't mind.

He'd needed that.

It made him come, too.

Corrado followed close behind.

Alessio saw stars, his breath gone as one by one, each of them stilled. He wasn't sure which one trembled, but it echoed in his *bones*. Ginevra fell forward, her forehead pressing against his chest as Corrado leaned over her to press a line of kisses up her spine. Gaze lifted, Alessio met Corrado's stare as their still-woven fingers squeezed together again.

"Chamomile, right?" Alessio asked.

Ginevra hummed a sweet sound. "What?"

"That's the tea you like before bed. They have some in the mansion, I'll go get you some and bring it back, hmm?"

"It is, but—"

"And a warm bath," Corrado added.

Ginevra sighed. "Is it spoiling me time now?"

Alessio chuckled.

Corrado smirked at him.

"For the rest of your life," Alessio said, "if that's what you want."

Ginevra made that happy, pleased hum again. "It is."

"Then, that's what you get," Corrado murmured.

EPILOGUE

Almost two months later …

Ginevra

"Greta?"

"What?"

Ginevra peeked over at her sister in the passenger seat of the SUV. Behind the wheel, she couldn't take her eyes off the road for too long, but all she needed was that quick look to know Greta was more interested in whatever she was looking at on her social media stream than whatever her older sister had to say.

"Could you come back to the real world for a second?"

Greta sighed, but set the phone down. "Better?"

"Slightly. Last day of classes before Christmas break, so try to make the best of it, and not get too bored. Also, did you finish that essay last night that you needed to hand in?"

"Yes."

"Last night at one in the morning," Giulia grumbled in the back seat.

"At least I did it."

"I could hear you clicking keys through the wall."

Ginevra focused her attention on the horrible traffic in front and wondered why she didn't just send the girls to their school in a fucking cab. She didn't remember bickering with her sisters as much as the other two did. Oh, she loved them to death, to be sure. Sometimes, they still got on her last nerve.

Especially when she was running late for her extra college class, had gotten halfway through her coffee that morning, and hadn't seen *either* of her men in two weeks. Ginevra needed a hell of a lot of things and listening to her sisters fight was not one.

"Can we hold off on the arguing until I drop you off?" she asked, not hiding the sarcasm in the slightest.

Greta rolled her eyes. Giulia stuck out her tongue when Ginevra checked the other girl in the rearview mirror. Nothing unusual for either of them, really.

Truth was, they were good girls. Normal teenagers, all things considered. They had their moments, and sometimes a bad attitude that made Ginevra squint. At the same time, they didn't get in trouble, took care of their business, and over the last couple of months, somehow realized on their own time that Ginevra had her own life she was trying to start and take care of them.

They were sensitive to that, never trying to take time away from Ginevra with Corrado and Alessio when they were around, even though they didn't have to worry about doing that at all. The guys *never* tried to take time from her sisters.

Thankfully, the girls quieted for the rest of the drive. Which was another forty-five fucking minutes for three goddamn blocks—New York traffic was terrible, and it reminded Ginevra daily that allowing Corrado to buy this stupid SUV was pointless. Oh, she loved it, to be sure. People got out of the way when something bigger was coming through, but that meant nothing when traffic was almost at a gridlock.

Every single day.

Ginevra was just pulling into the drop-off line when she noticed a familiar black Porsche parked along the side of the street. Cutting back out onto the street, she turned a hard left, and swung in beside Alessio's car. Standing beside it looking like absolute sin and *love* in his usual black jeans, and leather jacket overtop a plain tee, he winked at her when she cut the engine.

When had he gotten back?

Where was Corrado?

"Siena is picking you two up today, I'll drop off your overnight bags for the weekend later," she told the girls as they all unbuckled. "Don't forget, okay?"

"Got it," Greta said, pushing out of the front of the vehicle.

"Yep," Giulia echoed.

Their similar greetings to Alessio sounded as Ginevra got out of her side of the SUV, and rounded the front, tightening her tweed jacket to keep out the late December cold from seeping into her bones. The beanie on her head with the pompom on top helped too, at least, keep her ears warm, but she'd forgotten mittens in her rush to leave. Her fingers felt like icicles, so she hid them by tucking her hands inside the pockets of her jacket.

Greta and Giulia, despite being almost late for school, seemed to forget all about classes at the sight of Alessio. They chatted away as Ginevra stood a few feet back, giving him the inquisition about where he had been, and what new thing they had planned to do with him this time.

Because … that's what they did.

Ginevra didn't understand how it happened, but she loved it. She couldn't be more grateful that Corrado and Alessio spent time with her sisters when they were with her. Alessio took them out—movies, a day out, whatever they wanted. Corrado was the one who always brought something back for them, be it a small item from wherever he had been, or a story to tell.

They loved it.

Ginevra realized, after a month, that the boys were kind of like big brothers the girls never had because they were certainly nothing like their dead half-brothers. But less annoying, and a hell of a lot more fun.

"The new Marvel one, then?" Alessio asked.

"Can Siena come?" Greta asked.

Alessio chuckled. "Of course."

"Deal."

"And Corrado will come for it, too," Alessio added.

"Is he back, too?" Ginevra asked, the first time she had spoken at all, actually. Alessio's gaze turned on her, and she swore that her heart stopped for a split second when he grinned, and all of his attention was only on her. "Hey."

"Hey," he murmured, "and if he isn't already, he will be. A surprise for us, I guess. All I was told is that I'm supposed to take you to a certain address he texted me this morning at a specific time."

"A surprise for what?"

That wasn't like Corrado at all. He planned *everything*. And everybody needed to be made aware of those plans. That way, everything would go off without a hitch. Alessio was the spontaneous one, doing things just because he wanted to, and he figured it would be fun.

Alessio shrugged. "I can only say what I was told, babe. And don't these two have classes?"

Greta opened her mouth to reply with something smartass, likely, but the ringing bell across the street at the high school stopped her from saying anything at all. He gave the two a look, they sighed, and said a quick goodbye before darting across the street.

That's all it took.

Just the girls to be gone.

Alessio closed the distance between him and Ginevra in a flash. She forgot all about the cold December wind, and her frozen fingertips when he locked her in his embrace and dotted her mouth with kisses.

Ginevra hummed against his mouth. "Missed you."

"Shit, me, too. Congo was good, though ... quick."

That's about all he or Corrado ever gave about a job for The League, and she tried not to ask for more details. It was simpler that way, and she worried less. Not that she didn't worry at all because she still did.

Still, the Congo assignment he had just come back from would be his last for a few months. He chose to take time off, a spread of months to spend with Corrado, and *her*. Corrado had already started his time off, but he'd needed to head back to Vegas for a couple of weeks to do things there.

Her tiny apartment would be *full*.

This thing of theirs wasn't easy.

No doubt about it.

They did their best, though.

And she couldn't ask for more.

"So, when is this surprise?" she asked.

Alessio smirked sinfully, using the tip of his finger to slide along her bottom lip as he murmured, "After your classes at the college today."

"Damn, I hoped for an excuse to get out of them."

"I can think of a few," he replied, "but then Corrado will bitch because *you chose education, and you should have it.*"

"He's not wrong, though."

"But we don't tell him that, Ginny. It makes his ego grow."

Where was the lie?

• • •

Corrado

"I can take the job," Corrado said to his brother on the phone. His voice echoed throughout the empty hall he walked down.

Although, it was partly a lie. He *could* take the job that Andino Marcello called through to The League, but for one, he didn't give a fuck about that man. And for two, it meant the break he took to focus on Ginevra and Alessio and their *life* would have to be put on hold.

Corrado wouldn't do that.

Les and Ginny didn't come second.

Not now.

They came first.

No exceptions.

"But I knew you wouldn't," Chris said, "and Dare called me with the offer because extractions are my specialty."

Corrado cleared his throat, coming to the end of the entrance hallway where he would wait closer to the front door for his lovers to arrive. It was just about the time when they needed to arrive, and Alessio had a habit of being on time, if not early.

"How long has it been since you took an independent job from The League?"

"Four years," Chris said.

"A while, then. Do you think—"

"They have the auctions coming up, from what Dad explained. And Cree's team is heading to Syria for a job I wasn't allowed to get the details for."

"Government involved," Corrado replied.

The League had their hand in everything.

"Anyway, they would have pulled someone from somewhere else to do the extraction job for Andino down in Mexico, but I happened to be there with Dad when Dare called, and when your name got brought up, I offered."

Corrado smiled.

His twin, still looking out for him.

"Thanks, man."

Chris made a dismissive noise under his breath. "Yeah, well … gives you some time to figure things out over there in New York, huh?"

Right.

The shadowy figures approaching the frosted glass of the front door drew Corrado's attention there instead of his phone call. As the door opened, and he said goodbye to his brother to give his time to the people who needed it, the only thing to drift through his mind was, *I don't need time to figure this out, I know what I want.*

Alessio and Ginevra.

Until the day he died.

• • •

Alessio

"Why is this stoop twice the size of a normal brownstone?" Ginevra asked.

Alessio opened the door without knocking—as per Corrado's earlier instructions. Although, he hadn't known until they pulled up to the place that it would be a brownstone, so he still wasn't sure why they were here. "I'm not sure, you'll need to ask Corrado that."

"Ask me what?"

Corrado stood just beyond the doorway, leaning against the wall like he had watched the two of them walk up the stoop together. He probably had. Smiling at the two, he winked.

"The stoop," Ginevra said, leaving Alessio's side to greet Corrado with a quick kiss, and a soft pat to his cheek with the tips of her fingers. "It's double the size."

"Because this brownstone is also double the size."

Ginevra looked around the empty hallway, the hardwood floors gleaming under their feet. Then, she peeked back at Alessio with an arched brow. "And *very* ... lonely without furniture, or anything on the walls."

Corrado chuckled. "Well, that's because you'll have to decorate it, or hire someone to do that for you."

Ginevra stilled.

Alessio looked to Corrado. "What?"

"It's double the size because double the people need space here what with the girls, and all of us. It's empty because I closed on it yesterday, and the only thing we can keep is the big oak desk in the office upstairs because the movers weren't able to take it apart to get it out of the door without compromising the structural integrity."

"You bought this?" Ginevra asked.

Corrado lifted a shoulder. "Well, I had to use private accounts separate from Les's, so he wouldn't have a clue what I did either—it's not often I get to surprise him, too."

He wasn't wrong.

Ginevra's apartment happened to be a good size for a New York place, but it still wasn't *that* big. And when you had two teenage girls, two grown men, and Ginevra trying to share the same spaces, it became ... crowded.

"Three bathrooms," Corrado murmured, "five bedrooms, a little backyard, and an underground garage that can fit three vehicles."

"How much?" Ginevra asked.

"A lot," he returned, "but worth every single penny."

"Corrado."

Having money that was disposable still seemed like a foreign concept to Ginevra. She couldn't throw away money like them, but she was getting better at accepting *they* would spend money.

A lot.

"You need a bigger space," Corrado said, "you can't keep studying in bed, or trying to find space at a tiny table when the girls have their books all over it. I don't like you're in an apartment building with hundreds of other people. And Les and I ... we're moving everything around to be here with you until we figure out something different, Ginevra. Because this is where we want to be—starting a *life*. That starts with somewhere to live."

She made a soft noise under her breath.

Alessio smiled. "This is a good surprise."

Corrado laughed. "You think?"

"Not what I expected."

"But it's perfect," Ginevra whispered, letting Alessio pull her in close to press a kiss to the middle of her forehead.

"A big enough grand gesture for both of you, then?"

Right.

Corrado had always been the one willing to take a step back from telling them what he wanted for the sake of his pride. Heaven forbid they understand he needed them as much as they needed him.

Not now, though.

He made it perfectly clear.

Ginevra left Alessio's embrace to lean in and press another quick kiss to Corrado's grinning lips. Alessio stepped forward, too, finding Corrado's hand with his own to squeeze tight before he wrapped his other arm around Ginevra's back.

They were better together.

"Yeah, more than big enough," Alessio told him.

Ginevra smiled at both. "I want a tour."

She said the magic word.

Want.

They were always quick to give.

CHRIS

THE GUZZI LEGACY, 3

1.

Beautiful distractions hid the worst of crimes.

The table, draped in silk, and filled with food cooked by a renown chef, welcomed their guests, in a dining room with walls covered in expensive art. It proved to Valeria that the other people sitting down at the table for dinner would forget the young lady—who was barely a woman—across from them had been in the papers just a few months ago.

They wouldn't remember her face had been on the news after her mother's murder—the wife of a prominent Mexican politician. They didn't seem to remember how just months later she walked down the aisle, not yet sixteen at that point, forced to marry the son of the man who had invited them to this dinner.

None of it mattered to them.

Money *talked.*

And it apparently said very nice things.

Like the silk linen, the coveted art, delicious food, and beautiful people dressed in their best with glittering diamonds showcased on their bodies to prove their status and wealth. All of it became a promise to them. Should these people keep quiet about the other issues at the table, like Valeria, then the Lòpezs would make a deal.

They liked that.

Deals.

Better known as bribes, or blackmail. It depended on her husband, and his father's, preference or their need. When it had been her father on the other side of this table, they had wanted a promise he would help them smuggle their illegal drugs into the United States where he had connections to border control.

Her father said no.

They killed his wife.

Her father then agreed.

And so, they took her, too, and forced her to marry the oldest son of the Lòpez cartel's leader. A way to drive the point home, she figured. Because that's all she had been.

And now, she was a trophy.

A beautiful *thing.*

Something to own.

"*Sonreírse,*" Jorge said to her left, his Spanish order for her to smile coming out dark, and harsh, even under his breath. He watched her constantly, and when she didn't behave as he wanted her to, he made her aware. His fingers curved around her thigh under the table, flexing enough to make her draw in a quick breath. "*Now,* Valeria."

Her gaze swept the people at the table, a *business* meeting, they told her. Right, more like a way to manipulate and gain what the Lòpez family needed to do their work without trouble. Tonight, it was cops in high positions of power. Officers that controlled the subordinates under them, which corrupted the system further, but allowed the cartel to breathe a little easier.

This was how it worked.

She smiled when the wife of one officer turned her attention away from Valeria's sister-in-law, Abril, to the ones at the other side of the table. The whole damn family sat there—from her father-in-law, Martín, to Jorge's younger brother, Samuel. They pulled out all the stops to draw these people into their traps without using violent means first—the cartel's usual way.

When someone denied them things turned bad. Valeria's family was a good example of that.

"Martín," the woman said to Valeria's father-in-law, smiling a little too widely, "you must be pleased, *sí?*"

What was her name again?

Missy?

More American than Mexican. A dual citizen of both countries, if she trusted what her husband told her about their guests earlier, which kept the conversation drifting back and forth between English and Spanish for most of the dinner.

Not that Valeria cared to engage.

"Pleased about what?" Martín asked, tipping his wine glass up for a drink.

Out of all the people at this table, Valeria hated Martín the most. A difficult task for him to accomplish, considering she married his son, a man who beat her to keep her in line. He had *suggested* the marriage after killing her mother, like they should have expected it.

Still, she blamed him.

For all of this.

Across the table, Missy nodded at Valeria with a subtle tilt of her chin. Her grin reached to her eyes, as though she held a secret, but for now, she was only hinting at it.

Martín seemed to understand.

"Ah, *el bebé*," Martín said, chuckling. Setting his glass to the table harder than necessary, proving just how much he had imbibed over the course of the dinner, he smiled and nodded. "Very pleased. We hoped it would be a *niño* for us. A *boy*. And yet, it seems it will be a girl, but that's okay, too."

Valeria had done her best throughout the dinner to not draw attention to herself. For the last several months, they had not allowed her out of the Lòpez's compound after her marriage. This was one of the first dinners she attended, and her greatest fears would be that someone would ask about her father, apologize for her mother's death, or even, like now, want to discuss her current life.

Valeria's hand lifted from the table to rest upon the swell of her stomach. Under her palm, she felt the baby girl shift from her mother's touch, but like the good baby she already seemed to be, the child settled, allowing Valeria little discomfort from the movement.

"Congratulations," the woman said to Valeria. "Babies are gifts."

"Blessings," the man next to her added.

Right.

Her husband created this baby through violent means and pain, but she wouldn't say so. Was raping her a *blessing?* And besides, she loved her daughter. She loved her enough that she sat at this table, kept her smile on, and shut her fucking mouth so that Jorge wouldn't beat her later in the evening when everyone left. Then, the baby wouldn't get hurt, too.

"Thank you," Valeria whispered.

Her first words at the dinner.

No one seemed to notice.

Next to her, Jorge gave Valeria a tight smile. Another warning, she figured, but without him speaking it out loud. She didn't need him to do that at all—she was aware what he expected of her, and what the punishment would be if she failed.

It used to scare her.

He terrified her.

Now, she just ... *worried.*

For this child she carried, mostly. Because what would happen to her once she made her presence known in the world. Valeria, all of sixteen years old, but she would be seventeen before this baby was born. Not that it mattered because what control did a girl of her age have against a man like her husband. Six years her senior, a criminal who had only taken her because of the status it would provide him, and far too power hungry for his own good.

What could she do?

How might she protect this baby from him?

From the rest of them?

"Val, would you like another drink of water?"

At the soft question from a familiar, kind voice, Valeria came out of her thoughts to see her sister-in-law standing from the seat on the other side of hers. Abril gave Valeria a small smile, but in her eyes she found the truth.

Concern warred in Abril's gaze.

Older than her by a few months, Abril was the only person in the Lòpez family that Valeria had made friends with, and sometimes, she even questioned it because she no longer trusted anyone. Abril had done nothing to prove she deserved that hesitation though. She helped.

And she had promised to help more.

"Water?" Abril asked again.

Valeria nodded. "Yes, thank you, that would be nice."

Abril passed Valeria's chair, her hand coming to rest on her shoulder as she bent down to whisper, "The plan happens tonight—I received the message."

As quickly as Abril had told her the words, ones that might promise her freedom, she was leaving the dining room and the rest behind. Valeria looked to the man at her side, finding her husband distracted, and grinning at the young wife of an official across the table from him.

That grin meant he wanted to fuck the woman.

Valeria didn't care.

The promise of freedom would make a person smile, no matter how dangerous, crazy, and even if there was no guarantee her plan to run away would work.

Still, she had to try.

For this child, she *had to.*

"Valeria."

She hoped the guilt didn't show on her face when she met Jorge's gaze. He never missed her distractions. Now didn't seem like a good time to play with fire.

The blank expression he wore said she was the last thing on his mind.

Good.

"Yes?"

"I'm sure you won't mind going home to the compound alone tonight, will you?" he asked.

He posed it like a question.

It wasn't.

"Of course, not," she said.

"I'll be home for breakfast. Take care of my baby. You got me?"

Better than he understood.

• • •

Valeria did her best to soothe the nerves running wild as she brushed down the colt, *Butter*, in the stables. Butter, only two months old, had given Valeria a reason to visit the stables on the compound more often over the last couple of months.

The compound itself, set on a good twenty acres of secluded, desolate land protected by armed guards, allowed the Lòpez family privacy. To the east, one would find cliffs leading out to choppy, dangerous ocean water. The guards and an electric fence secured the only road leading out of the compound. Two larger barns, used like warehouses and full of drugs to smuggle, sat further west of the compound, while their homes and stables made up a small village right in the center.

There was no way out.

Or so they thought …

One simply needed enough time, and the means to make it happen. Not that they ever gave her the opportunity to run before. She could rarely do anything without a guard or her husband nearby to watch her do … whatever.

The stables, however, were her free time. Or, that's how Jorge liked to put it. He didn't have much interest in the horses, it was more of a pet project for his siblings, and some guards that stayed on the property.

Valeria took a liking to the horses *because* her husband didn't care. He wouldn't follow her into the stables to look after the horses, and he didn't mind her taking one out for a ride—like she did after arriving back to the compound that night—as long as someone was with her to keep an eye on her.

But when she looked after the horses in the stables?

No one cared.

No one watched her, then.

The sound of boots crunching against dried grass, and the hay that fell around the outside of the stables during the last delivery, made Valeria slow the strokes of her brush against the colt's hind end. She peered up over the back of the colt in just enough time to see Abril slip into the stables.

Dressed in riding boots, a helmet in hand, jeans molded to her legs, and a shawl that would keep her warm on a ride, Abril looked ready to take a horse out.

"Ready?" she asked.

Valeria swallowed hard. "Did they see you?"

"One or two."

God.

That just made Valeria nervous. Her heart threatened to jump into her throat. Was this possible? Would this even *work*?

She didn't know.

But she had to try.

"Stop worrying," Abril whispered, coming closer to the colt, and Valeria. "We have it all worked out, right? You went out on a horse and came back with a guard. They saw you do it. And like usual, you're in here taking care of the horses—nothing strange."

Right, right.

"But—"

"But nothing. They'll see *me* go out on a horse," Abril said, shrugging, "and they won't think anything strange when they see you go into the house."

Valeria nodded.

Except it wouldn't be Abril taking a horse out, and it wouldn't be Valeria heading back to the house. The girls were close enough in age, and in some ways, appearance given their olive-toned skin was the same, their stark, straight black hair both reached mid-back, and as long as someone was looking at them from behind while they sat on a horse, no one would tell the difference.

Abril had an inch of height on Valeria. Her eyes were a shade deeper brown than Valeria's russet gaze. Her sister-in-law took after her family in appearance. Sharp, angular jaws, elongated features. Whereas Valeria had a softer, rounder face, and lower cheekbones that always showed the apples of her cheeks when she smiled.

Looking at them face to face, it was clear the two looked nothing alike. But from behind, and on a horse, at a distance?

No one would be able to tell.

"Someone has to see *you* come back, though," Valeria pointed out. "Or they'll believe you helped me get away."

Abril shrugged as she dropped the riding helmet to the floor of the stables and kicked off her riding boots. "And they will."

"How?"

"You know Juan?"

"Samuel's guard?"

Her brother-in-law had a friend—*friend* being a loose term because Valeria wasn't sure any of the people in this family had someone they cared about, except for Abril. Point was, Samuel preferred one guard amongst the many that looked after them at the compound.

"What about him?" Valeria asked.

Abril smirked up at Valeria. "He'll do me a favor, okay? Tit for tat, I gave him something he wanted, and he'll make sure someone *saw me* come back tonight on foot after the horse threw me off. Now, are you going to get dressed and switch clothes with me, or keep wasting time?"

Valeria had so many more questions.

What kind of favor?

What had Abril done?

"All right," Valeria muttered.

The two of them stepped into a stable corner and made quick work of shedding their clothes. Abril dressed in the clothing from Valeria, and she took her sister-in-law's stuff to slip on. Before long, they came out of the corner, and Valeria turned to head for the horse she preferred to ride on toward the end of the stables.

"No, take Maple," Abril said, "he's my horse, and that's the one they expect me to ride."

"But he won't come back."

And Abril *loved* Maple.

"It's okay," Abril said, "he will be taken care of once you get to where you're supposed to go. I know that."

Valeria hesitated to move for the other horse who was blowing them his special kisses because his favorite human was close, and it meant a ride was coming. Turning to Abril, Valeria let the first tear fall, and she didn't bother to brush it away.

"Thank you for doing this."

She understood well just how much Abril was risking.

What it could mean if someone caught them …

"Take care of my niece," Abril replied, "and stay away so he can't hurt you anymore, Val."

"I will."

Or she would try.

It was all going to fall on a hope, a wish, and a damn prayer, though. She didn't doubt for a second that once Jorge knew she had run away, he would come after her. He would never stop tracking her down.

She was his trophy.

His thing.

He *won* her.

She belonged to him, and only he decided when to toss her away like trash on the sidewalk. But that was okay because Valeria would keep running. As long as it meant her baby was safe, and Jorge couldn't hurt their child, then she would keep going.

To the ends of the fucking earth.

Abril checked the watch on her wrist, and said, "You only have three hours, now. Do you remember the spot where you're supposed to meet Cruz? He has the fake papers you'll need with him, and he can get you across the border, but only for a small window of time, Val."

"Can I even trust him?"

"Papá killed his father—he'd do anything that went against my father or brothers. It's only because he was my … it doesn't matter," Abril whispered, shaking her head. In a flash, the emotion she had showed speaking about her lost love, something she guarded even from Valeria unless she slipped up like now, to cold in a blink. "He will be at the meeting place, but he will not wait past the time we agreed. You need to go, so *go*."

"Right," Valeria said. "Now or never."

"Good luck."

Those words—*good luck*—echoed in Valeria's mind long after she had taken Maple from the stables and headed out toward the cliffs to the east of the compound. Two hours later, when her back ached, her legs felt like pins and needles had settled into her bloodstream, and her stomach cramped, she still thought about those words.

Maple never slowed.

The darkness turned black.

Valeria thought about those words.

Good luck.

Luck hadn't found her yet.

And while she could taste the promise of freedom with every gallop of Maple's hooves against the ground, it still felt temporary.

How long could she run?

How long would it be before Jorge found her?

2.

Seven years later …

For a man like Christopher Guzzi, comfort came easy. *Usually.* He was most comfortable when surrounded by people he trusted—or better, those he loved. His family, for starters. When it was just them, his brothers and father or mother, and him, then Chris didn't put on his mask.

The one *all* Guzzi sons wore.

The Don's child.

A made man.

A proper Guzzi.

It never failed to amaze him that from the outside looking in, people had a perspective of his family that they shaped and perfected over the years. Untouchable. Vastly wealthy. *Dangerous.* They needed to be that way to everyone else, a formidable wall of a mafia Don and his army of sons lined up to protect their organization and legacy.

Because otherwise, they all realized what would happen. If someone couldn't have what they had, then they needed to be what they were. *Famiglias* like theirs didn't stay on top being weak, and God knew the Guzzis were anything but that.

Unless they were all alone, the doors closed, and it was just a father and his sons in private, the rules shifted. The masks left, and the walls dropped. Chris, at only twenty-three years old, enjoyed his position as a young made man in his father's Cosa Nostra, no doubt about it.

He also liked this.

Easy conversation with his father about *anything* but business. His oldest brother, Marcus, laughing where he sat on the corner of their father's oak desk—because fuck, it was rare for Marcus to let loose anymore, not when he was too busy being their father's understudy.

Sometimes it seemed like the Mafia took over every aspect of their lives, controlling how they needed to behave even with each other, and blurring the lines between business, and blood. And then there were moments like these when they were all brought back down to earth, reminded of why they were all here.

They were *family.*

And this was when they were at their best.

God save the soul who thought to ruin it.

Gian's—his father—laughter faded at the joke Marcus told before his gaze turned on Chris at the other side of the desk. "Have you talked to your brother?"

Chris had four brothers, and yet, when someone asked him a question like that, it meant they were asking about his identical twin, Corrado. Out of all his brothers, his twin had been the only one who decided not to join the family business. Not that Corrado headed straight in his life when it came to the law—he still very much worked on the illegal side of their life, but it wasn't within their mafia rankings.

"I did, he was just catching his flight to New York," Chris said. "He didn't say too much, distracted, possibly."

Marcus chuckled. "I bet."

Chris shot his brother a look.

Marcus only shrugged.

"Now, now," Gian murmured.

"I'm still trying to figure out how that works, is all."

"As long as it works for them, then that's what matters," Chris returned to Marcus.

"I don't share well," Marcus noted. "Not sure that would work for me."

Chris thought about that one.

"Yeah, me either," he muttered.

Somehow, his twin found himself in love and in a relationship with *two* people. Alessio, and Ginevra. Knowing how his brother's sexual preferences followed Corrado through most of his life, haunting him because he never seemed like he fit in with the rest of his family or their life, Chris was happy he found the people with whom he belonged. What else needed to be said?

Did he understand how that three-person relationship worked?

No.

Did he want to?

Again, no.

It wasn't his life, his home, or his bed.

Simple as that.

And he didn't want other people discussing it where Corrado, Alessio, or Ginevra weren't around to be a part of the discussion. Good manners, and all.

Right?

"Besides, if there's something you want to ask Corrado," Chris told Marcus, "then you could, oh, *ask* him. Or Les—he's pretty open to talk."

Marcus blinked. "Probably not."

"Then, don't speculate."

"That's fair," Gian said, jumping into the discussion as the phone on his desk rang. He gave his two sons a look, pointing a finger at both, a silent *quiet*, before he picked up the call, and put the phone to his ear. "*Bonjour, ciao*, Gian here."

It took Gian just long enough to hear who was on the other line before he reached over, hit the speaker button on the phone, and set it back down to the cradle. The voice that filled the office was one Chris hadn't heard in a while, and he still wasn't sure how he felt when he heard it.

A mixture of things, he supposed.

Only a couple of them any good.

"Do you have a minute to chat, Gian?" Dare asked.

"A few—two of the boys are here."

"Which ones?"

"Marcus, and Chris. What can we do for you?"

Chris never asked for details about how his father came in to contact or all the finer details of Gian's business with Dare—no one seemed to be aware of his last name—but somehow, he had. Gian ended up as one investor who fronted *a lot* of cash to finance a business venture Dare and his partner now controlled.

They called it The League.

An organization which trained assassins, like his brother, Corrado, and then sold them at an auction to the highest bidder. Sure, The League also had their own teams of assassins that worked *only* for The League, and independent contractors, again, like Chris's twin, and one of Corrado's lovers, Alessio.

But mostly, they made real money in the auctions. Selling skilled individuals who could kill someone in a hundred different ways on demand.

Chris had been one of those people once—he trained with Corrado because *fuck*, he couldn't imagine leaving his twin to something like The League without someone there to watch his back. He'd always looked after his twin.

The League wasn't for him, and he realized that rather quickly, but he stuck out his contract. He did the one-year training, stayed for another year to work on a team with his brother and the others they had placed him with, and then he came back home at nineteen.

He wasn't like them.

Chris wanted to be a made man.

And so, he did.

"I have an issue," Dare said, "and I thought getting your opinion on what I should do about it might help to clear up my thoughts, Gian."

"Do tell."

"A job came in. The client isn't *new*, or rather, the family isn't."

"Who?"

"New York—Marcellos."

Gian dragged in a heavy breath and rested back in his chair to steeple his fingers together. He didn't look at either of his sons, but Chris didn't need to see his father's eyes to understand what he was thinking when that name came into play. Oh, sure, their family was on friendly terms with the Marcello Cosa Nostra in New York. The largest mafia organization in North America, it was always better to be on their good side.

His father's reaction, no doubt, was because he wondered *what* the issue was. With the Marcellos, it couldn't be something small. They went all in, or nothing at all. There was no in between for them, and it was one reason Chris respected them as much as he did in the grand scheme.

"And?" Gian asked.

"They need a retrieval done," Dare said, "which seems simple on the surface—it's my team's specialty, right?"

"It seems to be their focus, yes."

"Except there are details that make it problematic for this job. And beyond *those* issues, I have another problem."

"Which is what?" Gian demanded. "Because my suggestion, Dare, would be to give the Marcello family whatever they want, and get them off your ass. They are not the types to be fucked around, and they won't stand for you to jerk on their chains, if you understand what I'm saying here. Take it into account when dealing with them."

"I *am*," Dare muttered, "that's not the issue."

"Well, what is?"

"The auctions, Gian."

"Ah," his father said in a sigh, massaging at his temples with his fingers. "Right, those are next month."

"And the main team—the one I'd use for this job—are being sent out to Russia next month for a prison assignment. We need someone to scope the target out first, and gain as much information as we can get before we gather who and what we need. Then, we can grab the target, but not before. Maybe two months, or a little less. I don't have someone who would be appropriate for this job except Corrado and Alessio."

"I can do it," Chris said.

He didn't regret saying the words, sure. All eyes in the room turned on him as soon as he said it. And even the man on the phone quieted at the declaration.

"What?" he asked.

"You haven't done a job for The League since you were nineteen," his father said.

"It's like riding a bike," Chris returned, "you fall off, and get back on."

Right.

Like riding a bike.

Mostly, Chris spoke up because he didn't want his twin to be bothered and that fucking ingrained need inside his being to take care of Corrado, and look out for him—even when his twin didn't have a clue he did it—was bred deep.

He blamed genetics.

And his father.

"That's … going to be my suggestion, actually," Dare said, his voice filtering through the speaker again. "Because with *your* influence and name, Gian, it would make it a hell of a lot easier to infiltrate the organization where we believe the target is located."

"What in the hell are you talking about?" Gian asked.

"When can you two get to Vegas for a proper briefing?"

Gian gave Chris a glance.

He shrugged.

"Christmas is soon," Gian said.

"Right after New Years?"

Chris nodded to his father. "After the new year is fine."

"Good. I will arrange it with the Marcellos."

The phone call ended before anyone said goodbye, not that Chris or his father seemed to mind. Marcus continued sipping on a glass of whiskey, not bothering to step in at all.

"Are you sure you want to take that assignment?" Gian asked Chris. "You have duties here to *la famiglia*, too, son. I am sure I could make do for a couple of months, but it's not about that. I want you to be certain this is what you want to do."

His father, always looking out for his boys.

Chris appreciated it.

"Why not?"

Yeah, *why not?*

That seemed to be the story of his life.

Might as well add another chapter.

• • •

The League ran their business out of a cluster of connected buildings deep within the desolate land of Nevada which they dubbed *the complex*. And frankly, Chris thought the name fit considering it's massive size. It had to be considering everything and anything The League needed to operate smoothly was inside the complex.

He trained here. *Broke* here. He lived here—ate, slept, and survived behind these walls. He was sure, despite the time he had stayed and worked for The League, he hadn't seen every single square inch of the place.

They also added to the place over the years, building on to the complex for whatever suited their purposes. It had been a while since Chris last visited the secluded cluster of connected buildings, so he hadn't known they added an Olympic-size pool until he stood in the doorway leading to it.

He stared across the calm blue water, unnerved by the black tiling design at the bottom of the pool. It gave the water a bottomless effect, and it sent his anxiety spiking through the roof.

If the water went over his fucking head, it was too deep. An almost drowning as a child left Chris with a paranoia and fear for water. He did his best to hide it from others, but his family knew.

And The League.

They had knowledge of it, too.

One of the many reasons he was conflicted on being back inside this building. Although he appreciated all they did for him here, and what it taught him, Chris still walked away from this place with more scars than he cared to count. Some, more than others, never too far away from his thoughts.

Their motto?

Break the body, break the mind.

They'd done that to him.

Again and again.

"Chris," Gian murmured.

For the first time, he looked away from the pool, realizing he had come to a complete stop before he passed the room to stare inside. His father, a few steps down the hall, raised a brow and waited for him to get over his … *thing*.

"Sorry," Chris blurted, "I'm coming."

Gian nodded, but said nothing about the water, or the obvious problem Chris had by being *near* it. His father was good in that way, and Chris respected it. "Dare is waiting with the others. Let's not keep them."

Right, right.

Their reason for being here.

Knowing his father made a good point, and the Marcellos had been kind enough to allow them to hold this meeting after the holidays passed, Chris forced his attention away from the goddamn pool. He followed behind his father in silence, walking through newer halls of the complex he wasn't familiar with as the owners added them over the last year.

Before long, they stood in the doorway of Dare's office. The group inside, four in total, turned to greet them, although none wore smiles.

That serious, huh?

Chris recognized all the men, but for different reasons. Dare, standing behind his desk, because he had been Chris's boss for a time, and he was his father's business partner with this place. Cree, the Native with his hands clasped at his back in front of a row of screens showcasing an aerial view of what looked to be a map, because he was one who trained Chris here.

The other two men, Dante and Andino Marcello, he knew from the business— *Cosa Nostra*. Rarely were they known to leave New York, but especially not to come to Nevada, so he figured this job was important to them.

"Gian, and Chris, right?" Dante asked, looking his way.

Chris nodded. "That's me."

"Not to be confused with his twin, who—"

"Isn't here," Chris interjected, giving Andino Marcello a stare that would silence the devil. He understood this man had issues with his twin, and he didn't care to hear them. Fucking *nobody*, regardless of what their last name happened to be, would bad mouth his twin, but not to his damn face. "And we have things to do, don't we?"

"We do," Dare said from behind his desk, "and we're waiting on you all before we start."

"Sorry to keep you waiting," Gian said, giving Chris a wave to enter the office first, "shall we get started?"

Dare picked up the remote on his desk and pointed it at the screen once Chris and his father entered the office. The picture changed when he pressed a button, showcasing Andino in a tux, a woman in a white wedding dress, and a little girl between them being held by a black-haired, *beautiful* woman with a wide smile.

And God, yeah, beautiful didn't do the woman justice. Her joyful smile brightened her delicate features, and her black hair had a glossy sheen under the sunlight. Tall, and curvy, the lavender dress she had picked for the day hugged her body and showed off all kinds of leg.

With only a picture, Chris thought whoever had taken it had captured the woman's beauty, her confidence, and her womanly appeal all at the same time.

Quite a feat.

"Valeria Lòpez," Cree said when Dare stayed quiet. "Formerly *Gomez*, but she changed it after a forced marriage to Jorge Lòpez at fifteen when the cartel killed her mother down in Mexico, it became a means to blackmail her father. Or, those are the details we have."

"That's all we had," Andino muttered.

"Right," Dare said, nodding at Andino, "and so this is what we're working on. Somehow, around sixteen from what we understand, Valeria was pregnant, and ran away from her husband, and the cartel. She found her way to the States, and we don't know how. What we do know is her daughter was born in the States, and at some point, she met Haven Murphy."

"Marcello, now," Andino added under his breath.

That name rang a bell.

Chris looked to Andino. "Your new wife?"

Andino nodded. "The two happened to be roommates for quite a while before I came along, Valeria worked for Haven, and one night she came home ... seemed like Val up and left and so did—"

Dare pressed a button, and the screen changed to a single picture of the little girl Valeria had been holding in the wedding picture. "Her daughter, Maria. Who is six. We cannot find anything for this little girl anywhere at the moment. No school records in Mexico, nothing for a doctor, and ... yeah."

Chris let out a heavy breath as he took in the black-haired, brown-eyed child. She looked all of maybe five on the screen if that. Cute, with a wide, toothy smile, and her arms high in the air as her yellow summer dress spun around her legs.

"Jorge Lòpez is her father," Dare said, "but what's important is ... Valeria ran from the cartel, we're aware she was forced into marriage, and at some point, they took her again. We have every reason to believe she is back with the cartel."

"Might she want to be there?" Chris asked.

"Possibly," the man returned, "but you must figure that out when you get inside, won't you?"

Gian hummed under his breath beside his son. "And that's why you want me here, isn't it? Being the boss of the Guzzis, I'm not affiliated to the Marcellos on paper as a business partner, they wouldn't expect me to go there for her, and I could use my status and territory as a transaction for them, correct?"

"They wouldn't suspect something's up, no."

Chris looked to the two Marcello men as this was *their* job. They had come here with it, and they wanted to retrieve the woman. "Why is she important? A cartel wife ... that's playing with fire. I'm familiar with details about the Lòpez cartel. Jorge, he's the oldest son, and has taken over more now that his father took a step back years ago. And you want to ... what, take his wife and child from him?"

Andino arched a brow, replying, "I respect the hesitance, but the woman never asked for the life they gave her. From what my wife explained, and I understood, Val stayed on the run and had been for years, which meant she had to be running from something."

"Or *someone*," Chris finished.

"Jorge, likely," Andino agreed. "Val and Haven ... she needs to know if Val is where she wants to be, is *safe*, and happy. And if she is, fine, we leave it alone. But if she isn't, and if she needs help, that's what you're here to do."

Chris cleared his throat and nodded once. "All right."

Dare passed him a glance. "The job's a go?"

"The job is a go."

3.

"Mamá, watch me!"

Valeria already had one eye on her daughter, but she tipped the rim of her large, pink summer hat higher so that Maria could see her. She smiled, refusing to allow her six-year-old to see her discomfort about where they were staying. Maria liked the pool at her grandfather, Martín's, mansion in Mexico City, but Valeria hated it.

Or better yet, she hated the people here.

Most of them.

"When did she learn to swim?"

The soft voice at Valeria's left didn't take her attention away from her daughter in the pool—safety first, and all—but she still answered Abril on the lounger. "Last summer. A friend and I took her twice a week to an indoor pool for lessons."

"A *friend?*"

Valeria did her best not to roll her eyes at her sister-in-law. Six years on the run, and Jorge had caught up to her. It wasn't Abril's fault, and no one had ever found out the truth about how she helped Valeria all those years ago. She had been back in Mexico, under Jorge's thumb, for a year now … and life was worse.

"Haven Murphy," Valeria said, her gaze darting to the marble steps leading to the back of the mansion's patio doors. It was a habit for her now—she looked for Jorge if she *dared* mention anything about her time when she ran away because if he was within hearing distance, or if someone else was that would tell on her, she would suffer for it later. "She thought it was a good idea."

In her stark white, one-piece bathing suit that contrasted against her deeply tanned skin, Abril shifted to face Valeria more on her lounger. Valeria still kept one eye on her little girl in the water, just in case Maria became tired, and needed her ma to jump in after her.

"I would think you might be … *furioso*—angry—with her, after everything."

Val blinked. "Why?"

"It was because of her that he found you, no?"

"I don't blame her. It wasn't her fault that someone leaked a picture from the private wedding to the public, and it was the one that Maria and I were also in, Abril. It was the circumstance, and nothing more."

Valeria never understood how she befriended Haven when she found herself in New York a good year after taking off from Mexico, but she had never been more grateful for the friendship. For years, Haven was the only person Valeria had to rely on—they lived together, for Christ's sake. And then when Haven met someone who was maybe as dangerous as Jorge had been for Valeria, she knew it was a risk to continue her friendship.

Except, she was scared to walk away.

She *loved* her friend.

Haven married that man.

Turned out, he wasn't awful like Jorge.

The rest, from the wedding to the leaked picture, all brought Valeria right back to this hellscape Jorge liked to call *home* for her. And oh, he had been so fucking pleased to watch his men drag her through the gates of the compound, messy and fighting, while another man carried his drugged, sleeping daughter to him.

"We shouldn't talk about that," Valeria said.

"Hmm."

Mostly, because it pissed Jorge off, and Valeria didn't feel like dealing with her husband later in the evening. But also, because it hurt Valeria in her heart to think about the people she had left behind.

Haven.

Her best friend.

Chances were, she would never see Haven again. That would be to Haven's best benefit, all things considered. Anything Valeria cared about, Jorge took note, and used it to keep her controlled, and to make her behave.

Even her daughter wasn't out of bounds for him, the bastard. Valeria had learned over the last year since her forceful return that it was better to do what the asshole wanted from her than to fight him every step of the way.

One hurt less.

"Well, at least he allowed you out of the compound for this weekend," Abril muttered, rolling to her back on the lounger, and tipping her matching white sunhat down enough to hide the sun's rays from her face. "That's a start."

Yes, but for *what?*

Jorge did nothing without reason.

Valeria assumed this was the same.

"Not too far, now," Valeria called to her daughter as Maria dared to head for the deep end. She could swim in it, but it still made Valeria a little too nervous for her liking. "Come back where you can still touch your feet, Maria."

"Okay, Mamá," her girl replied.

She watched as Maria swam closer to the edge of the pool on the shallow side, her tanned legs kicking up a storm and splattering the tiled edge with droplets of water. It was only then that Valeria noticed the man approaching, and because Maria happened to splash him with water from the pool.

Not that he seemed to care.

Dressed in beige slacks, his leather shoes hit the tiles soundlessly as he rolled up the sleeves of his silk dress shirt around his elbows, showing off skin darkened by the sun. He'd left the top two buttons of his shirt undone at his throat and seemed comfortable approaching them.

Roberto García.

Son of a rival cartel leader.

Enemy of *theirs*.

In peace talks.

And also—

"Ah, dove, you're getting too much sun," Roberto murmured as he came to a stop beside Abril's lounger.

Abril took a deep breath, but didn't move her sunhat to peer up at the man who should be her intended husband sometime over the next few months. Or, that's what Valeria had understood. According to Jorge, it was one of the many attempts at making peace between the rival cartels. Although, she wasn't sure they should trust anything that came out of his rotten mouth.

"I am fine, but *gracias*," Abril replied, not unkindly.

Still, a bite lingered in her tone.

Roberto didn't miss it if the slight narrowing of his eyes was any sign to his lessening patience. His gaze darted to Valeria, and he offered her a tight smile. "You two look like twins today—*almost*."

Yes, her in a pale pink one-piece.

Abril in her white one.

Valeria shrugged. "Only from behind, though."

That made Abril laugh.

Roberto didn't understand.

Valeria grinned.

Her amusement didn't last long when a familiar figure came to stand on the marble steps. She swore she distinguished his gaze nailing into her from thirty feet away. She couldn't see his eyes from behind the dark aviator sunglasses he wore, their weight was still palpable.

"Valeria, clean Maria up and come inside," Jorge called out to her, "we're about ready to sit down for dinner."

She didn't reply, simply moved to do as she was told, slipping off the lounger to approach the side of the pool. As she pulled Maria from the water, a towel already waiting for her to dry her daughter off, and get her dressed, Roberto murmured something to Abril behind her before he headed for the mansion.

Valeria turned around with a towel-wrapped Maria in just enough time to watch Abril *glower* at the man's back as he walked away. "Be careful," she told her sister-in-law, "because they won't like seeing your face looking like that about him."

Abril's jaw tightened before her hateful expression morphed into a blank slate. "I refuse to marry that man."

"He isn't a bad man."

"He isn't the man I want, Val."

Yes, well … she knew how that worked.

How this life of theirs worked.

Look at her.

Valeria said nothing.

Abril didn't seem to mind.

• • •

Spanish flowed around the table between the men, but the women at their sides kept quiet, and focused on the meal. It was what the Lòpez men expected from their wives, or sister, in Abril's case. They weren't interested in hearing a woman's perspective on their business, and they didn't want opinions.

Valeria didn't care.

She used that time to make sure Maria ate enough of her food that she wouldn't be asking for a snack every five minutes after dinner ended. And when her attention was on her daughter, which she didn't get often because Jorge was an asshole, no one seemed to pay any mind to Valeria.

She considered that a win.

Right?

Maria sat between her mother, and Jorge. She called him Papá because Jorge refused to answer to anything else, but God knew Maria didn't like the man who had helped to give her life. It didn't help that the child had a front-row seat to the horrible treatment her mother received from her father daily.

Not to mention, until this last year, Maria hadn't known her father at all. So, they forced the girl out of America, put her in front of some *man* who behaved like a monster, and expected the six-year-old to love him.

Okay.

Valeria did her best to make sure Maria behaved and gave her father the attention he wanted. It was easier on all of them that way, but in private, she let her daughter hug her tight, cry, and beg to go back to America, and Haven. Away from these people who she said were mean and hurt her mom.

What else could she do?

"Is it good?" Valeria asked.

Maria nodded. "I like it."

"Good."

"This will be a good deal," Martín, her father-in-law, said with a pointed finger moving between Abril and Roberto sitting side by side across from Valeria and Jorge. "It is a good match, and it will bring our organizations closer ... more money, more power, *sí?*"

Jorge smiled tersely. "Absolutely, Papá."

Across the table, Roberto chuckled. "The Garcías never thought we would see the day when we made peace with the Lòpez family, but as they say, all wars must come to an eventual end, right?"

"That's what they say," the man next to Roberto muttered.

Samuel.

The other Lòpez son.

No one paid him any mind.

Valeria was a little distracted by trying to ignore the hand that came to rest behind her chair. Jorge's fingers curved around her shoulder, his fingers digging in painfully. Still, she managed a smile across their daughter between them, just enough to make him assume she was fine with his touch.

She wanted to *puke.*

Still, Jorge's hand flexed against her shoulder again when his father smiled at the man who was now arranged to be his future son-in-law because of the upcoming marriage to Abril. Even if she didn't sense that tension in her husband's hand, she would know the truth. In private, Jorge didn't *shut up.*

His father had taken a step down from running the cartel a while back. Jorge was the one who had the major control of the operation, but that didn't stop his father from stepping in occasionally, to remind everyone that the king wasn't truly dead.

Like this deal with their enemy.

This *marriage.*

Jorge despised it all.

"Good things are happening to us all," Jorge murmured to the table, lifting a glass of red wine for the others to follow his lead. He tipped his glass toward his father, "To power, Papá, by whatever means we can get it, no?"

Martín smiled and raised his own glass. "To power."

Jorge tipped his drink back and swallowed it in one gulp. Valeria knew if he kept that up, by the time they got up to their room later, he would be drunk and unpleasant. To say the least ... more like *violent* and wanting her.

Something else to make her sick.

"And we have more things to look forward to," Jorge added, setting his glass down to the table hard. "More business—starting next week. Everyone will benefit if it goes right."

Across the table, Roberto asked, "*Everyone?*"

He meant their side of things, too. Because now, if the two cartels merged, even if Jorge didn't like it, what benefitted them should also benefit Roberto's father's organization. That was how it should work, but Valeria didn't believe for a second Jorge would agree.

Jorge didn't reply.

Valeria doubted the other man missed it.

· · ·

Valeria tightened the silk robe around her body, using the ties to cinch the fabric at the trim curve of her waist. She sensed his presence the moment he opened the bedroom door.

Jorge had that effect.

"Why would you dress in *that?*" he asked.

It was by his tone she knew he had polished off the bottle of red wine from the table after dinner finished. *Great.* He was always worse when he was a little too drunk, and his lips were loose.

Not only did she have to deal with his pawing in bed but also his fucking mouth which never shut the hell up. It was a losing battle.

"*Val,*" he mumbled.

She turned around to face him, only to find him circling the foot of the bed to come closer to her. Maybe her attention should have been on the door because she always found it easier to handle him when she could see him coming.

Valeria hated being surprised.

Like now.

As she assumed, he was drunk. *Thoroughly.* Bloodshot eyes, a slack mouth, and a sheen of perspiration dotting the lines in his forehead as his gaze narrowed in on her. Not that she had much time to react because she didn't.

He reached for her before she might refuse him—*lie* and say she was on her cycle, which turned him off like nothing else. Pulling the robe she had just tightened away from her body with his rough hand, it allowed him access to the silk short and camisole set she wore underneath.

He picked her clothes, too.

"Jorge," she started to say.

His hand found her breast, sliding under the silk before clamping down tight enough to take her breath and words away as he muttered, "Next week, when the Canadians come down to make that deal, we won't need the fucking Garcías for *anything*. And then my father will understand that I can do this without merging. Smart, aren't I?"

Valeria swallowed hard, ignoring the bile rising in her throat as his hand slid from one of her breasts to the other, and then climbed higher on her neck to rest against her throat. If she flinched, he would become rough. She didn't need more bruises to hide with makeup.

It never worked, anyway.

"Of course, you are," she lied. "But might he be mad?"

"I don't *care* what he'll be!"

She flinched.

Except, the high level of his shout made their daughter wake up in the room she used across the hall from theirs inside the mansion.

Maria's tired cries were muffled, but Valeria still heard them. She fixed her sleep clothes, but Jorge didn't remove his hand from her body.

"She's *six*," he snapped, "and is fine—she'll go back to sleep on her own."

"It's a new place, and it might scare her."

"You can't *baby* her forever."

No, but she would right now.

Maria needed her.

And she needed to get away from Jorge.

Win-win.

"Please," Valeria whispered, "I'll just get her back to sleep, and then I'll come to bed."

Jorge sighed, and rolled his eyes, letting his hand drop from her throat as he took a step back. "*Fine*. Whatever. Go."

She didn't need to be told again. Hopefully, by the time she got back to bed, he would be passed out. Sometimes the universe worked for her, and other times, it only seemed to want to laugh in her face.

Valeria didn't glance back as she exited the bedroom and crossed the hall. Once she was inside her daughter's room, Maria reached for her from the sheets that were nothing like the ones she had loved so much in her pink bed back in New York.

Nothing here was like New York.

"Mamá," Maria breathed, "someone *yelled*."

"It's okay," Valeria murmured, slipping under the blankets with her daughter, and holding her tight. "Mamá's here, *bebita*. I love you."

4.

Chris checked the watch on his wrist as the jet jumped when the landing gear first touched down on the ground. He found that was the most nerve-wracking part of flying. He didn't mind takeoff, or even being in the air. It was landing that always had his heart jumping into his damn throat.

Their flight was on time, according to his watch. Across the aisle from his seat on the private jet, his father cleared his throat as the pressure in the cabin became bearable, and their voices didn't sound like an echo to each other's ears.

"Not anymore settled about this, are you?" Gian asked.

In a tailored suit, unbothered and relaxed sitting in the white leather seat, Gian smirked in Chris's direction, like he had known the whole time what was running through his quiet son's mind. His father always seemed to have a good grasp on the complexities of his boys although Chris never understood why.

Sometimes, it felt like a curse.

Others, a gift.

"I don't see the point in *you* coming along for this," Chris replied, shrugging his broad shoulders under his own suit. He was thinking his choice of attire would be a mistake once they stepped off the temperature-controlled jet into the dry, Mexican heat. Not that it mattered. Guzzis were who they were, suits and class included, even when the weather called for board shorts and a dip in the ocean. "All I'm saying, is I can do this all without you needing to come along, Dad."

Gian nodded and turned to stare out the port window as the plane slowed. Soon, it would taxi into the private gate at the international airport. According to their contact, guards would greet them although they arrived at a public airport.

It showed how far the cartel reached, and Chris refused to allow that thought very far from his mind. When people forgot who they were dealing with, they underestimated them at the same time.

He wouldn't be doing that.

Not here.

They couldn't afford to.

"It is a show of faith for me to be here for this first meeting," Gian said, never turning back to give Chris his full attention as he spoke, "and you know that. In this life, this *business*, it is better when bosses sit down for a proper face to face, and then we go from there. It extends a friendly hand, and people are less likely to question our intentions. That is what we need here, isn't it?"

Gian made all good points.

He wasn't wrong.

Still, Chris watched his father from the side, and all he thought about was his mother back home in Canada. They were all at a rather comfortable place with *la famiglia*, and the family business. It had been a good while since the mafia touched their family violently, and Chris didn't want this cartel job for The League to be the first thing in a while to remind their family—but especially not his mother—that this was dangerous.

They knew.

All of them did.

It didn't change the fact that, sometimes, people became relaxed in their positions, and believed nothing would touch them in their lives.

Cartels were notoriously vicious, and risky, when doing business with them. A true statement whether someone learned it firsthand, or not. That, more than anything else, was what kept Chris on edge since they were using business as a front to get their *in* to the goddamn cartel here. Not only was he looking for a woman he wasn't sure wanted to leave Mexico, but he also had to consider his father's safety.

Like fuck would he leave here needing to tell his mother that her husband wouldn't be coming home to her alive. That just would not happen. Not if Chris had any say.

Chris could have done this job alone without his father, but yes, it would be easier with his presence here to defer to until the leaders of the cartel trusted him. But as soon as that fucking happened, Gian was gone.

No questions asked.

"Did you call Ma?" Chris asked.

Gian's lips lifted with a small smile. "I will call her once we're off the plane, Chris."

"You should call her now."

"Stop worrying. You sound like her."

Right.

Chris forced himself to shut up and let his annoying thoughts stay tucked away in his mind. There were a lot of reasons he could think of for why he shouldn't have taken this job, but it was too late to back out now.

The phone in Chris's pocket buzzed, and he took it out to check the text rolling across the screen. A simple message from his twin, but it calmed his overacting nerves. Corrado's text only read, *Call me if you need anything.*

Chris would keep that in mind.

He might need it.

The private jet took a good twenty minutes to taxi to the correct gate where they could finally unbuckle and grab their bags from the cupboards at the front. Chris grabbed his own, a larger bag, than his father's overnight travel duffle. If all went right, the overnight bag was all his father would need here, because Gian wouldn't be staying more than a day or two.

They had to play their cards right.

"*Merci,*" Gian thanked the pilot at the front in French.

It was a toss-up with his father, and even his twin, or their oldest sibling, Marcus, which language they might use to talk. Chris was handy with English and Italian, but he had never picked up on French, for whatever reason.

Chris exited the plane after his father, giving the pilot a nod as he passed. He didn't know where the flight attendant had disappeared to, but he didn't care, either. At the bottom of the stairs, assault rifles in hand, stood three men dressed in matching outfits of denim jeans, and black shirts.

"Ah, good," Gian muttered under his breath, "the cartel followed through."

Chris swallowed the discomfort in his throat. "Good."

It was unnerving when someone realized just how much control the cartels in Mexico— there were two major organizations that had long been in battle against one another—had in the country. From the government, to small businesses in the towns they used to make or smuggle their drugs through, it didn't matter.

Blackmail.

Bribery.

Violence.

Cartels were not a game.

And here the Guzzis were, ready to play one with them.

Fun.

"Gian Guzzi?" the man standing ahead of the other two asked, his accent heavy.

"That would be me," Chris's father returned.

The man nodded. "We'll walk you through customs, sir, and take you to the drop."

The drop.

Huh.

They weren't even calling it a meeting today.

Good to know.

• • •

"This is not the compound."

Chris's declaration to his father was quiet and said before the guards who had already stepped out of the vehicle opened the back door for them to exit the car. He had to say it while he had the chance because he wasn't sure what to expect here. Sure, the Lòpez cartel had not offered many details about where or how they would do business, but that didn't mean he was comfortable going in blind, either.

"Let's get the pleasantries out of the way first," Gian said quickly, "and then we'll worry about what is going on here, *oui?*"

Chris sighed. "All right."

He only knew the yellow brick mansion with the terracotta roof, surrounded by a large stone fence where armed guards stood staring down at their vehicle, wasn't the Lòpezs' infamous compound because of The League. The aerial views The League had provided of the cartel's home base was neither in the middle of a busy city, nor were there any mansions on the property. Small homes, stables, barns, and a few other buildings out in the middle of nowhere, but not *this*.

"Step out," one of the guard's said when he came to open the rear passenger door for Gian and Chris. "And they will open the gate for you to enter the grounds."

Chris had a million and one questions to ask, but he stayed silent because this wasn't *his* show. His father was the one who had come here as the front man, so to speak. He was the boss, the one wanting to make a deal with the cartel, and Chris was nothing more than muscle at his father's side.

For now.

He needed to keep the act up.

The guard hadn't lied.

Chris stared up at the almost white-blue sky, the sun so bright, it still hurt his eyes behind the dark sunglasses he wore. His distraction only lasted as long as it took for the creak of metal to bring his attention back to what was important.

The guards stepped aside as the gate opened.

Gian moved forward first, but Chris was fast to follow behind. Just beyond the wrought metal gate, a pathway made of red stone and lined with towering trees led them toward the front of the mansion. Waiting on white marble steps were two men, both of whom Chris recognized, although he kept that to himself.

Still needed to keep up that act …

"Gian Guzzi, and … son, correct?" the man standing just beyond the other asked.

Jorge Lòpez.

In his head, Chris did a mental inventory of the man and also what he knew about him. From the yellow silk dress shirt he wore, with the sleeves rolled up around his elbows, to the black slacks that looked pressed from an iron. This was the man they forced Valeria to marry, according to the information they had, and he was also the oldest son of the cartel's former leader.

Well, that's what they assumed. No one had a clue if the former leader was a *former*, but from all public appearances, Jorge ran the show now.

"Chris," Gian said, "my son's name is Chris. We were not sure what to expect today, but this home is a lovely spot for a meeting."

"Our father's," the man just behind Jorge stated.

Samuel.

Second son of the Lòpez leader. Brother to Jorge. Chris wouldn't concern himself with Samuel, except for the fact he was a Lòpez, and *there*. Part of it all and possibly keeping Valeria hidden somewhere.

Or was she even hidden here?

Yet to be determined.

Gian continued his greetings with the Lòpez brothers while Chris took in his surroundings. He blamed that on his training at The League, and not so much the fact he was a made man. They had taught him to find what he needed to deal with first. To take in his surroundings, and everything else, too.

Then, there were as little surprises as possible. Although, should a surprise come up on him, he would handle that knowing everything else around him. It was all in the details, really.

"And," Gian said to Chris's left as he noted the white trim around the windows of the mansion, "once we hammer down the main details, I will take a step back because I have business to attend to at home. I can't leave it for long."

"Which is where your son will come in, *sí?*" Jorge asked, his accent thickening his English.

"Chris will take over whatever you need here for my side of things. I intend to involve myself in all of this, even if it is from afar and I want to understand how things will work, where everything will be held, and how you intend to smuggle the cocaine over. I hope you understand, but I am a *details* man."

Jorge chuckled. "As am I, Gian."

"*Oui*, well, when I am guaranteeing you the ability to supply to all of Canada through my organization and contacts, I am sure you won't be uncomfortable with allowing us a stay here, and time to understand your business, and process, Mr. Lòpez."

"We'll make it work," Samuel muttered, "although we're not accustomed to someone who wants *all* the details. We rarely work that way."

"Except we will in this case," Jorge added, "a deal with you ensures we will be the largest producing and supplying cartel in Mexico."

Chris didn't miss the way the two brothers passed a look between them, something unsaid lingering in their stares. He tucked it into the back of his mind and returned to surveying the grounds.

"And you won't take issue with my son doing the majority of the work and passing word back then?" Gian asked.

"Is that why he's currently scoping us out?"

Chris didn't miss the sharpness of Jorge Lòpez's tone. He came back to the conversation, smiling carefully to make sure the man didn't think he was malicious in his perusal of the grounds.

He was all too aware in that moment of certain things he needed to be careful to do for this plan of theirs to work. Things he needed to portray to allow him inside the cartel's top echelon to get closer to Valeria—wherever she was here, because no one saw her yet.

They needed to trust him, at all costs. He was to be no better or worse than them, in their eyes, and willing to indulge in whatever they asked of him to make sure they didn't question his reasoning for being here. "It's a beautiful home. Almost reminds me of my parents' mansion."

Jorge eyed Chris for a moment, his silence stretching on a beat too long before he said, "Large, is it?"

"Two wings. More acres than someone cares to count."

"Not as protected, I bet."

Chris shrugged. "Better not to make a show, in our part of the world."

Jorge nodded. "I can understand that, I suppose."

Gian cleared his throat. "Shall we begin this process, then?"

"Yes, let's get comfortable inside. We figured … a quick lunch, and then maybe a drink later in the back by the pool before a proper dinner. If that works for you, Gian?"

"It does," Gian replied.

"Good. Lunch will be ready soon. Later, the rest of our family will join us for dinner."

Oh?

Chris kept that question inside, but barely. Did the rest of the *family* mean Jorge's supposed wife—Valeria—and his daughter, Maria, too? Because that would answer a lot of things that were still unknown here.

"I hope you like bourbon," Jorge said, "as that is our drink of choice for *business* deals."

"I do," Gian said.

Chris smiled when the men turned their backs to him and his father. The Guzzis were *in*.

For now.

• • •

Lunch went well, and as Chris assumed, his father took over the majority of the conversation with Jorge. Chris and Samuel sat at opposite ends of the table, enjoying their meal and sharing a word when asked for it, but otherwise, staying out of the dealings between the other two.

Not that Chris minded.

He enjoyed being the silent one in a conversation more than he liked to be the one who talked. It allowed him to learn a hell of a lot more when he wasn't concerned about what might slip out of his mouth.

Once lunch finished, and Jorge and Gian seemed fine with the *specifics* of their arrangement, with one supplying the other cocaine, the four moved outside.

Well, three, he supposed.

Samuel disappeared after lunch. He stepped outside with them for a moment, but left soon after, re-entering the mansion through the back without as much as a word why.

It didn't matter.

Chris had other things on his mind.

The *pool*, for starters.

His anxiety picked up as he, his father, and Jorge walked along the side of the pool, each with a glass of bourbon in their hands to sip from. He wouldn't enjoy the drink this close to water even if the fear seemed unfounded.

Chris could *swim*.

He learned to do that.

The pool on one end was not deep.

He could touch the bottom.

Even hearing those thoughts in his mind, a constant mantra that played on repeat whenever he faced water, it only helped a little. Not enough for him to forget what it felt like to have water rushing into his lungs with every breath he attempted to take in. It didn't stop the memory of his garbled shouts as he tried to call for help as the water pulled him under the docks at his uncle's vacation home.

"Chris," his father said quietly.

His gaze snapped away from the pool, drifting to where his father had stepped out of his conversation with Jorge to bring Chris out of his head. A knowing glint in his father's eye—that familiar concern—stared back at him.

"Do you like the bourbon?" his father asked.

Jorge, who seemed confused at the question, not to mention hadn't noticed Chris's distraction, glanced between the two men. Gian brought him out of a state of panic but also did it without making the other man aware of his son's deepest fear.

It was never good to hand someone your weakness.

They used it when you did that.

"Yes," Chris said, keeping the nerves out of his tone, "it's fine."

"It better be," Jorge muttered, "I paid enough for the import."

"Forgive me for being forward," Gian said, bringing Jorge's attention away from Chris for the moment, "but I can't help noticing this is your father's home, and yet, we haven't seen him. They told me, although I don't trust everything said in passing, that your father stepped back from the cartel a while ago, yes?"

Jorge raised a brow and brought the lit cigar between his fingers to his lips for a heady drag. Grey smoke lifted toward the darkening sky, telling them night would fall soon.

"He has stepped back," Jorge said, passing the house behind them a look, "but he still puts his opinion and influence in whenever he wants."

A bite colored his tone.

Gian didn't miss it.

"And what, he doesn't agree with us being here?"

Jorge tipped his cigar in Gian's direction. "*Almost* correct—not quite, though. He's of the opinion the business will be good, but he's currently attempting a merger between our cartel, and the only rival we have. Something I think is a mistake, and with you Canadians on my books, we won't need to merge at all."

"Is he aware?"

"He stepped back."

"But did he?"

"It doesn't matter once it's all said and done, does it?"

They didn't get the chance to reply to the man because a door closing had Jorge's attention turning away. His brow lifted in contemplation before he smiled. Not a *fond* smile.

"Ah, there they are. Which means the rest have already arrived, and we can begin a proper dinner." Jorge lifted a hand to wave, and called out, "*Hermosa*, bring the *princesa* over for a proper hello to our new friends."

Chris turned to see who had come out on the back steps of the mansion, not familiar with Spanish but having heard just enough in his lifetime to understand those affectionate terms that left Jorge's mouth. In a white dress, holding the hand of a small girl at her side, Chris found the answer to one of their unknowns standing on marble steps.

Yes, Valeria was very much alive.

Yes, the cartel had her.

And yes, she was beautiful as that picture of her at the Marcello wedding had shown. Shockingly so. The image on the screen he had seen before now had not done the woman justice.

Tanned, golden skin. Pin-straight, black hair that fell to her mid-back. Tall, and womanly. Her soft features, accentuated with a touch of makeup, seemed more natural than dolled up. The dress she chose draped over her curves loosely, yet still allowed him an appreciation for her body.

None of which he had any right to notice. Nor should he.

"My wife, and daughter," Jorge said to them, although Valeria had not yet left the stairs with little Maria at her side. "Val is shy, so don't mind if she doesn't talk a lot. It's her nature."

Or, Chris wondered, could she not talk? That's what he was here to find out.

5.

"*Hermosa*, bring the *princesa* over for a proper hello to our new friends."

Valeria heard Jorge's call to her, but her attention was on someone far more important. Surely, he could wait two minutes. Maria attempted to pull the bow from her dark ponytail, and as much and Valeria sympathized with her daughter's annoyance, she was still quick to kneel and fix the ribbon. She gave her girl a smile and winked.

"Remember what I said?" she asked.

Maria sighed, her dark gaze darting to the side as two kids came out of the back of the mansion, their squeals chasing them down the steps. Valeria thought they were the children of Jorge's men—the ones privileged enough to dine with them during business, or otherwise. She couldn't talk to people on the payroll, unless it was Maria's nanny, and so she couldn't say for sure.

"Maria," Valeria murmured, letting her fingers twist into the ends of her daughter's soft curls. "What did I say this morning, huh?"

"To be good today. We must look pretty. *Be quiet.*"

God.

She hated this.

Those weren't things a child Maria's age should have to worry about at all. Valeria knew, however, if her child misbehaved that she wouldn't hear the end from Jorge. He'd given her more than enough warnings leading up to this dinner for the last week about what he expected from her, and Maria.

Sure, she could handle his moods, even if it was the last thing she wanted to do, but it wasn't fair for her daughter, either. Even if Jorge didn't shout and smack Maria around, she would still have to watch the asshole do it to her mother.

Valeria tried to avoid that.

"Mamá, can I go play with them?" Maria pointed at the kids running down the grassy pathway leading away from the pool. "Please?"

Frankly, Valeria couldn't find a reason to tell her daughter no. At least, playing with the kids would keep her out from beneath her father's feet for a while, or until dinner. It wasn't like the girl could find trouble when there happened to be a small army of guards all around the damn mansion to look after them.

Jorge had asked for her to bring Maria over, but what did it matter?

"Sure," Valeria told Maria. "Be kind and don't get your dress *too* dirty."

Maria grinned and swished the skirt of yellow dress like she had when her mother put it on her earlier. "I'll *try.*"

"That's my girl."

"Val!"

She tensed at Jorge's shout for her, gave Maria a quick kiss, and stood up when her daughter raced down the steps to chase after the other children. Air filled her lungs in a heavy inhale, the one extra second she needed to be ready to face her husband, and put on that fake smile he seemed to like so much for his guests.

Everything was fake here.

444

Nothing was true.

Settled enough in her heart that Valeria thought she might pretend to give a fuck about what Jorge wanted, she turned to see her husband still staring expectantly at her—although, with annoyance tugging his lips down at the edges. *Great.*

It wasn't Jorge that her attention turned to though. He was a background thought, never leaving and always a reminder for her to behave. Rather, it was the two men standing near Jorge, one ahead of him, and another behind him at the wet bar beside the pool.

A father and a son, maybe?

Valeria thought the older gentleman, and younger—but he had to be close to her age, at least—shared a lot of similar features. Their strong, square-cut jaws, brown, short-cropped hair, dark eyes, and high, defined cheekbones. The slight differences in the shapes of their faces didn't detract from the fact it was obvious they were family.

What had Jorge told her today?

Business meeting—new partners.

Right.

Valeria was hyperaware of the men's gazes locked on her as she came down the stairs and walked along the edge of the pool to approach them. She was careful in her heels not to step on any wet spot, lest she slip, and fall into the water. Wouldn't that be just perfect?

It was the man ahead of Jorge by a step—the younger of the two—that didn't drop Valeria's stare as she came closer. He was handsome, strikingly so with his piercing gaze, and rugged features that seemed carved from stone. He didn't smile, but he also didn't have to considering his lips naturally curved in such a way they pulled into the hint of a smirk, anyway. His form, fit under a tailored suit, rested confidently in his stance.

Valeria shook her head, turning her gaze away from the man that was still watching her with every step she took closer to him, her husband, and the other unknown gentleman. God knew she didn't need Jorge thinking she was staring a beat too long at another man even if said man *was* decent to stare at.

That was her first thought about him, too, which was strange. Looks were the last thing Valeria noticed about a man. His appearance only hid what was beneath the handsome package. A lesson she had, unfortunately, learned firsthand, and not one she cared to learn again.

"I wanted you to bring Maria over to say hello," Jorge said, nothing hiding his displeasure in the slightest once Valeria was close enough for him to speak. He reached for her, and while it killed her to put on this act for the newcomers, she allowed his arm to snake around her waist, and pull her into his side. Cigar smoke clung to the air, and it became worse when Jorge lifted the lit cigar in his other hand for a heady drag. "And now look at her."

Valeria's gaze searched for her girl, and she found her. "She's having fun with the other children, let her play. She's a child."

"It's good for children to play," the older gentleman said, "because it lets them burn out all that energy they can't seem to get rid of otherwise."

Jorge tipped his cigar in the man's direction and nodded. "You make a good point, Gian."

Gian.

Was that Italian?

She thought so, but the man had a strange accent. It had a hint of Italian, but also something else, too. Something as equally smooth, maybe. French?

Valeria couldn't be sure.

Gian chuckled. "Been a while since any of my boys were that young, however. Isn't that right, Chris?"

"It is, Papa."

So, she had been right.

Father and son.

Jorge's hand tightened on Valeria's waist, bringing her attention back to him. Heaven forbid her eyes weren't always on him, waiting for the next moment when he would snap his fingers, and demand something new.

"Valeria," he said, "meet my new business partners. Gian and Christopher—although, he likes Chris, they told me—Guzzi. From Canada."

Business partners.

Right.

The cartel had one business.

Jorge tipped his head toward her, saying to Gian, "And this is the wife I may have mentioned once or twice."

"Yes, Valeria, correct?"

She nodded. "That's me."

Gian smiled, but said nothing.

Jorge didn't notice, continuing with, "We had a rough patch for a while, but somehow, Valeria found her way home, didn't you, *hermosa?*"

Her heart thundered in her throat. Yeah, *she* found her way home. As though it had been her choice to come back to Mexico, and not like Jorge hunted her down as though she were an animal that deserved what it got. She wondered if her choosing to come home also meant watching Jorge's man point a rifle at her daughter's head, and calmly explaining that if she didn't go with them, they would kill Maria?

She swallowed those words, knowing damn well nothing good would come from her letting it slip out of her mouth. Instead, she took the safe route, even if every single part of her screamed to do the opposite.

So was her life, now.

"Yes, right where I belong," Valeria agreed.

All lies.

The younger man—Chris—had said nothing at all, and he didn't then, either. Gian chuckled as though he understood Jorge fine.

"You should go watch Maria while I discuss details here," Jorge told her.

Fine with me.

"Sure," Valeria replied.

He didn't let her go, so she didn't move. She understood what Jorge expected; she gave him a quick kiss on the corner of his mouth, swallowing back the bile that flooded her tongue, before giving the other two men a smile. One she had practiced time and time again in the mirror. That way, no one had a clue it was a fake.

"Very nice to meet both of you," Valeria said.

The men greeted her in kind, not that she cared for small talk, or whatever business they had come here to do. She still counted down the seconds when she could get away from her husband for the evening though. Jorge had that effect on people.

• • •

Tiptoeing out of the room Maria would use to sleep in for the night at her grandfather's mansion, Valeria carefully closed the door without making more noise that might wake her daughter up. She could stay upstairs for a bit—a few minutes more, safely—and Jorge would know nothing different, but she wasn't stupid.

He expected her to put their child to sleep after dinner and come right back down. He would send someone up after her, if he figured she was taking too long, and no one needed that problem.

Mostly, dinner had gone well. The Canadians kept conversation on everything *but* business, although Jorge hadn't seemed to mind indulging their chattiness, for once. She figured because he banked on being able to supply their territory in order to get out of the arrangement his father had made with the García cartel. If they wanted to talk about the sky, he would probably do it as long as it got him what he wanted, no doubt.

Valeria didn't care either way. She liked it when Maria didn't have to hear about all of that nonsense, anyway. Wasn't it bad enough that the girl had a front-row seat to her father being horrible against her mother, did she also need the cartel spelled out for her, too?

Maria wouldn't be young forever.

Eventually, she would understand.

Not now, though.

Valeria navigated the halls of the upstairs, walking down the grand spiral stairs where at the bottom, she listened to the echoing voices of the men inside the large sitting room. She edged closer to the doorway, but stayed hidden beyond view to peek inside.

With dinner over, business took its place.

"You expect to need that many kilos a *month*?" Jorge asked.

Gian stared at Chris. "*Oui?*"

"We can supply Canada-wide through our connections with the gangs, and other organizations. We've had the stronghold over most organized crime in Canada for … longer than I have been alive," Chris added.

"He isn't wrong," Gian added. "So yes, monthly."

"The smuggle runs will have to go in through several ports of entry," Jorge muttered, his gaze narrowing on the glass of liquor in his hand, "to avoid detection. We'll have that covered, but once it gets over the border, it's your problem."

"We can handle that."

"Now, on the *money* side of things."

Valeria tuned their conversation out. What did it matter? She concluded that anyone working with Jorge, or the cartel, was likely no fucking better than him at the end of the day.

Did they understand how the family built the cartel?

How they became so strong?

On the backs of the weak and the ignorant, breaking down a country's justice, legal, and political systems piece by piece until nothing was left but *corruption*. With the blood of innocents, spilled across crate after crate of every shipment of cocaine that crossed the borders.

There was nothing good here.

Even thinking these Canadians couldn't be any better or worse than her husband and his family, her gaze still drifted to the younger of the two.

Chris.

She didn't understand why, but she enjoyed looking at him, even if she had no business doing it, and that would be a dangerous game for her to play. He was just another *good-looking* man, nothing special, right? He'd barely spoken two words to her, so she didn't need to be staring at him, not like she might want to know more *about* him. She didn't get curious about men, not when she had neither the time, the give a damn, nor the ability to do something with it.

Valeria was going crazy.

Yet, as she stared across the room from her hidden position in the shadows of the doorway, it seemed Chris recognized someone was looking at him. His attention left the conversation, and his gaze drifted upward, finding the spot where Valeria hid, watching him and the others. She stiffened, her heart picking up pace with its beats, as his stare lingered her way. A heat danced over her skin when those thin lips of his twitched before curving into a sensual smile.

Did he see her?

"Careful," a soft voice said behind her.

Valeria jerked in her heels. "Jesus, Abril. Make a noise."

Her sister-in-law laughed under her breath, a single dark eyebrow lifting in what seemed like a challenge. "Like you're doing?"

"Well ..."

She had a point.

Abril stepped in beside Valeria in the shadows but didn't glance her way. Instead, she stared across the room, looking at the men, and specifically, the one man who still had his attention focused in their direction.

"Don't let Jorge see you staring at one of his new friends," Abril said under her breath, "lest he get in his feelings about it, and wonder if something is going on, *sí?*"

"What might go on?"

"Nothing. He only needs to think there is. We both know what happens then, Val."

Right.

Valeria stepped back from the entryway, needing five minutes to breathe alone, and far away from her confusion. "Tell Jorge I wanted to take a walk outside—it's hot in here, and I'm not feeling well."

She might as well take the chance to get away even if her husband would come looking for her soon enough. He always did; it was one thing she counted on with

Jorge although she wished he would find someone else to focus his attention on.

Well, he did that, too.

Any woman pretty enough he wanted to stick his dick in, he did exactly that. Not that Valeria complained. If he fucked someone else, then he wasn't raping her night after night.

Win some, lose some.

"Tell him for me, if he asks," she said again.

Abril nodded. "Sure."

• • •

Valeria sensed the presence join her on the back stairs of the mansion before he even said a word. She hadn't heard him open the door, or his steps as he came to stand next to her while she stared up at the stars dotting the inky sky, but she felt him.

Somehow.

"Christopher," she said, not *unkindly*.

"I prefer Chris," he returned.

Valeria did her best to keep her gaze on the sky overhead, and not the handsome man next to her. She wasn't sure why he had come out here. Had he seen her in the shadows and followed her?

If so, what did that mean?

Nothing decent, she imagined. Her heart stuttered at the idea, and she liked it too much. *Not good.*

"Care to take a walk?" he asked.

Valeria looked at him then, surprised at his offer. Earlier, when they met, and even at dinner, she hadn't spoken more than a few careful sentences to him. It wouldn't be enough for him to assume they were friendly, or otherwise. And yet, he smiled at her as though he already had her answer.

"As long as it's where the guards can see," she finally replied.

Chris nodded, peering around to survey the grounds where they could be seen. His gaze lingered on the walkway around the pool for a second, and then two. "Sure. How about around the pool?"

Was that a walk, then?

What did it matter?

"Sure," she said.

Chris remained quiet as they strolled down the pathway and stayed alongside the pool. Valeria noticed the way he continued to glance towards the calm water at the surface, but not in a way that said he cared for the pool.

"Swimming isn't your thing?" she dared to ask.

His head snapped in her direction. "Pardon?"

"You stare at the water like it might bite you."

She didn't miss the way his throat jumped at her statement, or how his Adam's apple bobbed reflexively.

"I almost drowned as a child," he murmured, his tone terse, "and it's followed me throughout my life. Water makes me nervous, that's all. Nonsensical, considering I can swim, but I swear I can taste the water in my lungs when I'm close enough."

Huh.

She wouldn't have guessed that.

"I'm sorry that happened," she whispered.

Chris shrugged and smiled again. "A long time ago, I suppose."

And yet, she bet it seemed like yesterday to him. Because he trusted her with the truth, Valeria would never breathe a word about it to anyone else.

Everyone needed their secrets, no?

That little detail about Chris made Valeria take a second glance at him, not that she needed to be doing that at all. Still, it made him seem different to her and almost easier to ignore the fact he was here to do business with her husband.

Their conversation during the walk around the pool stayed on safe topics, and she still looked for the guards to make sure *they* kept an eye on her. That way, later when Jorge no doubt asked where she left to, he would confirm nothing nefarious had been going on when his back was turned.

The paranoid *bastard.*

Although, Chris kept a distance between them. He didn't get too close to Valeria throughout their stroll, and his hands remained clasped at his back while he did his best to ignore the pool beside them.

"Do you like it here?" he asked.

Random, she thought.

"What do you mean?"

Chris shrugged under the nice fit of his suit jacket. "Here, *Mexico.* Being the wife of a cartel leader, tucked away from the rest of the world, you know? All these beautiful things surrounding you, and you must have status in your position. Do you like it?"

Not at all.

Not one fucking bit.

Valeria asked for none of those things, and instead, they forced it upon her regardless if she wanted them. When she made it clear, this was not the life for her, she faced the wrath of a man she didn't think was worthy enough to kiss her shoes.

What choice did she have, though?

"People who live in gilded cages," Valeria said, tone soft, "often forget that's where they are after a while. Or we learn we need to forget it to survive."

Chris looked her way, but she was already staring ahead at the man who had come out to stand on the back steps. Like when Chris had joined her on the steps earlier, she sensed his presence the same way she did Jorge's now. Except his had been fine, and her husband's was not.

Jorge looked her way, his face a mask of calm, and his arms folded over his broad, silk-covered chest. He said nothing, but she saw the tilt of his head, a silent demand for her to come his way, and not to say a thing about it. He was famous for his silent commands, and she had learned to fear those more than his outbursts. It was when he was quiet she didn't know what might come next.

"Thank you for the walk," Valeria told Chris, "but I think this is the end for me tonight."

Chris noticed Jorge then, too. "Thank you for indulging me."

"Of course."

As much as Val wanted to look over her shoulder as she left Chris behind to head for Jorge on the steps, she didn't. Jorge hadn't once looked away from her, after all. While he appeared fine outside, she doubted that he was on the inside.

"Head inside," he told her as she climbed the stairs, "and stay there for the evening, Val."

"I only needed a breather."

She attempted to move past him, but his arm struck out fast, and he caught her at the elbow. To anyone else, she was sure his hand on her body would appear innocent from afar, but his fingers dug in hard, leaving marks behind. Tomorrow, she would have to wear something with longer sleeves to hide the bruises he was creating on her body, not that it was anything new. She had become good at hiding things Jorge didn't want the rest of the surrounding people to see.

Valeria swallowed hard, knowing better than to tell him to let her go. He would only hurt her worse later. "Do you want me to go inside, or not?"

"*Just* a breather?"

His gaze burned into hers, searching for the lie.

He would find none.

Not yet, anyway.

"Just a breather," she echoed. "The house was getting stuffy."

Jorge let her go. "Head inside, as I told you."

Like she had a choice?

Valeria went.

6.

"Papa."

Chris slid in beside his father where Gian seemed comfortable to stand next to a window overlooking the garden on the north side of the property. Quite a large garden, too, and one his mother would appreciate, had she been here to see it.

"Chris," Gian replied in kind.

"Did they leave you on your own?"

Gian raised his brows, and lifted the drink in his hand for a sip. "I wandered off, but no one bothered to follow me. I figured something else must have taken their attention for a time."

Possibly.

Or, at least Jorge's attention.

"I approached her outside," Chris said, lowering his tone to above a murmur. If he believed Jorge to be paranoid, then even if they assumed they were alone, they likely were not. "We took a walk around the pool."

Gian cleared his throat. "Do you think that's smart at this moment?"

"We have to know, don't we?"

"Know what?"

"Whether this is where she wants to be," Chris said, shrugging. "I know all signs point to her being taken by force, given what we know, but there was still a possibility that she wanted to be here with him."

"Was," his father noted. "Past tense."

Right.

"She's controlled here, isn't she?"

"To be fair, they all are," Gian replied. "Fear is the first tactic a cartel uses to keep people in line, even their own."

"Sure, but so much so that to take a short walk with me, she asked that we stay in view of the guards?"

"Some women don't want even a suggestion of impropriety, Chris."

His father wasn't wrong, and he knew Gian was playing the devil's advocate for him right now. Gian was of the mindset that Valeria didn't want to be here, and there was nothing to figure out. Chris wasn't as simple, and needed to be one-hundred percent sure before he started this plan of theirs, and did something crazy.

"I asked her if she liked it here," Chris added, "and while her response was … meant to distract me, I still heard what she didn't say."

"Hmm. What, then?"

"The husband came out. She went back in the house."

Chris didn't mention how, while it may have seemed like he was staring at the sky when Valeria joined Jorge on the steps earlier, he had been keeping one eye on them. He saw it all—the way Jorge grabbed her, like she was property to him, and even the flash of fear in Valeria's face before she slipped inside the house.

"Tell me," Gian said, turning to face Chris, but keeping his head tilted down, "why, even with all the details we had on this situation, that you thought the woman might be here willingly, son."

That seemed obvious enough, didn't it?

"I don't pretend to understand the complexities of other people's relationships," Chris replied, "and if people think she would be the first woman to fall in love with her captor, then they would be wrong. I wanted to be *sure*."

Gian sighed, nodding. "And you're convinced now?"

"Undoubtedly. She's not here because she wants to be."

Which meant, it was time for them to get to work. Or rather, for Chris to get to work. He needed to get his father out of this country, and work out a plan to get Valeria, and little Maria, out of here, too.

Without Jorge coming after them.

That would be the hardest part.

Jorge chased after Valeria once—hunted her down like a dog. He took years to find her hiding out in New York, but patience and perseverance paid off. That's what would happen the next time, too. Chris wanted to make sure that wasn't a possibility for the man when it was all said and done.

So, what did that mean?

Someone would have to die, likely.

It was the approach of footsteps that had Gian and Chris turning to see who found them away from the rest of people at the mansion. Samuel, the youngest Lòpez son, came to stand at the end of the hallway, but didn't come closer to intrude on their space. Out of the two brothers, Chris preferred this one.

In the single day they had been in the Lòpezs' presence, Samuel seemed like the easier, more rational of the two that he would need to deal with. Appearances were also deceiving, and Chris wasn't stupid enough to trust the man, either. He would also keep that in mind.

"Yes?" Gian asked him.

Samuel smiled. "Jorge made your accommodations for the night at a hotel in the city."

"Thank him for me."

"Of course. Jorge would like to complete any last details—he hears you want to head out tomorrow, Gian, and won't have time to do it before you leave. So, if we could do that soon, then we can end this night on a good note."

"Right, well, we'll be out in a moment."

The man gave them a nod before he turned, and left them in private once again. Chris turned to his father, giving him a look.

"What?" Gian asked.

"What are these last *details*?"

His father chuckled. "A contract, is all."

Ah, yeah.

Because even criminals took their contracts seriously. It was something Chris had never understood because despite the honor they toted in their oath to Cosa Nostra, there was little amongst the men in the underworld of crime.

"What will happen with that contract once this is over, and we've fucked them around?"

Gian grinned, and tipped his glass up to swallow the last of his drink before sitting it down with a loud clink to the nearby stand. "Deal with that when we come to it, *fils.*"

That sounded easy.

Chris doubted it would be.

• • •

Standing next to his father, just beyond the iron wrought gate that had given them entrance to the Lòpez mansion, Chris tried not to be unnerved by the amount of guards standing around. Sure, he had seen the men over the course of the day, and even when they first arrived, but he didn't remember there being *so many*.

Or, perhaps more came out to play when nighttime fell.

Not that it mattered.

He noticed them now.

A good ten guards stood on the stone wall, and some behind Chris and Gian on the sidewalk as they waited for the car Jorge had sent for them. They said nothing and given neither of the Lòpez brothers had come out to wait with them while they left, it put Chris on edge.

He wondered if that was the point.

To his benefit, Chris did his best to ignore the guards, and instead, stared up at the inky sky overhead. There was nothing like looking at the sky when you were in a country that wasn't your own. He swore it allowed a person a different view—this time was no different for him, watching the stars streak the sky with their brilliance against a dark backdrop.

If anything, that settled him.

But not by much.

Gian checked his phone, unbothered about their current circumstances. "Your mother has been messaging me all day."

"Worried, I bet."

"No, she wanted me to bring her back a special treat she likes here. I'll grab it before I head for the jet tomorrow morning."

Chris rolled his eyes.

Typical.

His father spoiled his wife to the ends of the earth and back. All his mother had to do was speak, and she would have whatever she wanted in the blink of an eye. No questions asked. Gian had made sure his sons understood that nothing less was acceptable for their mother, and he expected them to treat their future wives, or *spouses*, in his twin's case, with the same respect.

A pair of headlights flashed at the end of the street, and a black car crawled to them. The guards all around them shifted their positions, letting Chris know the vehicle was theirs. Once the town car stopped at the curb, Chris didn't bother to wait for the driver to get out and open his father's door for him.

Chris did it for Gian.

"Ah, good, I didn't miss the two of you leaving," came a voice from behind.

Chris kept one hand on the back passenger door, ready to close his father inside the vehicle should he need to, as he turned to greet the approaching man. Jorge slipped through the slight opening in the gate, his smile friendly as he nodded to

Gian in the car.

"I look forward to working with you, *amigo*," Jorge said.

Gian replied in kind. "And you, as well."

Jorge came close enough to clap a hand on Chris's shoulder, grabbing tightly when he added, "And I am sure your son here can take care of all the details you need, but I will keep you informed in the meantime."

"*Perfetto.*"

"Have a good night, Gian, and a safe flight tomorrow."

"Thank you," his father replied.

Gian gave Chris a glance, and so, he closed his father inside the vehicle. Jorge had let go of Chris's shoulder, but when he moved to round the vehicle and get in his side, the man blocked his path.

Jorge's smile dissipated. In its place rested a blank mask, and cold eyes. He stared Chris down like he meant for it to be intimidating, but it was merely annoying. Not that he showed it.

"Yes?" Chris asked. "Is there something I can do for you?"

Jorge's lips quirked up at the edges.

A *hint* of a smile.

It wasn't kind, though.

No, it kind of felt threatening.

"There is," Jorge said.

"Do tell."

Chris didn't wonder *what* people saw in Jorge Lòpez. He didn't assume what the man had done, or was capable of, that made people terrified of him. Hell, his family had control of a good thirty percent of Mexico—from small businesses, to entire towns, and even the goddamn government.

No one became *that* powerful by being nice or playing fair. This man had spilled a lot of blood to get here and would spill as much as he needed to get whatever he still wanted to go.

That, primarily, was what made Jorge more dangerous than people could understand. His unstable mindset, his uncaring attitude, and his willingness to be irrational to get what he wanted made him tricky to deal with. Chris needed to consider all those things on this job, or it would be his life that ended before his time was up.

Chris understood fine and well why he should be afraid of this man, and yet, he still figured … Jorge Lòpez was just a man. Another man in this criminal world of theirs with a big fucking ego, and a gun to match it. And like all men who assumed they couldn't be beat; it only took the right man coming up against him to get it done.

Chris would be that man.

Just not tonight.

"Well?" Chris asked when Jorge stayed silent.

"I tried to find the right way to phrase this, but perhaps being blunt is the better option, *sí?*"

"I prefer a man who is frank rather than one that hides his issues or intentions behind the guise of politeness."

Jorge nodded. "I will remember that, then."

"And?"

Because he didn't think this man had approached him for *that* exchange, to be honest. He wasn't disappointed.

"For future reference, Christopher, if I catch you with my wife where the guards cannot see you, I will cut off your hands, and have them delivered to your mother in a box lined with satin. I hope I have made myself clear."

Well, okay.

He always had appreciated a good threat, even if it was leveled on him. Maybe there was a broken part of him, but he always took them as challenges. Undoubtedly, his twin would tell him to be careful here, to be mindful of where he stepped with the man in front of him. His twin wouldn't be wrong, either.

"That so?" Chris asked.

"It is."

"Hmm."

Jorge arched a brow. "Are we *clear*?"

Chris's jaw tightened.

Jorge never looked away.

"Crystal clear," Chris murmured.

"Perfect. Have a good night, and I look forward to working with you in the coming weeks when we get things settled for you to come in again. Next time we meet, I suspect it'll be at the ranch, although most of us call it the compound."

Yes, and he looked forward to that.

Not that Chris said it out loud.

"Of course."

All at once, Jorge stepped back from Chris, that kind—but *fake*—smile firmly back in place as he gestured at the car. "Safe travels to the hotel, *amigo*."

Friend.

Right.

They wouldn't ever be friends.

Chris didn't reply, simply nodded to the man, and turned his back to him. The one and only time he would ever put his back to Jorge, all things considered. Rounding the car to get in the back with his father, he looked over the roof of the vehicle in just enough time to see Jorge head back through the gate.

He swallowed hard, realizing something.

Jorge would go to Valeria.

Chris could leave, but she could not. Her torment continued. What would happen to her tonight? Had his little trick of taking her on a walk caused her more pain?

The idea made his heart ache.

Fuck.

Feelings didn't work well in business, or a job. It would be hard to turn off. He was human, after all.

So was she.

Yanking open the back passenger door, Chris climbed in the vehicle, and before he had even buckled up, tires squealed against the pavement. Next to him, his father looked his way.

"And what's that about?" Gian asked.

"A pissing contest—what else?"

Gian made a noise under his breath. "If you think someone else might be better to do this job, then I am sure we can come up with a solution to make it happen, son."

"No, I'll do it."

That, he understood for sure.

Not even a question.

At all.

7.

"Maria is still asleep, then?"

Valeria had expected no one else to be in the kitchen when she walked in, but at least it was just Samuel. He wasn't as difficult to deal with as Jorge, but she also didn't feel like she could trust him very much.

"She is—thought I should check because it's been a long night," she said.

Her brother-in-law nodded and lifted a bottle of wine. "A drink?"

"Sure."

Not that she would say it, but that was why she had come down here. Once the late dinner, and party after, died down, the guests had left, and the servants went to their quarters for the night, Jorge disappeared, too. Valeria wasn't sure where her husband went, but while she had the chance, she planned on taking advantage.

Or rather, five minutes alone.

Soon, Jorge would be back.

That was a guarantee.

Samuel grabbed two long-stemmed glasses from the cupboard and made quick work of uncorking the bottle of wine. Once he had the wine poured through a decanter he'd found under the kitchen island, he held a glass out for her to take.

"Here, *chica*."

Valeria took the drink, and sipped, letting the heady flavors soak her palate. "Thanks."

Samuel didn't invite her for more conversation as he drank his wine, but Valeria didn't mind, either. She had other things to worry about, and silence was better than the alternative for these men.

She was almost through her glass, enjoying the silence of the large mansion, when the hair on the back of her neck stood on end. It wasn't a good sensation, not when dread accompanied it, climbing up her spine with punishing steps.

That was how she knew Jorge was behind her.

Samuel confirmed it by looking over her shoulder and nodding at someone. His words only added to what she knew when he said, "Brother."

"The Canadians left."

"Hmm."

"The deal is good, Samuel," Jorge said, his voice coming closer to Valeria. She did her best to stay put, drink her wine, and hopefully, her husband would leave her alone for the night. Not that it had ever worked for her in the past, but she wasn't about to give up hope just yet. "And once it's done, we won't need the fucking Garcías for shit."

"And then what happens when the Garcías realize we fucked them over?"

"You're asking pointless questions."

"Or is it you don't have the answers?"

The pregnant, loaded silence stretched on in the kitchen, making Valeria wish she was anywhere but there. It was rare for Samuel and Jorge to disagree about things, but especially with the cartel. When they did, however, it rarely ended well.

She did not want to be the idiot in the middle.

"Who is running this operation?" Jorge asked.

He was right behind Valeria, now. She didn't need to turn around to *feel* the heat of his body too close to hers, or the way it made her sick just from proximity alone.

So was her life.

"Papá," Samuel replied.

"Wrong answer, brother."

Samuel sighed. "Jorge—"

"He oversees *details*," Jorge spat. "Says yes or no, or makes demands. He isn't on the front lines. He isn't making the *money*. I do all of that, and because this is the right choice, whether he likes it, then it is what we will do. The Canadian deal will get rid of our García issue, or at the least, it will negate the problem altogether. It's a win-win."

"Right," Samuel replied, "a win-win."

Satisfied with his brother conceding to his point, Jorge turned his attention on Valeria by stroking the back of her neck where she had pushed her hair over her right shoulder. It was a light graze of his fingertips along the ridge of her spine, almost daring to dip below the neckline of her dress. Nothing *violent*. Certainly not this man's usual motives, and yet, it still burned.

She didn't want his touch.

"Val," Jorge murmured.

"Hmm?"

"Would you care to tell me what happened earlier with that man?"

She closed her eyes. Honestly, she had been waiting for this, but Jorge had incredible patience at times. Hadn't six years of him chasing her taught her anything at all?

Apparently, not.

"I don't understand what you mean," she said, choosing her words carefully.

Again, his fingers drifted over her neck, along the line of her shoulder, and then he tucked in a few strands of her hair that had fallen out of place. He stepped in a little closer to her back, his mouth coming down to press a soft kiss to the side of her throat before he murmured, "You were outside *alone* with him."

The lump came back in her throat.

Across the island, Samuel turned his gaze away from them. None of Jorge's family ever cared to indulge his nonsense, but especially not with Valeria. She suspected because, if they did, they wouldn't like what happened after.

Jorge and his lessons were infamous.

"I took a moment to breathe on the steps," she said, keeping her tone level to *not* poke the monster. "He came out after and asked if I wouldn't mind taking a walk around the pool. I didn't want to be rude, and the guards watched."

She figured that was important to point out to him. The guards *had* been watching—Valeria made sure. She understood how to play this game with her husband, and she was quick enough on her feet to make sure she didn't step in any trouble with him. At least, none that would leave her with permanent damage.

Some other things, however, were unavoidable.

Jorge proved that time and time again.

Against her jaw, his lips curved into a sneer before he *bit* her. Not an easy bite—not even *playful*. His teeth cut into her skin, and she sucked in a sharp breath when his hand came up to grab the back of her neck with a rough grasp.

"And for that," he muttered against her jawline, "you are *lucky*. If not for the guards, we would have been having a very different discussion."

"I did nothing wr—"

"And you're also a lying whore, Val. You already got out of my hands once, but I promise it won't happen again. I will have you put in a shipping container and sent to the highest bidder who will keep you under lock and key until they tire of *fucking* you before you'll ever get away from me again. Do you understand me?"

She squeezed her eyes shut.

Samuel cleared his throat. "Excuse me."

Valeria didn't open her eyes again until she heard the footsteps recede from the kitchen and fade away down the hall. She might have been mad that Samuel left her alone with Jorge when, his intentions were bad, but why bother?

No one else would save her here.

She had to do that alone.

Somehow.

Jorge's hand tightened on Valeria's neck, and without a word, he spun her around so the two faced one another. He barricaded her against the island, his one hand sliding around to grip the front of her throat while his other played with the hem of her dress, twisting it between his fingers like he considered ripping it off her.

It wouldn't be the first time.

"Did you enjoy coming into the city again?" he asked.

No.

Because she was with him.

She lied. "I did."

"See, if you behaved yourself more, and showed an effort to care about this marriage of ours, and what I want from you, I might let you have more freedom."

No, he wouldn't.

Whether it was one of his vacation homes, the ranch, or the city … if she had to be with him, then it was all the same fucking prison to her.

She didn't have to say anything to Jorge because he leaned in close, and pressed a kiss that tasted like aged bourbon against her lips. His sneer deepened into a smirk that promised she would not like what happened next.

"Get upstairs," he uttered, "and make sure you're naked when I join you."

• • •

"Are you going to tell me where we're going now?"

Next to her in the backseat of the Cadillac, Jorge kept his gaze locked on the window. That didn't bother Valeria as much, seeing as how his attention focused elsewhere. What bothered her was the fact she had to dress up, leave her daughter at the ranch, and without a reason.

"Does it matter? A night out is good for you, Val."

"Curiosity, is all."

"Women are better when they're not curious," he returned, "because you're more interesting to look at that way, and less problematic."

Perfect.

Not that it helped to sedate her worries. Usually, when Jorge took her out, he made her aware of what to expect, and what he expected from her. Because those were two different things.

"It's a dinner," Jorge muttered to her left, "that's all. I thought the Canadian might like to sit down with me before he arrives at the ranch in a few days. His father headed back to his own country. He has details to share about the deal we hadn't hammered out."

Chris?

Huh.

She tried not to show how that only made her *more* curious. She didn't need to admit that thoughts about Chris Guzzi lingered in her mind more than they should since their first meeting. His question to her during that walk—*did she like it here?*—played on repeat in the back of her mind. Alongside the image of his face, that handsome profile she had no business admiring.

He didn't have to care about her, or ask about her welfare, so to speak. And yet he had, which made her wonder about him.

All dangerous things.

"So, why am I here?" she asked.

Jorge passed her a cold, dismissive glance. "Because he asked for you to come along. Thought I might enjoy bringing you. I didn't want to seem rude. Don't disappoint me tonight and do something I'll deal with later. Understand?"

Valeria nodded.

"I got it."

Better than he understood.

The rest of the drive passed in silence. That continued even after they had parked, and the driver opened their doors for them to exit the vehicle. Her husband only spoke to tell her to *smile* before they entered the traditionally decorated restaurant, one she hadn't visited before. It wasn't a business owned or controlled by her husband or one of his men, considering the woman working the front desk said they had to wait until their guest wanted them at his table.

"This *shit*," Jorge uttered under his breath. "Anywhere else would have been suitable."

Or, she thought, *he's showing you that you don't have a stronghold everywhere.*

Once they entered the back of the restaurant where Chris waited, standing next to a table spread out with a buffet of food already prepped to eat on gold-plated dishes, Jorge still hadn't relaxed.

"Guzzi," he said, gruffly.

Chris smiled, his gaze darting to Valeria even as he said, "Jorge, thank you for indulging me tonight."

"Better make it worth it, that's all I have to say. Is the food here any good? I don't trust people I am not paying to make me anything I have to put inside my mouth."

"It's a buffet. We're all eating from the same plates. A true sign of friendship, yes? And trust."

Smart again.

Valeria shouldn't notice those things.

Or the way Christopher looked in his suit.

Still, she did.

Maybe a part of her recognized ... this man would be a problem for her. It didn't matter he looked at her like he was looking into her soul, searching for something she was keeping well hidden. Or that she liked his handsome features, and the way his form filled out the very expensive Armani he wore.

There was something else ...

And she liked it.

"Fine," Jorge muttered. "Let's sit, and we'll—"

A sharp *Boss* from behind them had Jorge turning before he approached the table to pull out a chair for himself, likely leaving her to fend for herself.

"What?" Jorge asked the man who kept a safe distance.

The section they were dining in had no other patrons.

A private area?

What strings had Chris pulled?

"Your father is on the phone."

Jorge grunted and waved a hand. "I will call him back."

"He's adamant that—"

"*Fine.*" Jorge gave Chris a nod, saying, "I will be a few minutes. I'm sure you can entertain yourself without me." He eyed the platters on the table, adding, "Begin eating without me, hmm? We eat, and then we do business."

"Right," Chris agreed. "No worries."

Jorge pivoted on his heel, unbothered with leaving Valeria there to fend for herself. She was stunned, however, when Chris was quick to come around to her side of the table, and the first thing he did was grab a chair to pull out.

For her.

This close, she smelled the distinct aroma of his cologne. It fit his personality, she thought. Understated, but with distinct notes. Complex. Like him.

Valeria ignored the heat in her gut, never mind the way her heart raced when his hand came to rest on her waist when his dark tenor urged her to, "Sit."

Lord.

Definitely a problem.

One she didn't expect to have.

She held onto the clutch in her hands tighter as she took the seat he offered, but didn't breathe any easier when his hand left her side. In fact, she wished for it to come back. "Thank you."

"Never thank a man for being a gentleman," he said, rounding the table to take his own seat, "because then they seem to think every kind act deserves a reward, hmm? It's better not to teach men that behaving means getting something in return."

Valeria stared across the table, unsure of what to say. Chris stared back, a sensual smile curving his lips. Finally, her brain worked.

"Why did you ask him to bring me here tonight?"

Chris shrugged. "Because I find you fascinating, and he's *slightly* more interesting when you're near. Also, it might keep him in line."

"Good luck with that. Jorge is … uncontainable."

To say the least.

"Well, he has to behave a little, if he wants my father's business. I thought I should remind him of that before I arrive at the ranch. And you, well, you can enjoy the meal. I paid a lot for this evening, but if you smile even once, it'll be worth it."

Valeria did just that.

Smile.

Chris winked back.

Damn.

• • •

Maria bounced at her mother's side, tugging on Valeria's hand with her excitement. "Can I ride Butter?"

Valeria smiled down at her girl. "Of course."

Butter, somehow, turned from a rowdy colt into a *very* tame riding horse. If there was one thing that had come out of Valeria being dragged back to this hell, it was the fact she put her daughter on a horse, and Maria took right to it like a fish to water. She *loved* the horses, but especially Butter.

"Come on, we have to tack them up," Valeria said, "and I bet they sense someone is coming to take them out for a ride, so they're as excited as you are."

Maria pumped a fist into the air, and Valeria let go of her daughter's hand. The girl darted down the steps, and headed for the large row of stables to the west of their home at the compound. It wasn't like she had to worry about someone taking her daughter here, considering how well-protected the family ranch was with all the guards, only one proper road leading in or out, and all the desolate land and cliffs surrounding them.

Her child wasn't going anywhere here.

Valeria followed behind Maria, but at a much slower speed. She passed the house that belonged to Abril, and Samuel. The siblings shared their one-level bungalow on the ranch until, according to Jorge, one of the two married and they moved off the property. Knowing how things were going, she suspected it would be Abril to leave first.

And she would miss her.

Jorge, having already left their two-level ranch home earlier that morning, was … somewhere. Between the three other small homes that the guards used to sleep, and do their business, or the many barns further out that served as makeshift warehouses when drugs needed to be stored before being smuggled out of the country.

Knowing he could be anywhere around kept Valeria on her best behavior, because not only were guards likely watching her, but her husband might be, too. Sure, she preferred being at the ranch compound rather than out in public with her husband, but that was only because here, she let her masks slip.

A little.

Not too much though.

Privacy meant a lot.

Once she had entered the stables, Valeria found Maria already standing on a stool, and leaning over the gate to feed Butter a small, thin slice of apple from the pail they used as treats. She smiled at her mother while Valeria got to work on pulling down the horse gear from the walls.

Since they were already dressed and ready to go in their riding boots, she only needed to find Maria's helmet, and her own. Then, they would get the horses tacked up, and the two of them could spend their morning *away* from the ranch.

Or as far as was safely possible.

Valeria turned the corner at the back of the stables where all the helmets sat on a shelf, and came to a full stop at the sight of Jorge leaning in the rear doorway. "Oh."

He smiled. "Going on a ride?"

"She asked after breakfast. You weren't there to—"

"I'll take her later," he said.

Valeria blinked. "What?"

Jorge shrugged. "If she wants to go on a ride, then I will take her later."

Not that Valeria wanted to point it out, but Jorge *hated* the horses. He didn't like riding, and he only kept the stables at the ranch full of horses because it kept up the appearance, and Abril would throw an unholy fit if someone took away her horses. He didn't keep the beautiful beasts because he ever took care of them or liked to ride the way the rest of them did.

"Do you want to explain to her that she can't go out when I told her she could?" Valeria asked.

"I can and will, yes. You wanted a ride, too?"

"I like riding in the mornings."

That wasn't news to him.

Riding was the one thing Jorge allowed Valeria even though it had been the way she escaped all those years ago. None of them had ever figured that out. They assumed someone smuggled her out of the ranch, likely in a vehicle. They killed a handful of guards for their troubles in an effort to figure it out.

Because her husband didn't know the truth, he never questioned allowing her to get on a horse, and go. Sometimes, she had to take someone with her, if she planned to go to the cliffs, or further out into the desolate land surrounding the ranch.

She didn't mind that.

They stayed far behind.

"You can go out," Jorge said, "but find someone to take with you. As for Maria, she can stay with me."

Anger flooded Valeria.

"Why?"

"Pardon?"

"Why can't she come with me for a ride like she does every other day?"

Jorge lifted his brow and smirked in that arrogant way again. "Because I said so. You forget occasionally, Val, that you have no control or say here. *I do.* And so, if I don't want my daughter going off with you on the horses, then she won't. Not to mention, if I want to make sure you come back, what better way to do that then to make sure you have a good damn reason to return, hmm?"

Fuck him.

She hated this man.

God knew she had a whole list of reasons to despise him. From his treatment of her, the abuse, how he enjoyed taking from her body when she didn't willingly give it to him, and *more* ... so much fucking more.

And yet, she hated him the most for this reason right here. Because he used their child as a way to manipulate Valeria and keep her in line.

"I won't go on a ride, then," Valeria said, "I wanted to go with her."

It might have been childish, but if she could find one way to tell Jorge to go fuck himself, then she would do that.

Her husband clicked his tongue. "No, you will go out on your ride. And you will go alone while she watches you go."

Ah.

Valeria got it, then.

It wasn't just about controlling her, but Maria, too. This way, he could make sure his daughter saw her mother leave her behind, make a promise, and not keep it ... because that's what he did.

That's what monsters did.

"Fine," Valeria murmured, "I'll take a ride."

"Have fun."

• • •

The first thing Valeria noticed when she arrived back at the stables after a quick ride to the cliffs—Jorge didn't say how long she had to stay out, after all—was the line of her husband's men walking the road as though they were meeting someone.

Maybe they were.

No one entered the gate before going through the guards.

The second thing Valeria noticed was that despite Jorge saying he would keep Maria with him, her daughter wasn't anywhere to be seen as she steered the horse toward the stables. She tried to keep the panic at a manageable level, but it was hard.

Jorge's threats lingered ...

She didn't doubt that, if needed, he would take her daughter away, and there would be nothing she could do about it. It's why she shut her mouth, behaved, and did as Jorge told her to do.

Who would protect Maria?

It had to be her.

Even if she sacrificed to do it.

The panic didn't last for too long, however. She had just steered the horse to the stable's entrance when across the ranch, the front door of their home flew open, and little Maria came flying down the steps, running in her mother's direction.

It made Val smile.

Fuck Jorge.

He thought he could control the amount of love her daughter had for her by pitting the two against each other, but there was a lot he didn't know about Maria.

And even her, in a way. He thought he was aware of everything about Valeria, but she kept a lot to herself.

Like her daughter.

Next to her friend, Haven, the only person Maria had for the last few years *was* her mother. It was Valeria who taught her to speak, to read, and to sing; *her* who spent long nights holding her child when she was sick.

She loved her *unconditionally*.

And no matter what Jorge tried to do, he couldn't erase those memories for Maria. Instead, every single time he raised his hand to strike the girl's mother, he was simply adding to the reasons she distrusted and disliked him.

He would have to figure that out on his own time, though. Valeria didn't plan to help him out in that regard.

"Mamá!" Maria shouted, still coming her way.

Valeria's smile dropped when a woman stepped out of the house. Maria was already halfway across the property. The *nanny*—Carla Nunez. Or, a nanny was what Jorge liked to call the woman he kept around to make sure his bed was warm with a variety when he felt the need to change scenery from raping Valeria.

According to Abril, Carla—a year younger than Valeria in age—had come around after Valeria took off years ago and had stuck around. Now, Jorge used the woman to keep an eye on Maria, and her, too. She took great satisfaction in refusing to allow Valeria choices regarding her daughter, and more.

On the ranch, Carla was always nearby.

It drove her crazy.

The woman was a rat, reporting back on her behavior, and the things she did with her daughter. Little was private when someone was always waiting to listen in, and that left her unsettled.

Valeria jumped down from the horse, grabbing the reins to steer the animal into the stables while Maria was still running to catch up with her mom. Abril came out of the stable entrance with leather gloves in one hand, and her riding boots already on.

"I would have waited for you," Valeria told her, "had I known you were going out."

Abril shrugged. "I wasn't going to, but then I heard we'll have a visitor, and I don't feel like being nice with Jorge while he plays with his friends."

"What?"

"The Canadians are back," Abril explained. "Or the one is—the younger one." *Chris.*

It had been a week since that first meeting, and a few days since the dinner, and Valeria almost forgot about him. Well, that was a lie. She couldn't forget the devastatingly handsome man who seemed far too interested in her, but she knew it would be better for her if she did. So, she put him out of her mind.

"He'll be staying a while," Abril added, "because according to Samuel, they want to know how *everything* will go down for this deal."

"Huh."

"Mamá," Maria huffed, out of breath as she came to a stop next to the horse Valeria had taken out, "was the water pretty today?"

Instantly, Valeria dropped to her knees. "It was. I'm sorry Papá said you couldn't come. Later, okay?"

"What?" Abril asked.

"It's nothing," Valeria was quick to say, seeing that Carla was fast approaching, and not wanting her to hear, "but I wanted to take her out on a ride, and Jorge wouldn't let me. You know how he is."

Abril made a disgusted grunt, her gaze following Carla as the woman came closer. "Then, I will take her out with me."

"You don't have—"

"What's he going to say, Val? *Nothing.*"

"Maria," Carla called, "we have to finish your studies."

Right, Valeria thought, *because you know anything about tutoring my daughter.*

"Actually," Abril told the woman, taking Maria's hand in her own to make her position clear, "she will go out on a ride with me, but thank you."

Carla scowled as she reached their spot. "Jorge said—"

"You're not Jorge."

Abril smiled.

Carla stiffened.

"And I am sure you can find better things to do for two hours," Abril added. "God knows you find enough to do at night when Valeria is the one putting her child to sleep, yes?"

Carla's face reddened. "Excuse me?"

"You heard what I said."

Valeria kept her mouth shut, knowing if she opened it, Carla would take that back to Jorge as this was her doing. She would pay for that later, so she knew better.

"Lunch is at one," Carla snapped.

"I will have her back before then."

That was that.

Valeria didn't know whether to be grateful for her sister-in-law, or terrified that in a lot of ways, Abril was the same as her brother. She was just as volatile, and twice as dangerous when she wanted to be.

Manipulative.

Cunning, and sly.

What would she do with it?

That was the real question.

8.

"Arms out, like a T," Jorge called, a smirk playing at the edges of his lips.

Chris gave the man on the other side of the gate cocked brow, but did as Jorge ordered. The gate opened, and two of the armed guards that had walked out the exit road from the Lòpez ranch came through to check him, patting him down and looking for any sign of a wire. It had to be that because they didn't seem to give a shit about the knife in his pocket.

He wouldn't get so irritated over being checked. It wasn't the first time he needed to do that, and God knew being who he was, he had enough run-ins with the cops over the years to be familiar with a pat down. It was more the fact that Jorge seemed to be enjoying Chris's annoyance.

The one man with the bandana covering his face grabbed the duffle bag Chris had brought along with his clothes, and other items, from the ground. He wasn't respectful about checking the bag.

"He's clean," one of the men said to Jorge.

"*Perfecto,*" Jorge praised. "As I thought he would be, ah, *amigo?*"

Chris jerked his arm out of the hold of the one man who still hadn't let him go, and fixed the front of his blazer, brushing off any invisible dust. He hated being handled like he was nothing more than a *dog*. "Offensive, is all."

Jorge waved a hand, dismissing that statement. "Can't be too safe, for one. And for two, I enjoy the show. Now, are you ready to see the ranch?"

"Which do you prefer to call it, the compound or the ranch?"

"Whichever one seems less illegal at the time."

Good point.

"I look forward to seeing it," Chris said.

"Come on, then."

Once the guards stepped back to give Chris room, he moved to follow Jorge who already had his back turned to the others as he walked down the road. Just how long was the road before they arrived at the ranch?

Chris stepped beyond the iron gate with the cursive *L* welded at the center, and a thought whispered through his mind at the same time. *No going back now.* The job had only kind of been in play before, but now it was go time. Well, his mind wasn't wrong, but he pushed it out of his head, so he could focus on the now.

From here on out, Chris would have to be careful. It was just him here—his father, as of a week ago, was back in Canada, and he didn't have a back up. Sure, he had a phone to call out if he needed help, but what good was that going to do? It would take people time to get here to him, and by then, it would be already too late.

"You'll see the barns first," Jorge said, "a couple of miles in. We use them for a lot of things, being we have actual animals on the ranch, but we also use them for storage before a drop, or if we have an oversupply at any given time. Depending on the circumstances before a smuggle run for your father, we'll be storing his on the property."

Gravel crunched under Chris's feet, and the hot sun overhead beat down on his back, reminding him why it had been a bad idea to wear his usual slacks and blazer. At least, he had been smart enough not to wear a fucking tie.

Still, as he shrugged off his jacket, he asked, "How far in is the main ranch?"

"Five miles."

"And we walk the whole way?"

Jorge chuckled. "We do."

Great.

"Has the ranch ever been stormed by officials, or—"

"No," Jorge interjected fast, "because I pay a lot of money to make sure that doesn't happen. Or, we divert their attention to somewhere else, give them *something* they want, and that's all."

"I don't understand."

The man glanced over his shoulder at Chris, grinning sardonically. "Here, it is all about who you know, and who you can blackmail or bribe. They *need* an arrest, or a bust, and so we give it to them, so they have something to flash on the news, and make it look like they're doing something important. The public thinks they're getting a hold on the cartels, the government looks good, and *la policía* appear like they're doing their job. Our main operation remains untouched, and we continue to operate as normal. Clear enough?"

More than, but Chris didn't bother to say it.

"I heard your wife was the daughter of a politician," Chris said, still keeping a few paces between him and Jorge just in case. He still didn't trust the man. "Does that play into your bribery and blackmail at all?"

"It did," Jorge muttered, "and then I had the man killed when he was no longer useful, so it didn't matter."

Yes, *after* Valeria had run off. Chris had enough information to know that. He wondered if that was because Jorge thought her father helped her to get away. He didn't ask because that wouldn't be smart, but he still wondered.

Sure enough, two large barns took form on the horizon. With the lack of animals around the fenced in sections around the barns, he had to wonder if the structures were being used to house something with a heartbeat, bricks of cocaine, or both.

Likely the latter.

"The barns are a good distraction, or ... ruse," Chris noted, trying to keep up the con of why he was here in the first damn place. For *business.* "Any aerial shots would only show the barns, and any animals or whatever else. Thermal imaging would show the heat of the animals and confuse the systems. It fits well with the ranch, and nothing looks out of place."

"Exactly."

At around three miles, the duffle bag hanging from Chris's grasp became heavier. He wasn't out of shape—at home, he went into a gym three times a week, and jogged every morning on a treadmill just to wake up before jumping in the shower. He maintained his image and body because he preferred to be healthy, but no fucking human should walk in the dead heat for this long.

"And the barns are only the beginning of the ranch," Jorge said, glancing back at him once more. "There is a great deal more to see, and my men will show you around for the tour tomorrow after you've settled in for the evening. I have something else I need to handle, but I will come around to check in throughout the day. You'll have lodging here—one of the smaller houses on the property—and full run of the place to look around and see what you think. Sound good?"

Chris nodded. "Sounds fine."

Time to get this job started.

• • •

"Are you lost?"

Feminine laughter, two distinct tenors, rang out in the darkness. The amusement at his expense didn't offend Chris, but he took a moment to figure out where the sound was coming from.

Apparently, following the fence line would not take him back to the main pathways of the Lòpez ranch that would lead to the houses, but rather, *behind* them. Or in this case, one house. Chris wasn't told to explore on his own after he settled into the residence he would use during his stay, but he also hadn't been told *not* to explore, either.

He figured, what was the harm?

This late at night, it seemed like the only people around were the guards. He wasn't going inside any of the houses, or other buildings. This wasn't snooping, and he enjoyed a good walk in the evenings and mornings.

He found the source of the laughter sitting on the back wraparound porch of a one-level bungalow. Sitting on a hanging swing, each with a wine glass in hand, two familiar women looked his way. Only one was smiling though.

"Abril," he greeted, stepping away from the fence to approach the house, "and Valeria. I wouldn't say I'm lost, no … more like looking around."

"Careful," Abril said, tipping her wine glass up to her lips as though she might take a drink, "my brother doesn't like it when people snoop."

"Does he also take a problem with people who like to walk?"

Abril made a noise under her breath. "Depends on what you're walking *toward.*"

Consciously, Chris's gaze drifted to the quieter woman sitting beside Abril on the bench. Valeria, that was. She didn't avoid his gaze, but he could see she wasn't going to engage him in a conversation like this, either.

That bothered him.

Valeria was, after all, the entire reason for him being here. He kind of needed her to talk to him, amongst other things. Like trust him, but that was a task for another day … or evening. It wasn't something he could do tonight, anyway.

"Care for a drink?" Abril asked after emptying her wine glass. "Liquor, water, or coffee, I mean."

Chris nodded. "Water would be great."

"I'll just be a minute."

The woman was quick to stand from the bench, giving Valeria a quiet word that Chris wasn't able to hear, before disappearing into the back of the house. He walked closer to the porch, coming to a stop on the bottom step, but not moving further. It was enough for him to let Valeria know he would engage her though.

That's all he wanted.

"You like wine?" he asked.

Valeria smiled, glancing down at the glass in her hand. "Not particularly, but I *do* like getting away from my house for an hour. Abril is one of the few people I can relax with like this without ... having to hear about it."

He heard what she didn't say.

Chris didn't call it out.

Shrugging, she was quick to add, "She *loves* wine, and likes to try new ones. I indulge her. This one isn't so bad."

Chris noted the color of the remaining liquid in her glass. "A white wine is good for a hot night under the stars, but hell, so is vodka."

Valeria laughed.

Freely.

She tossed her head back with a laugh, surprised by his frank statement. To be fair, the way the woman looked in the moonlight as she laughed equally shocked him. The russet tones in her golden skin were more clear, her dimmed gaze brightened, and those pretty lips of hers curved in the most beautiful way in her easy joy.

He wondered if she didn't get to do that enough.

Laugh, that was.

Not wanting to make her uncomfortable with his staring when she quieted, Chris cleared his throat, and glanced up at the inky sky. "I don't think I can appreciate the size of this place at night, but by the time I settled in after arriving, it was already dark."

"They haven't given you a proper tour yet?"

"Tomorrow."

"I'm sure you'll appreciate what they've done here. Men who visit typically do."

He didn't miss the edge to her tone.

"And that's what you assume I am, then? A man like them?"

Valeria's gaze darted to his.

Chris arched a brow, challenging her to say whatever was on her mind instead of alluding to it. Absolutes, he could work with. Hints, not so much.

"You know what my husband is—what he *does*," Valeria said quietly, "and because I know why you're here, to make a deal with him, there's only one thing for me to assume about you, too."

"Shame you think that, then."

Valeria's throat jumped when she swallowed. "Why is that?"

"Appearances are deceiving. And bad men don't always do bad things. Sometimes, they do good things, too."

"Don't they?"

How simple that question seemed.

The answer was anything but.

Unfortunately, Chris's life had taught him that no matter what he said here, she would find it most difficult to believe him. Because her experiences were not the same as his. Her life taught her one thing, and that's what she understood.

It was his duty to show her differently.

That was the thing, right?

Actions spoke louder than words.

"We'll see," he said.

Valeria opened her mouth as though she would reply, but all it took was Abril coming back out from the rear of the house for her to quiet. Abril came down the stairs, a glass of water for Chris in one hand, and a refill of wine in the other for her.

"Thank you," he said.

Abril nodded. "You know, in my experience, it's always what *motivates* a man that determines whether his actions are justifiable. What do you think, Chris?"

Huh.

Seems someone had been listening.

He smirked. "I would say you're right."

"I usually am."

• • •

Although Chris was in Mexico with the Lòpez cartel for a reason, he could still appreciate and respect the set up they had here. The ranch itself was almost a small community. In the middle, a cluster of homes sat in a large circle, all connected by pathways and gravel driveways. Another two barns also sat further in the property, along with stables.

For horses, apparently.

The cocaine, the man showing Chris around explained, they made and packaged it for shipping in Colombia where the cartel had gained control over production. They moved the substance between several locations—the ranch being one—to store before a smuggle run, which was a different story, and something Chris would get details on later.

"It's important," the man—Jesús, was it?—said as they stepped out of the house that Chris would use for his stay, "that the cartel maintains its control over territory, and distribution. Territory is the issue we've been having for a while, because of the García organization."

Right.

The cartel that controlled the lower portion of Mexico, and for a while, had tried to take control of the production in Colombia.

"We're working on that," the man said before Chris could ask further.

He wasn't *that* interested in the cartel, or their business. Cartels were complex criminal organizations, but he had a good enough grasp on the details to know how they worked. The lengths the family went to in order to maintain their privacy and control fascinated him, but he didn't really *care*.

Yet, he had to pretend to.

Fun.

Chris's entire purpose here rested on a ruse, and him being able to keep it up. The longer he could stay in the Lòpezs' presence, gather as much information about their lives and business, the better chance he had at getting Valeria and her daughter out of here alive. So, he continued to ask questions, and allow the man to take him around the ranch when what he wanted was a goddamn nap.

As far as the Lòpez family, and Jorge, understood … Chris was here because his father was anal on every single detail in business. Most, if not all, organizations would not be willing to indulge the demands Gian had made for this *deal*, but because the Lòpez cartel needed something from the Guzzis—the arrangement for a cocaine supply between them would be in the hundreds of millions a year—they would play along.

But for how long?

That was the real question.

As they walked along a pathway leading toward the biggest house on the property, something in the corner of his eye caught Chris's attention. A familiar woman came out of the stables with a saddle in her hands that she tossed onto a fence to hold it up before turning back to disappear inside the building.

Valeria.

For a second, Chris felt as though he could breathe a little better. Sure, he had seen her the night before, but he hadn't felt safe asking her questions about her safety here when prying ears were nearby. All week, he had worried about that woman, and what might happen to her. It left him with little sleep, and more restless nights than he cared to admit. And when he slept, images of her beautifully sad face filled his mind.

Not that he needed to be dreaming about that woman at all, or how she had looked with her curves filling out a dress, heels to show off long, golden legs, and black hair pin-straight falling down her back. Because *no*, he didn't need those images in his mind alongside the concern he already had for her.

This was a problem waiting to happen.

Obviously.

It was a little relieving for him to see her looking well and happy in the daylight. He still wanted to *speak* to her—get close, look her in the eyes, and make sure things were okay. It wasn't a game he should play, and nothing good would come out of the fact he had a growing emotional attachment to this job, but whatever.

Chris was who he was.

Someone who *cared*.

He gave a fuck.

Before he reconsidered, he asked the man ahead of him, "Can we go inside the stables?"

"Didn't you want a drink?"

"Sure, soon. The stables?"

"Why not?"

He expected his current guard to follow him inside the stables, as that had been his entire tour today in a nutshell, but someone called the guy's name just as they came up to the entrance where one could hear the horses hooves scuffing the floor inside.

"*Jesús, venir!*"

Chris had no idea what the man across the way was shouting to his guard, but whatever it was, Jesús was quick to give him a nod before he said, "I'll be back in a moment—you're good to look around, *sí?*"

"Perfectly fine," Chris replied.

Even better that he got to do it alone, now.

"Do not wander off."

"Of course, not."

He was right where he wanted to be.

As soon as Jesús's back was turned, Chris headed inside the stables. His gaze swept the space, taking in the horses, and the equipment lining one wall. A bucket of apple slices rested on the floor near one station, and the scent of animals and hay clung to the air with every breath he drew in.

Another time, and he might have admired the stables, and the beautiful creatures it housed. He always had a healthy appreciation for horses and had gone riding a time or two in the past. But as he was running low on time, and couldn't chance getting caught alone with Valeria, he didn't bother to enjoy the stables.

Instead, he found the woman in question down the corridor stepping into a stall beside a white and beige speckled horse.

"Ah, *caballo*," Valeria said as the sounds of a brush being dragged over the horse's hide echoed from the stall, "you're a *bonito* boy today. You like the brush, huh?"

Chris didn't even hesitate, simply headed down the corridor, and slipped into the stall where Valeria was brushing the horse down. Her gaze flew to him, her eyes widening as her pink lips fell open in a perfect *O* at the sight of him. No, he certainly didn't have time to admire the stables, or to have small talk, but he enjoyed the sight of this woman in front of him in her surprise.

There was something beautiful about that.

About *her*.

"You can't be in here," she blurted, her breath gone.

Chris leaned back enough to peek out the stall which gave him a perfect view of the stable doors that were still wide open. "No one is here to stop me."

His stare went back to her.

She swallowed hard.

"What do you want?"

"To talk," he replied.

Valeria took a little step back, but she didn't have very far to go. The horse next to them pranced in place wanting his attention back with that brush. "Do you understand that my husband will hurt—"

"Oh, he's made it clear what he intends to do if I get too close to you, yes."

She chewed on her bottom lip, those dark brown eyes of hers—like melting pools of russet—drifting over him like she wasn't sure what to do with Chris. "That's fine and great for you," she returned, "but I am more concerned about what he might do to me."

That made Chris stiffen.

"He hurts you?"

Valeria's cheek twitched. "I … I shouldn't talk about it."

"Yeah," he said, taking one step closer to her as he spoke, "I'm not at all worried about your husband, Val. He's a problem—an issue for me to take care of. I'm not even here for him, not *really*."

Her gaze locked onto his.

Chris stepped close enough to her that her back hit the wall of the stall, and she needed to stare up at him. There was no getting away now, and he wanted something to be very clear to her. For one, because he needed for her to trust him. And for two, because this would only work if she understood what was about to happen.

"W-what are you doing?" she whispered.

Chris hadn't intended to crowd Valeria because he wanted to make her uncomfortable, but because he needed to make sure she wouldn't run, not when he had the chance to do this. The funny thing?

She wasn't uncomfortable.

Not in the *slightest*.

Staring at him, those pupils of hers blew wide, showcasing his own reflection back to him. Her tongue peeked out to wet the seam of her lips, the action making his chest grow tight with something unusual—*lust*. That was before he noticed the way she looked him over, curious, yet wary, and still with *interest*. He bet if he touched her pulse point at her throat, he'd find her sweet heart racing like crazy.

What are you doing?

Get out of your head, asshole.

Focus.

His thoughts brought him back to the present, but barely. Because now, he concerned himself with the way Valeria's skinny jeans molded to her shapely legs, and the low dip of her flimsy blouse that gave a peek at the valley between her breasts. Her skin, the golden sheen dotting it, pebbled from his attention, and he had the greatest urge to *touch* her, or God forbid … fucking taste her.

Wow.

Valeria made a small noise.

Chris's gaze flew back up to hers. "What's that for?"

"*Me?* What is that for?"

"I beg your pardon?"

"The way you stare at me …"

Chris's brow furrowed. "You're an exceptionally beautiful woman. Does no one tell you that?"

"*You* shouldn't."

Hadn't she learned, yet?

"But I still did."

She sucked in a shaky breath. "It has been a long time since someone looked at me like that."

"Shame, that," he murmured. "Beautiful things should be admired by the ones who care for them, and they should be told often of their worth and value."

Valeria dropped his stare. "I'm not worth very much *here*."

"Or is it you aren't valued?"

Their stares met again.

Chris inched closer, because he wanted her pressed against the wall, and also because something at the neckline of her shirt had caught his attention. A mark that marred her skin, but he had to be sure. Lifting his hand, a shiver that raced through Valeria when his fingertips glided along the fabric of her blouse to move it aside.

Sure enough …

He found three bruises there, a dark red that told him they were recent. He made a rough noise under his breath, though it came out thick between them and loaded with things he wasn't sure he should say yet. Perhaps a part of him had still assumed this woman might want to be here, but he doubt she wanted to also be abused.

Now, he didn't wonder at all.

"I'm not here for your husband," Chris said quietly, meeting Valeria's stare again, but not dropping his hand to stop from touching her. He liked the heat of her body, and the silkiness of her skin, and considering the way she trembled, and her breaths came out harder while she watched him, he could tell she liked it, too. "Despite what they might say, I didn't come here for them. I came for you."

"What does that mean?"

He didn't have time.

It was a long story, and they didn't have the minutes needed to tell it. Time was already running out for their little moment here.

"Who did this?" he asked, his fingers sweeping over the bruises.

"Take a guess."

"Jorge?"

"Regularly."

"Last night?"

"This morning," she breathed.

The dark, violent urge that swept through him seemed destructive, and *reckless*. He wanted nothing more than to feed into it and hurt the man who put his hands on his wife. Whether she was property to Jorge didn't factor in at all—*no man* should hurt their spouse, ever.

Full stop.

"I'm sorry," Chris said, his thumb sweeping to the side, across her collarbone. That shiver in her body followed the same path, and her lips parted again like she might say something to him. All he wondered was what it might be like to kiss this woman—something else he had no business doing.

Well, so much for *that*.

He had broken all the rules, now.

"I want to kiss you," he said. "Can I?"

She sucked in a hard breath, but nodded once. Chris closed the distance between them in a blink, catching Valeria's mouth with his own in a soft, yet still *burning* kiss. She never hesitated to kiss him back, her lips working against his, like she found something that was pure heaven to her senses. His tongue struck against the seam of her lips, demanding more, and she gave it to him willingly.

Beautifully.

Her fist found his shirt, and she dragged him closer as a war raged on between them. It was strange, in a way. Kissing someone had never been a battle before, to hand over himself to her, and see what happened after that.

And yet, that's what it seemed like. She tasted of cherries, and vanilla. Sweetness, and sin.

Chris backed Valeria into the stable wall again, the horse shifting beside them as her palms found his jaw, and he dragged her closer with his. There was something intoxicating about this woman, and he wanted to find out what. Not that he had enough time to do it.

The sound of boots crunching against gravel had Chris taking a wide step back from Valeria. He didn't have a clue what came over him, but as he stared at her still pressed to the wall, her fingertips hovering over her lips like she wanted to feel his kiss, he didn't regret what just happened.

Even if it was dangerous … and *stupid*.

The questions in her eyes stared back at him. He couldn't answer them now. "Chris?"

He gave her a pointed stare and took two steps backwards out of the stall to find the man from earlier—Jesús—glancing down the stables. He smiled at the man, thankful that he learned how to mimic his twin's, Corrado, natural ability to remain calm in all situations. Even when his heart raged out of control.

"Just admiring the horse," Chris said. "Can we get that drink, now?"

Jesús nodded. "Absolutely, and Jorge called, too. He invited you to dinner with him if you're hungry."

Chris headed for the man, forcing himself not to glance back into the stall at Valeria as he did so. "Food would be great."

And so was the flavor of Valeria Lòpez still lingering in his mouth.

Fuck.

9.

"Easy, *easy*."

Valeria's attempt to soothe the broken horse worked. Abril came out here in the field and worked with the horse to make it rideable, but after a bad fall from the horse throwing her from the saddle … well, she was hesitant to approach the animal so soon.

Horses were like people. Sometimes, they didn't always connect with someone else. Human, or animal. And other times, they needed a bit to come around. Valeria figured that was the problem with Duke, the horse she was trying to work with on his riding skills, so she tried to take him out while Abril took a break from working with him.

At least this way, he didn't have long spells of little to no activity with a human. Something beyond being fed, brushes, or having his stall cleaned. He would be a riding horse, and so someone needed to ride him.

Simple as that.

"That's a good boy, Duke," Valeria said, reaching down to pat his muscular neck. "One more trip around the fence line, huh? Let's go."

She pulled the reins on the right side, a silent command for the animal to turn in that direction. It took a harder tug for him to listen to her command, though, which spoke to his stubbornness. That was another issue with him. He didn't like to do what others wanted him to do when he would much rather do what he wanted.

Horses with stubborn streaks kept them even after being trained. She figured Duke would be an adult's horse, and not appropriate for children to ride. Which was fine, honestly. Some horses were better suited to adults because they needed that strong, dominant hand.

They were halfway around the fence line of the field that the horses used to graze when she first noticed *him*. Chris, that was.

It was impossible for her to ignore the way her heart raced in her chest from nothing more than sight alone. He seemed so calm, unbothered, and confident leaning against the post of the wooden fence, his gaze locked on her as she came closer to his spot riding Duke.

After their moment in the stables the other day, Valeria had done her best to avoid him because she didn't know how to deal with the strange emotions the Canadian invoked in her. Not to mention, there was just something about the way he *looked* at her. She couldn't explain what it was, but she swore he was looking right into her soul, seeing all of those secrets she tried damn hard to hide, with very little effort at all.

Chris raised a hand, a small wave urging her closer to him.

Damn.

Now, she couldn't pretend like she hadn't seen him. Although, if she were being an honest woman, she didn't want to avoid him at all. That would probably end badly for her in one way or another.

"Enjoying a ride?" he asked when Duke trotted closer to his spot at the fence post.

Valeria kept a good fifteen feet between her, and him. *Just in case.* Surely, no one would see them out here in the field and think something inappropriate might go on, but she couldn't be too careful.

Jorge had acted on lesser beliefs.

He shouldn't be tested.

Besides, *something* had happened.

In the stables …

Valeria couldn't forget it.

Neither could her body.

"Training Duke, actually," she replied. "Have you taken a horse out yet?"

"Considering it." Chris flashed her a grin one might consider sinful. God knew she did if the way her thighs clenched around the body of the horse was any sign. She was not used to *this*—to feeling attraction for someone else. Not at all. "Although, I have to say I am enjoying watching you ride a horse far more."

There was no hiding the suggestion in his tone.

He didn't even make the attempt.

Why did she like that?

Because she shouldn't.

At all.

Valeria swallowed thickly. "You shouldn't do that."

"Pardon?"

"*Flirt* with me."

Chris shrugged one shoulder, almost uncaringly even though he looked damn good doing it. "When *you* say you don't want me to, then I won't. See, telling me I shouldn't do something isn't the same as telling me not to do it because you don't like it, Val."

Goddamn him for being right.

Valeria, out of an instinctual need to be safe and nothing more, peeked back to the ranch, and stables. Here, all she ever did was look over her shoulder to see who was spying, and might report back to Jorge about her behavior. She hadn't realized how often she did it until Chris was nearby.

Sad thing, that.

"No worries, no one is watching," Chris said, amusement coloring his tone.

Valeria was quick to snap around to glare at him, then. "Don't treat this like a *joke.* I might like your attention, but that doesn't mean I can always *accept* it."

His playful smile never faltered.

God.

Why did he have to be so *cocky?*

So damn confident?

Arrogant men were not Valeria's first choice, that was for sure, and yet she found it was a good look on Chris. She was not used to the heat traveling lower between her thighs, making an ache settle deep in her bones.

Jesus.

And that *want?*

Clawing at her chest?

It was too much.

"Don't you have questions for me?" he asked.

She did.

Too many.

And yet, all she could say was, "You will get me killed."

"Quite the opposite, Valeria."

What?

Again with that *suggestion*. Like he was here for her—he said it as though that's what he meant, but she couldn't be sure that's what it was.

She didn't even trust herself.

"Would you let me do it again?"

Valeria sucked in a shaky breath, a flush traveling down her throat. She could feel the heat crawling over her skin though she did her best to ignore it. She asked, although she was sure she knew his answer, "Do what?"

"Kiss you."

"*Valeria!*"

The shout of Abril coming from the stables had her rearing the horse back, already turning to head for the stables and leaving Chris behind.

"Will you?" he called after her.

His tone was still dark with wicked promises that made her skin pebble, and her thighs clench. She couldn't miss it, not that she wanted to.

"Not if I value my life."

He probably didn't hear her.

That was okay.

Even she didn't believe it.

• • •

The week following Valeria's encounter with Chris in the field could only be described as hell. Not because anyone had caught them, although it came close, or because anyone suspected something had happened. Rather, she couldn't help the paranoia that seemed to creep up her spine whenever the memory of Chris kissing her against that wall, or him asking her if he could do it again as he leaned against the fence, would flood her mind.

It was made worse whenever she would be close enough for Jorge to be looking at her when the memories came rushing into her mind, intent on driving her crazy, making her hot, *and* scared for her life all at the same time.

Because that's what her husband would do, she knew. Undoubtedly, he would kill her for even *thinking* about another man, let alone kissing one. Jorge was terribly jealous when a man was staring at Valeria for too long because he thought of her as a prize he had won. And not once, but twice, when he caught her after running. He was not giving her up, and instead of treating her like something prized, he behaved like she was shit under his shoe.

The more troubling part?

Valeria couldn't stop thinking about it.

About Chris.

That moment replayed in her mind daily—on fucking repeat. It woke her up at night when Jorge was beside her, and she didn't need to be thinking about it, all things considered. The taste of him seemed like it lingered on her lips whenever she sipped on a glass of water because it reminded her of him. *Crisp*, and fresh.

Like the way his kiss and simple touch had made her body light up with barely any effort on his part at all.

God.

She didn't need that.

None of it.

Worse was the fact she thought a huge part of her might want to do it again, and that was terrifying. Valeria spent her days at the side of a man who raped and beat her simply for being his wife. And a random man shows up with strange words coming out of his mouth about being there for her, and she's kissing him in a stable? Entertaining his flirting while she rode a horse?

Stupid.

That's what she was.

A stupid little *niña*.

Because only a girl would behave the way she did, so recklessly and dumbly. It was the only excuse she could come up with to justify why she had done what she did, and why she wanted to do it again.

Or you are so starved for love and affection that a kind man with care in his eyes reminded you that you are both alive, and a woman.

Fuck her thoughts, too.

Valeria had done her best to avoid Chris over the last week. He had occasionally joined them at their table for a meal, but he made a careful effort not to talk to her in her husband's presence, which she was sure Jorge appreciated, as he usually did for other men. And if there was a chance for her to speak with Chris, she was quick to take herself out of the situation so they couldn't talk.

She didn't need the trouble.

Right?

So, why did her body think differently?

"Don't let the kitten get too far from you," Valeria called to her daughter from the porch.

Sitting on the steps with her sister-in-law, she watched as Maria chased after a kitten she sneaked from a barn. It was normal for the cats to mate and have a batch of kittens on a ranch. Cats kept the vermin down with their hunting habits.

Somehow, Maria convinced her father to let her keep the kitten she had snuck away from the litter when it was big enough, and no longer needed its mother. Valeria figured Jorge had only allowed her to take the gray and white kitten because it was something for him to use to bribe their child, not because she seemed to love the kitten. Whenever he thought she misbehaved, he threatened to send the kitten back to the barn, or worse …

Valeria did her best to assure Maria that wouldn't happen, but she also seemed like she made promises she wouldn't be able to keep. And that, more than anything, killed her. She was never more aware of how little control she had over her life until it was her daughter, and nothing was for her to decide.

Even if it was just a kitten.

"Oh, no!" Maria shouted when the kitten darted away from her and went around the house. "Come back, Kitty!"

Kitty.

Yep, that's what she had named it.

Valeria let her.

What else could she do?

"Hurry and grab it before it goes back to the barn," Abril told Maria, "because that's probably what she wants to do."

Maria darted after the kitten, almost going out of Valeria's line of sight, but stopped just short. Her head tilted back as a shadow drifted over her form, and she stared up at whoever had come around the side of the house.

"Better hold on to her good so she doesn't get away again," a familiar voice said.

Valeria felt that voice through every part of her body.

Every single fucking part.

Chris.

"Thank you very much," Maria said, smiling.

They both came into view around the side of the house, standing beside a garden bed of roses that Abril liked to maintain. She had one for every house although she only lived in her own.

Chris passed a look toward the house, his gaze landing on Valeria before it went back to her daughter. Kneeling down, he handed the squirming kitten to her daughter with a soft smile. His voice lowered as he spoke to her daughter, and pet the kitten between her ears with the pad of his finger.

It didn't matter.

Maria smiled, looking back at her mom, and then nodding at whatever Chris had told her. Pointing at a flower, he waited for Maria to give him the okay before he pulled a small pocketknife from his slacks. He cut the rose that the kitten had jumped on at the stem, dragging the blade down the length to remove any small thorns. Then, he tucked the pink rose into her daughter's hair, right above Maria's ear.

"Beautiful, like your Ma," he said just loud enough for Valeria to hear.

Her throat tightened.

In her chest, her heart thundered.

Chris must have asked Maria something else because his head tilted to the side. Her child's happy smile faded when she shrugged in her dress. She understood well enough what Chris said next because his lips moved to say, "I'm sorry, Maria."

He said something else, and Maria quickly bounced on her feet, happy all over again as though nothing was wrong. The two of them laughed, and Chris pointed between himself, and then her daughter with a firm nod. Then, he pointed at Valeria, too, and gave Maria a wink that had her smile growing wide all over again.

"You understand?" she heard him ask.

Maria grinned. "I understand."

"Good—I promise. I don't break those."

"Do you pinky promise?"

Chris shot Valeria another look from the side, but his stare didn't linger long before it went right back to her daughter. Unquestioningly, he brought his hand out, and popped his pinky out for her daughter to catch with her own. Maria hooked their pinkies and tugged.

"Pinky promise," he said.

"That's the most *important* one, you know."

"I know."

Valeria wanted to know what they talked about—so badly. What was it the man said to her daughter that had her frowning and sad, but then had her smiling like the entire world watched and loved her in the next second?

The sight was sweet, really.

Maria didn't take to strangers, but especially not men. Valeria blamed that on the fact there hadn't been a lot of men in her daughter's life when they stayed on the run for the last few years, but also because the man who should adore and treat her well made it his mission to ensure she saw his vile treatment of her mother. Her *mom*—someone she loved more than anyone else in the world. Her little girl with a heart of gold wouldn't soon forget that, Valeria knew.

For whatever reason though ... Maria liked Chris.

"He's good with kids," Abril noted at her side, "and she's not even his, huh?"

Valeria let out a sigh. "Hmm."

"And stop staring, Val. You look like a woman who has found something she likes."

Well, *shit.*

She averted her stare.

So much for avoiding him.

Not that it mattered, and her attempt to look away didn't last for long, either. Chris stood, after giving Maria a one-armed hug and a kiss to the top of her head, and looked their way again. She sensed his gaze on her, even though she was trying to make it seem like she was looking out at the land beyond him, and not at him.

"Have a good day, ladies," he murmured.

That was it.

He walked off.

The confusion, and heaviness in Valeria's heart became worse. This—whatever was happening here—would lead nowhere good.

She was sure.

• • •

The next evening found everyone on the ranch celebrating a successful smuggle run into Texas that had been touch and go for a good month or more due to changes at the ports of entry. Valeria wasn't interested in the flowing alcohol, or the laughter of her husband's men that filled their house, and spilled out into the backyard where they had gathered in a large group.

She hung back on the rear porch of their home, forgotten by Jorge as he swallowed back more whiskey, and laughed at whatever the man next to him had said. It wasn't like she would complain about his lack of attention, but that wasn't what bothered Valeria at the moment.

Other things stuck to the back of her mind like sticky tar, dark and *thick*, promising it would stay there forever unless she handled it, and soon. *Chris.* And his little show the day before with her daughter.

For whatever reason, it wouldn't leave her mind. Like his kiss that day in the stables, or that whenever he was within visual distance of her, he stared at her when no one else did.

All bad things.

And yet, *good*, too.

Even if it was crazy and dangerous. If Valeria were a smart woman, she would tell the man to stop. To leave her be and go his way.

Except he'd said something to her in the stables …

He came here for her.

What did that mean?

This might be one of the few times she would be able to deal with the thoughts that plagued her, so she decided to at least try. Now or never because it was likely she wouldn't get another chance soon.

And Chris came to Jorge's impromptu celebration. He hung back like she did, but never stepped in on their conversations unless they invited him, or otherwise.

He didn't want to be there.

Clearly.

With everyone's attention on the row of fireworks that Samuel was setting off, while Abril kept an exhausted Maria safely away, Chris slipped inside the house. He had to pass by Valeria to do it, and met her gaze unashamed as he did so, arching a brow before he disappeared inside.

Without saying anything at all, his silent challenge sounded like, *Well, are you coming?*

Did the man read her mind?

She would soon find out.

It was foolish, no doubt about it. At least, inside the house, Valeria would be able to slip into another room should someone come inside, or even run upstairs. There were variables that worked to her favor here, and she figured it should be safe enough to at least try to have a private conversation with the man.

Valeria ducked into the house but she found the back hallway empty. Not knowing where Chris had gone, she walked further down the hall, a shriek dying in her throat when a hand snapped out to grab her at her elbow before someone yanked her into the downstairs bathroom.

"What—"

Valeria didn't even get to finish her sentence before he slammed the bathroom door shut, leaving her in darkness. A form pressed her against the counter. She knew it was Chris who pulled her inside by the *scent* of him.

Intoxicating, she thought, like his taste, too. Crisp and fresh like a freshly fallen snow.

"Turn the light on," Valeria said, air rushing with her words, trying to ignore the rushing desire in her bloodstream. "Please."

Chris did just that, the space lighting up although it took a second for her eyes to adjust to the brightness. He backed up a bit, giving her enough room to breathe, but that was all he afforded her in the small bathroom. It wasn't made for two people, and her body knew it given his proximity.

"We have, what, ten minutes before the fireworks stop?" he asked.

Valeria wet her lips. "About that. I have questions."

"About what?"

"Whatever you said to my daughter yesterday."

Chris blinked, the hard lines of his handsome face softening as a smile fettered over his lips. "*That's* what you want to ask?"

"Yes."

"Not about what I said to you in the stables? I figured that would be on your mind."

"It is," Valeria blurted, "but my daughter comes first for me ... *always*. No exceptions, and so if something about you might put her in danger, even unknowingly, then I have to handle that. Surely, you can understand."

Chris's throat jumped at her words, like maybe he swallowed something back before he muttered, "Hurting her—accidentally, or not—is the last thing on my mind, trust that."

"Still, what did you say to her?"

"Val—"

"I want you to tell me."

His gaze darted away, but his tone came out low when he said, "I asked her about Haven ... and New York. I needed to give her something she *understood*. Something that would resonate with her, right, because she needs to believe I'm not like the rest of the people here. I'm *different*. She misses Haven and her school in New York. She doesn't like you crying a lot, or that her father hurts you."

That was not what Valeria expected. A mixture of things had a lump growing in her throat, the emotions lodging there to take her breath away, and make her want to sob at the same time. Her eyes stung with unshed tears, and she clenched her fists into tight balls at her sides.

The mention of Haven—her only friend they forced her to leave behind when Jorge found her—made her emotional, but the rest just drove the knife in deeper, and twisted until everything was *pain*.

"You're aware Haven got married," Chris added, "to Andino Marcello since you were there. That's who hired me. To come here, and figure out a way to get you the fuck out of here, in case you wondered. That's why I'm here."

God.

That wasn't possible.

She didn't dare say it though, because a brief flutter of hope danced through her heart, swelling to epic proportions, and threatened to drown her with the emotion. It had been so goddamn long since she felt anything akin to hope. How sad was that?

"She told me you're unhappy," Chris murmured. "Your daughter, I mean."

"Don't put her in danger by asking—"

"You don't give her enough credit, Val. She is young, but she is *not* stupid."

Valeria met his gaze, unsure and wary. "You made her a promise. I heard you say that. What was it?"

His grin deepened. "I shouldn't tell. I made a pinky promise—"

"Stop it."

"Relax," he said, one of his hands coming up to stroke the line of her jaw with his thumb and forefinger. The soft touch made her sigh and tilt her head into his hand a little more, not that she had any business doing that at all. "I promised you would be happy soon, and no one would hurt you. All she wants is for her mom to be happy again, okay?"

Fuck him.

For doing that, and telling her, even if she asked. For giving her hope.

A tear fell from the corner of Valeria's eye, but Chris quickly wiped it away before it got very far. He did the same for the other side of her face when she blinked, and more tears threatened to fall.

"Why did you do that in the stables ... kiss me, I mean?"

"Not sure," Chris murmured, his thumb sweeping her cheekbone as he spoke. "It's not something I was *supposed* to do. I asked first, you nodded."

"I did," she agreed softly, "although I'm not sure why."

"Then, we're in the same position."

And what a position.

"Not part of the job, then?"

His stare snapped down to her mouth. "No. I just ..."

"What? Because I don't think you understand how dangerous this is for me."

"I do, Val. I promise I do, and if you don't—or didn't—want me to do that, all you have to do is say."

She sucked in a sharp breath, her back straightening at the directness of his tone. "I don't, no."

Chris frowned. "What?"

"Get a *say*. About sex. Or I never have, and I realized you're right, too."

His hands dropped to her thighs overtop the skirt of her dress, and his fingers flexed gently. As supportive as it seemed, his silent acknowledgement of her truth, it also reminded her all he had to do was push up her dress around her thighs, spread her wide, and he would have her.

She *wanted* it.

"Sex ... anything like it," she whispered, "has always been used against me, and I've never wanted someone else before. Not *him*, not a stranger—no one."

"Except me," he murmured.

Valeria peeked up at him through her lashes, only then realizing she had been staring at the corded band of muscles lining his broad shoulders, and the way his throat jumped when his gaze dropped to her lips.

Desire.

Lust..

Always the possession; the *thing* Jorge won. Used because her husband wanted to. Coveted for his pride.

Men around her husband desired her for their own selfish reasons or gains. Because they saw her as the perfect *cartel* wife, their belief they too would be a king with a queen they handpicked and demanded. Or to others because they believed her unworthy of her status after running—a traitor to *break*.

And yet ...

"No one has ever looked at me the way you are right now," she said, her voice almost unrecognizable to herself with the heat she found there. "I've never been wanted—not like this."

"And you never wanted—until now."

That's why this had seemed so confusing to her. From the walk around the pool with an almost flirting, but very charming man, to the kiss in the stables had all seemed foreign to her in a way. She played a game she had never needed the rules to before now.

"Val," he said, tone thick.

"Yeah?"

Chris leaned in close enough so if she wanted—because he had made it clear this was on her terms, she had the *say*—moving forward would let her capture his kiss. His lips quirked up at the edges, sexy as ever, when he told her, "Has a man never loved your body the way it deserves to be, sweetheart?"

God.

If it were possible, she felt his voice everywhere. At the apex of her thighs, in between the beats of her heart, and straight to her mind. All the parts of her attention that a single man *never* caught of hers before.

Chris didn't give her the chance to respond before he added quieter, "Not with his cock—not while he's *fucking* you. Just him, Val, and his hands or his mouth. Touching you with parts of his body that makes it more intimate than just his cock. Has no one done that the way you want them to—the way they *should*?"

She swallowed hard.

Shook her head.

"No," she breathed.

"Fucking shame," he muttered, arching a brow. "Can I?"

Valeria blinked, the word slipping from her mouth before she even understood she had said it because staring at him was intoxicating. "Yes."

"Which do you want, then? My fingers, my mouth—*both*? Because we don't have a lot of time, and as much as I would like to spend hours showing how you should be fucked and adored, I only have a few minutes before someone realizes we're not out back where we should be."

He also had a way of reminding her about reality.

Damn.

"Just ..."

He leaned an inch closer. "*Which one?*"

Valeria moved in, too, whispering against his lips as she kissed him, "*Both.*"

She kissed him hard, and fast, the sharp flavor on his tongue from the rum he'd been nursing earlier blooming across her palate. His fingers drifted between her thighs, his hard lines crowding her to the mirror when he came closer. He stroked her over the line of her lace panties first, making her hips rock into his touch with each soft swipe.

"*There*, yeah? You want me there?" he asked, his lips ghosting over her cheek. "That's what we need to do, Val. Wake up your pussy first, little by little, and then when you're nice and wet from this, I will treat you like a *feast*."

His words, and the way they sounded coming out of his mouth, lit up a fire inside Valeria like she had never felt before. His fingers flamed it as they worked between her thighs, now slipping under the gusset of her panties to stroke her bare flesh and the short-trimmed hair above the hood of her clit.

"Jesus," she breathed.

Chris chuckled. "Wait, it gets better."

She didn't doubt it.

Valeria couldn't imagine *how*.

This was already more than she understood—more than she experienced before. Overwhelmed. Sensitive. Her body became a live wire snapping with every encouraging, tantalizing touch.

"I bet you're pussy tastes as hot as you are on my fingers," he told her.

Valeria's head tipped back to the mirror as she dragged in a hard breath. "*Oh, my God.* Keep doing *that.*"

He did; his two fingers stroking in and out of her sex before coming up to circle the tight bud of her clit. A rhythmic, perfect beat. Her legs trembled as she lifted them higher out of a deep need to spread herself wider for him.

She bet she was quite a sight.

Spread open.

A man between her thighs whom she had not spoken vows to … even if her husband had broken his vows to her more times than she was aware, and in more ways than she would ever care to count.

Begging like she did.

"*Please, please, please,*" she heard herself say.

Although for what she asked for, Valeria didn't know. For the building need to continue, but for it to become *more*. For him to give her it because he *had* to see she needed relief. Or for things she didn't understand.

She would beg for it though.

All of it.

Chris pressed one quick kiss to her trembling lips, his own tugging into a sinfully wicked smirk that had her gulping, before he lowered between her thighs. The beat of his fingers thrusting into her wet pussy before coming back up to rub at her clit stopped.

Only for his tongue to take the place of his fingertips on her clit with a faster, harsher beat than before. Those two fingers in her sex became three, filling her deliciously as his tongue moved back and forth from licking at her clit to lapping at his fingers fucking her and covered in her cum.

She had to watch.

Chris looked like a man enthralled—eating her while he watched her, and his fingers worked her pussy until she teetered on an edge like never before. Valeria hadn't been ready to fall, then, hadn't known what it would be like when it wasn't forced, and she craved it—willing to let a man have her like this.

And then she fell.

Her bliss became a cliff.

She stifled the noises crawling from her throat as the orgasm tore through her core and rippled across all of her nerves. Shouting into the heel of her palm as she watched Chris replace his fingers inside her still-pulsing sex with his tongue to lick her essence right from the source.

Valeria never saw anything hotter.

Never been higher.

Chris caught her when the trembling started in her legs, his tongue drifting from her sex to lap at her inner thigh before he raised up. She didn't even think about it, just seeing his mouth wet with her arousal made her want to taste herself on his lips.

So, she did just that.

Valeria didn't know who this woman was—this person here, doing this with him. This *man* who came into her life without warning, saying things to give her hope, and terrified her to death at the same time.

She had no clue who she became around Christopher Guzzi, but she liked it. That was a dangerous thing.

10.

"Where did you go off to?" Jorge asked.

Do not look that woman's way, Christopher.

He could feel Valeria's stare burning into his back from across the backyard. She exited through the rear of the home, but he decided it would be smarter if he didn't take the same way back to the party she did.

Better not to play with fire.

Hadn't they already risked a lot?

Chris thought so.

Stuffing his hands in his pockets, Chris came closer to Jorge, making sure his posture was light, and easy. "Fireworks always give me a headache, so I took a walk. Thought it might be nice."

"Ah, yes. They bother the horses, too. You'll make friends with those beasts."

Had he compared Chris to animals?

Well, whatever.

Chris took the clipped cigar Jorge offered him but used his own lighter to get it smoking. Jorge turned his back to Chris for the moment, watching the men who had gathered in a slight circle, and the two in the middle who were sharing punches. A bareknuckle match, it looked like.

Another time or place, and Chris might have joined in just because. Not here, though, and not with these men. These people weren't his family or friends, and he could not afford to forget that fact.

This job was already dangerous before he came here and got stuck in his head about a woman he needed to get the fuck out of this place. Now, he couldn't get her out of his head, and that made it worse.

Emotional attachments were bad.

Even if they felt good.

Speaking of which …

Chris could still feel Valeria's stare on him, and with Jorge's back turned, it allowed him to check her way. Sure enough, she watched him from her position on the porch, looking no better or worse than she had before their little encounter in the house. Frankly, looking at her wasn't any good for his side of things, either.

The woman was a siren.

She called to him.

He didn't know what to do with that.

Knowing he should turn his stare away from her before someone noticed his attention, he gave Valeria a quick nod, and looked away. It was all he could do although he wished he didn't have to do that at all.

She needed someone to care. That much was painfully obvious with her. The woman was strong as hell, no doubt about it. Look at all she had gone through and was still dealing with regularly. No one could ever say she hadn't done all she could and still held her head high while she did it.

Simple as that.

Valeria was still human though. And very much a woman. Her mind, heart, and soul needed things, whether she craved it or it felt good. Affection, *touch* ... attention. All of it, those were basic human needs. He knew she wasn't getting those things from the man they forced her to marry, and he wasn't sure what to do with the fact he wanted to give it to her instead.

Yeah.

This was a mess.

A dangerous one.

"What's next, hmm?" Chris asked Jorge.

He needed to get his thoughts away from Valeria, what had happened in the house, and how he felt about her. If not, someone would notice his distraction, and he doubted it would take them long to put two and two together to make four.

No one needed that.

"For what?" Jorge replied over his shoulder.

"Me being here—what do I get to see next?"

Jorge turned, giving Chris a smile as he did so. "The tunnels, I think. There's a good chance part of your father's run will go through the tunnels, especially if ports of entry are too hot, or we can't take it across an unwatched part of the border for whatever reason. The easiest way for me to show you the tunnels is to take you to one we don't use a lot but was also one of the first ones my father ever had built."

Huh.

"And when are we doing that?"

"A few days, likely," Jorge replied, shrugging.

"Not sooner?"

"You forget that you are here on my time." Jorge turned back to the fighting men, the bonfire glowing bright with flickering flames a few feet away from their position. "Which means, I also have work to do, and so I will deal with you and what your father wants when I have time to do it, Christopher."

"I prefer Chris."

"I don't care."

Yeah, he was aware.

Clearly.

He left the conversation alone if only because he didn't think it would get him anywhere to keep needling Jorge about it. He lost any chance at civility with the man the first night they met when Jorge felt Chris had overstepped his bounds with his wife, anyway, and he doubted it would get better now.

Not that he gave a fuck.

He wasn't here to make friends with Jorge.

Chris was getting antsy even though this job could take a while to complete. He hadn't expected to be in Mexico for any more than two weeks, maybe three, at the most. Already, he had been here for two, and he didn't see an end in sight. He didn't have a way to get Valeria the hell out of here, but might those tunnels help his plan along?

Who knew?

His bigger problem was what would happen if the ruse ran its course, he had to leave, and he still didn't have a way out for Valeria? What the fuck was he going to do?

"I think you'll like the tunnels," Jorge said absently.

Chris looked Valeria's way again. Now, she wasn't looking at him. That was okay, he only needed to see her. If she was okay that's what he wanted to know. The rest, he would deal with as he could, or should.

What else could he do?

"I look forward to it," Chris replied.

• • •

The bay window of the small living room in the house Chris was using on the Lòpez ranch during his stay allowed him a good view of the rest of the houses on the property, and all the walkways connecting them. It was a nice, practical design, if someone admired that sort of thing, but mostly, he felt the need to imprint it to memory.

If something happened, he would need to know *all the* things about this place. Should something cause chaos, and it was his only chance to get Valeria and Maria out, then he wanted to walk it with his fucking eyes closed.

No questions asked.

That was why, every single morning, he took an hour-long jog around the property. He went out, took pathways, and sometimes didn't, and then came back to his house again. To the guards, or the family, it looked like nothing was amiss. He was focusing on his fitness, and little else.

That was fine.

It's what he wanted them to think.

The ring of a cell phone took Chris's attention away from the window, and the scenery outside. He didn't bother to check the caller ID when he reached for the phone on the coffee table behind him, simply picked it up and answered it, thinking it would be his father, or twin.

Although, Corrado had been careful not to call since Chris was here. So was his brother's way—always erring on the side of caution, rather than unpredictability. It was something he appreciated about his twin.

"Chris here," he murmured into the phone, going back to the window.

The voice on the other end of the call was not who he expected, and it put him on edge. "Chris, it's Andino."

"Why?"

"Excuse me?"

"Why are you calling me?"

Andino chuckled. "For an update to give to my wife, who asks about her missing friend nonstop, that's why. Good enough answer for you, or no?"

Well …

Chris sighed. "You shouldn't be calling me, it's risky. You have no idea what I am doing here at any given time, and I usually have someone nearby. What if they saw the name on the phone, or heard me say your name? The Lòpez family are aware Valeria was with your new wife before they grabbed her again, and you want to play that kind of game?"

"I don't want to, no, but your father didn't have news. He thought a call to you—"

"Don't do this again."

Andino cleared his throat. "All right, noted. What can you tell me if you're able I mean? Do you have a plan to get the woman and her child out of there?"

"It's complicated."

"How so?"

"She's incredibly isolated away from the public," Chris said, "for fucking starters. Their compound in the middle of nowhere—yeah, that's where he keeps her. And when she may leave, he has a small army to keep her in line. She's not treated well here, but she keeps up a good façade. As of now, she knows why I am here, but I don't think she trusts me yet, which is a problem."

"Hmm."

"What was that noise for?"

"Sounds like you should figure out a way to make her trust you, doesn't it?"

"Thanks for the memo. Let me jot it down."

Andino grunted. "You and your twin ... you are both a lot alike, yes?"

"We are *twins*. Identical in many ways."

In fact, he and his twin were different, too. The most obvious being the way they lived their lives, things they enjoyed, and what they wanted for their future. On the surface, to people who didn't know them well—like Andino—the twins seemed more similar than opposite. All people saw first were the things that made Chris and Corrado the same, but they missed the more important bits.

The shit that made them unique.

"And what does my twin have to do with this?" Chris asked.

"I find him as equally bothersome as you."

"Sounds like an issue you should handle, no?"

Andino made another one of those annoyed noises. "Back to Valeria, and her daughter, if you wouldn't mind. I suspect you don't have all day to chat."

Right.

"The situation here is not as easy as I hoped it would be, and I don't have a clear path forward yet. When I do, however, you will be one of the first ones I tell. Also, have you considered what comes *after*?"

"I beg your pardon?"

"Jorge Lòpez came after her once when she ran, Andino," Chris intoned, wanting the man to hear every single word, "and chances are, when we get her out of here this time, he will hunt her down again. For as horribly as he seems to treat her, he's obsessed with keeping her at all costs. What then, huh?"

"We'll make sure he *can't* come after her."

"How?"

Because his focus was getting Valeria and Maria *out*. Nothing more, and nothing less. If he added the hit of a cartel leader onto this job, then they would have a hell of a lot more problems than they could handle.

Did he need to spell it out?

"We'll figure it out," Andino was quick to mutter.

Chris rolled his eyes. "Sure, sure."

He didn't like *what ifs*.

He hated unanswered questions.

Flying by the seat of his pants?

493

No fucking thanks.

He would have to roll with it whether he wanted to or not.

Great.

Out of the corner of his eye, he noticed a man stepping out of the house on the far left to his that the guards used. One of several. The man headed toward Chris's home, which meant his day was about to get started. For the last few days, the focus had been on transferring crates of product out of the barns, and onto trucks, all the while, they prepped for the trip to the tunnels this weekend.

It never stopped here, it seemed.

"I have to go," Chris told Andino, "and don't call again."

"I got it—get the job done, yeah?"

"Yeah."

That was the plan.

As unknown as it was.

• • •

"Right here, *amigo*," the Lòpez man said, pulling the back of a Jeep wide open for Chris. "Toss that bag in, we're just waiting on the boss, and his wife."

Chris nodded, pleased that Valeria was coming along for the weekend trip. He knew better than to show that on his face, however. "Thanks."

With his weekend bag thrown in the back of the Jeep on top of the other couple of bags piled there, the man closed the hatch with a slam. Chris settled on leaning against the back of the vehicle while the guard—or driver, whatever his designated job was for the day—headed for the house closest to them.

It was funny in that the only vehicles Chris had seen come this far into the ranch were all ones the guards and Jorge used to come in and out. Even the man's siblings weren't allowed to take a vehicle in and out of the place.

He filed that information away for later.

Vehicles were a no-go.

The slam of a screen door had Chris pushing off the side of the Jeep to look around the side of the vehicle. Jorge stood on the porch with Valeria where the two talked fast. She tried to remain calm and pleasant. It didn't matter; her husband was animated and irritated enough for the both of them.

Chris's irritation picked up a notch.

The more he observed the two together, the clearer it became to him that Valeria was neither happy with Jorge, nor safe. She carefully measured her behavior, and words. Even if she hadn't told him the truth when he asked, it wouldn't take a genius to figure out that marriage was a steaming pile of shit.

It didn't help he had somehow got into his feelings about Valeria, and whenever he saw her being dismissed or mistreated by the bastard she called a husband … it took everything in him not to kill Jorge right then and there with his bare hands.

Chris's gaze slipped past the two on the porch to the little girl peering out the screen door, watching her parents' quiet argument. Well, it was only quiet from Valeria's side of things. Jorge didn't seem to give a shit, to be honest.

Maria saw Chris looking her way, and the worry on her features morphed into a bright smile. She waved, and he returned the gesture with a wink. For whatever reason, the girl slipped out of the screen door, and headed past her parents. They didn't even note her leaving the house or coming down the stairs.

Maria came to stand in front of him. Chris kneeled to the ground to be closer to eye-level with her, uncaring that he was dirtying the knees of his slacks. He always thought it ignorant for adults to loom above kids when they talked to them. How would they like it to have someone much larger than them hanging overtop of them while they talked?

Not well, he bet.

"Hey," he said.

Maria beamed. "*Hey*. I made you something."

Chris blinked. "Did you?"

"Yes." Digging in the pocket of her dress, she added, "We're friends, right? Friends make promises, and you made me a promise."

Kids, man.

They had a way of simplifying everything. Of taking any kind of gesture and turning it into something *more*, innocent or otherwise. It reminded him of the good in the world when he was surrounded by things others might consider immoral, or even evil, sometimes.

"We are friends."

Maria glanced up at him, her hand stilling in its quest to find whatever item she wanted in her pocket. "*Best* friends? Like Mamá and me?"

Chris grinned. "We can be, Maria. But you didn't have to make me anything to be that, okay? Friends are just friends because they want to be—we don't have to give anything to our friends to keep them. Just our kindness, and the goodness in our hearts, huh? That's what counts."

She shrugged tiny shoulders. "But I *wanted* to. You'll wear it, won't you?"

"Wear what?"

She found the item she had been searching for. Pulling it from her pocket, she held it high for him to admire. A woven bracelet made from a dark, thin leather cord. She smiled, her eyes glimmering with pride as he stared at it.

"That's amazing," he said.

"Aunt Abril showed me how to braid it. Do you like it?"

Chris took the bracelet and held it flat in his palm. "So much, thank you."

"Put it on!"

He laughed but did as she said. It was a little too loose, but she showed him how to pull on one of the two end cords to tighten it firm to his wrist.

"It shouldn't get wet," she said.

"Okay, I'll make sure it doesn't."

"But you'll wear it always, anyway, right?"

Her genuine request had his chest tightening.

Chris nodded. "Absolutely. *Always*. I won't take it off."

"Good."

Maria darted forward, and gave him a tight hug, her little arms snaking around his neck so hard, he almost lost his breath. He didn't get the chance to hug her back before she stepped away from him and turned to dart back to the house.

She didn't get far.

Valeria stood two feet behind her daughter, now, surveying the scene with a soft gaze. She gave them a small smile, and then said to Maria, "Better get back in the house. Jorge forgot something and had to go back in to get it. We don't want him getting angry that you didn't listen when he told you to stay inside, right?"

Maria peeked over her shoulder at Chris, but turned back to her mother. "Okay, Mamá."

"I'll see you soon. Love you. *Behave.*"

"I will."

Once Maria had disappeared back inside the house, Chris stood up straight again. Valeria climbed into the back of the Jeep without a word.

He followed her lead.

· · ·

Whenever he saw a Jeep in Toronto, Chris always wondered what in the fuck their purpose was for their owner. They almost always had mud on the tires, too. Where in the hell had they even found mud in a city?

Now, driving in a Jeep as Jorge's driver took a sharp turn onto a dirt road that took their vehicle down a winding path, deeper into a forested area with little population, Chris understood the appeal. The Jeep handled the terrain just fine, and with the doors and top pulled off, the wind kept them cool.

Beside him in the back, Valeria sat quiet and still, her gaze drawn to the blur of trees at their sides, instead of Chris. He would much rather have her gaze on him, but that was perilous territory that neither of them needed to play in at the moment.

Especially not with her husband sitting in the front.

"Have they caught up?" Jorge asked, his laughter disappearing into the wind.

Chris peered over his shoulder, seeing the front of another Jeep coming over the hill behind them as they reached the end. "Almost."

"Ah, have to make this fun for them. It's a long drive, *amigo.*"

Apparently.

They had been driving for two hours now.

"You will enjoy this tunnel we'll show you," Jorge explained, his attention going back to the dirt road ahead of them. "My father had the tunnel built in first, but when the authorities became suspicious over the activity out this way, he had a permit made for a house."

Chris blinked. "A house?"

Jorge smirked over his shoulder. "Yes."

Valeria sighed beside Chris, as though she had heard this story a million and one times before. If Jorge took note of her annoyance, he said nothing. The sunhat in her lap hid the clenching of her fists from her husband's view, but Chris saw the action given she had to hold on to the item to keep it from flying away.

Was there something else on her mind?

Something other than her husband's conversation?

"And so," Jorge continued, his voice bringing Chris back to the present, although he didn't think he had missed much from the conversation, "my father had the tunnels built into the basement. Or rather, he built the home *around* the

496

tunnel with no one any wiser. They simply assumed the work we had been doing before was us digging the basement out of the rock and then pouring cement. Brilliant, hmm?"

"Smart, yes," Chris agreed. "And they have never found the tunnel."

"Once, almost. We had to dynamite a connecting tunnel when aerial surveillance found the entrance, and we didn't want it leading back to the house a few miles away. The vacation home tunnel is still the closest one we have to the border, and while we don't use it as much as we used to, well ..."

"It's good to have."

"Just in case," Jorge said, nodding.

The man's attention went back to the road ahead of them, but he continued talking. Chris had no interest in a lot of things Jorge had to say, but he listened because the man gave details that sometimes helped him along here in this plan to get Valeria and her daughter out.

"I brought Val along for the weekend," Jorge said, even though no one had asked, "because it's good for her to get out of the house, and she needs a break occasionally. Isn't that right, *hermosa*?"

Valeria's jaw tensed, but she forced a smile—a fake one—on her face when she turned to nod at Chris. "*Sí*, that's what they told me."

Told, he noted.

Not *wanted*.

"And our daughter gets to stay at home with the nanny, to keep her out of trouble," Jorge added after a moment.

Chris kept an eye on Valeria out of the corner of his eye, and that's how he witnessed the flash of sadness and worry that passed over her features before she hid it by looking away. That was it, then. Not Jorge's story, or the fact Chris sat beside her in the backseat.

Had Jorge *made* Maria stay home?

Was this purposeful beyond what the man said?

Chris wouldn't put it past him.

"Almost there," Jorge said. "Another twenty minutes, or so. The men I sent ahead of us will already have the generators up and running. This will be a good weekend away for us all, even if you are here for the tunnels, Chris. We all need a break, no?"

"A break is good for the soul," Chris replied.

His attention was still on Valeria though.

Reaching over, he placed his hand on her jean-covered thigh. She tensed from the sudden touch and then relax. He swept his thumb over the denim, her shiver reverberating through her body, and into his palm.

Something else he shouldn't be doing.

Still, he wanted her to be aware.

It would be okay.

It would.

He would make sure.

Even if it killed him.

11.

The vacation home, as Jorge dubbed it, sat tucked away in isolation, as much as their ranch did. Perhaps, more so. Dry, desert land surrounded the ostentatious house from all directions, with no neighbor or civilization in sight.

Valeria had never understood the draw of the vacation home—could it really be that when it was in the same country as their usual home? It was the same size as her father-in-law's mansion, except out in the middle of nowhere, and without power unless all six generators were running, which caused a racket when one was trying to sleep.

Besides that, the house was just … *big*. Three levels, reaching toward the sky, a separate wing for whatever men Jorge brought along, and the servants that kept the house running when no one was around to live within its walls. There was no guest house like the ones at the ranch. That meant *everyone* would sleep in the same house, walking the same halls, and eating at the same table all weekend.

Didn't that sound fun?

Valeria thought not.

A large pool in the back stretched across dry land, and while landscapers had come out to decorate, Valeria still felt the place was ugly, and lonely. Or maybe that was the projection because of her own emotions, and current situation. She couldn't be sure, but she didn't like it here.

Valeria walked through the home—watching servants scatter into the closest room whenever they heard Jorge's boots coming down the hallway—at her husband's side while he gave Chris a tour. She had other things to do, like hide away in her room, and go back to her daughter at the end of the weekend.

Jorge made it clear this weekend was nonnegotiable for her. Valeria was coming along whether she wanted to, and Maria wouldn't. Simple as that. It put her on edge to think of her daughter alone with that *nanny* all weekend.

Although, she knew Maria was also safe because nothing would save the woman from Jorge—certainly not his affection for her—if she thought to put her hands on their child. That didn't mean she liked her daughter spending more time with Carla than was necessary. Not that she cared to explain it to Jorge because this was just another way for the bastard to keep Valeria in line.

"And now," Jorge said, taking the stairs leading into the basement slowly as they sloped sharply, "the tunnel."

The keys in Jorge's hand jangled with every step he took. Valeria had to walk carefully in her heels, more so than the man in front of her. Jorge didn't notice, or if he did, then he didn't care. A hand came to rest on Valeria's back, and while it shocked her, her body only relaxed from the soft touch.

Chris.

His hand on her back let her know she was safe, and if she missed a step, then he would be right there to catch her. For whatever reason, and she blamed poor planning, they situated the light switch at the bottom of the stairs. She had seen the tunnel before, so there wasn't very much about this tour that was new or amazing

498

to her.

Jorge flicked the light on, illuminating a stark, white hallway that led to a set of double steel doors at the end, a good twenty feet away.

"There's nothing else down here?" Chris asked.

Jorge waved a hand for them to stay where they were at the bottom of the stairs as he headed for the doors at the end. "Cement in this section. We filled the rest of the space in because we didn't need it. The basement is finished and furnished in other areas—bedrooms, and whatever else. Some storage, too."

Chris shot Valeria a look, but for what, she didn't know. So, she shrugged as a non-response. He didn't seem to mind.

Using the keys he'd brought along, Jorge unlocked the metal doors at the end of the corridor. It took an effort for him to pull the doors open to showcase what rested behind. Once he did, Jorge stepped back with a smile and a nod at the dank-smelling, dark tunnel the metal doors kept hidden.

Chris made a noise under his breath. "How is it ventilated?"

"A couple of different ways." Jorge shrugged. "A few pipes here and there that come out of the ground, and when someone is working in the tunnels, we force air through them."

"And this is the closest one to the American border?"

"We're still quite a ways away, but *sí.*" Jorge gestured at the dark hole, asking, "Care to inspect?"

"Not particularly."

That earned a chuckle out of Jorge.

"Don't blame you, *amigo.* I won't go inside them, either."

"I take it this isn't where I will sleep for the weekend," Chris said, his attempt at a joke flying way over Jorge's head when the man gave him a pensive look at the other end of the hall. "I'd like to relax. It was a long drive."

Jorge nodded. "One of my men will show you which rooms you can use for the weekend. Find one and ask."

"Thank you."

Chris gave Valeria a quick smile, but didn't linger. If Jorge witnessed the exchange between the two, he didn't say. The receding footsteps echoed up the stairwell until a door opened and clicked shut. By the time she turned around to wait for Jorge to lock the doors back up, he was already down the hall and coming her way.

The doors at the end?

Closed.

That was how distracted Valeria became whenever Chris was in the picture. She knew, without a doubt, that wasn't a good thing for either of them. It would likely get them both in a world of trouble.

It scared her to death.

Jorge, though?

He terrified her more.

"I would like to call Maria," she told him, "once we're settled in."

Her husband chuckled, his arm coming to snake around her waist. To someone else, that hold might seem affectionate, but to her … it felt like another kind of prison. One she would never escape.

"No," he said.

"But—"

"Maria is fine where she is for the weekend, Val."

"I want to tell her goodnight, and to be a good girl while we're away."

When she couldn't get what she wanted from being honest, then she had to try another route. What she really wanted to do was make sure her daughter was being treated fairly by that bitch he forced her to leave Maria with.

"Come on," Jorge said, his arm tugging her up the stairs with him, "let's get settled in, and have something made to eat. I am starved."

"And then I can call Maria?"

"No."

"Jorge—"

In the stairwell, Valeria found herself slammed into the wall. Her spine ached from the force of her husband shoving her before he was quick to crowd her with his presence. She stared into his cold, dark eyes as his lips pulled down into a scowl that would rival the devil's. It frightened her, sure, but she refused to show it.

"You're too close to her, I think."

Valeria sucked in a sharp breath. "She's my child. I raised her."

"Yes, *without* me. Because what did you do, hmm?"

She refused to entertain *that* conversation. It always ended the same way, and that wasn't a game she wanted to play with this man today. One person lost every single time—*her*. That loss came in the form of a sore body, and bruises she needed to be creative to hide. She wasn't in the mood for it.

Her silence was not what he wanted though.

Jorge leaned in close, baring his teeth as he spoke in a hissed tone. "You spend *far* too much time filling that girl's head full of shit about me, Valeria."

"I do not."

On that, she wouldn't budge.

Valeria never told Maria anything bad about her father. Why would she when she didn't need to? Jorge poisoned his daughter against him all on his own, and with little to no effort on her part. If he couldn't see that, then how was that her problem?

"I think it would do her—and *you*—good to spend time apart."

"What does that mean?"

Jorge smiled. "Behave this weekend, Val, or she won't be there when you get home. The tutoring works well enough for her, doesn't it? I can't say how long that'll last, and there are quite a few private schools she can attend instead. Ones that will keep her away for weeks at a time. Do you hear me?"

Valeria swallowed the lump in her throat and nodded. "I hear you."

"Make sure."

• • •

The crack of a gunshot slicing through the air had Valeria jerking on the spot. She glanced upward in just enough time to see a skeet fly into the air by a mechanical arm before it exploded into shards of ruined ceramic. This little game of Jorge's and his men was now getting tiring, but she knew better than to go out there and tell him to knock it off.

Not that it mattered.

The sky was darkening as Valeria could see from her position on the bench seat at the large bay window in the sitting room. Soon, they would drink—let's be honest, they already had—and that would take importance over playing stupid shooting games with their rifles.

"You seem annoyed."

Valeria gave a look over her shoulder, and a small smile when her sister-in-law joined her at the window. "Decided to come along, did you?"

Abril waved a dainty hand. "Someone needs to keep you company, no?"

"Oh, was that it?"

"I had nothing better to do back at the ranch."

"Did you see Maria with—"

Abril's smile grew cold in an instant. "Carla knows what will happen to her should she step out of line with my niece."

Of course.

No question, Abril *was* just like her brothers. They didn't realize it, which was their mistake, Valeria supposed.

The raucous laughter from outside drew their attention to the window again. Valeria didn't wonder for long what had caused the men's uproar when she found her husband pawing at a woman while he stuck his tongue down her throat.

Valeria blinked.

The woman, wearing a gray dress with white buttons down the front, was a servant at the house. She couldn't be any older than twenty, if that, but she didn't seem to have a problem with the way Jorge groped her in front of a crowd of men while he licked the goddamn taste right out of her mouth.

She made a noise in the back of her throat, unsure of how she felt about the entire scene happening outside. Annoyed, maybe, but only because if the woman was bothered by the attention, she was far better at hiding it than Valeria.

"Better her than you tonight," Abril murmured beside her.

"That's cold, don't you think?"

Abril sighed. "I have learned that we all have to sacrifice to survive in this world, Val. And that means sometimes, thinking about yourself and what is best for you, even if that means someone else must hurt for it. You have too caring of a heart—you worry too much about people who wouldn't give a damn about you, and that's why you're an easy target for him, and whoever else wants to break your back on the way to the top."

Ouch.

That stung.

Abril wasn't wrong though.

"It's bad I care?" she asked quietly.

"It's bad you care so much, you would sacrifice yourself for someone else, yes. Women like us that's not how we make it in our life."

"Abril?"

"Hmm?"

Valeria glanced at her sister-in-law from the side, weighing her next words because she didn't want to offend the one person from her husband's family who gave a shit, and looked out for her. Then again, Abril had always appreciated Valeria's honesty, so she chose to say was on her mind.

"I don't want to be like you," Valeria whispered, "I'm *not* like you, or them. I never was."

Abril cleared her throat, her gaze drawing down to the ledge of the bench seat where Valeria sat, and she stood next to her. "I know, which is why I never understood his obsession with keeping you when you didn't fit him."

"I'm a trophy. Something he won. Nothing else."

"Shame, that."

Valeria let out a hard exhale and put her attention on the scene outside. "He told me earlier that if I didn't behave, Maria wouldn't be there when I returned home."

Abril made a dismissive noise. "He wouldn't bother. That's too much energy to spend for a *girl*, Val. And that's all she is to him, a girl. What he wants more is a boy, and so if he can keep you in your place long enough to get what he wants from you, then that's what he'll do. Even if it means using her, and your fears about her, to get it."

She swallowed hard.

Abril didn't miss it.

"What?"

"He will not get that boy," Valeria muttered.

"That's not how sex works, is it?"

"IUD, two years ago. A *just in case*. I have another four years before it must be replaced."

Abril whistled low. "Do *not* let him find out about that."

Yeah.

Valeria got it.

"But for her—Maria—he doesn't care," Abril said, "and if you were a smart woman, you would use that to your advantage more than you do."

"I don't understand."

"Because you're not like me, right?"

Valeria gave her a glance.

Abril cocked her brow. "Not a lie."

"Not a lie," she echoed. "What do you mean, though?"

"If he's willing to use her to manipulate you into *behaving*, then use her as a way to make him believe you're willing *to* behave."

Valeria blinked. "Do you mean—"

"He's a man, Val, and not a complex one to begin with. Should he think letting you have her and do what you want with her will make you react and behave better than his way, which do you think he'll use?"

Huh.

At the dawning realization in Valeria's eyes, Abril smirked.

"Keep it in mind." With that said, Abril turned to leave, but not before saying, "It's rude to spy. Or hasn't anyone told you that, yet?"

Valeria's head snapped sideways at Abril's chiding only to find the reason for it leaning in the sitting room's doorway room like he didn't have a care in the world. Chris shrugged when Abril strolled on past him, but his attention turned on her once Abril left.

Sadness.

That's what she found in his gaze.

How long had he been listening?

What did it matter?

• • •

Valeria avoided going to bed, but as the house grew quiet and the sky blackened but for the moon and stars, she no longer had a choice except to go to her room. It was always easier when she went willingly rather than Jorge needing to come and find her to drag her to bed.

The bedroom was empty and dark when she made her way upstairs, but she wasn't mad about it. At least, it gave her a few more minutes to be alone with her thoughts, and *without* her husband.

Everything was always easier without him.

Valeria also learned what she had to do to make her experience in bed with Jorge less traumatic and painful. As long as she seemed submissive, and unwilling to fight, even if every piece of her *wished* she didn't have to be there, doing what he forced her to do, then she walked away from nights with her husband in the morning less sore, and with fewer bruises.

Sad as that was.

So, Valeria readied for her night, sick to her stomach the entire time. Undressing from her day clothes, and slipping into something more appropriate for nighttime, and moved on to set out her clothes for the next day, the minutes ticked by.

Jorge still didn't come upstairs.

The longer she waited, the more nervous Valeria became sitting on the edge of the bed. There, she had a full view of the door, and what kind of monster might come through it.

Jorge had been in a mood all day, and that was going to translate into the man who entered the bedroom. She much preferred to be ready to deal with it right away instead of being surprised by it.

Valeria had time to consider her life during moments like these, and everything that happened until this point. All the choices she made, and the things she might have done differently so that this wasn't where she ended up night after night.

She didn't want to blame herself.

Easier said than done.

Sighing at the sounds of footsteps in the hallway, approaching the bedroom, Valeria glanced down at the clenched hands in her lap. Her fingernails manicured to perfection because that's what her husband liked, but she was more concerned with the stiffness in her hands that reflected in the rest of her body.

She willed it to calm.

To relax.

It didn't work—it never did.

The doorknob jiggled, before it turned, and the door pushed open. For the split second she took to peek up, ready to deal with yet another nightmare in her daily life … only for her to freeze on the bed at the man who slipped into the room.

It wasn't Jorge at all.

"Chris."

12.

Valeria's shock at seeing Chris slip into her room only lasted long enough for him to close the door before she shot up off the bed like a bullet coming out of a gun. Her hands were already up, palms facing him as she came toward him, reading to push him back.

"You can't be in here," she hissed, "you *can't*—he'll be up any minute. You have to go!"

"Val—"

"Get out. This isn't funny anymore, Chris!"

"*Valeria.*"

She wasn't hearing him at all. Her hands hit his chest, and with all her might, she pushed him back toward the door. Or rather, she *tried*. Chris was a wall, tough as fucking brick, and unmovable. That didn't mean she wasn't willing to give her all, which he had to appreciate either way, as cute as it was.

Cute.

Yeah, that wasn't the right word.

Chris had seen Valeria go through a gamut of emotions and situations since his arrival in Mexico. He'd seen her sweet and loving with her child. Sad and scared with her husband. Indifferent when no one thought she was looking, and she was alone with her thoughts. The woman was a spectrum of feelings—never settling on one thing for too long before she had to put on yet another mask to satisfy her husband, and whatever he was demanding of her for the moment.

But anger?

He'd never seen her with that.

Until now.

Chris had to admit, she looked damn good angry. A red flush colored her golden-brown skin and brightened her eyes more than they already were. Sure, that beautiful smile he loved faded, but that didn't change his desire to kiss those full, sexy lips of hers at all.

Not in the slightest.

"Do you know what he'll do to me?" Valeria demanded.

Her hands came up to shove against him again, but Chris was quick to grab her wrists that time. Locking her in place with his fingers like bars around her wrists, he dragged her into his chest without warning, and tipped his head down to press a fast kiss to her lips.

He had control.

Always.

Chris was the one who, in the middle of chaos, would be as calm as the eye of a storm. No matter what, he took great pains to ensure that was the case.

Except with her, it seemed.

There was something about Valeria, something in her soul, he thought, that called out to him, and shredded any sense of self-preservation or restraint he had left. He swore that he could sense her sadness and loneliness from across a

505

crowded room, and he hated that. This woman should never feel those things—
ever.

The second his mouth touched to hers, Valeria answered him back. She kissed
him hard, her lips moving against his in a way that seemed familiar although it
couldn't be—he had barely touched this woman, and yet, a part of him felt like he
had known her for his entire life.

How was that possible?

It was *crazy*.

Chris let Valeria's wrists go just so he could cup her jaw and draw her even
closer to him as his tongue teased the seam of her lips. He wanted *in*—wanted to
taste her, and if that meant handing over his soul to this woman to get what he
wanted, then *fine*.

So fucking be it.

Their tongues clashed, a war in a kiss, if that were possible. Her fingers found
the neckline of his shirt, curling tight, and holding close. She seemed determined to
lick the taste of him right from his mouth with her kiss, and as much as he liked
that, he still needed to talk to her.

As he was learning, there were few times when he could get Valeria alone like
this—she was so protected, so *sheltered*. Someone was almost always around to keep
an eye on her, and that put Chris in a bad position when he needed as much time
with this woman as he could get.

And *not* just for this.

Not for moments like these, even though he needed them, too. No, because
this plan—which he hadn't even figured out yet—would not work unless she
trusted him. Inexplicably, and *completely*. This woman needed to trust him.

"Shhh," he whispered against the seam of Valeria's lips when he pulled away,
and she opened her mouth to speak. "Just relax, yeah?"

Valeria let out a shaky breath, her dark eyes darting up to his. "Kind of hard, so
excuse me."

He grinned crookedly, a thumb sweeping the line of her jaw. There was
something silky about her skin—warm and *inviting*. She had to feel the hard ridge of
his erection pressing against her body tucked into his, but she said nothing about it.
That was the proof, though, about just how much this woman affected him, even if
he didn't understand why.

All it took was kissing her.

Stroking her jaw.

And all of him wanted to discover as much as he could about the rest of her.
Peel off these thin, soft bed clothes she had put on, lay her back, and *explore*. With
his mouth, and his hands, and his cock. Learn how she enjoyed being loved, and
the kinds of sounds she would make when he found what she liked the most.

"You shouldn't *be* here," she mumbled, her bottom lip trembling when he
dropped a soft kiss to her mouth again. "What are you doing?"

"I shouldn't be, you're right."

He could do the job without *this*. God knew he had no business messing
around with a married woman, even if said woman didn't want to be married, or in
her current situation. There were vows in life a man didn't need to break, and this
was one of those.

The problem for him was that it wasn't the forbidden that drew him back to Valeria, or even the thrill. No, it was simply *her*.

Something about her had him coming back, wanting more, and willing to risk it all.

Was it stupid?

Entirely.

It also might be worth it.

Chris would chance it.

"Jorge took off in one of the Jeeps with a woman," Chris said, still stroking the line of Valeria's jaw with his thumbs as he spoke to keep her calm, "and said he wouldn't be back until morning, likely."

Her gaze drifted away from his. "The servant?"

"Seemed so."

"Hmm."

"Sorry," he said quickly.

Valeria barked out a laugh, her dark stare coming back to his with a fire lingering there. "*Look at me*—in a bedroom with a man who isn't my husband, with his hands on me, and still able to taste him in my mouth. What are you apologizing for?"

"That look in your eyes," Chris responded, "that sadness I wish you didn't feel."

She stiffened, her chin quivered, but just as fast as that threat of her vulnerability came on, it left. Replaced instead by something colder, and stronger. Life had a funny way of doing that to people—of shaping them into a better version of themselves, even if it hurt a lot along the way to get to the end result.

Chris was proof of that.

"There are still people—*guards*—in this house that could get me in trouble for this," she said.

Chris shrugged. "They're busy."

"What does that mean?"

"Seems like when the king is away, the court will play."

Valeria's gaze burned. "He is no king."

"Agreed." Chris sighed, tipping Valeria's head back so he could stare down at her, and enjoy the sight of this woman in his hands for a moment. "You understand, don't you?"

"Understand what, Chris?"

Her words were a whisper.

A caress.

"That you're safe with me, Val—I'm not like him, and I won't hurt you, or take from you when you don't want to give it to me. I'm not a perfect man, but I am a good one."

"I like to think I do understand that."

Chris smiled. "But?"

"Life has taught me to be wary."

Right.

He would be concerned otherwise.

"But I think I always knew anyway," Valeria said, her tongue snaking out to wet the seam of her lips as she spoke. "You were soft and sweet with my daughter, and I saw it in how you treated me. So, I *do* get it, but—"

"Life," he interjected.

"I have to be careful."

"I want you to be."

"Oh?"

He nodded. "And I also want you to trust me. This can't work otherwise, Val."

She let out a hard breath. "I'm not convinced it will work at all, if I'm being honest."

"Why?"

"You see my life, don't you?" A bitter laugh fell from her lips, and he instantly wanted to kiss it away. Somehow, he refrained, but it was *hard*. "Don't blame me for thinking freedom is a dream I'll never see come true, Chris."

"Except it will, and it starts with tonight."

"What does that mean?"

Chris chuckled. "Well, it means whatever you want. You run this show, sweetheart."

Valeria gave him a sly smile. "Does that mean you'll share all your secrets with me?"

"I don't have many of those, but what do you want to know?"

A quick shake of her head answered his question, and she looked away. "I was kidding, I didn't—"

"I have four siblings—*all* brothers," Chris said. "We're French-Italian Canadians, but only a couple of us can speak fluent French. All of us are fluent in Italian. My twin, well, this job was almost his, but he's … married isn't the right word, but he needed time off, and so I took the job for him instead."

Valeria's brow lifted. "A *twin?*"

"Identical, too."

"Like … the same?"

Chris made a noise under his breath. "On the outside, yeah. Corrado. He's always been my best friend, so I have to look out for him, that's all."

"Like taking this job?"

"Yeah, like this. We're one set of two twins, and we have an older brother who was the only singleton of our siblings. My mother was also an identical twin."

"It's a genetic thing, then?"

Chris laughed. "Seems so."

Valeria's smile softened. "And you love them. I can hear it in your voice."

"All of my family," he agreed, "to the ends of the earth and back. I would do anything for them, and they would do the same for me. That's how our parents raised us."

Chris shook his head, thinking about his family, but more specifically, his twin. "I joined The League—an organization that trains assassins—because I didn't want my twin to go it alone. I thought he needed me there to watch his back. That's what my family taught me; no matter what, we look out for each other."

"And did he need you?"

"Not for that, but it didn't change what I felt. It's like this, too, though. I need to *fix* things. It's what I do, it's who I am. All I want to do is fix this for you, to make it better, so you can be happy again. *Safe* again."

"I was happy once."

"When?"

"In New York."

"Not before?"

Valeria sighed. "When I was a girl, too, I guess."

"Were your parents good to you?"

That earned him another smile, but it faded fast. Chris hated that, and wanted to get her smiling again, but she was already talking.

"I was an only child, but my papa and mama spoiled me. We didn't have a lot when I was younger, and my father had grand ideas about all the changes he thought our country needed."

"That's why he went into politics?"

Valeria shrugged one shoulder, her gaze dimming. "I don't know if he thought he would be untouchable because he made it clear his loyalties didn't lie with those who could buy him, but it didn't matter, did it? The cartel got what they wanted when they went after the things that meant the most to him. And what good did it do to him—he's dead, too."

"I'm sorry."

"I … don't want that to be the lesson my daughter learns."

"She won't because her mother is *better*."

Maybe it was the strength in his tone—the truth ringing out—but Valeria was quick to nod before meeting his gaze again. "I want to be, yeah. Know, no matter what happens here, or how this ends up … if I am put in a position where I have to leave without my daughter, I won't go. I *can't*."

His hands that had slid down to her waist tightened. "I would never put you in that position. If it can't be done my way, then we will figure out another way."

"And what is your way?"

Well, that, he hadn't figured out yet. Chris figured now was not the time to say that.

"And he'll kill Maria," Valeria added when Chris stayed silent, "if he even *thinks* I am planning to leave with her. It would mean hurting me, but also teaching me that if he cannot have me, no one can. She doesn't matter to him. She is a pawn for him to use."

"Not for much longer."

"You say that, but—"

"I get that, Val." Chris leaned in, and pressed a featherlight kiss to Valeria's lips as he murmured, "I made a promise to her—and to you, in a way—and I intend to *keep it*. But trust me. Just trust me."

With each graze of his lips against hers, her kisses answered him back. Soft, at first. Tentative, before each one of her kisses became more and more *hungry*. He hadn't intended to come to her room for this, but her demand was a loud echo—despite their silence—as her hands grabbed at his shirt with enough force to pull the buttons from the loops.

Chris didn't need to stop and ask Valeria if this was what she wanted with him, or if she was just reacting from her high emotions. This woman had been gaslighted and abused enough in her one relationship—he hadn't forgotten what she told him that first time she let him touch her, after all—that she didn't need another man to make her wonder if he was underhandedly second-guessing her.

She was a woman.

Capable of attraction, lust, and desire.

If she wanted to *fuck*, then that's what she would do. He was more than happy to give her whatever she wanted because that meant he was fucking her.

It was a win-win, really.

"I … I want you," Valeria mumbled against his mouth, her voice a needy whine that had his cock hardening, "*please*."

"Abso-fucking-lutely," he told her in a groan.

He pulled the six-pack of condoms he had bought for this trip to keep on him as a *just in case* from the back of his slacks, tossing them to the bed while kissing Valeria with enough force to have her walking backward. She only stopped when the backs of her knees hit the edge of the bed.

He'd never seen someone be as graceful or *sexy* as she was undressing him one piece of clothing at a time. Her intent, as heady as her determination, had Chris checking his more dominant nature to be the one to control during sex.

And then, as she pushed his boxer-briefs down his hips, the last stich of clothing on him, she stilled when his hard cock jerked out in her direction. Chris grinned at the color flooding her cheeks—a delicious red, innocent in some ways, and yet that want in her eyes made it seem so fucking sinful, too.

He thought, *a walking complex.*

That's what this woman was.

She was many things.

Alone, or together.

Sinful and innocent.

Harsh, and soft

It amazed him.

And turned him all the way *on.*

"What do you want, huh?" he asked. "You get whatever you want, Valeria, I need you to use your words, and tell me. I'll always give it, if you tell me. So, what is it, babe? I can lay you back on this bed, feast on your pussy, and then fuck you until you can't take it anymore … or I can let you climb on me, and ride until your heart is content. You can bend over this bed, and let me worship your pussy and your ass, or you can—"

"I want to touch you."

Chris audibly swallowed.

Damn.

He didn't mind making this all about her. Regardless of what other men liked to bullshit about when it meant busting a nut during sex, he got off on getting someone *else* off. And yet, to hear her ask to pleasure him almost had his fucking knees buckling.

What was she doing to him?

"Yeah, Val," he murmured, "fucking touch me. Get what you want, woman."

She did, deft fingers curling around his length after he'd stepped out of those boxer-briefs. Light tugs *really* stroked him awake, but it was the way she tightened and loosen her grip with a faster speed that had his head falling back for a moan to drag from his lips.

"You look so good like that."

Her whisper woke up his senses.

Every fucking one.

"All for you," he rumbled.

She did just that, taking her time to tease him into a tight ball of hot need with her hands while she watched him with hooded, lustful eyes. He about fucking died when she leaned in to press a featherlight kiss to the middle of his chest before subsequent touches of her lips lowered with each one.

"Fucking *hell*."

Valeria's light laughter lasted only long enough for her to get the head of his dick in her mouth. And if there was a heaven, it was Christopher watching this woman on her knees for him, learning the way he liked for her to suck his dick, while his hand tangled into her hair, and her gaze locked on him.

"Look at you, huh?" he uttered, jaw clenching from the way her lips kept tightening around the head of his cock when she came back up to the tip. "So fucking pretty on your knees for me. Do you like that, Val, do you want my load down your throat, babe?"

He swore her throat flexed at the head of his dick, an instinctual swallow, that about had him coming. He wasn't a fourteen-year-old boy getting his first pussy here—he would not bust a nut in two minutes—but she sure as fuck made him feel like it.

His hand left her hair long enough to snake in under her jaw. He held her still, his cock still stretching out those pretty lips of hers, as wide eyes looked up at him with the need to please, and *be* pleased.

"Let me fuck you," he whispered.

Valeria released his cock from her mouth, the heat of her breath a contrast to the sensitive skin of his length when she breathed, "Please do."

"God, yes."

It took Chris all of a minute to have her standing naked in front of him after he'd stood her up and pulled every piece of clothing keeping her from him off her body.

Had he mentioned how beautiful she was?

All her lines, and curves.

Hips that spoke of a woman who carried a child, shapely and *sinful*, and a round ass that made him want to take a bite. Golden skin with undertones of red and brown that made his fucking mouth water. That dark hair of hers fell over her shoulders in a wave, still a contrast to her skin, and shiny under the dim lights of the bedroom.

An angel.

Wicked as she was.

"You're beautiful," he told her, "it fucking *hurts*, Val. That's how beautiful you are."

She sucked in a jerky breath, breathing, "Show me. Show me how beautiful."

He said nothing, only moved forward to get Valeria to her back on the bed. His hands slid under her thighs, lifting her legs high and wide as his head dipped between her legs. Oh, he'd spend lots of time eating the juices from her slit later after he'd had her coming on his cock for a while, but right then he wanted her flavor on his tongue.

Chris licked her from her slit to her clit.

One tease.

Then, his lips worked up her body, past her navel, her stomach, and the valley of her breasts. He reached for the condoms he'd tossed aside earlier as he hovered above her, breaking open cardboard to get to the foil packets inside. Valeria panted beneath him, chest rising and falling while he sheathed his cock in latex.

Her hands found her knees, and she pulled her legs up, and open for him as he leaned back, and her head fell to the pillow to give him a beautiful view of her willingly spread out for him. He teased her with his fingers for a moment, enjoying the sight of her moaning into the pillow while her slick arousal coated his hand.

"Feel how fucking wet you are for me?" Chris asked. "I can't wait to get another taste of this after you've been praying to my name."

"*Please …*"

This sweet woman.

He didn't deny himself, or her, longer.

The sound she made when he worked his cock into her tight pussy was *raw*. So hot, and needy all rolled into one sexy woman. When he seated himself deep inside her walls, Valeria let out a hard breath, those lips of hers a perfect *O* while she stared up at him.

His hand pressing into her lower stomach kept her trembling hips from being able to seek more of him as she tried to move against him. "You like that?"

"Oh, God, so much."

"You want more?"

"*Please.*"

He loved how the word slipped from her lips. Airless, and yet so sure. Desperate in her want, but assured in her need.

Chris fucked her slow at first, his hands flattening to her sides to grab tight and pull her into every flex of his hips. And then when she whined, the broken cries she tried to hide muffled into the pillow, he fucked her faster.

A little harder.

Deeper.

Until she trembled, her skin flushed, and her lips a bitten-red from her teeth as she shook through her first orgasm from his dick. And just as fast, before she had even finished shaking through that orgasm, he moved them on the bed.

Him on his back.

Her on top.

"Ride me until you come again," he told her, thrusting his hips up, so she sat deeper onto his cock while her breaths burst out of her chest, "use me like you want to Val, and I'll get what I need, too. Fuck me, woman."

She did.

So damn good, too.

• • •

As much as Chris didn't want to leave that bedroom, or Valeria's side, he still

THE GUZZI LEGACY: VOL 1

pushed out of the bed slowly. Once the two had cleaned up, redressed, and he tucked her into his side in the bed, she fell into a deep sleep.

Small blessings, he supposed.

A quick look out the window told him the sky was still dark, and would be for a while. If all went well, the house would be quiet, and the rest of the people would be asleep, or damn close to it. No one would look sideways at him coming down the hallway in the middle of the night, not if they were already drunk, or sleepy.

An easy excuse—he had to use the bathroom.

Who would question it?

Still, Chris didn't want to risk running into anyone at all. One or two incidents he might be able to brush off, but if caught in a compromising position with Valeria, then this whole thing would be over.

That was not a risk he wanted to take.

A check of the clock on the bedside table told him it was three in the morning—lucky he hadn't fallen asleep, too. It would be a long day for him tomorrow with only a couple of hours of sleep, but with Valeria still pressed against him, her taste lingering on his tongue, and the sounds of her bliss echoing in his mind ...

Worth it.

This had been worth it.

Leaning over the bed, he tangled his fingers in the stray waves of Valeria's black hair that had fallen over her shoulder. Tucking the strands back, he let his fingertips glide over her delicate shoulder, and down her arm. She slept on, unbothered by his attention, lost in her dreams.

Like this, she was peaceful.

He wanted her to have more of that.

Peace.

Someone who gave a fuck.

He wanted to be that person.

Carefully, he dropped a soft kiss to her shoulder, and the corner of her mouth. He swore he saw her lips quirk into a smile in her dreams, but he couldn't linger any longer than he already had.

"See you soon, sweetheart," he murmured.

Before he found another reason to stay—wasn't the woman sleeping in the bed reason enough?—Chris headed out of the bedroom, checking the hallway first. An empty hall stared back at him, thankfully. He closed the bedroom door behind him without making a sound.

Down the hall though?

Another door *clicked.*

Chris looked that way, but saw nothing.

Someone going back to bed?

God.

He fucking hoped so.

13.

The next morning, Valeria stepped into the large dining room, surprised at how quiet it was considering how many people were staying at the home with them for the weekend. She didn't have to wonder for long what caused the stillness when her gaze landed on the man sitting at the head of the table.

Jorge scowled at the older man who brought his breakfast to him. "Took long enough, don't you think?"

"Sorry, sir. Would you like your coffee—"

"*Now.*"

His voice, slurred and harsh, told the truth. Jorge was hung over, and that *rarely* spelled good things for anyone else in his direct vicinity. The man loved to drink, but hated to deal with the morning after because of it, too.

The only good thing about his hangover?

Jorge barely paid Valeria any mind.

She joined them at the table, willing to ignore she hadn't seen her husband at all the night before, and had no idea when he returned to the home. It meant she spent her entire evening and morning without him, and that wasn't a bad thing.

Not that she had been lonely.

Across the table, Chris worked on buttering a bagel as one servant poured him a cup of coffee. He smiled up at the woman pouring his coffee, nodding. "That's good, thank you. I'll prepare it the way I like it."

"If you're sure …"

"No worries, I have it."

"Where is my *cream?*"

Jorge's bellow echoed down the table and silenced the rest of the people trying to enjoy their breakfast. A lot of them weren't any better or worse than Jorge if Valeria was to believe what Chris had told her the night before.

He had no reason to lie.

She might have been sorry for them and the headaches they had, but she didn't give a shit. And given her husband was busy snapping at anyone who didn't move fast enough for his liking, or dared to breathe in his direction, she also had better things to do.

Like stare at Chris.

He looked back.

It was insane.

Foolish.

His wink from across the table was enough to make her crazy, and hot all at the same time. God knew she had spent more than enough hours the night before beneath this man, letting him learn all the parts of her body he wanted, and still … somehow, she wanted more.

Definitely insane.

There was no other explanation for why Valeria seemed willing and ready to get Chris between her thighs as soon as she could. Not when she knew each time was yet one step closer to being caught, which meant the end of her life.

Not that it mattered.

No one noticed her staring.

Or his.

Chris's lips quirked up at the edges, and Valeria had to glance down at the empty plate in front of her because of it. The flood of heat that traveled straight down to her pussy, making her thighs clench under the table as she tried to soothe that sudden ache, was dangerous.

And *addicting*.

She had forgotten what sex should be until Chris. A part of her thought it would never be good again—that she wouldn't *want* for it, or a man, again because of the hell Jorge put her through. She had forgotten about the things she wanted, and *deserved*, because she was too busy trying to survive. Or even, taking care of someone else's needs, like her child. Although, she didn't regret that. Ever.

With little effort at all, Chris reminded her that she was very much a woman with needs, and one who wanted them fulfilled. She should be grateful for that, and she *was* … but it also scared her.

Everything about this terrified her.

Trust me.

His words rang in her mind.

Valeria wouldn't soon forget them.

She couldn't.

Glancing across the table again, she found Chris tipping his coffee up for a drink. Over the rim of the mug, while everyone else around them was trying to avoid Jorge's morning wrath, Chris watched her with a knowing glint in his eye.

That look said *soon*.

It murmured beautiful things.

It promised, too.

Hope, Valeria realized.

That's what she was feeling in those moments—*hope*. As traitorous as it was, and as destructive as it might be. Because what might happen, she wondered, if she did get that freedom Chris promised her.

What would happen with him?

With her?

For her child?

She had never dared to hope before.

Now, it was all she felt.

Because of him.

• • •

"But have you explained to Papá what you're planning yet?"

"Why, so he can ruin the Canadian deal?"

"Jorge—"

"Samuel, I told you how this will work. Didn't I?"

The Spanish between the Lòpez brothers flowed fast, and while Valeria was fluent, her years away from Mexico and not needing to speak her mother tongue sometimes made it difficult for her to follow along when two or more people spoke quickly. Her steps slowed coming down the stairs of their ranch home, so she could focus on *just* the conversation happening between Jorge and his brother in the kitchen.

"He's already planned Abril's wedding to Roberto García," Samuel said, a sigh following his words. "If you think by ruining this arrangement, he's made with our rivals will only piss them off, then you are mistaken, brother."

"Have you considered that's what I want?"

"Excuse me?"

Jorge let out a bitter laugh. Valeria shivered. Her husband was a lot of things, and a bastard was at the top of the list. He didn't care who he had to hurt on his way to the top as long as that's where he landed at the end of it all.

His family?

People he should care for?

Those he proclaimed to love?

Fodder.

That's all they were to him.

Things to use.

"That's what I want, Samuel," Jorge said, his tone thick with pleasure at his plan coming together. "*Finally*, this will be the message I need to send for it to be clear where Papá and I stand—he is no longer running this organization. *I am.*"

"You're looking for a problem, then."

Valeria knew better than to spy, and yet, she stayed right where she was. Sometimes, eavesdropping was the only way she got any information. No one ever thought to inform her because what did it matter? She was a woman, nothing more. Jorge's wife—his *thing* to do with what he wanted, whether anyone cared what happened to her.

A part of her figured she needed to listen to Abril more and take the woman's advice. If she planned to make it out of here alive, then she would use everything to her advantage.

"He's old, and his ways show it," Jorge snapped. "What is he going to do at his age? Step back—that is his only option, now. To step back and see my way is the better way. And if we have to tear apart the García cartel when this is all said and done to finish it, then so be it."

"You don't understand the issue with that at all, do you?"

"No, I don't understand *your* issues."

"They are the same things!"

Jorge's annoyance came out in a dark grunt. The sound told Valeria that Samuel was walking a thin line with Jorge's patience. A dangerous thing, no matter which way someone tried to spin it.

Mostly, she tried to stay out of her husband's way when he was in this kind of mood. Come to think of it, he had been like this for the last week. Ever since they returned to the ranch from the vacation home. She had seen little of Chris throughout the week, other than his occasional walk around the property.

Here, Jorge sheltered her.

It made things hard.

"This is *done*," Jorge hissed to his brother, "and nothing you say to sway my decisions will work, so quit before it becomes an annoyance I will have to deal with, Samuel. Do you hear me? *Stop*."

"I'm only trying to make you look at the bigger picture. All you see is what you *want*, but not what will happen because of it, or who will suffer *for* it, Jorge."

"I'm done discussing this. The deal with the Canadians will be completed soon. Once it is, and we have the full supply control or all of Canada, we won't need Papá, or his fucking deal with the Garcías to merge our organizations. And with that much territory behind our name, it won't matter what the García cartel tries to do to us—it won't leave a dent."

"How soon until it's finalized?"

"Chris will leave by mid-week, or that's what he explained," Jorge replied, "so I assume before then."

What?

Valeria's heart stopped.

Chris was leaving?

That soon?

Within a couple of days?

Maybe less?

What did that mean for her? Or ... for Maria?

She didn't give a single shit about the rest of Jorge's plans—nothing he planned against his own father, or the rival cartel, helped her. It would not get her out of here, and would only force him to seclude her and his child further away from the public while his manufactured wars raged on.

That's how this life worked.

The conversation continued in the kitchen with her husband and his brother unaware that the fluttering hope she had allowed herself to feel now seemed like shards of glass inside her chest. Her legs became weak, and she slipped down to sit on the step, drawing her knees to her chest as she realized this was over.

They would never get free.

How could they if he left?

Her last hope.

What was hope good for, anyway?

Nothing.

That's what.

Hope is for the fucking weak. It's why she had never bothered before now because it all ended the same. So, why did this hurt so much?

● ● ●

"What are you do—"

Valeria scooped her daughter up from the ground where she had been playing with the kitten that her father still threatened to take from her. She ignored the nanny's shout at her back as she turned and headed toward the stables while Maria's wild black curls flew in every direction.

"Careful, my kitty!"

"Hold him tight," Valeria told her girl.

Maria did just that, tucking the squirming kitten into her arms, cradling it like a baby doll. Behind them, Carla shouted louder.

"You can't just *take* her, Valeria!"

"She is my child. I can do whatever I want."

"I'll tell Jorge you said that."

Fuck it.

"Do so," Valeria snapped over her shoulder.

Carla's fish-mouthed stare almost made her laugh. The bitch also wasn't as important as she tried to seem to be, so Valeria didn't give her another thought.

Oh, sure, she would pay for this.

Jorge would make her aware.

Valeria didn't give a shit.

Not right now.

"Where are we going?" Maria asked.

"For a horse ride."

Away, she wanted to say,

Just ... God, away from here, and this place, and these people. Away from pain, and fear, and the hell that would someday catch up with her. Not that it mattered. Eventually, she would have to come back, and if she didn't, then someone would come find her.

For right now, though, she was going.

She needed to.

Once she had calmed down earlier after overhearing Jorge's conversation with his brother, Valeria's only wanted to *get away*. It screamed in her heart—to *go*. *Somehow.*

Knowing she didn't have much time, Valeria took the one horse that someone already tacked up. That way, she didn't have to waste time getting their favorite riding horses ready.

She put Maria on the horse first, tucking the kitten into a rucksack for her daughter to carry close to her chest, before heaving herself onto the animal, too. They came out of the stables in a slow trot.

"Don't look back at the house," she told her daughter.

Maria frowned, tipping her head back to peeked up at her mom. "Why?"

"Because if they know we see them, then we can't lie later when we come back."

"Not supposed to lie, Mamá."

Valeria struggled the most with these moments. She wanted her child to be a *good* human being—a person with values, and morals. And with one white lie came more white lies, right?

Still ...

"Sometimes, we have to lie, Maria."

Her daughter blinked. "To Jorge?"

She didn't miss how it wasn't *Papá* when someone couldn't hear Maria. That just proved to Valeria that her daughter understood what she said even if she wanted her mother to explain it better.

"To him, and people that help him," she agreed.

Maria nodded. "Okay, Mamá."

Valeria checked behind them, though she told Maria not to. No one watched them leave, and even Carla had disappeared. No one saw them take the horse out.

It didn't matter.

Valeria pressed her heels into the sides of the horse and clicked her tongue. That slow trot became a gallop, and she continued looking over her shoulder until the ranch disappeared. Still, no one saw them go.

The ride to the cliffs went by quickly. She should have planned the ride better—attempted to grab food to take with them so that Maria could have a supper.

Her daughter didn't seem to mind.

Maria busied herself with wildflowers and her kitten. She didn't notice her mother sitting along the edges of the cliffs. Valeria watched the horizon, and the choppy waters down below. They stayed like that, Valeria staring, and Maria playing, and before long, she heard hooves hitting the ground in a gallop.

Approaching.

She just knew.

It wasn't someone coming after her.

Not to take her back.

It wasn't Jorge, or his men.

Valeria peeked over her shoulder. She could tell who it was by the way he sat atop the animal, both comfortable and confident.

She also sensed him.

Chris.

Apparently, her heart hadn't finished breaking.

14.

The risk of following Valeria on horseback to the cliffs was high, but Chris weighed it before he left. Given he was already out on a horse, one he took out around noon when the guards were doing their shift change, nobody saw him leave, and so they wouldn't expect him to be returning soon, either.

Chris often came and went on the property. After a spread of time on the ranch, it almost seemed like the guards and the family had become accustomed to Chris doing his own thing, and as he didn't interrupt their business, they didn't bother his.

That worked in his favor.

Like now.

It wasn't seeing Valeria on a horse that concerned Chris, as she often took the animals out to ride, but rather, the look on her face. If sadness had a picture in the dictionary next to the word, it would have been of Valeria. A deep ache settled in his heart at the sight, and before he knew what was happening, he had turned his horse around in the field as he had been approaching the ranch, and followed behind.

He'd noticed Maria, too, but the girl didn't seem to be in the same state her mother was, and she rode on her own horse whenever she took one out. Not today, though. This time, she was riding with her mother.

Chris's anxiety spiked when he realized Valeria was heading for the cliffs. Since his arrival, he had only visited the cliffs once on a ride. Their proximity to the water, and the obvious danger, kept him from taking the horses out that way. He didn't need to be urging his fears on more than he already did whenever he felt the need to test himself.

He did his best to ignore that Valeria was sitting on the edge, overlooking the water, when he approached. She glanced back at him, dark eyes filled with a line of water that had his chest clenching.

Something was wrong.

But what?

"Chris!"

"Hey, *bambina*," he said to Maria, slowing the horse to a stop before jumping down to the ground. The animals were well-trained and didn't wander off as he learned, so he dropped the horse's reins and didn't give it a second thought. Maria peered up at him from her spot in a patch of wildflowers where her kitten napped in her lap. "Out for a ride?"

The girl shrugged. "Mamá wanted to."

Chris nodded. "Stay away from the edge of the cliffs, okay?"

"I will." Then, Maria held up a white wildflower, offering it to him with a brilliant smile. "Here, a gift."

How could he refuse that?

Chris took the flower from the girl, twirling the fragile stem between his fingers as he looked it over before putting it in the breast pocket of his jacket for safekeeping. "It's beautiful—like you, hmm? Thank you."

Maria's cheeks pinked, but when she looked back at her mother who stared out across the cliffs and not paying them attention, her happiness faded. "Mamá is sad."

He was quick to bend down, reaching out to soothe the girl because he wondered how many people thought to stop and do that for her. She was still a *child*—small, and young. He bet she faced adult issues far more than she should.

Next to her mother, Maria was one of the few people on the ranch that Chris found himself drawn to, and she was *just* a child. Her smile lit up a room, and the way she cared about things—from her mother to the kitten in her lap—was as sweet as could be.

This job had turned out to be far more than what he expected, but Chris would not complain about it. How could he when he met these two wonderful souls because of it? He no longer wondered why Valeria's friend was so willing to approach an organization like The League to get her home where she belonged.

He wanted them home, too.

Chris wondered if home might be with him.

"Let's see if I can make your ma happy, okay?" he told the girl.

Maria grinned. "Okay."

He gave her a quick pat on the top of her black curls before standing. Valeria said nothing as Chris came to sit next to her on the edge of the cliffs. He swallowed back the discomfort the position caused and kept his gaze on her instead of the water down below. She spoke before he did, giving him the exact reason for her sadness.

It was not what he expected.

"You're leaving," she whispered.

Yeah.

He didn't bother to ask how she knew that. It didn't matter.

"The business side of things have run their course here," he explained, although it wouldn't help her feelings on the matter. "I can't stay just because I want to. Jorge has wanted me gone since I arrived."

"Right."

"Val."

She refused to look at him.

Chris tried not to let that hurt.

"*Val.*

"What?" she asked.

"Hey," he murmured, reaching for her.

The second his palm came in contact with her cheek, Valeria blinked, and the tears she had been holding back tracked lines down from the corners of her eyes. He could handle a lot of things from this woman, but crying did not seem to be one. When the tears started, all he wanted to do was make them stop.

Now.

"Don't cry, don't cry," he said, his arm snaking around her waist to pull her into his lap. He wiped the tears from her face, and met her gaze. Although, when that didn't work to make her stop crying, he did the next best thing. *Kissed her.* His lips touched to hers, he tasted the salt from her tears, and the rest of the world faded away. Still, he breathed against her mouth, "Please, don't cry. It's not over, I promise."

Somewhere behind him, he heard Maria's little gasp.

Then, her *giggle*.

Kids.

Valeria pushed away from him, but not very far. She couldn't get away when he was holding her locked in his arms. "Maria might tell—"

"She won't."

That, he was most sure of.

All little Maria wanted was for her mother to be happy. She was tired of seeing her mother sad and hurting. That's all Valeria ever was here.

Chris used the pad of his thumb to wipe away the last bit of wetness from under Valeria's eye. "Hey, look at me."

Valeria did, but he wasn't sure he liked what he found staring back. "I was *never* going to be free. I never will be. Hope was a lie."

"What?"

"I can't even protect my daughter because she is the sacrifice he's willing to use to punish me. And now you're *leaving*. What am I going to do?"

Those tears had started again.

Her voice climbed higher.

Chris kissed her quiet. Her fingers tightened into the collar of his jacket as their lips moved in a familiar rhythm. Soft, and sweet. A heat spreading between the two of them he had never known existed before this woman.

Against her lips, he said, "I didn't want to leave until I had a clear way out for you—that won't happen with the way he has this place run, but I know that now. Which means as soon as I am out of here, I will gather a team, and they'll come in to get you out. Do you understand?"

"That's not poss—"

"It is, and that's what will happen. I don't want you to stay here a second longer than you need to, but this is my only way to make it work."

Unless something else came up.

As of now, nothing had.

Chris grabbed Valeria's chin and tipped her head back so she was staring at him again. "Don't you want a chance?"

"W-what?"

"A chance to do whatever you want—to live, or to *love*? To be whoever you want to be, and not who someone else demands from you?"

Fire rushed her stare. "Of course, I do."

"Then, don't give up. You can't." Chris sighed, glancing over his shoulder to scan the land in case someone was coming. Although, they would have heard the horses approaching. "Did anyone see you leave?"

"Carla—the nanny—knew I was going, but she didn't see us leave the stables."

"No one else? Jorge?"

Valeria shook her head.

Chris nodded. "Okay, go back before he sends someone out after you and her. Don't make him angry—keep the peace, however you can."

"I can't do this anymore. I can't keep letting him use me and hurt me."

He didn't have the right words for that.

Nothing to make it better.

"I'm sorry," he whispered.

Valeria's shoulders lifted and sank with her heavy breaths. "I just ... I want that chance, Chris."

"You'll get it," he promised. "I'll make sure."

"I don't want to go back."

"Yeah."

The unspoken words hung between them—*but you have to.*

Valeria climbed out of his lap with help, and then Chris stood too after brushing off his clothes. Silently, his hand found hers, their fingers wove together, and he squeezed before letting go.

"Jorge said you would leave mid-week."

"Probably tomorrow."

He got a flight.

Valeria made a heartbroken noise.

"Shh," Chris hushed, tugging her close to his side to press a kiss to the top of her head, and hide her away from the rest of the world while he was able. "It will be *fine.*"

"It won't."

"Let me show you."

Then, another thought popped into his mind.

"The stables," he said, "at midnight. That's when the second shift change happens for the guards—every twelve hours. They meet at the gate for an hour before heading back to their posts. If you're there, that's where I'll be tonight. Okay?"

She nodded.

Chris gestured at the horse she brought along. "Go ahead. Get back before he sends someone out for you."

Maria glanced up from the kitten in her lap. "You have Butter."

He smiled at the girl and passed a glance at the horse he brought along. Butter, that was. "Butter is a great horse."

"My *favorite.*"

Oh?

"You can take him back for me," Chris said, knowing it would be a five-mile walk back to the ranch, "as long as you promise to keep this a secret."

Maria stood up from the ground, packing her kitten away in the rucksack hanging across her small body. "Deal."

He helped Valeria to get the horses ready for the ride back, but before she left him behind at the cliffs, he grabbed her wrist. Her gaze met his, and he tugged to make her lean down. One more kiss between them, and he held her gaze.

"I always keep my promises, Val."

That fire was back in her stare.

He liked it better, now.

"You better," she said.

He *would.*

Chris watched the girls and the horses fade in the distance. Pulling that flower

Maria had given him from his breast pocket, he fished out his wallet, too. He flipped the wallet open to a spot in the back, and laid the flower on the leather before closing it up, pressing firmly to keep it in place. Once he had the chance, he would take it out and press it safely between the pages of a book he kept on his desk at home.

Someday, he wanted to show Maria that he kept it, and her mother, too. Because this day? It felt like it changed everything.

· · ·

The sky had blackened by the time Chris walked those five miles back to the ranch. Not that he minded—walking hurt nobody, and he used the time to clear his head. The weather had stayed decent during his stay in Mexico, so he wouldn't say anything bad about that, either.

He wasn't at all surprised to find the ranch quiet when he returned. The one guard walking the pathways between the houses gave him a nod as he passed, but the man didn't even realize Chris wasn't out for one of his normal strolls. That had become normal to them, and so they didn't even question it, now.

A blessing, really.

Chris intended on heading to the house he was using on the ranch, having a quick shower, and then making his way to Jorge's home to sign off on the deal for his father, even if was still a ruse. A throat clearing to his left stopped his walk up short.

Sitting on the porch of the small bungalow she and her brother used, Abril Lòpez raised an eyebrow when Chris's gaze landed on her.

"Good walk?" she asked.

Chris nodded, careful with his words because he wasn't sure what to make of this woman. She went along with her brothers, and their plans more often than she didn't. After watching her for a while, he found that she followed the rules, even if she seemed to enjoy pushing the boundaries around her.

A complex.

Nothing like Valeria.

She had been easy to figure out.

Abril ... not so much.

"It was nice," he said.

Abril leaned forward on the steps, a sly smile curving her lips as a glint twinkled in her russet gaze. "I thought you took out a horse earlier? I was in the stables, remember? Butter."

Shit.

Chris forgot about that.

A mistake he couldn't afford.

"You didn't see me come back?"

He hoped to distract the woman with a lie, but perhaps he should have known better than to even try. There was something about Abril that was not the same as her brothers although *what* it was, he wasn't sure. She was quiet, always sticking to the shadows, but never inserting herself into conversations.

However, Chris understood it was the silent ones someone had to watch more than the others. They were the people who saw things, but never said a word. They heard conversations and filed them away in their minds for a later date.

He doubted Abril was different.

"No, I didn't see you come back," Abril said, resting her arms over her jean-covered knees, and tipping her head to the side. "But I saw Val leave with one horse, and her daughter, and then come back with two horses. Maria was riding Butter."

Chris cleared his throat.

Abril smiled.

"You're playing a dangerous game, Christopher Guzzi, and I want you to tell me exactly what kind it is."

"I'm not sure what you're talking—"

"Cut the shit. I've seen you dancing around her since you arrived. Last weekend? You got out of her room just in time because Jorge got home an hour later and passed out in the hallway before his men came up and put him in a spare bedroom."

Fuck.

"The door closing," Chris murmured.

Abril shrugged one bare shoulder where her flimsy blouse had fallen down. "I don't trust new people, and I had every reason to wonder about you."

"Why?"

"I'm aware of *just enough* about the cocaine trade in Canada to say your father has a good supplier, and he didn't need to come here. Jorge and my father? They think I'm a pretty face to give to whoever the fuck they want, but that's their mistake."

He didn't miss how she didn't say her other brother. The one that stayed in this house with her.

Chris didn't point it out.

"I like Val," Abril said, "and I don't like very many people, so that says a lot. And my niece? She didn't ask to be here, either."

"What do you want?" he asked outright.

Abril smirked. "Not much … just a guarantee. Tell me what you want, and then we'll see what I can do for you."

"I'm not sure you can help me."

"Don't make the same mistakes they do. Those who underestimate me tend to get what they deserve. Do you want to fall into that category, too?"

Well, all right, then.

"Valeria, and her daughter."

Abril's expression didn't change, and she gave nothing away when she replied, "What about them?"

"What do you think?"

"I think if you came here to remove them from my brother, then you will have an uphill battle to make it happen."

Chris laughed darkly. "That's not news."

"What if I help with it?"

"How so?"

Abril glanced up at the stars overhead. "I love this place. It's *mine*. Always has been, always will be, but they've changed it over the years. And now, they want to give me to someone who will take me away from it."

"Your arranged marriage to the García man?"

"Mmm."

Her hum was the only agreement to his question.

Chris didn't mind.

"Do you have the capability to take the two out of here?" Abril asked.

"Within reason."

"What *reason?*"

"Time to get it done."

"I need the night to do what I have to," Abril said, "and I'm sure it'll then give you some *time*, as you say you need."

"How?"

The woman smiled at him.

Coldly.

"How about you follow along, Christopher? Things always go better when someone just does what I tell them to."

"You haven't told me anything yet."

Abril nodded. "By the morning, you'll have everything you need to do what you have to." The woman picked up the wine glass at her side and winked as she tipped it up for a drink. After, she let the stem dangle from the tips of her fingers as she asked, "Do you know in English my name means April?"

"I didn't."

"Have you heard the saying—about the showers, and the flowers?"

Chris's brow furrowed. "What does that have to do with anything?"

"Do you know it?"

"Sure. April showers bring May flowers."

Abril grinned wickedly. "I think it's about time for some rain."

What did that mean?

He still wasn't even sure he should trust this woman, but what choice did he have?

15.

"Mamá?"

Valeria looked up from the book she had been reading to her daughter to find Maria peering over at her from just under the edge of her comforter. "Yeah, *niña?*"

"Jorge was angry we took the horse today."

Well, *sort of.*

Mostly, Jorge got pissed that Valeria took her daughter away from the nanny and did so without telling him. Which meant she had to listen to him rant and rage for a good hour after she arrived back at the ranch.

The good thing?

He didn't realize what happened out on the cliffs. No one picked up on the fact Valeria had taken out one horse but came back with two. They didn't seem to notice Chris wasn't around, either. Then again, Jorge had a one-track mind, and since Valeria took his focus when she stepped out of line, that's all he cared about.

He calmed down.

After a while.

"Don't worry about Papá and what he says," Valeria told her daughter, lowering her tone even as her gaze drifted to the open doorway of the bedroom. She could take care of Maria without someone looking over her shoulder in the evenings. Meaning, the *nanny.* Or Jorge. Even still, she had to leave the bedroom door open, and she didn't trust that someone wouldn't listen down the hall. "He was angry with me, not you, Maria."

"But—"

"But *nothing,*" she assured, leaning over in the bed to kiss her sweet girl in the middle of her forehead. "You don't have to worry about that stuff, okay? All you have to worry about is you and being happy."

Maria glanced down at her comforter. "But I don't like it here, Mamá. I am *not* happy."

God, yeah.

Didn't she know it?

Rolling over in the bed, Valeria tossed the book aside—she'd almost finished it, anyway—and slipped under the blankets with her daughter. Jorge would ready for bed soon, and expect her in their room, but she took five extra minutes with her child. She didn't get enough time with Maria now.

She hated that.

Once she had her arms locked around her child, Maria settled, closing her eyes as her mother kissed her temple, and sung a sweet lullaby she remembered her own mama singing to her long ago. As she finished the song, Maria sighed.

"Do you remember the promise you made to Chris today?" she whispered to her daughter.

Maria nodded. "I will not tell."

"That's a good girl."

She didn't want to put her daughter in that position, but she also didn't think she gave Maria enough credit, either. Maria was smart—quick as a whip. She recognized when something didn't seem right, or rather, when something *was*.

Chris was right.

Just in different ways.

"Do you like Chris?" Maria asked.

Valeria blinked. "I … that's not an easy question."

"Why not?"

Because it was complex.

Difficult.

Dangerous.

Yes, she liked that man. She more than liked him. With nothing more than his presence, and attention, he showed her good men existed. He reminded her she deserved care, and adoration by someone like him. He made her *want* him more than anything … she wanted happiness, and if possible, she wanted to find it with him. She knew happiness because he had given her glimpses. And at night, when it was just the two of them away from the rest of the world, he'd given her back the ability to be her own woman, too, although she didn't think he understood that.

She loved seeing him with her daughter because he never dismissed her child. He didn't walk past Maria without at the least, stopping to speak to her. He handled Maria with kindness, grace, and a tender heart, as a good man should.

She cared for Chris because of many reasons, and wanted him.

And she had more reasons why she couldn't have him. At least, not right now. Valeria wasn't the type to punish herself. So, she forced herself not to think about him at all because that was easier.

For now.

"It just isn't," she told her daughter.

Maria shrugged in her mother's hold. "I like him."

Valeria smiled. "Oh?"

"Yep."

"Why is that?"

"Because he doesn't hurt you," Maria said, "and he likes you. That's why I like him."

"That's all?"

Maria nodded. "That's all, Mamá."

Huh.

Children were still children. The only people on the earth who looked past the surface to see what was underneath. Children saw bad things, and yet, still found the good, too.

That was their innocence.

The beauty of kids.

They found hope.

Possibility.

Even when no one else did.

"I like him," Valeria murmured into her daughter's hair.

Although, if Maria heard it, she didn't acknowledge it. Valeria was fine with that because she wasn't sure how to deal with this herself. Away from this place, at a different time, had she met Chris … it would have been amazing.

They could be wonderful.

And maybe—*God*, maybe—if she had the chance he promised her to get away from here, and live her life the way she wanted, then she might let herself feel all those things she kept holding at bay. For now, though, she didn't dare.

Heartache was one thing.

Heartbreak was quite another.

Valeria was not ready for that. Giving her heart to a man she couldn't be with would only bring her pain.

Someday, that might change.

Her thoughts were a whisper.

They reminded her hope wasn't dead.

Not yet.

• • •

Valeria had closed the door to her daughter's bedroom when Jorge came stumbling *drunk* down the hall. His drinking had become more regular, and that concerned her if only because he was a mean drunk, and she always seemed to be right in his fucking line of fire.

"*Hermosa*," Jorge slurred, coming closer to her. "We need to celebrate, woman."

Valeria took a careful step backward. "Why?"

She ignored the red lipstick stain on the collar of his shirt, and the undone buttons because she didn't give a fuck who put it there as long as it wasn't her. The strands of his hair stuck up everywhere. Sweat dotted his forehead and wrinkles covered his slacks.

It wasn't like Jorge to be messy.

Except lately, he was more often than not.

He reached out for her when she was close enough and grabbed onto her. Valeria didn't have the chance to react before his disgusting mouth came down on hers. The taste of the rum he had been drinking flooded her tongue, making her want to gag. Her hands hit his chest, ready to push him away even though that would cause her more trouble.

She didn't get the chance.

In a flash, the two of them stumbled into their bedroom. Jorge stepped back from her, realizing where they were, and grinned. He pointed a finger at her while pulling his shirt down his arms, and nodding.

"Ah, now get undressed for me, *sí*?" He winked, as stupid as that looked. "*Slowly*, Val. I like that, don't you?"

God.

"You're too drunk," she told him.

Jorge rolled his eyes and fell back to the foot of the bed to get his shoes off. "I am *not*. Get undressed, or I will cut the fucking clothes off you."

She didn't doubt it.

She also didn't lie.

He struggled to pull the leather loafers from his feet, almost falling face first to the floor. Another night, and she might have laughed at him. Except, the time closed in on eleven-thirty, and in a half an hour, she needed to meet Chris in the stables. She hadn't forgotten about that.

If she could help it, she would not let her husband touch her one more fucking time. She searched for a way out of this situation while Jorge continued to struggle with his shoes, and his socks, too, when he finally removed the loafers.

"What are you standing there for?" he snapped up at her.

Jesus Christ.

The last thing she wanted was this drunk pig hauling his body on top of hers to get himself off—whiskey dick was a real thing, and not specific to only whiskey, either. Sex with Jorge was bad enough when he stayed sober although she didn't think of him raping her as *sex*. When he was drunk, though, it became a whole different horror.

"Did you remember to let the kitten in?" she asked, hoping for a distraction.

Jorge's brow furrowed, and sleepy eyes stared up at her.

Hazy eyes, too, she noticed. Drunk as fuck. She might have asked him how much he drank downstairs before coming up to bed if she cared. Except she didn't, and really, if he gave himself alcohol poisoning, she would not cry about it.

Damn.

Might he fall asleep if she gave him the chance?

Pass right out?

"What kitten?" he slurred again.

"Never mind," she blurted, "I will use the bathroom—freshen up, okay? I'll be right back out. Lay back and take a break. You deserve it."

Right.

That's what he deserved.

Jorge sighed, pleased with her submissiveness. That's all this bastard ever wanted. To *believe* Valeria was willing and capable of going along with whatever he needed and demanded. He was easier to handle but shit … it killed her to do it.

No point in lying.

"All right," he mumbled, folding his arms behind his head, "but don't be too long. I need a good sleep. Big things happening tomorrow."

"Oh, like what?"

She asked the question over her shoulder as she headed for the bathroom. Moving around inside the space, turning on the taps and lifting the toilet seat to make it seem like she was doing something, he wouldn't know the difference if he stayed resting on the bed. Knowing Jorge like she did, when he was drunk, if he stayed on his back for long enough, he would fall asleep.

A win-win for her.

Stupid, yes.

Risky, absolutely.

Valeria didn't care. Not right now. Not knowing soon, Chris would leave, and tonight was the last chance she would have to be with him. She would do what she needed to do.

"Business, Val," he muttered, "with the Canadian."

"Chris?"

"Mmm, I don't like him."

"Why?"

"He looks at you too much."

Valeria stiffened near the sink.

How often did Jorge watch when she didn't pay attention?

"Does he? I never noticed."

"They all look at you, woman … but they're smart about it. He doesn't care, and I don't … like that."

His words came slower, now, so Valeria kept talking as she pretended to wash her hands.

"I don't notice," she admitted. "What are you celebrating?"

"The deal is …"

"Hmm?"

"Completed," Jorge mumbled. A beat of silence passed before he asked almost unintelligibly, "Are you finished?"

"Just about."

She took a minute to dry her hands, and brushed her teeth, a familiar sound echoed into the bathroom.

Snoring.

Valeria smiled at her reflection.

It worked.

She came out of the bathroom, and sure enough, Jorge had passed out on the bed with his arms still acting as a pillow beneath his head. Using the blanket that acted as a decoration on the chair in the corner, she covered him. Not because she cared should he become cold, but because he slept better when he was warm, and she needed him to stay asleep for as long as possible.

Should he wake up, and realize she wasn't in the room, that wouldn't be good for her. She also turned on the small radio … just in case someone came to knock on the door, it was unlikely the noise would even disturb him.

Valeria glanced over her shoulder as she closed the bedroom door behind her when she left, only to see Jorge snoring away.

Alcohol was good for that.

She used it enough to sleep next to that man.

• • •

Valeria tiptoed through the stables, her heart in her throat as she passed stall after stall, realizing Chris wasn't there at all. She'd not expected him to be out in the open but it seemed like he hadn't been here.

She almost passed the final stall, resolving herself to sneak back to the house—their chance at a stolen moment gone, when someone yanked her into that last stall of the stables on the right. They used it to store care items, feed, and other things for the horses. Including *blankets*, if a terrible night or a storm came through unexpectedly.

Valeria barely had the chance to catch her breath before Chris's lips found the back of her neck as her chest met the stall wall. *God*, she didn't even care that the rough wood might leave a splinter in her palms when his hands fisted into the skirt of the wrap dress she had thrown on to leave the house.

"Val," he started.

"Just fuck me," she breathed, "and we'll talk later."

If they had the chance.

That's what made desperate sex the best kind of sex. She was sure.

Chris never made her feel even the smallest bit unsafe. Not when his touches came rougher, and her cheek pressed to the wood. Not when his teeth dragged across the racing pulse in her throat while his hands shoved her dress high before slipping between her thighs to cup her sex. He *squeezed* her pussy, fingers sliding through her wetness to prove how fucking much she wanted his.

Valeria drowned out the sounds of her pleasure into her palm as Chris worked her pussy open with his fingers first. Wet sounds filled the stall as his fingers pushed and pulled, twisting into her G-spot with every curl of the tips. Her hips jerked, a sensation like she had never experienced before spiraling through her gut when his lips danced across her ear lobe.

His words?

A dark *promise*.

"Feel that?" he asked, "You're about to rain all over my hand, Val. You'll leave a fucking puddle in this stall. I bet you haven't done that before, huh?"

"No, never."

It almost embarrassed her. The very idea.

Yet, she didn't have time to think about it before she came. And not *just* an orgasm that seemed so fucking good, but one that almost brought her to her knees from the intensity. It started deep within her womb and flared outward with violent intent. The rush of wetness between her legs, hot and *slick*, came fast. It ruined her panties, but that didn't seem to matter to Chris as he pulled his hands free from her pussy only to yank the soaked undies down her legs.

He was back on her, fast with those same dirty words promising she would *see stars* and *gonna be so fucking good when I'm done, babe* while his hands went back to working on getting her dress off entirely. Valeria only had time to catch her breath while Chris stepped back from her to take care of himself, shedding his clothes, and sheathing his cock in latex before he was back behind her.

One hand slid under her right thigh, lifting it high and the head of his dick slid through her sensitive slit. That wet sound came back, a reminder of her own arousal and how hot she was for him.

"*Breath*," he demanded.

She did, sucking in a hard breath. He thrust in, seating himself all the way inside her pussy with one flex of his hips. She'd been so ready to take him, her need indescribable, until he was filling her full and stretching her open.

"Oh, my *God*," Valeria whimpered.

"Hold on," Chris murmured along the column of her throat.

She did, finding purchase with one hand on the wall, and the other reaching back to grasp onto his hips as he pounded into her from behind. His lips found her neck, kissing and tasting and biting her into bliss while his cock drove her crazy with every fast, deep stroke.

It was too much, and not enough.

"I c-can't—I can't …"

Valeria couldn't form words, or explain that she hovered right on the precipice of an orgasm that would leave her in shattered pieces on the ground, if only he gave her a bit more. The words wouldn't come, and yet it didn't even matter.

Chris knew.

How to work her ...

How to play her body ...

All of it.

His hand on her hip slid around to the front of her body, drifting between her thighs, so his fingertips rubbed tight circles into her clit while his other arm wrapped tight around her chest. The air exploded out of her chest in a high cry. Probably *too loud* for their current circumstances as the orgasm tore through her body with devastating intent.

It was heaven.

And she would die happily like that.

"Fuck, yeah," Chris said, his words a hoarse murmur along her throat, "that's what I wanted, babe. Come all over that cock—fucking now. Take it all, Valeria."

Each thrust that followed his words came deeper and harder inside her pussy, accompanied by the jerking of his hands against her body with his own orgasm.

Her air wouldn't come, or her thoughts.

And that was okay.

It meant, for that moment with him, she didn't have to feel anything at all.

But especially not the pain.

16.

"What do I do now?"

Valeria's voice was a whisper, her gaze locked on the stall instead of him where he wanted it. Chris didn't mind because he figured everyone had to protect themselves, and Valeria's way was like this. He didn't take offense, even if he wished this woman knew he was doing everything in his power to get her away from this place, and happy again.

"You give me time, and before you know it, I'll be back to—"

"No, *me*, I mean. What am I supposed to do now?"

Chris tipped his head down and pressed a kiss to the line of Valeria's naked shoulder. He couldn't resist her on his lips—her scent had mixed with his, and it reminded him of woman, sex, and *heaven*. "I don't understand, love."

Two blankets he grabbed from the stable shelves kept the hay-covered floor of the stall soft enough for them to rest comfortably on. The other, he'd used to wrap around his shoulders before he tightened the ends around them both. The high stall door allowed them to remain unseen from the stables, and other than the six-inch space at the bottom where he saw out into the main corridor, no one had a view of them unless they opened the door.

No one came into the stables this late though.

He knew because he watched.

"*You*," she whispered.

Chris made a noise under his breath, thick and unsure. "Val—"

She sighed. "You know, before when I was on the run, I went years without being in a relationship—but is that what we can call this? *Should* we call it that?"

Huh.

"I don't know," he admitted, "but we can call it whatever you want to call it. I want what you want that's all."

Hadn't she figured that out yet?

Chris didn't think it needed to make sense, but frankly, why should it? They hadn't met under normal circumstances. She wasn't the average woman, and he wasn't every other man, either. They couldn't simplify anything they did together down to one label, but he didn't care. As long as he still had moments like this with her, rather it be now or when she was away from here, then that was all that mattered to him at the end.

Valeria tipped her head back and rested it against the crook in his shoulder. It gave Chris the perfect chance to kiss her cheek, and then the corner of her mouth. So, he did just that. He thought about this woman, and all the things he wanted to do with her—*to her*—far more often than he should.

This job turned out to be more than he expected, but he wouldn't complain. How could he when, he'd found an angel?

Someone was looking out for him.

"I meant …" Valeria gave him a sweet smile when he used the pad of his thumb to trace the line of her cheekbone while he watched her. She didn't possibly know it, but he found her most fascinating like this. She didn't have to pretend to be someone else. Happy, pleased, and content. All his. As she should be, he decided. "I tried to date, but I didn't. I didn't want to."

"Nothing wrong with that," he rumbled.

Not that he would tell her, but Chris was a jealous motherfucker. Even the thought of Valeria spending time with another man—before him, it didn't matter—had his green monster beating at the bars of its cage. He kept the bastard in place if only because he didn't think she would appreciate it. Hadn't she put up with enough bullshit from a man who thought he owned her?

Chris would not be another.

Valeria peered up at him, her pink lips curving into a soft smile as he stroked two fingers up and down her arm under the blanket. "I was young when they forced me to marry Jorge, but you know that, don't you?"

"I do, yes."

"He was the first man …" She flinched, but added, "He was the first for me. And then I ran, stayed running for years, and kept busy raising my daughter because she was always most important."

Ah.

Chris thought he might understand what Valeria had been trying to tell him, but he remained quiet, and allowed her the chance to say it without his input. This woman didn't use her voice enough, and when she did, God knew she watched every single word that came out of her mouth.

Shame, that.

She said beautiful things.

People were missing out.

Their loss, he supposed.

His gain.

"I never learned what it meant to enjoy being with someone emotionally, or physically. Love was always abusive. Sex only hurt. I never had the chance to figure out what I wanted and what was good for me until you, and this isn't even a *thing*. It's not right, we shouldn't have done this, but I'm not sure what I'm supposed to do when you go. I can't let him *touch* me, anymore. I can't—"

"Shhh," Chris murmured, leaning down just enough to press a kiss to her forehead. Valeria's eyes fluttered closed, and her frown melted away. That was better. "Val, listen—"

"I don't want you to leave."

Yeah.

There it was.

"I don't want to go, either," he muttered.

He needed to be here. Someone had to keep an eye on this woman because no one else was doing it. Undoubtedly, leaving would kill him inside when it meant she would face hell alone. Yes, she had been doing it for years before him, but that didn't matter to him at all.

She shouldn't *have* to.

"What do you want?" he asked.

Valeria looked away from him. "I don't understand."

"When this is over, and you can do whatever you want to do, what is it you want?"

"Still not sure when that'll happen, Chris."

Right.

"Part of hope is having something to hope *for,*" he murmured against her cheek, letting his nose nuzzle her soft, warm skin. "So, what are you hoping for, Val?"

She stayed quiet.

He waited her out.

"You," she said. "I'm hoping for you, and what you gave me here. I don't want to forget it when you're gone, I don't think I can because I'm hoping for something better, and that's you."

Chris tightened his arms around her trembling form because, all too soon, he would let her go again. "You'll have that. I promise."

He didn't break those.

He wouldn't.

"Will I? *How?*"

Asking her to trust him again—how many times had he said that now?—didn't seem like it was what she wanted, and so Chris said nothing at all. Actions were still louder than words, and he was working on making this a reality one fucking step at a time. It was the best he could do right now.

His silence wasn't the response she wanted either. Valeria turned in his lap, the blanket around them falling to the stall floor before she was straddling him. Her hands found his face, and those sharp fingernails of her dragged teasingly against his skin as she pulled him in for a hard kiss. There was no *give* to it—only her taking.

He didn't care.

She wanted it?

Have it.

In the back of his mind, Chris recognized they were running out of time here. She needed to head back to the house before someone noticed she left. Or even, before a guard made a trip through the stables just because.

And yet, all those thoughts faded away when her hands fell between them. Her palms found his cock, grabbing tight and stroking him alive in a few firm pulls. He didn't speak the truth—that she needed to *go*—when her lips still crushed against his, and her tongue seemed intent to lick his flavor straight from his fucking mouth.

God.

It was so damn good though.

He swore, over the notes of the hay and the horses, of old wood and dirt floor, he still smelled the lingering whiff of their sex in the air. Of her fresh, yet warm perfume that reminded him of a summer rain in the dead heat.

"Again, once more before you go," she whispered. "*Please.*"

Her words danced along his lips, sinful and tantalizing. Who could say no to that? It's what he wanted, too. If he could keep this woman with him forever, he would do exactly that.

Chris reached for his discarded pants, digging through the pocket to find the last fucking condom he had. She took the foil packet from his fingertips, ripping it open before making quick work of sheathing his hard length in latex. Air hissed between his teeth when she settled on top of him, hovering with the head of his cock sliding between the fleshy lips of her sex while she watched him.

Perfect.

She was so fucking perfect.

When she came down on his length, he swore he found heaven. Even if it was his personal brand of hell, too. After all, it only reminded him that she wasn't entirely his.

Not yet.

"You made me trust you," she breathed against his mouth, but it almost seemed like something else. It almost sounded like *you made me love you*, and fuck, he felt that inside his bones. He heard that louder, echoing in his heart with the beats it pumped, and spreading like a wildfire ready to devastate his soul. Not that he had a soul anymore because he gave it to this fucking woman, and he had no idea when that happened. "And now you're *leaving*."

"Not for long. I swear, not for long."

That hurt.

It hurt him, too.

• • •

The day Chris would leave the ranch came far too soon for his liking. Despite having a ticket bought, and a time he had to be at the airport to make his flight, he still took his time packing up his bag in the guest house he used during his stay. One thing at a time—*slowly.*

Soon, he'd packed his bags, and set them on the front porch of the small house. Crossing his arms over his chest, he stared out over the property and the houses connected by small pathways.

Time to say goodbye.

Even if wasn't a goodbye.

It still seemed like it.

Chris picked up the bag at his feet, settling his raging heart to finish this. The quicker he left, the faster this plan—even if he didn't understand everything, and still had more yet to figure out on his end—would get started. And that's what he wanted and needed more than anything, right?

To get Val, and Maria, away from here.

It sucked he had to leave first.

Chris hadn't expected Jorge to be waiting in front of his house, a handful of men loitering within shouting distance, as he came down the pathway. While the man had been mostly respectful during his stay here, Chris understood it wasn't because Jorge wanted to be. Rather, it was because he *had* to be.

He wanted that deal.

Now, he had it.

He thought.

"Ready to head out?" Jorge asked, his foot kicking out at Maria's striped gray and white kitten that jumped over his boot. "Damn *cat*. Maria! Get out here and put this goddamn thing somewhere before I throw it off the cliffs!"

Chris tried not to show his annoyance at hearing the little girl he cared a great deal for be yelled at in that way. And by her own father, no less. She was such a sweet child, but her father didn't seem to care.

"I am heading out," Chris said as the screen door on the porch pushed open. Little Maria came out, but wouldn't meet anyone's gaze as she came down the steps. Not too far behind her was her mother. Valeria stayed in the doorway, arms folded over her chest, and watched Chris from a safe distance. "Have to catch that flight, or I will never hear the end from my mother when I don't show up for her dinner tomorrow."

Jorge made a noise under his breath. "*Women.* They're all the fucking same. More trouble than they're worth." Then, to his daughter who picked up the kitten, he snapped, "And keep the fucking thing out of my sight, got it?"

Maria looked over her shoulder and nodded. Still, her gaze drifted to Chris for a moment, meeting his. He swore, in the depths of her irises, he saw the little girl's secrets, all the things she had seen and known, staring back at him.

"Remember," she said to him, "you promised."

His heart ached.

All over, so painful, and unrelenting.

It hurt.

Chris nodded. "I did, Maria, and I'll keep it."

In the doorway, Valeria called for her daughter, the flash of worry on her face disappearing when Jorge looked her way. "Come on, Maria, and we'll get the kitty milk in a bowl, so she'll be sleepy."

"Okay, Mamá."

Maria darted up the stairs, and into her mother's waiting arms. It killed Chris to look away from them, but he did it. He was not good at hiding his affections. One of his only flaws, but he couldn't afford for it to be on display.

Jorge shifted on his feet, shoving his hands into his pockets as his attention came back to Chris. "And what did you promise my daughter?"

He chuckled.

Dry and tense as it was.

"Just that I would come back and say hello someday," Chris murmured. "She's a sweet child. You should be proud of her—fathers and their daughters, hmm?"

Jorge arched a brow. "Proud, *sure.*"

Fuck him.

He didn't deserve that child, or her mother. Jorge might have helped to create Maria's life, but he had nothing more to do with it than that. He provided the sperm, but Maria didn't reflect the man.

She deserved a good man in her life—a father who would show her what real love and care was between a daughter, and her dad. She needed someone to show her how she deserved to be treated by the men in her life, so she didn't go looking for it somewhere else.

Jorge understood nothing about that; his reaction wasn't shocking. It still annoyed Chris to no fucking end, and only strengthened his resolve to make sure Maria, and her mother, found the happiness they deserved far away from this place, and the people here.

Including Jorge.

Any man could be a father.

All it took was the spunk from his balls.

Being a *dad* was not the same.

"A car will meet you at the gate," Jorge said, nodding toward the dirt road, "like when you arrived."

Right.

Because the only vehicles allowed this far into the ranch brought the family back to their homes, or ones carrying drugs. Jorge's rules never changed, not even for a guest who had promised to make him billions on a smuggling deal.

Whatever.

Chris didn't mind the walk.

"Pleasure doing business with you and your father," Jorge said. "Have a good flight, Chris."

He smiled. "Oh, I don't think it's finished yet."

Chris didn't allow Jorge the chance to question him on what he meant because he had already spun on his heels and headed for the road. He figured … *let him wonder*. It would be good for him even if he wouldn't see what came next.

• • •

Chris took in the darkening sky as the town car crawled through a busy section of the city. His driver, one of the Lòpez grunts, kept quiet throughout the drive. The man in the passenger seat, only there for decoration because he did nothing else, also remained silent throughout the drive.

Not that Chris cared.

He had other things on his mind.

A few miles from the airport, the two men in the front conversed back and forth in Spanish. It still left Chris out of the conversation, mostly. He had picked up a few words and phrases since his time here, and some language was close to Italian—or rather, close enough he made do.

"Happy … gone," he caught from one.

"It is who Jorge is," he understood better from the other.

Chris almost chuckled, understanding they were talking about him, and that Jorge wanted to see him go. He was fine with that, too, but he would be a hell of a lot better once he took Valeria and Maria from the man's clutches.

Soon, he told himself.

It would happen soon.

"What time is the flight again?"

The quick switch to English had Chris looking forward to meet the driver's stare in the rear-view mirror. A brow raised in question to his silence, but Chris said, "Five-twenty."

"Ah, we're making good time, then."

Chris checked his Rolex, saying as he tilted his head down, "Looks like it."

"*What the fuck*—Juan!"

He didn't get the chance to find out *what* the other man in the passenger seat shouted about because the impact of something hitting their car sent Chris flying across the back of the vehicle. He hadn't buckled in. A mistake. His head cracked against the glass of the rear passenger window, but that was the least of his worries.

Tires screeched and crunched.

Metal *crashed*.

One man cursed, another yelled.

Chris's ears rang as he flipped over in the backseat again, unable to stop his body from rolling all the way to the other side of the car. This time, his shoulder snapped hard against the plastic of the door, an ache spreading.

He didn't focus on the pain.

Not when adrenaline coursed through his system, making him hyper aware of the bits of debris flying all around his head, and the force of the rolling car sending him flying to the roof on his back. *Holy shit*.

He should have buckled up.

The car came to a stop, but on its *top*. Chris rolled over to his knees, the pressure in his ears making the men's voices from the front sound like they mumbled under water. His hands scraped against the shards of glass that had littered the roof of the car, but he barely even felt the sting when it cut his palms.

"*Fuck*," he mumbled, still trying to figure out what happened.

What had happened?

That hit he took to the head made his vision cloudy, and his mind slow. *Too slow*. He lifted his head, nausea filling him as his hearing came back with an almost painful clarity. Outside of the car, an alarm sounded.

Their vehicle?

Maybe.

The alarm didn't concern him.

The three men coming for the car did.

Shit.

The men said nothing, and the fools in the front of their overturned vehicle didn't even have time to react before they had leaned in the car with guns aimed. Guns with silencers already attached.

Pop.

Pop.

Two shots.

Two men dead.

The three men didn't even speak together as they worked. This had been planned, obviously, and they understood what they had to do. Simple as that.

Chris blinked, seeing the blood that sprayed against the side of the windshield that hadn't broken into little pieces like the rest. The rusty tang of the blood filled the car, and gunpowder, freshly fired, mixed with it. He'd smelled that before. It still made his stomach roll into knots all the same.

The third man, the one who hadn't fired his gun, kneeled to stare in the back seat where Chris remained on all fours, trying to figure out his next move. Any other time, and he would have already been dead.

"April showers bring May flowers," the man murmured, his English decent, but his accent still thick, and clear. Chris heard the words, and understood what they meant, but his shock still hadn't died yet. "Tell the Lòpez family the Garcías aren't going anywhere, *Canadian*, and because of their deal with you, the war is on."

17.

"Val, come in here, *now*."

Maria peered up at her mother from the pile of wooden blocks they had used to build a *school* for her three Barbie dolls. Valeria was quick to give her daughter a smile, not wanting the girl to worry herself over Jorge, and whatever he wanted. His sharp tone had likely caused Maria's concern, but then again, the man was always harsh.

He didn't have a concept of kindness.

"I'll be right back," Valeria said, "and by then, you can decide what we will build next, okay?"

Maria nodded. "Okay, Mamá."

Valeria wouldn't waste time, so she headed to the rear of the house where Jorge worked in his office. Although working on what, she didn't know, and she didn't care to ask. Coming to stand in the doorway, she didn't walk inside the office because that was yet another one of his rules.

This space was his.

Not hers.

"Yes?" she asked.

Behind the desk, Jorge kept his head down on the paperwork in front of him that he shuffled into a folder. He didn't bother to glance up at her entrance, nor to greet her before he said, "I am heading out for a week—I need a break after these last few."

Great.

She didn't want to be here, but she also didn't want to be elsewhere with her husband, either. That sounded like a problem waiting to happen, and not at all one she wanted to deal with, all things considered.

Still, Valeria kept her attitude in check. That way, Jorge would keep his fucking moods, and his hands, to himself.

"What will we need?"

He chuckled. "No, *me*, Val. I am going away for the week. You will be fine here with the guards, Maria, and Abril to keep you company, I am sure."

Well, *yes.*

She didn't show her happiness at his news. That wouldn't do her any good.

"Where are you going?"

Jorge glanced up, dark eyes nailing her to the floor with his displeasure. "Does it matter?"

"No, of course, not. I wonder—"

"Don't bother."

Valeria nodded. "When are you coming back, then?"

"When I feel like it, *hermosa.*"

Fine with her.

"Okay," she said quietly, "I hope it's a good trip."

And that you never come back.

Valeria forced a smile on her face when Jorge looked her way again. He arched a brow, lifted a finger, and pointed at the doorway, saying, "Leave now."

She didn't need to told again.

Spinning on her heel, mind reeling over the fact she would have at least an entire week without this man looking over her shoulder, Valeria moved to leave Jorge's sight.

"Well, wait a second," he said behind her.

Valeria's shoulders dropped.

She knew it was too good to be true.

All day, she had focused on keeping her emotions under control. From the moment Chris had disappeared down the road leading out of the ranch, she had all she could do to keep from having a mental breakdown. She distracted herself with her child, and work around the house. Not to mention, staying the hell out of Jorge's way.

What could he want now?

Turning around, she asked, "What else can I do for you?"

He tipped his head to the side, his gaze roving over her slowly like he was drinking her up. Had that been another man looking at her that way—*Chris*—she would have shivered, filled with anticipation about what might come next. Not this man though.

It made her shiver, sure.

But in *disgust*.

"Maria," Jorge said.

"What about her?"

"That private school I had mentioned. I think it's time we—"

Valeria opened her mouth, ready to plead if that's what this asshole wanted, to keep her daughter with her, but the ringing phone on the desk saved her the trouble. For now, anyway. There was no way in hell she was allowing him to send Maria away.

"A moment," Jorge muttered, giving her a glare as he reached for the landline. He didn't even bother to pick the phone up, instead hitting a button that put the call on speaker phone as he answered with, "*Hola, casa de López.*"

The man on the other end of the line spoke fast, his Spanish coming out jumbled, making it hard for Valeria to follow along. Although, she managed to catch a few bits and pieces. Not that she needed to.

The expression on Jorge's face told it all.

He'd moved from annoyed with her to *stunned* in a blink. And then, just as fast, his gaze darkened as his lips pulled into a sneer when he snarled, "*What?*"

"Attacked, they attacked the car," the man muttered.

"*How?*"

"I don't know ... I—"

"You better figure it out!"

"Sorry, sorry," the man rushed to say, stumbling over his Spanish yet again when he added, "T-the one, boss, they left him alive. The Canadian."

"Christopher?"

"Yes, him. That one. He asked for a hospital, they told me. After the police arrived, and had called for an ambulance, he asked—"

"Which hospital?"

Valeria's heart thundered in her chest. Her fingernails bit into the palms of her hands when she squeezed her fists into tight balls. All that relief she had over Jorge leaving fled in an instant. Instead, a fear replaced it—a fear like never before.

Chris, her heart whispered.

Chris, Chris … Chris.

It had become a mantra.

Repeating with the beats of her heart.

God.

What happened?

She didn't dare ask.

Really, she shouldn't be standing there at all. The second Jorge realized she was still there listening to his conversation, he would snap at her to leave. Until then, however, she planned to stay right where she fucking was because she couldn't move.

Her feet had become cemented to the floor with panic.

"Which hospital?" Jorge demanded again.

"Hospital de Jesús Nazareno," the man said, "but I sent a man over, and they checked him out."

"Where the fuck is he?"

"I'm not sure."

"You're *not sure?*"

Jorge's voice slithered across the room to Valeria's spot in the doorway. Deathly calm, and a little too quiet. That tone meant violence was about to happen.

"Someone attacked the Canadian on the way to the airport, with my men inside the car, and now he is missing, but you don't know where he is?"

"It was the Garcías, boss. They did it."

Jorge stiffened behind his large desk. "Why—"

"The deal with the Canadians, I heard. Word is going around. They're letting it be known they are aware you planned to use that deal to ruin the merger."

"*Fuck.* Who let that information out?"

"I don't—"

"I don't care what you don't know!"

Another day, and the sound of Jorge's growing rage would have sent Valeria running. A part of her wasn't as scared of it as she had used to be. Oh, she needed to be careful, and to watch her step when he was in a mood, but it didn't leave her paralyzed with fear anymore.

"You best find out where the Canadian is, because if that man dies before we can get him the fuck out of Mexico, his father will *never* go through with the deal. As for the fucking Garcías, fuck the bastards. The deal is done, we don't need the merger now. Let them have their tantrums."

"It's more than that … they said something else, boss. The officials at the scene—one of them is on our payroll, and he said the Canadian told him the war with the Garcías is on. They're coming for us. We have to get ready."

Jorge noticed Valeria in the doorway, or rather, that she was still standing there. His glowering scowl landed on her before he snapped, "What are you still there for? Don't you have a child to take care of? Get the fuck out of my face!"

She didn't want to move.

She wanted to ask about Chris.

Jorge cocked an eyebrow at her, his stupid mouth already opening to bark at her again like she was a dog who couldn't be trained. Valeria didn't bother to give him that satisfaction before she turned on her heels and headed down the hallway. And even still, his rage continued to flow out of the office, chasing her even after she sat with Maria in the living room again to play.

Her daughter looked to her for an explanation to the man's rage. Valeria said nothing. She couldn't; her heart was still breaking.

She didn't have answers, either.

• • •

Jorge said they would handle the Garcías.

He could *not*.

That had never been more apparent to Valeria as she watched the chaos between brothers unfurl in a mess of shoves and shouts between Jorge and Samuel.

"I told you—*I fucking told you!*" Samuel pointed a finger in his brother's face, for once refusing to back down when he had always been willing to do it for Jorge before. "We lost *two* storage facilities the night after they attacked the Canadian on the way to the airport, and—"

"They attacked our father's home," Abril whispered, coming to stand beside Valeria on the porch. She tried to follow along with the newest fight between Jorge, and Samuel, but her curiosity peaked about what Abril had just told her. At her raised brow, the woman nodded. "This morning—he's in bad shape, unlikely to come out of it."

"No one told me."

"Jorge doesn't care," Abril murmured, "that's what he planned to do when all this was said and done, anyway. Kill our father and take over. Samuel tried to go along with other parts of the plan, but it didn't work out."

She sounded so cold.

So … *unbothered*.

As though Abril expected this to happen.

It had only been a couple of days, but already, the García cartel was hitting them in every single place where it would hurt the most. Valeria had woken up the night before only to hear Jorge raging down the hall about the fact police raided one of the Lòpez businesses they used as a front to smuggle, but also to launder dirty money. According to what she understood, those weren't things the Garcías should be aware of without someone on the inside helping them.

So, who was it?

And what did it mean for her?

Or for *Maria*?

"Mamá?"

Valeria turned to find her daughter stood on the threshold of the front door. Her wide, tearful eyes stared up at her mother. She rushed to soothe her girl, not wanting her to see the mess happening outside.

Not that it mattered.

Maria was not stupid.

Something was happening. Things weren't right. Jorge didn't care who listened to his fits, or his phone calls.

"It's all right," Valeria told her daughter, kneeling to open her arms so she could bring her child in for a hug. Once Maria was in her arms, she felt like she might hide her from the rest of the word, and the unknowns. It was a wish, though, and not at all real. "It'll be okay. Aren't you supposed to be in bed?"

It was a little early for bedtime, but it kept Maria out of trouble.

Her daughter shrugged. "I heard yelling."

Valeria plastered on a smile. "They're just having a disagreement, that's all. Nothing to worry—"

"Open the gates! Open the fucking gates!"

At Jorge's shouts, Valeria was quick to scoop her daughter up from the porch when she stood. Turning fast, she watched the whole group of gathered men head for the dirt road. Except Jorge, and his brother.

Abril, however, stayed on the porch.

"What's happening?" she asked.

Her sister-in-law smiled. "Good things."

"*What?*"

Abril glanced sideways, anticipation lighting up her gaze. "I said, *good things* are happening, Val."

It terrified her to ask if Abril said that because she might have had her hand in causing this chaos. Had she? Was that even possible?

"Who is at the gates?"

Abril shrugged. "Chris, they said. Your Canadian."

Valeria would have noted the *your Canadian* comment, but she was a little busy with the fact Abril said it was Chris.

"Are you sure?" she demanded.

"That's what they said before they took off."

Valeria stared out into the distance, watching the men disappear down the darkening dirt road. Jorge and Samuel stared in the same direction; their fight forgotten for the moment.

Was it him?

Was it Chris?

God.

She hoped so.

She needed it to be so.

Maria's arms tightened around her mother's neck. "Mamá?"

She couldn't speak or smile for her child.

Valeria looked to Abril who was far calmer, and ready. Although, for what, she didn't have a clue. "What do we do now?"

"We get a bag ready for you and her."

"A bag—"

Abril nodded. "Quickly, before they get back or Jorge notices something is up. Wouldn't want to ruin his part of the plan when mine went off without a hitch, no?"

What was happening?

Valeria didn't dare ask.

Right now, it was just better to do what she was told.

• • •

Valeria came back out of the house, although she had to make Maria stay tucked away in her bedroom with the little pink book bag hidden under her bed, as the men appeared on the darkened road. They walked in a line, with one moving slower than the rest in front.

Her heart ached.

"Is that him?" Jorge asked. "Is it?"

Samuel grunted under his breath the closer the men came. "It looks like it."

Abril, who had now taken a seat on the wicker chairs on the porch, stood and gave Valeria a quick nod. "You good?"

"Yeah, Abril."

"Good. Keep up, okay?"

What?

Valeria didn't get the chance to ask, her attention going back to the men as their boots crunched against the gravel road. One guard picked up his pace, jogging past the slower man heading the group to dart in Jorge and Samuel's direction. Overhead, the blackened sky twinkled with stars, but for whatever reason, it seemed foreboding to Valeria.

Night always held secrets.

Didn't it?

"Chris says they're coming, boss," the man told Jorge. "*Here*—the Garcías got a hold of him and then let him go to send us a message. They will storm the ranch."

Valeria went cold all over.

They were secluded.

It was a strength as much as it was a weakness out here. There was no way out of this fucking ranch except the road. The miles and miles of desolate land surrounding them only led to the cliffs, or more fucking *land*.

How were they supposed to get out?

Or … was that the point?

Jorge stared over his shoulder to the women on the porch. "So, we fight back. We've got the artillery, and—"

"The girls need to go," Samuel muttered. "They can't be here for a fucking *gun fight*, Jorge. You were the one who demanded we stay on the ranch while the Garcías were tearing us apart outside of here because it would be *safer*. That's what you said, but it's not fucking safe anymore. They need to go if the Garcías are coming here. Don't be stupid."

"I'm *not*, I'm—"

"You won't have time," came a quiet, yet still strong, voice.

Valeria's gaze drifted to the bruised, sore-looking man approaching the group with the rest of the guards at his back. He looked like Chris, sure. From the browns of his eyes, to the shape of his face. He wore the same clothes, although now they were dirty, tattered, and bloodied, that he had when he left. Everything about him reflected a man she fell in love with through stolen moments and heated stares.

With only a passing glance, one wouldn't be able to see he *wasn't* Chris.

She sensed it in her *heart*.

His raising hand, empty of a familiar woven leather band, only confirmed what her heart and soul already recognized. He swore to Maria he wouldn't take that band off his wrist, and he didn't break his promises. *Ever.* The man standing in front, the one who sounded and looked just like Chris, was not Chris at all.

His twin, she realized.

Valeria was looking at Corrado Guzzi.

She had another striking understanding. She was the only one who saw the difference. He had never mentioned his twin to anyone else there—never spoke about his life, family, or siblings.

The man—*Corrado*—passed her a glance, but didn't linger. There was no familiarity in his stare beyond recognizing her face, perhaps because someone had told him who she was. She wasn't sure, but he didn't stare at her the way Christopher did.

His eyes didn't hold love for her.

Because this man didn't love her.

"What does that mean?" Jorge snapped.

"They dropped me off just far enough away to walk in," Corrado said, wiping at the blood on the corner of his mouth with the sleeve of his jacket, "but they weren't waiting. If they're not already coming in on the ranch, they will be soon. You won't have time to get out of here. And not the women, or your daughter."

Abril stepped forward, taking the front stairs on the porch two at a time until she reached the ground, interjecting herself into the conversation with, "The horses. We can take the horses out with a couple of men, yes? We'll be safe as long as we're away—they won't think to search for us out there, Jorge."

"I don't kn—"

"Let them take the fucking horses," Samuel snarled. "We don't have time for this shit!"

The roar of an engine punctuated Samuel's statement in the distance. Following that came the sound of rapid fire shattering the silent night.

Pat, pat, pat, pat.

Jorge was already turning to head for one guard homes where they kept the guns, and whatever else they needed to defend the land. "Take the horses, then. And a man for Val, and one for Abril. *Go.*"

He didn't glance back as he left.

Because he didn't care, Valeria realized.

Jorge never had.

It didn't even sting.

Abril wasted no time looking Valeria's way. "Get Maria ... the horses are already tacked up."

Right.

Because anyone who had been to this place would understand that there was no way out ... without a horse, and a fucking boat. Someone like *Abril.*

That should have been another clue.

Nothing here was as it seemed.

"What's happening, Mamá? Why is it so loud?"

Valeria hushed her daughter as she shoved the girl up into the saddle. "Just hold tight, okay. We're going to go on a little—" Gunfire cut through the air, far enough away from the stables, sure, but loud enough to take her breath away. Maria's eyes widened further, but she was determined to get on these horses, and leave, *now*. "Come on, move up for me."

Maria did.

Valeria mounted the horse, too.

"Abril—"

"Let's go! We don't have time to fuck around in here!"

One of the two guards that had been waiting out by the stable doors came around the corner just as Valeria turned to tell her sister-in-law to hurry. She saw the way Abril bent down, her fingers sliding into the leg of her riding boot—she had already been dressed to ride, although Valeria only noticed it now—before standing straight with a knife in her hands.

That blade swung around and embedded deep into the neck of the guard. Valeria sucked in a sharp breath, her arm swinging around to cover Maria's eyes as the man dropped to the ground, and Abril yanked the blade out.

Blood *sprayed*.

The man choked.

Abril looked her way. "*Go.*"

"Not without you," she said just as fast.

"What the fuck was that back there?"

Abril's attention flew around the corner of the stable, the knife in her hand flipping around so she had a good grasp on the hilt. "Valeria, *go.*"

"But—"

They already had the two horses ready for her, and Abril to ride. Standing in the stable's middle floor, the horses tacked up, and edgy because of the noise of gunfire and shouting men outside the building, but ready to go.

Ready to run.

Abril reached out and slapped the thigh of Valeria's horse with a loud *crack*. "Heeyah!"

She had time to grab hold of her daughter, and the reins before the horse reared back from the slap, and jerked forward. They came out of the stable doors in a full gallop, the man coming back toward them barely got out of the way.

Valeria looked back in just enough time to see Abril kill that man, too. Which meant no guards would follow them off the ranch, she realized. It was just them, and the horses, now. Abril was quick to jump on the horse waiting for her, wasting no time coming out of the stables at full speed.

Her horse was fast, but skittish from the noise. She managed well enough to get the animal steered toward the fields behind the house that would take them further away from the chaos behind them. It took Abril no time at all to catch up with Valeria, her horse coming alongside hers as she glanced over.

"We're going to the cliffs," Abril said, her voice faint, the words almost disappearing in the wind. "We don't have a lot of time."

"Why is that where we have to go ... or how do you kn—"

Abril smiled. "Who do you think helped to start this war, Val?"

"But why?"

She was *so* grateful.

So much.

Was this her freedom?

It seemed like it.

Tasted like it.

"Why?" Valeria asked again.

Abril would have sacrificed so much for what she did here tonight. Most certainly.

"I needed to be free, too," Abril said. "Just differently than you."

What could she say to that?

"Mamá," Maria whispered before the girl peered up at her mother. "I smell *fire.*"

She did, too.

Whispering in the wind.

What was burning?

Her arm tightened around Maria's waist, and her heels pressed hard into the horse's hind end. "Keep looking forward, *niña.*"

Because they weren't ever going back.

Not now.

18.

Someone slammed a Kevlar vest into Chris's chest, and he barely caught the item before it fell to the ground. His mouth opened to thank the man who had given him the protective item, but Alessio Sorrento had already turned to move onto the next waterproof storage crate they had brought along for this assault.

The tension in Alessio's back—his twin's lover, one of two people that Corrado spent his life with—said the man wasn't in the mood to talk. On a good day, Alessio's moods regularly swung one way or another. Today, however, he was swinging toward the bad side of things, and it all had to do with Chris.

Or rather, the plan Chris and Corrado came up with over the phone during a late night call after the morning Abril told him what she would do to help. Chris had to figure out the rest, how to *get in* the ranch without coming in through the front—the cliffs would be the only way, he knew. Then, he needed people. He couldn't do this alone, and so he called his twin, who made more phone calls. Amid all that, Corrado thought switching out the two of them—because his twin was far better in an assault-type situation one-on-one than he was—would be a good idea.

Alessio did not agree.

"Les," Chris said.

"Just get fucking dressed. We don't have time."

The man's sharp order wasn't just for Chris, and it slithered through the small crowd that had gathered on the edge of the cliffs. It was a handful of men—the three that The League spared for this mission, a couple from his father's organization that had skills in retrievals or assaults, and the handful Andino Marcello gave to them to use.

It wasn't much.

Still a team though.

Dressed in tactical gear, with assault weapons that would mow down a crowd, if needed, this job should be easy. Get in once the girls were out, clear the ranch, and hightail it back to the cliffs where they would all leave like this had never even happened.

Simple, right?

Yeah, Chris hoped so.

This all came down to a prayer.

Down below, three boats waited. Speed boats that one of their guys had got a hold of when he called through to a contact he had in Mexico. Alessio scaled the wall, his years of rock climbing coming in handy when they needed to secure a rope ladder with metal steps down the cliffs.

There should be only one way into the ranch.

Just one.

They were wrong.

Someone just needed the means and the mode.

His means were Valeria and Maria.

His mode was The League.

Two days.

That was all he had to put this plan together, get these eight men into the country and *here*, and make this fucking shit work. It had been a toss-up whether they pulled it off. No one would say it might work, and but for the grace of God, they were here.

Now, it was Abril's turn.

Half of this plan had been Chris's. The other side of things belonged to her. None of it would work if she didn't get her part of the plan in order, and so now he waited beside cliffs and water that made his heart race. He'd just come up from there, and one way or the other, he was going back down those cliffs to get in a boat before the night was over. That fear of water would never leave him.

Of that, he was most sure.

Chris had never been more grateful for his father forcing him to get in water after the almost drowning incident, and making him learn to swim because *you have to learn, Chris, you have to.* Never had he thought he hated his father more than he did when Gian dunked his head under water at only aged seven, apologizing because he knew it scared his son, but still determined to make him work through the terror.

He had.

It still made him fucking edgy.

Chris turned to the readying men, wanting to go over the plan just one more time—everyone needed to be on the same page, and while The League members likely already were, it was the men who came from outside of their organization that concerned Chris. No one needed to be a fucking hero here. It wouldn't help.

His speech stopped at the galloping in the distance. The unmistakable *clip-clop* of hooves hitting soil hard. With the sky a blank canvas of black, it was hard to see into the dense stretch of forest that separated a small portion of the desolate land before one came out to the cliffs.

His gaze strained.

Heart *thundering.*

Chris forgot everything he would say, everything he wanted, as his world came to a standstill. *Now or never.* Either those horses would carry a woman he had somehow fallen hopelessly in love with during the process of trying to save her life, and her child, or all of this had been for nothing.

He didn't think that way though.

Those thoughts were *poison.*

Time slowed when the horses broke through the tree line, and even in the darkness, he recognized how she rode the animal. As the animals came closer, he distinguished little Maria in front of her mother with Valeria's arm keeping her safe, and her pink book bag tight in her small hands.

Chris rushed forward before the horses had even come to a stop. The clock in his mind ticked down again. They were running out of time, surely. How long would it be before someone realized the fight between the rival cartels had been a manufactured war, only meant to distract just long enough for them to finish all of this?

They needed to get out of here.

"Come on, let me help you down," Chris said, coming alongside the horse to reach for Maria first. Unsurprisingly, she reached back, and he almost laughed when a little gray head with two pointed ears peeked out of her backpack. *That kitten of hers.* "Snuck her out, did you?"

Maria grinned in Chris's arms. "She's my kitty, I *had* to."

Right.

Goddammit.

He would get her a million kittens if that's what she wanted.

Just not tonight.

Chris kneeled down when he had Maria's feet on the ground, and Valeria hauled herself off the horse, too. Turning, he pointed at Alessio who was tying safety lines to the stakes he had beat into the ground for when they took the girls down the cliffs to return to the boats. The ladders were fine, and they would use them, too, but the lines were just for added protection.

His demand.

"See that man right there?"

Maria nodded.

Chris smiled her way. "He's my brother's ..." Okay, that was a difficult one to explain, but he managed with, "My brother's spouse, yeah? He will take you down the cliffs, and you hold on tight, okay? Listen to everything he says, make sure you keep a tight hold on your kitten, and—"

"We're going down the cliffs?"

He glanced up at Valeria, seeing the worry in her eyes. "It's the safest way out of here without drawing attention. It's how we came in, and it's how we planned to leave, too."

He didn't miss the way her throat jumped at that statement.

"What?" he asked.

"You came up from the water?"

Oh.

It wasn't her that she worried about, he realized. It was *him.*

"You do what you gotta do, sweetheart." Chris went back to Maria, giving her a playful wink, so she didn't feel as scared. "Think you can handle it?"

Maria shrugged. "It's very dark."

"The boats will shine lights up."

"There're boats?"

Her surprise made him laugh.

"They go *really* fast, too."

"*Wow.*"

"Les?" Chris called.

Alessio didn't waste time coming over with harnesses ready in his hands— three. One for Maria, Valeria, and Abril who still hadn't gotten down from her horse. Chris figured he would deal with that one after he handled Valeria.

Maria went to Alessio with no arguments.

Chris turned to Valeria as he stood.

It took their gazes meeting in the darkness for his world to slow again. Two days he had been in pain because he had left her, punishing himself second by second for the suffering she endured behind closed doors with no one to help. And yet, here she was, as beautiful and perfect and *strong* as ever.

While people moved all around them, unpacking AKs from waterproof cases, and getting the finishing touches ready for their oncoming assault on the ranch—Corrado needed to make it out alive, after all—Chris took a moment to step forward. His arm linked around Valeria's neck, tightening to pull her close to him until he hid her away from the rest as she folded into his chest.

Closer was better.

He needed her closer *always*.

Chris tipped his head down and pressed a kiss to the top of her head. Her fingers curled around the edge of the Kevlar vest he'd thrown on, and he breathed her life in.

Because she was ...

Alive.

"He'll take you down the cliffs, too," he whispered.

Valeria looked up, eyes dimmed with confusion. "Aren't you coming?"

"Later. We have to get my brother out first."

"But that means you're not coming with—"

"Soon, okay? I will follow you soon."

"*Chris.*"

"Don't make this hard, Val. Argue with me another day. Tell me this was crazy some night when you're next to me in bed. Give me the silent treatment over dinner because I didn't follow you like you wanted me to. Right now, though, let Alessio put the harness on you, and take you down the cliffs to the boats. Because that means you can do all those things someday. And that's what you wanted, right?"

She nodded, bottom lip trembling. "A chance, yeah."

"Here's your chance, babe."

Her grip on his vest flexed tighter. "But you're coming *right after?*"

"As soon as I can."

Valeria made a soft noise in the back of her throat before standing on her tiptoes to press a fast, burning kiss to Chris's lips. She didn't linger, not nearly as long as he wanted her to, but it was enough to remind him why he was here doing this.

And that was worth *everything*.

Her hand patted his chest over the Kevlar vest. "I'll ... see you soon, then?"

Chris grinned. "Absolutely."

"Okay," she said in a breath.

He didn't watch her walk to the cliffs because that was easier, and while he wasn't at all scared to run into a gunfight between rival cartels for his twin ... watching that woman walk away was the hardest thing he would ever have to do in his life.

He wasn't ready for it.

Instead, he looked to Abril still on the horse.

"You're next," he told her.

Abril arched a brow. "I'm not leaving."

"I beg your pardon?"

"This is my home—*my family*. I have a place here, a purpose here. I can do what they can't, and I can do it better."

The cartel, he knew.

"Abril—"

"Do you have an extra gun for me?" she asked.

There would be no argument. Her tone made it clear.

"Pink?" he called to the Marcello enforcer handling the guns.

The man's attention flew his way. "Yeah?"

"Toss me a gun that's ready."

An AK was in his hands in ten seconds, and he handed it up to Abril on the horse. She used the strap to secure the weapon at her back before nodding at the horse Valeria had brought along.

"That's Butter—it's a good horse. I want to keep it. You'll ride it back."

Well, all right, then.

"I take it, the plan has changed?" he asked.

Abril laughed airily. "For the cartel, plans *always* change."

"And the new plan is …?"

"I walk out of here on top. The rest of you have to follow along."

Chris nodded.

Seemed simple enough.

Truth was, some women didn't need to be saved. They didn't *want* to be saved. Not when they would do it themselves and do it better. Abril was one of those women.

Chris was fine with that—she wasn't *his* woman. She could do whatever she wanted as long as he got what he needed.

He had that now.

• • •

On horseback, Chris and Abril arrived back at the ranch first. The group, in their tactical gear and with guns ready, wouldn't be too far behind them, though. That was the least of his concerns when the property line of the infamous Lòpez compound came into view.

Flames licked at the sky.

Smoke clung to the air.

"Oh, my God," Abril whispered.

The ranch was burning. From what he saw, a barn, three of the houses, part of the stables, and a good portion of the land. The Garcías came in hard, and they weren't fucking around here. The whines of the horses echoed from where they were stuck in the stables, and unable to get out of their stalls. The loud smack of their hooves crashing against the wood walls told him the animals were panicking, and rightfully so.

Around the corner of one building, Chris caught sight of a man peeking around the side with a gun aimed across the property at one house that wasn't burning. Gunfire lit up the sky, from several directions, although it all seemed aimed right at that house. With the windows blown out, he figured they'd been shooting at it for a while, now.

That's where he needed to go.

"My horses," Abril said, her tone growing frantic when she added, "*they will die!*"

Chris pulled his shirt high to cover his mouth and give him the ability to breathe cleaner air. Abril did the same when he nodded over at her. "Head for the stables, and get the animals out," he said, "be fucking *careful*, and quick. That house they're shooting at, I bet it's where Jorge is, and the rest."

His brother, too?

Maybe.

"How long?" she asked.

"Ten minutes," Chris said, "because that's how long the team estimated it would take for them to run in—what's your plan *now*?"

"White flag it."

He raised a brow. "Really?"

Abril shrugged. "I have to make it look good, don't I?"

"You play a dangerous game."

"I intend to *win*."

Chris tipped his chin down, a silent agreement to her statement. "Ready, then?"

"So ready."

She pressed her heels into the horse and took off. He did the same to Butter although he felt the animal's hesitance to approach the chaos in front. No animal—none with any instinct—wanted to walk into a smoky blaze with this much noise. Still, the horse went as it'd been trained, it's trot turning into a gallop with Chris's encouragement.

He swung that gun at his back around to his hands, a tight grip on the reins with his other as his finger wrapped the trigger. All he needed to do was keep pulling back that trigger, fast and repeated, and a bullet would come out each time. It was his aim while on a horse that concerned him.

Apparently, for no reason.

Coming around the side of the building that one man was using as a shield, he caught the fucker in the side of his face when he turned to look at the approaching horse. Blood and matter sprayed the wood of the wall before the body hit the ground.

Chris snapped his heels into the horse, a *heeyah* coming through his clenched teeth to urge the animal closer to the gunfire around the west side of the property. Aiming that gun as the horse jumped over a six inch line of fire snaking along the dried grass on the pathway between the houses, his distraction stopped the sounds of whizzing bullets just long enough for attention to turn on him.

His finger pulled back on the trigger fast—*pat, pat, pat, pat*. Rapid fire, or rather, as fast as his finger pulled on the fucking trigger. He knew how many bullets were in his clip, and until the rest of the team came onto the property, he needed to be conservative with his ammo.

Although, by the time the men from the García cartel realized what was happening, Chris had already gotten his horse around the side of the house under attack. He rolled off the animal, hitting the ground with his feet, as bullets sprayed the corner of the home, sending wood splintering and flying past the horse's hind end.

Abril would find the horse.

They wouldn't go far.

Chris let his hand drift over the shuddering coat of the animal before he patted it. "*Merci,*" he told the horse. A quick slap and a shout to *go* from him, and the horse took off, hooves beating against the ground fast to get far away from the noise.

More bullets hit the side of the house.

Fuck.

Chris darted for the back porch, flinging himself over the railing and rolling to the back door that looked like someone kicked it open. The dead body in the hallway—a Lòpez guard he recognized—was a grisly sight he stepped over as he headed deeper into the back of the house. His gun was already back in his hands and aimed in front of him. He didn't put on as much tactical gear as the rest of the team, like covering his face, because he had plans here.

He wanted Jorge to *understand.*

He never said whether he would kill the man to Abril—it felt more like an unspoken agreement between the two. Jorge needed to go. Not only for what he did to his wife and child, but because Abril needed *no question* to her place here once it was all said and done.

A man popped his head around the corner, down the hall. Near the staircase that led into the upstairs of the home. They used this house for the guards, and servants on the property. He didn't recognize the man's face, although even if he had, he still would have fired.

The more gone, the better.

Less work when the team got here.

Chris pulled back the trigger before the man even realized what was happening and stepped over the corpse when the noise started upstairs. The shouts in Spanish, orders, he thought, although he wasn't sure.

Didn't matter.

He recognized that voice.

Jorge.

A spray of bullets came in through a broken window five feet to his left, peppering the wall with *more* bullet holes. It looked like swiss cheese.

Damn.

Chris took the stairs two at a time, keeping that gun in front of him and ready for whatever was coming next. He took no time at all to find where the group upstairs hid themselves in a back bedroom with three large windows. With the glass gone, they were using the windows to rest their own assault weapons.

Four, he counted.

One glanced over his shoulder.

Chris grinned.

It was like staring into a fucking mirror.

Corrado.

"Brother," he murmured.

Corrado returned his smile. "Chris."

Their quiet exchange drew the attention of the other three men. Two, guards for the family that Chris recognized, and the other ... *Jorge.* Corrado was quick to lean back along the windowsill, readjusting the aim of his gun before he pulled back the trigger twice in quick succession. Just like that, the two guards were *done.*

Jorge turned with his gun already aimed for Christopher. His eyes widened, shifting between Chris in the doorway, and Corrado on the other side of the room.

"Figured it out yet?" Chris asked, his own gun ready, blinking red light from the sights nailed to the spot between Jorge's eyes. "Meet my *twin*. The Marcellos say hello, but me? I only want to say fuck you."

He pulled back the trigger.

He didn't care to let the man talk.

Jorge just needed to *die*.

Chris watched the bullet rip through the man's head, sending him flying back into the windowsill where he'd been standing to shoot. His body damn near flipped out the window, but instead, hung there.

"How far are they away?" he heard his twin ask.

"Not far now, I imagine. And thanks."

Chris looked Corrado's way.

His twin shrugged.

"Wasn't a big thing," Corrado murmured.

That was a lie.

This was a *huge* thing.

"Sometimes, let me watch your back," Corrado said. "It can't always be you looking out for me, man. That's all."

Chris nodded. "Sometimes. We have to wait, now."

"For what?"

"The white flag."

A false surrender.

• • •

"*Alto—para!*"

The command cut through the air when a figure, womanly in her shape with a white rag held high, emerged through the smoke in the middle of the dirt road. With her head tilted down, the darkness behind her form made her quite a sight with the gray cloud lingering in the air.

The shouts for the firing to stop came again, louder the second time. Through the broken windows of the house, the men of the García cartel passed verbal orders between them, one at a time.

Stop.

Stop the firing.

Halt.

Repeatedly until the bullets stopped flying, and a silence settled over the ranch. Oh, there was still noise, sure. Hooves clattering in the distance, and the crackle of flames from buildings that were still burning to the ground.

The war, though?

All at once, it stopped.

"Where is Samuel?" Chris asked.

Corrado glanced his way. "What?"

"The other brother—*Samuel* Lòpez."

"Never saw him."

Chris wasn't even sure his brother knew what the man looked like, but perhaps Jorge had been so distracted in the gunfight he'd forgotten about his other sibling.

It didn't matter as he had other things to focus on right now.

Like the woman outside.

Abril kept her head tilted down low as she walked the road, one slow step at a time. Still, she kept her hand and that white rag high, a clear signal that the Lòpezs were giving up. During his time in the house, he pinned down where the leader of the other side had been hiding out—in a barn that didn't burn—because the García men flanked the structure from all directions, never turning back to retreat, but only facing forward to keep anyone from getting too close.

Chris hadn't been wrong.

The man that emerged from the barn, hands free of a weapon, dressed differently than the rest. He carried himself differently even in his steps—confident and sure. A war had been raging all around him, and yet the man's suit looked tailored to his form and without even a speck of dust on the dark fabric.

He tipped his head back as he came closer to Abril, a pleased smirk curving his lips as though he just caught his prey.

"Abril," the man—Roberto García, the man Abril would have to marry through an arrangement made by her father—called about thirty feet away from the approaching woman, "Thank you for helping me."

Abril said nothing.

She kept walking.

"What's happening?" Corrado asked.

Chris made a noise under his breath. "With her, you never know."

It wasn't a lie.

The García men gathered behind their leader, allowing Chris a quick count of the remaining men on their side of things. About twenty, he thought. How many were here before?

Twenty wasn't a large number though.

Easily handled.

Twenty also wasn't the *entire* cartel, but Chris bet Roberto had been smart enough to bring what would be more than he needed to strong-arm the ranch under his control. His mistake to assume, however.

He'd learn soon enough.

Abril and Roberto stood face to face before they spoke again. Abril stared up at him, her face a mask of nothingness. She gave nothing away—the calm in the eye of a hurricane.

Chris thought … *God help the souls who come up against her.*

She would be a force.

"You've given me all I wanted, *princesa*," Roberto said clearly, his voice traveling over the silent ranch to reach even Chris's spot in the window, "I have the cartels, and I have *you*."

Abril laughed light and sweet, her lips curving salaciously at what he implied. "Is that really what you think?"

Roberto stiffened. "I don't—"

"I only needed to make this easy," Abril interjected, her gaze burning as she dropped that white rag to the ground, "and round you up like *dogs*."

Roberto took a step back.

Abril dropped to the ground, body flat on the dirt as a line of figures came out of the smoky darkness where she first emerged. The team arrived, it seemed, and Chris finally figured out where Samuel Lòpez had gone.

It looked like he'd been waiting on his sister. Everyone had loyalties. Rarely did others know what they were though.

The Garcías made it easy on the team by gathering behind their leader. Samuel fired his AK first, peppering Roberto García with at least fifteen bullets before the man's bloodied body fell back to the ground.

Abril covered her head.

The team moved in.

Chris looked to Corrado. "Time to go."

"We should stay out of Mexico for a while, huh?"

"Oh, yeah."

Most certainly.

19.

Valeria thought she knew what exhaustion was, but she had no idea until she was in the backseat of a town car, driving through dark streets, and feeling like if she closed her eyes, she would instantly fall asleep. She didn't know where Alessio was driving to, and he didn't answer many questions once he had guided their boat to a port where he paid a waiting man a bribe to look the other way.

Still, Valeria forced her eyes to stay peeled open even as her daughter had fallen asleep with her head in her mother's lap. The kitten—she still wasn't sure how Maria snuck the cat into her bag—slept happily on the floor of the car near her feet, unbothered by the occasional swaying of the vehicle.

"Not long now," she heard Alessio say from the front.

"Oh?"

"We'll be staying at a hotel for just long enough to get the jet in the air."

Valeria glanced up, confused. "The jet?"

"Compliments of your friend. They also brought papers along—forged, mind you—that will get the two of you through customs without problems when the time comes. We need to keep moving. The others will follow, but through their own plans."

She still didn't understand.

Her tired brain again.

"They will be okay, right?" she asked.

Alessio's gaze darted to the rear-view mirror, meeting hers for a moment before he put his attention back on the road ahead of them where it needed to be. "They better be."

His underlying threat couldn't be missed.

It reminded Valeria of what she had heard Chris say about Alessio to her daughter. *Spouse* was the word he used, but to her, he had also told her that *married* was not the right way to describe his twin's relationship.

"How long have you been with Corrado?"

Alessio's stare darted back to the mirror. "Straight to the point, aren't you?"

"I need to talk or I will fall over."

"It's okay to sleep."

"It's okay to talk, too."

The man chuckled. "Many years—we have been together many years. However, we have only been with Ginevra for a little over a half a year."

Valeria blinked.

He *laughed.*

"Wait, it's *three* of you? Together? *All of you?*"

A part of her had thought Chris's twin was gay. This man suggested something else, with an extra twist, and she had to process that to respond appropriately.

Alessio nodded. "Poly. New concept?"

She thought about that for a moment.

"Well, if it works for you."

"It does," he murmured. "For us, it is perfect."

"That's what counts."

Silence drifted through the car for the rest of the drive. She was grateful that Alessio had been telling the truth, and the hotel wasn't far away. Another ten minutes of driving, and he pulled the vehicle into the underground garage.

She would have carried Maria inside, but Alessio stepped forward to take the girl before she could even try to get her out of the car.

Valeria wouldn't say it out loud, but she doubted she had the strength or energy to carry her daughter inside the building. She was happy to follow behind Alessio as he strolled through the main lobby of the hotel as though he knew where he was going, and he had been here before.

Maybe he had.

How long were they planning this?

Valeria knew better than to ask.

It didn't matter.

She was *free*.

"We should get a call soon," he said as they stepped into an elevator.

"From who?"

"Whoever is still alive at the ranch."

Valeria stiffened.

A cold dread slipped down her spine.

Alessio chuckled, passing her a look. "Mmm, and now you know what I have been thinking for the last several hours. It was me, or Corrado, though, and since he is the only one who looks like Christopher, it made sense for him to go in. Which meant, no matter what, I had to stay behind … our—*Ginevra*, well, at least one of us has to go home. That's what we promised her. This time, it's me."

Valeria smiled, as faint as it was. "Him, too, I'm sure."

"He better."

She heard it loud and clear in his tone—that threat *again*. Only this time, she realized he wasn't only making it for the woman in his life, but because he loved someone back at the ranch, too. She understood that feeling all too well.

It ached in her chest, too.

Soon, the elevator reached the floor that Alessio had chosen, the structure jumping before the doors slid open to expose a hallway that led to only one door at the end. At her questioning glance, he shrugged.

"Marcellos have expensive taste," he said. "And he wanted the best for his wife while she waited. I guess she didn't want to stay in New York … she wanted to see you as soon as she could."

Valeria froze. "Do you mean—"

"Val? *Oh, my God, Val!*"

Haven.

Valeria found her best friend coming out of the door down the hall. The person who had helped to protect her for years when she was hiding from Jorge, who helped to raise her daughter … the woman who helped to teach Maria how to speak English, who read her daughter nighttime stories when Valeria had to work late nights, and couldn't be there to put her child to bed.

Haven.

She hadn't been able to think much about her friend after Jorge caught and took her back if only because she didn't want to draw attention to Haven. God forbid the cartel go after Haven when all she had done was *help*.

"Haven," Valeria said, her voice faint, locking gazes with the blonde-headed woman down the hall. "Why did you do all of this for me?"

Haven, in her skinny jeans and silk blouse, tall and confident, head high because she had always been proud, came forward with arms already opened. "It was nothing … nothing you wouldn't have done for me. I'm sorry it took so long."

She shook her head.

"Don't be sorry for that … *don't be.*"

It was all she said before her beautiful friend came all the way down the hall to wrap her in a hug that reminded her of home. That was the thing—Valeria never had a home for so many years, and then she stumbled upon this woman. Who gave her a place to live, fed her, taught her how to survive, and helped her raise her child.

She *adored* Haven.

Loved her so fucking much.

Valeria let out a hard breath when her friend's arms tightened harder around her frame, but it was so fucking good, too. Down the hall, a man came to stand in the hotel's doorway room. His familiar face, still stone cold, and his frame, filling up the doorway as though he should be on a defensive line for a football team and not the head of a major crime family, watched them from a distance without intruding.

Andino.

Haven's new husband.

Valeria just kept hugging her friend.

"Come on," Haven murmured in her ear, "we'll get food into you. We have enough time for that before the jet will be ready for us to leave. It's not safe to stay here—it won't be long before people find out where we are. Apparently, bribes only last so long in this country before someone else's bribe becomes more interesting. Maybe we can wake Maria up so she can eat, too? I miss her so much."

She nodded, but Haven still hadn't let go.

That was okay.

Home almost seemed like home again.

Except it was missing one person, now.

Chris.

• • •

The plan to remove Valeria and Maria from Mexico was in motion long before Chris came on the scene, she came to learn on the long flight back to New York. It was *how* they would retrieve the two from the clutches of Jorge and the rest of the cartel they needed help with.

Removing them from the country?

Protecting them after?

Easy, Andino explained.

Valeria had no reason not to believe them, although she didn't think it was as easy as the man said in his dismissive way, but it still stunned her. They only stayed at the hotel long enough to get food in their stomachs before they were on the road again. A Marcello-owned jet waited at a private gate for them to board at an international airport with agents that barely glanced at the fake passports Andino gave her.

Although, they looked kindly upon the envelop of cash Andino passed to them when he walked through first. It worked the same way when they entered the states after landing in New York at a small airport outside of the city where apparently, the Marcellos had connections and didn't mind pulling them to get their business handled.

It all happened so fast.

Simple.

Valeria still felt like she was floating.

Once in New York, they moved to a hall of suites in the Manhattan Waldorf where she found more people waiting. She tried to keep track of her daughter, but let Maria run freely amongst the rooms with Haven when she figured out that the woman looking her in the face was Chris's mother.

How did she know that?

Alessio.

"Cara," Alessio said, smiling as he leaned in to kiss the pretty, red-headed woman with lines around her eyes that appeared whenever she grinned. "No phone calls from your boys yet, but they told me some phones ended up in the water on the way down the ladder."

Cara frowned. "As long as *they* didn't end up in the water."

"Chris can swim."

The statement came from the man who approached behind Cara, making Valeria's eyes widen in familiarity when he smiled her way. "Been a minute since the two of us had the chance to speak, *oui?*"

"Gian," Valeria said, taking the hand he offered when he came to stand beside his wife. "had I known that first day your intentions for being there were to help me—"

Gian shook his head. "No need to say anything or wish for different things. We're here, now, all of us."

"Most of us," Alessio corrected.

Cara gave him a smile. "Still in that mood, hmm?"

"I didn't like the *plan.*"

"He's headstrong."

Alessio made a noise under his breath but said nothing.

Cara's gaze turned back on Valeria in an instant. "You must be exhausted."

"Very. And ... still in shock."

"I bet."

"I want Chris, and the rest, to get back safely."

At that statement, all eyes turned back on her. It was only them in the small sitting room at the Waldorf that connected to a larger bedroom, sure, but it still seemed like she suddenly had a huge audience that became enraptured with whatever she might say or do next.

Gian gave Alessio a glance. "Something we should be told ... on *that?*"

Alessio arched a brow. "I'd say so, but we'll wait for him to say it."

"What did I miss?" Valeria asked.

Cara reached out, taking her hands with a warm smile that reminded her of the mother she lost years ago. "*Nothing*—it means nothing. We're so *thrilled* to meet you, Valeria. I would love to spend time with your daughter if that's okay with you?"

Valeria was quick to nod. "Sure, she loves people. Always wants to make them smile."

"I bet she's an angel."

"She's certainly been mine."

One of *several*, Valeria realized.

Her daughter was one of many angels in her life.

• • •

"Thank you."

Haven smiled as Valeria took the mug of tea. "You really should try for more than an hour-long nap, Val. Being tired will not make him get here any fast—"

"*There they are! There's the cars! Mamá, look!*"

Valeria peered around Haven's side to see Maria standing on the edge of a chaise at the window, her hands gesturing at whatever was down below. "Maria, it could just be guests coming to the hotel."

"No, it's *Chris*. It is!"

Maria hopped down from the window, the dress Valeria packed for her daughter flying wide around her legs as she darted for the doorway.

At the window, Andino who entertained Maria, smirked back at them. "She's not wrong—they're coming in now."

What?

Valeria no longer cared about her tea, or the fact she was exhausted. She didn't bother to glance at the people milling between the rooms as she followed her shouting, excited daughter as the girl headed out of their room, and down the hall of the hotel. She caught up with Maria before she pressed the button on the elevator for it to open.

She grabbed Maria around her waist, pulling her back as she kneeled to say, "Just wait ... let them come up, okay?"

Sure, she said that.

Didn't mean she meant it.

Valeria's heart thundered as she watched the elevator, and the little sign above it that said the doors opened on the ground floor. The Marcellos closed down the corridor of the hotel, renting every single room for the night to make sure they had all the privacy they needed for whatever might happen.

Footsteps approached behind them.

Their *voices*.

Valeria continued watching the elevator.

"I *saw* him, I did," Maria whispered.

"I bet," she said, believing her daughter. "Just a minute, okay?"

Still, the girl practically vibrated in her mother's arms. It was only in that moment that Valeria realized … she was not the only person caught in Chris's snare. His caring nature, sweet and yet still firm, caught her daughter's heart, too.

Maria looked up at her mom by tilting her head. "We never have to go back, right?"

Valeria met her daughter's stare, so the girl understood she was telling the truth. "Never. *Ever.*"

"Good."

The elevator dinged as the two of them broke their staring contest. The first men out of the elevator weren't faces that Valeria recognized, but she was still quick to stand, and keep her daughter out of the way so they were able to come through.

And then there Chris was.

At the back with his twin.

"*Chris!*"

Maria's squeal, punctuated by her jumping in place, had him turning with a wide smile in their direction. Valeria let her girl go, and Maria wasted no time darting forward. Corrado slipped out of the elevator first, but her daughter didn't seem to have an issue differentiating who was who between the identical twins. She gave him a smile, sure, but the man Maria wanted was the only one she reached for.

Chris came out of the elevator with arms open, already kneeling to hug Maria. The girl's arms locked around his neck, and he stood, holding her tight all the while. He pressed a kiss to her temple, murmuring something to Maria.

"You still have it?" Maria asked.

Chris grinned and flashed his wrist with the woven leather bracelet. "Of course, *bambina*. Never take it off if I can help it."

"Better not."

"Be nice," she told her smartass child.

At her quiet admonishment, Chris's gaze came her way, and she swore the world stopped. Like her ability to breathe, and the beats of her heart.

It all just … *stopped.*

For him.

"I love you," she whispered.

Chris's features softened. "Do you?"

She was very aware of the people behind her. Of the family that gathered, and the others saying hello to men who arrived back. None of that mattered to her though. Better people be aware now.

Was it crazy?

Yes.

Was it true?

More than anyone understood.

"I do," Valeria said quickly, "I love you."

Chris came forward, still holding Maria—although he shifted her to one arm instead of two—and reached for Valeria. Once his arm locked around her neck, he pulled her in close, his mouth finding hers for a soft, long kiss that made her heart restart all over again.

Damn.

She would have preferred he kept kissing her, but she didn't mind when he pulled away just long enough to touch their noses together, his eyes locking onto hers. Softly, he said, *"Ti amo—sempre.* I love you *always.* As long as you want me."

That was perfect.

Because she wanted him forever.

20.

"You went to Mexico for a *job*."

Chris chuckled as he poured a small glass of whiskey at the wet bar. "I did."

His father came to stand next to him with a knowing smile. "Seems you came back with more than you intended to, Christopher."

"And?"

Gian sighed, his gaze drifting across the room to where Cara was helping Valeria settle Maria for the evening. Once she was in bed, his parents had promised they would leave them be to relax for the night, or as much as they could.

"Bit ... rushed," Gian murmured. "What is it about you boys of mine *rushing* into love, hmm?"

"Don't you know?"

Gian shook his head. "I don't, so tell me."

Chris thought it was simple.

Obvious.

"You taught us not to be afraid of love, Papa. You and Ma—watching the two of you growing up showed us what love is supposed to be. Not perfect. Not always easy, or *given* to us. We earn it, we nurture it, and we do that so we can keep it. That's the wonderful part, or I thought so, anyway."

Gian made a soft noise in the back of his throat, turning so that his back was to the wet bar, and he could watch the women across the room as he spoke. "So, what you're telling me is not to worry, yes?"

Chris smiled. "Not about this. I have it handled."

"You always have everything handled. You were not the one of my five boys I had to worry about *that*. Trust me."

He did.

"And I am proud of you," Gian added after a moment.

Chris tipped his glass up for a drink, letting the spices of the heady liquor rove over his tongue before he swallowed it back. Setting the lowball down, he asked, "For what?"

"Doing the impossible. And finding something you wanted, I suppose." Gian glanced his way, that soft expression of his father's turning into something else. The Don was in the room—just like that. All it took was his father flipping a switch, and his mood changed. "As for the cartel ..."

"What about it?"

"I would appreciate knowing what we're looking at now where they are concerned." Gian shrugged his broad shoulders under his tailored, black blazer. "I let you go into Mexico with little plans, or even understanding how all of this would play out."

"To be fair," Chris replied, amused, "even my plans got fucked up. Someone else had her own plans, and she did what she wanted do whether anyone else cared."

"And who is this *someone*?"

"Abril Lòpez. The youngest daughter—same age as Val, but nothing like her, if we're being honest here. And that's not a bad thing, let me say."

"She helped?"

"Helped … caused a war." Chris made a dismissive noise and waved a hand in the air. "What do the details matter if it's all the same, yeah?"

Gian grunted under his breath. "And what, I assume a surviving male will now take over the cartel? Will we have to be concerned about retribution for our part we played down there, or not?"

"Oh, no. I assume nothing. Abril is now a new queen on a very broken throne, and that's fine, she likes it there."

His father blinked.

Chris nodded.

What else could he do?

He had not planned for Abril, and when he *decided* to use her help … the woman had her own schemes running. She was dangerous, a lot like the rest of her family, but a hell of a lot less obvious about it, too.

"We should stay out of Mexico as much as possible," Chris said. "Entirely. I suspect she will be busy tearing down what remains of her father's cartel to rebuild it in the image she prefers, while—"

"Warring with her rivals."

"Mmm."

Gian folded his arms over his chest, considering those words. "You think she would … use us to her advantage, if we were to return, even for vacation?"

"I think anyone—man or woman—who thinks to assume to underestimate Abril Lòpez will deserve everything they get, and our family should not be the ones who she makes an example out of."

That seemed to be enough for his father.

"I will pass the information along to Andino, then. I am sure the Marcellos won't be welcome down that way, either."

"To be safe," he agreed, "yeah."

Gian glanced his way again, the kinder smile replacing his stony expression. "As for *you* …"

"What about me?"

"I hope you will settle down, now. I've never said one way or the other, Chris, on *famiglia* or The League because I thought you had decided long ago."

He cleared his throat. "I thought I did, too."

"And now?"

A laugh burst from his chest.

"This was enough for me. I am a made man, and nothing more. That's where I need to be, and where I want to be. Corrado and I, well, we're old enough now we don't need to be looking over each other's backs all the time, I think."

"You're not wrong." Gian nodded, reaching over to clap his son on the shoulder. "And on the made bit, *good.*"

"What would you have said, if I chose the other option?"

"The same thing, son."

Right.

Because that was his father in a nutshell.

And his mother, too.

Speaking of which …

Across the room, Cara took a hug from Maria before the girl darted to take her mother's outstretched hand. Valeria shot Chris a smile over her shoulder before the two disappeared into the connected bedroom of the hotel room. Once the door was shut behind them, Cara looked her son's way with a familiar smile that had his chest growing tight.

He loved his ma.

All the Guzzi boys did.

"She is a sweet child," Cara said, crossing the room to stand in front of Chris. She patted his cheek with a soft palm, pride and support shining through in her actions, and in her eyes. "I was worried about you."

"Sorry, Ma."

"You didn't call enough."

"It wasn't safe, really."

Cara's thumb stroked his unshaven cheek. "And just what do you plan to do with the two of them now, hmm?"

Chris smiled. "We have all the time in the world to figure it out."

Inside, though?

He already knew.

Keep them forever.

• • •

"That's *three* books," Valeria said, laughing.

Chris grinned to himself in the doorway when Maria gave her mother a dramatic sigh. The girl wasn't at all spoiled, but she still had her mom wrapped right around her pinky finger, as cute as that was.

"But—"

"And we had to get the concierge of the hotel to find the books, Maria."

"Just one more?"

Valeria was trying to get her daughter to fall asleep, but Chris figured the events of the past couple of days had been a bit much. They all needed time to absorb what happened, calm down, and get back to a normal routine. Maria included.

Behind him, the echo of water running into a tub reminded him of what Valeria had been trying to do before Maria crawled out of the bed meant for her, and found them in the bedroom as they talked.

"I'll read her another book," he said, "and you can go have your bath."

Valeria gave him a look. "I don't mind—"

"Neither do I."

"Yes, Chris can read," Maria said. "I want *him* to read me a book now."

He hid his chuckles when Valeria shook her head and tossed the handful of children's books to the bed.

"Anything to get out of bedtime," she teased, strolling past him in the doorway.

He caught her with his hand to her wrist before she could leave. Dropping a quick kiss to her mouth, he murmured, "Enjoy your bath, okay? She's fine with me."

"She is."

That was all she said before leaving him alone in the bedroom with Maria. Chris gave the little girl dwarfed by the big bed and huge blankets a look.

"One book," he said.

"Three," she shot back.

Oh, now they were bartering.

Kids were great.

"Two," he countered.

Maria considered that before nodding once. "Fine, two. Chris?"

"Hmm?" he asked as he crossed the room. "What, *bambina*?"

"Do we get to stay with you now?"

He hesitated as he sat on the edge of the bed, already reaching for the books. "Do you want to stay with me?"

"You kept your promise."

"I did, yes."

"No one except Mamá keeps her promises."

Chris shrugged. "I always will."

"Can we make a new promise?"

"What is that?"

"That you won't leave."

"I don't need to make that promise." He smiled, leaning back on the bed with the book already opened in his hands. "I can't leave, *bambina*."

"Why not?"

"People don't leave things they love, Maria. That's all."

"Oh."

Her soft exclamation echoed in the quiet bedroom.

"Promise to be ours, then?"

Chris nodded as he flipped the page to the beginning in the book. "I can definitely promise that."

She suckered him into *four* reads of two books, but he didn't mind. And by the time he finished, Maria snored away in the bed's middle, unaware when he slipped out of the bedroom to find her mother.

Valeria made it easy for him, considering she left the bathroom door wide open.

"You know," Chris murmured, leaning in the doorway to enjoy the sight of Valeria's tanned legs spattered with bubbles and hanging over the ledge of the tub, "my mother asked me a question earlier."

"Oh?"

"Yes, about you and Maria."

A sly, yet still sweet, smile curved her pouty lips when her gaze darted up to his. It was taking every ounce of his willpower to stay where he was, and not slam the door shut, go to her, and take what he wanted.

Somehow, this woman who had once been so confused about her lust and need for sex because of the constant abuse she suffered, could now look like his personal minx ready to torture him with seduction. Chris was more than willing to let her do that, too.

"And what was that question she asked?"

Chris cleared his throat, refusing to let thoughts of his mother into his mind when this beautiful woman was just across the room, naked but for the water and bubbles hiding her curves from his view. "What I planned to do with the two of you, actually."

Valeria arched a perfect brow. "What does that mean?"

"Better question," he returned, "what do you plan to do?"

"You."

"Pardon?"

Her tongue peeked out to wet the seam of her lips as her hand came up from the water, covered in bubbles and dribbling water down her throat as she pointed a delicate finger at him. "*You*, Chris. I plan to be with you as long as you want me. That's what you told me on the cliffs, right?"

"It was."

"And that still stands?"

"Absolutely, Val."

She grinned. "Then, that's all I care about. Although, I would like to hear your plans."

"With you?"

"Anything. I enjoy hearing you talk. Do you know how long it has been since I wanted to sit and have a conversation with a man? A man that *wanted* to hear me talk, too?"

He blinked.

Swallowed thickly, too.

"You can do anything, and I will be here to help you do that," he said, shrugging. "If you want to put Maria back in her old school, let's do it. Come to Canada with me, or travel back and forth—all right. Maybe I can take you out on a proper date, too."

Valeria winked. "*Maybe?*"

His gaze lifted to meet hers when he murmured, "Yeah, and someday, you might let me marry you. Because that's the thing about this. I don't care what we do as long as you let me love you while we do it."

She sucked in a quick breath.

Chris smiled.

"I see you, and her, and it's all possibilities now. Unending possibilities, sweetheart. We can do anything—everything. You're both looking for something, but I'm right here. You can stop looking now, Val, you found me."

"Yeah, we did, huh?"

"I just wanna learn."

"Learn what?"

He came further into the bathroom, closing the door behind him to quiet the noise so it didn't wake up Maria in the next room. Crossing the space between him and Valeria, he kneeled beside the tub, resting his arms along the ledge so that the two of them were eye-level.

"This," he said, tipping his head to the side when she leaned a little closer to him. Almost close enough that her lips pressed to his if she wanted that. "*Us*. Love, but without everything else, too. That's what I want to do now."

Her dark eyes drifted over his face, pleasure and happiness curving her lips as her wet fingers came to draw a line along the edge of his jaw. "That sounds like the best plan."

"You think?"

"Perfect."

"Like you, then."

She dragged in a quick breath, her top teeth catching her bottom lip as she mumbled, "You always say the right things, you know?"

"Honest things, babe."

"*Still.*"

"And only for you," he promised.

Valeria nodded. "Just me."

She closed the distance between them, her soft lips moving against his in a slow, tantalizing kiss that had his cock hardening under his slacks, and his chest pounding in his chest. Her tongue teased at the seam of his lips, ready and willing to take more of what she wanted from him. Chris wanted to give it, too.

Just kissing this woman was intoxicating.

A *privilege.*

It's what he wanted to spend the rest of his life doing, too. Kissing her first thing in the morning, and right before he fell asleep. Love was strange like that, but he didn't mind. He would happily spend the rest of his days at the mercy and whims of this woman if that's what God had planned for him.

She reached for him, soaking wet and dampening his already ruined dress shirt. He hadn't even changed his clothes after arriving back. Which was fine, because she was in a perfect position—wet, in a warm bubble bath—to help fix that little problem of his.

Chris stood, stripping out of his dirty clothes faster than he thought possible. All the while, Valeria's sexy laughter colored up the bathroom, fading once he stepped into that large bathtub, already reaching for her to get what they both wanted the most.

For the first time, he didn't think about needing a condom to be with this woman. He didn't *care*—he fucking wanted her. All of her, and to have her be his. To mingle with her in a way only he would for the rest of their lives.

Nothing was better than that.

As soon as he was sitting in the tub, Valeria climbed into his lap. Her hands found his semi-hard cock—a permanent state for him now whenever he was near her—to stroke him alive until his chest burned with every breath while her hips and ass did this slow, grinding dance, making the water slosh along the tub.

"Did you know," she whispered to him, a sinful grin curving her sexy lips, "that I used to dance?"

Chris blinked. "What?"

Her body kept moving, a sensual beat that had his gaze following all her lines and curves as she moved to a beat he couldn't hear, but swore he sensed it in his bones. Her hands jerking him off was enough to drive him insane, but the memorizing sway of her body had his attention split between the two things.

"What do you mean, *dance?*"

"Stripped," she said simply, "for Haven's club. I used to dance a lot when I first started, but then I moved into helping her more with the business, and only danced occasionally after. It was what taught me I *could* be sexy, and desired, but it was just a *thing*. You made it real for me … tangible."

"Fuck."

He was still trying to picture the image of her dancing on a stage, a thrill shooting through him, but Valeria gave him a good, real life view right there in the large tub. She let him go, turning around in his lap so that her ass rested halfway above the water, her hands steady on the edge of the tub, keeping her up. She shook her ass beautifully, and there was something primal curling through him as he reached out to grab her while she danced for him, the sliver of her wet pussy peeking out from the water when she lifted high enough.

Her dancing turned into something more erotic—if that were possible—when his hand slipped between her thighs to rub against her pussy. Her hips ground into his palm and fingers. A tremor worked its way through her body because of it.

"Get off," he murmured. "Get off for me and then let me fuck you."

His words only urged her on to grind harder against his hand, letting him feel the pulsing of her pussy when her orgasm approached. Her soft, desperate cries climbed higher until shudders raced through her body all at once, and a gasp rushed from her.

Chris was already pulling Valeria back into his lap before she had even finished shaking from the force of her orgasm. He spread her thighs wide, tucking her back into his chest as he slid his cock into her flexing pussy.

Damn.

"So fucking *tight*," he rumbled against her throat. "Got you milking me, Val, *God*."

His hand slid along the side of her neck, tipping her head to the side to suck and bite at her racing pulse while she rode his cock like that. He was sure they were making a mess, the sounds of the sloshing water hitting the side of the tub mingling with their hard breaths and his groans.

This right here.

Always.

That's what he wanted.

"Make me come again," she whined, the demand clear even in her neediness. "Please, Chris … *please*, I want to come."

There was something about his name in her mouth.

It always fucking did it for him.

Jesus.

His arms locked around her like bars as her hips kept that fast tempo. Sliding a hand between her thighs, he worked her clit while she moved her body against him to get what she wanted. His fucking balls ached with a base need to just *empty* into her.

It was only when she was breathing his name like a prayer when she came again that he finally let go, holding her tight to his cock as he released deep inside her shuddering pussy.

"Holy fuck, I love you," he mumbled against her damp skin.

Valeria's breathless laugh filled him with satisfaction because that's what it sounded like, too. "You *better*."

He shifted her in the tub, allowing her to turn around and curl up into his lap as his raging heart settled.

Pleased there, Valeria's breathing came out slow, and steady. His fingers traced lazy, wet circles across her shoulders, and down her back. Each swipe of his fingertips had her shivering and sighing. Minutes passed—too many to count. Long enough for the steam to leave the bathroom, and the hot water to turn only *warm*.

They were content to stay like that, together, still humming from sex, and almost ready to fall asleep, but a quiet call from outside the bathroom had Chris perking up. Little Maria's cry for her mom came again, and Valeria stiffened before she pushed up from his arms.

"Stay in the bath, enjoy it," she said, "she's probably just scared because she woke up in a new place, and—"

Chris leaned in, quieting her words with a kiss. "I'll come, too. You don't have to do anything alone anymore. You know that, right?"

Valeria pulled him in for another burning kiss, whispering, "Yeah, I do."

21.

"Is it weird to have two homes?"

Valeria tipped her head sideways, careful not to interrupt the kind woman who was removing the curling rollers from her hair. "You're asking me that?"

Haven's brow dipped. "Well, yeah. Why not?"

"*You*, Haven."

"What?"

"Doesn't Andino have two vacation homes on the west coast?"

Soft laughter floated throughout the hotel room, reminding Valeria that they weren't alone. It was easy to get lost in the pampering she was experiencing, considering it had started the moment she opened her eyes that day.

It was, after all, her wedding day.

"I think," Ginevra said, the roundness of her twenty-week pregnancy swell coming into view of Valeria's gaze as she stepped between the two women's chairs, "what Val means, is that Andino still has the brownstone, doesn't he? Oh, and the vacation homes. The mansion in the—"

"I don't *use* those," Haven said.

Ginevra winked at Valeria, and she grinned back. This was nice. The easy banter between friends, no topic off-limits, and no worries. She couldn't remember a time in her life when she had more than one friend to count on, and now it felt like she had a small army around her at all times.

Between the people Haven brought into her life from the Marcello side of the things, and with Chris's family ... Sure, her circle was still small in a lot of ways, but it was wider than it had ever been.

That's what counted.

"And you actually live between your two homes," Haven continued. "Weekends in New York, and the week in Toronto. I wondered if that gets tiring."

The travel could be annoying.

Also, very much worth it.

"You let Maria choose, didn't you?" Ginevra asked.

Valeria nodded. "I did. I knew she missed her school in New York, but she also liked Chris's home in Toronto, and the private school she would attend there. As long as I promised she could visit Haven every weekend, she decided Toronto was where she wanted to stay."

Chris, bless his heart, hadn't said a thing. Oh, Valeria knew he wanted to ... more than anything, that man wanted her and Maria with him as much as possible. Yet, he kept quiet for those two weeks it took Maria to decide what she wanted to do.

Really, Valeria had always known what her daughter's decision would be. Chris didn't realize it, but Maria loved him *inexplicably*. He was the exact opposite of the men that had been forced upon her as male influences, including her—may he

575

enjoy his place in hell—dead father.

And to give credit where it was due, Chris loved her little girl. He would spend hours with Maria doing whatever she wanted just because. Bedtimes were spent reading a dozen books because he couldn't seem to tell her no. He learned how to manage her thick, unruly hair because Maria liked their conversations in the mornings while Valeria cooked, and Chris styled it for school.

It was painfully sweet.

Everything she thought they wouldn't have.

Some people didn't understand how, in just a few months, Valeria went from not knowing a man, to living with him and marrying him, but it was an easy choice for her. The *right* one. Because that's what Chris was.

The right man.

The perfect one.

Hers.

And her child's.

"I thought, after a couple of months, you might have felt differently about weekends in New York, and the rest of the time spent there," Haven said, bringing Valeria back to the conversation. "That's all."

"Or are you slyly asking me to spend more time in New York with you?"

Before Haven responded, the stylist pulled the final curler from Valeria's hair, and urged her to tip her head over. A brush was dragged through her thick strands, leaving it wild, and wavy. Once she was sitting straight again, the woman nodded.

"Let me get the hair piece, and I'll work on the style you wanted, Valeria."

"Thank you," she told the stylist.

"And I am *loving* this," the woman added, pointing a finger at the gold lettering on her silk robe.

Mrs. Guzzi, it read.

She wasn't a Guzzi yet. A few more hours had to pass before she would walk down the aisle to meet Christopher waiting at the end, but still … she loved the robe, too.

"It's great, isn't it?"

"I'll let Corrado know his gift is appreciated," Ginevra said, sneaking a piece of cheese from the tray next to Valeria's chair. "This is good, I need more."

The stylist went off to do her own thing.

Valeria went back to the conversation with Haven. "Well, which is it?"

Haven laughed. "Neither. I *would* like to see you more, but we're both busy, and it's not like we can't make time, right?"

"Right."

"Oh," Ginevra whispered.

Valeria shot her a look, but the young woman's hand drifted down to rest atop her swell covered by a pale pink, silk robe. "You okay?"

A wedding day was stressful. Her future in-laws did every single thing to make today easy for her, not to mention wonderful and beautiful. Valeria barely needed to lift a finger to plan this wedding from the moment she said yes when Chris asked her at his father's birthday celebration.

The most she had to do was sit down with an event coordinator and pick out things she liked. They delivered everything else for her approval.

The most difficult decision she had to make was picking her wedding dress, and deciding whether she should choose her girls' dresses, or if they should. Haven picked her own dress. Ginevra ended up bringing Corrado and Alessio along last minute for her final fitting because she didn't like the way hers looked with her pregnancy starting to show ... and those men calmed her about the dress, *and* the way she wore it.

Valeria smiled at the memory.

Yet another reminder she wasn't alone anymore. She had a whole family, now, spread out amongst many people. Three months ago, she had not realized how much her entire life would change when she rested in a bathtub with Chris, and told him, yes, she wanted to be with him.

It moved fast.

Kind of like them.

Valeria didn't mind.

A wedding day was still ... stressful.

She didn't want Ginevra to experience any stress today. Not when she was carrying her niece, halfway through her pregnancy, and should only be glowing.

Which she was.

Mostly.

"It's good," Ginevra said at Valeria's worried expression. "Here ..."

Ginevra took Valeria's hand and pressed her palm into the side of her stomach. The soft movement of the baby girl turned into a hard jab. She remembered those hard movements from her long-passed pregnancy with Maria.

"Ouch," Valeria said to Ginevra.

"Right?" She sighed. "I like the cheese—baby girl doesn't."

"Well, she doesn't know what she's missing out on," Haven said, laughing as she grabbed a piece of cheese from the tray before popping it into her mouth. "Just saying."

They were still laughing when the stylist came back into the room, followed by Cara, and little Maria who was already dressed up to the nines in her pretty flower girl gown. She danced over to her mother, doing a little twirl at Cara's urging who beamed.

Already a proud grandmother. Or, that's what Cara said when Maria asked if she could call her *Nonny*.

"She wanted to show you her dress," Cara explained.

"Little early to put that on."

Cara shrugged. "I'll bribe it off her with something."

Valeria shook her head. "Well, if it works."

"Do you like my dress, Mamá?" Maria asked.

Valeria leaned down to kiss her smiling princess. "*Love it.*"

"Come on, now," Ginevra muttered, rubbing circles into the side of her swell. Cara didn't miss it, a concerned frown growing when her attention turned on the woman. Ginevra was quick to explain, "The baby won't relax—the cheese didn't agree with her, I guess. I think I'll find Corrado and let him calm her down."

"Not Alessio?"

Ginevra laughed. "*No*, he makes her dance."

"Ah," Valeria replied, "well, we're okay. We've got lots of time."

"Thanks."

Ginevra was quick to slip out of the hotel room. Valeria didn't worry because Ginny would find Corrado soon enough, undoubtedly. Their entire wedding party had the whole room block booked for the weekend at the tucked away, private villa-styled bed-and-breakfast. It was one of the few things she wanted. A small wedding. The people she cared about the most.

And the man of her dreams.

Valeria had him.

"Mamá, it's not raining," Maria said, climbing up in her mother's lap to sit. "I *checked*."

Valeria laughed.

Yes.

Her *one* worry for today.

Canadian weather was tricky.

"That's great," she said, kissing Maria's cheek. "It's a beautiful day to get married."

Cara nodded.

Haven, too.

"It is," they echoed.

• • •

Haven made quick work of smoothing out the lace train of Valeria's wedding gown. She held tight to the bouquet of white roses in her hands, staring at the double doors still closed in front. *Almost time.*

"Now?" Maria asked, bouncing on the spot.

Ginevra laughed. "Not yet."

Haven came to stand in front of Valeria, and for a moment, the rest of the surrounding distractions seemed to disappear. "You okay?"

"So good."

"That's what matters. This dress ... *wow*, babe. Banging, huh?"

Valeria grinned. "You think?"

The form-fitted, sleeveless, heavy lace gown wasn't what she had envisioned when she first thought about her wedding dress. She found the gown hanging on a back rack in a dress shop. It fit almost perfectly although they had needed to take the fabric in at her sides to make it tight to her curves. The ivory lace, decorated with pearls, covered the gown from top to bottom where the skirt flared out. The three-foot train was just enough, but not too much.

Regal.

Beautiful.

Like Valeria wearing it.

"It's perfect, Val," Haven said.

"It's not at all like my first."

Haven's smile slipped. "No?"

She hadn't talked a lot about her first—*forced*—marriage, but especially not to Haven. Not even when she was on the run and had lived with Haven for years. It was something she didn't bring up because she figured ... then she wasn't putting

Haven in danger unwittingly.

"No, that was some stupid princess ... God, it was an ugly thing."

Haven grinned. "Yeah?"

"Not what I wanted."

"And this is?"

That's what she was trying to say.

The emotions made it difficult.

"All of this is exactly what I want," Valeria whispered. "I'm still trying to convince myself that it's real, you know?"

"This is so fucking real, Val. That man loves you. His family *loves you*. Your kid? She's theirs, now. You did *good*, okay? You will not wake up tomorrow and find out this was all a lie, I promise. This is real life—your life as long as you want it. Got it?"

Valeria nodded, dragging in a shaky breath to keep the tears lining her eyes at bay, lest she ruin her makeup. What a mess that would be, and they couldn't fix it when she was a couple minutes away from walking to her future.

"Yeah, I understand," Valeria whispered.

"Good. Sometimes, we need to hear it, right?"

"Right, Haven."

Her best friend winked. "You are worthy of this, never forget that. Him? These people? *Me*? They *deserve* you. We are lucky to have you, and we are better because we know you."

"I think it's the other way around, too."

"Maybe," Haven agreed, "but today isn't their day, either. It's yours."

"Yeah."

"Ready to get married?"

"More than ready."

"Then, let's get you married."

Haven's pep talk came at the right time because beyond the double oak doors lined with waves of white and red tulle, the music changed to a familiar tune. Ginevra shot a wide smile over her shoulder and lifted her bouquet of red roses high.

"That's me," she said.

The doors opened a little. Not enough to show the rest, but it allowed Ginevra to walk through first. Haven gave Valeria a wink.

"Me next. You're not sad, right?"

"For what?"

"Well, I'm not sure. Maybe because your side of the aisle might be a little ... empty."

Valeria shook her head. "Not at all. The people who count are already here, and the only other person I might like to see ... well, my parents are dead, and Abril called to congratulate before she asked after Maria. I'm not sad."

"Good. I love you, huh?"

Valeria nodded. "I love you, too. Thank you ... for everything."

When she had nothing, Haven was there. Against all odds, Haven had been the one who never gave up on Valeria. Now she had everything, and she was so glad she could share this with her best friend. That was the beauty of life.

"We're just getting started, Val."

"Absolutely."

A minute later, Haven slipped through the doors when they opened for her. That left Valeria and Maria waiting in the corridor. Gian, Chris's father, had offered to walk her down the aisle, and while it meant the world to her ... she still asked to do this alone.

So much of her life was forced upon her. She wasn't given any choice, and she had never been free to do something *willingly*.

More than anything, she wanted to do this.

Gian understood.

"Almost time, Mamá," Maria whispered, smiling.

She looked so beautiful in her red and white gown.

"Almost," she echoed.

Maria would walk first, spreading her rose petals down the aisle. When the song changed to the one she chose for her walk, then she would go, too.

"And then we get to keep Chris forever, right?"

"Yeah, baby, we get to keep him forever."

Maria turned with her basket ready when the doors opened for her. Instead of walking in, she *skipped*. Chuckles murmured down the line of chairs before the doors closed again, leaving her to her thoughts.

She wouldn't be alone for long.

Chris promised.

She didn't have to do anything alone now. And hadn't he proven that he always kept his promises?

Soon, the song changed behind the closed doors, and Valeria dragged in a heavy breath. Lifting her head to smile, the doors opened wide open to expose her waiting behind them.

Every guest stood.

Valeria smiled wider behind her veil.

She should have taken the time to admire the way the decorations had come together in the hotel's hall where they chose their venue. All the reds and whites, melding together with the roses as accents, and centerpieces. The silk aisle runner dotted with red and white rose petals, compliments of her daughter. The event planner and the small army she brought in to decorate the place had worked so hard to get it ready for this moment.

She looked over the people, noting familiar faces; some she had only recently met, and others she had known for months now, smiling back at her.

And then, she stared forward.

At *him*.

Chris waited at the end of the aisle, his twin at his left, wearing a custom, tailored tux he filled perfectly. It reminded her how lucky she was to have this gorgeous man waiting on her—smiling *for* her. Well, he reminded her of that every time he woke her up in the morning, and each night before she fell asleep with him next to her. His white silk vest and tie was a stark contrast to the red set his twin, and other brothers wore for the day.

The chiseled line of his jaw softened when his grin deepened, and his dark gaze drifted down her dress to take her in. The proud glint in his eye said he liked what he saw waiting for him. Just like that, she was the only woman in the world, and he was the one man made for her. She'd been careful to do that for this day. Ensure he didn't see her dress—that it would be a complete surprise.

Chris had been more than willing to play along.

Whatever she wanted.

He loved her too much.

She understood.

She loved him the same.

From all the way across the room, she sensed his stare. The way he drank her in and appreciated her. *Adored* her. He never hid it. Not from her, or from anyone else. She couldn't wait to spend the rest of her life being loved by this amazing man.

Maria waved at her mom from her spot next to Haven, reminding her they still had a whole ceremony to get through. Valeria stopped wasting time standing at the end of the aisle when where she wanted to be next to Chris far more.

That's where she belonged.

Forever.

EPILOGUE

"Whatever it is," Chris said when he answered the ringing phone while heading up the stairs, lest it wake up his sleeping wife or Maria, "make it good, and fast. I have better things to do this morning than talk on the phone."

"Is that how you greet your father?"

"Well ... no."

"Good," Gian said, "I was worried you forgot your manners in your new married life."

"I've been married almost two months. You don't think it might take longer?"

Gian made a noise under his breath. "I'll be honest, I might as well have forgotten the rest of the world existed for the first six months of mine and your mother's marriage. That was a wonderful time."

"And that's enough of that," Chris muttered.

"Anyway," Gian said, "I called for a reason. Happy birthday."

"Who did you tell first this year, me or Corrado?"

"Both of us," came the new voice on the call.

A three-way call.

Nice.

Chris chuckled. "Ah, Papa got smart this year."

"Wouldn't want either of you feeling left out," Gian returned, his amusement clear.

A long running joke between Chris and his twin on their birthday was whoever got called first by their parents—mother or father—was clearly loved the most. It was only a couple of years ago that their parents caught onto the joke which they didn't find all that funny. Or rather, their mother didn't find it as cute as they did.

Their father played along.

They couldn't say the same for their ma.

"And now can I go back to bed?" Corrado mumbled. "It was way too early for this."

Chris checked his watch. "It's nine."

"Thank you for that information. I will let a *very* pregnant Ginevra and an extremely anxious Alessio know that their nightly habits of walking the halls and worrying about every little thing isn't an acceptable excuse to keep me awake until two in the morning. Care to be here while I do that, brother? Or to lend me a couch when they kick my ass out?"

Gian laughed.

Chris was quick to say, "No, you're on your own there."

"Thanks for that, really."

"I do what I can," Chris replied.

"Go back to sleep, Corrado," Gian said, "and call your mother later. Alessio isn't the only anxious one lately."

"Right, right. Later."

One call clicked off, and Chris knew he was left with only his father. During his conversation, he had climbed the two levels of stairs in his three-level home and stood in the doorway of their master bedroom. Across the large space, Valeria slept happily under gray and white striped sheets, only a peek of her bare shoulders and a splash of black hair could be seen on her pillow.

God.

He loved this woman.

So much.

More every day.

"Someone asked Ginevra who the father was when she went to the salon the other day with your mother," Gian said.

Chris frowned. "What?"

"The boys were *very* angry."

"I mean … I understand the curiosity someone might have," Chris said, "but not the ignorance to outright *ask*. That's nobody's business."

From the moment his twin had announced Ginevra's pregnancy to their family, the expectation of how to act and receive it was undoubtedly clear. It was *we* are pregnant. It was *they* were expecting a baby. *Their* daughter. From the start, neither Corrado nor Alessio had differentiated, and Ginevra was the same way.

Everyone fell in line because, sure, while the circumstances of a poly relationship might be strange to some, it was his twin's everyday *normal*. What was Corrado's life didn't have to fit into everyone else's box—they didn't have to live it. They did, however, have to respect it.

"What did Ma do?" Chris asked. "You said she was there, right?"

Gian chuckled. "Had all her future appointments cancelled and found a new salon before lunch."

"Easy when her last name is Guzzi."

"Easy when she is who she is, you mean."

"That, too."

"Nonetheless, I thought you might want to know for later today when we're having the birthday dinner at the mansion," Gian said. "In case they're sensitive about the baby and the pregnancy, that might be why."

"Yeah, thanks. I'll let Val know."

"And how is she, hmm?"

"Pardon?"

"Valeria. How is she?"

"Perfect. She's perfect."

"I bet. I know she's been busy prepping for the fall semester to start. Has she settled on a major after her bachelor's?"

"Not yet," he said, "but she's got all the time in the world."

Chris had promised her that.

He intended to keep it.

"Well," his father drawled, "I will let you get back to your morning. I'm sure you have plans, and I didn't mean to interrupt them. Living that good life, huh?"

Maria was still sleeping.

Valeria, too.

Still, his father wasn't wrong.

He wasn't sure what that *good life* was his father spoke about, or if this was it, but it was the perfect life for Chris. That's what mattered most to him.

"I will see you later, Papa."

"You, too. Happy birthday, son."

Oh, it was about to be *very* happy.

• • •

"Oh, my *God*."

Chris's dark chuckles whispered along his wife's naked skin as he raised from between her thighs, dropping hot kisses to her trembling stomach, up to the valley between her breasts, and finally along the damp column of her throat.

Valeria's heavy breaths, thick from her orgasm, panted into the bedsheets. There was nothing he liked more than waking this woman up by loving her. Usually, with him between her thighs because *fuck* …

That was a win-win for him, too.

Her taste was still tart on his tongue, and she all but sucked the flavor of her arousal off his tongue when he kissed her. Her soft moans were swallowed by his kiss, but he was already lost in the way she had widened her legs for him. The slickness of her pussy grinded against his bare length while her fingernails dragged burning lines down the muscles of his back.

"*Fuck*," he breathed.

"Yes, yes."

He was a lucky fuck.

Every morning, this woman was in his bed.

She arched into his hands that slid down her body, and he leaned up to hover above her while she licked her lips. Sinful and inviting. *Begging* and ready.

God, he loved it.

His fingers flexed around her waist, loving that he knew this woman never missed a fucking meal. He was fit, and toned, but her curves drove him crazy. From the expanse of her hips, to the roundness of her ass when she was backing into his thrusts. Every part of her was perfect, and he wanted her to know it every morning she woke up, and each night before she fell asleep.

That was his job.

He did it.

"You want that dick, huh?"

Valeria laughed breathlessly. "So bad."

See, and now he had wakened her up with his tongue between her thighs, it only made her want more. That was the *win-win* for him.

It was only once Chris slid home inside Valeria's clenching pussy, feeling her tightening around him in the best way, that he kissed her again. He loved to feel the way her lips trembled against his when he stretched her open one inch at a time, slow but so fucking good, too. She was always so shameless, her hips rising to meet his while her hands pulled him closer to her.

"*Stop teasing* …"

Because she knew.

And he loved that, too.

His control snapped when her heels dug into his back, and her fingernails found the best spot to dig in along his sides. He couldn't fuck her hard enough, then, or *fast enough*. He would never get enough of this woman, no matter what.

But wasn't that the beauty of it?

Chris lost himself in the way Valeria worked her body against his, fast to seek her own bliss while he was chasing his. Her noises muffled against his kiss until he felt that climax rush through her again as she froze beneath him. He followed soon after, holding her tight as he thrust deep, and came hard.

"*God, I fucking love you.*"

Valeria's laughter, so high and sweet, was better than a morning prayer. Hell, maybe it *was* his new prayer. He tangled his arms around her, flipped them over so they were both on their sides, and he could bury his face into the mess of her hair, and *sighed*.

"Happy birthday," he heard her say. "I love you, too."

"Best fucking birthday yet."

"You wait," she whispered, "it will get *way* better."

He didn't know how.

Chris was willing to find out though.

• • •

"Can I get it for Daddy now, Mamá?"

Hearing Maria call him *daddy* never failed to make Chris smile. It didn't matter if she was saying it because it annoyed her that he refused to let her wear her pink, sparkly running shoes on a rainy day, or because she was asking for five more minutes of storytelling at bedtime. He wasn't sure when she thought of him as her father, but he vividly remembered when she asked if she could call him that.

You're kind of like my daddy, right?

Kind of?

It's all he wanted to be.

She all out refused to call him papa or father, and Chris understood why. She related those titles to a man whose name they didn't speak because it upset her, and of a time in her life which was still all too recent, and traumatic.

So, instead, he got to be her daddy.

That was better.

Because her daddy didn't let her down.

Ever.

Her daddy loved her unconditionally.

No exceptions.

"Okay," Valeria said, "you can go get it, but hurry before Uncle Les gets up there to take his bat."

Chris shot her a look across the backyard of the mansion where she sat beside Cara and Ginevra. There, they could watch the rest of the Guzzi men—well, most, as the younger Guzzi twins had been sent off to Chicago after their twenty-first birthday—and the other guests who wanted to join from their birthday dinner play their game of baseball from a safe distance. Valeria *pretended* like she didn't see Chris glancing her way with his questioning stare about just what she was hiding from him, but he knew she did.

Alessio came up to bat after Maria darted for the back of the mansion, and from the spot they'd chosen as the pitcher's mound, Corrado grinned. "You want that curve ball, Les?"

The man tapped the metal bat against the heel of his shoe before pointing it at Chris's twin, saying, "I'm up for whatever—you know that."

"*Right.*"

Sitting on third base, Chris just wanted to hit home so he could sneak over to Valeria and find out why Maria disappeared into the mansion. She had already given him a birthday present earlier after they cut the cake. A damn nice Rolex, custom-made with the Guzzi *G* designed in diamonds on the face.

What else was there?

"I mean, we've already won," Corrado added. "There's no way you will get those two runs, and this is your last bat."

"Stop gloating," Alessio returned. "That's your one warning."

"That's what makes it *fun.*"

"Throw the goddamn ball."

"Language," Cara called out.

"Sorry."

Corrado threw the pitch when he thought he distracted Alessio with his apology, but he should have known better. He got his two runs when the metal bat connected with the ball and sent it flying past the tree line on the back property—their designated space for a *home run*. Because no one wanted to go searching for balls in the small patch of forest.

Alessio only stepped off the home plate as Chris came jogging across it, tossing his bat so it flipped around in the air before landing back in his waiting palm. He pointed the bat at Corrado, smirking wickedly.

"I think I'm gonna *walk it*," he said. "Remind you who you're trying to better, yeah?"

Corrado shook his head, grinning. "Who's gloating now?"

"And who likes it, huh?"

Chris would have enjoyed the banter between his twin, and Alessio, but he was already heading toward Valeria who was smiling his way.

"Where did Maria go?" he asked his wife.

Valeria peered up at him. "In the house. And congrats on winning."

"Why?"

"Because you won the game."

"No, why did she go in the house?"

"For a surprise."

"For me?"

"Since when are you nosy?"

"Just because it's your birthday, son," his father called as he crossed the backyard with Maria skipping at his side, "doesn't mean you get everything you want ... or does it?"

He might have questioned his father on that statement, but he was more interested in his girl, and the gift in her hands. A white box, maybe twelve inches long, and wrapped with a big, golden bow. She held onto it like it was a lifeline.

"What's this?"

Maria smiled. "It's for you. And me."

Chris shot Valeria a look. She only shrugged.

"Open it?" Maria asked.

Chris took the chair his father pulled out so he could sit beside his wife, with his mother on the other side of him. Gian came to stand behind his chair while Maria placed the box in his lap. Sweet as could be, she bounced on the spot while she waited for him to reach for the gift.

"Any hints?" he asked Valeria.

She shook her head. "It's better if you … understand all at once, I think."

"Definitely," Gian added.

His brow dipped. "They know what it is?"

"We needed help with—"

"Details," Cara was quick to interject. "Don't give him too much to go on."

Valeria laughed. "Yeah, that. Open your gift."

Well, okay.

Maria's excitement only grew like her huge smile when Chris pulled the satin ribbon from the top of the box. He gave her a laugh before opening the top, and then he looked down.

His whole world *stopped.*

Application for Adoption.

The papers were ready. All filled out, and it appeared a lawyer could file them anytime. It only needed one thing. A little arrow pointed to a space where his signature needed to go.

Chris grabbed a little tighter to the box, unable to speak.

Maria did it for him. "Because you're already my daddy, right?"

His father's hands found his shoulders and squeezed. Valeria reached over to stroke his cheek with her warm palm.

Yeah.

This was most definitely the best birthday of his life.

"Right?" Maria asked again, quieter the second time.

He looked up to meet her gaze.

Her smile never faltered.

"That's right," he said, keeping his tone level, although he didn't know how. "I promise."

Maria darted forward when he opened his arms to bring her in for a hug. Someone pulled the box from his lap just in time, so the papers inside didn't get crushed.

He didn't know who. It didn't matter.

Everything he wanted was right in his arms and sitting beside him.

All around him.

His father had been right. This was the good life.

• • •

Grab *The Guzzi Legacy: Vol 2* and fall in love with three more Guzzi brothers!

XO.

BK

ABOUT THE AUTHOR

Bethany-Kris is a Canadian author, lover of much, and mother to four sons, three cats, and four dogs. A small town in Eastern Canada where she was born and raised is where she has always called home. With her boys under her feet, a snuggling cat, barking dogs, and a spouse calling over his shoulder, she is nearly always writing something ... when she can find the time.

Find her at www.bethanykris.com

OTHER BOOKS

The After Another Trilogy

One Step After Another
One Breath After Another
One Second After Another

Boykov Bratva

Fractured Ties
Essence of Fear

The Guzzi Legacy

Corrado
Alessio
Chris
Beni
Bene
Marcus
The Firsts
The Guzzi Legacy: Vol 1
The Guzzi Legacy: Vol 2

Renzo + Lucia

Privilege
Harbor
Contempt
Forever
Cusp
Renzo + Lucia: The Complete Trilogy

Andino + Haven

Duty
Vow
One Last Time
Andino + Haven: The Complete Duet

BETHANY-KRIS

John + Siena

Loyalty
Disgrace
John + Siena: The Complete Duet
John + Siena: Extended

Cross + Catherine

Always
Revere
Unruly
The Companion
Naz & Roz

Guzzi Duet

Unraveled, Book One
Entangled, Book Two
Cara & Gian: The Complete Duet

DeLuca Duet

Waste of Worth: Part One
Worth of Waste: Part Two

Standalone Titles

Pink
Pretty Lies
Dirty Pool
Effortless
Inflict
Cozen
Captivated
Dishonored

Donati Bloodlines

Thin Lies
Thin Lines
Thin Lives
Behind the Bloodlines
The Complete Trilogy

THE GUZZI LEGACY: VOL 1

Filthy Marcellos

Antony
Lucian
Giovanni
Dante
Legacy
A Very Marcello Christmas
The Complete Collection

Seasons of Betrayal

Where the Sun Hides
Where the Snow Falls
Where the Wind Whispers
Seasons: The Complete Seasons of Betrayal Series

Gun Moll Trilogy

Gun Moll
Gangster Moll
Madame Moll

The Chicago War

Deathless & Divided
Reckless & Ruined
Scarless & Sacred
Breathless & Bloodstained
The Complete Series
Maldives & Mistletoe

The Russian Guns

The Arrangement
The Life
The Score
Demyan & Ana
Shattered
The Jersey Vignettes

FANTASY ROMANCE

The Hunted: A 9INE REALMS Novel

Find more on Bethany-Kris's website at www.bethanykris.com.

www.ingramcontent.com/pod-product-compliance
Lightning Source LLC
Chambersburg PA
CBHW051054030726
47504CB00006B/1625